GREAT

DETECTIVE

STORIES

Selected by the Editors of Reader's Digest

The Reader's Digest Association Limited

LONDON SYDNEY AUCKLAND MONTREAL CAPE TOWN HONG KONG

FIRST EDITION 1998

Published by The Reader's Digest Association Limited
11 Westferry Circus, Canary Wharf, London E14 4HE.

The stories in this volume are used by permission of and by
special arrangement with the holders of the respective copyrights.
(For further information see pages 527–8.)

ISBN 0 276 42418 2

Origination by Rodney Howe Limited
Printed and bound by
Caledonian International Book Manufacturing Limited, Glasgow

Contents

Introduction

'A murder occurs; many are suspected; all but one suspect, who is the murderer, are eliminated; the murderer is arrested or dies.' This was how W. H. Auden summed up the plot of a typical detective story and neatly identified the main ingredients that make up the form. Detective stories deal with murders and their punishment, with puzzles and their solution. They begin with a mysterious crime: the baronet found dead on the library carpet, a dagger planted between his shoulder blades, with the door and all the windows firmly locked. They end by nailing the culprit: the butler did it, not the greedy heir or the discarded mistress or the passing tramp, and he contrived to leave the door and windows locked behind him by this or that ingenious device. In effect, detective stories begin by posing a question and, after a certain amount of deliciously tantalising delay, they end by answering it.

Fans of the old school, who prize detective fiction in its classic, most rigorous form, would rush to add that there are rules governing how the question is asked and the answer given. Both must be fair. The solution cannot emerge arbitrarily, pulled like a rabbit from the conjuror's hat at the last minute. It should develop in a logical fashion from evidence available to us, the readers, as well as to the detective in charge of the investigation. We need to know that we could solve the mystery for ourselves before we reach the explanation on the last page. The story is thus a compelling challenge. Readers will devour all the titles by Agatha Christie they can find in the vain hope that this time they'll manage to beat her at her game. Many people reread their favourite Sherlock Holmes stories for the pleasure of dwelling on the clues they overlooked or, like the reassuringly obtuse Dr Watson, misinterpreted on first reading.

The appeal of the detective story, then, can seem as irresistible as the urge to scratch an itch. Many fans of the genre describe themselves as 'addicts', and they are not just joking. W. H. Auden, for one, was willing to invoke the psychology of addictive behaviour in explaining his own love of the form. Others, more grandly, speak of its appeal as at once noble and fundamental, a world apart from the vulgar fascination that the blood and guts of violent crime hold for readers of the tabloids. Detective stories, they argue, are a proving-ground for our innate love of order and our innate attachment to the power of reason in creating order from circumstances that at first look baffling or even frightening.

The argument is seductive, if only because it gives so flattering an account of why we read detective fiction. But it is surely misleading. Our love of order and attachment to reason may well be innate, but we managed to get along for most of our recorded history without the need for detective stories. The stories you will find in this collection were all written within the last hundred and fifty years, and most of them were written in the twentieth century. The earliest is Charles Dickens's *Hunted Down*, from the 1850s. Scholars, to be sure, like to point to episodes in the Bible or to the puzzle tales of the eighteenth century or, more substantially, to Edgar Allan Poe's tales about his amateur detective Dupin, written in the 1840s, as significant precursors. But even they admit that they are hunting out prehistory, and that the real history starts with Sir Arthur Conan Doyle at the end of the nineteenth century.

The Sherlock Holmes stories fixed the formula that later writers lovingly elaborated and critics like W. H. Auden admiringly described. Doyle, it is true, took hints from Poe and generously acknowledged the debt. But in his hands the result had a flair for which nothing that had gone before prepared his readers. Doyle enjoyed an unprecedented popularity for his tales of Holmes and Watson that best-selling detective writers of today might well envy. However much we love our current detective heroes, we are not going to throng the streets wearing black armbands in their memory, as Doyle's readers did when he tried to kill Sherlock Holmes off. He made the attempt in the pages of *Strand* magazine and it was there, in the confines of the short story, that Holmes always seemed most comfortable and became best loved. We should not really be surprised if the novels about Holmes look broken-backed by comparison. In grasping the essential formula of the detective story, Doyle also discovered the pitfalls that lie in its middle section: parading a gallery of suspects or a range of alternative solutions to be eliminated from consideration requires special inventiveness if it is not going to annoy, or just bore, the reader. Usually detective fiction works best when it proceeds as economically as possible from intriguing question to satisfying answer. It belongs naturally in the short story.

Doyle's example certainly ensured that the short story rather than the novel would carry the essential history of the form for many years to come. Hence the embarrassment of riches which a collection like the present anthology has to choose from. Indeed, it is hard to find a distinguished detective novel from the period immediately following the success of Sherlock Holmes, unless it be E. C. Bentley's *Trent's Last Case*. The real achievement lies in shorter work, not just by Bentley himself but also by G. K. Chesterton in his Father Brown stories and R. Austin Freeman in his Dr Thorndyke stories——not to mention writers often overlooked such as Baroness Orczy, Ernest Bramah and H. C. Bailey.

Together they ushered in what fans like to call the 'Golden Age' of detective fiction, by which they mean the great flowering of talent between the two World Wars. You will find it represented in this volume by a roster of famous names: Agatha Christie, Dorothy L. Sayers, Margery Allingham, John Dickson Carr, Ngaio Marsh and Michael Innes. We immediately associate them with a distinctive milieu and a distinctive hero. The murder mystery might be bizarre or even grisly, but the detective who solves it—whether an amateur, a professional private investigator or a policeman—is usually carefree in his behaviour and almost always impeccably genteel in his background. His well-bred and light-hearted manner helps him look thoroughly at home in the country houses, Oxbridge colleges, picturesque villages and other favourite settings of the Golden Age.

Nowadays we can feel nostalgia for this world or, if we are sensible enough to remember it never actually existed, we can relish its innocent charm. At the time it could provoke irritation, and nowhere more strongly than among the writers and readers of the American 'pulp' magazines. Living in the United States amid the Depression, Prohibition and the rise of the mobs, they found what Agatha Christie——or even an American like Ellery Queen——had to offer irrelevant to their understanding of crime. The true voice of American crime writing between the wars came from Dashiell Hammett and later from Raymond Chandler. Together they established the 'hard-boiled' school, in which the detective is a down-at-heel private eye inhabiting the 'mean streets' of the city and solving his cases less by reasoned deduction than by invincible toughness.

These differences announced a radical break with the conventions that had served writers, largely British, from Sir Arthur Conan Doyle to Agatha Christie. The familiar process of question and answer, ingenious problem and elegant solution, could disappear out of the window with the well-cut suits and top-drawer accents. The possibilities of detective fiction, it seemed, were too many and too inviting to be captured in one simple formula or contained in one hard and fast definition. Indeed, for the last fifty years writers have been busy showing that the variety of which the form is capable goes far beyond even the opposition between the Golden Age and hard-boiled schools. Georges Simenon showed how an ordinary policeman—previously the disregarded Cinderella of crime writing—could be made into an Everyman probing fundamental questions of justice and humanity. His work helped give heart to other approaches outside the familiar formulas: the 'police procedural' (as practised by Ed McBain) with its emphasis on the technical and bureaucratic side of investigation; and the tradition of crime writing, stretching from Somerset Maugham to Julian Symons, which finds its real matter in the tortuous mazes of the human heart. And recently, just as the Golden Age was challenged by the hard-boiled school, so the male—if not macho—attitudes of Hammett and Chandler have been challenged by a new generation of broadly feminist writers, represented in this anthology by Marcia Muller, Sue Grafton and Linda Barnes.

No wonder, then, that the stories in this collection should encompass a much broader range than their brief chronological span might lead us to expect. And no wonder that this range should broaden steadily as we approach the present, when writers seem more than ever determined to draw on all the different possibilities that examples from the past have put at their disposal. Variety and eclecticism, not repetition or subservience to orthodoxy, have always been what has kept detective fiction alive and kept it popular. They look like doing so for some time to come.

The Editors

Margery Allingham
1904–1966

THE LONGER VIEW

O N THE DAY that the entrancing Beatrix Lea married her famous leading man, Mr Albert Campion took Mr Lance Feering to re-visit the happy scenes of Mr Feering's youth.

The expedition was purely remedial. Throughout their long luncheon Lance had remained mildly depressed. After all, as he said, a broken heart takes at least twenty-four hours in which to mend without a seam and, while he was perfectly prepared to believe that life with a young woman of Miss Lea's uncontrolled and vituperative tongue might drive a man to suicide, he yet needed a day or two to get used to his merciful deliverance.

Campion, who had known Lance long before he had become one of the leading designers of stage *décor* in Europe, was ready to agree, but it occurred to him that a little gentle exercise, judiciously coupled with a rival sentimental regret, might possibly speed up the recovery.

He was rewarded. As they turned into the web of little streets which floats out like a dusty cap round the neck of the Museum, Lance began to brighten visibly.

'I used to live round here once,' he remarked casually. 'Four of us existed in a hovel on the top floor of a house in Duke's Row. We were all under twenty. Berry was there, and Jorkins, and old Salmon, the poster chap. We were all broke and completely happy. We used to slave away like lunatics, all striving and dreaming of the glorious future when our respective geniuses would be recognised, and we should be rich and eat three times a day. It's tragic, you know, Campion. Look at us now. All recognised, all successful, and all damned miserable. We've got the apple off the top of the tree and the cursed thing's sour.'

Campion experienced a sensation of relief. The man was becoming recognisable. Once Lance got going on his time-honoured 'futility of endeavour' the next stage, 'self-expression, the comforter', was close at hand, and after that it was but a step to that mood of light-hearted good temper laced with high excitement which was his normal state.

'What we all miss now is adventure,' Lance continued, absent-mindedly crossing the road to reach a familiar turning. 'When we lived down here it was an adventure to be alive at all. Here we are. That's the place. Wonderful architecture. Look at that porch and those windows. Look at them!'

Campion surveyed the row of dusty houses, but even the rose-coloured spectacles of Lance Feering's reawakening enthusiasm could not restore Duke's Row to any sort of splendour. The backwater was forlorn and shabby. Fine doors hung open under the ragged elegance of graceful porches, betraying glimpses of bare and dirty communal hallways within. It was a sad street of decayed mansions, whose rooms were now let out unfurnished at a few shillings a week. Lance strolled down the road.

'I haven't been here for ten years,' he said regretfully. 'All the old crowd must have gone, of course. No one stayed here long. It was a sort of half-way house. If you lived here you were either going up or coming down. I wonder who's got our old hovel now?'

He had paused before an open doorway as he spoke and, after a moment's contemplation, suddenly dived through it and hurried up the fine but unsteady flight of wooden stairs inside. Campion followed dubiously, catching up with him just as he was shamelessly engaged in trying the handle of the door on the top landing.

'I say, is this wise?' Campion put out a restraining hand, but the door swung open and Feering grinned.

'Empty, by George!' he said delightedly. 'This is an omen, Campion. Who knows, it may be the will of Providence that we take this place, and, turning our backs resolutely on the fleshpots, settle down to adventure and art for art's sake.'

Campion remained polite but unimpressed. The crumbling attic with the discoloured walls, the wobbling floorboards, and the one dusty window did not attract him. But Feering was his old volatile self again.

'It's a hole, Campion, I admit,' he said. 'It's a dirty little hole, twice as dark and half the size I thought it was. Yet we all worked in here and slept in this bedroom. Lord, look at it! It's a cupboard. Salmon, Berry and I shared this.'

He had thrown open an inner door and they stepped gingerly into a tiny room in which there was nothing but a broken chair, a cup without a handle, and a portrait of a film star torn from one of the weekly illustrated magazines. Feering's enthusiasm sagged before this scene of desolation.

'I wouldn't like to see us trying it now,' he remarked. 'You haven't met old Salmon lately, have you? He's grown very pompous since his success, poor chap. We used to make Jorkins sleep in this cupboard over here. He was short enough to lie down in it.'

He was still laughing as he opened the small door in the wall. Campion did not follow him immediately. An empty cigarette carton on the window sill had caught his attention and he had gone across to look at it. He still had it in his hand when Feering's voice came sharply from the cupboard.

'I say, Campion, come here. Look at this.'

Campion put his head into the little cell and glanced round its dingy walls through his horn-rimmed spectacles. The place was less than six feet square and was lit by a small window in the roof. It was quite devoid of furnishing, but possessed one startling feature. All round the rough plaster walls, about a foot above the wainscot, ran a string of six-inch crimson letters. They made out the words with difficulty.

'Let me out,' they read. 'O let me out let me out let me out let me out let me out.'

The writing was shaky and irregular, but there was no mistaking the message. It sprang out at them from the little den like a cry and sent an unaccustomed thrill down Campion's spine. On and on the message went, all round the tiny room. Sometimes it was in a double row. Sometimes it staggered up the wall.

'Let me out o let me out let me out let me out.'

Very low down on the back of the door was the single word 'Janey' repeated half a dozen times.

The two men stared at each other for an instant and finally Feering laughed.

'It's mad, of course,' he said. 'Some sort of joke. It gave me a shock, though, almost a superstitious thrill. "Let me out" written in blood on the walls of a prison. As soon as one's mind works one realises it's a false effect. If anyone had been imprisoned here he would have shouted the words, not scribbled them. How attractively absurd!'

Campion was silent. He was kneeling down on the floor, peering at the inscription. Presently he rubbed one of the letters with an inquisitive finger and the colour came off on his hand. He moved under the skylight to examine it.

'It's recent work, anyway,' he observed at last. 'Wait a minute. Get out of the light, can you, old boy? Stand in the doorway while I have a look round.'

Feering moved obligingly and stood watching.

'I like to see the veteran sleuth sleuthing,' he remarked cheerfully. 'It's very instructive. Look out for the trouser knees. Hullo, have you got something? What is it? The clue the great man knew was there?'

'The clue the great man hoped was there,' corrected Campion modestly. He prised something small and bright from beneath the wainscot board, and rose, holding the treasure in the palm of his hand. 'There you are,' he said. 'There's half the explanation of the blood-stained handwriting. All done while you wait.'

'Lipstick!' Lance took the small gilt holder from which practically all the cosmetic had been worn away, and turned it over curiously. 'Sample size,' he commented. 'What's the little bit of green thread for? That's amateur work.'

'I shouldn't pull it off.' Campion spoke hastily, an urgency in his tone which made the other man glance at him inquiringly.

'Taking it seriously?' he asked. 'It is a joke of some sort, isn't it? Have we stumbled on a crime?' He almost sounded hopeful, and Campion shrugged his shoulders. He was laughing.

'My dear chap, I don't know,' he said. 'I admit it doesn't seem likely, and even if we have it's hardly anything to do with us. Yet it's odd that any woman should waste a whole lipstick writing "*let me out*" all round the wainscot of an empty room.'

'Perhaps it wasn't empty then?'

'In that case it's curiouser and curiouser. Why should she move the furniture away from the walls in order to write behind it?'

'I say, there is that.' Lance Feering's black eyes were growing sharper. 'Still, why write it? Why not shout it?' he insisted. 'And anyway, why so low down?'

Campion hesitated. 'I don't want to be melodramatic,' he said, 'but if she were lying on the floor she could just reach as high as that, and I can imagine a frightened woman writing like that if she was prevented from shouting.'

'Good Lord!' Feering was staring at the little cell in blank astonishment. 'Gagged!' he ejaculated. 'Bound and gagged.'

'Hardly. If she was bound she couldn't write, and if she wasn't bound she'd hardly remain gagged. But she might have been frightened. It's very curious.'

'It's incredible.' Lance was frankly excited. 'What shall we do? Call a bobby?'

'Oh, no, I shouldn't do that.' Campion was firm. 'He might not be amused. We've got to account for ourselves being here at all, you see. We walked in off the street without being asked. There isn't even a "To Let" sign anywhere. We're on enclosed premises. If you call the police we shall spend the rest of the day making statements. It's interesting, though. I should say it had been written within the last forty-eight hours. The stuff isn't dry, you see.'

Lance grimaced. 'I came up here on a silly sentimental impulse, hoping to recapture some of the old spirit of adventure,' he remarked. 'Now I seem to have found it, and hang it, Campion, it's a responsibility. Look at it. "*Let me out o let me out.*" It's pathetic, poignant. It must be answered. I don't see what we're going to do, though, apart from making discreet inquiries from the people downstairs.'

'Wait a moment.' Campion was examining the lipstick holder. 'All in good time. Let's do the thing in proper academic style. First we learn all we can from the scene. Then we take the statements. I'll tell you something, young sir. This is not ordinary lipstick. Not only is it a sample but it has an inscription. Look. "*Prince Pierrot, Inc. 'Maiden Voyage'.*" What does that tell you? Nothing, I suppose. However, the experienced sleuth deduces instantly that Prince Pierrot is an American firm of high-class cosmetic manufacturers; American because he's "Inc." and not "and Co." and high-class because the smell of the stuff is not offensive but rather pleasing. Moreover, it's a nice expensive-looking colour. The "Maiden Voyage" provokes a longer shot, I admit, but there has been a pretty important maiden voyage from the US just lately.'

'The *Eire*!' Lance swung round. 'I say, that's about it. That boat is the last word in floating hotels and I believe the advertising tie-ups were incredible. Probably these Pierrot people control the beauty parlours on board and ran off a few special samples with the complimentary name. There you are. This poor girl Janey—her name must be Janey—came over on the *Eire*. We're on to something highly peculiar. They were all first-class passengers on that trip.

What's an American socialite doing in a dive like this less than a week after she lands in England? We must find her. Hang it, it's up to us!'

Campion smiled, but his eyes were still serious.

'Don't be disappointed,' he said warningly.

'Disappointed?' Lance was hurt. 'My dear chap, I'm not a ghoul. I only hope it is a joke. I don't want any beautiful young woman to have had a beastly time. What are you laughing at?'

'I was wondering if she was beautiful and if she was young,' murmured Campion. 'There's absolutely no guarantee of that.'

Lance grinned. 'Poor, ugly little beast, then,' he said. 'I don't care. I've got my adventure. Her name is Janey and I am her knight-errant. We've got all eternity before us. Where do we go from here?'

THEIR PRELIMINARY INVESTIGATIONS were unexpectedly profitable. To Feering's delight he discovered that the old charwoman who had lived in the basement in the days of his youth was still in occupation. After a glorious reunion, which could not have been more hearty had he been her long-lost son, she told them all she knew of the ex-tenants of the top floor. This was not a great deal, but the story had points of interest.

There had been two of them, she said, 'flash boys, a little too smart to be trusted'. They had been living there for the best part of a month, and had seemed to her experienced eyes to be none too flush with money, even according to the standards of the neighbourhood. However, two days before there had come a change. The tenants of the attic had received visitors of an unusual kind. The strangers had arrived late one night. Out of her basement window she had caught a glimpse of their limousine, and afterwards had heard the sound of trampling feet on the uncarpeted stairs. The following evening the car had called again, and this time everyone had gone off in it, carrying bundles and packages.

The old lady suspected a moonlight flit but had been surprised in the morning to discover one of the tenants still in possession. Even more to her astonishment, he had fetched in a junk dealer and disposed of the entire furnishings for a few shillings. Then, after leaving a week's rent for the landlord, he had walked out quietly into the blue.

That was all Mrs Sadd had to report, and she hardly liked to take the treasury note which Feering pressed upon her, but she came running after them to tell them that one of the 'flash boys' had spoken with an American accent.

'No girl,' Lance remarked dubiously, as he followed Campion into a cab. 'No mention of a girl at all. No screams. Nothing. The only corroboration we have is that one of the tenants had an American accent.'

'He liked American cigarettes too,' Campion observed. 'There was an empty "Camel" carton on the mantelshelf. They're expensive over here. Perhaps the visitors brought him a packet. It may be a wild-goose chase, but I think we'll try the shipping office.'

'Janey,' said Feering, leaning back in the cab. 'I see her as a dazzling blonde with dark eyes.'

Since Beatrix was a brunette with blue eyes, Campion took the observation to be a favourable sign.

Lance waited in the cab while Campion negotiated the somewhat delicate line of inquiry in the shipping office. It was a long vigil, but he was rewarded. The tall man in the horn-rimmed spectacles came striding out of the impressive doorway wearing that vacant expression which indicated that he was on the track of something interesting. He directed the taxi-man to the offices of one of the newspapers and climbed in beside his friend.

'Miss Janey Lobbet, travelling with her mother, Mrs Fran Lobbet, of Boston, Mass.,' he said briefly. 'That's all I can find out about her. Passenger lists aren't very communicative. But she was the only Janey on the boat, so far as I can find out. There's one other point. You were perfectly right. Messrs Prince Pierrot Inc. had the monopoly of the beauty trade on the ship and they did run a special line in "Maiden Voyage" samples, exclusive to the trip. How's that?'

Lance whistled. 'What an extraordinary thing!' he said at last. '"*Let me out o let me out*" . . . what on earth does it mean? There's been nothing in the papers. What's happened, Campion?'

'I don't know.' The other man spoke with a seriousness unusual in him. 'I don't know at all, but I don't like the feel of it and I rather think it's something I ought to find out.'

At the newspaper office Campion's call was on Miss Dorothea Azores, well known as the most industrious gossip-writer of the day. The lady herself was out, unfortunately, but her secretary was able to give them at least the bare bones of the information they sought. Mrs Fran Lobbet was the widow of Carl Lobbet, the paper magnet, and she and her only daughter, Janey, were staying at the Aragon Hotel, overlooking the Park. The secretary apologised that she had no photographs and so little information about the pair, but explained gently that there were a great many Americans in London.

'Well, what do we do?' inquired Lance as they came out through the bronze-and-glass doors into Fleet Street again. 'Do we barge in on these good ladies and ask if either of them has spent a bad half-hour in Duke's Row?'

Campion hesitated. 'No,' he said, the anxious expression still lingering behind his spectacles. 'No, hardly that. But we might dine at the Aragon to-night if you're not doing anything. I think I shall go myself, in any case.'

'No, you don't,' said Lance firmly. 'No poaching. This is my adventure. I found it and I'm sticking to it. The dinner's mine. I'll meet you in the restaurant at a quarter to eight. Don't look so dubious. This is going to be good.'

'I hope so.' But Campion did not sound sanguine.

THE ARAGON was fashionable that year, and the big dining-room with the fine windows opening on to the Park was crowded with the usual noisy, well-dressed crowd when Lance arrived. He found Campion already installed at a table at the far end of the room, on the edge of the little dais which was part of the orchestra platform. It was a most advantageous position, giving him a clear view of the entire gathering.

'Any luck?'

'It all depends.' Campion was cautious. 'I'm not sure. I've been talking to Baptiste. He's the *maître d'hôtel* here. I cultivate a line in *maîtres d'hôtel*. He's an old friend. The Lobbets are here all right, or rather Madame is. Mademoiselle is away for a few days, staying with friends. That's the table, the little one down there by the window. She's expected any moment now.'

'Staying with friends?' Lance repeated, his eyebrows rising. 'That's suggestive, isn't it? This is damned silly and exciting. Don't be so blasé—or is this an everyday affair for you?'

'I'm not blasé.' Campion resented the accusation. 'I don't like the look of the thing. If I'm on the right track, and I'm afraid I may be, I'm appalled by it. Hullo, here she is.'

Feering followed his glance across the room to where the portly Baptiste was settling a newcomer at the little table by the window.

'It's Janey.' Lance turned to Campion. 'What did I tell you? A dazzling blonde with dark eyes. I'm the seventh child of a seventh child: I've got prophetic vision. She looks a little pale, a little sad, doesn't she? Momma has been very trying and she doesn't know anybody in London. By George, she's lovely! Look at her.'

Campion was looking at her. He saw a pale slender girl of twenty-eight or so, with ash-blonde hair and enormous dark eyes, the shadows beneath them enhancing their sombre loveliness. She was delightfully dressed, and from the clasp on her shoulder came the unmistakable watery gleam of real diamonds, yet he thought he had never seen anyone who looked so forlorn and miserably unhappy in his life. Lance drew a card from his wallet and began to scribble on it.

'One can only be snubbed,' he observed philosophically. ' "Faint heart", "nothing venture", likewise "fain would I climb". Give me that lipstick-holder. The green thread may touch a chord.'

He pushed the card across the table so that Campion could read the message.

I think this is yours. May I tell you where I found it and how I know? It's a good story.

'Yes, that'll do, I think.' Campion produced the lipstick-holder as he spoke. 'I wonder, though,' he went on. 'It's not fair to spring it on her like this unless . . .'

His voice trailed away. Lance was no longer listening to him. He had signalled a waiter and was dispatching his message.

Together the two friends watched the man cross the room. He paused before the table in the window, and said something to the girl. She looked surprised and almost, it seemed to Lance, a little frightened, but she glanced across at him and took the card as the waiter placed the holder on the white table-cloth beside her plate. The card fluttered from her hand as she caught sight of it and even from that distance they saw all trace of colour creep slowly from her face. She grew paler and paler and her eyelids drooped. Campion rose.

'Look out, she's going to faint,' he said.

He was too late. The girl swayed sideways and crumpled to the ground.

Instantly there was commotion all round her, and the two men on the other side of the room had the uncomfortable experience of seeing her assisted to the door, Baptiste fluttering behind the procession like a scandalised duenna.

Lance turned to Campion. In any other circumstances the bewildered regret upon his face would have been comic.

'Ghastly,' he said. 'How did that happen? Was it coincidence or the sight of that confounded thing?'

Campion put his napkin on the table. 'We're going to find out,' he said briefly.

Baptiste, solemn and reproachful, was bearing down upon them. He paused before the table and gave the message in a tone in which respectful deference was subtly mingled with deep disapproval.

'Mrs Lobbet will be glad to see the two gentlemen who sent her the card in her private sitting-room.'

IT WAS NOT SO MUCH an invitation as a royal command, and Lance said afterwards that he followed Campion to the suite on the first floor feeling as if he were bound for the headmaster's study. At any rate, five minutes later they stood side by side, looking helplessly at the pale, unsmiling woman who waited to receive them with courage and dignity as well as terror in her dark eyes.

As the door closed behind the servant who had conducted them she spoke. Her voice was unexpectedly deep, and its trace of New England accent made it very attractive.

'Well?' she said. 'Has the price gone up again? Or couldn't you wait until to-morrow?'

They gaped at her and Lance tugged at his collar uncomfortably.

'I'm afraid there's some mistake,' he began awkwardly. 'You see, we had no idea that you were Mrs Lobbet. We—that is, I—was looking for Janey.'

The name was too much for the woman. She remained for a moment struggling to master herself and then, with a gesture of complete helplessness, collapsed into a chair and hid her face.

'Don't,' she whispered. 'Oh, please don't. I've told you I'll meet any demands you like to make, but don't torture us like this. Is she all right? Please, please tell me. Don't you understand, she's my baby? Is she all right?'

Lance glanced sharply at Campion and met the other man's eyes.

'A child!' he said huskily. 'Good Lord, I never guessed.'

Campion did not reply to him. His mouth was grim as he went across the room and looked down at the woman.

'Mrs Lobbet, you should have gone to the police,' he said quietly. 'When did you miss your daughter?'

The young widow sprang up. Before she had been broken-hearted; now she was terrified.

'Who are you?' she demanded. 'I tell you I don't know anything. I——I don't want to discuss anything with you. Please go away.'

He shook his head.

'You're making a great mistake,' he said gently. 'This is England, you know. Conditions are rather different over here. I know when someone dear is kidnapped in America it is often safest not to go to the authorities for fear of reprisals, but over here, believe me, it's not the same.'

The girl did not speak. There was a light of pure desperation in her eyes and her lips remained obstinately closed. He stood watching her for a little while and finally shrugged his shoulders.

'I'm sorry,' he said. 'You could have trusted us.'

He had reached the door before she called him back.

'If only I knew what to do,' she said brokenly. 'If only I knew what to do.'

Lance went suddenly across the room and took her hand. He looked young for his years and very handsome as he peered down into her face.

'We are both reputable people, my dear girl,' he said. 'We'll give you our credentials if you'll let us. We found that holder in such very odd circumstances that it made us curious, and quite by chance we were able to trace it to you. Won't you tell us all about it? We'll help you if we can.'

It was a sincere little speech and gradually the tenseness round her mouth slackened, although her eyes were still afraid.

'Where did you get it?' she whispered. 'Did you see her? Do you know where she is?'

It took them the best part of an hour to convince her that they were genuinely disinterested parties in the affair. Lance left the description of the scribbled message, which had now taken on such a new and pathetic significance, to Campion, who managed it very tactfully, without frightening the young mother unduly.

'So you see,' he finished at last, 'we were curious and just a little apprehensive. How old is Janey?'

'Only six.' Fran Lobbet's voice quivered. 'She's just a baby. I've never let her out of my sight before, but this new nurse seemed so sensible and trustworthy that I let them both go out into the Park. When they didn't return I was paralysed with fear. Then the telephone message from these——these people came.'

'Oh, they phoned you, did they? What did they say?'

'The usual thing. I nearly fainted when I heard the warning. I've read about the same sort of thing in our newspapers. I wasn't to tell anyone or——or I'd never see her again. I was to go to Oxborough Racecourse and put ten thousand dollars to win on a certain horse with a certain bookmaker. Then they promised she'd be returned to me.'

'Did you do it?'

'Oh, yes, of course. That was the day before yesterday. I did everything they told me, but there was no sign of her when I got back here. I waited by the telephone all day and this morning, when I was half out of my mind, they rang again. They swore that she was safe but they made another demand. They may be playing with me. She may be dead. But what can I do? What *can* I do?'

The appeal was too much for Lance.

'My poor, dear, good girl,' he said, forgetting himself completely, 'ring up the police instantly. This is frightful. You poor child, you must be in agony. See to it, Campion. Get on the telephone.'

'No, no, please don't! Please. They'll kill her if I do that. I know they will. They so often do. There are hundreds of cases of it back home.' She was clutching his coat imploringly, and Campion intervened.

'You're not back home now,' he said. 'Look here, it's not as bad as you think, or at least I think not, thank God. This is a smaller country and the law is tighter, but I think you may be right about not calling in the police at this juncture. Tell me, did the man you spoke to on the phone have an American accent?'

'Yes, a slight one.'

'I see. Then that's what's happened. Probably the whole thing's engineered from the other side, with confederates in this country. The nurse is in it, of course. When did you engage her?'

'Just before we sailed. She came to me with wonderful references and she seemed so placid and sensible that I never dreamed—'

Mrs Lobbet's voice trembled and she broke off, fighting with her tears.

'I'm alone,' she said. 'I daren't trust anyone. Even now I don't know about you. Forgive me, but you come to me out of the air with something that Janey had with her. How can I trust you? I oughtn't to talk. Oh, my God, I oughtn't to talk!'

'Wait a minute,' said Lance, who was still puzzled. 'What was a child of six doing with a lipstick?'

In spite of her anxiety a faint smile passed over Fran Lobbet's beautiful face.

'It belonged to her doll,' she said. 'Janey has a very grand French doll with a green belt, and on the boat, when they were giving away those little samples, she got hold of one because it was a doll's size. I tied it on to the belt for her with a piece of green thread. That's how I recognised it. Look, the thread's still there.'

'I see. And when she was too scared to shout she used it to write her name on the door. She's a clever kid for six.' Lance's black eyes had grown bleak. 'They're swine,' he said softly. 'They deserve what's coming to them. Now look here, Mrs Lobbet, you've got to allow us to manage this. We'll get her back, I promise you. We'll get her back safely if it's the last thing we do. You can rely on us.'

Campion did not echo the impulsive promise. Long experience of criminals had made him cautious. But there was a rare spark of anger in the shadows behind his eyes.

'Suppose you tell us about this latest demand,' he said quietly.

Mrs Lobbet glanced from one to the other of the two men. She seemed pathetically young and tragic and, to Lance at any rate, one of the loveliest women he had ever seen.

'It's so impressed on us back home that complete silence is the only hope,' she said, 'but I can't help it. They've lied to me once and they may go on doing it. I feel I'm taking her life in my hands, but I'll tell you, and please God I'm doing the right thing. This is what they've told me to do.'

As Campion listened to the instructions his opinion of the organising powers of the gang increased. It was a pretty little plan, evidently devised by someone with a proper appreciation of English laws and police procedure. Janey's captors required her mother to attend Thursday's Oxborough meeting alone. She was to seek out a bookie called Fred Fitz, whose stand would be among the others, but she was not to speak to him until the second race was actually being run. Then she was to walk over and place two thousand pounds in one-pound notes on *Flyaway* to win the two-thirty.

The simplicity of the scheme was exquisite. Here was no clumsy passing of notes in narrow lanes, no leaving of mysterious boxes on churchyard walls. A bookmaker is the only man on earth who can receive large sums of money for nothing from perfect strangers in the open light of day without occasioning suspicion or even interest. Moreover, in the event of a police trap what man could have a better story? Any tale which she might tell about mysterious telephone messages could always come as a complete surprise to him, and who could argue? No charge could be preferred against him, for he had done nothing to offend.

'I've got the money ready and I shall do exactly what they say.' The girl spoke stiffly, as if her lips were set. 'You mustn't come with me. I mustn't jeopardise her chances in any way. I daren't. I just daren't.'

'Mrs Lobbet is right,' said Campion hastily before Lance could interrupt. 'For her own peace of mind she must keep her bargain with the crooks. She must go to the meeting and pay the ransom money alone.'

'But we shall be there,' Lance insisted.

Campion cocked an eye at him. 'Oh, dear me, yes,' he said and his precise voice was almost caressing. 'We shall be there.'

THEY WERE THERE. Lance Feering in chauffeur's uniform drove Fran Lobbet to the meeting in his own car.

Campion went racing alone. Apart from an hour's intensive telephoning in the morning, his day might have borne the scrutiny of the most suspicious of shadowing crooks. He had an early lunch at the celebrated White Hart Hotel in Oxborough Wool Market and drove gently down to the car park as though he had no care in the world. He watched the first race from the stand, won a little money, and afterwards wandered down to the bookies' ring to collect it and place another trifling stake.

He did not bet with Fred Fitz. Indeed, he scarcely looked at the wizened little man who was shouting so lustily. He did not recognise his face and did not expect to. The morning's careful inquiries had identified him as a small man of no reputation, nor of sufficient importance to be of any great interest to the police. After discussing him on the telephone with Superintendent Stanislaus Oates of Scotland Yard, Campion had been moved once more to admire the organising abilities of the men who had engineered the kidnapping of the little American girl. Fitz was one of those men who float round the edge of the underworld, doing odd jobs for larger and more whole-hearted crooks. Since nothing definite was known against him the police were bound to treat him as an honest man, whatever their private opinions might be.

The man who was acting as his clerk, however, was a different person altogether. As soon as Campion set eyes upon that sharp white face his own expression became an amiable blank and he never glanced again in his direction. There was no mistaking Fingers Hawkins. Once seen never forgotten, and Campion had not only seen but had dealt before with that little crook, whose reputation was not admired even by his own kind.

He returned to the stand in thoughtful mood. If Fingers was a typical member of the gang with whom he had to deal, things could hardly be more unpromising.

He took up his position and reviewed the scene through his glasses. The meeting was not a very popular one and the crowds were not enormous, although there were enough people to make the gathering interesting. The racecourse is just outside the town, which lies in a hollow, and beyond the red rooftops the rolling green hills, dotted with country houses, rise up to the sky-line. It was a sunny day, and as Campion's powerful glasses swept the country they brought him little intimate glimpses of manors and farms and villas nestling in their surrounding greenery. He spent some time apparently lost in the beauties of the scene, and dragged his attention back to the course almost with reluctance.

Just before the second race started, when the stand was full and the crowd was moving steadily towards the rails, he caught sight of Fran Lobbet. She was wearing the red hat on which they had agreed, and was quite alone, he was relieved to notice. Through his glasses he watched her edging her way towards the ring, clutching an enormous white handbag with both hands. She made a very small and pathetic figure in her loneliness, and his indignation rose to boiling-point. He did not notice the horses coming up to the start, and it was not until the roar from the crowd told him that they were off that he was ever aware of their existence.

As the crowd swept past Fran in a last-minute rush, the bookies and their stands were temporarily deserted, and Campion saw her walk resolutely forward. His glasses left the girl and focused upon the ignoble features of Fingers Hawkins. The little crook appeared to be employed in something which looked at first like amateur tic-tac work. His arms rose above his head and dropped again. Then Fran came into the circle. A package passed and she received her slip. Still Campion did not follow her. Fingers made his entry and then, stepping up on the box, raised his arms once again. Afterwards he too raised glasses and looked steadfastly out across the course.

Campion remained where he was for a few seconds and for a while appeared to watch the race, but he did not stay to see the finish. At the very moment when the horses passed the post he was forcing his way out through the excited throng, and two minutes later climbed into a solid-looking black car containing five expressionless men, all of whom appeared to favour the same particular type of nondescript raincoat.

'Over there, on the brown hill,' he said briefly to the man at the wheel. 'A modern white villa with a flat roof. Take the London road and branch off by a church with a spire.'

THE SHORT FAT MAN with the American accent, who was known to the Federal Police as Louis Greener, was still standing on the flat roof of the white villa, his glasses trained on the racecourse which lay, a patterned ribbon of colour, in the valley below him, when one police car, followed by another, swung quietly up the steep drive and debouched its swarming cargo before it reached a standstill.

Mr Greener was engrossed in his vigil and was not disturbed from it until a shout from the room below him, followed by a volley of revolver shots, brought him back to present emergencies with a rush. He dropped his glasses and fled to the stairhead just as a lean figure appeared through the hatchway, an automatic in its hand.

'I should come very quietly if I were you,' said Campion.

Twenty minutes later the villa was calm and peaceful again, and the drive was empty. Fingers Hawkins drove up in a small car, a tremendous smile on his unbeautiful face, and a suspicious bulkiness about his coat pockets. He was not alone. Two men accompanied him, each betraying a certain careful solicitude for his safety which could hardly be accounted for by mere affection. Fingers was jaunty. He sounded the horn two or three times.

'You come be'ind me,' he said to his bodyguard. 'I deserve a committee of welcome for this lot. Now let's see how his American Nibs treats a bloke who's done 'alf his work for him.'

He strolled up to the front door and kicked it open.

'Anyone at 'ome?' he shouted as he passed into the hall. 'No 'anging about, if you please. Oi! Shop!'

His companions followed him, and as soon as they came into the hall the door closed quietly behind them. The little click which the latch made as it shot home brought them all round, the hair bristling on their necks. There was a moment of uncomfortable silence and the police closed in on them.

Meanwhile, in a private sitting-room at the White Hart, Fran Lobbet sat in an arm-chair clasping a grubby little bundle, while tears of pure relief streamed down her face. From the other side of the room Lance Feering beamed at her.

'She's all right,' he said. 'I believe she enjoyed it.'

'No, I didn't.' Janey Lobbet's bright eyes peered at him from a tangle of hair. 'Sometimes I was frightened. After Nurse left me I was frightened.'

'But you're not frightened now, are you, darling?' Fran put the question anxiously and the child chuckled.

'No,' she said. 'Not now. I'm *tough*.'

They laughed and Fran smiled at the man.

'I'll never be able to thank you.'

'Don't thank me. Campion worked the oracle.' Feering nodded towards the fourth occupant of the room, who sat on the edge of a table, an expression of mild satisfaction on his thin face. 'I don't see now how you spotted the house. What was it? Second sight?'

'In a way, yes. I did it with my little binoculars,' said Campion modestly. 'Fingers takes full credit for the rest. As soon as I saw his little weasel snout quivering pinkly through the undergrowth I thought, "Hullo, my lad, you're not handling two thousand pounds of anybody's money without a pretty close watch being kept on you, I'll bet." I saw he had two attendants in the background, but neither of them looked exactly like the foreman of the sort of outfit we had been led to expect. I was completely in the dark until I noticed Fingers signal to someone apparently in the middle of the course. Then he put his glasses up and I saw he wasn't watching the race. Since he was taking a longer view, naturally I did the same myself and caught sight of a person whom I now know to be a most unpleasant bird called Louis Greener, standing on a flat roof and waving his arms about in reply.

'That was really quite enough in the circumstances. The police were waiting, as they had promised, so off we went and there was the gang and there was Janey. She and I came away and we left the boys waiting for Fingers and the loot. There should be a happy family party down at the police station by this time.'

His voice died away. Neither Fran nor Lance was listening to him. He watched them for some seconds, but they appeared to be having a satisfactory, if wordless, conversation of their own, so presently he wandered off to find the Inspector in charge of the raid. That good-tempered man was comforting.

'Fingers has been talking about you, sir,' he said cheerfully as Campion appeared. 'I've had it all took down. I'm thinking you might like a copy. Coming from him it's a regular testimonial. If it wasn't so highly coloured that some might think it vulgar, you could almost have it framed.'

H. C. Bailey
1878–1961

THE LITTLE HOUSE

MRS PEMBERTON always calls it providential. She is not the only one. But when he hears her say so Mr Fortune looks at her with a certain envy. It is one of the few cases which have frightened him.

The hand of providence, Mrs Pemberton is convinced, sent her to Mr Fortune: and she only just caught him. He was, with reluctance, leaving his fire to go to Scotland Yard about the man who died in Kensington Gardens when her card was brought to him. 'I was to tell you Mrs Warnham sent her, sir,' the parlourmaid explained.

Mr Fortune went down to receive a little old lady dressed like Queen Victoria. She had a rosy round face and a lot of white hair. Her manner was not royal but very feminine. 'Mr Fortune! How good of you to help me! Mrs Warnham said you would.' She clasped his hands. 'You were so beautiful with her.'

'Mrs Warnham is too kind—'

'You saved her dear boy's life.'

'I hope it's nothing like that,' said Mr Fortune anxiously.

Mrs Pemberton wiped her eyes and the white lilac on her black bonnet shook. 'No, indeed. My darling Vivian is quite well. But she has lost her kitten, Mr Fortune!'

Mr Fortune controlled his emotions. 'I'm so sorry. I'm afraid kittens aren't much in my way.'

Her nice face looked distress. 'I know. That's what I said to Mrs Warnham. I told her you wouldn't want to be bothered with it, you would only laugh at me, like the police.'

'But I'm not laughing,' said Reggie.

'Please don't.' Her nice voice was anxious. 'She said I was to go and tell you I was really troubled and you would listen.'

'She was quite right.'

'I'm dreadfully troubled.' She wrung her little hands. 'You see, it's the strange way it went and the people next door are so peculiar and I know the police don't take it seriously. The officer was quite civil and attentive, but he smiled, you know, Mr Fortune, he just smiled at me.'

'I know,' said Reggie. 'They do smile. I've felt it myself.'

'Don't they,' Mrs Pemberton sighed. 'Mrs Warnham said you would understand.'

'Yes. Yes. She's very kind. Perhaps if you began at the beginning.'

Mrs Pemberton had difficulty over that. Her nice mind worked on the theory that everybody knew all about her. The facts when patiently extracted and put in order by Reggie took this shape. She was a widow, her only son was a general commanding in India. She lived in Elector's Gate, one of those streets of big Victorian houses by the park. Her granddaughter Vivian, aged six, had lately come to live with her and brought a grey Persian kitten. With care and pains a garden had been persuaded to bloom behind the house. There Vivian and her kitten were playing when the kitten went over the wall. Vivian scrambled up high enough to look over and saw it in the paved yard of the house next door, saw a little girl run out of that house, snatch up the kitten and run in again. Vivian called to her and was not answered. Vivian came weeping to Mrs Pemberton. Mrs Pemberton put on her bonnet and called at the house next door. She was told that nobody had been out at the back, no kitten had come in, they had no kitten, her granddaughter must have made a mistake. They were not at all nice about it.

'Who are they?' said Reggie.

It was Miss Cabot. Miss Cabot and her father lived there. She did not really know them, only to bow to. But they had been there quite a long while, a dozen years or more, very quiet people, perfect neighbours, never the least trouble till this dreadful thing. But of course Mrs Pemberton couldn't let them take Vivian's kitten. She went to the police station and complained. And the police wouldn't take it seriously at all.

Mr Fortune, with her innocent blue eyes upon him, contrived to do that. It has been remarked by the envious that he has great success with old ladies. Mrs Pemberton went away murmuring that he had been so kind. He was left wondering how long she would think so. It did not seem to him a case over which the police would be persuaded to lose much sleep. But it had points which occupied his mind as he drove down to Scotland Yard.

He was late for his appointment. 'Ye gentlemen of England who sit at home at ease!' the Chief of the Criminal Investigation Department rebuked him. 'This luncheon habit is growing on you, Fortune!' He pointed an accusing finger at Reggie's girth.

'It wasn't lunch,' said Reggie with indignation. 'I've had a most difficult and interestin' case.'

Lomas sat up. 'Difficult, was it? Come along then. Avery's full of ideas about it. What was the cause of death?'

Reggie stared at him. Reggie looked at Inspector Avery and murmured: 'How are you?' Reggie stared again at Lomas. 'Cause of death? Oh, ah. You mean the man found in Kensington Gardens.'

'That is what I'm talking about,' said Lomas with some bitterness. 'That happens to be what we're here for.'

'Nothing in it. He died from exposure.'

'Exposure, sir?' Inspector Avery was disappointed. 'Just being out on a spring night?'

'Takin' the winds of March,' Reggie shrugged. 'He wasn't a good life. Badly nourished. Rotten heart. Nothing much good about him. Drug habits—and other errors. Who was he?'

'In the foreign restaurant business, sir. Lots of money. Quite a big man in his own line. Why he should go and lie down in the gardens to die beats me.'

Reggie shrugged again. 'He just got there and got no farther. No vitality in him. He'd go out at a breath.'

'You said something about drugs, sir?'

'Oh, he wasn't drugged when he died. Probably he had run out of his dope and life wasn't worth living. And the night frost finished him.'

Lomas lay back. 'That clears him up, Avery. You can go home to tea.'

But Inspector Avery was not satisfied. 'Mr Fortune was worried about something, sir?'

'Yes, yes. Most interesting case. Is Elector's Gate in your division?'

'That's right, sir.'

'What do you know about Mrs Pemberton's Persian kitten?'

Lomas put up his eyeglass. 'My dear fellow!' he protested.

Inspector Avery also felt a shock to his dignity. 'They don't come to me about kittens, sir.'

'They come to me,' said Reggie sadly. 'It wasn't you that smiled, then?'

'Sir?'

'Mrs Pemberton says she went to the station and they only smiled. Quite sweet but smiling. It hurts her.'

'I do remember hearing talk of it,' Inspector Avery admitted. 'The lady was so pathetic. But they did the usual, sir, sent a sergeant round to the house where the kitten was supposed to have gone in. The lady there said they hadn't got it. Her little niece did try to catch it, but it got away. We couldn't do any more.'

Reggie lit a cigar. '"Her little niece did try to catch it,"' he repeated slowly. 'Now that's very interesting.' He gazed at the puzzled inspector through smoke.

'It might be if I knew anything about it,' Lomas grumbled. 'Why this devotion to kittens, Reginald?'

So Reggie told him the story Mrs Pemberton had told.

'Very, very sad,' Lomas sighed. 'But kittens will be cats. What do you want me to do? Leave a card with deep sympathy and regret?'

Reggie shook his head. 'Not one of our good listeners,' he said sadly. 'Didn't you notice anything? You're not taking this seriously, Lomas. When Mrs Pemberton called about the kitten, Miss Cabot said no one had been out at the back. When the police called, she said her little niece did try to catch it.'

Lomas put up his eyeglass. 'Aha! The case looks black indeed!' said he. 'Miss Cabot didn't know about the little niece at first and found out afterwards. A deep, dark woman, Fortune,' and he smiled.

'Yes. A facetious force, the police force.' Reggie nodded. 'That's what annoyed

Mrs Pemberton. And now do you mind thinking? A dear old lady calls very distressed and says Miss Cabot's little girl has caught her kitten and Miss Cabot says there wasn't any little girl and bundles her out. Why so curt? Because there was a little girl and there was a kitten.' He turned on Inspector Avery. 'Did your sergeant see the little girl?'

'No, sir. No occasion. He saw Miss Cabot, who was quite definite the kitten got away.'

'Yes. Marked anxiety to know nothing about the kitten. Elusive little girl.'

'My dear Reginald!' Lomas protested. 'There're a dozen obvious explanations. The woman doesn't like cats. The little girl is a naughty little girl. The woman doesn't want to be bothered.'

'No. She doesn't want to be bothered. That's what struck me.'

'I fear your dear Mrs Pemberton is a little fussy, Reginald.'

'That isn't your complaint, Lomas,' Reggie said sharply. 'Well, well. Sorry I don't interest you.' He nodded to Avery and went out.

Avery looked at Lomas with some concern. 'That's all right,' Lomas laughed. 'Wonderful fellow. But he will see things that aren't there.'

'I wish he'd been more interested in that death in the Gardens,' said Avery sadly.

'Too ordinary, my dear fellow, too ordinary for Mr Fortune.'

'This kitten business rather put me off.' Avery was thoughtful. 'I suppose we did ought to have seen the little girl.'

'Good gad!' said Lomas. 'You run along home and have a nice quiet night. I don't want my inspectors seeing things.'

But Inspector Avery did not go home. He had a conscience. He went back to the police station of his division. Mr Fortune is not at Scotland Yard thought to resemble the prim little inspector. But he also has an active conscience. He went to Elector's Gate.

It is maintained by Superintendent Bell and others of his devoted admirers that he has a queer power of divining the people behind facts, a sort of sixth sense. At this he would jeer. His own account of himself is that he is so ordinary anything which isn't ordinary disturbs him. From the first he felt the vanishing of the kitten was queer. But the only credit he takes for the case, which they call one of his best, is that he brought to it a perfectly open mind. The rest was merely obedience to the rule of scientific inquiry, that one ought to try everything.

What there was to try in Elector's Gate, he had no notion. He left his car by the park and strolled down that majestically Victorian street. The range of stucco fronts was broken on one side by an opening which led to a dead wall. In this recess two little red-brick houses faced each other, neat and prim, hiding behind the solemn mansions of the rest of Elector's Gate. At one corner of the opening stood Mrs Pemberton's house. Then Miss Cabot's next door—Miss Cabot's was that little house behind it in the recess. Reggie rubbed his chin. So

Miss Cabot did not live in the way suggested by an address in Elector's Gate. Quite a small place, a one-or-two servant house. Nice and quiet too. No traffic. No neighbours on one side. Retiring folk, the Cabots.

Reggie rang Mrs Pemberton's bell. He had hardly been shown into her dowdy comfortable drawing-room when she hurried in crying: 'Dear Mr Fortune! But how good of you! Have you found out anything?'

'No. I came to see what I could find here.'

'Oh, but I'm so glad! Such a queer thing has happened. Let me show you.' She led him away into a little sitting-room and took from a drawer in the writing-table a piece of coarse blue paper. 'Look! When I came back from you that was lying in the garden.'

Reggie laid it on the table. It was a queer shape, it had a rough black line round the edges.

'You see! It's meant for a kitten!'

'Yes. It's meant for a kitten,' said Reggie gravely. 'Somebody drew a kitten on packing paper—with a piece of coal—and then tore the paper along the line—so as to make a paper kitten. Somebody who's not very old.' He shivered a little. 'Has your little granddaughter seen it?'

'No, Vivian was out when we found it. She has gone to a party. I was rather glad, you know. It seemed meant to tease her.'

Reggie folded the paper and put it in his pocket-book. His round face was pale and angry.

'Oh, did you want to talk to her about it?' Mrs Pemberton fluttered.

'I don't want anyone to talk to her about it.'

'I'm so glad. Vivian is only six, you see, and—'

'And nobody but Vivian has ever seen the little girl next door?'

'Why no. I never thought of it like that. No, indeed. We didn't know there was a little girl. Oh, but Mr Fortune, I'm sure there was if Vivian said so.'

'Did Vivian notice what she was like?'

'Poor child, she was so distressed,' Mrs Pemberton apologised for her. 'She said it was a nasty, dirty little girl. Children will talk like that, you know, when they're upset. It doesn't mean anything.'

Reggie did not answer. He walked to the window. Mrs Pemberton's garden was a pleasant place of crazy paving and rock plants. The little house next door had a bare, paved yard.

'Oh, wouldn't you like to go out?' Mrs Pemberton cried. 'I could show you just where the paper fell.'

'No, I won't go out.' Reggie turned away. 'Good-bye, Mrs Pemberton. Don't let anyone talk to anybody. Don't let anybody know who I am. Don't let Vivian think about the business.'

'Mr Fortune! You mean there's something dreadful?'

'The worst of it for Vivian is that she's lost a kitten. There's nothing else to trouble you.'

'But you're troubled about something.'

'Yes, that's what I'm for,' said Mr Fortune. 'Good-bye.'

It was an hour which Lomas is wont to give to his club. He was before the smoking-room fire, he was pronouncing the doom of the last new play, when Reggie looked round the door, caught his eye and vanished. Lomas went after him at leisure. He was in the hall, tapping an impatient foot. 'My dear fellow, what's the matter? Has the kitten had foul play?'

'Come on,' said Reggie.

Lomas came on with his usual studied jauntiness, to be thrust into a car and driven away at Reggie's side. 'Why this stealthy haste, Reginald?' he protested. 'Why thus abduct my blameless youth? Miserable man, where are you taking me?'

Mr Fortune·was not amused. 'We're going to Avery's damned police station,' he said. He spread out on his knee the blue paper. 'That's why.'

'Good gad!' Lomas groaned. 'A kitten! An infant's effort at creating a kitten. Oh, my dear Reginald!'

'Yes. An infant's effort at creating a kitten,' Reggie repeated. 'Exactly that. That's what frightened me. It was flung over into Mrs Pemberton's garden this afternoon.'

'Tut, tut. Not quite nice. Designed, I fear, to harrow the feelings of the bereaved.'

Reggie drew a long breath. 'Do you mind not being funny?' he said in a low voice. 'I'm scared.'

'My dear fellow! Oh, my dear fellow! What on earth for?'

'For the child who made that.' Reggie put it away again. 'My God, don't you feel it? There's something devilish in that little house.'

Lomas was shaken. Strong language is very rare on the lips of Reggie Fortune. 'I can't say I feel anything,' he said slowly. 'What do you want to do?'

'See Avery about the people. Here we are.'

Inspector Avery was still at the station. Inspector Avery showed no surprise at seeing them. 'I told you to go home, young fellow,' said Lomas.

'Yes, sir. I know. I was a bit worried about that kitten case.'

'Oh, you were, were you? Mr Fortune's got it very bad.'

Avery's keen face turned to Reggie. 'About the little girl, sir?' he said eagerly.

'Yes, yes. What do you know about the little girl?'

'Nobody knows anything. That's just it. It don't look right to my mind.'

'No. It isn't right,' said Reggie. 'Send two men to watch the house.'

'I've put one there, sir.'

'The deuce you have!' Lomas exclaimed.

'Good. But we'll have two, please. One to follow if the child's taken away. One to stand by whatever happens. The constable on the beat must keep in touch with them.'

'Right, sir. Just a moment.' Avery went out with visible satisfaction to give the orders.

'You won't mind me, will you?' said the Chief of the Criminal Investigation

Department with some bitterness. 'But aren't you going rather fast, Fortune?'

'No. We're going far too slow.'

'I can't let you commit the police to anything, you know.'

'I know. You like a crime finished before you begin. Mr Lomas, his theory of police work. Well, I've committed you to watching a suspected house. Ever heard of that being done before?'

Lomas, however, kept his temper. 'You can have it watched, if it amuses you. But there's no reasonable ground for suspicion.'

'Oh my aunt!' Reggie murmured.

Avery bustled in. 'I've got that done, sir. Now is there anything else?'

'Yes, I'm not satisfied there's anything in it,' said Lomas sharply. 'What have you got against these people, Avery?'

'Mr Lomas touches the spot.' Reggie nodded. 'Who are these people, Avery?'

'Ah, that's what I'd like to know,' said Inspector Avery with relish. 'Very retiring people, sir. Kind of secluded.'

'Retiring be hanged,' Lomas cried. 'You've nothing against them but this stuff about a kitten and a girl.'

'Pretty queer stuff, isn't it, sir? Girl is seen taking a kitten, owner of the kitten is told nobody there saw it, we're told the girl did see it, like I said. But there's more to it than that. Nobody round there knew there was a little girl in that house, nobody's ever seen her, nobody's heard of her.'

'Why should they?'

'Ever lived next door to a house with a child, Lomas?' said Reggie wearily. 'You notice it. But Mrs Pemberton lives next door and she didn't know there was a child in that house.'

'Nobody knew. They won't hardly believe it,' said Avery.

'How the deuce can you tell?'

Avery smiled. 'The men get to know the servants in their beats, sir. I've had some inquiries made. That house, there's Miss Cabot, handsome lady not so young as she was, and her father and an old married couple o' servants very stand-offish. Been there a dozen years, living very quiet, never any guests and as for a child— well, the servants in Elector's Gate laugh at it. If there is a child, they keep her in the cupboard, one of 'em said. But there is, Miss Cabot owned up to her.'

'There was a child,' said Reggie gravely, and took out the blue paper kitten.

Inspector Avery gasped at it. 'Kind of uncanny, sir.' He puzzled over it. 'I don't know what to make of it, sir.'

'There was a child in that little house wanted to create a kitten. She only had packing paper, she only had a bit of coal to draw with, she had no scissors to cut it out. This was the best she could do. She wanted to tell that other child next door something about her kitten. She threw this over the wall.'

'I don't like it, sir.'

'What's it all come to?' Lomas cried. 'There's a lonely child playing tricks.'

Reggie turned on him. 'There's a child in that little house living a queer life.

And the only paper she can get hold of came off a parcel. It happened to be a parcel of scientific apparatus.'

'Are you sure about that, sir?' Avery cried eagerly.

'This is the sort of stuff they always use for glass.' Reggie fingered it. 'Look at the scrap of a label : "ette & Co." That's Burette's. First-class firm. What are the Cabots doing in that little house that they want glass from Burette's and keep a child shut up and squalid and miserable?'

'Squalid?' Lomas took up the word.

'The Pemberton child saw her. She was dirty.'

'The house is kept as clean as a pin, they say,' Avery frowned.

'Yes. Quite clean. And the hidden child is nasty and dirty.'

'And they're at some scientific work. Do you think they're doing experiments on the child, sir?'

'I don't know. I don't know anything. But I'm frightened.'

'We've got 'em all right, whatever their game is,' Avery said fiercely.

'And the child?' Reggie murmured.

Lomas stood up. 'You win,' he said. 'Sorry, Reginald. My error. Well, I haven't wasted much time. We'll go through with it now. First points to work on, who are the Cabots and what is it that Burette's send them? They're to be watched wherever they go, Avery—and their servants. I'll put Bell on to the case to-night. Report to him. We can deal with Burette's in half an hour in the morning. Anything else, Reginald?'

'Yes. You might find out if anybody lost a little girl some time ago.'

Lomas shrugged. 'We can look up the records. Rather an off-chance, isn't it? Whoever she is, they'd get hold of her quietly, these quiet people.'

'Oh, it isn't ordinary kidnapping,' Reggie said wearily. 'I say, Avery, for God's sake don't let the Cabots know they're being watched. They might do the child in to-night.'

'Good Lord, sir! No, I don't think it. If they know they're watched they'd know they couldn't get away with a murder.'

'We might not be able to prove murder. He's a man of science, Mr Cabot is. Warn your men to be careful.'

'We can't have a search-warrant on this evidence,' Lomas frowned. 'We can't do anything to-night. Begad, I'll have somebody get into the house in the morning.'

'Yes, I'm going,' said Reggie.

'My dear fellow!'

'You want a doctor to see that child.'

That night lives in the memory of Mr Fortune. He could not sleep. It is a condition otherwise unknown to him. He drove early to Scotland Yard and found Superintendent Bell fresh and hearty from a night watch.

'You've got something, Mr Fortune. They're queer folk, these Cabots. Where do you think they went last night? Night club, if you please. The Doodah Club. Yes, the old man and the woman living in that quiet style, they go off to the

Doodah which is about as hot as we've got. Well, as soon as I heard they were there, I sent round one of the night club experts. He knew the Cabots by sight right enough. They're pretty regular at the Doodah. He made out that Cabot is known there as Smithson and runs some sort of an accountant's business in Soho. Nothing on our books against him. But we're looking into Smithson & Co., of course.'

'Yes. Have you found anything about a lost child?'

Bell shook his head. 'We've got no record of any to fit this little girl. Not many children get lost nowadays. I'm still looking about. But it's a bit of a long shot, sir.'

'I know. And Burette's?'

'Harland's on that, sir. We'll know all about their end of the business before lunch.'

'Now who's going with me to the house? I want some fellow with a nerve and lots of chat.'

Superintendent Bell looked at him with solicitude. 'Are you set on going yourself, sir? If you don't mind my saying so—'

'I do,' Reggie smiled.

'Well, I knew you would,' Bell sighed. 'You can't do better than Avery, sir. He's a little bull-terrier.'

'Yes. I thought that myself. But is he chatty?'

'He can keep it up. He's a politician.'

'Oh my aunt!' said Reggie.

Some time later two men in the uniform of the inspectors of the Metropolitan Water Board strolled into Elector's Gate. A street sweeper asked one of them for a match and over his cigarette remarked: 'All out but the woman servant. Cabot and Miss Cabot went off together. The manservant's gone to the pub.'

The water inspectors strolled on. 'That's a bit of luck, sir,' said Avery.

'No. That's Bell making a fuss down at Smithson & Co. I thought he would draw 'em. Your fellows said the manservant was in the pub till it closed. I thought he'd be on the doorstep when it opened—if master was out of the way. Now then. Lots of patter, please.'

Avery rang the tradesmen's bell of the little house. After some minutes the side door opened to display a gaunt woman in black who scowled. Avery was sorry to trouble her, but they were going over the water fittings. She objected. Avery was very sorry, regular inspection, must go through with it, the law was the law.

'Constable over there, mum, go and ask him if you like.' They were admitted. 'All the taps, please, then the run of the pipes, then the cistern. All fittings. Now then, where's the main?' He listened professionally. 'Ah, I thought so. Just have a look at the scullery, mate. Now, mum, upstairs if you please.' He swept her on before him, still talking about water and the law.

Reggie went into the kitchen, crossed to the scullery and turned on taps so that a noise of splashing water arose and came back to the kitchen. He called out, 'Taps running, mate,' and was answered: 'Right-o! Stand by the main,' and heard Avery in continuous eloquence and the servant grumbling. He went swiftly from room to room, such rooms as upholsterers furnish to their own taste, and saw no child's gear nor any mark that a child would make. He could hear Avery moving about upstairs arguing about the lead of pipes and having doors opened. Avery was not missing anything. 'Hallo, mate!' Avery called. 'Try the main tap. Now up to the cistern if you please, mum.' Talking, he climbed.

Reggie stood in the hall. There was a cupboard under the stairs. He opened that, saw darkness and in darkness the gleam of eyes. He went in. 'My dear,' he said gently. 'What's your name?'

There was no answer but panting breath.

He switched on an electric torch and saw a little girl cowering in the corner. Her face was pinched and dirty, she seemed to have no body so she was huddled shrinking from him.

'I'm friends,' said Reggie and reached for her hand. 'It's all right.' His fingers moved along the lean bare arm, about her neck. 'Where's the kitten?'

Her face shook. 'It died. It did. It's in the dust,' she gasped.

'I'm friends,' Reggie said again. 'Wait: just wait. It's all right.'

He shut off the torch and slipped out of the cupboard. The feet of Avery were heavy on the stair.

'I say, mate. Waste pipes at the back,' Reggie called.

'Have a look at 'em, Bill. Have a look at 'em,' said Avery and held the gaunt woman in conversation in the hall.

Reggie went out to the paved yard. While he watched the scullery window his arm slid into the dustbin and brought out a bass basket. He buttoned that into his jacket and came back calling, 'That's all right, mate. Shall I shut off the taps?'

'Shut 'em off, Bill. Come on. Good day, mum. Sorry to trouble you. Duty is duty.'

The gaunt woman grumbling about a lot of fuss and nonsense slammed the door on them.

A chauffeur came out of the bonnet of his car as they passed him.

'Watch it. Watch it,' Avery muttered and hurried on. It was hard work to keep up with Reggie.

He made for a post office and telling Avery to get a taxi shut himself into the telephone box. 'Superintendent Bell? Fortune speaking. What have you got about the Cabots? Somebody interviewing them at the Smithson & Co. Office? Let him keep 'em busy. Child in the house in danger of foul play. Yes. Death. Instant danger. I want a search-warrant quick. Right. At my house.' He joined Avery in the taxi and they drove away.

'No sign of the child, sir,' Avery began. 'But there was—'

'I saw the child,' said Reggie. 'She's still alive. I got the kitten too. He isn't.' The bass basket was produced and from it the stiff cold body of a Persian kitten.

'Dead, eh? Looks all right too. Did it die natural, sir?'

Reggie pointed to the eyes. 'No. Not natural. There isn't much natural in that house.' He shivered.

'What did they want to kill it for?'

'What do they want to keep the child in a dark cupboard for?'

'Had her there when we came, I reckon.'

'Yes. She's out sometimes. But she's used to the dark.'

'The devils,' said Avery heartily. 'But what is the game, sir? Scientific experiments? There was a room I couldn't get into. The woman said the master had the key. But I made out it had water laid on.'

'Yes. Laboratories have.' The taxi turned into Wimpole Street and stopped. 'You go on to the Yard and see Bell. I've got to look into the kitten.' But he went first to the telephone and talked to his hospital and asked for a certain nurse.

He was in his own clothes again, he was eating lunch without appetite when Bell came. 'Got the warrant?' He started up. 'Good. Where are the Cabots?'

'I couldn't say for the moment, sir. Our fellows had orders to keep 'em talking as long as they could. But there wasn't anything much to go on. That business looks all right. They do accountants' work for the foreign restaurants.'

'The man who died in Kensington Gardens,' Reggie murmured.

'Good Lord, sir!' Bell stared. 'He was in the restaurant trade, sure enough. And he was a drug fiend, you said.'

'Come on, come on. I want to get back to that child before the Cabots.'

But as soon as the car was moving Bell returned to his point. 'About the drugs, sir. What did you make of the house this morning? Avery said there was a room might be a laboratory. Burette's say they've been supplying Mr Cabot with laboratory glass ware for years.'

'Yes. I think we shall find a laboratory. The kitten has been drugged. The little girl has been drugged.'

'What's their game, sir? Some kind of scientific experiments with drugs?'

Reggie shuddered. 'They've been making experiments. Not for science. For the devil. They killed the kitten because she liked it. And she made her paper kitten to tell the other little girl it was gone. Silly, isn't it?' He laughed nervously. 'This car's damned slow, Bell.'

'We're almost there, sir.'

'Almost! Nice word, almost! My God!'

'Steady, sir, steady.' Bell laid an anxious hand on his arm. 'I want you, you know. I'll ask for the child first.'

The car swung into Elector's Gate and stopped just short of the recess in which the little house stood. As Bell sprang out a large man on the pavement met him. 'Both of 'em drove straight here from the office, sir. Only just gone in.'

Bell strode on to the house and rang and rang again. It was some while before the door moved. Then it opened only a little way and a man's flabby face with watery eyes looked round it.

'I am a police officer. I have a warrant to enter this house.' Bell pushed the door back and went in with Reggie and on their heels two large men followed. Silent and adroit they took the manservant and put him into the street where careful hands received him, and shut the door.

Bell stood still in the hall listening. There was a murmur of voices in one of the rooms. Its door opened. The gaunt woman came out. 'Well?' she said defiantly. 'Who may you be?'

The large men swept her aside. Bell and Reggie went into the room.

Two people were in it. A plump old man, neatly professional in his clothes, with a large brown face under his white hair, the face of a clever fellow who enjoyed his life, a woman darker than he, black-haired, black-browed, a woman on a large scale who might have been handsome before she was full-blown. She looked at them with gleaming eyes, and the lines were deep about her big mouth. She laughed, a shrill sound that began suddenly and suddenly ended.

'What is all this, gentlemen?' the man said.

'Mr and Miss Cabot, alias Smithson?' Bell inquired.

'My name is Cabot and this is my daughter. The name of my firm is Smithson & Co. But you have the advantage of me.'

'I am Superintendent Bell. I have a warrant to search your house.'

'Very good of the police to take this interest in me. May I ask why?'

'I want the child you have here.'

Mr Cabot looked at his daughter. 'Oh, our poor little darling,' he said slowly.

'What's her name?' Bell snapped.

'I beg your pardon?' Mr Cabot suddenly became aware of him. 'Her name? Why Grace of course.'

'Grace of course?'

'Grace Cabot, sir. I see that you don't know our family tragedy. My poor son's child is mentally defective. Practically imbecile. It has—'

'Since she came here or before?'

Mr Cabot licked his lips. 'I see that you have picked up some scandal. She was—'

'Where is she?'

'Oh, I'll find her for you,' Miss Cabot cried.

But Reggie was at the door first. He went before her into the hall. Miss Cabot followed him and calling 'Grace, Grace,' ran upstairs.

A moment he stood, then pointed and one of the large men went heavily after her. Reggie moved to the cupboard under the stairs and unlocked it and looked into the dark. 'I'm friends,' he said very gently. 'Come, dear. I'm friends.' And above Miss Cabot's shrill voice called 'Grace! Grace!'

He could see something faintly white. He heard a moan. 'It's all over now,' he said. 'All right now. Friends, just friends.'

'Grace! Grace!' the shrill voice came nearer.

'No, no, no,' the child sobbed in the dark.

Reggie went in, groped for her and gathered her into his arms. She was very frail. 'My dear,' he whispered. She was carried out into the light, shaking, trying to hide into her dirty dress.

Miss Cabot ran down the stairs. 'So you've found the dear creature!' she cried. Her arms shot out.

Reggie swung on his heel, offering her a solid shoulder. 'Hold her wrist,' he said.

The large man behind her had both arms in a grip that brought a scream out of her. A syringe fell tinkling to the floor. And Miss Cabot began to swear.

'Take the child out of this,' Reggie said fiercely. 'Take her to my place.' But she nestled up against him and moaned. 'All right. All right. Get the woman off.' Handcuffs snapped upon Miss Cabot's wrists while she bit and struggled and blasphemed. She was thrust out to the ready hands in the street.

'A beauty, she is,' one of the large men muttered.

And then silence came down upon the house. The child felt it, raised her wan starved face from Reggie's shoulder. 'Is she gone?' she murmured, looked about her, saw nothing but those solid, comfortable men and listened again to the silence. 'Weally, weally gone?'

'Really gone. She'll never hurt you any more,' Reggie said. 'There's only friends for you now. You're coming home with me. Nice home. But just wait a minute. This man will hold you quite safe.' He persuaded her to go to the arms of one of the detectives. 'Take her out into the air at the back. I shan't be long, dear.'

He picked up the syringe carefully, he turned into the room where Bell watched Cabot. The old man stood by the window looking out. His face was yellow. But he had control of his nerves and his voice. 'Perhaps you will tell me what all this means, superintendent?' he was saying.

'You'll hear what it means all right,' Bell growled.

'I see my daughter arrested—'

'Yes. She didn't like it, did she?' Reggie spoke to hurt.

The old man swung round. 'Who is this person, pray?'

'That's Mr Fortune.'

'Oh, the great Mr Fortune! Why trouble him with our poor affairs?'

'A pleasure,' said Reggie.

'So happy to interest you! And will you be good enough to tell me why you have arrested my daughter?'

'We've found a child in your house who has been tortured.'

'I suppose she told you so,' the old man chuckled. 'Good evidence you have found, Mr Fortune. The child's an imbecile.'

'We shan't use her evidence,' said Reggie. 'You won't torture her any more, Mr Cabot.'

The old man grinned. 'Is the child dead, sir?' Bell cried.

. Reggie did not answer for a moment. He was watching the old man's face. 'No,' he said slowly. 'Oh no. Miss Cabot tried to kill her just now. But it didn't happen.'

The old man was breathing hard. 'A poor story, isn't it?' he sneered. 'You won't make much of it in court, Mr Fortune. Is that all, pray?'

'No. I should like to see your laboratory.'

'My laboratory? Oh, that's too kind of you! A very humble little place where I play with chemical experiments. Do you really want to see it?'

'We're going to see it,' said Bell.

'But I shall be delighted to show you.'

Bell looked at Reggie who nodded. The old man went upstairs between them. He unlocked a door and they came into a room fitted with a long bench and shelves and sink and much chemical apparatus. Reggie moved to and fro looking at the array of bottles, opening cupboards. There were many things which interested him.

'Ah, do you like that?' The old man came forward as he lingered by an arrangement of flasks and glass tube. 'It's a method of my own.' He became technical, skilled fingers moved demonstrating. 'And here'—he turned away and opened a drawer and bent over it—'here you see—'

'Yes. I see,' said Reggie and caught the hand that was going to his mouth.

Bell took the old man in his solid grip. The hand was opened and produced a white pellet.

'Not that way, Mr Cabot,' said Reggie. 'Not yet.'

'You go where your daughter's gone,' said Bell and called to the detective in the hall.

'I shall have some things to think of, gentlemen,' the old man grinned as he was led away.

'You will. And plenty of time to think. In this world and the next,' said Bell fiercely.

The old man laughed.

Reggie and Bell looked at each other and Reggie shivered and 'Thank God,' he said. He went to the window and leaned out to see the child with the big detective in the free air below.

'What was it the old scoundrel was doing here, sir? Kind of vivisecting the child?'

'Oh no, no. The little girl was a side line. He was making narcotic drugs— dope. Very neat plant.'

'Turning out dope? He's been doing that for years?'

'Yes, yes. Prosperous industry.'

'But why the child? For testing the drugs?'

'No. He wouldn't need her for tests. No. They drugged her for fun. You haven't got to the child's story yet. Lots of work to do yet.'

'What did you want me to work on, sir?'

'Go over this place. Go over the Cabots' past. Go and look for somebody that's lost a child. Good-bye.'

The big detective in the yard, nursing the little girl with awkward gentleness, grinned embarrassment at Reggie. 'I'm not much of a hand at this, sir. But she don't seem to like me to put her down.'

'No. Nice to have somebody to hold on to, isn't it, shrimp?' Reggie touched her cheek. 'Come and hold on to me.' He held out his arms. For the first time he saw something like a smile on that pinched face. She swayed towards him. 'Come along. We're going to a pretty house and a kind jolly lady and everybody there is waiting to love you.'

She was wrapped in a rug in Superintendent Bell's car, she sat on Reggie's knee watching the trees in the park rush by, the busy, gay streets. Suddenly she clutched at him. 'Is it weal?' she cried. 'Weally weal?'

'Yes. It's all real now,' Reggie said and put his hand over hers. 'Jolly things, real things.'

When the car stopped at his house, his parlourmaid had the door open before he reached it and watched him carry the child in with benign amusement which yielded to pity. 'Shall I take her, sir?' she said eagerly.

'She's all right, thanks. Has Nurse Cary come?'

'Here I am, Mr Fortune,' a small buxom woman ran down the stairs. 'Well!' She looked at the child. 'I'm going to like you ever so much. Please like me.'

It was difficult not to like those pretty pink and white cheeks, that kind voice. Again something like a smile came on the pinched, wan face.

'Oh, my dear,' said Nurse Cary with tears in her voice and her eyes. She gave a glance at Mr Fortune.

'Yes, I know,' he said quickly.

'I'm going to make you so beautifully cosy,' said Nurse Cary. 'You just come and try.' She took the child to her comfortable bosom.

Upstairs in the bathroom filthy clothes were stripped from the starved little body. But it was marked with something worse than dirt, punctured marks on the arms and here and there a rash. Nurse Cary looked at Mr Fortune.

'Yes, I know,' he said softly. 'They've been giving her drugs.'

'But why?'

'For fun.'

'Devils,' said Nurse Cary under her breath.

'Yes. I think so,' said Mr Fortune. He was handling the filthy clothes. They had been good honest stuff once. He looked close, made out a bit of tape with a name in stitched letters—Rose Harford. He turned to the child lying in the steaming water, Nurse Cary's hands busy upon her. 'Well, isn't it jolly, Rose?'

'So you're Rose, are you?' Nurse Cary smiled. 'My little Rose.'

'Mummy's Wose,' the child murmured.

Mr Fortune went out. The telephone called to Scotland Yard. 'Is that Lomas? Fortune speaking. The child is Rose Harford. There's a mother—or was. Get on to it.'

THE SMALL ROSE in golden pyjamas was among many pillows watching Mr Fortune and Nurse Cary set out a farm on her bed. They were being very funny about the hens, but she did not laugh, she watched with grave, tranquil eyes and sometimes stroked her beautiful pyjamas. Mr Fortune was called away.

At Scotland Yard he found a conference, Lomas, Bell, Avery.

'My dear fellow! How's the patient?'

'She'll come through with luck. But it's a long job. They've made a vile mess of her.'

'Hanging's too good for that pair,' Bell sighed. 'And we can't even hang 'em.'

'No, no. I hope not. They'll feel what they get, quite a lot, the family Cabot.'

'They've done enough to be hanged more than once,' said Avery fiercely. 'You remember that fellow who died in Kensington Gardens, Mr Fortune? He used to get his drugs from Smithson & Co.'

'Yes. You were right about him, Avery. I ought to have seen there was something to work on there.'

Avery laughed. 'You're the one that's been right, sir. Do you remember how we made fun of you about the kitten? If you hadn't taken that up, the Cabots would be playing at hell now quite happy and comfortable.'

'Don't recall my awful past, Avery,' Lomas said. 'It's not respectful. My dear Reginald, you're a disturbing fellow. You're sapping the foundations of the criminal courts of this country.'

'No flowers, by request,' Reggie murmured.

'You don't work by evidence, like a reasonable man.'

'My only aunt!' Reggie was annoyed. 'I use nothing but evidence. That's why I don't get on with lawyers and policemen. I believe evidence, Lomas, old thing. That's what bothers you.'

'You do bother me. And now will you kindly tell me the whole history of the Cabot affair.'

'Quite clear, isn't it? Cabot was a skilled chemist. The trouble in the dope trade is always to get supplies. He solved that by getting raw materials and making the stuff. He found his customers at the night clubs and the restaurants he was in touch with through the Smithson & Co. accountant business. He distributed probably by post from Smithson & Co.'

'That's right, sir,' Bell nodded. 'We've got on the track of that now. Big trade he did. Lots of poor fools he must have sent to the devil.'

'Very neat, Reginald,' Lomas smiled. 'You omit to explain the little girl.'

'Oh, that's revenge. Revenge on somebody. Probably her father and mother.'

'Did you get that out of the child?' said Lomas quickly.

'No. The child mustn't be asked anything about the past. Haven't you got that clear? No evidence from her. She mustn't come into court.'

'My dear fellow, we don't want her. There's two of you to swear to attempted murder and your medical evidence. That's all right. I only wanted to know how you arrived at the mother.'

'Have you found her at last?'

'Three months ago George and Rose Harford were convicted of dealing in drugs. The man is a young accountant, the woman an actress. They lived in a Bloomsbury flat and often went to one of the Soho restaurants. A waiter there gave information that the woman had been offering drugs. They were arrested. Dope was found in the pockets of the man's coat and the woman's cloak. More dope in their flat. A clear case and they were both convicted. Some time after they were in prison the woman complained that she had heard nothing of her daughter, whom another actress in the flats had promised to look after. Well, the prison people had inquiries made for her. It took time. The actress had gone on tour. When they found her, her story was that Mrs Harford's sister had called and taken the child away. The prison authorities told Mrs Harford and she said she had no sister extant. So at last it worked round to us.'

'Yes. At last. And you've had the mother in jail three months—wondering.'

'Wondering if there was a God,' said Bell solemnly.

'Well—it's a black business,' Lomas shrugged. 'See your way, Reginald?'

'Oh, I suppose the Cabot woman wanted George Harford herself. When he married, she looked for a chance to make the wife suffer. She bided her time. And sent father and mother to prison and took the child and tortured her. Patient woman.'

'The Harfords have been out of England. The man had a job for his firm in France. They hadn't been back long before this happened to them.'

'What evidence have you got?'

'That drunken dog of a manservant wants to turn King's evidence. He says he was under the thumb of his wife—'

'I dare say he was. Have you seen her? Born brute.'

'His story is that his wife was turned on to plant the dope in the Harford flat. The waiter put the stuff in their coat pockets while they were at dinner. We can't lay our hands on the waiter. Several people have vanished since the Cabots were taken. George Harford says he knew Miss Cabot at a night club, never knew her well, just danced with her. His wife had never seen her. Both of them always declared they knew nothing of the dope.'

'Yes. Gross miscarriage of justice, Lomas.'

'Clear case,' Lomas shrugged. 'Nobody's fault.'

'Yes. That's very gratifying. Great consolation for the Harfords. Cheering for the child.'

'We'll do all we can, of course. Put 'em right before the world, set 'em on their feet again and all that. An unfortunate affair. Shakes confidence in police work.'

Mr Fortune stared at him. Mr Fortune drew a long breath. 'Yes. That is one way of looking at it,' he murmured.

'Thank God for the kitten, sir,' Bell said.

Mr Fortune turned large grave eyes on him. 'Yes, that's another,' he said.

'I'd call it all providential,' Bell said earnestly. 'Just providential.'

Wonder grew in Mr Fortune's eyes. 'Providential!' he said. 'Well, well.'

Linda Barnes

b. 1949

LUCKY PENNY

LIEUTENANT MOONEY MADE ME dish it all out for the record. He's a good cop, if such an animal exists. We used to work the same shift before I decided—wrongly—that there was room for a lady PI in this town. Who knows? With this case under my belt, maybe business'll take a 180-degree spin, and I can quit driving a hack.

See, I've already written the official report for Mooney and the cops, but the kind of stuff they wanted: date, place, and time, cold as ice and submitted in triplicate, doesn't even start to tell the tale. So I'm doing it over again, my way.

Don't worry, Mooney. I'm not gonna file this one.

THE THAYLER CASE was still splattered across the front page of the *Boston Globe*. I'd soaked it up with my midnight coffee and was puzzling it out—my cab on automatic pilot, my mind on crime—when the mad tea party began.

'Take your next right, sister. Then pull over, and douse the lights. Quick!'

I heard the bastard all right, but it must have taken me thirty seconds or so to react. Something hard rapped on the cab's dividing shield. I didn't bother turning around. I hate staring down gun barrels.

I said, 'Jimmy Cagney, right? No, your voice is too high. Let me guess, don't tell me—'

'Shut up!'

'*Kill* the lights, *turn off* the lights, OK. But *douse* the lights? You've been tuning in too many old gangster flicks.'

'I hate a mouthy broad,' the guy snarled. I kid you not.

'*Broad*,' I said. 'Christ! *Broad*? You trying to grow hair on your balls?'

'Look, I mean it, lady!'

'*Lady*'s better. Now you wanna vacate my cab and go rob a phone booth?' My heart was beating like a tin drum, but I didn't let my voice shake, and all the time I was gabbing at him, I kept trying to catch his face in the mirror. He must have been crouching way back on the passenger side. I couldn't see a damn thing.

'I want all your dough,' he said.

Who can you trust? This guy was a spiffy dresser: charcoal-gray three-piece suit and rep tie, no less. And picked up in front of the swank Copley Plaza. I looked like I needed the bucks more than he did, and I'm no charity case. A woman can make good tips driving a hack in Boston. Oh, she's gotta take precautions, all right. When you can't smell a disaster fare from thirty feet, it's time to quit. I pride myself on my judgment. I'm careful. I always know where the police checkpoints are, so I can roll my cab past and flash the old lights if a guy starts acting up. This dude fooled me cold.

I was ripped. Not only had I been conned, I had a considerable wad to give away. It was near the end of my shift, and like I said, I do all right. I've got a lot of regulars. Once you see me, you don't forget me—or my cab.

It's gorgeous. Part of my inheritance. A '59 Chevy, shiny as new, kept on blocks in a heated garage by the proverbial dotty old lady. It's the pits of the design world. Glossy blue with those giant chromium fins. Restrained decor; just the phone number and a few gilt curlicues on the door. I was afraid all my old pals at the police department would pull me over for minor traffic violations if I went whole hog and painted 'Carlotta's Cab' in ornate script on the hood. Some do it anyway.

So where the hell were all the cops now? Where are they when you need 'em?

He told me to shove the cash through that little hole they leave for the passenger to pass the fare forward. I told him he had it backwards. He didn't laugh. I shoved bills.

'Now the change,' the guy said. Can you imagine the nerve?

I must have cast my eyes up to heaven. I do that a lot these days.

'I mean it.' He rapped the plastic shield with the shiny barrel of his gun. I checked it out this time. Funny how big a little .22 looks when it's pointed just right.

I fished in my pockets for change, emptied them.

'Is that all?'

'You want the gold cap on my left front molar?' I said.

'Turn around,' the guy barked. 'Keep both hands on the steering wheel. High.'

I heard jingling, then a quick intake of breath.

'OK,' the crook said, sounding happy as a clam, 'I'm gonna take my leave—'

'Good. Don't call this cab again.'

'Listen!' The gun tapped. 'You cool it here for ten minutes. And I mean frozen. Don't twitch. Don't blow your nose. Then take off.'

'Gee, thanks.'

'Thank *you*,' he said politely. The door slammed.

At times like that, you just feel ridiculous. You *know* the guy isn't going to hang around, waiting to see whether you're big on insubordination. *But*, he might. And who wants to tangle with a .22 slug? I rate pretty high in insubordination. That's why I messed up as a cop. I figured I'd give him two minutes to get lost. Meantime I listened.

Not much traffic goes by those little streets on Beacon Hill at one o'clock on a Wednesday morn. Too residential. So I could hear the guy's footsteps tap along the pavement. About ten steps back, he stopped. Was he the one in a million who'd wait to see if I turned around? I heard a funny kind of whooshing noise. Not loud enough to make me jump, and anything much louder than the ticking of my watch would have put me through the roof. Then the footsteps patted on, straight back and out of hearing.

One minute more. The only saving grace of the situation was the location: District One. That's Mooney's district. Nice guy to talk to.

I took a deep breath, hoping it would have an encore, and pivoted quickly, keeping my head low. Makes you feel stupid when you do that and there's no one around.

I got out and strolled to the corner, stuck my head around a building kind of cautiously. Nothing, of course.

I backtracked. Ten steps, then whoosh. Along the sidewalk stood one of those new 'Keep Beacon Hill Beautiful' trash cans, the kind with the swinging lid. I gave it a shove as I passed. I could just as easily have kicked it; I was in that kind of funk.

Whoosh, it said, just as pretty as could be.

Breaking into one of those trash cans is probably tougher than busting into your local bank vault. Since I didn't even have a dime left to fiddle the screws on the lid, I was forced to deface city property. I got the damn thing open and dumped the contents on somebody's front lawn, smack in the middle of a circle of light from one of those snooty Beacon Hill gas streetlamps.

Halfway through the whiskey bottles, wadded napkins, and beer cans, I made my discovery. I was doing a thorough search. If you're going to stink like garbage anyway, why leave anything untouched, right? So I was opening all the brown bags—you know, the good old brown lunch-and-bottle bags—looking for a clue. My most valuable find so far had been the moldy rind of a bologna sandwich. Then I hit it big: one neatly creased bag stuffed full of cash.

To say I was stunned is to entirely underestimate how I felt as I crouched there, knee-deep in garbage, my jaw hanging wide. I don't know what I'd expected to find. Maybe the guy's gloves. Or his hat, if he'd wanted to get rid of it fast in order to melt back into anonymity. I pawed through the rest of the debris. My change was gone.

I was so befuddled I left the trash right on the front lawn. There's probably still a warrant out for my arrest.

District One Headquarters is off the beaten path, over on New Sudbury Street. I would have called first, if I'd had a dime.

One of the few things I'd enjoyed about being a cop was gabbing with Mooney. I like driving a cab better, but, face it, most of my fares aren't scintillating conversationalists. The Red Sox and the weather usually covers it. Talking to Mooney was so much fun, I wouldn't even consider dating him. Lots of guys are good at sex, but conversation—now there's an art form.

Mooney, all six-foot-four, 240 linebacker pounds of him, gave me the glad eye when I waltzed in. He hasn't given up trying. Keeps telling me he talks even better in bed.

'Nice hat,' was all he said, his big fingers pecking at the typewriter keys.

I took it off and shook out my hair. I wear an old slouch cap when I drive to keep people from saying the inevitable. One jerk even misquoted Yeats at me: 'Only God, my dear, could love you for yourself alone and not your long red hair.' Since I'm seated when I drive, he missed the chance to ask me how the weather is up here. I'm six-one in my stocking feet and skinny enough to make every inch count twice. I've got a wide forehead, green eyes, and a pointy chin. If you want to be nice about my nose, you say it's got character.

Thirty's still hovering in my future. It's part of Mooney's past.

I told him I had a robbery to report and his dark eyes steered me to a chair. He leaned back and took a puff of one of his low-tar cigarettes. He can't quite give 'em up, but he feels guilty as hell about 'em.

When I got to the part about the bag in the trash, Mooney lost his sense of humor. He crushed a half-smoked butt in a crowded ashtray.

'Know why you never made it as a cop?' he said.

'Didn't brown-nose enough.'

'You got no sense of proportion! Always going after crackpot stuff!'

'Christ, Mooney, aren't you interested? Some guy heists a cab, at gunpoint, then tosses the money. Aren't you the least bit *intrigued*?'

'I'm a cop, Ms Carlyle. I've got to be more than intrigued. I've got murders, bank robberies, assaults—'

'Well, excuse me. I'm just a poor citizen reporting a crime. Trying to help—'

'Want to help, Carlotta? Go away.' He stared at the sheet of paper in the type-writer and lit another cigarette. 'Or dig me up something on the Thayler case.'

'You working that sucker?'

'Wish to hell I wasn't.'

I could see his point. It's tough enough trying to solve any murder, but when your victim is *the* Jennifer (Mrs Justin) Thayler, wife of the famed Harvard Law prof, and the society reporters are breathing down your neck along with the usual crime-beat scribblers, you got a special kind of problem.

'So who did it?' I asked.

Mooney put his size twelves up on the desk. 'Colonel Mustard in the library with the candlestick! How the hell do I know? Some scumbag housebreaker. The lady of the house interrupted his haul. Probably didn't mean to hit her that hard. He must have freaked when he saw all the blood, 'cause he left some of the ritziest stereo equipment this side of heaven, plus enough silverware to blind your average hophead. He snatched most of old man Thayler's goddam idiot artworks, collections, collectibles—whatever the hell you call 'em—which ought to set him up for the next few hundred years, if he's smart enough to get rid of them.'

'Alarm system?'

'Yeah, they had one. Looks like Mrs Thayler forgot to turn it on. According to the maid, she had a habit of forgetting just about anything after a martini or three.'

'Think the maid's in on it?'

'Christ, Carlotta. There you go again. No witnesses. No fingerprints. Servants asleep. Husband asleep. We've got word out to all the fences here and in New

York that we want this guy. The pawnbrokers know the stuff's hot. We're checking out known art thieves and shady museums—'

'Well, don't let me keep you from your serious business,' I said, getting up to go. 'I'll give you the collar when I find out who robbed my cab.'

'Sure,' he said. His fingers started playing with the typewriter again.

'Wanna bet on it?' Betting's an old custom with Mooney and me.

'I'm not gonna take the few piddling bucks you earn with that ridiculous car.'

'Right you are, boy. I'm gonna take the money the city pays you to be unimaginative! Fifty bucks I nail him within the week.'

Mooney hates to be called 'boy.' He hates to be called 'unimaginative.' I hate to hear my car called 'ridiculous.' We shook hands on the deal. Hard.

Chinatown's about the only chunk of Boston that's alive after midnight. I headed over to Yee Hong's for a bowl of wonton soup.

The service was the usual low-key, slow-motion routine. I used a newspaper as a shield; if you're really involved in the *Wall Street Journal*, the casual male may think twice before deciding he's the answer to your prayers. But I didn't read a single stock quote. I tugged at strands of my hair, a bad habit of mine. Why would somebody rob me and then toss the money away?

Solution Number One: He didn't. The trash bin was some mob drop, and the money I'd found in the trash had absolutely nothing to do with the money filched from my cab. Except that it was the same amount—and that was too big a coincidence for me to swallow.

Two: The cash I'd found was counterfeit and this was a clever way of getting it into circulation. Nah. Too baroque entirely. How the hell would the guy know I was the pawing-through-the-trash type?

Three: It was a training session. Some fool had used me to perfect his robbery technique. Couldn't he learn from TV like the rest of the crooks?

Four: It was a frat hazing. Robbing a hack at gunpoint isn't exactly in the same league as swallowing goldfish.

I closed my eyes.

My face came to a fortunate halt about an inch above a bowl of steaming broth. That's when I decided to pack it in and head for home. Wonton soup is lousy for the complexion.

I checked out the log I keep in the Chevy, totaled my fares: $4.82 missing, all in change. A very reasonable robbery.

By the time I got home, the sleepiness had passed. You know how it is: one moment you're yawning, the next your eyes won't close. Usually happens when my head hits the pillow; this time I didn't even make it that far. What woke me up was the idea that my robber hadn't meant to steal a thing. Maybe he'd left me something instead. You know, something hot, cleverly concealed. Something he could pick up in a few weeks, after things cooled off.

I went over that back seat with a vengeance, but I didn't find anything besides old Kleenex and bent paperclips. My brainstorm wasn't too clever after all. I mean, if the guy wanted to use my cab as a hiding place, why advertise by pulling a five-and-dime robbery?

I sat in the driver's seat, tugged my hair, and stewed. What did I have to go on? The memory of a nervous thief who talked like a B movie and stole only change. Maybe a mad toll-booth collector.

I live in a Cambridge dump. In any other city, I couldn't sell the damned thing if I wanted to. Here, I turn real estate agents away daily. The key to my home's value is the fact that I can hoof it to Harvard Square in five minutes. It's a seller's market for tarpaper shacks within walking distance of the Square. Under a hundred thou only if the plumbing's outside.

It took me a while to get in the door. I've got about five locks on it. Neighborhood's popular with thieves as well as gentry. I'm neither. I inherited the house from my weird Aunt Bea, all paid for. I consider the property taxes my rent, and the rent's getting steeper all the time.

I slammed my log down on the dining room table. I've got rooms galore in that old house, rent a couple of them to Harvard students. I've got my own office on the second floor, but I do most of my work at the dining room table. I like the view of the refrigerator.

I started over from square one. I called Gloria. She's the late-night dispatcher for the Independent Taxi Owners Association. I've never seen her, but her voice is as smooth as mink oil and I'll bet we get a lot of calls from guys who just want to hear her say she'll pick 'em up in five minutes.

'Gloria, it's Carlotta.'

'Hi, babe. You been pretty popular today.'

'Was I popular at one-thirty-five this morning?'

'Huh?'

'I picked up a fare in front of the Copley Plaza at one-thirty-five. Did you hand that one out to all comers or did you give it to me solo?'

'Just a sec.' I could hear her charming the pants off some caller in the back-ground. Then she got back to me.

'I just gave him to you, babe. He asked for the lady in the '59 Chevy. Not a lot of those on the road.'

'Thanks, Gloria.'

'Trouble?' she asked.

'Is mah middle name,' I twanged. We both laughed and I hung up before she got a chance to cross-examine me.

So. The robber wanted my cab. I wished I'd concentrated on his face instead of his snazzy clothes. Maybe it was somebody I knew, some jokester in mid-prank. I killed that idea; I don't know anybody who'd pull a stunt like that, at gunpoint and all. I don't want to know anybody like that.

Why rob my cab, then toss the dough?

I pondered sudden religious conversion. Discarded it. Maybe my robber was some perpetual screwup who'd ditched the cash by mistake.

Or . . . maybe he got exactly what he wanted. Maybe he desperately desired my change.

Why?

Because my change was special, valuable beyond its $4.82 replacement cost.

So how would somebody know my change was valuable?

Because he'd given it to me himself, earlier in the day.

'Not bad,' I said out loud. 'Not bad.' It was the kind of reasoning they'd bounced me off the police force for, what my so-called superiors termed the 'fevered product of an overimaginative mind.' I leapt at it because it was the only explanation I could think of. I do like life to make some sort of sense.

I pored over my log. I keep pretty good notes: where I pick up a fare, where I drop him, whether he's a hailer or a radio call.

First, I ruled out all the women. That made the task slightly less impossible: sixteen suspects down from thirty-five. Then I yanked my hair and stared at the blank white porcelain of the refrigerator door. Got up and made myself a sandwich: ham, Swiss cheese, salami, lettuce and tomato, on rye. Ate it. Stared at the porcelain some more until the suspects started coming into focus.

Five of the guys were just plain fat and one was decidedly on the hefty side; I'd felt like telling them all to walk. Might do them some good, might bring on a heart attack. I crossed them all out. Making a thin person look plump is hard enough; it's damn near impossible to make a fatty look thin.

Then I considered my regulars: Jonah Ashley, a tiny blond southern gent; muscle-bound 'just-call-me-Harold' at Longfellow Place; Dr Homewood getting his daily ferry from Beth Israel to MGH; Marvin of the gay bars; and Professor Dickerman, Harvard's answer to Berkeley's sixties radicals.

I crossed them all off. I could see Dickerman holding up the First Filthy Capitalist Bank, or disobeying civilly at Seabrook, even blowing up an oil company or two. But my mind boggled at the thought of the great liberal Dickerman robbing some poor cabbie. It would be like Robin Hood joining the sheriff of Nottingham on some particularly rotten peasant swindle. Then they'd both rape Maid Marian and go off pals together.

Dickerman *was* a lousy tipper. That ought to be a crime.

So what did I have? Eleven out of sixteen guys cleared without leaving my chair. Me and Sherlock Holmes, the famous armchair detectives.

I'm stubborn; that was one of my good cop traits. I stared at that log till my eyes bugged out. I remembered two of the five pretty easily; they were handsome and I'm far from blind. The first had one of those elegant bony faces and far-apart eyes. He was taller than my bandit. I'd ceased eyeballing him when I noticed the ring on his left hand; I never fuss with the married kind. The other one was built, a weight lifter. Not an Arnold Schwarzenegger extremist, but built. I think I'd have noticed that bod on my bandit. Like I said, I'm not blind.

That left three.

OK. I closed my eyes. Who had I picked up at the Hyatt on Memorial Drive?

Yeah, that was the salesman guy, the one who looked so uncomfortable that I'd figured he'd been hoping to ask his cabbie for a few pointers concerning the best skirt-chasing areas in our fair city. Too low a voice. Too broad in the beam.

The log said I'd picked up a hailer at Kenmore Square when I'd let out the salesman. Ah, yes, a talker. The weather, mostly. Don't you think it's dangerous for you to be driving a cab? Yeah, I remembered him, all right: a fatherly type, clasping a briefcase, heading to the financial district. Too old.

Down to one. I was exhausted but not the least bit sleepy. All I had to do was remember who I'd picked up on Beacon near Charles. A hailer. Before five o'clock, which was fine by me because I wanted to be long gone before rush hour gridlocked the city. I'd gotten onto Storrow and taken him along the river into Newton Center. Dropped him off at the Bay Bank Middlesex, right before closing time. It was coming back. Little nervous guy. Pegged him as an accountant when I'd let him out at the bank. Measly, undernourished soul. Skinny as a rail, stooped, with pits left from teenage acne.

Shit. I let my head sink down onto the dining room table when I realised what I'd done. I'd ruled them all out, every one. So much for my brilliant deductive powers.

I retired to my bedroom, disgusted. Not only had I lost $4.82 in assorted alloy metals, I was going to lose fifty dollars to Mooney. I stared at myself in the mirror, but what I was really seeing was the round hole at the end of a .22, held in a neat, gloved hand.

Somehow, the gloves made me feel better. I'd remembered another detail about my piggy-bank robber. I consulted the mirror and kept the recall going. A hat. The guy wore a hat. Not like my cap, but like a hat out of a forties gangster flick. I had one of those: I'm a sucker for hats. I plunked it on my head, jamming my hair up underneath—and I drew in my breath sharply.

A shoulder-padded jacket, a slim build, a low slouched hat. Gloves. Boots with enough heel to click as he walked away. Voice? High. Breathy, almost whispered. Not unpleasant. Accentless. No Boston *r*.

I had a man's jacket and a couple of ties in my closet. Don't ask. They may have dated from as far back as my ex-husband, but not necessarily so. I slipped into the jacket, knotted the tie, tilted the hat down over one eye.

I'd have trouble pulling it off. I'm skinny, but my build is decidedly female. Still, I wondered—enough to traipse back downstairs, pull a chicken leg out of the fridge, go back to the log, and review the feminine possibilities. Good thing I did.

Everything clicked. One lady fit the bill exactly: mannish walk and clothes, tall for a woman. And I was in luck. While I'd picked her up in Harvard Square, I'd dropped her at a real address, a house in Brookline: 782 Mason Terrace, at the top of Corey Hill.

JoJo's garage opens at seven. That gave me a big two hours to sleep.

I took my beloved car in for some repair work it really didn't need yet and sweet-talked JoJo into giving me a loaner. I needed a hack, but not mine. Only trouble with that Chevy is it's too damn conspicuous.

I figured I'd lose way more than fifty bucks staking out Mason Terrace. I also figured it would be worth it to see old Mooney's face.

She was regular as clockwork, a dream to tail. Eight-thirty-seven every morning, she got a ride to the Square with a next-door neighbor. Took a cab home at five-fifteen. A working woman. Well, she couldn't make much of a living from robbing hacks and dumping the loot in the garbage.

I was damn curious by now. I knew as soon as I looked her over that she was the one, but she seemed so blah, so *normal*. She must have been five-seven or eight, but the way she stooped, she didn't look tall. Her hair was long and brown with a lot of blond in it, the kind of hair that would have been terrific loose and wild, like a horse's mane. She tied it back with a scarf. A brown scarf. She wore suits. Brown suits. She had a tiny nose, brown eyes under pale eyebrows, a sharp chin. I never saw her smile. Maybe what she needed was a shrink, not a session with Mooney. Maybe she'd done it for the excitement. God knows, if I had her routine, her job, I'd probably be dressing up like King Kong and assaulting skyscrapers.

See, I followed her to work. It wasn't even tricky. She trudged the same path, went in the same entrance to Harvard Yard, probably walked the same number of steps every morning. Her name was Marcia Heidegger and she was a secretary in the admissions office of the college of fine arts.

I got friendly with one of her coworkers.

There was this guy typing away like mad at a desk in her office. I could just see him from the side window. He had grad student written all over his face. Longish wispy hair. Gold-rimmed glasses. Serious. Given to deep sighs and bright velour V necks. Probably writing his thesis on 'Courtly Love and the Theories of Chrétien de Troyes.'

I latched onto him at Bailey's the day after I'd tracked Lady Heidegger to her Harvard lair.

Too bad Roger was so short. Most short guys find it hard to believe that I'm really trying to pick them up. They look for ulterior motives. Not the Napoleon type of short guy; he assumes I've been waiting years for a chance to dance with a guy who doesn't have to bend to stare down my cleavage. But Roger was no Napoleon. So I had to engineer things a little.

I got into line ahead of him and ordered, after long deliberation, a BLT on toast. While the guy made it up and shoved it on a plate with three measly potato chips and a sliver of pickle you could barely see, I searched through my wallet, opened my change purse, counted out silver, got to $1.60 on the last five pennies. The counterman sang out, 'That'll be a buck eighty-five.' I pawed through my pockets, found a nickel, two pennies. The line was growing restive. I concentrated on looking like a damsel in need of a knight, a tough task for a woman over six feet.

Roger (I didn't know he was Roger then) smiled ruefully and passed over a quarter. I was effusive in my thanks. I sat at a table for two, and when he'd gotten his tray (ham-and-cheese and a strawberry ice cream soda), I motioned him into my extra chair.

He was a sweetie. Sitting down, he forgot the difference in our height, and decided I might be someone he could talk to. I encouraged him. I hung shamelessly on his every word. A Harvard man, imagine that. We got around slowly, ever so slowly, to his work at the admissions office. He wanted to duck it and talk about more important issues, but I persisted. I'd been thinking about getting a job at Harvard, possibly in admissions. What kind of people did he work with? Were they congenial? What was the atmosphere like? Was it a big office? How many people? Men? Women? Any soulmates? Readers? Or just, you know, office people?

According to him, every soul he worked with was brain dead. I interrupted a stream of complaint with 'Gee, I know somebody who works for Harvard. I wonder if you know her.'

'It's a big place,' he said, hoping to avoid the whole endless business.

'I met her at a party. Always meant to look her up.' I searched through my bag, found a scrap of paper and pretended to read Marcia Heidegger's name off it.

'Marcia? Geez, I work with Marcia. Same office.'

'Do you think she likes her work? I mean I got some strange vibes from her,' I said. I actually said 'strange vibes' and he didn't laugh his head off. People in the Square say things like that and other people take them seriously.

His face got conspiratorial, of all things, and he leaned closer to me.

'You want it, I bet you could get Marcia's job.'

'You mean it?' What a compliment—a place for me among the brain dead.

'She's gonna get fired if she doesn't snap out of it.'

'Snap out of what?'

'It was bad enough working with her when she first came over. She's one of those crazy neat people, can't stand to see papers lying on a desktop, you know? She almost threw out the first chapter of my thesis!'

I made a suitably horrified noise and he went on.

'Well, you know, about Marcia, it's kind of tragic. She doesn't talk about it.'

But he was dying to.

'Yes?' I said, as if he needed egging on.

He lowered his voice. 'She used to work for Justin Thayler over at the law school, that guy in the news, whose wife got killed. You know, her work hasn't been worth shit since it happened. She's always on the phone, talking real soft, hanging up if anybody comes in the room. I mean, you'd think she was in love with the guy or something, the way she . . .'

I don't remember what I said. For all I know, I may have volunteered to type his thesis. But I got rid of him somehow and then I scooted around the corner of Church Street and found a pay phone and dialed Mooney.

'Don't tell me,' he said. 'Somebody mugged you, but they only took your trading stamps.'

'I have just one question for you, Moon.'

'I accept. A June wedding, but I'll have to break it to Mother gently.'

'Tell me what kind of junk Justin Thayler collected.'

I could hear him breathing into the phone.

'Just tell me,' I said, 'for curiosity's sake.'

'You onto something, Carlotta?'

'I'm curious, Mooney. And you're not the only source of information in the world.'

'Thayler collected Roman stuff. Antiques. And I mean old. Artifacts, statues—'

'Coins?'

'Whole mess of them.'

'Thanks.'

'Carlotta—'

I never did find out what he was about to say because I hung up. Rude, I know. But I had things to do. And it was better Mooney shouldn't know what they were, because they came under the heading of illegal activities.

When I knocked at the front door of the Mason Terrace house at 10.00am the next day, I was dressed in dark slacks, a white blouse, and my old police department hat. I looked very much like the guy who reads your gas meter. I've never heard of anyone being arrested for impersonating the gasman. I've never heard of anyone really giving the gasman a second look. He fades into the background and that's exactly what I wanted to do.

I knew Marcia Heidegger wouldn't be home for hours. Old reliable had left for the Square at her usual time, precise to the minute. But I wasn't 100 percent sure Marcia lived alone. Hence the gasman. I could knock on the door and check it out.

Those Brookline neighborhoods kill me. Act sneaky and the neighbors call the cops in twenty seconds, but walk right up to the front door, knock, talk to yourself while you're sticking a shim in the crack of the door, let yourself in, and nobody does a thing. Boldness is all.

The place wasn't bad. Three rooms, kitchen and bath, light and airy. Marcia was incredibly organised, obsessively neat, which meant I had to keep track of where everything was and put it back just so. There was no clutter in the woman's life. The smell of coffee and toast lingered, but if she'd eaten breakfast, she'd already washed, dried, and put away the dishes. The morning paper had been read and tossed in the trash. The mail was sorted in one of those plastic accordion files. I mean, she folded her underwear like origami.

Now coins are hard to look for. They're small; you can hide 'em anywhere. So this search took me one hell of a long time. Nine out of ten women hide things that are dear to them in the bedroom. They keep their finest jewelry closest to the bed, sometimes in the nightstand, sometimes right under the mattress. That's where I started.

Marcia had a jewelry box on top of her dresser. I felt like hiding it for her. She had some nice stuff and a burglar could have made quite a haul with no effort.

The next favorite place for women to stash valuables is the kitchen. I sifted through her flour. I removed every Kellogg's Rice Krispy from the giant economy-sized box—and returned it. I went through her place like no burglar ever will. When I say thorough, I mean thorough.

I found four odd things. A neatly squared pile of clippings from the *Globe* and the *Herald*, all the articles about the Thayler killing. A manila envelope containing five different safe-deposit-box keys. A Tupperware container full of superstitious junk, good luck charms mostly, the kind of stuff I'd never have associated with a straight-arrow like Marcia: rabbits' feet galore, a little leather bag on a string that looked like some kind of voodoo charm, a pendant in the shape of a cross surmounted by a hook, and, I swear to God, a pack of worn tarot cards. Oh, yes, and a .22 automatic, looking a lot less threatening stuck in an ice cube tray. I took the bullets; the unloaded gun threatened a defenseless box of Breyers' mint chocolate-chip ice cream.

I left everything else just the way I'd found it and went home. And tugged my hair. And stewed. And brooded. And ate half the stuff in the refrigerator, I kid you not.

At about one in the morning, it all made blinding, crystal-clear sense.

The next afternoon, at five-fifteen, I made sure I was the cabbie who picked up Marcia Heidegger in Harvard Square. Now cabstands have the most rigid protocol since Queen Victoria; you do not grab a fare out of turn or your fellow cabbies are definitely not amused. There was nothing for it but bribing the ranks. This bet with Mooney was costing me plenty.

I got her. She swung open the door and gave the Mason Terrace number. I grunted, kept my face turned front, and took off.

Some people really watch where you're going in a cab, scared to death you'll take them a block out of their way and squeeze them for an extra nickel. Others just lean back and dream. She was a dreamer, thank God. I was almost at District One Headquarters before she woke up.

'Excuse me,' she said, polite as ever, 'that's Mason Terrace in *Brookline*.'

'Take the next right, pull over, and douse your lights,' I said in a low Bogart voice. My imitation was not that good, but it got the point across. Her eyes widened and she made an instinctive grab for the door handle.

'Don't try it, lady,' I Bogied on. 'You think I'm dumb enough to take you in alone? There's a cop car behind us, just waiting for you to make a move.'

Her hand froze. She was a sap for movie dialogue.

'Where's the cop?' was all she said on the way up to Mooney's office.

'What cop?'

'The one following us.'

'You have touching faith in our law-enforcement system,' I said.

She tried a bolt, I kid you not. I've had experience with runners a lot trickier than Marcia. I grabbed her in approved cop hold number three and marched her into Mooney's office.

He actually stopped typing and raised an eyebrow, an expression of great shock for Mooney.

'Citizen's arrest,' I said.

'Charges?'

'Petty theft. Commission of a felony using a firearm.' I rattled off a few more charges, using the numbers I remembered from cop school.

'This woman is crazy,' Marcia Heidegger said with all the dignity she could muster.

'Search her,' I said. 'Get a matron in here. I want my four dollars and eighty-two cents back.'

Mooney looked like he agreed with Marcia's opinion of my mental state. He said, 'Wait up, Carlotta. You'd have to be able to identify that four dollars and eighty-two cents as yours. Can you do that? Quarters are quarters. Dimes are dimes.'

'One of the coins she took was quite unusual,' I said. 'I'm sure I'd be able to identify it.'

'Do you have any objection to displaying the change in your purse?' Mooney said to Marcia. He got me mad the way he said it, like he was humoring an idiot.

'Of course not,' old Marcia said, cool as a frozen daiquiri.

'That's because she's stashed it somewhere else, Mooney,' I said patiently. 'She used to keep it in her purse, see. But then she goofed. She handed it over to a cabbie in her change. She should have just let it go, but she panicked because it was worth a pile and she was just babysitting it for someone else. So when she got it back, she hid it somewhere. Like in her shoe. Didn't you ever carry your lucky penny in your shoe?'

'No,' Mooney said. 'Now, Miss—'

'Heidegger,' I said clearly. 'Marcia Heidegger. She used to work at Harvard Law School.' I wanted to see if Mooney picked up on it, but he didn't. He went on: 'This can be taken care of with a minimum of fuss. If you'll agree to be searched by—'

'I want to see my lawyer,' she said.

'For four dollars and eighty-two cents?' he said. 'It'll cost you more than that to get your lawyer up here.'

'Do I get my phone call or not?'

Mooney shrugged wearily and wrote up the charge sheet. Called a cop to take her to the phone.

He got Jo Ann, which was good. Under cover of our old-friend-long-time-no-see greetings, I whispered in her ear.

'You'll find it fifty well spent,' I said to Mooney when we were alone.

Jo Ann came back, shoving Marcia slightly ahead of her. She plunked her prisoner down in one of Mooney's hard wooden chairs and turned to me, grinning from ear to ear.

'Got it?' I said. 'Good for you.'

'What's going on?' Mooney said.

'She got real clumsy on the way to the pay phone,' Jo Ann said. 'Practically fell on the floor. Got up with her right hand clenched tight. When we got to the phone, I offered to drop her dime for her. She wanted to do it herself. I insisted and she got clumsy again. Somehow this coin got kicked clear across the floor.'

She held it up. The coin could have been a dime, except the color was off: warm, rosy gold instead of dead silver. How I missed it the first time around I'll never know.

'What the hell is that?' Mooney said.

'What kind of coins were in Justin Thayler's collection?' I asked. 'Roman?'

Marcia jumped out of the chair, snapped her bag open, and drew out her little .22. I kid you not. She was closest to Mooney and she just stepped up to him and rested it above his left ear. He swallowed, didn't say a word. I never realised how prominent his Adam's apple was. Jo Ann froze, hand on her holster.

Good old reliable, methodical Marcia. Why, I said to myself, *why* pick today of all days to trot your gun out of the freezer? Did you read bad luck in your tarot cards? Then I had a truly rotten thought. What if she had two guns? What if the disarmed .22 was still staring down the mint chocolate-chip ice cream?

'Give it back,' Marcia said. She held out one hand, made an impatient waving motion.

'Hey, you don't need it, Marcia,' I said. 'You've got plenty more. In all those safe deposit boxes.'

'I'm going to count to five—' she began.

'Were you in on the murder from day one? You know, from the planning stages?' I asked. I kept my voice low, but it echoed off the walls of Mooney's tiny office. The hum of everyday activity kept going in the main room. Nobody noticed the little gun in the well-dressed lady's hand. 'Or did you just do your beau a favor and hide the loot after he iced his wife? In order to back up his burglary tale? I mean, if Justin Thayler really wanted to marry you, there is such a thing as divorce. Or was old Jennifer the one with the bucks?'

'I want that coin,' she said softly. 'Then I want the two of you'—she motioned to Jo Ann and me—'to sit down facing that wall. If you yell, or do anything before I'm out of the building, I'll shoot this gentleman. He's coming with me.'

'Come on, Marcia,' I said, 'put it down. I mean, look at you. A week ago you just wanted Thayler's coin back. You didn't want to rob my cab, right? You just didn't know how else to get your good luck charm back with no questions asked. You didn't do it for money, right? You did it for love. You were so straight you threw away the cash. Now here you are with a gun pointed at a cop—'

'Shut up!'

I took a deep breath and said, 'You haven't got the style, Marcia. Your gun's not even loaded.'

Mooney didn't relax a hair. Sometimes I think the guy hasn't ever believed a word I've said to him. But Marcia got shook. She pulled the barrel away from Mooney's skull and peered at it with a puzzled frown. Jo Ann and I both tackled her before she got a chance to pull the trigger. I twisted the gun out of her hand. I was almost afraid to look inside. Mooney stared at me and I felt my mouth go dry and a trickle of sweat worm its way down my back.

I looked.

No bullets. My heart stopped fibrillating, and Mooney actually cracked a smile in my direction.

So that's all. I sure hope Mooney will spread the word around that I helped him nail Thayler. And I think he will; he's a fair kind of guy. Maybe it'll get me a case or two. Driving a cab is hard on the backside, you know?

Arnold Bennett

1867–1931

MURDER

I

MANY GREAT ONES of the earth have justified murder as a social act, defensible, and even laudable in certain instances. There is something to be said for murder, though perhaps not much. All of us, or nearly all of us, have at one time or another had the desire and the impulse to commit murder. At any rate, murder is not an uncommon affair. On an average, two people are murdered every week in England, and probably about two hundred every week in the United States. And forty per cent of the murderers are not brought to justice. These figures take no account of the undoubtedly numerous cases where murder has been done but never suspected. Murderers and murderesses walk safely abroad among us, and it may happen to us to shake hands with them. A disturbing thought! But such is life, and such is homicide.

II

TWO MEN, NAMED respectively Lomax Harder and John Franting, were walking side by side one autumn afternoon, on the Marine Parade of the seaside resort and port of Quangate (English Channel). Both were well-dressed and had the air of moderate wealth, and both were about thirty-five years of age. At this point the resemblances between them ceased. Lomax Harder had refined features, an enormous forehead, fair hair, and a delicate, almost apologetic manner. John Franting was low-browed, heavy-chinned, scowling, defiant, indeed what is called a tough customer. Lomax Harder corresponded in appearance with the popular notion of a poet—save that he was carefully barbered. He was in fact a poet, and not unknown in the tiny, trifling, mad world where poetry is a matter of first-rate interest. John Franting corresponded in appearance with the popular notion of a gambler, an amateur boxer, and, in spare time, a deluder of women. Popular notions sometimes fit the truth.

Lomax Harder, somewhat nervously buttoning his overcoat, said in a quiet but firm and insistent tone:

'Haven't you got anything to say?'

John Franting stopped suddenly in front of a shop whose façade bore the sign: 'Gontle. Gunsmith.'

'Not in words,' answered Franting. 'I'm going in here.'

And he brusquely entered the small, shabby shop.

Lomax Harder hesitated half a second, and then followed his companion.

The shopman was a middle-aged gentleman wearing a black velvet coat.

'Good afternoon,' he greeted Franting, with an expression and in a tone of urbane condescension which seemed to indicate that Franting was a wise as well as a fortunate man in that he knew of the excellence of Gontle's and had the wit to come into Gontle's.

For the name of Gontle was favourably and respectfully known wherever triggers are pressed. Not only along the whole length of the Channel coast, but throughout England, was Gontle's renowned. Sportsmen would travel to Quangate from the far north, and even from London, to buy guns. To say: 'I bought it at Gontle's', or 'Old Gontle recommended it', was sufficient to silence any dispute concerning the merits of a fire-arm. Experts bowed the head before the unique reputation of Gontle. As for old Gontle, he was extremely and pardonably conceited. His conviction that no other gunsmith in the wide world could compare with him was absolute. He sold guns and rifles with the gesture of a monarch conferring an honour. He never argued; he stated; and the customer who contradicted him was as likely as not to be courteously and icily informed by Gontle of the geographical situation of the shop-door. Such shops exist in the English provinces, and nobody knows how they have achieved their renown. They could exist nowhere else.

''d afternoon,' said Franting gruffly, and paused.

'What can I do for you?' asked Mr Gontle, as if saying: 'Now don't be afraid. This shop is tremendous, and I am tremendous; but I shall not eat you.'

'I want a revolver,' Franting snapped.

'Ah! A revolver!' commented Mr Gontle, as if saying: 'A gun or a rifle, yes! But a revolver—an arm without individuality, manufactured wholesale! . . . However, I suppose I must deign to accommodate you.'

'I presume you know something about revolvers?' asked Mr Gontle, as he began to produce the weapons.

'A little.'

'Do you know the Webley Mark III?'

'Can't say that I do.'

'Ah! It is the best for all common purposes.' And Mr Gontle's glance said: 'Have the goodness not to tell me it isn't.'

Franting examined the Webley Mark III.

'You see,' said Mr Gontle. 'The point about it is that until the breech is properly closed it cannot be fired. So that it can't blow open and maim or kill the would-be murderer.' Mr Gontle smiled archly at one of his oldest jokes.

'What about suicides?' Franting grimly demanded.

'Ah!'

'You might show me just how to load it,' said Franting.

Mr Gontle, having found ammunition, complied with this reasonable request.

'The barrel's a bit scratched,' said Franting.

Mr Gontle inspected the scratch with pain. He would have denied the scratch, but could not.

'Here's another one,' said he, 'since you're so particular.' He simply had to put customers in their place.

'You might load it,' said Franting.

Mr Gontle loaded the second revolver.

'I'd like to try it,' said Franting.

'Certainly,' said Mr Gontle, and led Franting out of the shop by the back, and down to a cellar where revolvers could be experimented with.

Lomax Harder was now alone in the shop. He hesitated a long time and then picked up the revolver rejected by Franting, fingered it, put it down, and picked it up again. The back-door of the shop opened suddenly, and, startled, Harder dropped the revolver into his overcoat pocket: a thoughtless, quite unpremeditated act. He dared not remove the revolver. The revolver was as fast in his pocket as though the pocket had been sewn up.

'And cartridges?' asked Mr Gontle of Franting.

'Oh,' said Franting, 'I've only had one shot. Five'll be more than enough for the present. What does it weigh?'

'Let me see. Four-inch barrel? Yes. One pound four ounces.'

Franting paid for the revolver, receiving thirteen shillings in change from a five-pound note, and strode out of the shop, weapon in hand. He was gone before Lomax Harder decided upon a course of action.

'And for you, sir?' said Mr Gontle, addressing the poet.

Harder suddenly comprehended that Mr Gontle had mistaken him for a separate customer, who had happened to enter the shop a moment after the first one. Harder and Franting had said not a word to one another during the purchase, and Harder well knew that in the most exclusive shops it is the custom utterly to ignore a second customer until the first one has been dealt with.

'I want to see some foils.' Harder spoke stammeringly the only words that came into his head.

'Foils!' exclaimed Mr Gontle, shocked, as if to say: 'Is it conceivable that you should imagine that I, Gontle, gunsmith, sell such things as foils?'

After a little talk Harder apologised and departed—a thief.

'I'll call later and pay the fellow,' said Harder to his restive conscience. 'No. I can't do that. I'll send him some anonymous postal orders.'

He crossed the Parade and saw Franting, a small left-handed figure all alone far below on the deserted sands, pointing the revolver. He thought that his ear caught the sound of a discharge, but the distance was too great for him to be sure. He continued to watch, and at length Franting walked westward diagonally across the beach.

'He's going back to the Bellevue,' thought Harder, the Bellevue being the hotel from which he had met Franting coming out half an hour earlier. He strolled slowly towards the white hotel. But Franting, who had evidently come up the face of the cliff in the penny lift, was before him. Harder, standing outside, saw Franting seated in the lounge. Then Franting rose and vanished down a long passage at the rear of the lounge. Harder entered the hotel rather guiltily. There was no hall-porter at the door, and not a soul in the lounge or in sight of the lounge. Harder went down the long passage.

III

AT THE END of the passage Lomax Harder found himself in a billiard-room—an apartment built partly of brick and partly of wood on a sort of courtyard behind the main structure of the hotel. The roof, of iron and grimy glass, rose to a point in the middle. On two sides the high walls of the hotel obscured the light. Dusk was already closing in. A small fire burned feebly in the grate. A large radiator under the window was steel-cold, for though summer was finished, winter had not officially begun in the small economically-run hotel: so that the room was chilly; nevertheless, in deference to the English passion for fresh air and discomfort, the window was wide open.

Franting, in his overcoat, and an unlit cigarette between his lips, stood lowering with his back to the bit of fire. At sight of Harder he lifted his chin in a dangerous challenge.

'So you're still following me about,' he said resentfully to Harder.

'Yes,' said the latter, with his curious gentle primness of manner. 'I came down here specially to talk to you. I should have said all I had to say earlier, only you happened to be going out of the hotel just as I was coming in. You didn't seem to want to talk in the street; but there's some talking has to be done. I've a few things I must tell you.' Harder appeared to be perfectly calm, and he felt perfectly calm. He advanced from the door towards the billiard-table.

Franting raised his hand, displaying his square-ended, brutal fingers in the twilight.

'Now listen to me,' he said with cold, measured ferocity. 'You can't tell me

MURDER / Arnold Bennett

anything I don't know. If there's some talking to be done I'll do it myself, and when I've finished you can get out. I know that my wife has taken a ticket for Copenhagen by the steamer from Harwich, and that she's been seeing to her passport, and packing. And of course I know that you have interests in Copenhagen and spend about half your precious time there. I'm not worrying to connect the two things. All that's got nothing to do with me. Emily has always seen a great deal of you, and I know that the last week or two she's been seeing you more than ever. Not that I mind that. I know that she objects to my treatment of her and my conduct generally. That's all right, but it's a matter that only concerns her and me. I mean that it's no concern of yours, for instance, or anybody else's. If she objects enough she can try and divorce me. I doubt if she'd succeed, but you can never be sure—with these new laws. Anyhow she's my wife till she does divorce me, and so she has the usual duties and responsibilities towards me—even though I was the worst husband in the world. That's how I look at it, in my old-fashioned way. I've just had a letter from her—she knew I was here, and I expect that explains how you knew I was here.'

'It does,' said Lomax Harder quietly.

Franting pulled a letter out of his inner pocket and unfolded it.

'Yes,' he said, glancing at it, and read some sentences aloud: '"I have absolutely decided to leave you, and I won't hide from you that I know you know who is doing what he can to help me. I can't live with you any longer. You may be very fond of me, as you say, but I find your way of showing your fondness too humiliating and painful. I've said this to you before, and now I'm saying it for the last time." And so on and so on.'

Franting tore the letter in two, dropped one half on the floor, twisted the other half into a spill, turned to the fire, and lit his cigarette.

'That's what I think of her letter,' he proceeded, the cigarette between his teeth. 'You're helping her, are you? Very well. I don't say you're in love with her, or she with you. I'll make no wild statements. But if you aren't in love with her I wonder why you're taking all this trouble over her. Do you go about the world helping ladies who say they're unhappy just for the pure sake of helping? Never mind. Emily isn't going to leave me. Get that into your head. I shan't let her leave me. She has money, and I haven't. I've been living on her, and it would be infernally awkward for me if she left me for good. That's a reason for keeping her, isn't it? But you may believe me or not—it isn't my reason. She's right enough when she says I'm very fond of her. That's a reason for keeping her too. But it isn't my reason. My reason is that a wife's a wife, and she can't break her word just because everything isn't lovely in the garden. I've heard it said I'm unmoral. I'm not all unmoral. And I feel particularly strongly about what's called the marriage tie.' He drew the revolver from his overcoat pocket, and held it up to view. 'You see this thing. You saw me buy it. Now you needn't be afraid. I'm not threatening you; and it's no part of my game to shoot you. I've nothing to do with your goings-on. What I have to do with is the goings-on of my wife. If she deserts me—for you or for anybody or for nobody—I shall follow her, whether it's to

Copenhagen or Bangkok or the North Pole, and I shall kill her—with just this very revolver that you saw me buy. And now you can get out.'

Franting replaced the revolver, and began to consume the cigarette with fierce and larger puffs.

Lomax Harder looked at the grim, set, brutal, scowling bitter face, and knew that Franting meant what he had said. Nothing would stop him from carrying out his threat. The fellow was not an argufier; he could not reason; but he had unmistakable grit and would never recoil from the fear of consequences. If Emily left him, Emily was a dead woman; nothing in the end could protect her from the execution of her husband's menace. On the other hand, nothing would persuade her to remain with her husband. She had decided to go, and she would go. And indeed the mere thought of this lady to whom he, Harder, was utterly devoted, staying with her husband and continuing to suffer the tortures and humiliations which she had been suffering for years—this thought revolted him. He could not think it.

He stepped forward along the side of the billiard-table, and simultaneously Franting stepped forward to meet him. Lomax Harder snatched the revolver which was in his pocket, aimed, and pulled the trigger.

Franting collapsed, with the upper half of his body somehow balanced on the edge of the billiard-table. He was dead. The sound of the report echoed in Harder's ear like the sound of a violin string loudly twanged by a finger. He saw a little reddish hole in Franting's bronzed right temple.

'Well,' he thought, 'somebody had to die. And it's better him than Emily.' He felt that he had performed a righteous act. Also he felt a little sorry for Franting.

Then he was afraid. He was afraid for himself, because he wanted not to die, especially on the scaffold; but also for Emily Franting who would be friendless and helpless without him; he could not bear to think of her alone in the world— the central point of a terrific scandal. He must get away instantly . . .

Not down the corridor back into the hotel-lounge! No! That would be fatal! The window. He glanced at the corpse. It was more odd, curious, than affrighting. He had made the corpse. Strange! He could not unmake it. He had accomplished the irrevocable. Impressive! He saw Franting's cigarette glowing on the linoleum in the deepening dusk, and picked it up and threw it into the fender.

Lace curtains hung across the whole width of the window. He drew one aside, and looked forth. The light was much stronger in the courtyard than within the room. He put his gloves on. He gave a last look at the corpse, straddled the window-sill, and was on the brick pavement of the courtyard. He saw that the curtain had fallen back into the perpendicular.

He gazed around. Nobody! Not a light in any window! He saw a green wooden gate, pushed it; it yielded; then a sort of entry-passage . . . In a moment, after two half-turns, he was on the Marine Parade again. He was a fugitive. Should he fly to the right, to the left? Then he had an inspiration. An idea of genius for baffling pursuers. He would go into the hotel by the main-entrance. He went slowly and deliberately into the portico, where a middle-aged hall-porter was standing in the gloom.

'Good evening, sir.'

'Good evening. Have you got any rooms?'

'I think so, sir. The housekeeper is out, but she'll be back in a moment—if you'd like a seat. The manager's away in London.'

The hall-porter suddenly illuminated the lounge, and Lomax Harder, blinking, entered and sat down.

'I might have a cocktail while I'm waiting,' the murderer suggested with a bright and friendly smile. 'A Bronx.'

'Certainly, sir. The page is off duty. He sees to orders in the lounge, but I'll attend to you myself.'

'What a hotel!' thought the murderer, solitary in the chilly lounge, and gave a glance down the long passage. 'Is the whole place run by the hall-porter? But of course it's the dead season.'

Was it conceivable that nobody had heard the sound of the shot?

Harder had a strong impulse to run away. But no! To do so would be highly dangerous. He restrained himself.

'How much?' he asked of the hall-porter, who had arrived with surprising quickness, tray in hand and glass on tray.

'A shilling, sir.'

The murderer gave him eighteenpence, and drank off the cocktail.

'Thank you very much, sir.' The hall-porter took the glass.

'See here!' said the murderer. 'I'll look in again. I've got one or two little errands to do.'

And he went, slowly, into the obscurity of the Marine Parade.

IV

Lomax Harder leant over the left arm of the sea-wall of the man-made port of Quangate. Not another soul was there. Night had fallen. The lighthouse at the extremity of the right arm was occulting. The lights—some red, some green, many white—of ships at sea passed in both directions in endless processions. Waves plashed gently against the vast masonry of the wall. The wind, blowing steadily from the north-west, was not cold. Harder, looking about—though he knew he was absolutely alone, took his revolver from his overcoat pocket and stealthily dropped it into the sea. Then he turned round and gazed across the small harbour at the mysterious amphitheatre of the lighted town, and heard public clocks and religious clocks striking the hour.

He was a murderer, but why should he not successfully escape detection? Other murderers had done so. He had all his wits. He was not excited. He was not morbid. His perspective of things was not askew. The hall-porter had not seen his first entrance into the hotel, nor his exit after the crime. Nobody had seen them. He had left nothing behind in the billiard-room. No fingermarks on the window-sill. (The putting-on of his gloves was in itself a clear demonstration that he had fully kept his presence of mind.) No footmarks on the hard, dry pavement of the courtyard.

Of course there was the possibility that some person unseen had seen him getting out of the window. Slight: but still a possibility! And there was also the possibility that someone who knew Franting by sight had noted him walking by Franting's side in the streets. If such a person informed the police and gave a description of him, inquiries might be made . . . No! Nothing in it. His appearance offered nothing remarkable to the eye of a casual observer—except his forehead, of which he was rather proud, but which was hidden by his hat.

It was generally believed that criminals always did something silly. But so far he had done nothing silly, and he was convinced that, in regard to the crime, he never would do anything silly. He had none of the desire, supposed to be common among murderers, to revisit the scene of the crime or to look upon the corpse once more. Although he regretted the necessity for his act, he felt no slightest twinge of conscience. Somebody had to die, and surely it was better that a brute should die than the heavenly, enchanting, martyrised creature whom his act had rescued for ever from the brute! He was aware within himself of an ecstasy of devotion to Emily Franting—now a widow and free. She was a unique woman. Strange that a woman of such gifts should have come under the sway of so obvious a scoundrel as Franting. But she was very young at the time, and such freaks of sex had happened before and would happen again; they were a widespread phenomenon in the history of the relations of men and women. He would have killed a hundred men if a hundred men had threatened her felicity. His heart was pure; he wanted nothing from Emily in exchange for what he had done in her defence. He was passionate in her defence. When he reflected upon the coarseness and cruelty of the gesture by which Franting had used Emily's letter to light his cigarette, Harder's cheeks grew hot with burning resentment.

A clock struck the quarter. Harder walked quickly to the harbour front, where was a taxi-rank, and drove to the station . . . A sudden apprehension! The crime might have been discovered! Police might already be watching for suspicious-looking travellers! Absurd! Still, the apprehension remained despite its absurdity. The taxi-driver looked at him queerly. No! Imagination! He hesitated on the threshold of the station, then walked boldly in, and showed his return ticket to the ticket-inspector. No sign of a policeman. He got into the Pullman car, where five other passengers were sitting. The train started.

V

He nearly missed the boat-train at Liverpool Street because according to its custom the Quangate flyer arrived twenty minutes late at Victoria. And at Victoria the foolish part of him, as distinguished from the common-sense part, suffered another spasm of fear. Would detectives, instructed by telegraph, be waiting for the train? No! An absurd idea! The boat-train from Liverpool Street was crowded with travellers, and the platform crowded with senders-off. He gathered from scraps of talk overhead that an international conference was about to take place at Copenhagen. And he had known nothing of it—not seen a word of it in the papers! Excusable perhaps; graver matters had held his attention.

Useless to look for Emily in the vast bustle of the compartments! She had her through ticket (which she had taken herself, in order to avoid possible complications), and she happened to be the only woman in the world who was never late and never in a hurry. She was certain to be in the train. But was she in the train? Something sinister might have come to pass. For instance, a telephone message to the flat that her husband had been found dead with a bullet in his brain.

The swift two-hour journey to Harwich was terrible for Lomax Harder. He remembered that he had left the unburnt part of the letter lying under the billiard-table. Forgetful! Silly! One of the silly things that criminals did! And on Parkeston Quay the confusion was enormous. He did not walk, he was swept, on to the great shaking steamer whose dark funnels rose amid wisps of steam into the starry sky. One advantage: detectives would have no chance in that multitudinous scene, unless indeed they held up the ship.

The ship roared a warning, and slid away from the quay, groped down the tortuous channel to the harbour mouth, and was in the North Sea; and England dwindled to naught but a string of lights. He searched every deck from stem to stern, and could not find Emily. She had not caught the train, or, if she had caught the train, she had not boarded the steamer because he had failed to appear. His misery was intense. Everything was going wrong. And on the arrival at Esbjerg would not detectives be lying in wait for the Copenhagen train? . . .

Then he descried her, and she him. She too had been searching. Only chance had kept them apart. Her joy at finding him was ecstatic; tears came into his eyes at sight of it. He was everything to her, absolutely everything. He clasped her right hand in both his hands and gazed at her in the dim, diffused light blended of stars, moon and electricity. No woman was ever like her: mature, innocent, wise, trustful, honest. And the touching beauty of her appealing, sad, happy face, and the pride of her carriage! A unique jewel—snatched from the brutal grasp of that fellow—who had ripped her solemn letter in two and used it as a spill for his cigarette! She related her movements; and he his. Then she said:

'Well?'

'I didn't go,' he answered. 'Thought it best not to. I'm convinced it wouldn't have been any use.'

He had not intended to tell her this lie. Yet when it came to the point, what else could he say? He told one lie instead of twenty. He was deceiving her, but for her sake. Even if the worst occurred, she was for ever safe from that brutal grasp. And he had saved her. As for the conceivable complications of the future, he refused to front them; he could live in the marvellous present. He felt suddenly the amazing beauty of the night at sea, and beneath all his other sensations was the obscure sensation of a weight at his heart.

'I expect you were right,' she angelically acquiesced.

VI

THE SUPERINTENDENT of Police (Quangate was the county town of the western half of the county), and a detective-sergeant were in the billiard-room of the Bellevue. Both wore mufti. The powerful green-shaded lamps usual in billiard-rooms shone down ruthlessly on the green table, and on the reclining body of John Franting, which had not moved and had not been moved.

A charwoman was just leaving these officers when a stout gentleman, who had successfully beguiled a policeman guarding the other end of the long corridor, squeezed past her, greeted the two officers, and shut the door.

The Superintendent, a thin man, with lips to match, and a moustache, stared hard at the arrival.

'I am staying with my friend Dr Furnival,' said the arrival cheerfully. 'You telephoned for him, and as he had to go out to one of those cases in which nature will not wait, I offered to come in his place. I've met you before, Superintendent, at Scotland Yard.'

'Dr Austin Bond!' exclaimed the Superintendent.

'He,' said the other.

They shook hands, Dr Bond genially, the Superintendent half-consequential, half-deferential, as one who had his dignity to think about; also as one who resented an intrusion, but dared not show resentment.

The detective-sergeant recoiled at the dazzling name of the great amateur detective, a genius who had solved the famous mysteries of 'The Yellow Hat', 'The Three Towns', 'The Three Feathers', 'The Gold Spoon', etc., etc., etc., whose devilish perspicacity had again and again made professional detectives both look and feel foolish, and whose notorious friendship with the loftiest heads of Scotland Yard compelled all police forces to treat him very politely indeed.

'Yes,' said Dr Austin Bond, after detailed examination. 'Been shot about ninety minutes, poor fellow! Who found him?'

'That woman who's just gone out. Some servant here. Came in to look after the fire.'

'How long since?'

'Oh! About an hour ago.'

'Found the bullet? I see it hit the brass on that cue-rack there.'

The detective-sergeant glanced at the Superintendent, who, however, resolutely remained unastonished.

'Here's the bullet,' said the Superintendent.

'Ah!' commented Dr Austin Bond, glinting through his spectacles at the bullet as it lay in the Superintendent's hand. 'Decimal 38, I see. Flattened. It would be.'

'Sergeant,' said the Superintendent. 'You can get help and have the body moved, now Dr Bond has made his examination. Eh, Doctor?'

'Certainly,' answered Dr Bond, at the fireplace. 'He was smoking a cigarette, I see.'

'Either he or his murderer.'

'You've got a clue?'

'Oh yes,' the Superintendent answered, not without pride. 'Look here. Your torch, sergeant.'

The detective-sergeant produced a pocket electric-lamp, and the Superintendent turned to the window-sill.

'I've got a stronger one than that,' said Dr Austin Bond, producing another torch.

The Superintendent displayed finger-prints on the window-frame, foot-marks on the sill, and a few strands of inferior blue cloth. Dr Austin Bond next produced a magnifying glass, and inspected the evidence at very short range.

'The murderer must have been a tall man—you can judge that from the angle of fire; he wore a blue suit, which he tore slightly on this splintered wood of the window-frame; one of his boots had a hole in the middle of the sole, and he'd only three fingers on his left hand. He must have come in by the window and gone out by the window, because the hall-porter is sure that nobody except the dead man entered the lounge by any door within an hour of the time when the murder must have been committed.' The Superintendent proudly gave many more details, and ended by saying that he had already given instructions to circulate a description.

'Curious,' said Dr Austin Bond, 'that a man like John Franting should let anyone enter the room by the window! Especially a shabby-looking man!'

'You knew the deceased personally then?'

'No! But I know he was John Franting.'

'How, Doctor?'

'Luck.'

'Sergeant,' said the Superintendent, piqued. 'Tell the constable to fetch the hall-porter.'

Dr Austin Bond walked to and fro, peering everywhere, and picked up a piece of paper that had lodged against the step of the platform which ran round two sides of the room for the raising of the spectators' benches. He glanced at the paper casually, and dropped it again.

'My man,' the Superintendent addressed the hall-porter. 'How can you be sure that nobody came in here this afternoon?'

'Because I was in my cubicle all the time, sir.'

The hall-porter was lying. But he had to think of his own welfare. On the previous day he had been reprimanded for quitting his post against the rule. Taking advantage of the absence of the manager, he had sinned once again, and he lived in fear of dismissal if found out.

'With a full view of the lounge?'

'Yes, sir.'

'Might have been in there beforehand,' Dr Austin Bond suggested.

'No,' said the Superintendent. 'The charwoman came in twice. Once just before Franting came in. She saw the fire wanted making up and she went for some coal, and then returned later with some coal. But the look of Franting frightened her, and she went back with her coal.'

'Yes,' said the hall-porter. 'I saw that.'

Another lie.

At a sign from the Superintendent he withdrew.

'I should like to have a word with that charwoman,' said Dr Austin Bond.

The Superintendent hesitated. Why should the great amateur meddle with what did not concern him? Nobody had asked his help. But the Superintendent thought of the amateur's relations with Scotland Yard, and sent for the charwoman.

'Did you clean the window here today?' Dr Austin Bond interrogated her.

'Yes, please, sir.'

'Show me your left hand.' The slattern obeyed. 'How did you lose your little finger?'

'In a mangle accident, sir.'

'Just come to the window, will you, and put your hands on it. But take off your left boot first.'

The slattern began to weep.

'It's quite all right, my good creature,' Dr Austin Bond reassured her. 'Your skirt is torn at the hem, isn't it?'

When the slattern was released from her ordeal and had gone, carrying one boot in her grimy hand, Dr Austin Bond said genially to the Superintendent:

'Just a fluke. I happened to notice she'd only three fingers on her left hand when she passed me in the corridor. Sorry I've destroyed your evidence. But I felt sure almost from the first that the murderer hadn't either entered or decamped by the window.'

'How?'

'Because I think he's still here in the room.'

The two police officers gazed about them as if exploring the room for the murderer.

'I think he's there.'

Dr Austin Bond pointed to the corpse.

'And where did he hide the revolver after he'd killed himself?' demanded the thin-lipped Superintendent icily, when he had somewhat recovered his aplomb.

'I'd thought of that, too,' said Dr Austin Bond, beaming. 'It is always a very wise course to leave a dead body absolutely untouched until a professional man has seen it. But *looking* at the body can do no harm. You see the left-hand pocket of the overcoat. Notice how it bulges. Something unusual in it. Something that has the shape of a—Just feel inside it, will you?'

The Superintendent, obeying, drew a revolver from the overcoat pocket of the dead man.

'Ah! Yes!' said Dr Austin Bond. 'A Webley Mark III. Quite new. You might take out the ammunition.' The Superintendent dismantled the weapon. 'Yes, yes! Three chambers empty. Wonder how he used the other two! Now, where's that bullet? You see? He fired. His arm dropped, and the revolver happened to fall into the pocket.'

'Fired with his left hand, did he?' asked the Superintendent, foolishly ironic.

'Certainly. A dozen years ago Franting was perhaps the finest amateur light-weight boxer in England. And one reason for it was that he bewildered his opponents by being left-handed. His lefts were much more fatal than his rights. I saw him box several times.'

Whereupon Dr Austin Bond strolled to the step of the platform near the door and picked up the fragment of very thin paper that was lying there.

'This,' said he, 'must have blown from the hearth to here by the draught from the window when the door was opened. It's part of a letter. You can see the burnt remains of the other part in the corner of the fender. He probably lighted the cigarette with it. Out of bravado! His last bravado! Read this.'

The Superintendent read:

'. . . repeat that I realise how fond you are of me, but you have killed my affection for you, and I shall leave our home tomorrow. This is absolutely final. E.'

Dr Austin Bond, having for the nth time satisfactorily demonstrated in his own unique, rapid way, that police-officers were a set of numskulls, bade the Superintendent a most courteous good evening, nodded amicably to the detective-sergeant, and left in triumph.

VII

'I MUST GET SOME mourning and go back to the flat,' said Emily Franting.

She was sitting one morning in the lobby of the Palads Hotel, Copenhagen. Lomax Harder had just called on her with an English newspaper containing an account of the inquest at which the jury had returned a verdict of suicide upon the body of her late husband. Her eyes filled with tears.

'Time will put her right,' thought Lomax Harder, tenderly watching her. 'I was bound to do what I did. And I can keep a secret for ever.'

E. C. Bentley
1875–1956

THE CLEVER
COCKATOO

'WELL, THAT'S MY SISTER,' said Mrs Lancey in a low voice. 'What do you think of her, now you've spoken to her?'

Philip Trent, newly arrived from England, stood by his hostess within the loggia of an Italian villa looking out upon a prospect of such loveliness as has enchanted and enslaved the northern mind from age to age. It was a country that looked good and gracious for men to live in. Not far below them lay the broad, still surface of a great lake, blue as the sky; beyond it, low mountains rose up from the distant shore, tilled and wooded to the summit, drinking the light and warmth, visibly storing up earthly energy, with little villages of white and red scattered about their slopes like children clustered round their mother's knees. Before the villa lay a long paved terrace, and by the balustrade of it a woman stood looking out over the lake and conversing with a tall grey-haired man.

'Ten minutes is rather a short acquaintance,' Trent replied. 'Besides, I was attending rather more to her companion. Mynheer Scheffer is the first Dutchman I have met on social terms. One thing about Lady Bosworth is clear to me though. She is the most beautiful thing in sight, which is saying a good deal. And as for that low velvety voice of hers, if she asked me to murder my best friend I should have to do it on the spot.'

Mrs Lancey laughed.

'But I want you to take a personal interest in her, Philip; it means nothing, I know, when you talk like that. I care a great deal about Isabel; she is far more to me than any other woman. That's rather rare between sisters, I believe. And it makes me wretched to know that there's something wrong with her.'

'With her health, do you mean? One wouldn't think so.'

'Yes, but I fear it is that.'

'Is it possible?' said Trent. 'Why, Edith, the woman has the complexion of a child and the step of a racehorse and eyes like jewels. She looks like Atalanta in blue linen.'

'Did Atalanta marry an Egyptian mummy?' inquired Mrs Lancey.

'It is true,' said Trent thoughtfully, 'that Sir Peregrine looks rather as if he had been dug up somewhere. But I think he owes much of his professional success to that. People like a great doctor to look more or less unhealthy.'

'Perhaps they do; but I don't think the doctor's wife enjoys it very much. Isabel is always happiest when away from him—if he were here now she would be quite different from what you see. You know, Philip, their marriage hasn't been a success—I always knew it wouldn't be.'

Trent shrugged his shoulders.

'Let us drop the subject, Edith. Tell me why you want me to know about Lady Bosworth having something the matter with her. I'm not a physician.'

'No; but there's something very puzzling about it, as you will see; and you are clever at getting at the truth about things other people don't understand. Now, I'll tell you no more. I only want you to observe Bella particularly at dinner this evening, and tell me afterwards what you think. You'll be sitting opposite to her, between me and Agatha Stone. Now go and talk to her and the Dutchman.'

'Scheffer's appearance interests me,' remarked Trent. 'He has a face curiously like Frederick the Great's, and yet there's a difference—he doesn't look quite as if his soul were lost for ever and ever.'

'Well, go and ask him about it,' suggested Mrs Lancey.

WHEN THE PARTY of seven sat down to dinner that evening Lady Bosworth had just descended from her room. Trent perceived no change in her; she talked enthusiastically of the loveliness of the Italian evening, and joined in a conversation that was general and lively. It was only after some ten minutes that she fell silent, and that a new look came over her face.

Little by little all animation departed from it. Her eyes grew heavy and dull, her lips were parted in a foolish smile, and to the high, fresh tint of her cheek there succeeded a disagreeable pallor. There was nothing about this altered appearance in itself that could be called odious. Had she been so always, one would have set her down merely as a beautiful and stupid woman of lymphatic type. But there was something inexpressibly repugnant about such a change in such a being; it was as though the vivid soul had been withdrawn.

All charm, all personal force had departed. It needed an effort to recall her quaint, vivacious talk of an hour ago, now that she sat looking vaguely at the table before her, and uttering occasionally a blank monosyllable in reply to the discourse that Mr Scheffer poured into her ear. It was not, Trent told himself, that anything abnormal was done. It was the staring fact that Lady Bosworth was not herself, but someone wholly of another kind, that opened a new and unknown spring of revulsion in the recesses of his heart.

An hour later Mrs Lancey carried Trent off to a garden seat facing the lake.

'Well?' she said quietly.

'It's very strange and rather ghastly,' he answered, nursing his knee. 'But if you hadn't told me it puzzled you I should have thought it was easy to find an explanation.'

'Drugs, you mean?'

He nodded.

'Of course everybody must think so. George does, I know. It's horrible!' declared Mrs Lancey, with a thump on the arm of the seat. 'Agatha Stone began hinting at it after the first few days. Gossiping cat! She loathes Isabel, and she'll spread it round everywhere that my sister is a drug fiend. Philip, I asked her point-blank if she was taking anything that could account for it. She was much offended at that; told me I had known her long enough to know she never had done, and never would do such a thing. And though Isabel has her faults she's absolutely truthful.'

Trent looked on the ground. 'Yes; but you may have heard—'

'Oh, I know! They say that kind of habit makes people lie and deceive who never did before. But, you see, she is so completely herself, except just at this time. I simply couldn't make up my mind to disbelieve her. And, besides, if Bella is peculiar about anything, it's clean, wholesome, hygienic living. She has every sort of carbolicky idea. She never uses scent or powder or any kind of before-and-after stuff, never puts anything on her hair; she is washing herself from morning till night, but she always uses ordinary yellow soap. She never touches anything alcoholic or tea or coffee. You wouldn't think she had that kind of fad to look at her and her clothes; but she has; and I can't think of anything in the world she would despise more than dosing herself with things.'

'Not any kind of cosmetic whatever? That is surprising. Well, it seems to suit her,' Trent remarked. 'When she isn't like this she is one of the most radiant creatures I ever saw.'

'I know, and that's what makes it so irritating for women like myself, who look absolute hags if they don't assist nature a little. She's always been as strong as a horse and bursting with vitality, and her looks have never shown the slightest sign of going off. And now this thing has come to her, absolutely suddenly and without warning.'

'How long has it been going on?'

'This is the seventh evening. I entreated her to see a doctor; but she hates the idea of being doctored. She says it's sure to pass off and that it doesn't make any difference to her general health. George, who has always been devoted to her, only talks to her now with an effort. Randolph Stone is just the same; and two days before you arrived the Illingworths and Captain Burrows both went earlier than they had intended—I'm certain, because this change in Isabel was spoiling their visit for them.'

'She seems to get on remarkably well with Scheffer,' remarked Trent.

'I know—it's extraordinary, but he seems more struck with her than ever.'

'Well, he is; but in a lizard-hearted way of his own. He and I were talking just now after you left the dining-room. He spoke of Lady Bosworth in a queer semi-scientific sort of way, saying she was very interesting to a medical man like himself. You didn't tell me he was one.'

'I didn't know. George calls him an anthropologist, and disagrees with him about the races of Farther India. It's the one thing George does know something about, having lived there twelve years governing the poor things. They took to each other at once when they met last year, and when I asked him to stay here he was quite delighted. He only begged to be allowed to bring his cockatoo, as it could not live without him.'

'Strange pet for a man,' Trent observed. 'He was showing off its paces to me this afternoon. Well, it seems he's greatly interested in these attacks of hers. He has seen nothing quite like it. But he is convinced the thing is due to what he calls a toxic agent of some sort. As to what, or how, or why, he is absolutely at a loss.'

'Then you must find out what, and how, and why, Philip. I'm glad Scheffer isn't so easily upset as the other men; it's so much better for Isabel. She finds him very interesting of course; not only because he's the only man here who pays her a lot of attention, but because he's really a wonderful person. He's lived for years among the most appalling savages in Dutch New Guinea, doing scientific work for his government, and according to George they treat him like a sort of god; he's somehow got the reputation among them that he can kill a man by pointing his finger at him, and he can manage the natives as nobody else can. He's most attractive and quite kind really, I think, but there's something about him that makes me afraid of him.'

'What is it?'

'I think it is the frosty look in his eyes,' replied Mrs Lancey, drawing her shoulders together in a shiver.

'Perhaps that is the feeling about him in Dutch New Guinea,' said Trent. 'Did you tell me, Edith, that your sister began to be like this the very first evening she came here?'

'Yes. And it had never happened before, she declares.'

'She came out from England with the Stones, didn't she?'

'Only the last part of the journey. They got on the train at Lucerne.'

Trent looked back into the drawing-room at the wistful face of Mrs Stone, who was playing piquet with her host. She was slight and pretty, with large appealing eyes that never lost their melancholy, though she was always smiling.

'You say she loathes Lady Bosworth,' he said. 'Why?'

'Well, I suppose it's mainly Bella's own fault,' confessed Mrs Lancey with a grimace. 'You may as well know, Philip—you'll soon find out, anyhow—the truth is she *will* flirt with any man that she doesn't actively dislike. She's so brimful of life she can't hold herself in—or she won't, rather; she says there's no harm in it, and she doesn't care if there is. Several times she has practised on Randolph and, although he's a perfectly safe old donkey if there ever was one, Agatha can't bear the sight of her.'

'She seems quite friendly with her,' Trent observed.

Mrs Lancey produced through her delicate nostrils a sound that expressed a scorn for which there were no words.

'Well, what do you make of it, Philip?' his hostess asked at length. 'Myself, I simply don't know what to think. These queer fits of hers frighten me horribly. There's one dreadful idea, you see, that keeps occurring to me. Could it perhaps be'—Mrs Lancey lowered her already low tone—'the beginning of insanity?'

He spoke reassuringly. 'Oh, I shouldn't cherish that fancy. There are other things much more likely and much less terrible. Look here, Edith, will you try to arrange certain things for tomorrow, without asking me why? And don't let anybody know I asked you to do it—not even George. Until later on, at least. Will you?'

'How exciting!' Mrs Lancey breathed. 'Yes, of course, mystery man. What do you want me to do?'

'Do you think you could manage things tomorrow so that you and I and Lady Bosworth could go out in the motor boat on the lake for an hour or two in the evening, getting back in time to change for dinner—just the three of us and the engineer?'

She pondered. 'It might be. George and Randolph are playing golf at Cadenabbia tomorrow. I might arrange an expedition in the afternoon for Agatha and Mr Scheffer, and let Bella know I wanted her to stay with me. You could lose yourself after breakfast with your sketching things, I dare say, and return for tea. Then the three of us could run down in the boat to San Marmette—it's a lovely little place—and be back before seven. In this weather it's really the best time of day for the lake.'

'That would do admirably, if you could work it. And one thing more—if we do go as you suggest, I want you privately to tell your engineer to do just what I ask him to do—no matter what it is.'

MRS LANCEY WORKED it without difficulty. At five o'clock the two ladies and Trent, with a powerful young man of superb manners at the steering-wheel, were gliding swiftly southward, mile after mile, down the long lake. They landed at the most picturesque, and perhaps the most dilapidated and dirtiest, of all the lakeside villages where, in the tiny square above the landing-place, a score of dusky infants were treading the measures and chanting the words of one of the immemorial games of childhood. While Mrs Lancey and her sister watched them in delight, Trent spoke rapidly to the young engineer, whose gleaming eyes and teeth flashed understanding.

Soon afterwards they strolled through San Marmette, and up the mountain road to a little church half a mile away where a curious fresco could be seen.

It was close on half past six when they returned, to be met by Giuseppe, voluble in excitement and apology. It appeared that while he had been fraternising with the keeper of the inn by the landing-place certain *tristi individui* had, unseen by anyone, been tampering maliciously with the engine of the boat, and had poured handfuls of dust into the delicate mechanism. Mrs Lancey, who had received a private nod from Trent, reproved him bitterly for leaving the boat, and asked how long it would take to get the engine working again.

Giuseppe, overwhelmed with contrition, feared that it might be a matter of hours. Questioned, he said that the public steamer had arrived and departed twenty minutes since; the next one, the last of the day, was not due until after nine. Their excellencies could at least count on getting home by that, if the engine was not ready sooner. Questioned further, he said that one could telephone from the post office, and that food creditably cooked was to be had at the *trattoria*.

Lady Bosworth was delighted. She declared that she would not have missed this occasion for anything. She had come to approve highly of Trent, who had made himself excellent company, and she saw her way to being quite admirable, for she was in dancing spirits. In ten minutes she was on the best of terms with the fat, vivacious woman at the inn. Trent, who had been dispatched to telephone their plight to George Lancey, and had added that they were enjoying it very much, returned to find Lady Bosworth in the little garden behind the inn, with her skirts pinned up, peeling potatoes and singing '*Il segreto per esser felice*', while her sister beat up something in a bowl, and the landlady, busy with cooking, laughed and screamed cheerful observations from the kitchen. Seeing himself unemployable, Trent withdrew; sitting on a convenient wall, he took a leaf from his sketch-book and began to devise and decorate a menu of an absurdity suited to the spirit of the hour.

It was a more than cheerful dinner that they had under a canopy of vine leaves on a tiny terrace overlooking the lake. Twilight came on unnoticed, and soon afterwards appeared the passenger boat, by which, Giuseppe advising it, they decided to return. It was as they sought for places on the crowded upper deck that Mrs Lancey put her hand on Trent's arm. 'There hasn't been a sign of it all the evening,' she whispered. 'What does that mean?'

'It means,' murmured Trent, 'that we got her away from the cause at the critical time, without anybody knowing we were going to do it.'

'Whom do you mean by "anybody"?'

'How on earth should I know? Here comes your sister.'

It was not until the following afternoon that Trent found an opportunity of being alone with his hostess in the garden.

'She is perfectly delighted at having escaped it last night,' said Mrs Lancey. 'She says she knew it would pass off, but she hasn't the least notion how she was cured. Nor have I.'

'She isn't,' replied Trent. 'Last night was only a beginning, and we can't get her unexpectedly stranded for the evening every day. The next move can be made now, if you consent to it. Lady Bosworth will be out until this evening, I believe?'

'She's gone shopping in the town. What do you want to do?'

'I want you to take me up to her room, and there I want you to look carefully through everything in the place—in every corner of every box and drawer and bag and cupboard—and show me anything you find that might—'

'I should hate to do that!' Mrs Lancey interrupted him, her face flushing.

'You would hate much more to see your sister again this evening, as she was every evening before last night. Look here, Edith; the position is simple enough. Every day about seven Lady Bosworth goes into that room in her normal state to dress for dinner. Every day she comes out of it apparently as she went in, but turns queer a little later. Now is there any other place than that room where the mischief could happen?'

Mrs Lancey frowned dubiously. 'Her maid is with her always.'

'I suppose so; but it doesn't make any difference to the argument. That room is the only place where Lady Bosworth isn't with the rest of us, doing what we are doing, eating the same food, breathing the same air, exposed to all the same influences as we are. Does anything take place in that room to account for those strange seizures?'

Mrs Lancey threw out her hands. 'I can't bear to think that Isabel should be deceiving me. And yet I know—it's a dreadful thing—and what else could happen there?'

'That is what we may find out, if we do as I say. You must decide, but remember that you must think of Lady Bosworth as one whom you are trying to save from a subtle evil. You can't shrink from a step merely because you wouldn't dream of taking it in the ordinary way.'

For a few moments she stood carefully boring a hole in the gravel with one heel. Then, 'Come along,' she said, and led the way towards the house.

'Unless we take the floor up,' said Mrs Lancey, seating herself emphatically on the bed in her sister's room twenty minutes later, 'there's nowhere else to look. I've taken everything out and pried into every hole and corner. There isn't a single lockable thing that is locked. There isn't a bottle or phial or pill-box of any sort to be found. So much for your suspicions. What interests you about that nail-polishing pad? You must have seen one before, surely.'

'This ornamental design on hammered silver is very beautiful and original,' replied Trent abstractedly. 'I have never seen anything quite like it.'

'The same design is on the whole of the toilet set,' Mrs Lancey observed tartly, 'and it shows to least advantage on the manicure things. You are talking rubbish; and yet,' she added slowly, 'you are looking rather pleased with yourself.'

Trent, his hands in his pockets, was balancing himself on his heels as he stared out of the window of the bedroom. His eyes were full of animation, and he was whistling almost inaudibly. He turned round slowly. 'I'm only thinking. Whose are the rooms on each side of this, Edith?'

'This side, the Stones's; that side, Mr Scheffer's.'

'Then I will go for a walk all alone and think some more. Goodbye.'

'Yes,' declared Mrs Lancey as he went out, 'it's plain enough you have picked up some scent or other.'

'It isn't scent exactly,' Trent replied, as he descended the stairs. 'Guess again.'

TRENT WAS NOT IN THE HOUSE WHEN, three hours later, a rousing tumult broke out on the upper floor. Those below in the loggia heard first a piercing scream, then a clatter of feet on parquet flooring, then more sounds of feet, excited voices, other screams of harsh, inhuman quality, and a lively scuffling and banging. Mr Scheffer, with a volley of guttural words of which it was easy to gather the general sense, headed the rush of the company upstairs.

'Gisko! Gisko!' he shouted at the head of the stairway. There was another ear-splitting screech, and the cockatoo came scuttling and fluttering out of Lady Bosworth's room, pursued by three vociferating women servants. The bird's yellow crest was erect and quivering with agitation; it screeched furious defiance again as it leapt upon its master's outstretched wrist.

'Silence, devil!' exclaimed Mr Scheffer, seizing it by the head and shaking it violently. 'I know not how to apologise, Lancey,' he declared. 'The accursed bird has somehow slipped from his chain away. I left him in my room secure just before we had tea.'

'Never mind, never mind!' replied his host, who seemed rather pleased than otherwise with this small diversion. 'I don't suppose he's done any harm beyond frightening the women. Anything wrong, Edith?' he asked as they approached the open door of the bedroom to which the ladies had already hurried. Lady Bosworth's maid was telling a voluble story.

'When she came in just now to get the room ready for Isabel to dress,' Mrs Lancey summarised, 'she suddenly heard a voice say something, and saw the bird perched on top of the mirror, staring at her. It gave her such a shock that she dropped the water-can and fled; then the two other girls came and helped her, trying to drive it out. They hadn't the sense to send for Mr Scheffer.'

'Apologise, carrion!' commanded Gisko's master. The cockatoo uttered a string of Dutch words in a subdued croak. 'He says he asks one thousand pardons, and he will sin no more,' Mr Scheffer translated. 'Miserable brigand! Traitor!'

Lady Bosworth hurried out of her room.

'I won't hear the poor thing scolded like that,' she protested. 'How was he to know my maid would be frightened? He looks so wretched! Take him away, Mr Scheffer, and cheer him up.'

It was half an hour later that Mrs Lancey came to her husband in his dressing-room.

'I must say Bella was very decent about Scheffer's horrid bird,' she began. 'Do you know what the little fiend had done?'

'No, my dear. I thought he had confined himself to frightening the maid out of her skin.'

'Not at all. He had been having the time of his life. Bella saw at once that he had been up to mischief, but she pretended there was nothing. Now it turns out he has bitten the buttons off two pair of gloves, chewed up a lot of hairpins and spoiled her pretty little manicure set. He's torn the lining out of the case, the silver handles are covered with beak-marks, two or three of the things he seems to have hidden somewhere, and the polishing pad is a ruin.'

'It's too bad!' declared Mr Lancey, bending over a shoe.

'I believe you're laughing, George,' said his wife coldly.

He began to do so audibly. 'You must admit it's funny to think of the bird going solemnly through a programme of mischief like that. I wish I could have seen the little beggar at it. Well, we shall have to get Bella a new nail outfit. I'm glad she held her tongue about it just now.'

'Why?'

'Because, my dear, we don't ask people to the house to make them feel uncomfortable—especially foreigners.'

'Bella wasn't thinking of your ideal of hospitality. She held her tongue because she's taken a fancy to Scheffer. But, George, how do you suppose the little pest got in? The window was shut, and Hignett declares the door was too when she went to the room.'

'Then I expect Hignett deceives herself. Anyway, what does it matter? What I am anxious about is your sister's little peculiarity. As I've told you, I don't at all like the look of her having been quite normal yesterday evening, the one evening when she was away from the house by accident. I really am feeling miserably depressed, Edith. What I'm dreading now is a repetition of the usual ghastly performance tonight.'

But neither that night, nor any night after, was that performance repeated. Lady Bosworth, free now of all apprehension, renewed and redoubled the life of the little company. And the lips of Trent were obstinately sealed.

THREE WEEKS LATER Trent was shown into the consulting-room of Sir Peregrine Bosworth. The famous physician was a tall stooping man of exaggerated gauntness, narrow-jawed and high-nosed. He was courteous of manner and smiled readily; but his face was set in unhappy lines.

'Will you sit down, Mr Trent?' said Sir Peregrine. 'You wrote that you wished to see me upon a private matter concerning myself. I am at a loss to imagine what it can be, but, knowing your name, I had no hesitation in making an appointment.'

Trent inclined his head. 'I am obliged to you, Sir Peregrine. The matter is really important, and also quite private—so private that no person whatever knows the material facts besides myself. I won't waste words. I have lately been staying with the Lanceys, whom you know, in Italy. Lady Bosworth was also a guest there. For some days before my arrival she had suffered each evening from a curious attack of lassitude and vacancy of mind. I don't know what it was. Perhaps you do.'

Sir Peregrine, immovably listening, smiled grimly. 'The description of symptoms is a little vague. I have heard nothing of this, I must say, from my wife.'

'It always came on at a certain time of the day, and only then. That time was a few minutes after eight, at the beginning of dinner. The attack passed off gradually after two hours or so.'

The physician laid his clenched hand on the table between them. 'You are not a medical man, Mr Trent, I believe. What concern have you with all this?' His voice was coldly hostile now.

'Lots,' answered Trent briefly. Then he added, as Sir Peregrine got to his feet with a burning eye, 'I know nothing of medicine, but I cured Lady Bosworth.'

The other sat down again suddenly. His open hands fell upon the table and his dark face became very pale. 'You—' he began with difficulty.

'I and no other, Sir Peregrine. And in a curiously simple way. I found out what was causing the trouble, and without her knowledge I removed it. It was—oh, the devil!' Trent exclaimed in a lower tone. For Sir Peregrine Bosworth, with a brow gone suddenly white and clammy, had first attempted to rise and then sank forward with his head on the table.

Trent, who had seen such things before, hurried to him, pulled his chair from the table, and pressed his head down to his knees. Within a minute the stricken man was leaning back in his chair. He inspired deeply from a small bottle he had taken from his pocket.

'You have been overworking, perhaps,' Trent said. 'Something is wrong. I think I had better not—'

Sir Peregrine had pulled himself together. 'I know very well what is wrong with me, sir,' he interrupted brusquely. 'It is my business to know. That will not happen again. I wish to hear what you have to say before you leave this house.'

'Very well.' Trent took a tone of colourless precision. 'I was asked by Lady Bosworth's sister, Mrs Lancey, to help in trying to trace the source of the disorder which attacked her every evening. I need not describe the signs of it, and I will not trouble you with an account of how I reasoned on the matter. But I found out that Lady Bosworth was, on these occasions, under the influence of a drug which had the effect of lowering her vitality and clogging her brain without producing stupefaction or sleep; and I was led to the conclusion that she was administering this drug to herself without knowing it.'

He paused, and felt in his waistcoat pocket. 'When Mrs Lancey and I were making a search for something of the kind in her room, my attention was caught by the fine workmanship of a manicure set on the dressing-table. I took up the little round box meant to contain nail-polishing paste, admiring its shape and decoration, and on looking inside it found it half full of paste. But I have often watched the process of beautifying finger-nails, and it seemed to me that the stuff was of a deeper red than the usual pink confection; and I saw next that the polish-pad of the set, though well worn, had never been used with paste, which leaves a sort of dark incrustation on the pad. Yet it was evident that the paste in the little box had been used. It is useful sometimes, you see, to have a mind that notices trifles. So I jumped to the conclusion that the paste that was not employed as nail-polish was employed for some other purpose; and when I reached that point I simply put the box in my pocket and went away with it. I may say that Mrs Lancey knew nothing of this, or of what I did afterwards.'

'And what was that?' Sir Peregrine appeared now to be following the story with an ironic interest.

'Naturally, knowing nothing of such matters, I took it to the place that called itself "English Pharmacy" in the town, and asked the proprietor what the stuff was. He looked at it, took a little on his finger, smelt it, and said it was undoubtedly lip-salve.

'It was then I remembered how, when I saw Lady Bosworth during one of her attacks, her lips were brilliantly red, though all the colour had departed from her face. That had struck me as very odd, because I am a painter, and naturally I could not miss an abnormality like that. Then I remembered another thing. One evening, when Lady Bosworth, her sister and myself were prevented from returning to the house for dinner, and dined at a country inn, there had been no sign of her trouble; but I had noticed that she moistened her lips again and again with her tongue.'

'You are observant,' remarked Sir Peregrine dispassionately, and again had recourse to his smelling-bottle.

'You are good enough to say so,' Trent replied with a wooden face. 'On thinking these things over, it seemed to me probable that Lady Bosworth was in the habit of putting on a little lip-salve when she dressed for dinner in the evening; perhaps finding that her lips at that time of day tended to become dry, or perhaps not caring to use it in daylight, when its presence would be much more easily detected. For I had learned that she made some considerable parade of not using any kind of cosmetics or artificial aids to beauty; and that, of course, accounted for her carrying it in a box meant for manicure-paste, which might be represented as merely a matter of cleanliness, and at any rate was not to be classed with paint and powder. It was not pleasant to me to have surprised this innocent little deception; but it was as well that I did so, for I soon ascertained beyond doubt that the stuff had been tampered with.

'When I left the chemist's I went and sat in a quiet corner of the museum grounds. There I put the least touch of the salve on my tongue and awaited results. In five minutes I had lost all power of connected thought or will; I no longer felt any interest in my own experiment. I was conscious. I felt no discomfort, and no loss of the power of movement. Only my intelligence seemed to be paralysed. For an hour I was looking out upon the world with the soul of an ox, placid and blank.'

Trent now opened his fingers and showed a little round box of hammered silver with a delicate ornamentation running round the lid. It was of about the bigness of a pill-box.

'It seemed best to me that this box should simply disappear, and in some quite natural, unsuspicious way. Merely to remove the salve would have drawn Lady Bosworth's attention to it and set her guessing. She did not suspect the stuff as yet, I was fully convinced; and I thought it well that the affair of her seizures should remain a mystery. Your eyes ask why. Just because I did not want a painful scandal in Mrs Lancey's family—we are old friends, you see. And now here I am with the box, and neither Lady Bosworth nor any other person has the smallest inkling of its crazy secret but you and I.'

He stopped again and looked in Sir Peregrine's eyes. They remained fixed upon him with the gaze of a statue.

'It was plain, of course,' Trent continued, 'that someone had got at the stuff immediately before she went out to Italy, or immediately on her arrival. The attacks began on the first evening there, two hours after reaching the house. Therefore any tampering with the salve after her arrival was practically impossible. When I asked myself who should have tampered with it before Lady Bosworth left this house to go out to Italy, I was led to form a very unpleasant conjecture.'

Sir Peregrine stirred in his chair. 'You had been told the truth—or part of the truth—about our married life, I suppose?'

Trent inclined his head. 'Three days ago I arrived in London, and showed a little of this paste to a friend of mine who is an expert analyst. He has sent me a report, which I have here.' He handed an envelope across the table. 'He was deeply interested in what he found, but I have not satisfied his curiosity. He found the salve to be evenly impregnated with a very slight quantity of a rare alkaloid body called "purvisine". Infinitesimal doses of it produce effects on the human organism which he describes, as I can testify, with considerable accuracy. It was discovered, he notes, by Henry Purvis twenty-five years ago; and you will remember, Sir Peregrine, what I only found out by inquiry—that you were assistant to Purvis about that time in Edinburgh, where he had the chair of medical jurisprudence and toxicology.'

He ceased to speak, and there was a short silence. Sir Peregrine gazed at the table before him. Once or twice he drew breath deeply, and at length began to speak calmly.

'I shall not waste words,' he said, 'in trying to explain fully my state of mind or my action in this matter. But I will tell you enough for your imagination to do the rest. My feeling for my wife was an infatuation from the beginning, and is still. I was too old for her. I don't think now that she ever cared for me greatly; but she was too strong-minded ever to marry a wealthy fool. By the time we had been married a year I could no longer hide from myself that she had an incurable weakness for philandering. She has surrendered herself to it with less and less restraint, and without any attempt to deceive me on the subject. If I tried to tell you what torture it has been to me you wouldn't understand. The worst was when she was away from me, staying with her friends. At length I took the step you know. It was undeniably an act of baseness, and we will leave it at that, if you please. If you should ever suffer as I do you will modify your judgment upon me. I knew of my wife's habit, discovered by you, of using lip-salve at her evening toilette. On the night before her departure I took what was in that box and combined it with a preparation of the drug purvisine. The infinitesimal amount which would pass into the mouth after the application of the salve was calculated to produce for an hour or two the effects you have described, without otherwise doing any harm. But I knew the impression that would be produced upon normal men and women by the sight of anyone in such a state. I wanted to turn her attractiveness into repulsiveness, and I seem to have succeeded. I was mad when I did it. I have been aghast at my own action ever since. I am glad it has been frustrated. And now I should like to know what you intend to do.'

Trent took up the box. 'If you agree, Sir Peregrine, I shall drop this from Westminster Bridge tonight. And so long as nothing of the sort is practised again, the whole affair shall be buried. Yours is a wretched story, and I don't suppose any of us would find our moral fibre improved by such a situation. I have no more to say.'

He rose and moved to the door. Sir Peregrine rose also and stood with lowered eyes, apparently deep in thought.

'I am obliged to you, Mr Trent,' he said formally. 'I may say, too, that your account of your proceedings interested me deeply. I should like to ask a question. How did you contrive that her box should disappear without its owner seeing anything remarkable in its absence?'

'Oh, easily,' Trent replied, his hand on the door-knob. 'After experimenting on myself I went back to the house before tea time, when no one happened to be in. I went upstairs to a room where a cockatoo was kept—a mischievous brute—took him off his chain, and carried him into Lady Bosworth's room. There I put him on the dressing-table, and teased him a little with the manicure things to interest him in them. Then I took away one of the pairs of scissors, so that the box shouldn't be the one thing missing, and left him shut in there to do his worst, while I went out of the house again. When I went he was ripping out the silk lining of the case, and had chewed up the silver handles of the things pretty well. After I had gone he went on to destroy various other things. In the riot that took place when he was found, the disappearance of the little box and scissors became a mere detail. Certainly Lady Bosworth suspected nothing.

'I suppose,' he added thoughtfully, 'that occasion would be the only time a cockatoo was of any particular use.'

And Trent went out.

Ernest Bramah

1868–1942

THE TRAGEDY AT BROOKBEND COTTAGE

'**M**AX,' SAID MR CARLYLE, when Parkinson had closed the door behind him, 'this is Lieutenant Hollyer, whom you consented to see.'

'To hear,' corrected Carrados, smiling straight into the healthy and rather embarrassed face of the stranger before him. 'Mr Hollyer knows of my disability?'

'Mr Carlyle told me,' said the young man, 'but, as a matter of fact, I had heard of you before, Mr Carrados, from one of our men. It was in connection with the foundering of the *Ivan Saratov*.'

Carrados wagged his head in good-humoured resignation.

'And the owners were sworn to inviolable secrecy!' he exclaimed. 'Well, it is inevitable, I suppose. Not another scuttling case, Mr Hollyer?'

'No, mine is quite a private matter,' replied the lieutenant. 'My sister, Mrs Creake—but Mr Carlyle would tell you better than I can. He knows all about it.'

'No, no; Carlyle is a professional. Let me have it in the rough, Mr Hollyer. My ears are my eyes, you know.'

'Very well, sir. I can tell you what there is to tell, right enough, but I feel that when all's said and done it must sound very little to another, although it seems important to me.'

'We have occasionally found trifles of significance ourselves,' said Carrados encouragingly. 'Don't let that deter you.'

This was the essence of Lieutenant Hollyer's narrative:

'I have a sister, Millicent, who is married to a man called Creake . . . She is about twenty-eight now and he is at least fifteen years older. Neither my mother (who has since died) nor I cared very much about Creake. We had nothing particular against him, except, perhaps, the moderate disparity of age, but none of us appeared to have anything in common. He was a dark, taciturn man, and his moody silence froze up conversation. As a result, of course, we didn't see much of each other.'

'This, you must understand, was four or five years ago, Max,' interposed Mr Carlyle officiously.

Carrados maintained an uncompromising silence. Mr Carlyle blew his nose and contrived to impart a hurt significance into the operation. Then Lieutenant Hollyer continued:

'Millicent married Creake after a very short engagement. It was a frightfully subdued wedding—more like a funeral to me. The man professed to have no relations and apparently he had scarcely any friends or business acquaintances. He was an agent for something or other and had an office off Holborn. I suppose he made a living out of it then, although we knew practically nothing of his private affairs, but I gather that it has been going down since, and I suspect that for the past few years they have been getting along almost entirely on Millicent's little income. You would like the particulars of that?'

'Please,' assented Carrados.

'When our father died about seven years ago, he left three thousand pounds. It was invested in Canadian stock and brought in a little over a hundred a year. By his will my mother was to have the income of that for life and on her death it was to pass to Millicent, subject to the payment of a lump sum of five hundred pounds to me. But my father privately suggested to me that if I should have no particular use for the money at the time, he would propose my letting Millicent have the income of it until I did want it, as she would not be particularly well off. You see, Mr Carrados, a great deal more had been spent on my education and advancement than on her; I had my pay, and, of course, I could look out for myself better than a girl could.'

'Quite so,' agreed Carrados.

'Therefore I did nothing about that,' continued the lieutenant. 'Three years ago I was over again but I did not see much of them. They were living in lodgings. That was the only time since the marriage that I have seen them until last week. In the meanwhile our mother had died and Millicent had been receiving her income. She wrote me several letters at the time. Otherwise we did not correspond much, but about a year ago she sent me their new address—Brookbend Cottage, Mulling Common—a house that they had taken. When I got two months' leave I invited myself there as a matter of course, fully expecting to stay most of my time with them, but I made an excuse to get away after a week. The place was dismal and unendurable, the whole life and atmosphere indescribably depressing.' He looked round with an instinct of caution, leaned forward earnestly, and dropped his voice. 'Mr Carrados, it is my absolute conviction that Creake is only waiting for a favourable opportunity to murder Millicent.'

'Go on,' said Carrados quietly. 'A week of the depressing surroundings of Brookbend Cottage would not alone convince you of that, Mr Hollyer.'

'I am not so sure,' declared Hollyer doubtfully. 'There was a feeling of suspicion and—before me—polite hatred that would have gone a good way towards it. All the same there *was* something more definite. Millicent told me this the day after I went there. There is no doubt that a few months ago Creake deliberately planned to poison her with some weed-killer. She told me the circumstances in a rather distressed moment, but afterwards she refused to speak of it again—even weakly denied it—and, as a matter of fact, it was with the greatest difficulty that I could get her at any time to talk about her husband or his affairs. The gist of it was that she had the strongest suspicion that Creake doctored a bottle of stout which he expected she would drink for her supper when she was alone. The weed-killer, properly labelled, but also in a beer bottle, was kept with other miscellaneous liquids in the same cupboard as the beer but on a high shelf. When he found that it had miscarried he poured away the mixture, washed out the bottle and put in the dregs from another. There is no doubt in my mind that if he had come back and found Millicent dead or dying he would have contrived it to appear that she had made a mistake in the dark and drunk some of the poison before she found out.'

'Yes,' assented Carrados. 'The open way; the safe way.'

'You must understand that they live in a very small style, Mr Carrados, and Millicent is almost entirely in the man's power. The only servant they have is a woman who comes in for a few hours every day. The house is lonely and secluded. Creake is sometimes away for days and nights at a time, and Millicent, either through pride or indifference, seems to have dropped off all her old friends and to have made no others. He might poison her, bury the body in the garden, and be a thousand miles away before anyone began even to inquire about her. What am I to do, Mr Carrados?'

'He is less likely to try poison than some other means now,' pondered Carrados. 'That having failed, his wife will always be on her guard. He may know, or at least suspect, that others know. No . . . The common-sense precaution would be for your sister to leave the man, Mr Hollyer. She will not?'

'No,' admitted Hollyer, 'she will not. I at once urged that.' The young man struggled with some hesitation for a moment and then blurted out: 'The fact is, Mr Carrados, I don't understand Millicent. She is not the girl she was. She hates Creake and treats him with a silent contempt that eats into their lives like acid, and yet she is so jealous of him that she will let nothing short of death part them. It is a horrible life they lead. I stood it for a week and I must say, much as I dislike my brother-in-law, that he has something to put up with. If only he got into a passion like a man and killed her it wouldn't be altogether incomprehensible.'

'That does not concern us,' said Carrados. 'In a game of this kind one has to take sides and we have taken ours. It remains for us to see that our side wins. You mentioned jealousy, Mr Hollyer. Have you any idea whether Mrs Creake has real ground for it?'

'I should have told you that,' replied Lieutenant Hollyer. 'I happened to strike up with a newspaper man whose office is in the same block as Creake's. When I mentioned the name he grinned. "Creake," he said, "oh, he's the man with the romantic typist, isn't he?" "Well, he's my brother-in-law," I replied. "What about the typist?" Then the chap shut up like a knife. "No, no," he said, "I didn't know he was married. I don't want to get mixed up in anything of that sort. I only said that he had a typist. Well, what of that? So have we; so has everyone." There was nothing more to be got out of him, but the remark and the grin meant—well, about as usual, Mr Carrados.'

Carrados turned to his friend.

'I suppose you know all about the typist by now, Louis?'

'We have had her under efficient observation, Max,' replied Mr Carlyle, with severe dignity.

'Is she unmarried?'

'Yes; so far as ordinary repute goes, she is.'

'That is all that is essential for the moment. Mr Hollyer opens up three excellent reasons why this man might wish to dispose of his wife. If we accept the suggestion of poisoning—though we have only a jealous woman's suspicion for it—we add to the wish the determination. Well, we will go forward on that. Have you got a photograph of Mr Creake?'

The lieutenant took out his pocket-book.

'Mr Carlyle asked me for one. Here is the best I could get.'

Carrados rang the bell.

'This, Parkinson,' he said, when the man appeared, 'is a photograph of a Mr—. What first name, by the way?'

'Austin,' put in Hollyer, who was following everything with a boyish mixture of excitement and subdued importance.

'—of a Mr Austin Creake. I may require you to recognise him.'

Parkinson glanced at the print and returned it to his master's hand.

'May I inquire if it is a recent photograph of the gentleman, sir?' he asked.

'About six years ago,' said the lieutenant, taking in this new actor in the drama with frank curiosity. 'But he is very little changed.'

'Thank you, sir. I will endeavour to remember Mr Creake, sir.'

Lieutenant Hollyer stood up as Parkinson left the room. The interview seemed to be at an end.

'Oh, there's one other matter,' he remarked. 'I am afraid that I did rather an unfortunate thing while I was at Brookbend. It seemed to me that as all Millicent's money would probably pass into Creake's hands sooner or later I might as well have my five hundred pounds, if only to help her with afterwards. So I broached the subject and said that I should like to have it now as I had an opportunity for investing.'

'And you think?'

'It may possibly influence Creake to act sooner than he otherwise might have done. He may have got possession of the principal even and find it very awkward to replace it.'

'So much the better. If your sister is going to be murdered it may as well be done next week as next year so far as I am concerned. Excuse my brutality, Mr Hollyer, but this is simply a case to me and I regard it strategically. Now Mr Carlyle's organisation can look after Mrs Creake for a few weeks, but it cannot look after her for ever. By increasing the immediate risk we diminish the permanent risk.'

'I see,' agreed Hollyer. 'I'm awfully uneasy but I'm entirely in your hands.'

'Then we will give Mr Creake every inducement and every opportunity to get to work. Where are you staying now?'

'Just now with some friends at St Albans.'

'That is too far.' The inscrutable eyes retained their tranquil depth but a new quality of quickening interest in the voice made Mr Carlyle forget the weight and burden of his ruffled dignity. 'Give me a few minutes, please. The cigarettes are behind you, Mr Hollyer.' The blind man walked to the window and seemed to look out over the cypress-shaded lawn. The lieutenant lit a cigarette and Mr Carlyle picked up *Punch*. Then Carrados turned round again.

'You are prepared to put your own arrangements aside?' he demanded of his visitor.

'Certainly.'

'Very well. I want you to go down now—straight from here—to Brookbend Cottage. Tell your sister that your leave is unexpectedly cut short and that you sail to-morrow.'

'The *Martian*?'

'No, no; the *Martian* doesn't sail. Look up the movements on your way there and pick out a boat that does. Say you are transferred. Add that you expect to be away only two or three months and that you really want the five hundred pounds by the time of your return. Don't stay in the house long, please.'

'I understand, sir.'

'St Albans is too far. Make your excuse and get away from there to-day. Put up somewhere in town, where you will be in reach of the telephone. Let Mr Carlyle and myself know where you are. Keep out of Creake's way. I don't want actually to tie you down to the house, but we may require your services. We will let you know at the first sign of anything doing and if there is nothing to be done we must release you.'

'I don't mind that. Is there nothing more that I can do now?'

'Nothing. In going to Mr Carlyle you have done the best thing possible; you have put your sister into the care of the shrewdest man in London.' Whereat the object of this quite unexpected eulogy found himself becoming covered with modest confusion.

'Well, Max?' remarked Mr Carlyle tentatively when they were alone.

'Well, Louis?'

'Of course, it wasn't worth while rubbing it in before young Hollyer, but, as a matter of fact, every single man carries the life of any other man—only one, mind you—in his hands, do what you will.'

'Provided he doesn't bungle,' acquiesced Carrados.

'Quite so.'

'And also that he is absolutely reckless of the consequences.'

'Of course.'

'Two rather large provisos. Creake is obviously susceptible to both. Have you seen him?'

'No. As I told you, I put a man on to report his habits in town. Then, two days ago, as the case seemed to promise some interest—for he certainly is deeply involved with the typist, Max, and the thing might take a sensational turn at any time—I went down to Mulling Common myself. Although the house is lonely it is on the electric tram route. You know the sort of market-garden rurality that about a dozen miles out of London offers—alternate bricks and cabbages. It was easy enough to get to know about Creake locally. He mixes with no one there, goes into town at irregular times but generally every day, and is reputed to be devilish hard to get money out of. Finally, I made the acquaintance of an old fellow who used to do a day's gardening at Brookbend occasionally. He has a cottage and a garden of his own with a greenhouse, and the business cost me the price of a pound of tomatoes.'

'Was it—a profitable investment?'

'As tomatoes, yes; as information, no. The old fellow had the fatal disadvantage from our point of view of labouring under a grievance. A few weeks ago Creake told him that he would not require him again as he was going to do his own gardening in future.'

'That is something, Louis.'

'If only Creake was going to poison his wife with hyoscyamine and bury her, instead of blowing her up with a dynamite cartridge and claiming that it came in among the coal.'

'True, true. Still—'

'However, the chatty old soul had a simple explanation for everything that Creake did. Creake was mad. He had even seen him flying a kite in his garden where it was bound to get wrecked among the trees. A lad of ten would have known better, he declared. And certainly the kite did get wrecked, for I saw it hanging over the road myself. But that a sane man should spend his time "playing with a toy" was beyond him.'

'A good many men have been flying kites of various kinds lately,' said Carrados. 'Is he interested in aviation?'

'I dare say. He appears to have some knowledge of scientific subjects. Now what do you want me to do, Max?'

'Will you do it?'

'Implicitly—subject to the usual reservations.'

'Keep your man on Creake in town and let me have his reports after you have seen them. Lunch with me here now. Phone up to your office that you are detained on unpleasant business and then give the deserving Parkinson an afternoon off by looking after me while we take a motor run round Mulling Common. If we have time we might go on to Brighton, feed at the "Ship", and come back in the cool.'

'Amiable and thrice lucky mortal,' sighed Mr Carlyle, his glance wandering round the room.

But, as it happened, Brighton did not figure in that day's itinerary. It had been Carrados' intention merely to pass Brookbend Cottage on this occasion, relying on his highly developed faculties, aided by Mr Carlyle's description, to inform him of the surroundings. A hundred yards before they reached the house he had given an order to his chauffeur to drop into the lowest speed and they were leisurely drawing past when a discovery by Mr Carlyle modified their plans.

'By Jupiter!' that gentleman suddenly exclaimed, 'there's a board up, Max. The place is to be let.'

Carrados picked up the tube again. A couple of sentences passed and the car stopped by the roadside, a score of paces past the limit of the garden. Mr Carlyle took out his notebook and wrote down the address of a firm of house agents.

'You might raise the bonnet and have a look at the engines, Harris,' said Carrados. 'We want to be occupied here for a few minutes.'

'This is sudden; Hollyer knew nothing of their leaving,' remarked Mr Carlyle.

'Probably not for three months yet. All the same, Louis, we will go on to the agents and get a card to view, whether we use it to-day or not.'

A thick hedge, in its summer dress effectively screening the house beyond from public view, lay between the garden and the road. Above the hedge showed an occasional shrub; at the corner nearest to the car a chestnut flourished. The wooden gate, once white, which they had passed, was grimed and rickety. The road itself was still the unpretentious country lane that the advent of the electric car had found it. When Carrados had taken in these details there seemed little else to notice. He was on the point of giving Harris the order to go on when his ear caught a trivial sound.

'Someone is coming out of the house, Louis,' he warned his friend. 'It may be Hollyer, but he ought to have gone by this time.'

'I don't hear anyone,' replied the other, but as he spoke a door banged noisily and Mr Carlyle slipped into another seat and ensconced himself behind a copy of *The Globe*.

'Creake himself,' he whispered across the car, as a man appeared at the gate. 'Hollyer was right; he is hardly changed. Waiting for a car, I suppose.'

But a car very soon swung past them from the direction in which Mr Creake was looking and it did not interest him. For a minute or two longer he continued to look expectantly along the road. Then he walked slowly up the drive back to the house.

'We will give him five or ten minutes,' decided Carrados. 'Harris is behaving very naturally.'

Before even the shorter period had run out they were repaid. A telegraph-boy cycled leisurely along the road, and, leaving his machine at the gate, went up to the cottage. Evidently there was no reply, for in less than a minute he was trundling past them back again. Round the bend an approaching tram clanged its bell noisily, and, quickened by the warning sound, Mr Creake again appeared, this time with a small portmanteau in his hand. With a backward glance he hurried on towards the next stopping-place, and, boarding the car as it slackened down, he was carried out of their knowledge.

'Very convenient of Mr Creake,' remarked Carrados, with quiet satisfaction.

'We will now get the order and go over the house in his absence. It might be useful to have a look at the wire as well.'

'It might, Max,' acquiesced Mr Carlyle a little dryly. 'But if it is, as it probably is, in Creake's pocket, how do you propose to get it?'

'By going to the post office, Louis.'

'Quite so. Have you ever tried to see a copy of a telegram addressed to someone else?'

'I don't think I have ever had occasion yet,' admitted Carrados. 'Have you?'

'In one or two cases I have perhaps been an accessory to the act. It is generally a matter either of extreme delicacy or considerable expenditure.'

'Then for Hollyer's sake we will hope for the former here.' And Mr Carlyle smiled darkly and hinted that he was content to wait for a friendly revenge.

A little later, having left the car at the beginning of the straggling High Street, the two men called at the village post office. They had already visited the house agent and obtained an order to view Brookbend Cottage, declining with some difficulty the clerk's persistent offer to accompany them. The reason was soon forthcoming. 'As a matter of fact,' explained the young man, 'the present tenant is under *our* notice to leave.'

'Unsatisfactory, eh?' said Carrados, encouragingly.

'He's a corker,' admitted the clerk, responding to the friendly tone. 'Fifteen months and not a doit of rent have we had. That's why I should have liked—'

'We will make every allowance,' replied Carrados.

The post office occupied one side of the stationer's shop. It was not without some inward trepidation that Mr Carlyle found himself committed to the adventure. Carrados, on the other hand, was the personification of bland unconcern.

'You have just sent a telegram to Brookbend Cottage,' he said to the young lady behind the brass-work lattice. 'We think it may have come inaccurately and should like a repeat.' He took out his purse. 'What is the fee?'

The request was evidently not a common one. 'Oh,' said the girl uncertainly, 'wait a minute, please.' She turned to a pile of telegram duplicates behind the desk and ran a doubtful finger along the upper sheets. 'I think this is all right. You want it repeated?'

'Please.' Just a tinge of questioning surprise gave point to the courteous tone.

'It will be fourpence. If there is an error the amount will be refunded.'

Carrados put down his coin and received his change.

'Will it take long?' he inquired carelessly, as he pulled on his glove.

'You will most likely get it within a quarter of an hour,' she replied.

'Now you've done it,' commented Mr Carlyle, as they walked back to their car. 'How do you propose to get that telegram, Max?'

'Ask for it,' was the laconic explanation.

And, stripping the artifice of any elaboration, he simply asked for it and got it. The car, posted at a convenient bend in the road, gave him a warning note as the telegraph-boy approached. Then Carrados took up a convincing attitude with his hand on the gate while Mr Carlyle lent himself to the semblance of a departing friend. That was the inevitable impression when the boy rode up.

'Creake, Brookbend Cottage?' inquired Carrados, holding out his hand, and without a second thought the boy gave him the envelope and rode away on the assurance that there would be no reply.

'Some day, my friend,' remarked Mr Carlyle, looking nervously towards the unseen house, 'your ingenuity will get you into a tight corner.'

'Then my ingenuity must get me out again,' was the retort. 'Let us have our "view" now. The telegram can wait.'

An untidy workwoman took their order and left them standing at the door. Presently a lady whom they both knew to be Mrs Creake appeared.

'You wish to see over the house?' she said, in a voice that was utterly devoid of any interest. Then, without waiting for a reply, she turned to the nearest door and threw it open.

'This is the drawing-room,' she said, standing aside.

They walked into a sparsely furnished, damp-smelling room and made a pretence of looking round, while Mrs Creake remained silent and aloof.

'The dining-room,' she continued, crossing the narrow hall and opening another door.

Mr Carlyle ventured a genial commonplace in the hope of inducing conversation. The result was not encouraging. Doubtless they would have gone through the house under the same frigid guidance had not Carrados been at fault in a way that Mr Carlyle had never known him fail before. In crossing the hall he stumbled over a mat and almost fell.

'Pardon my clumsiness,' he said to the lady. 'I am, unfortunately, quite blind. But,' he added, with a smile, to turn off the mishap, 'even a blind man must have a house.'

The man who had eyes was surprised to see a flood of colour rush into Mrs Creake's face.

'Blind!' she exclaimed, 'oh, I beg your pardon. Why did you not tell me? You might have fallen.'

'I generally manage fairly well,' he replied. 'But, of course in a strange house—'
She put her hand on his arm very lightly.

'You must let me guide you, just a little,' she said.

The house, without being large, was full of passages and inconvenient turnings. Carrados asked an occasional question and found Mrs Creake quite amiable without effusion. Mr Carlyle followed them from room to room in the hope, though scarcely the expectation, of learning something that might be useful.

'This is the last one. It is the largest bedroom,' said their guide. Only two of the upper rooms were fully furnished and Mr Carlyle at once saw, as Carrados knew without seeing, that this was the one which the Creakes occupied.

'A very pleasant outlook,' declared Mr Carlyle.

'Oh, I suppose so,' admitted the lady vaguely. The room, in fact, looked over the leafy garden and the road beyond. It had a French window opening on to a small balcony, and to this, under the strange influence that always attracted him to light, Carrados walked.

'I expect that there is a certain amount of repair needed?' he said, after standing there a moment.

'I am afraid there would be,' she confessed.

'I ask because there is a sheet of metal on the floor here,' he continued. 'Now that, in an old house, spells dry-rot to the wary observer.'

'My husband said that the rain, which comes in a little under the window, was rotting the boards there,' she replied. 'He put that down recently. I had not noticed anything myself.'

It was the first time she had mentioned her husband; Mr Carlyle pricked up his ears.

'Ah, that is a less serious matter,' said Carrados. 'May I step out on to the balcony?'

'Oh, yes, if you like to.' Then, as he appeared to be fumbling at the catch, 'Let me open it for you.'

But the window was already open, and Carrados, facing the various points of the compass, took in the bearings.

'A sunny, sheltered corner,' he remarked. 'An ideal spot for a deck-chair and a book.'

She shrugged her shoulders half-contemptuously.

'I dare say,' she replied, 'but I never use it.'

'Sometimes, surely,' he persisted mildly. 'It would be my favourite retreat. But then—'

'I was going to say that I had never even been out on it, but that would not be quite true. It has two uses for me, both equally romantic; I occasionally shake a duster from it, and when my husband returns late without his latchkey he wakes me up and I come out here and drop him mine.'

Further revelation of Mr Creake's nocturnal habits was cut off, greatly to Mr Carlyle's annoyance, by a cough of unmistakable significance from the foot of the stairs. They had heard a trade cart drive up to the gate, a knock at the door, and the heavy-footed woman tramp along the hall.

'Excuse me a minute, please,' said Mrs Creake.

'Louis,' said Carrados, in a sharp whisper, the moment they were alone, 'stand against the door.'

With extreme plausibility Mr Carlyle began to admire a picture so situated that while he was there it was impossible to open the door more than a few inches. From that position he observed his confederate go through the curious procedure of kneeling down on the bedroom floor and for a full minute pressing his ear to the sheet of metal that had already engaged his attention. Then he rose to his feet, nodded, dusted his trousers, and Mr Carlyle moved to a less equivocal position.

'What a beautiful rose-tree grows up your balcony,' remarked Carrados, stepping into the room as Mrs Creake returned. 'I suppose you are very fond of gardening?'

'I detest it,' she replied.

'But this *Gloire*, so carefully trained—?'

'Is it?' she replied. 'I think my husband was nailing it up recently.' By some strange fatality Carrados' most aimless remarks seemed to involve the absent Mr Creake. 'Do you care to see the garden?'

The garden proved to be extensive and neglected. Behind the house was chiefly orchard. In front, some semblance of order had been kept up; here it was lawn and shrubbery, and the drive they had walked along. Two things interested Carrados: the soil at the foot of the balcony, which he declared on examination to be particularly suitable for roses, and the fine chestnut-tree in the corner by the road.

As they walked back to the car Mr Carlyle lamented that they had learned so little of Creake's movements.

'Perhaps the telegram will tell us something,' suggested Carrados. 'Read it, Louis.'

Mr Carlyle cut open the envelope, glanced at the enclosure, and in spite of his disappointment could not restrain a chuckle.

'My poor Max,' he explained, 'you have put yourself to an amount of ingenious trouble for nothing. Creake is evidently taking a few days' holiday and prudently availed himself of the Meteorological Office forecast before going. Listen: *"Immediate prospect for London warm and settled. Further outlook cooler but fine."* Well, well; I did get a pound of tomatoes for *my* fourpence.'

'You certainly scored there, Louis,' admitted Carrados, with humorous appreciation. 'I wonder,' he added speculatively, 'whether it is Creake's peculiar taste usually to spend his week-end holiday in London.'

'Eh?' exclaimed Mr Carlyle, looking at the words again, 'by gad, that's rum, Max. They go to Weston-super-Mare. Why on earth should he want to know about London?'

'I can make a guess, but before we are satisfied I must come here again. Take another look at that kite, Louis. Are there a few yards of string hanging loose from it?'

'Yes, there are.'

'Rather thick string—unusually thick for the purpose?'

'Yes; but how do you know?'

As they drove home again Carrados explained, and Mr Carlyle sat aghast, saying incredulously: 'Good God, Max, is it possible?'

An hour later he was satisfied that it was possible. In reply to his inquiry someone in his office telephoned him the information that 'they' had left Paddington by the four-thirty for Weston.

It was more than a week after his introduction to Carrados that Lieutenant

Hollyer had a summons to present himself at The Turrets again. He found Mr Carlyle already there and the two friends awaiting his arrival.

'I stayed in all day after hearing from you this morning, Mr Carrados,' he said, shaking hands. 'When I got your second message I was all ready to walk straight out of the house. That's how I did it in the time. I hope everything is all right?'

'Excellent,' replied Carrados. 'You'd better have something before we start. We probably have a long and perhaps an exciting night before us.'

'And certainly a wet one,' assented the lieutenant. 'It was thundering over Mulling way as I came along.'

'That is why you are here,' said his host. 'We are waiting for a certain message before we start, and in the meantime you may as well understand what we expect to happen. As you saw, there is a thunderstorm coming on. The Meteorological Office morning forecast predicted it for the whole of London if the conditions remained. That was why I kept you in readiness. Within an hour it is now inevitable that we shall experience a deluge. Here and there damage will be done to trees and buildings; here and there a person will probably be struck and killed.'

'Yes.'

'It is Mr Creake's intention that his wife should be among the victims.'

'I don't exactly follow,' said Hollyer, looking from one man to the other. 'I quite admit that Creake would be immensely relieved if such a thing did happen, but the chance is surely an absurdly remote one.'

'Yet unless we intervene it is precisely what a coroner's jury will decide has happened. Do you know whether your brother-in-law has any practical knowledge of electricity, Mr Hollyer?'

'I cannot say. He was so reserved, and we really knew so little of him—'

'Yet in 1896 an Austin Creake contributed an article on "Alternating Currents" to the American *Scientific World*. That would argue a fairly intimate acquaintanceship.'

'But do you mean that he is going to direct a flash of lightning?'

'Only into the minds of the doctor who conducts the post-mortem, and the coroner. This storm, the opportunity for which he has been waiting for weeks, is merely the cloak to his act. The weapon which he has planned to use—scarcely less powerful than lightning but much more tractable—is the high voltage current of electricity that flows along the train wire at his gate.'

'Oh!' exclaimed Lieutenant Hollyer, as the sudden revelation struck him.

'Some time between eleven o'clock to-night—about the hour when your sister goes to bed—and one-thirty in the morning—the time up to which he can rely on the current—Creake will throw a stone up at the balcony window. Most of his preparation has long been made; it only remains for him to connect up a short length to the window handle and a longer one at the other end to tap the live wire. That done, he will wake his wife in the way I have said. The moment she moves the catch of the window—and he has carefully filed its parts to ensure perfect contact—she will be electrocuted as effectually as if she sat in the executioner's chair in Sing Sing Prison.'

'But what are we doing here!' exclaimed Hollyer, starting to his feet, pale and horrified. 'It is past ten now and anything may happen.'

'Quite natural, Mr Hollyer,' said Carrados, reassuringly, 'but you need have no anxiety. Creake is being watched, the house is being watched, and your sister is as safe as if she slept to-night in Windsor Castle. Be assured that whatever happens he will not be allowed to complete his scheme; but it is desirable to let him implicate himself to the fullest limit. Your brother-in-law, Mr Hollyer, is a man with a peculiar capacity for taking pains.'

'He is a damned cold-blooded scoundrel!' exclaimed the young officer fiercely. 'When I think of Millicent five years ago—'

'Well, for that matter, an enlightened nation has decided that electrocution is the most humane way of removing its superfluous citizens,' suggested Carrados, mildly. 'He is certainly an ingenious-minded gentleman. It is his misfortune that in Mr Carlyle he was fated to be opposed by an even subtler brain—'

'No, no! Really, Max!' protested the embarrassed gentleman.

'Mr Hollyer will be able to judge for himself when I tell him that it was Mr Carlyle who first drew attention to the significance of the abandoned kite,' insisted Carrados, firmly. 'Then, of course, its object became plain to me—as indeed to anyone. For ten minutes, perhaps, a wire must be carried from the overhead line to the chestnut-tree. Creake has everything in his favour, but it is just within possibility that the driver of an inopportune tram might notice the appendage. What of that? Why, for more than a week he has seen a derelict kite with its yards of trailing string hanging in the tree. A very calculating mind, Mr Hollyer. It would be interesting to know what line of action Mr Creake has mapped out for himself afterwards. I expect he has half a dozen artistic little touches up his sleeve. Possibly he would merely singe his wife's hair, burn her feet with a red-hot poker, shiver the glass of the French window, and be content with that to let well enough alone. You see, lightning is so varied in its effects that whatever he did or did not do would be right. He is in the impregnable position of the body showing all the symptoms of death by lightning shock and nothing else but lightning to account for it—a dilated eye, heart contracted in systole, bloodless lungs shrunk to a third the normal weight, and all the rest of it. When he has removed a few outward traces of his work Creake might quite safely "discover" his dead wife and rush off for the nearest doctor. Or he may have decided to arrange a convincing alibi, and creep away, leaving the discovery to another. We shall never know; he will make no confession.'

'I wish it was well over,' admitted Hollyer. 'I'm not particularly jumpy, but this gives me a touch of the creeps.'

'Three more hours at the worst, Lieutenant,' said Carrados, cheerfully. 'Ah-ha, something is coming through now.'

He went to the telephone and received a message from one quarter; then made another connection and talked a few minutes with someone else.

'Everything working smoothly,' he remarked between times over his shoulder. 'Your sister has gone to bed, Mr Hollyer.'

Then he turned to the house telephone and distributed his orders.

'So we,' he concluded, 'must get up.'

By the time they were ready a large closed motor car was waiting. The lieutenant thought he recognised Parkinson in the well-swathed form beside the driver, but there was no temptation to linger for a second on the steps. Already the stinging rain had lashed the drive into the semblance of a frothy estuary; all round the lightning jagged its course through the incessant tremulous glow of more distant lightning, while the thunder only ceased its muttering to turn at close quarters and crackle viciously.

'One of the few things I regret missing,' remarked Carrados, tranquilly; 'but I hear a good deal of colour in it.'

The car slushed its way down to the gate, lurched a little heavily across the dip into the road, and, steadying as it came upon the straight, began to hum contentedly along the deserted highway.

'We are not going direct?' suddenly inquired Hollyer, after they had travelled perhaps half a dozen miles. The night was bewildering enough but he had the sailor's gift for location.

'No; through Hunscott Green and then by a field path to the orchard at the back,' replied Carrados. 'Keep a sharp look-out for the man with the lantern about here, Harris,' he called through the tube.

'Something flashing just ahead, sir,' came the reply, and the car slowed down and stopped.

Carrados dropped the near window as a man in glistening waterproof stepped from the shelter of a lich-gate and approached.

'Inspector Beedel, sir,' said the stranger, looking into the car.

'Quite right, Inspector,' said Carrados. 'Get in.'

'I have a man with me, sir.'

'We can find room for him as well.'

'We are very wet.'

'So shall we all be soon.'

The lieutenant changed his seat and the two burly forms took places side by side. In less than five minutes the car stopped again, this time in a grassy country lane.

'Now we have to face it,' announced Carrados. 'The inspector will show us the way.'

The car slid round and disappeared into the night, while Beedel led the party to a stile in the hedge. A couple of fields brought them to the Brookbend boundary. There a figure stood out of the black foliage, exchanged a few words with their guide and piloted them along the shadows of the orchard to the back door of the house.

'You will find a broken pane near the catch of the scullery window,' said the blind man.

'Right, sir,' replied the inspector. 'I have it. Now who goes through?'

'Mr Hollyer will open the door for us. I'm afraid you must take off your boots and all wet things, Lieutenant. We cannot risk a single spot inside.'

They waited until the back door opened, then each one divested himself in a similar manner and passed into the kitchen, where the remains of a fire still burned. The man from the orchard gathered together the discarded garments and disappeared again.

Carrados turned to the lieutenant.

'A rather delicate job for you now, Mr Hollyer. I want you to go up to your sister, wake her, and get her into another room with as little fuss as possible. Tell her as much as you think fit and let her understand that her very life depends on absolute stillness when she is alone. Don't be unduly hurried, but not a glimmer of a light, please.'

Ten minutes passed by the measure of the battered old alarm on the dresser shelf before the young man returned.

'I've had rather a time of it,' he reported, with a nervous laugh, 'but I think it will be all right now. She is in the spare room.'

'Then we will take our places. You and Parkinson come with me to the bed-room. Inspector, you have your own arrangements. Mr Carlyle will be with you.'

They dispersed silently about the house. Hollyer glanced apprehensively at the door of the spare room as they passed it, but within was as quiet as the grave. Their room lay at the other end of the passage.

'You may as well take your place in the bed now, Hollyer,' directed Carrados when they were inside and the door closed. 'Keep well down among the clothes. Creake has to get up on the balcony, you know, and he will probably peep through the window, but he dare come no farther. Then when he begins to throw up stones slip on this dressing-gown of your sister's. I'll tell you what to do after.'

The next sixty minutes drew out into the longest hour that the lieutenant had ever known. Occasionally he heard a whisper pass between the two men who stood behind the window curtains, but he could see nothing. Then Carrados threw a guarded remark in his direction.

'He is in the garden now.'

Something scraped slightly against the outer wall. But the night was full of wilder sounds, and in the house the furniture and the boards creaked and sprung between the yawling of the wind among the chimneys, the rattle of the thunder and the pelting of the rain. It was a time to quicken the steadiest pulse, and when the crucial moment came, when a pebble suddenly rang against the pane with a sound that the tense waiting magnified into a shivering crash, Hollyer leapt from the bed on the instant.

'Easy, easy,' warned Carrados, feelingly. 'We will wait for another knock.' He passed something across. 'Here is a rubber glove. I have cut the wire but you had better put it on. Stand just for a moment at the window, move the catch so that it can blow open a little, and drop immediately. Now.'

Another stone had rattled against the glass. For Hollyer to go through his part was the work merely of seconds, and with a few touches Carrados spread the dressing-gown to more effective disguise about the extended form. But an unforeseen and in the circumstances rather horrible interval followed, for Creake, in accordance with some detail of his never-revealed plan, continued to shower missile after missile against the panes until even the unimpressionable Parkinson shivered.

'The last act,' whispered Carrados, a moment after the throwing had ceased. 'He has gone round to the back. Keep as you are. We take cover now.' He pressed behind the arras of an extemporised wardrobe, and the spirit of emptiness and desolation seemed once more to reign over the lonely house.

From half a dozen places of concealment ears were straining to catch the first guiding sound. He moved very stealthily, burdened, perhaps, by some strange scruple in the presence of the tragedy that he had not feared to contrive, paused for a moment at the bedroom door, then opened it very quietly, and in the fickle light read the consummation of his hopes.

'At last!' they heard the sharp whisper drawn from his relief. 'At last!'

He took another step and two shadows seemed to fall upon him from behind, one on either side. With primitive instinct a cry of terror and surprise escaped him as he made a desperate movement to wrench himself free, and for a short second he almost succeeded in dragging one hand into a pocket. Then his wrists slowly came together and the handcuffs closed.

'I am Inspector Beedel,' said the man an his right side. 'You are charged with the attempted murder of your wife, Millicent Creake.'

'You are mad,' retorted the miserable creature, falling into a desperate calmness. 'She has been struck by lightning.'

'No, you blackguard, she hasn't,' wrathfully exclaimed his brother-in-law, jumping up. 'Would you like to see her?'

'I also have to warn you,' continued the inspector impassively, 'that anything you say may be used as evidence against you.'

A startled cry from the farther end of the passage arrested their attention.

'Mr Carrados,' called Hollyer, 'oh, come at once.'

At the open door of the other bedroom stood the lieutenant, his eyes still turned towards something in the room beyond, a little empty bottle in his hand.

'Dead!' he exclaimed tragically, with a sob, 'with this beside her. Dead just when she would have been free of the brute.'

The blind man passed into the room, sniffed the air, and laid a gentle hand on the pulseless heart.

'Yes,' he replied. 'That, Hollyer, does not always appeal to the woman, strange to say.'

John Dickson Carr
1906–1977

THE SILVER CURTAIN

THE CROUPIER'S WRIST moved with such fluent ease as to seem boneless. Over the green baize its snaky activity never hesitated, never wavered, never was still. His rake, like an enormous butter-pat, attracted the cards, flicked them up, juggled them, and slid them in a steady stream through the slot of the table.

No voice was raised in the Casino at La Bandelette. There was much casualness; hardly any laughter. The tall red curtains and the padded red floors closed in a sort of idle concentration at a dozen tables. And out of it, at table number six, the croupier's monotone droned on.

'Six mille. Banco? Six mille. Banco? Banco?'

'Banco,' said the young Englishman across the table. The cards, white and grey, slipped smoothly from the shoe. And the young man lost again.

The croupier hadn't time to notice much. The people round him, moving in hundreds through the season, were hardly human beings at all. There was a calculating machine inside his head; he heard its clicks, he watched the run of its numbers, and it was all he had time for. Yet so acutely were his senses developed that he could tell almost within a hundred francs how much money the players at his table still retained. The young man opposite was nearly broke.

(Best to be careful. This perhaps means trouble.)

Casually the croupier glanced round his table. There were five players, all English, as was to be expected. There was the fair-haired girl with the elderly man, obviously her father, who had a bald head and looked ill; he breathed behind his hand. There was the very heavy, military-looking man whom someone had addressed as Colonel March. There was the fat, sleek, swarthy young man with the twisty eyebrows (dubious English?), whose complacency had grown with his run of luck and whose wallet stuffed with *mille* notes lay at his elbow. Finally, there was the young man who lost so much.

The young man got up from his chair.

He had no poker face. The atmosphere about him was so desperately embarrassed that the fair-haired girl spoke.

'Leaving, Mr Winton?' she asked.

'Er—yes,' said Mr Winton. He seemed grateful for that little help thrown into his disquiet. He seized at it; he smiled back at her. 'No luck yet. Time to get a drink and offer up prayers for the next session.'

(Look here, thought Jerry Winton, why stand here explaining? It's not serious. You'll get out of it, even if it does mean a nasty bit of trouble. They all know you're broke. Stop standing here laughing like a gawk, and get away from the table. He looked into the eyes of the fair-haired girl, and wished he hadn't been such an ass.)'

'Get a drink,' he repeated.

He strode away from the table with (imagined) laughter following him. The sleek young man had lifted a moon-face and merely looked at him in a way that roused Jerry Winton's wrath.

Curse La Bandelette and baccarat and everything else.

'There,' reflected the croupier, 'is a young man who will have trouble with his hotel. *Banco? Six mille. Banco?*'

In the bar, which adjoined the casino-rooms, Jerry Winton crawled up on one of the high stools, called for an Armagnac, and pushed his last hundred-franc note across the counter. His head was full of a row of figures written in the spidery style of France. His hotel-bill for a week would come to—what? Four, five, six thousand francs? It would be presented to-morrow, and all he had was his return ticket to London by plane.

In the big mirror behind the bar a new image emerged from the crowd. It was that of the fat, sleek, oily-faced young man who had cleaned up such a packet at the table, and who was even now fingering his wallet lovingly before he put it away. He climbed up on a stool beside Jerry. He called for mineral water: how shrewd and finicky-crafty these expert gamblers were! He relighted the stump of a cigar in one corner of his mouth.

Then he spoke.

'Broke?' he inquired off-handedly.

Jerry Winton glared at his reflection in the mirror.

'I don't see,' Jerry said, with a slow and murderous choosing of words, 'that that's anybody's business except mine.'

'Oh, that's all right,' said the stranger, in the same unpleasantly off-handed tone. He took several puffs at his cigar; he drank a little mineral water. He added: 'I expect it's pretty serious, though? Eh?'

'If the matter,' said Jerry, turning round, 'is of so much interest to you: no, it's not serious. I have plenty of money back home. The trouble is that this is Friday night, and I can't get in touch with the bank until Monday.' Though this was quite true, he saw the other's fishy expression grow broader. 'It's a damned nuisance, because they don't know me at the hotel. But a nuisance is all it is. If you think I'm liable to go out in the garden and shoot myself, stop thinking it.'

The other smiled sadly and fishily, and shook his head.

'You don't say? I can't believe that, now can I?'

'I don't care what you believe.'

'You should care,' said his companion, unruffled. As Jerry slid down from the stool, he reached out and tapped Jerry on the arm. 'Don't be in such a rush. You say you're a boy Croesus. All right: you're a boy Croesus. *I* won't argue with you. But tell me: how's your nerve?'

'My what?'

'Your nerve. Your courage,' explained his companion, with something like a sneer.

Jerry Winton looked back at the bland, self-assured face poised above the mineral water. His companion's feet were entangled with the legs of the bar-stool; his short upper lip was lifted with acute self-confidence; and a blank eye jeered down.

'I thought I'd ask,' he pursued. 'My name is Davos, Ferdie Davos. Everybody knows me.' He swept his hand towards the crowd. 'How'd you like to make ten thousand francs?'

'I'd like it a whole lot. But I don't know whether I'd like to make it out of any business of yours.'

Davos was unruffled. 'It's no good trying to be on your dignity with me. It don't impress me and it won't help you. I still ask: how would you like to make ten thousand francs? That would more than cover what you owe or are likely to owe, wouldn't it? I thought so. Do you or don't you want to make ten thousand francs?'

'Yes, I do,' Jerry snarled back.

'All right. See a doctor.'

'*What?*'

'See a doctor,' Davos repeated coolly. 'A nerve tonic is what you want: pills. No, I'm not wise-cracking.' He looked at the clock, whose hands stood at five minutes to eleven. 'Go to this address—listen carefully while I tell you—and there'll be ten thousand in it for you. Go to this address in about an hour. No sooner, no later. Do your job properly, and there may be even more than ten thousand in it for you. Number two, Square St Jean, Avenue des Phares, in about an hour. We'll see how your nerve is then.'

LA BANDELETTE, 'the fillet', that strip of silver beach along the channel, is full of flat-roofed and queerly painted houses which give it the look of a town in a Walt Disney film. But the town itself is of secondary consideration. The English colony, which is of a frantic fashionableness, lies among great trees behind. Close to the Casino de la Forêt are three great hotels, gay with awning and piling sham Gothic turrets into the sky. The air is aromatic; open carriages clop and jingle along broad avenues; and the art of extracting money from guests has become so perfected that we find our hands going to our pockets even in sleep.

This sleep is taken by day. By night, when La Bandelette is sealed up except for the Casino, the beam of the great island lighthouse sweeps the streets. It daz-zles and then dies, once every twenty seconds. And, as Jerry Winton strode under the trees towards the Avenue of the Lighthouses, its beam was beginning to be blurred by rain.

Square St Jean, Avenue des Phares. Where? And why?

If Davos had approached him in any other way, Jerry admitted to himself, he would have paid no attention to it. But he was annoyed and curious. Besides, unless there were a trick in it, he could use ten thousand francs. There was probably a trick in it. But who cared?

It was the rain that made him hesitate. He heard it patter in the trees, and deepen to a heavy rustling, as he saw the signboard pointing to the Avenue des Phares. He was without hat or coat. But by this time he meant to see the thing through.

Ahead of him was a street of fashionable villas, lighted by mere sparks of gas. An infernally dark street. Something queer, and more than queer, about this. Total strangers didn't ask you how strong your nerves were, and then offer you ten thousand francs on top of it, for any purpose that would pass the customs. Which was all the more reason why . . .

Then he saw Davos.

Davos did not see him. Davos was ahead of him, walking fast and with little short steps along the dim street. The white beam of the lighthouse shone out overhead, turning the rain to silver; and Jerry could see the gleam of his polished black hair and the light tan topcoat he was now wearing. Pulling up the collar of his dinner-jacket, Jerry followed.

A few yards farther on Davos slackened his pace. He peered round and up. On his left was the entrance to a courtyard, evidently the Square St Jean. But to call it a 'square' was noble overstatement; it was only a cul-de-sac some twenty feet wide by forty feet deep.

Two of its three sides were merely tall, blank brick walls. The third side, on the right, was formed of a tall flat house all of whose windows were closely shuttered. But there was at least a sign of life about the house. Over its door burned a dim white globe, showing that there was a doctor's brass name-plate beside the door. A sedate house with blue-painted shutters in the bare cul-de-sac—and Davos was making for it.

All this Jerry saw at a glance. Then he moved back from the cul-de-sac. The rain was sluicing down on him, blurring the dim white globe with shadow and gleam. Davos had almost reached the doctor's door. He had paused as though to consider or look at something; and then . . .

Jerry Winton later swore that he had taken his eyes off Davos only for a second. This was true. Jerry, in fact, had glanced back along the Avenue des Phares behind him and was heartened to see the figure of a policeman some distance away. What made him look quickly back again was a noise from the cul-de-sac, a noise that was something between a cough and a scream, bubbling up horribly under the rain; and afterwards the thud of a body on asphalt.

One moment Davos had been on his feet. The next moment he was lying on his side on the pavement, and kicking.

Overhead the beam of the lighthouse wheeled again. Jerry, reaching Davos in a run of half a dozen long strides, saw the whole scene picked out by that momentary light. Davos's fingers still clutched, or tried to clutch, the well-filled wallet Jerry had last seen at the Casino. His tan topcoat was now dark with rain. His heels scraped on the pavement, for he had been stabbed through the back of the neck with a heavy knife whose polished metal handle projected four inches. Then the wallet slipped out of his fingers, and splashed into a puddle, for the man died.

JERRY WINTON LOOKED, and did not believe his own eyes. Mechanically he reached down and picked up the wallet out of the puddle, shaking it. He backed away as he heard running footfalls pound into the cul-de-sac, and he saw the flying waterproof of a policeman.

'Halt there!' the law shouted in French. The policeman, a dim shape under the waterproof, pulled up short and stared. After seeing what was on the pavement, he made a noise like a man hit in the stomach.

Jerry pulled his wits together and conned over his French for the proper phrases.

'His—this wallet,' said Jerry, extending it.

'So I see.'

'He is dead.'

'That would appear obvious,' agreed the other, with a kind of snort. 'Well! Give it to me. Quick, quick, quick! His wallet.'

The policeman extended his hand, snapping the fingers. He added: 'No stupidities, if you please! I am prepared for you.'

'But I didn't kill him.'

'That remains to be seen.'

'Man, you don't think—?'

He broke off. The trouble was that it had happened too rapidly. Jerry's feeling was that of one who meets a super-salesman and under whirlwind tactics is persuaded to buy some huge and useless article before he realises what the talk is all about.

For here was a minor miracle. He had seen the man Davos stabbed under his eyes. Davos had been stabbed by a straight blow from behind, the heavy knife entering in a straight line sloping a little upwards, as though the blow had been struck from the direction of the pavement. Yet at the same time Davos had been alone in an empty cul-de-sac as bare as a biscuit-box.

'It is not my business to think,' said the policeman curtly. 'I make my notes and I report to my commissaire. Now!' He withdrew into the shelter of the dimlit doorway, his wary eye fixed on Jerry, and whipped out his notebook. 'Let us have no nonsense. You killed this man and attempted to rob him. I saw you.'

'No!'

'You were alone with him in this court. I saw as much myself.'

'Yes, that is true.'

'Good; he admits it! You saw no one else in the court?'

'No.'

'*Justement.* Could any assassin have approached without being seen?'

Jerry, even as he saw the bleak eye grow bleaker, had to admit that this was impossible. On two sides were blank brick walls; on the third side was a house whose door or windows, he could swear, had not opened a crack. In the second's space of time while he looked away, no murderer could have approached, stabbed Davos, and got back to cover again. There was no cover. This was so apparent that Jerry could not even think of a reasonable lie. He merely stuttered.

'I do not know what happened,' he insisted. 'One minute he was there, and then he fell. I saw nobody.' Then a light opened in his mind. 'Wait! That knife there—it must have been thrown at him.'

Rich and sardonic humour stared at him from the doorway. 'Thrown, you say? Thrown from where?'

'I don't know,' admitted Jerry. The light went out. Again he stared at blank brick walls, and at the house from whose sealed front no knife could have been thrown.

'Consider,' pursued his companion, in an agony of logic, 'the position of the knife. This gentleman was walking with his back to you?'

'Yes.'

'Good; we progress.' He pointed. 'The knife enters the back of his neck in a straight line. It enters from the direction where you were standing. Could it have been thrown past you from the entrance to the court?'

'No. Impossible.'

'No. That is evident,' blared his companion. 'I cannot listen to any more stupidities. I indulge you because you are English and we have orders to indulge the English. But this goes beyond reason! You will go with me to the Hôtel de Ville. Look at the note-case in his hand. Does he offer it to you and say: "Monsieur, honour me by accepting my note-case"?'

'No. He had it in his own hand.'

'He had it in his own hand, say you. Why?'

'I don't know.'

Jerry broke off, both because the story of his losses at the Casino must now come out with deadly significance, and because they heard the rattle of a door being unlocked. The door of the doctor's house opened; and out stepped the fair-haired girl whom Jerry had last seen at the Casino.

Beside the door the brass name-plate read, 'Dr Edouard Hébert', with consulting hours inscribed underneath, and an aggressive, 'Speaks English'. Behind the girl, craning his neck, stood a bristly middle-aged man of immense dignity. His truculent eyeglasses had a broad black ribbon which seemed to form a kind of electrical circuit with the ends of his brushed-up moustache.

But Jerry Winton was not looking at Dr Hébert. He was looking at the girl. In addition to a light fur coat, she now wore a cream-coloured scarf drawn over her hair; she had in one hand a tiny box, wrapped in white paper. Her smooth, worried face, her long, pale-blue eyes, seemed to reflect the expression of the dead man staring back at her from the pavement. She jerked back, bumping into the policeman. She put her hand on Dr Hébert's arm. With her other hand she pointed sharply to Davos.

'That's the man!' she cried.

M. GORON, PREFECT OF POLICE, was a comfortable man, a round, cat-like amiable sort of man, famous for his manners. Crime, rare in La Bandelette, distressed him. But he was also an able man. At one o'clock in the morning he sat in his office at the town hall examining his finger-nails and creaking back and forth in a squeaky swivel chair whose noise had begun to get on Jerry Winton's nerves.

The girl, who for the tenth time had given her name as Eleanor Hood, was insistent.

'M. Goron!'

'Mademoiselle?' said the prefect politely, and seemed to wake out of a dream.

Eleanor Hood turned round and gave Jerry Winton a despairing look.

'I only wish to know,' she urged, in excellent French, 'why we are here, Dr Hébert and I. And Mr Winton too, if it comes to that.' This time the look she gave Jerry was one of smiling companionship: a human sort of look, which warmed that miscreant. 'But as for us—why? It is not as though we were witnesses. I have told you why I was at Dr Hébert's house.'

'Mademoiselle's father,' murmured M. Goron.

'Yes. He is ill. Dr Hébert has been treating him for several days, and he had another attack at the Casino to-night. Mr Winton will confirm that.'

Jerry nodded. The old boy at the table, he reflected, had certainly looked ill.

'I took my father back to our hotel, the Brittany, at half-past eleven,' the girl went on, speaking with great intensity. 'I tried to communicate with Dr Hébert by telephone. I could not reach him. So I went to his house; it is only a short distance from the hotel. On the way I kept seeing that man—the man you call Davos. I thought he was following me. He seemed to be looking at me from behind every tree. That is why I said, "That's the man," when I saw him lying on the pavement with his eyes open. His eyes did not even blink when the rain struck them. It was a horrible sight. I was upset. Do you blame me?'

M. Goron made a sympathetic noise.

'I reached Dr Hébert's house at perhaps twenty minutes to twelve. Dr Hébert had retired, but he consented to go with me. I waited while he dressed. We went out, and on the doorstep we found—what you know. Please believe that is all I know about it.'

She had a singularly expressive voice and personality. She was either all anxiety or all persuasiveness, fashioning the clipped syllables. When she turned her wrist, you saw Davos lying in the rain and the searchlight wheeling overhead. Then she added abruptly in English, looking at Jerry:

'He was a nasty little beast; but I don't for a moment believe you killed him.'

'Thanks. But why?'

'I don't know,' said Eleanor simply. 'You just couldn't have.'

'Now there is logic!' cried M. Goron, giving his desk an admiring whack.

M. Goron's swivel chair creaked with pleasure. There were many lights in his office, which smelt of creosote. On the desk in front of him lay Davos's sodden wallet and (curiously) the tiny round box, wrapped in a spill of paper, which

Eleanor Hood had been carrying. M. Goron never spoke to Jerry, never looked at him; ignored him as completely and blandly as though he were not there.

'But,' he continued, growing very sober again, 'you will forgive me, mademoiselle, if I pursue this matter further. You say that Dr Hébert has been treating your father?'

'Yes.'

M. Goron pointed to the small box on the table.

'With pills, perhaps?'

'Ah, my God!' said Dr Hébert, and slapped his forehead tragically.

For several minutes Jerry had been afraid that the good doctor would have an apoplectic stroke. Dr Hébert had indicated his distinguished position in the community. He had pointed out that physicians do not go out in the middle of the night on errands of mercy, and then get dragged off to police stations; it is bad for business. His truculent eyeglasses and moustache bristling, he left off his stiff pacing of the room only to go and look the prefect in the eye.

'I *will* speak,' he said coldly, from deep in his throat.

'As monsieur pleases.'

'Well, it is as this lady says! Why are we here? Why? We are not witnesses.' He broke off, and slapped at the shoulders of his coat as though to rid himself of insects. 'This young man here tells us a story which may or may not be true. If it is true, I do not see why the man Davos should have given him *my* address. I do not see why Davos should have been knifed on my doorstep. I did not know the man Davos, except as a patient of mine.'

'Ah!' said the prefect. 'You gave him pills, perhaps?'

Dr Hébert sat down.

'Are you mad on the subject of pills?' he inquired, with restraint. 'Because this young man'—again he looked with disfavour at Jerry—'tells you that Davos made some drunken mention of "pills" at the Casino to-night, is that why you pursue the subject?'

'It is possible.'

'It is ridiculous,' said Dr Hébert. 'Do you even question my pills on the desk there? They are for Miss Hood's father. They are ordinary tablets, with digitalin for the heart. Do you think they contain poison? If so, why not test them?'

'It is an idea,' conceded M. Goron.

He picked up the box and removed the paper.

The box contained half a dozen sugar-coated pellets. With great seriousness M. Goron put one of the tablets into his mouth, tasted it, bit it, and finally appeared to swallow it.

'No poison?' asked the doctor.

'No poison,' agreed M. Goron. The telephone on his desk rang. He picked it up, listened for a moment with a dreamy smile, and replaced it. 'Now this is really excellent!' he beamed, rubbing his hands. 'My good friend Colonel March, of the English police, has been making investigations. He was sent here when a certain form of activity in La Bandelette became intolerable both to the French and English authorities. You perhaps noticed him at the Casino to-night, all of you?'

'I remember,' said Jerry suddenly. 'Very large bloke, quiet as sin.'

'An apt description,' said the prefect.

'But—' began Dr Hébert.

'I said "all of you", Dr Hébert,' repeated the prefect. 'One small question is permitted? I thank you. When mademoiselle telephoned to your house at eleven-thirty to-night, you were not there. You were at the Casino, perhaps?'

Dr Hébert stared at him.

'It is possible. But—'

'You saw M. Davos there, perhaps?'

'It is possible.' Still Dr Hébert stared at him with hideous perplexity. 'But, M. Goron, will you have the goodness to explain this? You surely do not suspect either mademoiselle or myself of having any concern with this business? You do not think that either mademoiselle or I left the house at the time of the murder?'

'I am certain you did not.'

'You do not think either mademoiselle or myself went near a door or window to get at this accursed Davos?'

'I am certain you did not,' beamed the prefect.

'Well, then?'

'But there, you see,' argued M. Goron, lifting one finger for emphasis, 'we encounter a difficulty. We are among thorns. For this would mean that M. Winton must have committed the murder. And that,' he added, looking at Jerry, 'is absurd. We never for a moment believed that M. Winton had anything to do with this; and my friend Colonel March will tell you why.'

Jerry sat back and studied the face of the prefect, wondering if he had heard aright. He felt like an emotional punching-bag. But with great gravity he returned the prefect's nod as a sergent de ville opened the door of the office.

'We will spik English,' announced M. Goron, bouncing up. 'This is my friend Colonel March.'

'Evening,' said the colonel. His large, speckled face was as bland as M. Goron's; his fists were on his hips. He looked first at Eleanor, then at Jerry, then at Dr Hébert. 'Sorry you were put to this inconvenience, Miss Hood. But I've seen your father, and it will be all right. As for you, Mr Winton, I hope they have put you out of your misery?'

'Misery?'

'Told you you're not headed for Devil's Island, or anything of the sort? We had three very good reasons for believing you had nothing to do with this. Here is the first reason.'

Reaching into the pocket of his dinner-jacket, he produced an article which he held out to them. It was a black leather note-case, exactly like the one already on M. Goron's desk. But whereas the first was stuffed with *mille* notes, this one had only a few hundred francs in it.

'We found this second note-case in Davos's pocket,' said Colonel March.

He seemed to wait for a comment, but none came.

'Well, what about it?' Jerry demanded, after a pause.

'Oh, come! Two note-cases! Why was Davos carrying two note-cases? Why should any man carry two note-cases? That is my first reason. Here is my second.'

From the inside pocket of his coat, with the air of a conjurer, he drew out the knife with which Davos had been stabbed.

A suggestive sight. Now cleansed of blood, it was a long, thin, heavy blade with a light metal handle and cross-piece. As Colonel March turned it round, glittering in the light, Jerry Winton felt that its glitter struck a chord of familiarity in his mind: that a scene from the past had almost come back to him: that, for a swift and tantalising second, he had almost grasped the meaning of the whole problem.

'And now we come to my third reason,' said Colonel March. 'The third reason is Ferdie Davos. Ferdie was a hotel thief. A great deal too clever for us poor policemen. Eh, Goron? Though I always told him he was a bad judge of men. At the height of the summer season, at hotels like the Brittany and the Donjon, he had rich pickings. He specialised in necklaces; particularly in pearl necklaces. Kindly note that.'

A growing look of comprehension had come into Eleanor Hood's face. She opened her mouth to speak, and then checked herself.

'His problem,' pursued Colonel March, 'was how to smuggle the stolen stuff over to England, where he had a market for it. He couldn't carry it himself. In a little place like La Bandelette, Goron would have had him turned inside out if he had as much as taken a step towards Boulogne. So he had to have accomplices. I mean accomplices picked from among the hordes of unattached young men who come here every season. Find some young fool who's just dropped more than he can afford at the tables; and he may grab at the chance to earn a few thousand francs by a little harmless customs bilking. You follow me, Mr Winton?'

'You mean that I was chosen—?'

'Yes.'

'But, good Lord, how? I couldn't smuggle a pearl necklace through the customs if my life depended on it.'

'You could if you needed a tonic,' Colonel March pointed out. 'Davos told you so. The necklace would first be taken to pieces for you. Each pearl would be given a thick sugar-coating, forming a neat medicinal pill. They would then be poured into a neat bottle or box under the prescription of a well-known doctor. At the height of the tourist rush, the customs can't curry-comb everybody. They would be looking for a pearl-smuggler: not for an obviously respectable young tourist with stomach trouble.'

Eleanor Hood, with sudden realisation in her face, looked at the box of pills on M. Goron's desk.

'So *that* is why you tasted my pills!' she said to the prefect of police, who made deprecating noises. 'And kept me here for so long. And—'

'Mademoiselle, I assure you!' said M. Goron. 'We were sure there was nothing wrong with those pills!' He somewhat spoiled the gallant effect of this by adding: 'There are not enough of them, for one thing. But, since you received them from Dr Hébert after office hours, you had to be investigated. The trick is neat, hein? I fear the firm of Hébert and Davos have been working it for some time.'

They all turned to look at Dr Hébert.

He was sitting bolt upright, his chin drawn into his collar as though he were going to sing. On his face was a look of what can only be called frightened scepticism. Even his mouth was half open with this effect, or with unuttered sounds of ridicule.

'We were also obliged to delay you all,' pursued M. Goron, 'until my men found Madame Fley's pearls, which were stolen a week ago, hidden in Dr Hébert's surgery. I repeat: it was a neat trick. We might never have seen it if Davos had not incautiously hinted at it to M. Winton. But then Davos was getting a bit above himself.' He added: 'That, Colonel March thinks, is why Dr Hébert decided to kill him.'

Still Dr Hébert said nothing.

It was, in fact, Jerry Winton who spoke. 'Sir, I don't hold any brief for this fellow. I should think you were right. But how could he have killed Davos? He couldn't have!'

'You are forgetting,' said Colonel March, as cheerfully as though the emotional temperature of the room had not gone up several degrees, 'you are forgetting the two note-cases. Why was Davos carrying two note-cases?'

'Well?'

'He wasn't,' said Colonel March, with his eye on Hébert. 'Our good doctor here was, of course, the brains of the partnership. He supplied the resources for Ferdie's noble front. When Ferdie played baccarat at the Casino, he was playing with Dr Hébert's money. And, when Dr Hébert saw Ferdie at the Casino to-night, he very prudently took away the large sum you saw in Ferdie's note-case at the tables. When Ferdie came to the doctor's house at midnight, he had only his few hundred francs commission in his own note-case, which was in his pocket.

'You see, Dr Hébert needed that large sum of money in his plan to kill Ferdie. He knew what time Ferdie would call at his house. He knew Mr Winton would be close behind Ferdie. Mr Winton would, in fact, walk into the murder and get the blame. All Dr Hébert had to do was take that packet of *mille* notes, stuff them into another note-case just like Ferdie Davos's, and use it as a trap.'

'A trap?' repeated Eleanor.

'A trap,' said Colonel March.

'Your presence, Miss Hood,' he went on, 'gave the doctor an unexpected alibi. He left you downstairs in his house. He went upstairs to "get dressed". A few minutes before Davos was due to arrive, he went quietly up to the roof of his house—a flat roof, like most of those in La Bandelette. He looked down over the parapet into that cul-de-sac, forty feet below. He saw his own doorstep with the lamp burning over it. He dropped that note-case over the parapet, so that it landed on the pavement before his own doorstep.

'Well?' continued Colonel March. 'What would Davos do? What would *you* do, if you walked along a pavement and saw a note-case bulging with thousand-franc notes lying just in front of you?'

Again Jerry Winton saw that dim cul-de-sac. He heard the rain splashing; he saw it moving and gleaming past the door-lamp, and past the beam of the light-house overhead. He saw the jaunty figure of Davos stop short as though to look at something—

'I imagine,' Jerry said, 'that I'd bend over and pick up the note-case.'

'Yes,' said Colonel March. 'That's the whole sad story. You would bend over so that your body was parallel with the ground. The back of your neck would be a plain target to anybody standing forty feet up above you, with a needle-sharp knife whose blade is much heavier than the handle. The murderer has merely to drop that knife: stretch out his fingers and drop it. Gravity will do the rest.

'My friend, you looked straight at that murder; and you never saw it. You never saw it because a shifting, gleaming wall of rain, a kind of silver curtain, fell across the door-lamp and the beam of the lighthouse. It hid the fall of a thin, long blade made of bright metal. Behind that curtain moved invisibly our inge-nious friend Dr Hébert, who, if he can be persuaded to speak—'

Dr Hébert could not be persuaded to speak, even when they took him away. But Eleanor Hood and Jerry Winton walked home through the summer dawn, under a sky coloured with a less evil silver; and they had discovered any number of mutual acquaintances by the time they reached the hotel.

Raymond Chandler
1888–1959

GOLDFISH

1

I WASN'T DOING any work that day, just catching up on my foot-dangling. A warm gusty breeze was blowing in at the office window and the soot from the *Mansion House Hotel* oil-burners across the alley was rolling across the glass top of my desk in tiny particles, like pollen drifting over a vacant lot.

I was just thinking about going to lunch when Kathy Horne came in.

She was a tall, seedy, sad-eyed blonde who had once been a policewoman and had lost her job when she married a cheap little check-bouncer named Johnny Horne, to reform him. She hadn't reformed him, but she was waiting for him to come out so she could try again. In the meantime she ran the cigar counter at the *Mansion House*, and watched the grifters go by in a haze of nickel cigar smoke. And once in a while lent one of them ten dollars to get out of town. She was just that soft. She sat down and opened her big shiny bag and got out a package of cigarettes and lit one with my desk lighter. She blew a plume of smoke, wrinkled her nose at it.

'Did you ever hear of the Leander pearls?' she asked. 'Gosh, that blue serge shines. You must have money in the bank, the clothes you wear.'

'No,' I said, 'to both your ideas. I never heard of the Leander pearls and don't have any money in the bank.'

'Then you'd like to make yourself a cut of twenty-five grand maybe.'

I lit one of her cigarettes. She got up and shut the window, saying: 'I get enough of that hotel smell on the job.'

She sat down again, went on:

'It's nineteen years ago. They had the guy in Leavenworth fifteen and it's four since they let him out. A big lumberman from up north named Sol Leander bought them for his wife—the pearls, I mean—just two of them. They cost two hundred grand.'

'It must have taken a hand truck to move them,' I said.

'I see you don't know a lot about pearls,' Kathy Horne said. 'It's not just size. Anyhow they're worth more to-day and the twenty-five-grand reward the Reliance people put out is still good.'

'I get it,' I said. 'Somebody copped them off.'

'Now you're getting yourself some oxygen.' She dropped her cigarette into a tray and let it smoke, as ladies will. I put it out for her. 'That's what the guy was in Leavenworth for, only they never proved he got the pearls. It was a mail-car job. He got himself hidden in the car somehow and up in Wyoming he shot the clerk, cleaned out the registered mail and dropped off. He got to BC before he was nailed. But they didn't get any of the stuff—not then. All they got was him. He got life.'

'If it's going to be a long story, let's have a drink.'

'I never drink until sundown. That way you don't get to be a heel.'

'Tough on the Eskimos,' I said. 'In the summertime, anyway.'

She watched me get my little flat bottle out. Then she went on:

'His name was Sype—Wally Sype. He did it alone. And he wouldn't squawk about the stuff, not a peep. Then after fifteen long years they offered him a pardon, if he would loosen up with the loot. He gave up everything but the pearls.'

'Where did he have it?' I asked. 'In his hat?'

'Listen, this isn't just a bunch of gag lines. I've got a lead to those marbles.'

I shut my mouth with my hand and looked solemn.

'He said he never had the pearls and they must have halfway believed him because they gave him the pardon. Yet the pearls were in the load, registered mail, and they were never seen again.'

My throat began to feel a little thick. I didn't say anything.

Kathy Horne went on:

'One time in Leavenworth, just one time in all those years, Wally Sype wrapped himself around a can of white shellac and got as tight as a fat lady's girdle. His cell mate was a little man they called Peeler Mardo. He was doing twenty-seven months for splitting twenty-dollar bills; Sype told him he had the pearls buried somewhere in Idaho.'

I leaned forward a little.

'Beginning to get to you, eh?' she said. 'Well get this. Peeler Mardo is rooming at my house and he's a coke-hound and he talks in his sleep.'

I leaned back again. 'Good grief,' I said. 'And I was practically spending the reward money.'

She stared at me coldly. Then her face softened. 'All right,' she said a little hopelessly. 'I know it sounds screwy. All those years gone by and all the smart heads that must have worked on the case, postal men and private agencies and all. And then a coke-head to turn it up. But he's a nice little runt and somehow I believe him. He knows where Sype is.'

I said: 'Did he talk all this in his sleep?'

'Of course not. But you know me. An old policewoman's got ears. Maybe I was nosy, but I guessed he was an ex-con and I worried about him using the stuff so much. He's the only roomer I've got now and I'd kind of go in by his door and listen to him talking to himself. That way I got enough to brace him. He told me the rest. He wants help to collect.'

I leaned forward again. 'Where's Sype?'

Kathy Horne smiled, and shook her head. 'That's the one thing he wouldn't tell, that and the name Sype is using now. But it's somewhere up North, in or near Olympia, Washington. Peeler saw him up there and found out about him and he says Sype didn't see *him*.'

'What's Peeler doing down here?' I asked.

'Here's where they put the Leavenworth rap on him. You know an old con always goes back to look at the piece of sidewalk he slipped on. But he doesn't have any friends here now.'

I lit another cigarette and had another little drink.

'Sype has been out four years, you say. Peeler did twenty-seven months. What's he been doing with all the time since?'

Kathy Horne widened her china-blue eyes pityingly. 'Maybe you think there's only one jailhouse he could get into.'

'OK,' I said. 'Will he talk to me? I guess he wants help to deal with the insurance people, in case there are any pearls and Sype will put them right in Peeler's hand and so on. Is that it?'

Kathy Horne sighed. 'Yes, he'll talk to you. He's aching to. He's scared about something. Will you go out now, before he gets junked up for the evening?'

'Sure—if that's what you want.'

She took a flat key out of her bag and wrote an address on my pad. She stood up slowly.

'It's a double house. My side's separate. There's a door in between, with the key on my side. That's just in case he won't come to the door.'

'OK,' I said. I blew smoke at the ceiling and stared at her.

She went towards the door, stopped, came back. She looked down at the floor.

'I don't rate much in it,' she said. 'Maybe not anything. But if I could have a grand or two waiting for Johnny when he came out, maybe—'

'Maybe you could hold him straight,' I said. 'It's a dream, Kathy. It's all a dream. But if it isn't you cut an even third.'

She caught her breath and glared at me to keep from crying. She went towards the door, stopped and came back again.

'That isn't all,' she said. 'It's the old guy—Sype. He did fifteen years. He paid. Paid hard. Doesn't it make you feel kind of mean?'

I shook my head. 'He stole them, didn't he? He killed a man. What does he do for a living?'

'His wife has money,' Kathy Horne said. 'He just plays around with goldfish.'

'Goldfish?' I said. 'To hell with him.'

She went on out.

2

THE LAST TIME I had been in the Gray Lake district I had helped a DA's man named Bernie Obis shoot a gunman named Poke Andrews. But that was higher up the hill, further away from the lake. This house was on the second level, in a loop the street made rounding a spur of the hill. It stood by itself high up, with a cracked retaining wall in front and several vacant lots behind.

Being originally a double house it had two front doors and two sets of front steps. One of the doors had a sign tacked over the grating that masked the peep window: Ring 1432.

I parked my car and went up right-angle steps, passed between two lines of pinks, went up more steps to the side with the sign. That should be the roomer's side. I rang the bell. Nobody answered it, so I went across to the other door. Nobody answered that one either.

While I was waiting a gray Dodge coupé whished around the curve and a small neat girl in blue looked up at me for a second. I didn't see who else was in the car. I didn't pay much attention. I didn't know it was important.

I took out Kathy Horne's key and let myself into a closed living-room that smelled of cedar oil. There was just enough furniture to get by, net curtains, a quiet shaft of sunlight under the drapes in front. There was a tiny breakfast room, a kitchen, a bedroom in the back that was obviously Kathy's, a bathroom, another bedroom in front that seemed to be used as a sewing-room. It was this room that had the door cut through to the other side of the house.

I unlocked it and stepped, as it were, through a mirror. Everything was backward, except the furniture. The living-room on that side had twin beds, didn't have the look of being lived in.

I went toward the back of the house, past the second bathroom, knocked at the shut door that corresponded to Kathy's bedroom.

No answer. I tried the knob and went in. The little man on the bed was probably Peeler Mardo. I noticed his feet first, because although he had on trousers and a shirt, his feet were bare and hung over the end of the bed. They were tied there by a rope around the ankles.

They had been burned raw on the soles. There was a smell of scorched flesh in spite of the open window. Also a smell of scorched wood. An electric iron on a desk was still connected. I went over and shut it off.

I went back to Kathy Horne's kitchen and found a pint of Brooklyn Scotch in the cooler. I used some of it and breathed deeply for a little while and looked out over the vacant lots. There was a narrow cement walk behind the house and green wooden steps down to the street.

I went back to Peeler Mardo's room. The coat of a brown suit with a red pin stripe hung over a chair with the pockets turned out and what had been in them on the floor.

He was wearing the trousers of the suit, and their pockets were turned out also. Some keys and change and a handkerchief lay on the bed beside him, and a metal box like a woman's compact, from which some glistening white powder had spilled. Cocaine.

He was a little man, not more than five feet four, with thin brown hair and large ears. His eyes had no particular color. They were just eyes, and very wide open, and quite dead. His arms were pulled out from him and tied at the wrists by a rope that went under the bed.

I looked him over for bullet or knife wounds, didn't find any. There wasn't a mark on him except his feet. Shock or heart failure or a combination of the two must have done the trick. He was still warm. The gag in his mouth was both warm and wet.

I wiped off everything I had touched, looked out of Kathy's front window for a while before I left the house.

It was three-thirty when I walked into the lobby of the *Mansion House*, over to the cigar counter in the corner. I leaned on the glass and asked for Camels.

Kathy Horne flicked the pack at me, dropped the change into my outside breast pocket, and gave me her customer's smile.

'Well? You didn't take long,' she said, and looked sidewise along her eyes at a drunk who was trying to light a cigar with the old-fashioned flint and steel lighter.

'It's heavy,' I told her. 'Get set.'

She turned away quickly and flipped a pack of paper matches along the glass to the drunk. He fumbled for them, dropped both matches and cigar, scooped them angrily off the floor and went off looking back over his shoulder, as if he expected a kick.

Kathy looked past my head, her eyes cool and empty.

'I'm set,' she whispered.

'You cut a full half,' I said. 'Peeler's out. He's been bumped off—in his bed.'

Her eyes twitched. Two fingers curled on the glass near my elbow. A white line showed around her mouth. That was all.

'Listen,' I said. 'Don't say anything until I'm through. He died of shock. Somebody burned his feet with a cheap electric iron. Not yours. I looked. I'd say he died rather quickly and couldn't have said much. The gag was still in his mouth. When I went out there, frankly, I thought it was all hooey. Now I'm not so sure. If he gave up his dope, we're through, and so is Sype, unless I can find him first. Those workers didn't have any inhibitions at all. If he didn't give up, there's still time.'

Her head turned, her set eyes looked toward the revolving door of the lobby entrance. White patches glared in her cheeks.

'What do I do?' she breathed.

I poked at a box of wrapped cigars, dropped her key into it. Her long fingers got it out smoothly, hid it.

'When you get home you find him. You don't know a thing. Leave the pearls out, leave me out. When they check his prints they'll know he had a record and they'll just figure it was something caught up with him.'

I broke my cigarettes open and lit one, watched her for a moment. She didn't move an inch.

'Can you face it down?' I asked. 'If you can't, now's the time to speak.'

'Of course.' Her eyebrows arched. 'Do I look like a torturer?'

'You married a crook,' I said grimly.

She flushed, which was what I wanted. 'He isn't! He's just a damn fool! Nobody thinks any the worse of me, not even the boys down at Headquarters.'

'All right. I like it that way. It's not our murder, after all. And if we talk now, you can say good-bye to any share in any reward—even if one is ever paid.'

'Darn tootin',' Kathy Horne said pertly. 'Oh, the poor little runt,' she almost sobbed.

I patted her arm, grinned as heartily as I could and left the *Mansion House*.

3

THE RELIANCE Indemnity Company had offices in the Graas Building, three small rooms that looked like nothing at all. They were a big enough outfit to be as shabby as they liked.

The resident manager was named Lutin, a middle-aged bald-headed man with quiet eyes, dainty fingers that caressed a dappled cigar. He sat behind a large, well-dusted desk and stared peacefully at my chin.

'Carmady, eh? I've heard of you.' He touched my card with a shiny little finger. 'What's on your mind?'

I rolled a cigarette around in my fingers and lowered my voice. 'Remember the Leander pearls?'

His smile was slow, a little bored. 'I'm not likely to forget them. They cost this company one hundred and fifty thousand dollars. I was a cocky young adjuster then.'

I said: 'I've got an idea. It may be all haywire. It very likely is. But I'd like to try it out. Is your twenty-five-grand reward still good?'

He chuckled. 'Twenty grand, Carmady. We spent the difference ourselves. You're wasting time.'

'It's my time. Twenty it is then. How much co-operation can I get?'

'What kind of co-operation?'

'Can I have a letter identifying me to your other branches? In case I have to go out of the State. In case I need kind words from some local law.'

'Which way out of the State?'

I smiled at him. He tapped his cigar on the edge of a tray and smiled back. Neither of our smiles was honest.

'No letter,' he said. 'New York wouldn't stand for it. We have our own tie-up. But all the co-operation you can use, under the hat. And the twenty grand, if you click. Of course you won't.'

I lit my cigarette and leaned back, puffed smoke at the ceiling.

'No? Why not? You never got those marbles. They existed, didn't they?'

'Darn right they existed. And if they still do, they belong to us. But two hundred grand doesn't get buried for twenty years—and then get dug up.'

'All right. It's still my own time.'

He knocked a little ash off his cigar and looked down his eyes at me. 'I like your front,' he said, 'even if you are crazy. But we're a large organisation. Suppose I have you covered from now on. What then?'

'I lose. I'll know I'm covered. I'm too long in the game to miss that. I'll quit, give up what I know to the law, and go home.'

'Why would you do that?'

I leaned forward over the desk again. 'Because,' I said slowly, 'the guy that had the lead got bumped off to-day.'

'Oh—oh.' Lutin rubbed his nose.

'I didn't bump him off,' I added.

We didn't talk any more for a little while. Then Lutin said:

'You don't want any letter. You wouldn't even carry it. And after your telling me that, you know damn well I won't dare give it to you.'

I stood up, grinned, started for the door. He got up himself, very fast, ran around the desk and put his small neat hand on my arm.

'Listen, I know you're crazy, but if you do get anything, bring it in through our boys. We need the advertising.'

'What the hell do you think I live on?' I growled.

'Twenty-five grand.'

'I thought it was twenty.'

'Twenty-five. And you're still crazy. Sype never had those pearls. If he had, he'd have made some kind of terms with us many years ago.'

'OK,' I said. 'You've had plenty of time to make up your mind.'

We shook hands, grinned at each other like a couple of wise boys who know they're not kidding anybody, but won't give up trying.

It was a quarter to five when I got back to the office. I had a couple of short drinks and stuffed a pipe and sat down to interview my brains. The phone rang.

A woman's voice said: 'Carmady?' It was a small, tight, cold voice. I didn't know it.

'Yeah.'

'Better see Rush Madder. Know him?'

'No,' I lied. 'Why should I see him?'

There was a sudden tinkling, icy-cold laugh on the wire. 'On account of a guy had sore feet,' the voice said.

The phone clicked. I put my end of it aside, struck a match and stared at the wall until the flame burned my fingers.

Rush Madder was a shyster in the Quorn Building. An ambulance-chaser, a small-time fixer, an alibi builder-upper, anything that smelled a little and paid a little more. I hadn't heard of him in connection with any big operations like burning people's feet.

4

It was getting toward quitting time on lower Spring Street. Taxis were dawdling close to the curb, stenographers were getting an early start home, street cars were clogging up, and traffic cops were preventing people from making perfectly legal right turns.

The Quorn Building was a narrow front, the color of dried mustard, with a large case of false teeth in the entrance. The directory held the names of painless dentists, people who teach you how to become a letter-carrier, just names, and numbers without any names. Rush Madder, Attorney-at-Law, was in Room 619.

I got out of a jolting open-cage elevator, looked at a dirty spittoon on a dirty rubber mat, walked down a corridor that smelled of butts, and tried the knob below the frosted glass panel of 619. The door was locked. I knocked.

A shadow came against the glass and the door was pulled back with a squeak. I was looking at a thick-set man with a soft round chin, heavy black eyebrows, an oily complexion, and a Charlie Chan mustache that made his face look fatter than it was.

He put out a couple of nicotined fingers. 'Well, well, the old dog-catcher himself. The eye that never forgets. Carmady is the name, I believe?'

I stepped inside and waited for the door to squeak shut. A bare carpetless room paved in brown linoleum, a flat desk and a rolltop at right angles to it, a big green safe that looked as fireproof as a delicatessen bag, two filing cases, three chairs, a built-in closet, and washbowl in the corner by the door.

'Well, well, sit down,' Madder said. 'Glad to see you.' He fussed around behind his desk and adjusted a burst-out seat cushion, sat on it. 'Nice of you to drop around. Business?'

I sat down and put a cigarette between my teeth and looked at him. I didn't say a word. I watched him start to sweat. It started up in his hair. Then he grabbed a pencil and made marks on his blotter. Then he looked at me with a quick darting glance, down at his blotter again. He talked—to the blotter.

'Any ideas?' he asked softly.

'About what?'

He didn't look at me. 'About how we could do a little business together. Say, in stones.'

'Who was the wren?' I asked.

'Huh? What wren?' He still didn't look at me.

'The one that phoned me.'

'Did somebody phone you?'

I reached for his telephone, which was the old-fashioned gallows type. I lifted off the receiver and started to dial the number of Police Headquarters, very slowly. I knew he would know that number about as well as he knew his hat.

He reached over and pushed the hook down. 'Now, listen,' he complained. 'You're too fast. What you calling coppers for?'

I said slowly: 'They want to talk to you. On account of you know a broad that knows a man had sore feet.'

'Does it have to be that way?' His collar was too tight now. He yanked at it.

'Not from my side. But if you think I'm going to sit here and let you play with my reflexes, it does.'

Madder opened a flat tin of cigarettes and pushed one past his lips with a sound like somebody gutting a fish. His hand shook.

'All right,' he said thickly. 'All right. Don't get sore.'

'Just stop trying to count clouds with me,' I growled. 'Talk sense. If you've got a job for me, it's probably too dirty for me to touch. But I'll at least listen.'

He nodded. He was comfortable now. He knew I was bluffing. He puffed a pale swirl of smoke and watched it float up.

'That's all right,' he said evenly. 'I play dumb myself once in a while. The thing is we're wise. Carol saw you go to the house and leave it again. No law came.'

'Carol?'

'Carol Donovan. Friend of mine. She called you up.'

I nodded. 'Go ahead.'

He didn't say anything. He just sat there and looked at me owlishly.

I grinned and leaned across the desk a little and said: 'Here's what's bothering you. You don't know why I went to the house or why, having gone, I didn't yell police. That's easy. I thought it was a secret.'

'We're just kidding each other,' Madder said sourly.

'All right,' I said. 'Let's talk about pearls. Does that make it any easier?'

His eyes shone. He wanted to let himself get excited, but he didn't. He kept his voice down, said coolly:

'Carol picked him up one night, the little guy. A crazy little number, full of snow, but way back in his noodle an idea. He'd talk about pearls, about an old guy up in the northwest of Canada that swiped them a long time ago and still had them. Only he wouldn't say who the old guy was or where he was. Foxy about that. Holding out. I wouldn't know why.'

'He wanted to get his feet burned,' I said.

Madder's lips shook and another fine sweat showed in his hair.

'I didn't do that,' he said thickly.

'You or Carol, what's the odds? The little guy died. They can make murder out of it. You didn't find out what you wanted to know. That's why *I'm* here. You think I have information you didn't get. Forget it. If I knew enough, I wouldn't be here, and if you knew enough, you wouldn't want me here. Check?'

He grinned, very slowly, as if it hurt him. He struggled up in his chair and dragged a deep drawer out from the side of his desk, put a nicely molded brown bottle up on the desk, and two striped glasses. He whispered:

'Two-way split. You and me. I'm cutting Carol out. She's too damn' rough, Carmady. I've seen hard women, but she's the blueing on armor plate. And you'd never think it to look at her, would you?'

'Have I seen her?'

'I guess so. She says you did.'

'Oh, the girl in the Dodge.'

He nodded, and poured two good-sized drinks, put the bottle down and stood up. 'Water? I like it in mine.'

'No,' I said, 'but why cut me in? I don't know any more than you mentioned. Or very little. Certainly not as much as you must know to go that far.'

He leered across the glasses. 'I know where I can get fifty grand for the Leander pearls, twice what you could get. I can give you yours and still have mine. You've got the front I need to work in the open. How about the water?'

'No water,' I said.

He went across to the built-in wash place and ran the water and came back with his glass half full. He sat down again, grinned, lifted it.

We drank.

5

So FAR I HAD only made four mistakes. The first was mixing in it at all, even for Kathy Horne's sake. The second was staying mixed after I found Peeler Mardo dead. The third was letting Rush Madder see I knew what he was talking about. The fourth, the whiskey, was the worst.

It tasted funny even on the way down. Then there was that sudden moment of sharp lucidity when I knew, exactly as though I had seen it, that he had switched his drink for a harmless one cached in the closet.

I sat still for a moment, with the empty glass at my fingers' ends, gathering my strength. Madder's face began to get large and moony and vague. A fat smile jerked in and out under his Charlie Chan mustache as he watched me.

I reached back into my hip pocket and pulled out a loosely wadded handkerchief. The small sap inside it didn't seem to show. At least Madder didn't move, after his first grab under the coat.

I stood up and swayed forward drunkenly and smacked him square on the top of the head.

He gagged. He started to get up. I tapped him on the jaw. He became limp and his hand sweeping down from under his coat knocked his glass over on the desk top. I straightened it, stood silent, listening, struggling with a rising wave of nauseous stupor.

I went over to a communicating door and tried the knob. It was locked. I was staggering by now. I dragged an office chair to the entrance door and propped the back of it under the knob. I leaned against the door panting, gritting my teeth, cursing myself. I got handcuffs out and started back toward Madder.

A very pretty black-haired, gray-eyed girl stepped out of the clothes closet and poked a .32 at me.

She wore a blue suit cut with a lot of snap. An inverted saucer of a hat came down in a hard line across her forehead. Shiny black hair showed at the sides. Her eyes were slate-gray, cold, and yet light-hearted. Her face was fresh and young and delicate and as hard as a chisel.

'All right, Carmady. Lie down and sleep it off. You're through.'

I stumbled toward her waving my sap. She shook her head. When her face moved it got large before my eyes. Its outlines changed and wobbled. The gun in her hand looked like anything from a tunnel to a toothpick.

'Don't be a goof, Carmady,' she said. 'A few hours' sleep for you, a few hours' start for us. Don't make me shoot. I would.'

'Damn you,' I mumbled. 'I believe you would.'

'Right as rain, toots. I'm a lady that wants her own way. That's fine. Sit down.'

The floor rose up and bumped me. I sat on it as on a raft in a rough sea. I braced myself on flat hands. I could hardly feel the floor. My hands were numb. My whole body was numb.

I tried to stare her down. 'Ha-a! L-lady K-killer!' I giggled.

She threw a chilly laugh at me which I only just barely heard. Drums were beating in my head now, war drums from a far-off jungle. Waves of light were moving, and dark shadows and a rustle as of a wind in tree-tops. I didn't want to lie down. I lay down.

The girl's voice came from very far off, an elfin voice.

'Two-way split, eh? He doesn't like my method, eh? Bless his big soft heart. We'll see about him.'

Vaguely as I floated off I seemed to feel a dull jar that might have been a shot. I hoped she had shot Madder, but she hadn't. She had merely helped me on my way out—with my own sap.

When I came around again it was night. Something clacked overhead with a heavy sound. Through the open window beyond the desk yellow light splashed on the high side walls of a building. The thing clacked again and the light went off. An advertising sign on the roof.

I got up off the floor like a man climbing out of thick mud. I waded over to the washbowl, splashed water on my face, felt the top of my head and winced, waded back to the door and found the light switch.

Strewn papers lay around the desk, broken pencils, envelopes, an empty brown whiskey bottle, cigarette ends, and ashes. The debris of hastily emptied drawers. I didn't bother going through any of it. I left the office, rode down to the street in the shuddering elevator, slid into a bar and had a brandy, then got my car and drove on home.

I changed clothes, packed a bag, had some whiskey, and answered the telephone. It was about nine-thirty.

Kathy Horne's voice said: 'So you're not gone yet. I hoped you wouldn't be.'

'Alone?' I asked, still thick in the voice.

'Yes, but I haven't been. The house has been full of coppers for hours. They were very nice, considering. Old grudge of some kind, they figured.'

'And the line is likely tapped now,' I growled. 'Where was I supposed to be going?'

'Well—you know. Your girl told me.'

'Little dark girl? Very cool? Name of Carol Donovan?'

'She had your card. Why, wasn't it—'

'I don't have any girl,' I said simply. 'And I bet that just very casually, without thinking at all a name slipped past your lips—the name of a town up North. Did it?'

'Ye-es,' Kathy Horne admitted weakly.

I caught the night plane North.

It was a nice trip except that I had a sore head and a raging thirst for ice-water.

6

THE SNOQUALMIE HOTEL in Olympia was on Capital Way, fronting on the usual square city block of park. I left by the coffee-shop door and walked down a hill to where the last, loneliest reach of Puget Sound dried and decomposed against a line of disused wharves. Corded firewood filled the foreground and old men pottered about in the middle of the stacks, or sat on boxes with pipes in their mouths and signs behind their heads reading: 'Firewood and Split Kindling. Free Delivery.'

Behind them a low cliff rose and the vast pines of the North loomed against a gray-blue sky.

Two of the old men sat on boxes about twenty feet apart, ignoring each other. I drifted near one of them. He wore corduroy pants and what had been a red and black mackinaw. His felt hat showed the sweat of twenty summers. One of his hands clutched a short black pipe, and with the grimed fingers of the other he slowly, carefully, ecstatically jerked at a long curling hair that grew out of his nose.

I set a box on end, sat down, filled my own pipe, lit it, puffed a cloud of smoke. I waved a hand at the water and said:

'You'd never think that ever met the Pacific Ocean.'

He looked at me.

I said: 'Dead end—quiet, restful, like your town. I like a town like this.' He went on looking at me.

'I'll bet,' I said, 'that a man that's been around a town like this knows everybody in it and in the country near it.'

He said: 'How much you bet?'

I took a silver dollar out of my pocket. They still had a few up there. The old man looked it over, nodded, suddenly yanked the long hair out of his nose and held it up against the light.

'You'd lose,' he said.

I put the dollar down on my knee. 'Know anybody around here that keeps a lot of goldfish?' I asked.

He stared at the dollar. The other old man nearby was wearing overalls and shoes without any laces. He stared at the dollar. They both spat at the same instant. The first old man turned his head and yelled at the top of his voice:

'Know anybody keeps goldfish?'

The other old man jumped up off his box and seized a big ax, set a log on end and whanged the ax down on it, splitting it evenly. He looked at the first old man triumphantly and screamed:

'I ain't neither.'

The first old man said: 'Leetle deef.' He got up slowly and went over to a shack built of old boards of uneven lengths. He went into it, banged the door.

The second old man threw his ax down pettishly, spat in the direction of the closed door and went off among the stacks of cordwood.

The door of the shack opened, the man in the mackinaw poked his head out of it.

'Sewer crabs is all,' he said, and slammed the door again.

I put my dollar in my pocket and went back up the hill. I figured it would take too long to learn their language.

Capitol Way ran north and south. A dull green street car shuttled past on the way to a place called Tum water. In the distance I could see the government buildings. Northward the street passed two hotels and some stores and branched right and left. Right went to Tacoma and Seattle. Left went over a bridge and out onto the Olympic Peninsula.

Beyond this right and left turn the street suddenly became old and shabby, with broken asphalt paving, a Chinese restaurant, a boarded-up movie house, a pawnbroker's establishment. A sign jutting over the dirty sidewalk said: 'Smoke Shop,' and in small letters underneath, as if it hoped nobody was looking, 'Pool.'

I went in past a rack of gaudy magazines and a cigar showcase that had flies inside it. There was a long wooden counter on the left, a few slot machines, a single pool table. Three kids fiddled with the slot machines and a tall thin man with a long nose and no chin played pool all by himself, with a dead cigar in his face.

I sat on a stool and a hard-eyed bald-headed man behind the counter got up from a chair, wiped his hands on a thick gray apron, showed me a gold tooth.

'A little rye,' I said. 'Know anybody that keeps goldfish?'

'Yeah,' he said. 'No.'

He poured something behind the counter and shoved a thick glass across. 'Two bits.'

I sniffed the stuff, wrinkled my nose. 'Was it the rye the "yeah" was for?'

The bald-headed man held up a large bottle with a label that said something about: 'Cream of Dixie Straight Rye Whiskey Guaranteed at Least Four Months Old.'

'OK,' I said. 'I see it just moved in.'

I poured some water in it and drank it. It tasted like a cholera culture. I put a quarter on the counter. The barman showed me a gold tooth on the other side of his face and took hold of the counter with two hard hands and pushed his chin at me.

'What was that crack?' he asked, almost gently.

'I just moved in,' I said. 'I'm looking for some goldfish for the front window. Goldfish.'

The barman said very slowly: 'Do I look like a guy would know a guy would have goldfish?' His face was a little white.

The long-nosed man who had been playing himself a round of pool racked his cue and strolled over to the counter beside me and threw a nickel on it.

'Draw me a drink before you wet yourself,' he told the barman.

The barman pried himself loose from the counter with a good deal of effort. I looked down to see if his fingers had made any dents in the wood. He drew a coke, stirred it with a swizzle-stick, dumped it on the bar top, took a deep breath and let it out through his nose, grunted and went away toward a door marked: 'Toilet.'

The long-nosed man lifted his coke and looked into the smeared mirror behind the bar. The left side of his mouth twitched briefly. A dim voice came from it, saying:

'How's Peeler?'

I pressed my thumb and forefinger together, put them to my nose, sniffed, shook my head sadly.

'Hitting it high, huh?'

'Yeah,' I said. 'I didn't catch the name.'

'Call me Sunset. I'm always movin' west. Think he'll stay clammed?'

'He'll stay clammed,' I said.

'What's your handle?'

'Dodge Willis, El Paso,' I said.

'Got a room somewhere?'

'Hotel.'

He put his glass down empty. 'Let's dangle.'

7

WE WENT UP to my room and sat down and looked at each other over a couple of glasses of Scotch and ginger ale. Sunset studied me with his close-set expressionless eyes, a little at a time, but very thoroughly in the end, adding it all up.

I sipped my drink and waited. At last he said in his lipless 'stir' voice:

'How come Peeler didn't come hisself?'

'For the same reason he didn't stay when he was here.'

'Meaning which?'

'Figure it out for yourself,' I said.

He nodded, just as though I had said something with a meaning. Then:

'What's the top price?'

'Twenty-five grand.'

'Nuts.' Sunset was emphatic, even rude.

I leaned back and lit a cigarette, puffed smoke at the open window and watched the breeze pick it up and tear it to pieces.

'Listen,' Sunset complained. 'I don't know you from last Sunday's sports section. You may be all to the silk. I just don't know.'

'Why'd you brace me?' I asked.

'You had the word, didn't you?'

This was where I took the dive. I grinned at him. 'Yeah. Goldfish was the password. The *Smoke Shop* was the place.'

His lack of expression told me I was right. It was one of those breaks you dream of, but don't handle right even in dreams.

'Well, what's the next angle?' Sunset inquired, sucking a piece of ice out of his glass and chewing on it.

I laughed. 'OK, Sunset. I'm satisfied you're cagey. We could go on like this for weeks. Let's put our cards on the table. Where is the old guy?'

Sunset tightened his lips, moistened them, tightened them again. He set his glass down very slowly and his right hand hung lax on his thigh. I knew I had made a mistake, that Peeler knew where the old guy was, exactly. Therefore I should know.

Nothing in Sunset's voice showed I had made a mistake. He said crossly: 'You mean why don't I put my cards on the table and you just sit back and look 'em over. Nix.'

'Then how do you like this?' I growled. 'Peeler's dead.'

One eyebrow twitched, and one corner of his mouth. His eyes got a little blanker than before, if possible. His voice rasped lightly, like a finger on dry leather.

'How come?'

'Competition you two didn't know about.' I leaned back, smiled.

The gun made a soft metallic blur in the sunshine. I hardly saw where it came from. Then the muzzle was round and dark and empty looking at me.

'You're kidding the wrong guy,' Sunset said lifelessly. 'I ain't no soft spot for chiselers to lie on.'

I folded my arms, taking care that my right hand was outside, in view.

'I would be—if I was kidding. I'm not. Peeler played with a girl and she milked him—up to a point. He didn't tell her where to find the old fellow. So she and her top man went to see Peeler where he lived. They used a hot iron on his feet. He died of the shock.'

Sunset looked unimpressed. 'I got a lot of room in my ears yet,' he said.

'So have I,' I snarled, suddenly pretending anger. 'Just what the hell have you said that means anything—except that you know Peeler?'

He spun his gun on his trigger finger, watching it spin. 'Old man Sype's at Westport,' he said casually. 'That mean anything to you?'

'Yeah. Has he got the marbles?'

'How the hell would I know?' He steadied the gun again, dropped it to his thigh. It wasn't pointing at me now. 'Where's this competish you mentioned?'

'I hoped I ditched them,' I said. 'I'm not too sure. Can I put my hands down and take a drink?'

'Yeah, go ahead. How did you cut in?'

'Peeler roomed with the wife of a friend of mine who's in stir. A straight girl, one you can trust. He let her in and she passed it to me—afterward.'

'After the bump? How many cuts your side? My half is set.'

I took my drink, shoved the empty glass away. 'The hell it is.'

The gun lifted an inch, dropped again. 'How many altogether?' he snapped.

'Three, now Peeler's out. If we can hold off the competition.'

'The feet-toasters? No trouble about that. What they look like?'

'Man named Rush Madder, a shyster down south, fifty, fat, thin down-curving mustache, dark hair thin on top, five-nine, a hundred and eighty, not much guts. The girl, Carol Donovan, black hair, long bob, gray eyes, pretty, small features, twenty-five to -eight, five-two, hundred twenty, last seen wearing blue, hard as they come. The real iron in the combination.'

Sunset nodded indifferently and put his gun away. 'We'll soften her, if she pokes her snoot in,' he said. 'I've got a heap at the house. Let's take the air Westport way and look it over. You might be able to ease in on the goldfish angle. They say he's nuts about them. I'll stay under cover. He's too stir-wise for me. I smell of the bucket.'

'Swell,' I said heartily. 'I'm an old goldfish fancier myself.'

Sunset reached for the bottle, poured two fingers of Scotch and put it down. He stood up, twitched his collar straight, then shot his chinless jaw forward as far as it would go.

'But don't make no error, bo. It's goin' to take pressure. It's goin' to mean a run out in the deep woods and some thumb twisting. Snatch stuff, likely.'

'That's OK,' I said. 'The insurance people are behind us.'

Sunset jerked down the points of his vest and rubbed the back of his thin neck. I put my hat on, locked the Scotch in the bag by the chair I'd been sitting in, went over and shut the window.

We started toward the door. Knuckles rattled on it just as I reached for the knob. I gestured Sunset back along the wall. I stared at the door for a moment and then I opened it up.

The two guns came forward almost on the same level, one small—a .32, one a big Smith and Wesson. They couldn't come into the room abreast, so the girl came in first.

'OK, hot shot,' she said dryly. 'Ceiling zero. See if you can reach it.'

8

I BACKED SLOWLY into the room. The two visitors bored in on me, either side. I tripped over my bag and fell backward, hit the floor and rolled on my side groaning.

Sunset said casually: 'H'ist 'm, folks. Pretty now!'

Two heads jerked away from looking down at me and then I had my gun loose, down at my side. I kept on groaning.

There was a silence. I didn't hear any guns fall. The door of the room was still wide open and Sunset was flattened against the wall more or less behind it.

The girl said between her teeth: 'Cover the shamus, Rush—and shut the door. Skinny can't shoot here. Nobody can.'

Then, in a whisper I barely caught, she added: 'Slam it!'

Rush Madder waddled backward across the room keeping the Smith and Wesson pointed my way. His back was to Sunset and the thought of that made his eyes roll. I could have shot him easily enough, but it wasn't the play. Sunset stood with his feet spread and his tongue showing. Something that could have been a smile wrinkled his flat eyes.

He stared at the girl and she stared at him. Their guns stared at each other.

Rush Madder reached the door, grabbed the edge of it and gave it a hard swing. I knew exactly what was going to happen. As the door slammed the .32 was going to go off. It wouldn't be heard if it went off at the right instant. The explosion would be lost in the slamming of the door.

I reached out and took hold of Carol Donovan's ankle and jerked it hard.

The door slammed. Her gun went off and chipped the ceiling.

She whirled on me kicking. Sunset said in his tight but somehow penetrating drawl:

'If this is it, this is it. Let's go!' The hammer clicked back on his Colt.

Something in his voice steadied Carol Donovan. She relaxed, let her automatic fall to her side and stepped away from me with a vicious look back.

Madder turned the key in the door and leaned against the wood, breathing noisily. His hat had tipped over one ear and the end of two strips of adhesive showed under the brim.

Nobody moved while I had these thoughts. There was no sound of feet outside in the hall, no alarm. I got up on my knees, slid my gun out of sight, rose on my feet and went over to the window. Nobody down on the sidewalk was staring up at the upper floors of the *Snoqualmie Hotel.*

I sat on the broad old-fashioned sill and looked faintly embarrassed, as though the minister had said a bad word.

The girl snapped at me: 'Is this lug your partner?'

I didn't answer. Her face flushed slowly and her eyes burned. Madder put a hand out and fussed:

'Now listen, Carol, now listen here. This sort of act ain't the way—'

'Shut up!'

'Yeah,' Madder said in a clogged voice. 'Sure.'

Sunset looked the girl over lazily for the third or fourth time. His gun hand rested easily against his hip bone and his whole attitude was of complete relaxation. Having seen him pull his gun once I hoped the girl wasn't fooled.

He said slowly: 'We've heard about you two. What's your offer? I wouldn't listen even, only I can't stand a shooting rap.'

The girl said: 'There's enough in it for four.' Madder nodded his big head vigorously, almost managed a smile.

Sunset glanced at me. I nodded. 'Four it is,' he sighed. 'But that's the top. We'll go to my place and gargle. I don't like it here.'

'We must look simple,' the girl said nastily.

'Kill-simple,' Sunset drawled. 'I've met lots of them. That's why we're going to talk it over. It's not a shooting play.'

Carol Donovan slipped a suede bag from under her left arm and tucked her .32 into it. She smiled. She was pretty when she smiled.

'My ante is in,' she said quietly. 'I'll play. Where is the place?'

'Out Water Street. We'll go in a hack.'

'Lead on, sport.'

We went out of the room and down in the elevator, four friendly people walking out through a lobby full of antlers and stuffed birds and pressed wildflowers in glass frames. The taxi went out Capitol Way, past the square, past a big red apartment house that was too big for the town except when the Legislature was sitting. Along car tracks past the distant capitol buildings and the high closed gates of the governor's mansion.

Oak trees bordered the sidewalks. A few largish residences showed behind garden walls. The taxi shot past them and veered onto a road that led toward the tip of the Sound. In a short while a house showed in a narrow clearing between tall trees. Water glistened far back behind the tree trunks. The house had a roofed porch, a small lawn rotten with weeds and overgrown bushes. There was a shed at the end of a dirt driveway and an antique touring car squatted under the shed.

We got out and I paid the taxi. All four of us carefully watched it out of sight. Then Sunset said:

'My place is upstairs. There's a schoolteacher lives down below. She ain't at home. Let's go up and gargle.'

We crossed the lawn to the porch and Sunset threw a door open, pointed up narrow steps.

'Ladies first. Lead on, beautiful. Nobody locks a door in this town.'

The girl gave him a cool glance and passed him to go up the stairs. I went next, then Madder, Sunset last.

THE SINGLE ROOM that made up most of the second floor was dark from the trees, had a dormer window, a wide day-bed pushed back under the slope of the roof, a table, some wicker chairs, a small radio, and a round black stove in the middle of the floor.

Sunset drifted into a kitchenette and came back with a square bottle and some glasses. He poured drinks, lifted one and left the others on the table.

We helped ourselves and sat down.

Sunset put his drink down in a lump, leaned over to put his glass on the floor and came up with his Colt out.

I heard Madder's gulp in the sudden cold silence. The girl's mouth twitched as if she were going to laugh. Then she leaned forward, holding her glass on top of her bag with her left hand.

Sunset slowly drew his lips into a thin straight line. He said slowly and carefully:

'Feet-burners, huh? Burned my pal's feet, huh?'

Madder choked, started to spread his fat hands. The Colt flicked at him. He put his hands on his knees and clutched his kneecaps.

'And suckers at that,' Sunset went on tiredly. 'Burn a guy's feet to make him sing and then walk right into the parlor of one of his pals. You couldn't tie that with Christmas ribbon.'

Madder said jerkily: 'All r-right. W-what's the p-pay-off?' The girl smiled slightly but she didn't say anything.

Sunset grinned. 'Rope,' he said softly. 'A lot of rope tied in hard knots, with water on it. Then me and my pal trundle off to catch fireflies—pearls to you—and when we come back—' he stopped, drew his left hand across the front of his throat. 'Like the idea?' he glanced at me.

'Yeah, but don't make a song about it,' I said. 'Where's the rope?'

'Bureau,' Sunset answered, and pointed with one ear at the corner.

I started in that direction, by way of the walls. Madder made a sudden thin whimpering noise and his eyes turned up in his head and he fell straight forward off the chair on his face, in a dead faint.

That jarred Sunset. He hadn't expected anything so foolish. His right hand jerked around until the Colt was pointing down at Madder's back.

The girl slipped her hand under her bag. The bag lifted an inch. The gun that was caught there in a trick clip—the gun that Sunset thought was inside the bag—spat and flamed briefly.

Sunset coughed. His Colt boomed and a piece of wood detached itself from the back of the chair Madder had been sitting in. Sunset dropped the Colt and put his chin down on his chest and tried to look at the ceiling. His long legs slid out in front of him and his heels made a rasping sound on the floor. He sat like that, limp, his chin on his chest, his eyes looking upward. Dead as a pickled walnut.

I kicked Miss Donovan's chair out from under her and she banged down on her side in a swirl of silken legs. Her hat went crooked on her head. She yelped. I stood on her hand and then shifted suddenly and kicked her gun clear across the attic. I sent her bag after it—with her other gun inside it. She screamed at me.

'Get up,' I snarled.

She got up slowly, backed away from me biting her lip, savage-eyed, suddenly a nasty-faced little brat at bay. She kept on backing until the wall stopped her. Her eyes glittered in a ghastly face.

I glanced down at Madder, went over to a closed door. A bathroom was behind it. I reversed a key and gestured at the girl.

'In.'

She walked stiff-legged across the floor and passed in front of me, almost touching me.

'Listen a minute, shamus—'

I pushed her through the door and slammed it and turned the key. It was all right with me if she wanted to jump out of the window. I had seen the windows from below.

I went across to Sunset, felt him, felt the small hard lump of keys on a ring in his pocket, and got them out without quite knocking him off his chair. I didn't look for anything else.

There were car keys on the ring.

I looked at Madder again, noticed that his fingers were as white as snow. I went down the narrow dark stairs to the porch, around to the side of the house and got into the old touring car under the shed. One of the keys on the ring fitted its ignition lock.

The car took a beating before it started up and let me back it down the dirt driveway to the curb. Nothing moved in the house that I saw or heard. The tall pines behind and beside the houses stirred their upper branches listlessly and a cold heartless sunlight sneaked through them intermittently as they moved.

I drove back to Capitol Way and downtown again as fast as I dared, past the square and the *Snoqualmie Hotel* and over the bridge toward the Pacific Ocean and Westport.

9

AN HOUR'S FAST driving through thinned-out timberland, interrupted by three stops for water and punctuated by the cough of a head gasket leak, brought me within sound of surf. The broad white road, striped with yellow down the center, swept around the flank of a hill, a distinct cluster of buildings loomed up in front of the shine of the ocean, and the road forked. The left fork was sign-posted: 'Westport—9 Miles,' and didn't go toward the buildings. It crossed a rusty cantilever bridge and plunged into a region of wind-distorted apple orchards.

Twenty minutes more and I chugged into Westport, a sandy spit of land with scattered frame houses dotted over rising ground behind it. The end of the spit was a long narrow pier, and the end of the pier a cluster of sailing boats with half-lowered sails flapping against their single masts. And beyond them a buoyed channel and a long irregular line where the water creamed on a hidden sandbar.

Beyond the sandbar the Pacific rolled over to Japan. This was the last outpost of the coast, the farthest west a man could go and still be on the mainland of the United States. A swell place for an ex-convict to hide out with a couple of somebody else's pearls the size of new potatoes—if he didn't have any enemies.

I pulled up in front of a cottage that had a sign in the yard: 'Luncheons, Teas, Dinners.' A small rabbit-faced man with freckles was waving a garden rake at two black chickens. The chickens appeared to be sassing him back. He turned when the engine of Sunset's car coughed itself still.

I got out, went through a wicket gate, pointed to the sign. 'Luncheon ready?'

He threw the rake at the chickens, wiped his hands on his trousers and leered. 'The wife put that up,' he confided to me in a thin, impish voice. 'Ham and eggs is what it means.'

'Ham and eggs get along with me,' I said.

We went into the house. There were three tables covered with patterned oilcloth, some chromos on the walls, a full-rigged ship in a bottle on the mantel. I sat down. The host went away through a swing door and somebody yelled at him and a sizzling noise was heard from the kitchen. He came back and leaned over my shoulder, put some cutlery and a paper napkin on the oilcloth.

'Too early for apple brandy, ain't it?' he whispered.

I told him how wrong he was. He went away again and came back with glasses and a quart of clear amber fluid. He sat down with me and poured. A rich baritone voice in the kitchen was singing 'Chloe' over the sizzling.

We clinked glasses and drank and waited for the heat to crawl up our spines.

'Stranger, ain't you?' the little man asked.

I said I was.

'From Seattle maybe? That's a nice piece of goods you got on.'

'Seattle,' I agreed.

'We don't git many strangers,' he said, looking at my left ear. 'Ain't on the way to nowheres. Now before repeal—' he stopped, shifted his sharp, woodpecker gaze to my other ear.

'Ah, before repeal,' I said with a large gesture, and drank knowingly.

He leaned over and breathed on my chin. 'Hell, you could load up in any fish stall on the pier. The stuff come in under catches of crabs and oysters. Hell, Westport was lousy with it. They give the kids cases of Scotch to play with. There wasn't a car in this town that slept in a garage, mister. The garages was all full to the roof of Canadian hooch. Hell, they had a coastguard cutter off the pier watchin' the boats unload one day every week. Friday. Always the same day.' He winked.

I puffed a cigarette and the sizzling noise and the baritone rendering of 'Chloe' went on in the kitchen.

'But hell, you wouldn't be in the liquor business,' he said.

'Hell, no, I'm a goldfish buyer,' I said.

'OK,' he said sulkily.

I POURED US ANOTHER round of the apple brandy. 'This bottle is on me,' I said, 'and I'm taking a couple more with me.'

He brightened up. 'What did you say the name was?'

'Carmady. You think I'm kidding you about the goldfish. I'm not.'

'Hell, there ain't a livin' in them little fellers, is there?'

I held my sleeve out. 'You said it was a nice piece of goods. Sure there's a living out of the fancy brands. New brands, new types all the time. My information is there's an old guy down here somewhere that has a real collection. Maybe would sell it. Some he's bred himself.'

I poured us another round of the apple brandy. A large woman with a mustache kicked the swing door open a foot and yelled: 'Pick up the ham and eggs!'

My host scuttled across and came back with my food. I ate. He watched me minutely. After a time he suddenly smacked his skinny leg under the table.

'Old Wallace,' he chuckled. 'Sure, you come to see old Wallace. Hell, we don't know him right well. He don't act neighborly.'

He turned around in his chair and pointed out through the sleazy curtains at a distant hill. On top of the hill was a yellow and white house that shone in the sun.

'Hell, that's where he lives. He's got a mess of them. Goldfish, huh? Hell, you could bend me with an eye-dropper.'

That ended my interest in the little man. I gobbled my food, paid off for it and for three quarts of apple brandy at a dollar a quart, shook hands and went back out to the touring car.

There didn't seem to be any hurry. Rush Madder would come out of his faint, and he would turn the girl loose. But they didn't know anything about Westport. Sunset hadn't mentioned the name in their presence. They didn't know it when they reached Olympia, or they would have gone there at once. And if they had listened outside my room at the hotel, they would have known I wasn't alone. They hadn't acted as if they knew that when they charged in.

I had lots of time. I drove down to the pier and looked it over. It looked tough. There were fishstalls, drinking dives, a tiny honky-tonk for the fishermen, a pool-room, an arcade of slot machines, and smutty peep-shows. Bait fish squirmed and darted in big wooden tanks down in the water along the piles. There were loungers and they looked like trouble for anyone that tried to interfere with them. I didn't see any law enforcement around.

I drove back up the hill to the yellow and white house. It stood very much alone, four blocks from the next nearest dwelling. There were flowers in front, a trimmed green lawn, a rock garden. A woman in a brown and white print dress was popping at aphids with a spray-gun.

I let my heap stall itself, got out and took my hat off.

'Mister Wallace live here?'

She had a handsome face, quiet, firm-looking. She nodded.

'Would you like to see him?' She had a quiet firm voice, a good accent.

It didn't sound like the voice of a train-robber's wife.

I gave her my name, said I'd been hearing about his fish down in the town. I was interested in fancy goldfish.

She put the spray-gun down and went into the house. Bees buzzed around my head, large fuzzy bees that wouldn't mind the cold wind off the sea. Far off like background music the surf pounded on the sandbars. The northern sunshine seemed bleak to me, had no heat in the core of it.

The woman came out of the house and held the door open.

'He's at the top of the stairs,' she said, 'if you'd like to go up.'

I went past a couple of rustic rockers and into the house of the man who had stolen the Leander pearls.

10

FISH TANKS WERE all around the big room, two tiers of them on braced shelves, big oblong tanks with metal frames, some with lights over them and some with lights down in them. Water grasses were festooned in careless patterns behind the algae-coated glass and the water held a ghostly greenish light and through the greenish light moved fish of all the colors of the rainbow.

There were long slim fish like golden darts and Japanese Veiltails with fantastic trailing tails, and X-ray fish as transparent as colored glass, tiny guppies half an inch long, calico popeyes spotted like a bride's apron, and big lumbering Chinese Moors with telescope eyes, froglike faces and unnecessary fins, waddling through the green water like fat men going to lunch.

Most of the light came from a big sloping skylight. Under the skylight at a bare wooden table a tall gaunt man stood with a squirming red fish in his left hand, and in his right hand a safety razor blade backed with adhesive tape.

He looked at me from under wide gray eyebrows. His eyes were sunken, colorless, opaque. I went over beside him and looked down at the fish he was holding.

'Fungus?' I asked.

He nodded slowly. 'White fungus.' He put the fish down on the table and carefully spread its dorsal fin. The fin was ragged and split and the ragged edges had a mossy white color.

'White fungus,' he said, 'ain't so bad. I'll trim this feller up and he'll be right as rain. What can I do for you, mister?'

I rolled a cigarette around in my fingers and smiled at him.

'Like people,' I said. 'The fish, I mean. They get things wrong with them.'

He held the fish against the wood and trimmed off the ragged part of the fin. He spread the tail and trimmed that. The fish had stopped squirming.

'Some you can cure,' he said, 'and some you can't. You can't cure swimming-bladder disease, for instance.' He glanced up at me. 'This don't hurt him, case you think it does,' he said. 'You can shock a fish to death but you can't hurt it like a person.'

He put the razor blade down and dipped a cotton swab in some purplish liquid, painted the cut places. Then he dipped a finger in a jar of white Vaseline and smeared that over. He dropped the fish in a small tank off to one side of the room. The fish swam around peacefully, quite content.

The gaunt man wiped his hands, sat down at the edge of a bench and stared at me with lifeless eyes. He had been good-looking once, a long time ago.

'You interested in fish?' he asked. His voice had the quiet careful murmur of the cell block and the exercise yard.

I shook my head. 'Not particularly. That was just an excuse. I came a long way to see you, Mister Sype.'

He moistened his lips and went on staring at me. When his voice came again it was tired and soft.

'Wallace is the name, mister.'

I puffed a smoke ring and poked my finger through it. 'For my job it's got to be Sype.'

He leaned forward and dropped his hands between his spread bony knees, clasped them together. Big gnarled hands that had done a lot of hard work in their time. His head tipped up at me and his dead eyes were cold under the shaggy brows. But his voice stayed soft.

'Haven't seen a dick in a year. To talk to. What's your lay?'

'Guess,' I said.

His voice got still softer. 'Listen, dick. I've got a nice home here, quiet. Nobody bothers me anymore. Nobody's got a right to. I got a pardon straight from the White House. I've got the fish to play with and a man gets fond of anything he takes care of. I don't owe the world a nickel. I paid up. My wife's got enough dough for us to live on. All I want is to be left alone, dick.' He stopped talking, shook his head once. 'You can't burn me up—not anymore.'

I didn't say anything. I smiled a little and watched him.

'Nobody can touch me,' he said. 'I got a pardon straight from the President's study. I just want to be let alone.'

I shook my head and kept on smiling at him. 'That's the one thing you can never have—until you give in.'

'Listen,' he said softly. 'You may be new on this case. It's kind of fresh to you. You want to make a rep for yourself. But me, I've had almost twenty years of it, and so have a lot of other people, some of 'em pretty smart people too. *They* know I don't have nothing that don't belong to me. Never did have. Somebody else got it.'

'The mail clerk,' I said. 'Sure.'

'Listen,' he said, still softly. 'I did my time. I know all the angles. I know they ain't going to stop wondering—long as anybody's alive that remembers. I know they're going to send some punk out once in a while to kind of stir it up. That's OK. No hard feelings. Now what do I do to get you to go home again?'

I shook my head and stared past his shoulder at the fish drifting in their big silent tanks. I felt tired. The quiet of the house made ghosts in my brain, ghosts of a lot of years ago. A train pounding through the darkness, a stickup hidden in a mail car, a gun flash, a dead clerk on the floor, a silent drop off at some water tank, a man who had kept a secret for nineteen years—almost kept it.

'You made one mistake,' I said slowly. 'Remember a fellow named Peeler Mardo?'

He lifted his head. I could see him searching in his memory. The name didn't seem to mean anything to him.

'A fellow you knew in Leavenworth,' I said. 'A little runt that was in there for splitting twenty-dollar bills and putting phony backs on them.'

'Yeah,' he said. 'I remember.'

'You told him you had the pearls,' I said.

I could see he didn't believe me. 'I must have been kidding him,' he said slowly, emptily.

'Maybe. But here's the point. He didn't think so. He was up in this country a while ago with a pal, a guy who called himself Sunset. They saw you somewhere and Peeler recognised you. He got to thinking how he could make himself some jack. But he was a coke-hound and he talked in his sleep. A girl got wise and then another girl and a shyster. Peeler got his feet burned and he's dead.'

Sype stared at me unblinkingly. The lines at the corners of his mouth deepened.

I waved my cigarette and went on:

'We don't know how much he told, but the shyster and a girl are in Olympia.

Sunset's in Olympia, only he's dead. They killed him. I don't know if they know where you are or not. But they will sometime, or others like them. You can wear the cops down, if they can't find the pearls and you don't try to sell them. You can wear the insurance company down and even the postal men.'

Sype didn't move a muscle. His big knotty hands clenched between his knees didn't move. His dead eyes just stared.

'But you can't wear the chiselers down,' I said. 'They'll never lay off. There'll always be a couple or three with time enough and money enough and meanness enough to bear down. They'll find out what they want to know some way. They'll snatch your wife or take you out in the woods and give you the works. And you'll have to come through . . . Now I've got a decent, square proposition.'

'Which bunch are you?' Sype asked suddenly. 'I thought you smelled of dick, but I ain't so sure now.'

'Insurance,' I said. 'Here's the deal. Twenty-five-grand reward in all. Five grand to the girl that passed me the info. She got it on the square and she's entitled to that cut. Ten grand to me. I've done all the work and looked into all the guns. Ten grand to you, through me. You couldn't get a nickel direct. Is there anything in it? How does it look?'

'It looks fine,' he said gently. 'Except for one thing. I don't have no pearls, dick.'

I scowled at him. That was my wad. I didn't have anymore. I straightened away from the wall and dropped a cigarette end on the wood floor, crushed it out. I turned to go.

He stood up and put a hand out. 'Wait a minute,' he said gravely, 'and I'll prove it to you.'

He went across the floor in front of me and out of the room. I stared at the fish and chewed my lip. I heard the sound of a car engine somewhere, not very close. I heard a drawer open and shut, apparently in a nearby room.

Sype came back into the fish room. He had a shiny Colt .45 in his gaunt fist. It looked as long as a man's forearm.

He pointed it at me and said: 'I got pearls in this, six of them. Lead pearls. I can comb a fly's whiskers at sixty yards. You ain't no dick. Now get up and blow—and tell your red-hot friends I'm ready to shoot their teeth out any day of the week and twice on Sunday.'

I didn't move. There was a madness in the man's dead eyes. I didn't dare move.

'That's grandstand stuff,' I said slowly. 'I can prove I'm a dick. You're an ex-con and it's felony just having that rod. Put it down and talk sense.'

The car I had heard seemed to be stopping outside the house. Brakes whined on drums. Feet clattered up a walk, up steps. Sudden sharp voices, a caught exclamation.

Sype backed across the room until he was between the table and a big twenty- or thirty-gallon tank. He grinned at me, the wide clear grin of a fighter at bay.

'I see your friends kind of caught up with you,' he drawled. 'Take your gat out and drop it on the floor while you still got time—and breath.'

I didn't move. I looked at the wiry hair above his eyes. I looked into his eyes. I knew if I moved—even to do what he told me—he would shoot.

Steps came up the stairs. They were clogged, shuffling steps, with a hint of struggle in them.

Three people came into the room.

11

MRS SYPE CAME IN FIRST, stiff-legged, her eyes glazed, her arms bent rigidly at the elbows and the hands clawing straight forward at nothing, feeling for something that wasn't there. There was a gun in her back, one of Carol Donovan's small .32s, held efficiently in Carol Donovan's small ruthless hand.

Madder came last. He was drunk, brave from the bottle, flushed and savage. He threw the Smith and Wesson down on me and leered.

Carol Donovan pushed Mrs Sype aside. The older woman stumbled over into the corner and sank down on her knees, blank-eyed.

Sype stared at the Donovan girl. He was rattled because she was a girl and young and pretty. He hadn't been used to the type. Seeing her took the fire out of him. If men had come in he would have shot them to pieces.

The small dark white-faced girl faced him coldly, said in her tight chilled voice: 'All right, Dad. Shed the heater. Make it smooth now.'

Sype leaned down slowly, not taking his eyes off her. He put his enormous frontier Colt on the floor.

'Kick it away from you, Dad.'

Sype kicked it. The gun skidded across the bare boards, over toward the center of the room.

'That's the way, old-timer. You hold on him, Rush, while I unrod the dick.'

The two guns swiveled and the hard gray eyes were looking at me now. Madder went a little way toward Sype and pointed his Smith and Wesson at Sype's chest.

The girl smiled, not a nice smile. 'Bright boy, eh? You sure stick your neck out all the time, don't you? Made a beef, shamus. Didn't frisk your skinny pal. He had a little map in one shoe.'

'I didn't need one,' I said smoothly, and grinned at her.

I tried to make the grin appealing, because Mrs Sype was moving her knees on the floor, and every move took her nearer to Sype's Colt.

'But you're all washed up now, you and your big smile. Hoist the mitts while I get your iron. Up, mister.'

She was a girl, about five feet two inches tall, and weighed around a hundred and twenty. Just a girl. I was five-eleven and a half, weighed one-ninety-five. I put my hands up and hit her on the jaw.

That was crazy, but I had all I could stand of the Donovan–Madder act, the Donovan–Madder guns, the Donovan–Madder tough talk. I hit her on the jaw.

She went back a yard and her popgun went off. A slug burned my ribs. She started to fall. Slowly, like a slow-motion picture, she fell. There was something silly about it.

Mrs Sype got the Colt and shot her in the back.

Madder whirled and the instant he turned Sype rushed him. Madder jumped back and yelled and covered Sype again. Sype stopped cold and the wide crazy grin came back on his gaunt face.

The slug from the Colt knocked the girl forward as though a door had whipped in a high wind. A flurry of blue cloth, something thumped my chest— her head. I saw her face for a moment as she bounced back, a strange face that I had never seen before.

Then she was a huddled thing on the floor at my feet, small, deadly, extinct, with redness coming out from under her, and the tall quiet woman behind her with the smoking Colt held in both hands.

Madder shot Sype twice. Sype plunged forward still grinning and hit the end of the table. The purplish liquid he had used on the sick fish sprayed up over him. Madder shot him again as he was falling.

I jerked my Lüger out and shot Madder in the most painful place I could think of that wasn't likely to be fatal—the back of the knee. He went down exactly as if he had tripped over a hidden wire. I had cuffs on him before he even started to groan.

I kicked guns here and there and went over to Mrs Sype and took the big Colt out of her hands.

It was very still in the room for a little while. Eddies of smoke drifted toward the skylight, filmy gray, pale in the afternoon sun. I heard the surf booming in the distance. Then I heard a whistling sound close at hand.

It was Sype trying to say something. His wife crawled across to him, still on her knees, huddled beside him. There was blood on his lips and bubbles. He blinked hard, trying to clear his head. He smiled up at her. His whistling voice said very faintly:

'The Moors, Hattie—the Moors.'

Then his neck went loose and the smile melted off his face. His head rolled to one side on the bare floor.

Mrs Sype touched him, then got very slowly to her feet and looked at me, calm, dry-eyed.

She said in a low clear voice: 'Will you help me carry him to the bed? I don't like him here with these people.'

I said: 'Sure. What was that he said?'

'I don't know. Some nonsense about his fish, I think.'

I lifted Sype's shoulders and she took his feet and we carried him into the bedroom and put him on the bed. She folded his hands on his chest and shut his eyes. She went over and pulled the blinds down.

'That's all, thank you,' she said, not looking at me. 'The telephone is downstairs.'

She sat down in a chair beside the bed and put her head down on the coverlet near Sype's arm.

I went out of the room and shut the door.

12

MADDER'S LEG was bleeding slowly, not dangerously. He stared at me with fear-crazed eyes while I tied a tight handkerchief above his knee. I figured he had a cut tendon and maybe a chipped kneecap. He might walk a little lame when they came to hang him.

I went downstairs and stood on the porch looking at the two cars in front, then down the hill toward the pier. Nobody could have told where the shots came from, unless he happened to be passing. Quite likely nobody had even noticed them. There was probably shooting in the woods around there a good deal.

I went back into the house and looked at the crank telephone on the living-room wall, but didn't touch it yet. Something was bothering me. I lit a cigarette and stared out of the window and a ghost voice said in my ears: 'The Moors, Hattie. The Moors.'

I went back upstairs into the fish room. Madder was groaning now, thick panting groans. What did I care about a torturer like Madder?

The girl was quite dead. None of the tanks was hit. The fish swam peacefully in their green water, slow and peaceful and easy. They didn't care about Madder either.

The tank with the black Chinese Moors in it was over in the corner, about ten-gallon size. There were just four of them, big fellows, about four inches body length, coal black all over. Two of them were sucking oxygen on top of the water and two were waddling sluggishly on the bottom. They had thick deep bodies with a lot of spreading tail and high dorsal fins and their bulging telescope eyes that made them look like frogs when they were head toward you.

I watched them fumbling around in the green stuff that was growing in the tank. A couple of red pond snails were window-cleaning. The two on the bottom looked thicker and more sluggish than the two on the top. I wondered why.

There was a long-handled strainer made of woven string lying between two of the tanks. I got it and fished down in the tank, trapped one of the big Moors and lifted it out. I turned it over in the net, looked at its faintly silver belly. I saw something that looked like a suture. I felt the place. There was a hard lump under it.

I pulled the other one off the bottom. Same suture, same hard round lump. I got one of the two that had been sucking air on top. No suture, no hard round lump. It was harder to catch too.

I put it back in the tank. My business was with the other two. I like goldfish as well as the next man, but business is business and crime is crime. I took my coat off and rolled my sleeves up and picked the razor blade backed with adhesive off the table.

It was a very messy job. It took about five minutes. Then they lay in the palm of my hand, three-quarters of an inch in diameter, heavy, perfectly round, milky white and shimmering with that inner light no other jewel had. The Leander pearls.

I washed them off, wrapped them in my handkerchief, rolled down my sleeves and put my coat back on. I looked at Madder, at his little pain- and fear-tortured eyes, the sweat on his face. I didn't care anything about Madder. He was a killer, a torturer.

I went out of the fish room. The bedroom door was still shut. I went down below and cranked the wall telephone.

'This is the Wallace place at Westport,' I said. 'There's been an accident. We need a doctor and we'll have to have the police. What can you do?'

The girl said: 'I'll try and get you a doctor, Mr Wallace. It may take a little time though. There's a town marshal at Westport. Will he do?'

'I suppose so,' I said and thanked her and hung up. There were points about a country telephone after all.

I LIT ANOTHER CIGARETTE and sat down in one of the rustic rockers on the porch. In a little while there were steps and Mrs Sype came out of the house. She stood a moment looking off down the hills, then she sat down in the other rocker beside her. Her dry eyes looked at me steadily.

'You're a detective, I suppose,' she said slowly, diffidently.

'Yes, I represent the company that insured the Leander pearls.'

She looked off into the distance. 'I thought he would have peace here,' she said. 'That nobody would bother him anymore. That this place would be a sort of sanctuary.'

'He ought not to have tried to keep the pearls.'

She turned her head, quickly this time. She looked blank now, then she looked scared.

I reached down in my pocket and got out the wadded handkerchief, opened it up on the palm of my hand. They lay there together on the white linen, two hundred grand worth of murder.

'He could have had his sanctuary,' I said. 'Nobody wanted to take it away from him. But he wasn't satisfied with that.'

She looked slowly, lingeringly at the pearls. Then her lips twitched. Her voice got hoarse.

'Poor Wally,' she said. 'So you did find them. You're pretty clever, you know. He killed dozens of fish before he learned how to do that trick.' She looked up into my face. A little wonder showed at the back of her eyes.

She said: 'I always hated the idea. Do you remember the old Bible theory of the scapegoat?'

I shook my head, no.

'The animal on which the sins of a man were laid and then it was driven off into the wilderness. The fish were his scapegoat.'

She smiled at me. I didn't smile back.

She said, still smiling faintly: 'You see, he once had the pearls, the real ones, and suffering seemed to him to make them his. But he couldn't have had any profit from them, even if he had found them again. It seems some landmark changed, while he was in prison, and he never could find the spot in Idaho where they were buried.'

An icy finger was moving slowly up and down my spine. I opened my mouth and something I supposed might be my voice said:

'Huh?'

She reached a finger out and touched one of the pearls. I was still holding them out, as if my hand was a shelf nailed to the wall.

'So he got these,' she said. 'In Seattle. They're hollow, filled with white wax. I forget what they call the process. They look very fine. Of course I never saw any really valuable pearls.'

'What did he get them for?' I croaked.

'Don't you see? They were his sin. He had to hide them in the wilderness, this wilderness. He hid them in the fish. And do you know—' she leaned toward me again and her eyes shone. She said very slowly, very earnestly:

'Sometimes I think that in the very end, just the last year or so, he actually believed they were the real pearls he was hiding. Does all this mean anything to you?'

I looked down at my pearls. My hand and the handkerchief closed over them slowly.

I said: 'I'm a plain man, Mrs Sype. I guess the scapegoat idea is a bit over my head. I'd say he was just trying to kid himself a bit—like any heavy loser.'

She smiled again. She was handsome when she smiled. Then she shrugged, quite lightly.

'Of course, you would see it that way. But me—' she spread her hands. 'Oh, well, it doesn't matter much now. May I have them for a keepsake?'

'Have them?'

'The—the phony pearls. Surely you don't—'

I stood up. An old Ford roadster without a top was chugging up the hill. A man in it had a big star on his vest. The chatter of the motor was like the chatter of some old angry bald-headed ape in the zoo.

Mrs Sype was standing beside me, with her hand half out, a thin, beseeching look on her face.

I grinned at her with sudden ferocity.

'Yeah, you were pretty good in there for a while,' I said. 'I damn near fell for it. And was I cold down the back, lady! But you helped. "Phony" was a shade out of character for you. Your work with the Colt was fast and kind of ruthless. Most of all Sype's last words queered it. "The Moors, Hattie—the Moors." He

141

wouldn't have bothered with that if the stones had been ringers. And he wasn't sappy enough to kid himself all the way.'

For a moment her face didn't change at all. Then it did. Something horrible showed in her eyes. She put her lips out and spat at me. Then she slammed into the house.

I tucked twenty-five thousand dollars into my vest pocket. Twelve thousand five hundred for me and twelve thousand five hundred for Kathy Horne. I could see her eyes when I brought her the check, and when she put it in the bank, to wait for Johnny to get paroled from Quentin.

The Ford had pulled up behind the other cars. The man driving spat over the side, yanked his emergency brake on, got out without using the door. He was a big fellow in shirt sleeves.

I went down the steps to meet him.

G. K. Chesterton
1874–1936

THE CHIEF MOURNER OF MARNE

A BLAZE OF LIGHTNING BLANCHED the grey woods tracing all the wrinkled foliage down to the last curled leaf, as if every detail were drawn in silver-point or graven in silver. The same strange trick of lightning by which it seems to record millions of minute things in an instant of time, picked out everything, from the elegant litter of the picnic spread under the spreading tree to the pale lengths of winding road, at the end of which a white car was waiting. In the distance a melancholy mansion with four towers like a castle, which in the grey evening had been but a dim and distant huddle of walls like a crumbling cloud, seemed to spring into the foreground, and stood up with all its embattled roofs and blank and staring windows. And in this, at least, the light had something in it of revelation. For to some of those grouped under the tree that castle was, indeed, a thing faded and almost forgotten, which was to prove its power to spring up again in the foreground of their lives.

The light also clothed for an instant, in the same silver splendour, at least one human figure that stood up as motionless as one of the towers. It was that of a tall man standing on a rise of ground above the rest, who were mostly sitting on the grass or stooping to gather up the hamper and crockery. He wore a pic-turesque short cloak or cape clasped with a silver clasp and chain, which blazed like a star when the flash touched it; and something metallic in his motionless figure was emphasised by the fact that his closely curled hair was of the burnished yellow that can be really called gold; and had the look of being younger than his face, which was handsome in a hard aquiline fashion, but looked, under the strong light, a little wrinkled and withered. Possibly it had suffered from wearing a mask of make-up, for Hugo Romaine was the greatest actor of his day. For that instant of illumination the golden curls and ivory mask and silver ornament made his figure gleam like that of a man in armour; the next instant his figure was a dark and even black silhouette against the sickly grey of the rainy evening sky.

But there was something about its stillness, like that of a statue, that distinguished it from the group at his feet. All the other figures around him had made the ordinary involuntary movement at the unexpected shock of light; for though the skies were rainy it was the first flash of the storm. The only lady present, whose air of carrying grey hair gracefully, as if she were really proud of it, marked her a matron of the United States, unaffectedly shut her eyes and uttered a sharp cry. Her English husband, General Outram, a very stolid Anglo-Indian, with a bald head and black moustache and whiskers of antiquated pattern, looked up with one stiff movement and then resumed his occupation of tidying up. A young man of the name of Mallow, very big and shy, with brown eyes like a dog's, dropped a cup and apologised awkwardly. A third man, much more dressy, with a resolute head, like an inquisitive terrier's, and grey hair brushed stiffly back, was no other than the great newspaper proprietor, Sir John Cockspur; he cursed freely, but not in an English idiom or accent, for he came from Toronto. But the tall man in the short cloak stood up literally like a statue in the twilight; his eagle face under the full glare had been like the bust of a Roman Emperor, and the carved eyelids had not moved.

A moment after, the dark dome cracked across with thunder, and the statue seemed to come to life. He turned his head over his shoulder and said casually:

'About a minute and half between the flash and the bang, but I think the storm's coming nearer. A tree is not supposed to be a good umbrella for the lightning, but we shall want it soon for the rain. I think it will be a deluge.'

The young man glanced at the lady a little anxiously and said: 'Can't we get shelter anywhere? There seems to be a house over there.'

'There is a house over there,' remarked the general, rather grimly; 'but not quite what you'd call a hospitable hotel.'

'It's curious,' said his wife sadly, 'that we should be caught in a storm with no house near but that one, of all others.'

Something in her tone seemed to check the younger man, who was both sensitive and comprehending; but nothing of that sort daunted the man from Toronto.

'What's the matter with it?' he asked. 'Looks rather like a ruin.'

'That place,' said the general dryly, 'belongs to the Marquis of Marne.'

'Gee!' said Sir John Cockspur. 'I've heard all about that bird, anyhow; and a queer bird, too. Ran him as a front-page mystery in the *Comet* last year. "The Nobleman Nobody Knows."'

'Yes, I've heard of him, too,' said young Mallow in a low voice. 'There seem to be all sorts of weird stories about why he hides himself like that. I've heard that he wears a mask because he's a leper. But somebody else told me quite seriously that there's a curse on the family; a child born with some frightful deformity that's kept in a dark room.'

'The Marquis of Marne has three heads,' remarked Romaine quite gravely. 'Once in every three hundred years a three-headed nobleman adorns the family tree. No human being dares approach the accursed house except a silent procession of hatters, sent to provide an abnormal number of hats. But'—and his voice took one of those deep and terrible turns, that could cause such a thrill in the theatre—'my friends, *those hats are of no human shape.*'

The American lady looked at him with a frown and a slight air of distrust, as if that trick of voice had moved her in spite of herself.

'I don't like your ghoulish jokes,' she said; 'and I'd rather you didn't joke about this, anyhow.'

'I hear and obey,' replied the actor; 'but am I, like the Light Brigade, forbidden even to reason why?'

'The reason,' she replied, 'is that he isn't the Nobleman Nobody Knows. I know him myself, or, at least, I knew him very well when he was an attaché at Washington thirty years ago, when we were all young. And he didn't wear a mask, at least, he didn't wear it with me. He wasn't a leper, though he may be almost as lonely. And he had only one head and only one heart, and that was broken.'

'Unfortunate love affair, of course,' said Cockspur. 'I should like that for the *Comet.*'

'I suppose it's a compliment to us,' she replied thoughtfully, 'that you always assume a man's heart is broken by a woman. But there are other kinds of love and bereavement. Have you never read "In Memoriam"? Have you never heard of David and Jonathan? What broke poor Marne up was the death of his brother; at least, he was really a first cousin, but had been brought up with him like a brother, and was much nearer than most brothers. James Mair, as the marquis was called when I knew him, was the elder of the two, but he always played the part of worshipper, with Maurice Mair as a god. And, by his account, Maurice Mair was certainly a wonder. James was no fool, and very good at his own political job; but it seems that Maurice could do that and everything else; that he was a brilliant artist and amateur actor and musician, and all the rest of it. James was very good-looking himself, long and strong and strenuous, with a high-bridged nose; though I suppose the young people would think he looked very quaint with his beard divided into two bushy whiskers in the fashion of those Victorian times. But Maurice was clean-shaven, and, by the portraits shown to me, certainly quite beautiful; though he looked a little more like a tenor than a gentleman ought to look. James was always asking me again and again whether his friend was not a marvel, whether any woman wouldn't fall in love with him, and so on, until it became rather a bore, except that it turned so suddenly into a tragedy. His whole life seemed to be in that idolatry, and one day the idol tumbled down, and was broken like any china doll. A chill caught at the seaside, and it was all over.'

'And after that,' asked the young man, 'did he shut himself up like this?'

'He went abroad at first,' she answered; 'away to Asia and the cannibal Islands and Lord knows where. These deadly strokes take different people in different ways. It took him in the way of an utter sundering or severance from everything, even from tradition and as far as possible from memory. He could not bear a reference to the old tie; a portrait or an anecdote or even an association. He couldn't bear the business of a great public funeral. He longed to get away. He stayed away for ten years. I heard some rumour that he had begun to revive a little at the end of the exile; but when he came back to his own home he relapsed completely. He settled down into religious melancholia, and that's practically madness.'

'The priests got hold of him, they say,' grumbled the old general. 'I know he gave thousands to found a monastery, and lives himself rather like a monk—or, at any rate, a hermit. Can't understand what good they think that will do.'

'Goddarned superstition,' snorted Cockspur; 'that sort of thing ought to be shown up. Here's a man that might have been useful to the Empire and the world, and these vampires get hold of him and suck him dry. I bet with their unnatural notions they haven't even let him marry.'

'No, he has never married,' said the lady. 'He was engaged when I knew him, as a matter of fact, but I don't think it ever came first with him, and I think it went with the rest when everything else went. Like Hamlet and Ophelia—he lost hold of love because he lost hold of life. But I knew the girl; indeed, I know her still. Between ourselves, it was Viola Grayson, daughter of the old admiral. She's never married either.'

'It's infamous! It's infernal!' cried Sir John, bounding up. 'It's not only a tragedy, but a crime. I've got a duty to the public, and I mean to see all this nonsensical nightmare . . . in the twentieth century—'

He was almost choked with his own protest, and then, after a silence, the old soldier said:

'Well, I don't profess to know much about those things, but I think these religious people need to study a text which says: "Let the dead bury their dead." '

'Only, unfortunately, that's just what it looks like,' said his wife with a sigh. 'It's just like some creepy story of a dead man burying another dead man, over and over again for ever.'

'The storm has passed over us,' said Romaine, with a rather inscrutable smile. 'You will not have to visit the inhospitable house after all.'

She suddenly shuddered.

'Oh, I'll never do that again!' she exclaimed.

Mallow was staring at her.

'Again! Have you tried it before?' he cried.

'Well, I did once,' she said, with a lightness not without a touch of pride; 'but we needn't go back on all that. It's not raining now, but I think we'd better be moving back to the car.'

As they moved off in procession, Mallow and the general brought up the rear; and the latter said abruptly, lowering his voice:

'I don't want that little cad Cockspur to hear but as you've asked you'd better know. It's the one thing I can't forgive Marne; but I suppose these monks have drilled him that way. My wife, who had been the best friend he ever had in America, actually came to that house when he was walking in the garden. He was looking at the ground like a monk, and hidden in a black hood that was really as ridiculous as any mask. She had sent her card in, and stood there in his very path. And he walked past her without a word or a glance, as if she had been a stone. He wasn't human; he was like some horrible automaton. She may well call him a dead man.'

'It's all very strange,' said the young man rather vaguely. 'It isn't like—like what I should have expected.'

Young Mr Mallow, when he left that rather dismal picnic, took himself thoughtfully in search of a friend. He did not know any monks, but he knew one priest, whom he was very much concerned to confront with the curious revelations he had heard that afternoon. He felt he would very much like to know the truth about the cruel superstition that hung over the house of Marne, like the black thundercloud he had seen hovering over it.

After being referred from one place to another, he finally ran his friend Father Brown to earth in the house of another friend, a Roman Catholic friend with a large family. He entered somewhat abruptly to find Father Brown sitting on the floor with a serious expression, and attempting to pin the somewhat florid hat belonging to a wax doll on to the head of a teddy bear.

Mallow felt a faint sense of incongruity; but he was far too full of his problem to put off the conversation if he could help it. He was staggering from a sort of set-back in a subconscious process that had been going on for some time. He poured out the whole tragedy of the house of Marne as he had heard it from the general's wife, along with most of the comments of the general and the newspaper proprietor. A new atmosphere of attention seemed to be created with the mention of the newspaper proprietor.

Father Brown neither knew nor cared that his attitudes were comic or commonplace. He continued to sit on the floor, where his large head and short legs made him look very like a baby playing with toys. But there came into his great grey eyes a certain expression that has been seen in the eyes of many men in many centuries through the story of nineteen hundred years; only the men were not generally sitting on floors, but at council tables, or on the seats of chapters, or the thrones of bishops and cardinals; a far-off, watchful look, heavy with the humility of a charge too great for men. Something of that anxious and far-reaching look is found in the eyes of sailors and of those who have steered through so many storms the ship of St Peter.

'It's very good of you to tell me this,' he said. 'I'm really awfully grateful, for we may have to do something about it. If it were only people like you and the general, it might be only a private matter; but if Sir John Cockspur is going to spread some sort of scare in his papers—well, he's a Toronto Orangeman, and we can hardly keep out of it.'

'But what will you say about it?' asked Mallow anxiously.

'The first thing I should say about it,' said Father Brown, 'is that, as you tell it, it doesn't sound like life. Suppose, for the sake of argument, that we are all pessimistic vampires blighting all human happiness. Suppose I'm a pessimistic vampire.' He scratched his nose with the teddy bear, became faintly conscious of the incongruity, and put it down. 'Suppose we do destroy all human and family ties. Why should we entangle a man again in an old family tie just when he showed signs of getting loose from it? Surely it's a little unfair to charge us both with crushing such affection and encouraging such infatuation. I don't see why even a religious maniac should be that particular sort of monomaniac, or how religion could increase that mania, except by brightening it with a little hope.'

Then he said, after a pause: 'I should like to talk to that general of yours.'

'It was his wife who told me,' said Mallow.

'Yes,' replied the other; 'but I'm more interested in what he didn't tell you than in what she did.'

'You think he knows more than she does?'

'I think he knows more than she says,' answered Father Brown. 'You tell me he used a phrase about forgiving everything except the rudeness to his wife. After all, what else was there to forgive?'

Father Brown had risen and shaken his shapeless clothes, and stood looking at the young man with screwed-up eyes and slightly quizzical expression. The next moment he had turned, and picking up his equally shapeless umbrella and large shabby hat, went stumping down the street.

He plodded through a variety of wide streets and squares till he came to a handsome old-fashioned house in the West End, where he asked the servant if he could see General Outram. After some little palaver he was shown into a study, fitted out less with books than with maps and globes, where the bald-headed, black-whiskered Anglo-Indian sat smoking a long, thin, black cigar and playing with pins on a chart.

'I am sorry to intrude,' said the priest, 'and all the more because I can't help the intrusion looking like interference. I want to speak to you about a private matter, but only in the hope of keeping it private. Unfortunately, some people are likely to make it public. I think, General, that you know Sir John Cockspur.'

The mass of black moustache and whisker served as a sort of mask for the lower half of the old general's face; it was always hard to see whether he smiled, but his brown eyes often had a certain twinkle.

'Everybody knows him, I suppose,' he said. 'I don't know him very well.'

'Well, you know everybody knows whatever he knows,' said Father Brown, smiling, 'when he thinks it convenient to print it. And I understand from my friend Mr Mallow, whom, I think, you know, that Sir John is going to print some scorching anti-clerical articles founded on what he would call the Marne Mystery. "Monks Drive Marquis Mad," etc.'

'If he is,' replied the general, 'I don't see why you should come to me about it. I ought to tell you I'm a strong Protestant.'

'I'm very fond of strong Protestants,' said Father Brown. 'I came to you because I was sure you would tell the truth. I hope it is not uncharitable to feel less sure of Sir John Cockspur.'

The brown eyes twinkled again, but the general said nothing.

'General,' said Father Brown, 'suppose Cockspur or his sort were going to make the world ring with tales against your country and your flag. Suppose he said your regiment ran away in battle, or your staff were in the pay of the enemy. Would you let anything stand between you and the facts that would refute him? Wouldn't you get on the track of the truth at all costs to anybody? Well, I have a regiment, and I belong to an army. It is being discredited by what I am certain is a fictitious story; but I don't know the true story. Can you blame me for trying to find it out?'

The soldier was silent, and the priest continued:

'I have heard the story Mallow was told yesterday, about Marne retiring with a broken heart through the death of his more than brother. I am sure there was more in it than that. I came to ask you if you know any more.'

'No,' said the general shortly; 'I cannot tell you any more.'

'General,' said Father Brown with a broad grin, 'you would have called me a Jesuit if I had used that equivocation.'

The soldier laughed gruffly, and then growled with much greater hostility.

'Well, I won't tell you, then,' he said. 'What do you say to that?'

'I only say,' said the priest mildly, 'that in that case I shall have to tell you.'

The brown eyes stared at him; but there was no twinkle in them now. He went on:

'You compel me to state, less sympathetically perhaps than you could, why it is obvious that there is more behind. I am quite sure the marquis has better cause for his brooding and secretiveness than merely having lost an old friend. I doubt whether priests have anything to do with it; I don't even know if he's a convert or merely a man comforting his conscience with charities; but I'm sure he's something more than a chief mourner. Since you insist, I will tell you one or two of the things that made me think so.

'First, it was stated that James Mair was engaged to be married, but somehow became unattached again after the death of Maurice Mair. Why should an honourable man break off his engagement merely because he was depressed by the death of a third party? He's much more likely to have turned for consolation to it; but, anyhow, he was bound in decency to go through with it.'

The general was biting his black moustache, and his brown eyes had become very watchful and even anxious, but he did not answer.

'A second point,' said Father Brown, frowning at the table. 'James Mair was always asking his lady friend whether his cousin Maurice was not very fascinating, and whether women would not admire him. I don't know if it occurred to the lady that there might be another meaning to that inquiry.'

The general got to his feet and began to walk or stamp about the room.

'Oh, damn it all,' he said, but without any air of animosity.

'The third point,' went on Father Brown, 'is James Mair's curious manner of mourning—destroying all relics, veiling all portraits, and so on. It does sometimes happen, I admit; it might mean mere affectionate bereavement. But it might mean something else.'

'Confound you,' said the other. 'How long are you going on piling this up?'

'The fourth and fifth points are pretty conclusive,' said the priest calmly, 'especially if you take them together. The first is that Maurice Mair seems to have had no funeral in particular, considering he was a cadet of a great family. He must have been buried hurriedly; perhaps secretly. And the last point is, that James Mair instantly disappeared to foreign parts; fled, in fact, to the ends of the earth.

'And so,' he went on, still in the same soft voice, 'when you would blacken my religion to brighten the story of the pure and perfect affection of two brothers, it seems—'

' Stop!' cried Outram in a tone like a pistol shot. 'I must tell you more, or you will fancy worse. Let me tell you one thing to start with. It was a fair fight.'

'Ah,' said Father Brown, and seemed to exhale a huge breath.

'It was a duel,' said the other. 'It was probably the last duel fought in England, and it is long ago now.'

'That's better,' said Father Brown. 'Thank God; that's a great deal better.'

'Better than the ugly things you thought of, I suppose?' said the general gruffly. 'Well, it's all very well for you to sneer at the pure and perfect affection; but it was true for all that. James Mair really was devoted to his cousin, who'd grown up with him like a younger brother. Elder brothers and sisters do sometimes devote themselves to a child like that, especially when he's a sort of infant phenomenon. But James Mair was the sort of simple character in whom even hate is in a sense unselfish. I mean that even when his tenderness turns to rage it is still objective, directed outwards to its object; he isn't conscious of himself. Now poor Maurice Mair was just the opposite. He was far more friendly and popular; but his success had made him live in a house of mirrors. He was first in every sort of sport and art and accomplishment; he nearly always won and took his winning amiably. But if ever, by any chance, he lost, there was just a glimpse of something not so amiable; he was a little jealous. I needn't tell you the whole miserable story of how he was a little jealous of his cousin's engagement; how he couldn't keep his restless vanity from interfering. It's enough to say that one of the few things in which James Mair was admittedly ahead of him was marksmanship with a pistol; and with that the tragedy ended.'

'You mean the tragedy began,' replied the priest. 'The tragedy of the survivor. I thought he did not need any monkish vampires to make him miserable.'

'To my mind he's more miserable than he need be,' said the general. 'After all, as I say, it was a ghastly tragedy, but it was a fair fight. And Jim had great provocation.'

'How do you know all this?' asked the priest.

'I know it because I saw it,' answered Outram stolidly. 'I was James Mair's second, and I saw Maurice Mair shot dead on the sands before my very eyes.'

'I wish you would tell me more about it,' said Father Brown reflectively. 'Who was Maurice Mair's second?'

'He had a more distinguished backing,' replied the general grimly. 'Hugo Romaine was his second; the great actor, you know. Maurice was mad on acting and had taken up Romaine (who was then a rising but still a struggling man), and financed the fellow and his ventures in return for taking lessons from the professional in his own hobby of amateur acting. But Romaine was then, I suppose, practically dependent on his rich friend; though he's richer now than any aristocrat. So his serving as second proves very little about what he thought of the quarrel. They fought in the English fashion, with only one second apiece; I wanted at least to have a surgeon, but Maurice boisterously refused it, saying the fewer people who knew, the better; and at the worst we could immediately get help. "There's a doctor in the village not half a mile away," he said; "I know him and he's got the fastest horse in the country. He could be brought here in no time; but there's no need to bring him here till we know." Well, we all knew that Maurice ran most risk, as the pistol was not his weapon; so when he refused aid nobody liked to ask for it. The duel was fought on a flat stretch of sand on the east coast of Scotland; and both the sight and sound of it were masked from the hamlets inland by a long rampart of sandhills patched with rank grass; probably part of the links, though in those days no Englishman had heard of golf. There was one deep, crooked cranny in the sandhills through which we came out on the sands. I can see them now; first a wide strip of dead yellow, and beyond, a narrower strip of dark red; a dark red that seemed already like the long shadow of a deed of blood.

'The thing itself seemed to happen with horrible speed; as if a whirlwind had struck the sand. With the very crack of sound Maurice Mair seemed to spin like a teetotum and pitch upon his face like a ninepin. And queerly enough, while I'd been worrying about him up to that moment, the instant he was dead all my pity was for the man who killed him; as it is to this day and hour. I knew that with that, the whole huge terrible pendulum of my friend's life-long love would swing back; and that whatever cause others might find to pardon him, he would never pardon himself for ever and ever. And so, somehow, the really vivid thing, the picture that burns in my memory so that I can't forget it, is not that of the catastrophe, the smoke and the flash and the falling figure. That seemed to be all over, like the noise that wakes a man up. What I saw, what I shall always see, is poor Jim hurrying across towards his fallen friend and foe; his brown beard looking black against the ghastly pallor of his face, with its high features cut out against the sea; and the frantic gestures with which he waved me to run for the surgeon in the hamlet behind the sandhills. He had dropped his pistol as he ran; he had a glove in one hand and the loose and fluttering fingers of it seemed to elongate and emphasise his wild pantomime of pointing or hailing for help. That is the picture that really remains with me; and there is nothing else in that picture, except the striped background of sands and sea and the dark, dead body lying still as a stone, and the dark figure of the dead man's second standing grim and motionless against the horizon.'

'Did Romaine stand motionless?' asked the priest. 'I should have thought he would have run even quicker towards the corpse.'

'Perhaps he did when I had left,' replied the general. 'I took in that undying picture in an instant and the next instant I had dived among the sandhills, and was far out of sight of the others. Well, poor Maurice had made a good choice in the matter of doctors; though the doctor came too late, he came quicker than I should have thought possible. This village surgeon was a very remarkable man, red-haired, irascible, but extraordinarily strong in promptitude and presence of mind. I saw him but for a flash as he leapt on his horse and went thundering away to the scene of death, leaving me far behind. But in that flash I had so strong a sense of his personality that I wished to God he had really been called in before the duel began; for I believe on my soul he would have prevented it somehow. As it was, he cleaned up the mess with marvellous swiftness; long before I could trail back to the sea-shore on my two feet his impetuous practicality had managed everything; the corpse was temporarily buried in the sandhills and the unhappy homicide had been persuaded to do the only thing he could do—to flee for his life. He slipped along the coast till he came to a port and managed to get out of the country. You know the rest; poor Jim remained abroad for many years; later, when the whole thing had been hushed up or forgotten, he returned to his dismal castle and automatically inherited the title. I have never seen him from that day to this, and yet I know what is written in red letters in the inmost darkness of his brain.'

'I understand,' said Father Brown, 'that some of you have made efforts to see him?'

'My wife never relaxed her efforts,' said the general. 'She refuses to admit that such a crime ought to cut a man off for ever; and I confess I am inclined to agree with her. Eighty years before it would have been thought quite normal; and really it was manslaughter rather than murder. My wife is a great friend of the unfortunate lady who was the occasion of the quarrel and she has an idea that if

Jim would consent to see Viola Grayson once again, and receive her assurance that old quarrels are buried, it might restore his sanity. My wife is calling a sort of council of old friends to-morrow, I believe. She is very energetic.'

Father Brown was playing with the pins that lay beside the general's map; he seemed to listen rather absent-mindedly. He had the sort of mind that sees things in pictures; and the picture which had coloured even the prosaic mind of the practical soldier took on tints yet more significant and sinister in the more mystical mind of the priest. He saw the dark-red desolation of sand, the very hue of Aceldama, and the dead man lying in a dark heap, and the slayer, stooping as he ran, gesticulating with a glove in demented remorse, and always his imagination came back to the third thing that he could not yet fit into any human picture: the second of the slain man standing motionless and mysterious, like a dark statue on the edge of the sea. It might seem to some a detail; but for him it was that stiff figure that stood up like a standing note of interrogation.

Why had not Romaine moved instantly? It was the natural thing for a second to do, in common humanity, let alone friendship. Even if there were some double-dealing or darker motive not yet understood, one would think it would be done for the sake of appearances. Anyhow, when the thing was all over, it would be natural for the second to stir long before the other second had vanished beyond the sandhills.

'Does this man Romaine move very slowly?' he asked.

'It's queer you should ask that,' answered Outram, with a sharp glance. 'No, as a matter of fact he moves very quickly when he moves at all. But, curiously enough, I was just thinking that only this afternoon I saw him stand exactly like that, during the thunderstorm. He stood in that silver-clasped cape of his, and with one hand on his hip, exactly and in every line as he stood on those bloody sands long ago. The lightning blinded us all, but he did not blink. When it was dark again he was standing there still.'

'I suppose he isn't standing there now?' inquired Father Brown. 'I mean, I suppose he moved sometime?'

'No, he moved quite sharply when the thunder came,' replied the other. 'He seemed to have been waiting for it, for he told us the exact time of the interval . . . is anything the matter?'

'I've pricked myself with one of your pins,' said Father Brown. 'I hope I haven't damaged it.' But his eyes had snapped and his mouth abruptly shut.

'Are you ill?' inquired the general, staring at him.

'No,' answered the priest; 'I'm only not quite so stoical as your friend Romaine. I can't help blinking when I see light.'

He turned to gather up his hat and umbrella; but when he had got to the door he seemed to remember something and turned back. Coming up close to Outram, he gazed up into his face with a rather helpless expression, as of a dying fish, and made a motion as if to hold him by the waistcoat.

'General,' he almost whispered, 'for God's sake don't let your wife and that other woman insist on seeing Marne again. Let sleeping dogs be, or you'll unleash all the hounds of hell.'

The general was left alone with a look of bewilderment in his brown eyes, as he sat down again to play with his pins.

Even greater, however, was the bewilderment which attended the successive stages of the benevolent conspiracy of the general's wife, who had assembled her little group of sympathisers to storm the castle of the misanthrope. The first surprise she encountered was the unexplained absence of one of the actors in the ancient tragedy. When they assembled by agreement at a quiet hotel quite near the castle, there was no sign of Hugo Romaine, until a belated telegram from a lawyer told them that the great actor had suddenly left the country. The second surprise, when they began the bombardment by sending up word to the castle with an urgent request for an interview, was the figure which came forth from those gloomy gates to receive the deputation in the name of the noble owner. It was no such figure as they would have conceived suitable to those sombre avenues or those almost feudal formalities. It was not some stately steward or major-domo, nor even a dignified butler or tall and ornamental footman. The only figure that came out of the cavernous castle doorway was the short and shabby figure of Father Brown.

'Look here,' he said, in his simple, bothered fashion. 'I told you you'd much better leave him alone. He knows what he's doing and it'll only make everybody unhappy.'

Lady Outram, who was accompanied by a tall and quietly dressed lady, still very handsome, presumably the original Miss Grayson, looked at the little priest with cold contempt.

'Really, sir,' she said; 'this is a very private occasion, and I don't understand what you have to do with it.'

'Trust a priest to have to do with a private occasion,' snarled Sir John Cockspur. 'Don't you know they live behind the scenes like rats behind a wainscot burrowing their way into everybody's private rooms. See how he's already in possession of poor Marne.' Sir John was slightly sulky, as his aristocratic friends had persuaded him to give up the great scoop of publicity in return for the privilege of being really inside a Society secret. It never occurred to him to ask himself whether *he* was at all like a rat in a wainscot.

'Oh, that's all right,' said Father Brown, with the impatience of anxiety. 'I've talked it over with the marquis and the only priest he's ever had anything to do with; his clerical tastes have been much exaggerated. I tell you he knows what he's about; and I do implore you all to leave him alone.'

'You mean to leave him to this living death of moping and going mad in a ruin!' cried Lady Outram, in a voice that shook a little. 'And all because he had the bad luck to shoot a man in a duel more than a quarter of a century ago. Is that what you call Christian charity?'

'Yes,' answered the priest stolidly; 'that is what I call Christian charity.'

'It's about all the Christian charity you'll ever get out of these priests,' cried Cockspur bitterly. 'That's their only idea of pardoning a poor fellow for a piece of folly; to wall him up alive and starve him to death with fasts and penances and pictures of hell-fire. And all because a bullet went wrong.'

'Really, Father Brown,' said General Outram, 'do you honestly think he deserves this? Is that your Christianity?'

'Surely the true Christianity,' pleaded his wife more gently, 'is that which knows all and pardons all; the love that can remember—and forget.'

'Father Brown,' said young Mallow, very earnestly, 'I generally agree with what you say; but I'm hanged if I can follow you here. A shot in a duel, followed instantly by remorse, is not such an awful offence.'

'I'll admit,' said Father Brown dully, 'that I take a more serious view of his offence.'

'God soften your hard heart,' said the strange lady speaking for the first time. 'I am going to speak to my old friend!'

Almost as if her voice had raised a ghost in that great grey house, something stirred within and a figure stood in the dark doorway at the top of the great stone flight of steps. It was clad in dead black, but there was something wild about the blanched hair and something in the pale features that was like the wreck of a marble statue.

Viola Grayson began calmly to move up the great flight of steps; and Outram muttered in his thick black moustache: 'He won't cut her dead as he did my wife, I fancy.'

Father Brown, who seemed in a collapse of resignation, looked up at him for a moment.

'Poor Marne has enough on his conscience,' he said. 'Let us acquit him of what we can. At least he never cut your wife.'

'What do you mean by that?'

'He never knew her,' said Father Brown.

As they spoke, the tall lady proudly mounted the last step and came face to face with the Marquis of Marne. His lips moved, but something happened before he could speak.

A scream rang across the open space and went wailing away in echoes along those hollow walls. By the abruptness and agony with which it broke from the woman's lips it might have been a mere inarticulate cry. But it was an articulated word; and they all heard it with a horrible distinctness.

'Maurice!'

'What is it, dear?' cried Lady Outram, and began to run up the steps; for the other woman was swaying as if she might fall down the whole stone flight. Then she faced about and began to descend, all bowed and shrunken and shuddering. 'Oh, my God,' she was saying. 'Oh, my God ... it isn't Jim at all ... it's Maurice!'

'I think, Lady Outram,' said the priest gravely, 'you had better go with your friend.'

As they turned, a voice fell on them like a stone from the top of the stone stair, a voice that might have come out of an open grave. It was hoarse and unnatural, like the voices of men who are left alone with wild birds on desert islands. It was the voice of the Marquis of Marne, and it said: 'Stop!'

'Father Brown,' he said, 'before your friends disperse I authorise you to tell them all I have told you. Whatever follows, I will hide from it no longer.'

'You are right,' said the priest, 'and it shall be counted to you.'

'Yes,' said Father Brown quietly to the questioning company afterwards. 'He has given me the right to speak; but I will not tell it as he told me, but as I found it out for myself. Well, I knew from the first that the blighting monkish influence was all nonsense out of novels. Our people might possibly, in certain cases, encourage a man to go regularly into a monastery, but certainly not to hang about in a mediaeval castle. In the same way, they certainly wouldn't want him to dress up as a monk when he wasn't a monk. But it struck me that he might himself want to wear a monk's hood or even a mask. I had heard of him as a mourner, and then as a murderer; but already I had hazy suspicions that his reason for hiding might not only be concerned with what he was, but with who he was.'

'Then came the general's vivid description of the duel; and the most vivid thing in it to me was the figure of Mr Romaine in the background; it was vivid because it was in the background. Why did the general leave behind him on the sand a dead man, whose friend stood yards away from him like a stock or a stone? Then I heard something, a mere trifle, about a trick habit that Romaine has of standing quite still when he is waiting for something to happen; as he waited for the thunder to follow the lightning. Well, that automatic trick in this case betrayed everything. Hugo Romaine on that old occasion, also, was waiting for something.'

'But it was all over,' said the general. 'What could he have been waiting for?'

'He was waiting for the duel,' said Father Brown.

'But I tell you I saw the duel!' cried the general.

'And I tell you you didn't see the duel,' said the priest.

'Are you mad?' demanded the other. 'Or why should you think I am blind?'

'Because you were blinded—that you might not see,' said the priest. 'Because you are a good man and God had mercy on your innocence, and he turned your face away from that unnatural strife. He set a wall of sand and silence between you and what really happened on that horrible red shore, abandoned to the raging spirits of Judas and of Cain.'

'Tell us what happened!' gasped the lady impatiently.

'I will tell it as I found it,' proceeded the priest. 'The next thing I found was that Romaine the actor had been training Maurice Mair in all the tricks of the trade of acting. I once had a friend who went in for acting. He gave me a very amusing account of how his first week's training consisted entirely of falling down; of learning how to fall flat without a stagger, as if he were stone dead.'

'God have mercy on us!' cried the general, and gripped the arms of his chair as if to rise.

'Amen,' said Father Brown. 'You told me how quickly it seemed to come; in fact, Maurice fell before the bullet flew, and lay perfectly still, waiting. And his wicked friend and teacher stood also in the background, waiting.'

'We are waiting,' said Cockspur, 'and I feel as if I couldn't wait.'

'James Mair, already broken with remorse, rushed across to the fallen man and bent over to lift him up. He had thrown away his pistol like an unclean thing; but Maurice's pistol still lay under his hand and it was undischarged. Then as the elder man bent over the younger, the younger lifted himself on his left arm and shot the elder through the body. He knew he was not so good a shot, but there was no question of missing the heart at that distance.'

The rest of the company had risen and stood staring down at the narrator with pale faces. 'Are you sure of this?' asked Sir John at last, in a thick voice.

'I am sure of it,' said Father Brown, 'and now I leave Maurice Mair, the present Marquis of Marne, to your Christian charity. You have told me something to-day about Christian charity. You seemed to me to give it almost too large a place; but how fortunate it is for poor sinners like this man that you err so much on the side of mercy, and are ready to be reconciled to all mankind.'

'Hang it all,' exploded the general; 'if you think I'm going to be reconciled to a filthy viper like that, I tell you I wouldn't say a word to save him from hell. I said I could pardon a regular decent duel, but of all the treacherous assassins—'

'He ought to be lynched,' cried Cockspur excitedly. 'He ought to burn alive like a nigger in the States. And if there is such a thing as burning for ever, he jolly well—'

'I wouldn't touch him with a bargepole myself,' said Mallow.

'There is a limit to human charity,' said Lady Outram, trembling all over.

'There is,' said Father Brown dryly; 'and that is the real difference between human charity and Christian charity. You must forgive me if I was not altogether crushed by your contempt for my uncharitableness to-day; or by the lectures you read me about pardon for every sinner. For it seems to me that you only pardon the sins that you don't really think sinful. You only forgive criminals when they commit what you don't regard as crimes, but rather as conventions. So you tolerate a conventional duel, just as you tolerate a conventional divorce. You forgive because there isn't anything to be forgiven.'

'But, hang it all,' cried Mallow, 'you don't expect us to be able to pardon a vile thing like this?'

'No,' said the priest; 'but *we* have to be able to pardon it.'

He stood up abruptly and looked round at them.

'We have to touch such men, not with a bargepole, but with a benediction,' he said. 'We have to say the word that will save them from hell. We alone are left to deliver them from despair when your human charity deserts them. Go on your own primrose path pardoning all your favourite vices and being generous to your fashionable crimes; and leave us in the darkness, vampires of the night, to console those who really need consolation; who do things really indefensible, things that neither the world nor they themselves can defend; and none but a priest will pardon. Leave us with the men who commit the mean and revolting and real crimes; mean as St Peter when the cock crew, and yet the dawn came.'

'The dawn,' repeated Mallow doubtfully. 'You mean hope—for *him*?'

'Yes,' replied the other. 'Let me ask you one question. You are great ladies and men of honour and secure of yourselves; you would never, you can tell yourselves, stoop to such squalid reason as that. But tell me this. If any of you had so stooped, which of you, years afterwards, when you were old and rich and safe, would have been driven by conscience or confessor to tell such a story of yourself? You say you could not commit so base a crime. Could you confess so base a crime?'

The others gathered their possessions together and drifted by twos and threes out of the room in silence. And Father Brown, also in silence, went back to the melancholy castle of Marne.

Agatha Christie
1890–1976

THE MYSTERY OF
THE BAGHDAD CHEST

THE WORDS MADE a catchy headline, and I said as much to my friend, Hercule Poirot. I knew none of the parties. My interest was merely the dispassionate one of the man in the street. Poirot agreed.

'Yes, it has a flavour of the Oriental, of the mysterious. The chest may very well have been a sham Jacobean one from the Tottenham Court Road; none the less the reporter who thought of naming it the Baghdad Chest was happily inspired. The word "mystery" is also thoughtfully placed in juxtaposition, though I understand there is very little mystery about the case.'

'Exactly. It is all rather horrible and macabre, but it is not mysterious.'

'Horrible and macabre,' repeated Poirot thoughtfully.

'The whole idea is revolting,' I said, rising to my feet and pacing up and down the room. 'The murderer kills this man—his friend—shoves him into the chest, and half an hour later is dancing in that same room with the wife of his victim. Think! If she had imagined for one moment—'

'True,' said Poirot thoughtfully. 'That much-vaunted possession, a woman's intuition—it does not seem to have been working.'

'The party seems to have gone off very merrily,' I said with a slight shiver. 'And all that time, as they danced and played poker, there was a dead man in the room with them. One could write a play about such an idea.'

'It has been done,' said Poirot. 'But console yourself, Hastings,' he added kindly. 'Because a theme has been used once, there is no reason why it should not be used again. Compose your drama.'

I had picked up the paper and was studying the rather blurred reproduction of a photograph.

'She must be a beautiful woman,' I said slowly. 'Even from this, one gets an idea.'

Below the picture ran the inscription:

A RECENT PORTRAIT OF MRS CLAYTON,
THE WIFE OF THE MURDERED MAN

Poirot took the paper from me.

'Yes,' he said. 'She is beautiful. Doubtless she is of those born to trouble the souls of men.'

He handed the paper back to me with a sigh.

'*Dieu merci*, I am not of an ardent temperament. It has saved me from many embarrassments. I am duly thankful.'

I do not remember that we discussed the case further. Poirot displayed no special interest in it at the time. The facts were so clear, and there was so little ambiguity about them, that discussion seemed merely futile.

Mr and Mrs Clayton and Major Rich were friends of fairly long standing. On the day in question, the tenth of March, the Claytons had accepted an invitation to spend the evening with Major Rich. At about seven-thirty, however, Clayton explained to another friend, a Major Curtiss, with whom he was having a drink, that he had been unexpectedly called to Scotland and was leaving by the eight o'clock train.

'I'll just have time to drop in and explain to old Jack,' went on Clayton. 'Marguerita is going, of course. I'm sorry about it, but Jack will understand how it is.'

Mr Clayton was as good as his word. He arrived at Major Rich's rooms about twenty to eight. The major was out at the time, but his manservant, who knew Mr Clayton well, suggested that he come in and wait. Mr Clayton said that he had no time, but that he would come in and write a note. He added that he was on his way to catch a train.

The valet accordingly showed him into the sitting-room.

About five minutes later Major Rich, who must have let himself in without the valet hearing him, opened the door of the sitting-room, called his man and told him to go out and get some cigarettes. On his return the man brought them to his master, who was then alone in the sitting-room. The man naturally concluded that Mr Clayton had left.

The guests arrived shortly afterwards. They comprised Mrs Clayton, Major Curtiss and a Mr and Mrs Spence. The evening was spent dancing to the phonograph and playing poker. The guests left shortly after midnight.

The following morning, on coming to do the sitting-room, the valet was startled to find a deep stain discolouring the carpet below and in front of a piece of furniture which Major Rich had brought from the East and which was called the Baghdad Chest.

Instinctively the valet lifted the lid of the chest and was horrified to find inside the doubled-up body of a man who had been stabbed to the heart.

Terrified, the man ran out of the flat and fetched the nearest policeman. The dead man proved to be Mr Clayton. The arrest of Major Rich followed very shortly afterward. The major's defence, it was understood, consisted of a sturdy denial of everything. He had not seen Mr Clayton the preceding evening and the first he had heard of his going to Scotland had been from Mrs Clayton.

Such were the bald facts of the case. Innuendoes and suggestions naturally abounded. The close friendship and intimacy of Major Rich and Mrs Clayton were so stressed that only a fool could fail to read between the lines. The motive for the crime was plainly indicated.

Long experience has taught me to make allowance for baseless calumny. The motive suggested might, for all the evidence, be entirely non-existent. Some quite other reason might have precipitated the issue. But one thing did stand out clearly—that Rich was the murderer.

As I say, the matter might have rested there, had it not happened that Poirot and I were due at a party given by Lady Chatterton that night.

Poirot, whilst bemoaning social engagements and declaring a passion for solitude, really enjoyed these affairs enormously. To be made a fuss of and treated as a lion suited him down to the ground.

On occasions he positively purred! I have seen him blandly receiving the most outrageous compliments as no more than his due, and uttering the most blatantly conceited remarks, such as I can hardly bear to set down.

Sometimes he would argue with me on the subject.

'But, my friend, I am not an Anglo-Saxon. Why should I play the hypocrite? *Si, si*, that is what you do, all of you. The airman who has made a difficult flight, the tennis champion—they look down their noses, they mutter inaudibly that "it is nothing". But do they really think that themselves? Not for a moment. They would admire the exploit in someone else. So, being reasonable men, they admire it in themselves. But their training prevents them from saying so. Me, I am not like that. The talents that I possess—I would salute them in another. As it happens, in my own particular line, there is no one to touch me. *C'est dommage!* As it is, I admit freely and without hypocrisy that I am a great man. I have the order, the method and the psychology in an unusual degree. I am, in fact, Hercule Poirot! Why should I turn red and stammer and mutter into my chin that really I am very stupid? It would not be true.'

'There is certainly only one Hercule Poirot,' I agreed—not without a spice of malice of which, fortunately, Poirot remained quite oblivious.

Lady Chatterton was one of Poirot's most ardent admirers. Starting from the mysterious conduct of a Pekingese, he had unravelled a chain which led to a noted burglar and housebreaker. Lady Chatterton had been loud in his praises ever since.

To see Poirot at a party was a great sight. His faultless evening clothes, the exquisite set of his white tie, the exact symmetry of his hair parting, the sheen of pomade on his hair, and the tortured splendour of his famous moustaches—all combined to paint the perfect picture of an inveterate dandy. It was hard, at these moments, to take the little man seriously.

It was about half-past eleven when Lady Chatterton, bearing down upon us, whisked Poirot neatly out of an admiring group, and carried him off—I need hardly say, with myself in tow.

'I want you to go into my little room upstairs,' said Lady Chatterton rather breathlessly as soon as she was out of earshot of her other guests. 'You know where it is, M. Poirot. You'll find someone there who needs your help very badly—and you will help her, I know. She's one of my dearest friends—so don't say no.'

Energetically leading the way as she talked, Lady Chatterton flung open a door, exclaiming as she did so, 'I've got him, Marguerita darling. And he'll do anything you want. You *will* help Mrs Clayton, won't you, M. Poirot?'

And taking the answer for granted, she withdrew with the same energy that characterised all her movements.

Mrs Clayton had been sitting in a chair by the window. She rose now and came toward us. Dressed in deep mourning, the dull black showed up her fair colouring. She was a singularly lovely woman, and there was about her a simple childlike candour which made her charm quite irresistible.

'Alice Chatterton is so kind,' she said. 'She arranged this. She said you would help me, M. Poirot. Of course I don't know whether you will or not—but I hope you will.'

She had held out her hand and Poirot had taken it. He held it now for a moment or two while he stood scrutinising her closely. There was nothing ill-bred in his manner of doing it. It was more the kind but searching look that a famous consultant gives a new patient as the latter is ushered into his presence.

'Are you sure, madame,' he said at last, 'that I can help you?'

'Alice says so.'

'Yes, but I am asking you, madame.'

A little flush rose to her cheeks.

'I don't know what you mean.'

'What is it, madame, that you want me to do?'

'You—you—know who I am?' she asked.

'Assuredly.'

'Then you can guess what it is I am asking you to do, M. Poirot—Captain Hastings'—I was gratified that she realised my identity—'Major Rich did *not* kill my husband.'

'Why not?'

'I beg your pardon?'

Poirot smiled at her slight discomfiture.

'I said, "Why not?"' he repeated.

'I'm not sure that I understand.'

'Yet it is very simple. The police—the lawyers—they will all ask the same question: Why did Major Rich kill M. Clayton? I ask the opposite. I ask you, madame, why did Major Rich *not* kill Mr Clayton.'

'You mean—why I'm so sure? Well, but I *know*. I know Major Rich so well.'

'You know Major Rich so well,' repeated Poirot tonelessly.

The colour flamed into her cheeks.

'Yes, that's what they'll say—what they'll think! Oh, I know!'

'*C'est vrai*. That is what they will ask you about—how well you knew Major Rich. Perhaps you will speak the truth, perhaps you will lie. It is very necessary for a woman to lie, it is a good weapon. But there are three people, madame, to whom a woman should speak the truth. To her Father Confessor, to her hairdresser and to her private detective—if she trusts him. Do you trust me, madame?'

Marguerita Clayton drew a deep breath. 'Yes,' she said. 'I do. I must,' she added rather childishly.

'Then, how well do you know Major Rich?'

She looked at him for a moment in silence, then she raised her chin defiantly.

'I will answer your question. I loved Jack from the first moment I saw him— two years ago. Lately I think—I believe—he has come to love me. But he has never said so.'

'*Épatant!*' said Poirot. 'You have saved me a good quarter of an hour by coming to the point without beating the bush. You have the good sense. Now your husband—did he suspect your feelings?'

'I don't know,' said Marguerita slowly. 'I thought—lately—that he might. His manner has been different . . . But that may have been merely my fancy.'

'Nobody else knew?'

'I do not think so.'

'And—pardon me, madame—you did not love your husband?'

There were, I think, very few women who would have answered that question as simply as this woman did. They would have tried to explain their feelings.

Marguerita Clayton said quite simply: 'No.'

'*Bien*. Now we know where we are. According to you, madame, Major Rich did not kill your husband, but you realise that all the evidence points to his having done so. Are you aware, privately, of any flaw in that evidence?'

'No. I know nothing.'

'When did your husband first inform you of his visit to Scotland?'

'Just after lunch. He said it was a bore, but he'd have to go. Something to do with land values, he said it was.'

'And after that?'

'He went out—to his club, I think. I—I didn't see him again.'

'Now as to Major Rich—what was his manner that evening? Just as usual?'

'Yes, I think so.'

'You are not sure?'

Marguerita wrinkled her brows.

'He was—a little constrained. With me—not with the others. But I thought I knew why that was. You understand? I am sure the constraint or—or—absent-mindedness perhaps describes it better—had nothing to do with Edward. He was surprised to hear that Edward had gone to Scotland, but not unduly so.'

'And nothing else unusual occurs to you in connection with that evening?'

Marguerita thought.

'No, nothing whatever.'

'You—noticed the chest?'

She shook her head with a little shiver.

'I don't even remember it—or what it was like. We played poker most of the evening.'

'Who won?'

'Major Rich. I had very bad luck, and so did Major Curtiss. The Spences won a little, but Major Rich was the chief winner.'

'The party broke up—when?'

'About half-past twelve, I think. We all left together.'

'Ah!'

Poirot remained silent, lost in thought.

'I wish I could be more helpful to you,' said Mrs Clayton. 'I seem to be able to tell you so little.'

'About the present—yes. What about the past, madame?'

'The past?'

'Yes. Have there not been incidents?'

She flushed.

'You mean that dreadful little man who shot himself. It wasn't my fault, M. Poirot. Indeed it wasn't.'

'It was not precisely of that incident that I was thinking.'

'That ridiculous duel? But Italians do fight duels. I was so thankful the man wasn't killed.'

'It must have been a relief to you,' agreed Poirot gravely.

She was looking at him doubtfully. He rose and took her hand in his.

'I shall not fight a duel for you, madame,' he said. 'But I will do what you have asked me. I will discover the truth. And let us hope that your instincts are correct—that the truth will help and not harm you.'

Our first interview was with Major Curtiss. He was a man of about forty, of soldierly build, with very dark hair and a bronzed face. He had known the Claytons for some years and Major Rich also. He confirmed the press reports.

Clayton and he had had a drink together at the club just before half-past seven, and Clayton had then announced his intention of looking in on Major Rich on his way to Euston.

'What was Mr Clayton's manner? Was he depressed or cheerful?'

The major considered. He was a slow-spoken man.

'Seemed in fairly good spirits,' he said at last.

'He said nothing about being on bad terms with Major Rich?'

'Good Lord, no. They were pals.'

'He didn't object to—his wife's friendship with Major Rich?'

The major became very red in the face.

'You've been reading those damned newspapers, with their hints and lies. Of course he didn't object. Why, he said to me: "Marguerita's going, of course."'

'I see. Now during the evening—the manner of Major Rich—was that much as usual?'

'I didn't notice any difference.'

'And madame? She, too, was as usual.'

'Well,' he reflected, 'now I come to think of it, she was a bit quiet. You know, thoughtful and faraway.'

'Who arrived first?'

'The Spences. They were there when I got there. As a matter of fact, I'd called round for Mrs Clayton, but found she'd already started. So I got there a bit late.'

'And how did you amuse yourselves? You danced? You played the cards?'

'A bit of both. Danced first of all.'

'There were five of you?'

'Yes, but that's all right, because I don't dance. I put on the records and the others danced.'

'Who danced most with whom?'

'Well, as a matter of fact the Spences like dancing together. They've got a sort of craze on it—fancy steps and all that.'

'So that Mrs Clayton danced mostly with Major Rich?'

'That's about it.'

'And then you played poker?'

'Yes.'

'And when did you leave?'

'Oh, quite early. A little after midnight.'

'Did you all leave together?'

'Yes. As a matter of fact, we shared a taxi, dropped Mrs Clayton first, then me, and the Spences took it on to Kensington.'

Our next visit was to Mr and Mrs Spence. Only Mrs Spence was at home, but her account of the evening tallied with that of Major Curtiss except that she displayed a slight acidity concerning Major Rich's luck at cards.

Earlier in the morning Poirot had had a telephone conversation with Inspector Japp of Scotland Yard. As a result we arrived at Major Rich's rooms and found his manservant, Burgoyne, expecting us.

The valet's evidence was very precise and clear.

Mr Clayton had arrived at twenty minutes to eight. Unluckily Major Rich had just that very minute gone out. Mr Clayton had said that he couldn't wait, as he had to catch a train, but he would just scrawl a note. He accordingly went into the sitting-room to do so. Burgoyne had not actually heard his master come in, as he was running the bath, and Major Rich, of course, let himself in with his own key. In his opinion it was about ten minutes later that Major Rich called him and sent him out for cigarettes. No, he had not gone into the sitting-room. Major Rich had stood in the doorway. He had returned with the cigarettes five minutes later and on this occasion he had gone into the sitting-room, which was then empty, save for his master, who was standing by the window smoking. His master had inquired if his bath were ready and on being told it was had proceeded to take it. He, Burgoyne, had not mentioned Mr Clayton, as he assumed that his master had found Mr Clayton there and let him out himself. His master's manner had been precisely the same as usual. He had taken his bath, changed, and shortly after, Mr and Mrs Spence had arrived, to be followed by Major Curtiss and Mrs Clayton.

It had not occurred to him, Burgoyne explained, that Mr Clayton might have left before his master's return. To do so, Mr Clayton would have had to bang the front door behind him and that the valet was sure he would have heard.

Still in the same impersonal manner, Burgoyne proceeded to his finding of the body. For the first time my attention was directed to the fatal chest. It was a good-sized piece of furniture standing against the wall next to the phonograph cabinet. It was made of some dark wood and plentifully studded with brass nails. The lid opened simply enough. I looked in and shivered. Though well scrubbed, ominous stains remained.

Suddenly Poirot uttered an exclamation. 'Those holes there—they are curious. One would say that they had been newly made.'

The holes in question were at the back of the chest against the wall. There were three or four of them. They were about a quarter of an inch in diameter and certainly had the effect of having been freshly made.

Poirot bent down to examine them, looking inquiringly at the valet.

'It's certainly curious, sir. I don't remember ever seeing those holes in the past, though maybe I wouldn't notice them.'

'It makes no matter,' said Poirot.

Closing the lid of the chest, he stepped back into the room until he was standing with his back against the window. Then he suddenly asked a question.

'Tell me,' he said. 'When you brought the cigarettes into your master that night, was there not something out of place in the room?'

Burgoyne hesitated for a minute, then with some slight reluctance he replied, 'It's odd your saying that, sir. Now you come to mention it, there was. That screen there that cuts off the draught from the bedroom door—it was moved a bit more to the left.'

'Like this?'

Poirot darted nimbly forward and pulled at the screen. It was a handsome affair of painted leather. It already slightly obscured the view of the chest, and as Poirot adjusted it, it hid the chest altogether.

'That's right, sir,' said the valet. 'It was like that.'

'And the next morning?'

'It was still like that. I remember. I moved it away and it was then I saw the stain. The carpet's gone to be cleaned, sir. That's why the boards are bare.'

Poirot nodded.

'I see,' he said. 'I thank you.'

He placed a crisp piece of paper in the valet's palm.

'Thank you, sir.'

'Poirot,' I said when we were out in the street, 'that point about the screen—is that a point helpful to Rich?'

'It is a further point against him,' said Poirot ruefully. 'The screen hid the chest from the room. It also hid the stain on the carpet. Sooner or later the blood was bound to soak through the wood and stain the carpet. The screen would prevent discovery for the moment. Yes—but there is something there that I do not understand. The valet, Hastings, the valet.'

'What about the valet? He seemed a most intelligent fellow.'

'As you say, most intelligent. Is it credible, then, that Major Rich failed to realise that the valet would certainly discover the body in the morning? Immediately after the deed he had no time for anything—granted. He shoves the body into the chest, pulls the screen in front of it and goes through the evening hoping for the best. But after the guests are gone? Surely, then is the time to dispose of the body.'

'Perhaps he hoped the valet wouldn't notice the stain?'

'That, *mon ami*, is absurd. A stained carpet is the first thing a good servant would be bound to notice. And Major Rich, he goes to bed and snores there comfortably and does nothing at all about the matter. Very remarkable and interesting, that.'

'Curtiss might have seen the stains when he was changing the records the night before?' I suggested.

'That is unlikely. The screen would throw a deep shadow just there. No, but I begin to see. Yes, dimly I begin to see.'

'See what?' I asked eagerly.

'The possibilities, shall we say, of an alternative explanation. Our next visit may throw light on things.'

Our next visit was to the doctor who had examined the body. His evidence was a mere recapitulation of what he had already given at the inquest. Deceased had been stabbed to the heart with a long thin knife something like a stiletto. The knife had been left in the wound. Death had been instantaneous. The knife was the property of Major Rich and usually lay on his writing table. There were no fingerprints on it, the doctor understood. It had been either wiped or held in a handkerchief. As regards time, any time between seven and nine seemed indicated.

'He could not, for instance, have been killed after midnight?' asked Poirot.

'No. That I can say. Ten o'clock at the outside—but seven-thirty to eight seems clearly indicated.'

'There *is* a second hypothesis possible,' Poirot said when we were back home. 'I wonder if you see it, Hastings. To me it is very plain, and I only need one point to clear up the matter for good and all.'

'It's no good,' I said. 'I'm not there.'

'But make an effort, Hastings. Make an effort.'

'Very well,' I said. 'At seven-forty Clayton is alive and well. The last person to see him alive is Rich—'

'So we assume.'

'Well, isn't it so?'

'You forget, *mon ami*, that Major Rich denies that. He states explicitly that Clayton had gone when he came in.'

'But the valet says that he would have heard Clayton leave because of the bang of the door. And also, if Clayton had left, when did he return? He couldn't have returned after midnight because the doctor says positively that he was dead at least two hours before that. That only leaves one alternative.'

'Yes, *mon ami*?' said Poirot.

'That in the five minutes Clayton was alone in the sitting-room, someone else came in and killed him. But there we have the same objection. Only someone with a key could come in without the valet's knowing, and in the same way the murderer on leaving would have had to bang the door, and that again the valet would have heard.'

'Exactly,' said Poirot. 'And therefore—'

'And therefore—nothing,' I said. 'I can see no other solution.'

'It is a pity,' murmured Poirot. 'And it is really so exceedingly simple—as the clear blue eyes of Madame Clayton.'

'You really believe—'

'I believe nothing—until I have got proof. One little proof will convince me.'

He took up the telephone and called Japp at Scotland Yard.

Twenty minutes later we were standing before a little heap of assorted objects laid out on a table. They were the contents of the dead man's pockets.

There was a handkerchief, a handful of loose change, a pocketbook containing three pounds ten shillings, a couple of bills and a worn snapshot of Marguerita Clayton. There was also a pocketknife, a gold pencil and a cumbersome wooden tool.

It was on this latter that Poirot swooped. He unscrewed it and several small blades fell out.

'You see, Hastings, a gimlet and all the rest of it. Ah! it would be a matter of a very few minutes to bore a few holes in the chest with this.'

'Those holes we saw?'

'Precisely.'

'You mean it was Clayton who bored them himself?'

'*Mais, oui—mais, oui!* What did they suggest to you, those holes? They were not to *see* through, because they were at the back of the chest. What were they for, then? Clearly for air? But you do not make air holes for a dead body, so clearly they were *not* made by the murderer. They suggest one thing—and one thing only—that a man was going to *hide* in that chest. And at once, on that hypothesis, things become intelligible. Mr Clayton is jealous of his wife and Rich. He plays the old, old trick of pretending to go away. He watches Rich go out, then he gains admission, is left alone to write a note, quickly bores those holes and hides inside the chest. His wife is coming there that night. Possibly Rich will put the others off, possibly she will remain after the others have gone, or pretend to go and return. Whatever it is, Clayton will *know*. Anything is preferable to the ghastly torment of suspicion he is enduring.'

'Then you mean that Rich killed him *after* the others had gone? But the doctor said that was impossible.'

'Exactly. So you see, Hastings, he must have been killed *during* the evening.'

'But everyone was in the room!'

'Precisely,' said Poirot gravely. 'You see the beauty of that? "Everyone was in the room." What an alibi! What *sangfroid*—what nerve—what audacity!'

'I still don't understand.'

'Who went behind that screen to wind up the phonograph and change the records? The phonograph and the chest were side by side, remember. The others are dancing—the phonograph is playing. And the man who does not dance lifts the lid of the chest and thrusts the knife he has just slipped into his sleeve deep into the body of the man who was hiding there.'

'Impossible! The man would cry out.'

'Not if he were drugged first?'

'Drugged?'

'Yes. Who did Clayton have a drink with at seven-thirty? Ah! Now you see. Curtiss! Curtiss has inflamed Clayton's mind with suspicions against his wife and Rich. Curtiss suggests this plan—the visit to Scotland, the concealment in the chest, the final touch of moving the screen. Not so that Clayton can raise the lid a little and get relief—no, so that he, Curtiss, can raise that lid unobserved. The plan is Curtiss's, and observe the beauty of it, Hastings. If Rich had observed the screen was out of place and moved it back—well, no harm is done. He can make another plan. Clayton hides in the chest, the mild narcotic that Curtiss had administered takes effect. He sinks into unconsciousness. Curtiss lifts up the lid and strikes—and the phonograph goes on playing "Walking My Baby Back Home".'

I found my voice. 'Why? But why?'

Poirot shrugged his shoulders.

'Why did a man shoot himself? Why did two Italians fight a duel? Curtiss is of a dark passionate temperament. He wanted Marguerita Clayton. With her husband and Rich out of the way, she would, or so he thought, turn to him.'

He added musingly:

'These simple childlike women . . . they are very dangerous. But *mon dieu!* what an artistic masterpiece! It goes to my heart to hang a man like that. I may be a genius myself, but I am capable of recognising genius in other people. A perfect murder, *mon ami*. I, Hercule Poirot, say it to you. A perfect murder. *Épatant!*'

Wilkie Collins
1824–1889

WHO KILLED ZEBEDEE?

A FIRST WORD FOR MYSELF

B EFORE THE DOCTOR left me one evening, I asked him how much longer I was likely to live. He answered: 'It's not easy to say; you may die before I can get back to you in the morning, or you may live to the end of the month.'

I was alive enough on the next morning to think of the needs of my soul, and (being a member of the Roman Catholic Church) to send for the priest.

The history of my sins, related in confession, included blameworthy neglect of a duty which I owed to the laws of my country. In the priest's opinion—and I agreed with him—I was bound to make public acknowledgement of my fault, as an act of penance becoming to a Catholic Englishman. We concluded, thereupon, to try a division of labour. I related the circumstances, while his reverence took the pen, and put the matter into shape.

Here follows what came of it:

I

WHEN I WAS a young man of five-and-twenty, I became a member of the London police force. After nearly two years' ordinary experience of the responsible and ill-paid duties of that vocation, I found myself employed on my first serious and terrible case of official inquiry—relating to nothing less than the crime of Murder.

The circumstances were these:

I was then attached to a station in the northern district of London—which I beg permission not to mention more particularly. On a certain Monday in the week, I took my turn of night-duty. Up to four in the morning, nothing occurred at the station-house out of the ordinary way. It was then springtime, and, between the gas and the fire, the room became rather hot. I went to the door to get a breath of fresh air—much to the surprise of our Inspector on duty, who was constitutionally a chilly man. There was a fine rain falling; and a nasty damp in the air sent me back to the fireside. I don't suppose I had sat down for more than a minute when the swinging-door was violently pushed open. A frantic woman ran in with a scream and said: 'Is this the station-house?'

Our Inspector (otherwise an excellent officer) had, by some perversity of nature, a hot temper in his chilly constitution. 'Why, bless the woman, can't you *see* it is?' he says. 'What's the matter now?'

'Murder's the matter!' she burst out. 'For God's sake come back with me. It's at Mrs Crosscapel's lodging-house, number 14, Lehigh Street. A young woman has murdered her husband in the night! With a knife, sir. She says she thinks she did it in her sleep.'

I confess I was startled by this; and the third man on duty (a sergeant) seemed to feel it too. She was a nice-looking young woman, even in her terrified condition, just out of bed, with her clothes huddled on anyhow. I was partial in those days to a tall figure—and she was, as they say, my style. I put a chair for her; and the sergeant poked the fire. As for the Inspector, nothing ever upset *him*. He questioned her as coolly as if it had been a case of petty larceny.

'Have you seen the murdered man?' he asked.

'No, sir.'

'Or the wife?'

'No, sir. I didn't dare go into the room; I only heard about it!'

'Oh? And who are you? One of the lodgers?'

'No, sir. I'm the cook.'

'Isn't there a master in the house?'

'Yes, sir. He's frightened out of his wits. And the housemaid's gone for the Doctor. It all falls on the poor servants, of course. Oh, why did I ever set foot in that horrible house?'

The poor soul burst out crying, and shivered from head to foot. The Inspector made a note of her statement, and then asked her to read it, and sign it with her name. The object of this proceeding was to get her to come near enough to give him the opportunity of smelling her breath. 'When people make extraordinary statements,' he afterwards said to me, 'it sometimes saves trouble to satisfy yourself that they are not drunk. I've known them to be mad—but not often. You will generally find *that* in their eyes.'

She roused herself, and signed her name—'Priscilla Thurlby'. The Inspector's own test proved her to be sober; and her eyes—of a nice light blue colour, mild and pleasant, no doubt, when they were not staring with fear, and red with crying—satisfied him (as I supposed) that she was not mad. He turned the case over to me, in the first instance. I saw that he didn't believe in it, even yet.

'Go back with her to the house,' he says. 'This may be a stupid hoax, or a quarrel exaggerated. See to it yourself, and hear what the Doctor says. If it *is* serious, send word back here directly, and let nobody enter the place or leave it till we come. Stop! You know the form if any statement is volunteered?'

'Yes, sir. I am to caution the persons that whatever they say will be taken down, and may be used against them.'

'Quite right. You'll be an Inspector yourself one of these days. Now, Miss!' With that he dismissed her, under my care.

Lehigh Street was not very far off—about twenty minutes' walk from the station. I confess I thought the Inspector had been rather hard on Priscilla. She was herself naturally angry with him. 'What does he mean,' she says, 'by talking of a hoax? I wish he was as frightened as I am. This is the first time I have been out at service, sir—and I did think I had found a respectable place.'

I said very little to her—feeling, if the truth must be told, rather anxious about the duty committed to me. On reaching the house the door was opened from within, before I could knock. A gentleman stepped out, who proved to be the Doctor. He stopped the moment he saw me.

'You must be careful, policeman,' he says. 'I found the man lying on his back, in bed, dead—with the knife that had killed him left sticking in the wound.'

Hearing this, I felt the necessity of sending at once to the station. Where could I find a trustworthy messenger? I took the liberty of asking the Doctor if he would repeat to the police what he had already said to me. The station was not much out of his way home. He kindly granted my request.

The landlady (Mrs Crosscapel) joined us while we were talking. She was still a young woman; not easily frightened, as far as I could see, even by a murder in the house. Her husband was in the passage behind her. He looked old enough to be her father; and he so trembled with terror that some people might have taken him for the guilty person. I removed the key from the street door, after locking it; and I said to the landlady: 'Nobody must leave the house, or enter the house, till the Inspector comes. I must examine the premises to see if anyone has broken in.'

'There is the key of the area gate,' she said, in answer to me. 'It's always kept locked. Come downstairs, and see for yourself.' Priscilla went with us. Her mistress set her to work to light the kitchen fire. 'Some of us,' says Mrs Crosscapel, 'may be the better for a cup of tea.' I remarked that she took things easy, under the circumstances. She answered that the landlady of a London lodging-house could not afford to lose her wits, no matter what might happen.

I found the gate locked, and the shutters of the kitchen window fastened. The back kitchen and back door were secured in the same way. No person was concealed anywhere. Returning upstairs, I examined the front parlour window. There again, the barred shutters answered for the security of that room. A cracked voice spoke through the door of the back parlour. 'The policeman can come in,' it said, 'if he will promise not to look at me.' I turned to the landlady for information. 'It's my parlour lodger, Miss Mybus,' she said, 'a most respectable lady.' Going into the room, I saw something rolled up perpendicularly in the bed curtains. Miss Mybus had made herself modestly invisible in that way. Having now satisfied my mind about the security of the lower part of the house, and having the keys safe in my pocket, I was ready to go upstairs.

On our way to the upper regions I asked if there had been any visitors on the previous day. There had been only two visitors, friends of the lodger—and Mrs Crosscapel herself had let them both out. My next enquiry related to the lodgers themselves. On the ground floor there was Miss Mybus. On the first floor (occupying both rooms) Mr Barfield, an old bachelor, employed in a merchant's office. On the second floor, in the front room, Mr John Zebedee, the murdered man, and his wife. In the back room, Mr Deluc; described as a cigar agent, and supposed to be a Creole gentleman from Martinique. In the front garret, Mr and Mrs Crosscapel. In the back garret, the cook and the housemaid. These were the inhabitants, regularly accounted for. I asked about the servants. 'Both excellent characters,' says the landlady, 'or they would not be in my service.'

We reached the second floor, and found the housemaid on the watch outside the door of the front room. Not as nice a woman, personally, as the cook, and sadly frightened of course. Her mistress had posted her, to give the alarm in the case of an outbreak on the part of Mrs Zebedee, kept locked up in the room. My arrival relieved the housemaid of further responsibility. She ran downstairs to her fellow-servant in the kitchen.

I asked Mrs Crosscapel how and when the alarm of the murder had been given.

'Soon after three this morning,' says she, 'I was woke by the screams of Mrs Zebedee. I found her out here on the landing, and Mr Deluc, in great alarm, trying to quiet her. Sleeping in the next room, he had only to open his door, when her screams woke him. "My dear John's murdered! I am the miserable wretch—I did it in my sleep!" She repeated those frantic words over and over again, until she dropped in a swoon. Mr Deluc and I carried her back into the bedroom. We both thought the poor creature had been driven distracted by some dreadful dream. But when we got to the bedside—don't ask me what we saw; the Doctor has told you about it already. I was once a nurse in a hospital, and accustomed, as such, to horrid sights. It turned me cold and giddy, notwithstanding. As for Mr Deluc, I thought *he* would have had a fainting fit next.'

Hearing this, I enquired if Mrs Zebedee had said or done any strange things since she had been Mrs Crosscapel's lodger.

'You think she's mad?' says the landlady. 'And anybody would be of your mind, when a woman accuses herself of murdering her husband in her sleep. All

I can say is that, up to this morning, a more quiet, sensible, well-behaved little person than Mrs Zebedee I never met with. Only just married, mind, and as fond of her unfortunate husband as a woman could be. I should have called them a pattern couple, in their own line of life.'

There was no more to be said on the landing. We unlocked the door and went into the room.

II

HE LAY IN BED on his back as the Doctor had described him. On the left side of his nightgown, just over his heart, the blood on the linen told its terrible tale. As well as one could judge, looking unwillingly at a dead face, he must have been a handsome young man in his lifetime. It was a sight to sadden anybody—but I think the most painful sensation was when my eyes fell next on his miserable wife.

She was down on the floor, crouched up in a corner—a dark little woman, smartly dressed in gay colours. Her black hair and her big brown eyes made the horrid paleness of her face look even more deadly white than perhaps it really was. She stared straight at us without appearing to see us. We spoke to her, and she never answered a word. She might have been dead—like her husband—except that she perpetually picked at her fingers, and shuddered every now and then as if she was cold. I went to her and tried to lift her up. She shrank back with a cry that well-nigh frightened me—not because it was loud, but because it was more like the cry of some animal than of a human being. However quietly she might have behaved in the landlady's previous experience of her, she was beside herself now. I might have been moved by a natural pity for her, or I might have been completely upset in my mind—I only know this, I could not persuade myself that she was guilty. I even said to Mrs Crosscapel, 'I don't believe she did it.'

While I spoke, there was a knock at the door. I went downstairs at once, and admitted (to my great relief) the Inspector, accompanied by one of our men.

He waited downstairs to hear my report, and he approved of what I had done. 'It looks as if the murder had been committed by somebody in the house.' Saying this, he left the man below, and went up with me to the second floor.

Before he had been a minute in the room, he discovered an object which had escaped my observation.

It was the knife that had done the deed.

The Doctor had found it left in the body—had withdrawn it to probe the wound—and had laid it on the bedside table. It was one of those useful knives which contain a saw, a corkscrew, and other like implements. The big blade fastened back, when open, with a spring. Except where the blood was on it, it was as bright as when it had been purchased. A small metal plate was fastened to the horn handle, containing an inscription, only partly engraved, which ran thus: 'To John Zebedee, from——' There it stopped, strangely enough.

Who or what had interrupted the engraver's work? It was impossible even to guess. Nevertheless, the Inspector was encouraged.

'This ought to help us,' he said—and then he gave an attentive ear (looking all the while at the poor creature in the corner) to what Mrs Crosscapel had to tell him.

The landlady having done, he said he must now see the lodger who slept in the next bedchamber.

Mr Deluc made his appearance, standing at the door of the room, and turning away his head with horror from the sight inside.

He was wrapped in a splendid blue dressing-gown, with a golden girdle and trimmings. His scanty brownish hair curled (whether artificially or not, I am unable to say) in little ringlets. His complexion was yellow; his greenish-brown eyes were of the sort called 'goggle'—they looked as if they might drop out of his face, if you held a spoon under them. His moustache and goat's beard were beautifully oiled; and, to complete his equipment, he had a long black cigar in his mouth.

'It isn't insensibility to this terrible tragedy,' he explained. 'My nerves have been shattered, Mr Policeman, and I can only repair the mischief in this way. Be pleased to excuse and feel for me.'

The Inspector questioned this witness sharply and closely. He was not a man to be misled by appearances; but I could see that he was far from liking, or even trusting, Mr Deluc. Nothing came of the examination, except what Mrs Crosscapel had in substance already mentioned to me. Mr Deluc returned to his room.

'How long has he been lodging with you?' the Inspector asked, as soon as his back was turned.

'Nearly a year,' the landlady answered.

'Did he give you a reference?'

'As good a reference as I could wish for.' Thereupon, she mentioned the names of a well-known firm of cigar merchants in the City. The Inspector noted the information in his pocket-book.

I would rather not relate in detail what happened next: it is too distressing to be dwelt on. Let me only say that the poor demented woman was taken away in a cab to the station-house. The Inspector possessed himself of the knife, and of a book found on the floor, called *The World of Sleep*. The portmanteau containing the luggage was locked—and then the door of the room was secured, the keys in both cases being left in my charge. My instructions were to remain in the house, and allow nobody to leave it, until I heard again shortly from the Inspector.

III

THE CORONER'S INQUEST was adjourned; and the examination before the magistrate ended in a remand—Mrs Zebedee being in no condition to understand the proceedings in either case. The surgeon reported her to be completely prostrated by a terrible nervous shock. When he was asked if he considered her to have been a sane woman before the murder took place, he refused to answer positively at that time.

A week passed. The murdered man was buried; his old father attending the funeral. I occasionally saw Mrs Crosscapel, and the two servants, for the purpose of getting such further information as was thought desirable. Both the cook and the housemaid had given their month's notice to quit; declining, in the interest of their characters, to remain in a house which had been the scene of a murder. Mr Deluc's nerves led also to his removal; his rest was now disturbed by frightful dreams. He paid the necessary forfeit-money, and left without notice. The first-floor lodger, Mr Barfield, kept his rooms, but obtained leave of absence from his employers, and took refuge with some friends in the country. Miss Mybus alone remained in the parlours. 'When I am comfortable,' the old lady said, 'nothing moves me, at my age. A murder up two pairs of stairs is nearly the same thing as a murder in the next house. Distance, you see, makes all the difference.'

It mattered little to the police what the lodgers did. We had men in plain clothes watching the house night and day. Everybody who went away was privately followed; and the police in the district to which they retired were warned to keep an eye on them, after that. As long as we failed to put Mrs Zebedee's extraordinary statement to any sort of test—to say nothing of having proved unsuccessful, thus far, in tracing the knife to its purchaser—we were bound to let no person living under Mrs Crosscapel's roof, on the night of the murder, slip through our fingers.

IV

IN A FORTNIGHT MORE, Mrs Zebedee had sufficiently recovered to make the necessary statement—after the preliminary caution addressed to persons in such cases. The surgeon had no hesitation, now, in reporting her to be a sane woman.

Her station in life had been domestic service. She had lived for four years in her last place as lady's-maid, with a family residing in Dorsetshire. The one objection to her had been the occasional infirmity of sleep-walking, which made it necessary that one of the other female servants should sleep in the same room, with the door locked and the key under her pillow. In all other respects the lady's-maid was described by her mistress as 'a perfect treasure'.

In the last six months of her service, a young man named John Zebedee entered the house (with a written character) as footman. He soon fell in love with the nice little lady's-maid, and she heartily returned the feeling. They might have waited for years before they were in a pecuniary position to marry, but for the death of Zebedee's uncle, who left him a little fortune of two thousand pounds. They were now, for persons in their station, rich enough to please themselves; and they were married from the house in which they had served together, the little daughters of the family showing their affection for Mrs Zebedee by acting as her bridesmaids.

The young husband was a careful man. He decided to employ his small capital to the best advantage, by sheep-farming in Australia. His wife made no objection; she was ready to go wherever John went.

Accordingly they spent their short honeymoon in London, so as to see for themselves the vessel in which their passage was to be taken. They went to Mrs Crosscapel's lodging-house because Zebedee's uncle had always stayed there when he was in London. Ten days were to pass before the day of embarkation arrived. This gave the young couple a welcome holiday, and a prospect of amusing themselves to their hearts' content among the sights and shows of the great city.

On their first evening in London they went to the theatre. They were both accustomed to the fresh air of the country, and they felt half stifled by the heat and the gas. However, they were so pleased with an amusement which was new to them that they went to another theatre on the next evening. On this second occasion, John Zebedee found the heat unendurable. They left the theatre, and got back to their lodgings towards ten o'clock.

Let the rest be told in the words used by Mrs Zebedee herself. She said:

We sat talking for a little while in our room, and John's headache got worse and worse. I persuaded him to go to bed, and I put out the candle (the fire giving sufficient light to undress by), so that he might the sooner fall asleep. But he was too restless to sleep. He asked me to read him something. Books always made him drowsy at the best of times.

I had not myself begun to undress. So I lit the candle again, and I opened the only book I had. John had noticed it at the railway bookstall by the name of *The World of Sleep*. He used to joke with me about my being a sleep-walker; and he said, 'Here's something that's sure to interest you'— and he made me a present of the book.

Before I had read to him for more than half an hour he was fast asleep. Not feeling that way inclined, I went on reading to myself.

The book did indeed interest me. There was one terrible story which took a hold on my mind—the story of a man who stabbed his own wife in a sleep-walking dream. I thought of putting down my book after that, and then changed my mind again and went on. The next chapters were not so interesting; they were full of learned accounts of why we fall asleep, and what our brains do in that state, and such like. It ended in my falling asleep, too, in my armchair by the fireside.

I don't know what o'clock it was when I went to sleep. I don't know how long I slept, or whether I dreamed or not. The candle and the fire had both burned out, and it was pitch dark when I woke. I can't even say why I woke—unless it was the coldness of the room.

There was a spare candle on the chimney-piece. I found the matchbox, and got a light. Then, for the first time, I turned round towards the bed; and I saw—

She had seen the dead body of her husband, murdered while she was unconsciously at his side—and she fainted, poor creature, at the bare remembrance of it.

The proceedings were adjourned. She received every possible care and attention; the chaplain looking after her welfare as well as the surgeon.

I have said nothing of the evidence of the landlady and the servants. It was taken as a mere formality. What little they knew proved nothing against Mrs Zebedee. The police made no discoveries that supported her first frantic accusation of herself. Her master and mistress, where she had been last in service, spoke of her in the highest terms. We were at a complete deadlock.

It had been thought best not to surprise Mr Deluc, as yet, by citing him as a witness. The action of the law was, however, hurried in this case by a private communication received from the chaplain.

After twice seeing, and speaking with, Mrs Zebedee, the reverend gentleman was persuaded that she had no more to do than himself with the murder of her husband. He did not consider that he was justified in repeating a confidential communication—he would only recommend that Mr Deluc should be summoned to appear at the next examination. This advice was followed.

The police had no evidence against Mrs Zebedee when the inquiry was resumed. To assist the ends of justice she was now put into the witness-box. The discovery of her murdered husband, when she woke in the small hours of the morning, was passed over as rapidly as possible. Only three questions of importance were put to her.

First, the knife was produced. Had she ever seen it in her husband's possession? Never. Did she know anything about it? Nothing whatever.

Secondly: Did she, or did her husband, lock the bedroom door when they returned from the theatre? No. Did she afterwards lock the door herself? No.

Thirdly: Had she any sort of reason to give for supposing that she had murdered her husband in a sleep-walking dream? No reason, except that she was beside herself at the time, and the book put the thought into her head.

After this the other witnesses were sent out of court. The motive for the chaplain's communication now appeared. Mrs Zebedee was asked if anything unpleasant had occurred between Mr Deluc and herself.

Yes. He had caught her alone on the stairs at the lodging-house; had presumed to make love to her; and had carried the insult still further by attempting to kiss her. She had slapped his face, and had declared that her husband should know of it, if his misconduct was repeated. He was in a furious rage at having his face slapped; and he said to her: 'Madam, you may live to regret this.'

After consultation, and at the request of our Inspector, it was decided to keep Mr Deluc in ignorance of Mrs Zebedee's statement for the present. When the witnesses were recalled, he gave the same evidence which he had already given to the Inspector—and he was then asked if he knew anything of the knife. He looked at it without any guilty signs in his face, and swore that he had never seen it until that moment. The resumed inquiry ended, and still nothing had been discovered.

But we kept an eye on Mr Deluc. Our next effort was to try if we could associate him with the purchase of the knife.

Here again (there really did seem to be a sort of fatality in this case) we reached no useful result. It was easy enough to find out the wholesale cutlers, who had manufactured the knife at Sheffield, by the mark on the blade. But they made tens of thousands of such knives, and disposed of them to retail dealers all over Great Britain—to say nothing of foreign parts. As to finding out the person who had engraved the imperfect inscription (without knowing where, or by whom, the knife had been purchased) we might as well have looked for the proverbial needle in the bundle of hay. Our last resource was to have the knife photographed, with the inscribed side uppermost, and to send copies to every police station in the kingdom.

At the same time we reckoned up Mr Deluc—I mean that we made investigations into his past life—on the chance that he and the murdered man might have known each other, and might have had a quarrel, or a rivalry about a woman, on some former occasion. No such discovery rewarded us.

We found Deluc to have led a dissipated life, and to have mixed with very bad company. But he had kept out of reach of the law. A man may be a profligate vagabond; may insult a lady; may say threatening things to her, in the first stinging sensation of having his face slapped—but it doesn't follow from these blots on his character that he has murdered her husband in the dead of the night.

Once more, then, when we were called upon to report ourselves, we had no evidence to produce. The photographs failed to discover the owner of the knife, and to explain its interrupted inscription. Poor Mrs Zebedee was allowed to go back to her friends, on entering into her own recognisance to appear again if called upon. Articles in the newspapers began to enquire how many more murderers would succeed in baffling the police. The authorities at the Treasury offered a reward of a hundred pounds for the necessary information. And the weeks passed, and nobody claimed the reward.

Our Inspector was not a man to be easily beaten. More enquiries and examinations followed. It is needless to say anything about them. We were defeated—and there, so far as the police and the public were concerned, was an end of it.

The assassination of the poor young husband soon passed out of notice, like other undiscovered murders. One obscure person only was foolish enough, in his leisure hours, to persist in trying to solve the problem of Who Killed Zebedee? He felt that he might rise to the highest position in the police force if he succeeded where his elders and betters had failed—and he held to his own little ambition, though everybody laughed at him. In plain English, I was the man.

V

WITHOUT MEANING IT, I have told my story ungratefully.

There were two persons who saw nothing ridiculous in my resolution to continue the investigation, single-handed. One of them was Miss Mybus; and the other was the cook, Priscilla Thurlby.

Mentioning the lady first, Miss Mybus was indignant at the resigned manner in which the police accepted their defeat. She was a little bright-eyed wiry woman; and she spoke her mind freely.

'This comes home to me,' she said. 'Just look back for a year or two. I can call to mind two cases of persons found murdered in London—and the assassins have never been traced. I am a person too; and I ask myself if my turn is not coming next. You're a nice-looking fellow—and I like your pluck and perseverance. Come here as often as you think right; and say you are my visitor, if they make any difficulty about letting you in. One thing more! I have nothing particular to do, and I am no fool. Here, in the parlours, I see everybody who comes into the house or goes out of the house. Leave me your address—I may get some information for you yet.'

With the best intentions, Miss Mybus found no opportunity of helping me. Of the two, Priscilla Thurlby seemed more likely to be of use.

In the first place, she was sharp and active, and (not having succeeded in getting another situation as yet) was mistress of her own movements.

In the second place, she was a woman I could trust. Before she left home to try domestic service in London, the parson of her native parish gave her a written testimonial, of which I append a copy. Thus it ran:

> I gladly recommend Priscilla Thurlby for any respectable employment which she may be competent to undertake. Her father and mother are infirm old people, who have lately suffered a diminution of their income; and they have a younger daughter to maintain. Rather than be a burden on her parents, Priscilla goes to London to find domestic employment, and to devote her earnings to the assistance of her father and mother. This circumstance speaks for itself. I have known the family many years; and I only regret that I have no vacant place in my own household which I can offer to this good girl.
>
> (Signed)
> HENRY DERRINGTON, Rector of Roth.

After reading those words, I could safely ask Priscilla to help me in reopening the mysterious murder case to some good purpose.

My notion was that the proceedings of the persons in Mrs Crosscapel's house, had not been closely enough enquired into yet. By way of continuing the investigation, I asked Priscilla if she could tell me anything which associated the housemaid with Mr Deluc. She was unwilling to answer. 'I may be casting suspicion on an innocent person,' she said. 'Besides, I was for so short a time the housemaid's fellow-servant—'

'You slept in the same room with her,' I remarked; 'and you had opportunities of observing her conduct towards the lodgers. If they had asked you, at the examination, what I now ask, you would have answered as an honest woman.'

To this argument she yielded. I heard from her certain particulars which threw a new light on Mr Deluc, and on the case generally. On that information I acted. It was slow work, owing to the claims on me of my regular duties; but with Priscilla's help, I steadily advanced towards the end I had in view.

Besides this, I owed another obligation to Mrs Crosscapel's nice-looking cook. The confession must be made sooner or later—and I may as well make it now. I first knew what love was, thanks to Priscilla. I had delicious kisses, thanks to Priscilla. And, when I asked if she would marry me, she didn't say No. She looked, I must own, a little sadly, and she said: 'How can two such poor people as we are ever hope to marry?' To this I answered: 'It won't be long before I lay my hand on the clue which my Inspector has failed to find. I shall be in a position to marry you, my dear, when that time comes.'

At our next meeting we spoke of her parents. I was now her promised husband. Judging by what I had heard of the proceedings of other people in my position, it seemed to be only right that I should be made known to her father and mother. She entirely agreed with me; and she wrote home that day, to tell them to expect us at the end of the week.

I took my turn of night-duty, and so gained my liberty for the greater part of the next day. I dressed myself in plain clothes, and we took our tickets on the railway for Yateland, being the nearest station to the village in which Priscilla's parents lived.

VI

THE TRAIN STOPPED, as usual, at the big town of Waterbank. Supporting herself by her needle, while she was still unprovided with a situation, Priscilla had been at work late in the night—she was tired and thirsty. I left the carriage to get her some soda-water. The stupid girl in the refreshment room failed to pull the cork out of the bottle, and refused to let me help her. She took a corkscrew, and used it crookedly. I lost all patience, and snatched the bottle out of her hand. Just as I drew the cork, the bell rang on the platform. I only waited to pour the soda-water into a glass—but the train was moving as I left the refreshment-room. The porters stopped me when I tried to jump on to the step of the carriage. I was left behind.

As soon as I had recovered my temper, I looked at the timetable. We had reached Waterbank at five minutes past one. By good luck, the next train was due at forty-four minutes past one, and arrived at Yateland (the next station) ten minutes afterwards. I could only hope that Priscilla would look at the timetable too, and wait for me. If I had attempted to walk the distance between the two places, I should have lost time instead of saving it. The interval before me was not very long; I occupied it in looking over the town.

Speaking with all due respect to the inhabitants, Waterbank (to other people) is a dull place. I went up one street and down another—and stopped to look at a shop which struck me; not from anything in itself, but because it was the only shop in the street with the shutters closed.

A bill was posted on the shutters, announcing that the place was to let. The out-going tradesman's name and business, announced in the customary painted letters, ran thus: *James Wycomb, Cutler, etc*.

For the first time, it occurred to me that we had forgotten an obstacle in our way, when we distributed our photographs of the knife. We had none of us remembered that a certain proportion of cutlers might be placed, by circumstances, out of our reach—either by retiring from business or by becoming bankrupt. I always carried a copy of the photograph about me; and I thought to myself, 'Here is the ghost of a chance of tracing the knife to Mr Deluc!'

The shop door was opened, after I had twice rung the bell, by an old man, very dirty and very deaf. He said: 'You had better go upstairs, and speak to Mr Scorrier—top of the house.'

I put my lips to the old fellow's ear-trumpet, and asked who Mr Scorrier was.

'Brother-in-law to Mr Wycomb. Mr Wycomb's dead. If you want to buy the business apply to Mr Scorrier.'

Receiving that reply, I went upstairs, and found Mr Scorrier engaged in engraving a brass door-plate. He was a middle-aged man, with a cadaverous face and dim eyes. After the necessary apologies, I produced my photograph.

'May I ask, sir, if you know anything of the inscription on that knife?' I said.

He took his magnifying glass to look at it.

'This is curious,' he remarked quietly. 'I remember the queer name—Zebedee. Yes, sir; I did the engraving, as far as it goes. I wonder what prevented me from finishing it?'

The name of Zebedee, and the unfinished inscription on the knife, had appeared in every English newspaper. He took the matter so coolly, that I was doubtful how to interpret his answer. Was it possible that he had not seen the account of the murder? Or was he an accomplice with prodigious powers of self-control?

'Excuse me,' I said, 'do you read the newspapers?'

'Never! My eyesight is failing me. I abstain from reading, in the interests of my occupation.'

'Have you not heard the name of Zebedee mentioned—particularly by people who do read the newspapers?'

'Very likely; but I didn't attend to it. When the day's work is done, I take my walk. Then I have my supper, my drop of grog, and my pipe. Then I go to bed. A dull existence you think, I dare say! I had a miserable life, sir, when I was young. A bare subsistence, and a little rest, before the last perfect rest in the grave—that is all I want. The world has gone by me long ago. So much the better.'

The poor man spoke honestly. I was ashamed of having doubted him. I returned to the subject of the knife.

'Do you know where it was purchased, and by whom?' I asked.

'My memory is not so good as it was,' he said; 'but I have got something by me that helps it.'

He took from a cupboard a dirty old scrap-book. Strips of paper, with writing on them, were pasted on the pages, as well as I could see. He turned to an index, or table of contents, and opened a page. Something like a flash of life showed itself on his dismal face.

'Ha! now I remember,' he said. 'The knife was bought of my late brother-in-law, in the shop downstairs. It all comes back to me, sir. A person in a state of frenzy burst into this very room, and snatched the knife away from me, when I was only half way through the inscription!'

I felt that I was now close on discovery. 'May I see what it is that has assisted your memory?' I asked.

'Oh yes. You must know, sir, I live by engraving inscriptions and addresses, and I paste in this book the manuscript instructions which I receive, with marks of my own on the margin. For one thing, they serve as a reference to new customers. And for another thing, they do certainly help my memory.'

He turned the book towards me, and pointed to a slip of paper which occupied the lower half of a page.

I read the complete inscription, intended for the knife that killed Zebedee, and written as follows:

'To John Zebedee, from Priscilla Thurlby.'

VII

I DECLARE THAT it is impossible for me to describe what I felt, when Priscilla's name confronted me like a written confession of guilt. How long it was before I recovered myself in some degree, I cannot say. The only thing I can clearly call to mind is, that I frightened the poor engraver.

My first desire was to get possession of the manuscript inscription. I told him I was a policeman, and summoned him to assist me in the discovery of a crime. I even offered him money. He drew back from my hand. 'You shall have it for nothing,' he said, 'if you will only go away and never come here again.' He tried to cut it out of the page—but his trembling hands were helpless. I cut it out myself, and attempted to thank him. He wouldn't hear me. 'Go away!' he said, 'I don't like the look of you.'

It may be here objected that I ought not to have felt so sure as I did of the woman's guilt, until I had got more evidence against her. The knife might have been stolen from her, supposing she was the person who had snatched it out of the engraver's hands, and might have been afterwards used by the thief to commit the murder. All very true. But I never had a moment's doubt in my own mind, from the time when I read the damnable line in the engraver's book.

I went back to the railway without any plan in my head. The train by which I had proposed to follow her had left Waterbank. The next train that arrived was for London. I took my place in it—still without any plan in my head.

At Charing Cross a friend met me. He said, 'You're looking miserably ill. Come and have a drink.'

I went with him. The liquor was what I really wanted; it strung me up, and cleared my head. He went his way, and I went mine. In a little while more, I determined what I would do.

In the first place, I decided to resign my situation in the police, from a motive which will presently appear. In the second place, I took a bed at a public house. She would no doubt return to London, and she would go to my lodgings to find out why I had broken my appointment. To bring to justice the one woman whom I had dearly loved was too cruel a duty for a poor creature like me. I preferred leaving the police force. On the other hand, if she and I met before time had helped me to control myself, I had a horrid fear that I might turn murderer next, and kill her then and there. The wretch had not only all but misled me into marrying her, but also into charging the innocent housemaid with being concerned in the murder.

The same night I hit on a way of clearing up such doubts as still harassed my mind. I wrote to the rector of Roth, informing him that I was engaged to marry her, and asking if he would tell me (in consideration of my position) what her former relations might have been with the person named John Zebedee.

By return of post I got this reply:

SIR—Under the circumstances, I think I am bound to tell you confidentially what the friends and well-wishers of Priscilla have kept secret, for her sake.

Zebedee was in service in this neighbourhood. I am sorry to say it, of a man who has come to such a miserable end—but his behaviour to Priscilla proves him to have been a vicious and heartless wretch. They were engaged—and, I add with indignation, he tried to seduce her under a promise of marriage. Her virtue resisted him, and he pretended to be ashamed of himself. The banns were published in my church. On the next day Zebedee disappeared, and cruelly deserted her. He was a capable servant; and I believe he got another place. I leave you to imagine what the poor girl suffered under the outrage inflicted on her. Going to London, with my recommendation, she answered the first advertisement that she saw, and was unfortunate enough to begin her career in domestic service in the very lodging-house to which (as I gather from the newspaper report of the murder) the man Zebedee took the person whom he married, after deserting Priscilla. Be assured that you are about to unite yourself to an excellent girl, and accept my best wishes for your happiness.

It was plain from this that neither the rector nor the parents and friends knew anything of the purchase of the knife. The one miserable man who knew the truth, was the man who had asked her to be his wife.

I owed it to myself—at least so it seemed to me—not to let it be supposed that I, too, had meanly deserted her. Dreadful as the prospect was, I felt that I must see her once more, and for the last time.

She was at work when I went into her room. As I opened the door she started to her feet. Her cheeks reddened, and her eyes flashed with anger. I stepped forward—and she saw my face. My face silenced her.

I spoke in the fewest words I could find.

'I have been to the cutler's shop at Waterbank,' I said. 'There is the unfinished inscription on the knife, completed in your handwriting. I could hang you by a word. God forgive me—I can't say the word.'

Her bright complexion turned to a dreadful clay-colour. Her eyes were fixed and staring, like the eyes of a person in a fit. She stood before me, still and silent. Without saying more, I dropped the inscription into the fire. Without saying more, I left her.

I never saw her again.

VIII

BUT I HEARD from her a few days later.

The letter has been long since burnt. I wish I could have forgotten it as well. It sticks to my memory. If I die with my senses about me, Priscilla's letter will be my last recollection on earth.

In substance it repeated what the rector had already told me. Further, it informed me that she had bought the knife as a keepsake for Zebedee, in place of a similar knife which he had lost. On the Saturday, she made the purchase, and left it to be engraved. On the Sunday, the banns were put up. On the Monday, she was deserted; and she snatched the knife from the table while the engraver was at work.

She only knew that Zebedee had added a new sting to the insult inflicted on her, when he arrived at the lodgings with his wife. Her duties as cook kept her in the kitchen—and Zebedee never discovered that she was in the house. I still remember the last lines of her confession:

The devil entered into me when I tried their door, on my way up to bed, and found it unlocked, and listened awhile, and peeped in. I saw them by the dying light of the candle—one asleep on the bed, the other asleep by the fireside. I had the knife in my hand, and the thought came to me to do it, so that they might hang *her* for the murder. I couldn't take the knife out again, when I had done it. Mind this! I did really like you—I didn't say Yes, because you could hardly hang your own wife, if you found out who killed Zebedee.

Since that past time I have never heard again of Priscilla Thurlby; I don't know whether she is living or dead. Many people may think I deserve to be hanged myself for not having given her up to the gallows. They may, perhaps, be disappointed when they see this confession, and hear that I have died decently in my bed. I don't blame them. I am a penitent sinner. I wish all merciful Christians goodbye for ever.

Edmund Crispin
1921–1978

WITHIN THE GATES

IT WAS IMMEDIATELY outside the entrance to an office building, within a stone's throw, almost, of New Scotland Yard, that the thing happened.

The Whitehall area is sacred—if that is the right word—to Government. Trade leads a hole-and-corner existence there, and a house given over to non-ministerial purposes is enough of a rarity in the district to attract fleeting attention from the idle passer-by. Thus it was that Gervase Fen, ambling with rather less than his usual vigour from St Thomas's Hospital, where he had been visiting a friend, towards St James's Park, through which he proposed strolling prior to dinner at the Athenaeum, paused to examine the brass plates and signboards flanking this particular doorway; and in so doing found himself shoulder to shoulder with a man who had just half a minute to live.

At this time—eight o'clock in the evening—the street was almost empty, a near-vacuum shut away from the Embankment traffic on one side and the Whitehall traffic on the other. A street-lamp gleamed on the brass and the white-lettered wood: trade journals mostly, Fen noted—*Copper Mining*, *Vegetation*, the *Bulb Growers' Quarterly*, *Hedging and Ditching*. A little beyond the doorway, an elderly woman had halted to rummage in her shopping-bag;

and immediately outside it, a neatly dressed man with a military bearing, who had been preceding Fen along the pavement, glanced up at the street-lamp, drew from a pocket three sheets of typewritten foolscap clipped together with a brass fastener, came to a stop, and began reading. Fen was beside him for no more than a moment, and had no cause to notice him particularly; leaving him still scanning his typescript, he walked on past the woman with the shopping-bag and so up to the end of the street. Behind him, he heard a car moving away from the pavement—presumably it was the black sedan which he had seen parked at the entrance to the street. But there was no way in which he could have anticipated the tragedy that followed.

The note of the car's engine altered; one of its doors clicked open and there were rapid footsteps on the pavement. Then, horribly, the woman with the shopping-bag screamed—and Fen, swinging round, saw the soldierly-looking man grapple with the stranger who had emerged from the waiting sedan. It was all over long before Fen could reach them. The assailant struck viciously at his victim's unprotected head, snatched the typescript from his hand as he fell, and scrambled back into the car, which slewed away from the kerb with a squeal of tyres, and in another instant was gone. Pausing only to note its number and direction, Fen ran on and bent over the huddled body at which the woman was staring in dazed, helpless incomprehension. But the skull was crushed; there was nothing, Fen saw, that he or anyone else could do. He stood over the body, allowing no one to touch it, until the police arrived.

And at eleven o'clock next morning: 'Very satisfactory,' said Detective-Inspector Humbleby of the Metropolitan CID. 'Very satisfactory indeed. Between you, you and that Ayres woman are going to hang Mr Leonard Mocatelli higher than Haman. And a good riddance, too.'

'The man must be quite mad.' As was allowable in an old and trusted friend of the Inspector's, Fen spoke somewhat petulantly. 'Mad, I mean, to commit murder under the noses of two witnesses. What *did* he expect?'

'Ah, but he hadn't got a record, you see.' Humbleby lit a cheroot with a new-fangled pocket-lighter which smelled of ether. '*He* didn't think Scotland Yard had ever heard of him, and it must have given him a nasty turn when we hauled him out of bed in the middle of the night, and brought him along here. He was the only member of the group whose viciousness was likely to extend to murder, and that being so—'

'Wait, wait,' Fen interposed fretfully. 'I don't understand any of this. Who *is* Mocatelli? Whom did he kill, and why? And what is the "group" you mentioned?'

At this, Humbleby's satisfaction diminished visibly; he sighed. 'It's not,' he said, 'that I'm *personally* unwilling to give you the facts. But there's a certain rather delicate matter involved, and . . .' His voice trailed away. 'Well, there you are.'

'Discretion,' said Fen with great complacency, 'is my middle name.'

'I dare say. But very few people *use* their middle names . . . Calm, now: because I think I shall tell you about it in spite of everything. It's possible you can help. And God knows,' said Humbleby seriously, 'this is a case where we can do with some help.'

He had been standing by the window. Now, with an air of decision, he turned and planted himself firmly in the swivel-chair behind the desk. His office, to which they had returned immediately after the identification parade, was high up, overlooking the river, in a corner of New Scotland Yard: a small overcrowded room with a large number of (illegal) gas and electric stoves over which you tripped every time you attempted to stir. Filing-cabinets lined the walls; queerly assorted books were piled in tottering heaps in the corners; and the decorations ranged from a portrait of Metternich to a photograph of an unattractive pet Sealyham which had passed to its reward, at an advanced age, in the year 1919. Scotland Yard is as strictly run as any other office, and more strictly than most. But Humbleby's position there was a peculiar one—in that for reasons which seemed good to him he had always refused to be promoted to Chief- Inspector—and so to a considerable extent he was allowed to legislate for himself in the matter of his surroundings. To that eyrie had come many who had allowed its untidy domesticity, and the tidy domesticity of its occupant, to make them over-confident. And not one of a long succession of Assistant Commissioners, on first introduction to it, had been short-sighted or stupid enough to do anything more than smile.

Sprawled in the one armchair, Fen waited. And presently Humbleby— having outlined on the blotter, to his own immense satisfaction, a fat bishop—said:

'We start, then, with this more than ordinarily cagey, more than ordinarily well-organised *gang*. It's two years now since we first became aware of its existence; and although we've got a complete, or almost complete, list of the members' names, together with a certain amount of good court-room evidence, we've been avoiding making arrests—for the usual reason that there's been nothing very damning so far against the man we know to be in charge, and we've been hoping that sooner or later his agents, if left to themselves, will incriminate *him*. In that respect we're not, even after last evening, very much better off than we were at the outset; and I think it's quite likely that in view of Mocatelli's arrest, which but for the murder we shouldn't have contemplated, the head man will pack it up and we'll never catch him. However, that remains to be seen.'

'Any speciality?' Fen asked.

'No. They've been very versatile: blackmail, smuggling, smash-and-grab, arson—all the fun of the fair. From our point of view it hasn't been any fun, though, and that for more reasons than one. So there was a good deal of rejoicing the other evening when one of the gang, a man named Stokes, got drunk, picked up one of these crazy children who start painting their faces and wearing high-heeled shoes at the age of fourteen, and attempted a criminal assault in an alley within five yards of a constable on his beat.

'We didn't rejoice at the actual *event*, of course: that was as nasty and depressing as these things always are. But it did enable us to arrest the man and to search his rooms. There, in due course, we came on a letter addressed to him and typewritten in code; and it wasn't exactly difficult to deduce that this letter had something to do with the operations of the gang.

'As you know, we've got a biggish Cipher Department here on the premises; and you're aware, too, that complex ciphers—such as this one obviously was—are dealt with by quite elaborate team-work, helped out by machines. That's as it should be, of course—but at the same time it tends to be rather a slow business: method, as opposed to intuition, always *is* slow. On the off-chance, then, of getting results more rapidly, I gave a copy of the cryptogram to Colonel Browley, and——'

'Browley?' Fen interrupted. 'You mean the man who ran the Cipher Department of MI5 during the war?'

'That's him. He retired in 1946 and went to live in Putney, where he's been spending most of his time on botany and scientific gardening and stuff like that. But we still used him as a consultant expert from time to time, because there's no doubt that he had a real flair for codes, and could sometimes solve them by a sort of inspired guess-work.'

Fen nodded. 'Putney,' he said. 'Direct Tube-line to Westminster—and that was about where I picked him up.'

'Oh yes: it was Browley who was murdered, unhappily. And having got that far, you'll easily see why.'

'You mean that he'd succeeded in decoding this letter; and that the letter was so important to the gang that they had to silence him and steal his report.'

'Exactly . . . I can't say'—here Humbleby wriggled uncomfortably—'I can't say that any of us *liked* Browley very much. He was one of those men who somehow contrive to be fussy and careless at one and the same time—an exhausting combination—and latterly his mind had been going to seed rather: he was getting on for seventy, you see, though admittedly he didn't look it . . . Well anyway, to get back to the point, Browley rang me up yesterday afternoon about this letter. I was out, as it happened; so he just mentioned his success and told the constable who answered the phone that he'd be coming here with his report during the evening—by which time I myself would be back. I'd warned him, you see, that the report was to be delivered to me and to me only.'

There was a brief silence; then:

'Oh,' said Fen, in a particular tone of voice.

'So that when the constable offered to have it collected from Putney, Browley said that he had to come in to Town in any case, on some private errand or other . . . with the result you witnessed. From what we knew of this gang, Mocatelli was by far the likeliest man to have done the job. So we picked him up, and you and the Ayres woman have now identified him as the murderer, and that's that.'

'The sedan,' said Fen, 'was *waiting* for Browley—not following him. It was *known* that he was coming.'

And reluctantly Humbleby inclined his head. 'Oh yes,' he said, 'there's a leak all right. There's a leak somewhere in this Department. That's half the reason why Mocatelli and his merry men have been getting away with it so easily— though since I first suspected a leak, some weeks ago, I've been keeping the more important information about the gang unobtrusively to myself; I imagine that if I hadn't done that, we'd hardly have found Mocatelli at home when we went to call on him last night . . . Well, there it is: not a nice situation. Rare, thank God—miraculously so, when you compare our salaries with what a well-heeled crook can afford to offer—but very bad when it *does* happen.' He glanced at his watch. 'I'm seeing the Assistant Commissioner about it in five minutes' time. If you'd like to wait till I get finished, we can have lunch together.'

Fen assented. 'And you've no notion,' he added, 'about what was in the stolen report? You didn't find any rough notes, for instance, in Browley's house?'

'None. His training had made him careful about *that* sort of thing, at least, and he'd certainly have destroyed anything at all revealing before leaving home to come here . . . There's this, of course.' Humbleby fished in a dossier and pro-duced a crumpled scrap of paper. 'It was evidently torn off the bottom of one of the pages of his report when the thing was snatched out of his hand.'

Fen raised his eyebrows. 'The blow came first, you know, and the snatching not till—' He checked himself. 'No, wait, I'm being stupid. Head injury: cadaveric spasm.'

'That's it. I had the devil of a job getting this fragment away from him, poor soul . . . But it doesn't help at all.'

Fen examined the line or two of typewriting on the paper. Literally tran-scribed, it ran: '. . . *so that x in the treatment of this var eetyof cryptogam care mut be taken to* . . .' 'Not,' Fen observed, 'one of the world's more expert typists, was he?'

'No. All his reports were like that. And he could never resist the temptation to incorporate sermons, on the basic principles of deciphering, in everything he sent us. If only he'd stuck to the point, that bit of paper might have been useful. As it is—' Humbleby broke off at a knock on the door. 'Come in!' he called, and a youthful, pink-cheeked Sergeant appeared. 'Yes, Robden? What is it?'

'It's about the contents of Colonel Browley's pockets, sir.'

'Oh yes, it was you who turned them out, wasn't it . . . All the stuff will have to go to his lawyer, as there aren't any relatives. I'll give you the address. And do *please* remember, this time, to get a detailed receipt.'

'I say, Humbleby'— Fen spoke pensively—'may I ask the Sergeant to do an errand for me? I've just developed the first symptoms of an idea—though it probably won't come to anything.'

'Well, provided it isn't anything too elaborate or lengthy—'

'No, just a phone-call.' Fen was scribbling some words on the back of an old envelope, which presently he handed to Robden. 'And from an *outside* phone, please, Sergeant. I don't want there to be any possibility of your being overheard.'

The Sergeant glanced at the envelope and then at Humbleby, who nodded; whereupon, collecting the address which Humbleby had jotted down for him, he took himself off. 'No questions for the moment,' said Humbleby, rising, 'because it's time I visited the AC. But I shall expect an explanation when I get back.'

Fen smiled. 'You shall have one.'

'And also I shall expect a conference about this business we've been speaking of. Over beer. It's been well said that salt, once it has lost its savour—'

'Do stop talking, Humbleby, and go.'

'Wait here, then, and try not to meddle with things. I shan't be long.'

IN FACT HE WAS NOT absent for much more than a quarter of an hour; and his return coincided with Robden's.

'No, sir,' said the Sergeant cryptically. 'Nothing of that sort. He *had* sent in one or two, but they'd always been rejected, and he was so angry about that that the Editor was positive he'd never try again. There was nothing commissioned, in any case.'

And Fen sighed. 'You're much too unsuspicious for a policeman, Robden,' he said mildly. 'And much too unsuspicious for a crook. And for the two things combined, quite hopelessly gullible.'

His tone altered. 'It apparently never occurred to you that I sent you to an outside phone in order to have time to ring the Editor of *Vegetation* before you did. And the story he told me—and which he assured me he would tell you also when you telephoned—was rather different from what *you've* just said.'

Robden had gone white, so that dark rings appeared round his normally candid brown eyes. He looked, and was, very young. But Fen, as he gazed out across the river at the expanses of South London, was thinking of old women in little shops who might one day go in intolerable fear because their protection against the thug and the delinquent had become a mockery and a sham; of pimps and bawds who might flourish at the cost of a few pounds slipped weekly into the right hands; of night-watchmen burned alive without hope of reprisal in well-insured warehouses, and of little girls violated by degenerates whose services were valuable to their bosses and whose immunity was therefore worth paying for. Robden's youth and folly, weighed in the scale against these possibilities, were no better than a pinch of sand, and so Fen hardened his heart, saying:

'It's possible, of course, that the Editor of *Vegetation* did in fact tell you a story different from the story he told me. But since he agreed to have witnesses listening to what he said—very friendly of him, that, in view of the fact that he didn't know me from Adam—that's not a point we need argue about for the moment.'

'*Vegetation?*' Humbleby echoed dreamily. He had already nudged his leg against a bell-push in the knee-hole of his desk, and now, as Robden backed abruptly towards the door, a revolver appeared, as if by some kind of noiseless magic, in his right hand; so that all at once Robden was rigid and motionless. '*Vegetation?*' Humbleby repeated.

'Just so,' said Fen. 'Here is a botanist with a private errand in Town. He is found standing outside the offices of *Vegetation* with an article on cryptogams in his hand.'

'Crypto*grams*.'

'No. Crypto*gams*. A class of plants without stamens or pistils. So it seemed worth while getting in touch with the Editor of *Vegetation* and finding out if he was expecting such an article from Browley. And he was.

'This article is what the murderous Mocatelli stole; and very disappointed he must have been when he found out what he'd got. But since, as we know, Browley definitely had the report on the gang's code-letter with him, what in the world became of *that*? Mocatelli simply grabbed the wrong typescript and ran— he didn't do any rifling of Browley's pockets. Nor did anyone else, subsequently, because I myself stood guard over the body and refused to allow it to be touched. Which leaves the police. *Someone* was a traitor—that much was already certain. So that when the Sergeant who turned out Browley's pockets failed to mention the code-report which must certainly have been there, I set a trap for him and he fell into it head first.'

Out of a dry mouth Robden said:

'Plenty of people had to do with Browley's body before I did.'

'No doubt. But you're the only person so far who's lied about the *Vegetation* article. And since you would come under immediate suspicion if the truth about that article were known, it's not difficult to see just why you lied.'

Behind Robden the door opened quietly, and at a nod from Humbleby the two constables advanced to grip their whilom colleague's arms. For an instant he seemed to contemplate resistance; but then all the valour went out of him, and he shrivelled like a dead leaf in a flame.

'He'll get a stiff sentence, I'm afraid,' said Humbleby when the party had gone. 'Much stiffer than he really deserves. That's always the way when one of *us* goes off the rails, and you can see why.' He brooded; then: 'Cryptogams,' he muttered sourly. '*Cryptogams . . .*'

'Like formication,' said Fen. 'Which, although you might not believe it, has no connection whatever with—'

'Quite so.' Humbleby was firm. 'Exactly so. And now let us get something to eat.'

Charles Dickens
1812–1870

HUNTED DOWN

I

MOST OF US see some romances in life. In my capacity of Chief Manager of a Life Assurance Office, I think I have within the last thirty years seen more romances than the generality of men, however unpromising the opportunity may, at first sight, seem.

As I have retired, and live at my ease, I possess the means that I used to want, of considering what I have seen, at leisure. My experiences have a more remarkable aspect, so reviewed, than they had when they were in progress. I have come home from the Play now, and can recall the scenes of the Drama upon which the curtain has fallen, free from the glare, bewilderment, and bustle of the Theatre.

Let me recall one of these Romances of the real world.

There is nothing truer than physiognomy, taken in connection with manner. The art of reading that book of which Eternal Wisdom obliges every human creature to present his or her own page with the individual character written on it, is a difficult one, perhaps, and is little studied. It may require some natural aptitude, and it must require (for everything does) some patience and some pains. That these are not usually given to it— that numbers of people accept a few stock commonplace expressions of the face as the whole list of characteristics, and neither seek nor know the refinements that are truest—that You, for instance, give a great deal of time and attention to the reading of music, Greek, Latin, French, Italian, Hebrew, if you please, and do not qualify yourself to read the face of the master or mistress looking over your shoulder teaching it to you—I assume to be five hundred times more probable than improbable. Perhaps a little self-sufficiency may be at the bottom of this; facial expression requires no study from you, you think; it comes by nature to you to know enough about it, and you are not to be taken in.

I confess, for my part, that I *have* been taken in, over and over again. I have been taken in by acquaintances, and I have been taken in (of course) by friends; far oftener by friends than by any other class of persons. How came I to be so deceived? Had I quite misread their faces?

No. Believe me, my first impression of those people, founded on face and manner alone, was invariably true. My mistake was in suffering them to come nearer to me, and explain themselves away.

II

THE PARTITION which separated my own office from our general outer office in the City was of thick plate glass. I could see through it what passed in the outer office, without hearing a word. I had it put up in place of a wall that had been there for years—ever since the house was built. It is no matter whether I did or did not make the change in order that I might derive my first impression of strangers, who came to us on business, from their faces alone, without being influenced by anything they said. Enough to mention that I turned my glass partition to that account, and that a Life Assurance Office is at all times exposed to be practised upon by the most crafty and cruel of the human race.

It was through my glass partition that I first saw the gentleman whose story I am going to tell.

He had come in without my observing it, and had put his hat and umbrella on the broad counter, and was bending over it to take some papers from one of the clerks. He was about forty or so, dark, exceedingly well dressed in black—being in mourning—and the hand he extended, with a polite air, had a particularly well-fitting black kid glove upon it. His hair, which was elaborately brushed and oiled, was parted straight up the middle; and he presented this parting to the clerk, exactly (to my thinking) as if he had said, in so many words: 'You must take me, if you please, my friend, just as I show myself. Come straight up here, follow the gravel path, keep off the grass, I allow no trespassing.'

I conceived a very great aversion to that man the moment I thus saw him.

He had asked for some of our printed forms, and the clerk was giving them to him and explaining them. An obliged and agreeable smile was on his face, and his eyes met those of the clerk with a sprightly look. (I have known a vast quantity of nonsense talked about bad men not looking you in the face. Don't trust that conventional idea. Dishonesty will stare honesty out of countenance, any day in the week, if there is anything to be got by it.)

I saw, in the corner of his eyelash, that he became aware of my looking at him. Immediately he turned the parting in his hair toward the glass partition, as if he said to me with a sweet smile, 'Straight up here, if you please. Off the grass!'

In a few moments he had put on his hat and taken up his umbrella, and was gone.

I beckoned the clerk into my room, and asked, 'Who was that?'

He had the gentleman's card in his hand. 'Mr Julius Slinkton, Middle Temple.'

'A barrister, Mr Adams?'

'I think not, sir.'

'I should have thought him a clergyman, but for his having no Reverend here,' said I.

'Probably, from his appearance,' Mr Adams replied, 'he is reading for orders.'

I should mention that he wore a dainty white cravat, and dainty linen altogether.

'What did he want, Mr Adams?'

'Merely a form of proposal, sir, and form of reference.'

'Recommended here? Did he say?'

'Yes, he said he was recommended here by a friend of yours. He noticed you, but said that, as he had not the pleasure of your personal acquaintance, he would not trouble you.'

'Did he know my name?'

'Oh yes, sir! He said, "There *is* Mr Sampson, I see!"'

'A well-spoken gentleman, apparently?'

'Remarkably so, sir.'

'Insinuating manners, apparently?'

'Very much so, indeed, sir.'

'Hah!' said I. 'I want nothing at present, Mr Adams.'

Within a fortnight of that day I went to dine with a friend of mine, a merchant, a man of taste, who buys pictures and books; and the first man I saw among the company was Mr Julius Slinkton. There he was, standing before the fire, with good large eyes and an open expression of face; but still (I thought) requiring everybody to come at him by the prepared way he offered, and by no other.

I noticed him ask my friend to introduce him to Mr Sampson, and my friend did so. Mr Slinkton was very happy to see me. Not too happy; there was no overdoing of the matter; happy in a thoroughly well-bred, perfectly unmeaning way.

'I thought you had met,' our host observed.

'No,' said Mr Slinkton. 'I did look in at Mr Sampson's office, on your recommendation; but I really did not feel justified in troubling Mr Sampson himself, on a point in the every-day routine of an ordinary clerk.'

I said I should have been glad to show him any attention on our friend's introduction.

'I am sure of that,' said he, 'and am much obliged. At another time, perhaps, I may be less delicate. Only, however, if I have real business; for I know, Mr Sampson, how precious business time is, and what a vast number of impertinent people there are in the world.'

I acknowledged his consideration with a slight bow. 'You were thinking,' said I, 'of effecting a policy on your life.'

'Oh dear no! I am afraid I am not so prudent as you pay me the compliment of supposing me to be, Mr Sampson. I merely enquired for a friend. But you know what friends are in such matters. Nothing may ever come of it. I have the greatest reluctance to trouble men of business with enquiries for friends, knowing the probabilities to be a thousand to one that the friends will never follow them up. People are so fickle, so selfish, so inconsiderate. Don't you, in your business, find them so every day, Mr Sampson?'

I was going to give a qualified answer; but he turned his smooth, white parting on me, with its 'Straight up here, if you please!' and I answered 'Yes.'

'I hear, Mr Sampson,' he resumed presently, for our friend had a new cook, and dinner was not so punctual as usual, 'that your profession has recently suffered a great loss.'

'In money?' said I.

He laughed at my ready association of loss with money, and replied, 'No, in talent and vigour.'

Not at once following out his allusion, I considered for a moment. '*Has* it sustained a loss of that kind?' said I. 'I was not aware of it.'

'Understand me, Mr Sampson. I don't imagine that you have retired. It is not so bad as that. But Mr Meltham—'

'Oh, to be sure!' said I. 'Yes. Mr Meltham, the young actuary of the "Inestimable".'

'Just so,' he returned in a consoling way.

'He is a great loss. He was at once the most profound, the most original, and the most energetic man I have ever known connected with Life Assurance.'

I spoke strongly; for I had a high esteem and admiration for Meltham; and my gentleman had indefinitely conveyed to me some suspicion that he wanted to sneer at him. He recalled me to my guard by presenting that trim pathway up his head, with its infernal 'Not on the grass, if you please—the gravel.'

'You knew him, Mr Slinkton?'

'Only by reputation. To have known him as an acquaintance, or as a friend, is an honour I should have sought if he had remained in society, though I might never have had the good fortune to attain it, being a man of far inferior mark. He was scarcely above thirty, I suppose?'

'About thirty.'

'Ah!' he sighed in his former consoling way. 'What creatures we are! To break up, Mr Sampson, and become incapable of business at that time of life!— Any reason assigned for the melancholy fact?'

('Humph!' thought I as I looked at him. 'But I won't go up the track and I will go on the grass.')

'What reason have you heard assigned, Mr Slinkton?' I asked point-blank.

'Most likely a false one. You know what Rumour is, Mr Sampson. I never repeat what I hear; it is the only way of paring the nails and shaving the head of Rumour. But, when *you* ask me what reason I have heard assigned for Mr Meltham's passing away from among men, it is another thing. I am not gratifying idle gossip then. I was told, Mr Sampson, that Mr Meltham had relinquished all his avocations and all his prospects, because he was, in fact, broken-hearted. A disappointed attachment, I heard—though it hardly seems probable, in the case of a man so distinguished and so attractive.'

'Attractions and distinctions are no armour against death,' said I.

'Oh, she died? Pray pardon me. I did not hear that. That, indeed, makes it very, very sad. Poor Mr Meltham! She died? Ah, dear me! Lamentable, lamentable!'

I still thought his pity was not quite genuine, and I still suspected an unaccountable sneer under all this, until he said, as we were parted, like the other knots of talkers, by the announcement of dinner:

'Mr Sampson, you are surprised to see me so moved on behalf of a man whom I have never known. I am not so disinterested as you may suppose. I have suffered, and recently too, from death myself. I have lost one of two charming nieces, who were my constant companions. She died young—barely three-and-twenty; and even her remaining sister is far from strong. The world is a grave!'

He said this with deep feeling, and I felt reproached for the coldness of my manner. Coldness and distrust had been engendered in me, I knew, by my bad experiences; they were not natural to me; and I often thought how much I had lost in life, losing trustfulness, and how little I had gained, gaining hard caution. This state of mind, being habitual to me, I troubled myself more about this conversation than I might have troubled myself about a greater matter. I listened to his talk at dinner, and observed how readily other men responded to it, and with what a graceful instinct he adapted his subjects to the knowledge and habits of those he talked with. As, in talking with me, he had easily started the subject I might be supposed to understand best, and to be the most interested in, so, in talking with others, he guided himself by the same rule. The company was of a varied character; but he was not at fault, that I could discover, with any member of it. He knew just as much of each man's pursuit as made him agreeable to that man in reference to it, and just as little as made it natural in him to seek modestly for information when the theme was broached.

As he talked and talked—but really not too much, for the rest of us seemed to force it upon him—I became quite angry with myself. I took his face to pieces in my mind, like a watch, and examined it in detail. I could not say much against any of his features separately; I could say even less against them when they were put together. 'Then is it not monstrous,' I asked myself, 'that because a man happens to part his hair straight up the middle of his head, I should permit myself to suspect, and even to detest him?'

(I may stop to remark that this was no proof of my sense. An observer of men who finds himself steadily repelled by some apparently trifling thing in a stranger is right to give it great weight. It may be the clue to the whole mystery. A hair or two will show where a lion is hidden. A very little key will open a very heavy door.)

I took my part in the conversation with him after a time, and we got on remarkably well. In the drawing-room I asked the host how long he had known Mr Slinkton. He answered, not many months; he had met him at the house of a celebrated painter then present, who had known him well when he was travelling with his nieces in Italy for their health. His plans in life being broken by the death of one of them, he was reading with the intention of going back to college as a matter of form, taking his degree, and going into orders. I could not but argue with myself that here was the true explanation of his interest in poor Meltham, and that I had been almost brutal in my distrust on that simple head.

III

ON THE VERY NEXT DAY but one I was sitting behind my glass partition, as before, when he came into the outer office, as before. The moment I saw him again without hearing him, I hated him worse than ever.

It was only for a moment that I had this opportunity; for he waved his tight-fitting black glove the instant I looked at him, and came straight in.

'Mr Sampson, good day! I presume, you see, upon your kind permission to intrude upon you. I don't keep my word in being justified by business, for my business here—if I may so abuse the word—is of the slightest nature.'

I asked, was it anything I could assist him in?

'I thank you, no. I merely called to enquire outside whether my dilatory friend had been so false to himself as to be practical and sensible. But, of course, he has done nothing. I gave him your papers with my own hand, and he was hot upon the intention, but of course he has done nothing. Apart from the general human disinclination to do anything that ought to be done, I dare say there is a speciality about assuring one's life. You find it like will-making. People are so superstitious, and take it for granted they will die soon afterwards.'

'Up here, if you please; straight up here, Mr Sampson. Neither to the right nor to the left.' I almost fancied I could hear him breathe the words as he sat smiling at me, with that intolerable parting exactly opposite the bridge of my nose.

'There is such a feeling sometimes, no doubt,' I replied; 'but I don't think it obtains to any great extent.'

'Well,' said he with a shrug and a smile, 'I wish some good angel would influence my friend in the right direction. I rashly promised his mother and sister in Norfolk to see it done, and he promised them that he would do it. But I suppose he never will.'

He spoke for a minute or two on different topics, and went away.

I had scarcely unlocked the drawers of my writing-table next morning, when he reappeared. I noticed that he came straight to the door in the glass partition, and did not pause a single moment outside.

'Can you spare me two minutes, my dear Mr Sampson?'

'By all means.'

'Much obliged,' laying his hat and umbrella on the table. 'I came early, not to interrupt you. The fact is, I am taken by surprise in reference to this proposal my friend has made.'

'Has he made one?' said I.

'Ye-es,' he answered, deliberately looking at me; and then a bright idea seemed to strike him—'or he only tells me he has. Perhaps that may be a new way of evading the matter. By Jupiter, I never thought of that?'

Mr Adams was opening the morning's letters in the outer office. 'What is the name, Mr Slinkton?' I asked.

'Beckwith.'

I looked out at the door, and requested Mr Adams, if there were a proposal in that name, to bring it in. He had already laid it out of his hand on the counter. It was easily selected from the rest, and he gave it me. Alfred Beckwith. Proposal to effect a policy with us for two thousand pounds. Dated yesterday.

'From the Middle Temple, I see, Mr Slinkton.'

'Yes. He lives on the same staircase with me; his door is opposite. I never thought he would make me his reference, though.'

'It seems natural enough that he should.'

'Quite so, Mr Sampson; but I never thought of it. Let me see.' He took the printed paper from his pocket. 'How am I to answer all these questions?'

'According to the truth, of course,' said I.

'Oh, of course!' he answered, looking up from the paper with a smile. 'I meant they were so many. But you do right to be particular. It stands to reason that you must be particular. Will you allow me to use your pen and ink?'

'Certainly.'

'And your desk?'

'Certainly.'

He had been hovering about between his hat and his umbrella for a place to write on. He now sat down in my chair, at my blotting-paper and inkstand, with the long walk up his head in accurate perspective before me, as I stood with my back to the fire.

Before answering each question he ran it over aloud, and discussed it. How long had he known Mr Alfred Beckwith? That he had to calculate by years upon his fingers. What were his habits? No difficulty about them; temperate in the last degree, and took a little too much exercise, if anything. All the answers were satisfactory. When he had written them all, he looked them over, and finally signed them in a very pretty hand. He supposed he had now done with the business. I told him he was not likely to be troubled any further. Should he leave the papers there? If he pleased. Much obliged. Good morning.

I had had one other visitor before him; not at the office, but at my own house. That visitor had come to my bedside when it was not yet daylight, and had been seen by no one else but my faithful confidential servant.

A second reference paper (for we required always two) was sent down into Norfolk, and was duly received back by post. This, likewise, was satisfactorily answered in every respect. Our forms were all complied with; we accepted the proposal, and the premium for one year was paid.

IV

FOR SIX OR SEVEN months I saw no more of Mr Slinkton. He called once at my house, but I was not at home; and he once asked me to dine with him in the Temple, but I was engaged. His friend's assurance was effected in March. Late in September, or early in October, I was down at Scarborough for a breath of sea air, where I met him on the beach. It was a hot evening; he came toward me with his hat in his hand; and there was the walk I felt so strongly disinclined to take in perfect order again, exactly in front of the bridge of my nose.

He was not alone, but had a young lady on his arm.

She was dressed in mourning, and I looked at her with great interest. She had the appearance of being extremely delicate, and her face was remarkably pale and melancholy; but she was very pretty. He introduced her as his niece, Miss Niner.

'Are you strolling, Mr Sampson? Is it possible you can be idle?'

It *was* possible, and I *was* strolling.

'Shall we stroll together?'

'With pleasure.'

The young lady walked between us, and we walked on the cool sea-sand, in the direction of Filey.

'There have been wheels here,' said Mr Slinkton. 'And now I look again, the wheels of a hand-carriage! Margaret, my love, your shadow, without doubt!'

'Miss Niner's shadow?' I repeated, looking down at it on the sand.

'Not that one,' Mr Slinkton returned, laughing. 'Margaret, my dear, tell Mr Sampson.'

'Indeed,' said the young lady, turning to me, 'there is nothing to tell—except that I constantly see the same invalid old gentleman at all times, wherever I go. I have mentioned it to my uncle, and he calls the gentleman my shadow.'

'Does he live in Scarborough?' I asked.

'He is staying here.'

'Do you live in Scarborough?'

'No, I am staying here. My uncle has placed me with a family here, for my health.'

'And your shadow?' said I, smiling.

'My shadow,' she answered, smiling too, 'is—like myself—not very robust, I fear; for I lose my shadow sometimes, as my shadow loses me at other times. We both seem liable to confinement to the house. I have not seen my shadow for days and days; but it does oddly happen, occasionally, that wherever I go, for many days together, this gentleman goes. We have come together in the most unfrequented nooks on this shore.'

'Is this he?' said I, pointing before us.

The wheels had swept down to the water's edge, and described a great loop on the sand in turning. Bringing the hoop back towards us, and spinning it out as it came, was a hand-carriage, drawn by a man.

'Yes,' said Miss Niner, 'this really is my shadow, uncle.'

As the carriage approached us, and we approached the carriage, I saw within it an old man, whose head was sunk on his breast, and who was enveloped in a variety of wrappers. He was drawn by a very quiet but very keen-looking man, with iron-grey hair, who was slightly lame. They had passed us, when the carriage stopped, and the old gentleman within, putting out his arm, called to me by my name. I went back, and was absent from Mr Slinkton and his niece for about five minutes.

When I rejoined them Mr Slinkton was the first to speak. Indeed he said to me in a raised voice, before I came up with him:

'It is well you have not been longer, or my niece might have died of curiosity to know who her shadow is, Mr Sampson.'

'An old East India Director,' said I. 'An intimate friend of our friend's, at whose house I first had the pleasure of meeting you. A certain Major Banks. You have heard of him?'

'Never.'

'Very rich, Miss Niner; but very old, and very crippled. An amiable man, sensible—much interested in you. He has just been expatiating on the affection that he has observed to exist between you and your uncle.'

Mr Slinkton was holding his hat again, and he passed his hand up the straight walk, as if he himself went up it serenely after me.

'Mr Sampson,' he said, tenderly pressing his niece's arm in his, 'our affection was always a strong one, for we have had but few near ties. We have still fewer now. We have associations to bring us together, that are not of this world, Margaret.'

'Dear uncle!' murmured the young lady, and turned her face aside to hide her tears.

'My niece and I have such remembrances and regrets in common, Mr Sampson,' he feelingly pursued, 'that it would be strange indeed if the relations between us were cold or indifferent. If I remember a conversation we once had together, you will understand the reference I make. Cheer up, dear Margaret. Don't droop, don't droop. My Margaret! I cannot bear to see you droop!'

The poor young lady was very much affected, but controlled herself. His feelings, too, were very acute. In a word, he found himself under such great need of a restorative, that he presently went away, to take a bath of sea-water, leaving the young lady and me sitting by a point of rock, and probably presuming—but that you will say was a pardonable indulgence in a luxury—that she would praise him with all her heart.

She did, poor thing! With all her confiding heart, she praised him to me, for his care of her dead sister, and for his untiring devotion in her last illness. The sister had wasted away very slowly, and wild and terrible fantasies had come over her toward the end, but he had never been impatient with her, or at a loss; had always been gentle, watchful, and self-possessed. The sister had known him, as she had known him, to be the best of men, the kindest of men, and yet a man of such admirable strength of character, as to be a very tower for the support of their weak natures while their poor lives endured.

'I shall leave him, Mr Sampson, very soon,' said the young lady; 'I know my life is drawing to an end; and, when I am gone, I hope he will marry and be happy. I am sure he has lived single so long, only for my sake, and for my poor, poor sister's.'

The little hand-carriage had made another great loop on the damp sand, and was coming back again, gradually spinning out a slim figure of eight, half a mile long.

'Young lady,' said I, looking around, laying my hand upon her arm, and speaking in a low voice, 'time presses. You hear the gentle murmur of that sea?'

She looked at me with the utmost wonder and alarm, saying:

'Yes!'

'And you know what a voice is in it when the storm comes?'

'Yes!'

'You see how quiet and peaceful it lies before us, and you know what an awful sight of power without pity it might be, this very night?'

'Yes!'

'But if you had never heard or seen it, or heard of it in its cruelty, could you believe that it beats every inanimate thing in its way to pieces without mercy, and destroys life without remorse?'

'You terrify me, sir, by these questions!'

'To save you, young lady, to save you! For God's sake, collect your strength and collect your firmness! If you were here alone, and hemmed in by the rising tide on the flow to fifty feet above your head, you could not be in greater danger than the danger you are now to be saved from.'

The figure on the sand was spun out, and straggled off into a crooked little jerk that ended at the cliff very near us.

'As I am, before Heaven and the Judge of all mankind, your friend, and your dead sister's friend, I solemnly entreat you, Miss Niner, without one moment's loss of time, to come to this gentleman with me!'

If the little carriage had been less near to us, I doubt if I could have got her away; but it was so near that we were there before she had recovered the hurry of being urged from the rock. I did not remain there with her two minutes. Certainly within five, I had the inexpressible satisfaction of seeing her—from the point we had sat on, and to which I had returned—half supported and half carried up some rude steps notched in the cliff, by the figure of an active man. With that figure beside her I knew she was safe anywhere.

I sat alone on the rock, awaiting Mr Slinkton's return. The twilight was deepening and the shadows were heavy, when he came round the point, with his hat hanging at his buttonhole, smoothing his wet hair with one of his hands, and picking out the old path with the other and a pocket-comb.

'My niece not here, Mr Sampson?' he said, looking about.

'Miss Niner seemed to feel a chill in the air after the sun was down, and has gone home.'

He looked surprised, as though she were not accustomed to do anything without him; even to originate so slight a proceeding.

'I persuaded Miss Niner,' I explained.

'Ah!' said he. 'She is easily persuaded—for her good. Thank you, Mr Sampson; she is better within doors. The bathing-place was further than I thought, to say the truth.'

'Miss Niner is very delicate,' I observed.

He shook his head and drew a deep sigh. 'Very, very, very. You may recollect my saying so. The time that has since intervened has not strengthened her. The gloomy shadow that fell upon her sister so early in life seems, in my anxious eyes, to gather over her, ever darker, ever darker. Dear Margaret, dear Margaret? But we must hope.'

The hand-carriage was spinning away before us at a most indecorous pace for an invalid vehicle, and was making most irregular curves upon the sand. Mr Slinkton, noticing it after he had put his handkerchief to his eyes, said:

'If I may judge from appearances, your friend will be upset, Mr Sampson.'

'It looks probable, certainly,' said I.

'The servant must be drunk.'

'The servants of old gentlemen will get drunk sometimes,' said I.

'The major draws very light, Mr Sampson.'

'The major does draw light,' said I.

By this time the carriage, much to my relief, was lost in the darkness. We walked on for a little, side by side over the sand, in silence. After a short while he said, in a voice still affected by the emotion that his niece's state of health had awakened in him:

'Do you stay here long, Mr Sampson?'

'Why, no. I am going away tonight.'

'So soon? But business always holds you in request. Men like Mr Sampson are too important to others, to be spared to their own need of relaxation, and enjoyment.'

'I don't know about that,' said I. 'However, I am going back.'

'To London?'

'To London.'

'I shall be there, too, soon after you.'

I knew that as well as he did. But I did not tell him so. Any more than I told him what defensive weapon my right hand rested on in my pocket, as I walked by his side. Any more than I told him why I did not walk on the sea side of him with the night closing in.

We left the beach, and our ways diverged. We exchanged good night, and had parted indeed, when he said, returning:

'Mr Sampson, *may* I ask? Poor Meltham, whom we spoke of—dead yet?'

'Not when I last heard of him; but too broken a man to live long, and hopelessly lost to his old calling.'

'Dear, dear, dear!' said he with great feeling. 'Sad, sad, sad! The world is a grave!' And so went his way.

It was not his fault if the world were not a grave; but I did not call that observation after him, any more than I had mentioned those other things just now enumerated. He went his way, and I went mine with all expedition. This happened, as I have said, either at the end of September or beginning of October. The next time I saw him, and the last time, was late in November.

V

I HAD A VERY particular engagement to breakfast in the Temple. It was a bitter north-easterly morning, and the sleet and slush lay inches deep in the streets. I could get no conveyance, and was soon wet to the knees; but I should have been true to that appointment, though I had to wade to it up to my neck in the same impediments.

The appointment took me to some chambers in the Temple. They were at the top of a lonely corner house overlooking the river. The name, MR ALFRED BECKWITH, was painted on the outer door. On the door opposite, on the same landing, the name MR JULIUS SLINKTON. The doors of both sets of chambers stood open, so that anything said aloud in one set could be heard in the other.

I had never been in those chambers before. They were dismal, close, unwholesome, and oppressive: the furniture, originally good, and not yet old, was faded and dirty; the rooms were in great disorder; there was a strong prevailing smell of opium, brandy, and tobacco; the grate and fire-irons were splashed all over with unsightly blotches of rust; and on a sofa by the fire, in the room where breakfast had been prepared, lay the host, Mr Beckwith, a man with all the appearances of the worst kind of drunkard, very far advanced upon his shameful way to death.

'Slinkton is not come yet,' said this creature, staggering up when I went in; 'I'll call him.—Halloa! Julius Caesar! Come and drink!' As he hoarsely roared this out, he beat the poker and tongs together in a mad way, as if that were his usual manner of summoning his associate.

The voice of Mr Slinkton was heard through the clatter from the opposite side of the staircase, and he came in. He had not expected the pleasure of meeting me. I have seen several artful men brought to a stand, but I never saw a man so aghast as he was when his eyes rested on mine.

'Julius Caesar,' cried Beckwith, staggering between us, 'Mist' Sampson! Mist' Sampson, Julius Caesar! Julius, Mist' Sampson, is the friend of my soul. Julius keeps me plied with liquor, morning, noon, and night. Julius is a real benefactor. Julius threw the tea and coffee out of window when I used to have any. Julius empties all the water-jugs of their contents, and fills them with spirits. Julius winds me up and keeps me going.—Boil the brandy, Julius!'

There was a rusty and furred saucepan in the ashes—the ashes looked like the accumulation of weeks—and Beckwith, rolling and staggering between us as if he were going to plunge headlong into the fire, got the saucepan out, and tried to force it into Slinkton's hand.

'Boil the brandy, Julius Caesar! Come! Do your usual office. Boil the brandy!'

He became so fierce in his gesticulations with the saucepan, that I expected to see him lay open Slinkton's head with it. I therefore put out my hand to check him. He reeled back to the sofa, and sat there panting, shaking, and red-eyed, in his rags of dressing-gown, looking at us both. I noticed then that there was nothing to drink on the table but brandy, and nothing to eat but salted herrings, and a hot, sickly, highly peppered stew.

'At all events, Mr Sampson,' said Slinkton, offering me the smooth gravel path for the last time, 'I thank you for interfering between me and this unfortunate man's violence. However you came here, Mr Sampson, or with whatever motive you came here, at least I thank you for that.'

'Boil the brandy,' muttered Beckwith.

Without gratifying his desire to know how I came there, I said quietly, 'How is your niece, Mr Slinkton?'

He looked hard at me, and I looked hard at him.

'I am sorry to say, Mr Sampson, that my niece has proved treacherous and ungrateful to her best friend. She left me without a word of notice or explanation. She was misled, no doubt, by some designing rascal. Perhaps you may have heard of it?'

'I did hear that she was misled by a designing rascal. In fact, I have proof of it.'

'Are you sure of that?' said he.

'Quite.'

'Boil the brandy,' muttered Beckwith. 'Company to breakfast, Julius Caesar. Do your usual office—provide the usual breakfast, dinner, tea, and supper. Boil the brandy!'

The eyes of Slinkton looked from him to me, and he said, after a moment's consideration:

'Mr Sampson, you are a man of the world, and so am I. I will be plain with you.'

'Oh no, you won't!' said I, shaking my head.

'I tell you, sir, I will be plain with you.'

'And I tell you you will not,' said I. 'I know all about you. *You* plain with any one? Nonsense, nonsense!'

'I plainly tell you, Mr Sampson,' he went on, with a manner almost composed, 'that I understand your object. You want to save your funds, and escape from your liabilities; these are old tricks of trade with you Office gentlemen. But you will not do it, sir; you will not succeed. You have not an easy adversary to play against, when you play against me. We shall have to enquire, in due time, when and how Mr Beckwith fell into his present habits. With that remark, sir, I put this poor creature, and his incoherent wanderings of speech, aside, and wish you a good morning and a better case next time.'

While he was saying this, Beckwith had filled a half-pint glass with brandy. At this moment, he threw the brandy at his face, and threw the glass after it. Slinkton put his hands up, half blinded with the spirit, and cut with the glass across the forehead. At the sound of the breakage, a fourth person came into the room, closed the door, and stood at it. He was a very quiet, but very keen-looking man, with iron-grey hair, and slightly lame.

Slinkton pulled out his handkerchief, assuaged the pain in his smarting eyes, and dabbled the blood on his forehead. He was a long time about it, and I saw that in the doing of it a tremendous change came over him, occasioned by the change in Beckwith—who ceased to pant and tremble, sat upright, and never took his eyes off him. I never in my life saw a face in which abhorrence and determination were so forcibly painted as in Beckwith's then.

'Look at me, you villain,' said Beckwith, 'and see me as I really am! I took these rooms to make them a trap for you. I came into them as a drunkard, to bait the trap for you. You fell into the trap, and you will never leave it alive. On the morning when you last went to Mr Sampson's office, I had seen him first. Your plot has been known to both of us all along and you have been counter-plotted all along. What! Having been cajoled into putting that prize of two thousand pounds in your power, I was to be done to death with brandy, and, brandy not proving quick enough, with something quicker? Have I never seen you, when you thought my senses gone, pouring from your little bottle into my glass? Why, you Murderer and Forger, alone here with you in the dead of night, as I have so often been, I have had my hand upon the trigger of a pistol, twenty times, to blow your brains out!'

This sudden starting up of the thing that he had supposed to be his imbecile victim into a determined man, with a settled resolution to hunt him down and be the death of him, mercilessly expressed from head to foot, was, in the first shock, too much for him. Without any figure of speech, he staggered under it. But there is no greater mistake than to suppose that a man who is a calculating criminal is, in any phase of his guilt, otherwise than true to himself, and perfectly consistent with his whole character. Such a man commits murder, and murder is the natural culmination of his course; such a man has to outface murder, and will do it with hardihood and effrontery. It is a sort of fashion to express surprise that any notorious criminal, having such crime upon his conscience, can so brave it out. Do you think that if he had it on his conscience at all, or had a conscience to have it upon, he would ever have committed the crime?

Perfectly consistent with himself, as I believe all such monsters to be, this Slinkton recovered himself, and showed a defiance that was sufficiently cold and quiet. He was white, he was haggard, he was changed; but only as a sharper who had played for a great stake, and had been outwitted and had lost the game.

'Listen to me, you villain,' said Beckwith, 'and let every word you hear me say be a stab in your wicked heart. When I took these rooms, to throw myself in your way and lead you on to the scheme that I knew my appearance and supposed character and habits would suggest to such a devil, how did I know that? Because you were no stranger to me. I knew you well. And I knew you to be the cruel wretch who, for so much money, had killed one innocent girl while she trusted him implicitly, and who was by inches killing another.'

Slinkton took out a snuff-box, took a pinch of snuff, and laughed.

'But see here,' said Beckwith, never looking away, never raising his voice, never relaxing his face, never unclenching his hand. 'See what a dull wolf you have been, after all! The infatuated drunkard who never drank a fiftieth part of the liquor you plied him with, but poured it away, here, there, everywhere—almost before your eyes; who bought over the fellow you set to watch him and to ply him, by out-bidding you in his bribe, before he had been at his work three days—with whom you have observed no caution, yet who was so bent on ridding the earth of you as a wild beast, that he would have defeated you if you had been ever so prudent—that drunkard whom you have, many a time, left on the floor of this room, and who has even let you go out of it, alive and undeceived, when you have turned him over with your foot—has, almost as often, on the same night, within an hour, within a few minutes, watched you awake, had his hand at your pillow when you were asleep, turned over your papers, taken samples from your bottles and packets of powder, changed their contents, rifled every secret of your life!'

He had had another pinch of snuff in his hand, but had gradually let it drop from between his fingers to the floor: where he now smoothed it out with his foot, looking down at it the while.

'That drunkard,' said Beckwith, 'who had free access to your rooms at all times, that he might drink the strong drinks that you left in his way, and be the sooner ended, holding no more terms with you than he would hold with a tiger, has had his master key for all your locks, his tests for all your poisons, his clue to your cipher-writing. He can tell you, as well as you can tell him, how long it took to complete that deed, what doses there were, what intervals, what signs of gradual decay upon mind and body; what distempered fancies were produced, what observable changes, what physical pain. He can tell you, as well as you can tell him, that all this was recorded day by day, as a lesson of experience for future service. He can tell you, better than you can tell him, where that journal is at this moment.'

Slinkton stopped the action of his foot, and looked at Beckwith.

'No,' said the latter, as if answering a question from him. 'Not in the drawer of the writing-desk that opens with a spring; it is not there, and it never will be there again.'

'Then you are a thief!' said Slinkton.

Without any change whatever in the inflexible purpose, which it was quite terrific even to me to contemplate, and from the power of which I had always felt convinced it was impossible for this wretch to escape, Beckwith returned:

'And I am your niece's shadow, too.'

With an imprecation Slinkton put his hand to his head, tore out some hair, and flung it to the ground. It was the end of the smooth walk; he destroyed it in the action, and it will soon be seen that his use for it was past.

Beckwith went on: 'Whenever you left here, I left here. Although I under-stood that you found it necessary to pause in the completion of that purpose, to avert suspicion, still I watched you close, with the poor confiding girl. When I had the diary, and could read it word by word—it was only about the night before your last visit to Scarborough—you remember the night? you slept with a small flat vial tied to your wrist—I sent to Mr Sampson, who was kept out of view. This is Mr Sampson's trusty servant standing by the door. We three saved your niece among us.'

Slinkton looked at us all, took an uncertain step or two from the place where he had stood, returned to it, and glanced about him in a very curious way—as one of the meaner reptiles might, looking for a hole to hide in. I noticed, at the same time, that a singular change took place in the figure of the man—as if it collapsed within his clothes, and they consequently became ill-shapen and ill-fitting.

'You shall know,' said Beckwith, 'for I hope the knowledge will be bitter and terrible to you, why you have been pursued by one man, and why, when the whole interest that Mr Sampson represents would have expended any money in hunting you down, you have been tracked to death at a single individual's charge. I hear you have had the name of Meltham on your lips sometimes?'

I saw, in addition to those other changes, a sudden stoppage come upon his breathing.

'When you sent the sweet girl whom you murdered (you know with what artfully made-out surroundings and probabilities you sent her) to Meltham's office, before taking her abroad to originate the transaction that doomed her to the grave, it fell to Meltham's lot to see her and to speak with her. It did not fall to his lot to save her, though I know he would freely give his own life to have done it. He admired her—I would say he loved her deeply, if I thought it possible that you could understand the word. When she was sacrificed, he was thoroughly assured of your guilt. Having lost her, he had but one object left in life, and that was to avenge her and destroy you.'

I saw the villain's nostrils rise and fall convulsively; but I saw no moving at his mouth.

'That man Meltham,' Beckwith steadily pursued, 'was as absolutely certain that you could never elude him in this world, if he devoted himself to your destruction with his utmost fidelity and earnestness, and if he divided the sacred duty with no other duty in life, as he was certain that in achieving it he would be a poor instrument in the hands of Providence, and would do well before Heaven in striking you out from among living men. I am that man, and I thank God that I have done my work!'

If Slinkton had been running for his life from swift-footed savages, a dozen miles, he could not have shown more emphatic signs of being oppressed at heart and labouring for breath than he showed now, when he looked at the pursuer who had so relentlessly hunted him down.

'You never saw me under my right name before; you see me under my right name now. You shall see me once again in the body when you are tried for your life. You shall see me once again in the spirit, when the cord is round your neck, and the crowd are crying against you!'

When Meltham had spoken these last words, the miscreant suddenly turned away his face, and seemed to strike his mouth with his open hand. At the same instant, the room was filled with a new and powerful odour, and, almost at the same instant, he broke into a crooked run, leap, start—I have no name for the spasm—and fell, with a dull weight that shook the heavy old doors and windows in their frames.

That was the fitting end of him.

When we saw that he was dead, we drew away from the room, and Meltham, giving me his hand, said, with a weary air:

'I have no more work on earth, my friend. But I shall see her again elsewhere.'

It was in vain that I tried to rally him. He might have saved her, he said; he had not saved her, and he reproached himself; he had lost her, and he was broken-hearted.

'The purpose that sustained me is over, Sampson, and there is nothing now to hold me to life. I am not fit for life; I am weak and spiritless; I have no hope and no object; my day is done.'

In truth, I could hardly have believed that the broken man who then spoke to me was the man who had so strongly and so differently impressed me when his purpose was before him. I used such entreaties with him as I could; but he still said, and always said, in a patient, undemonstrative way—nothing could avail him—he was broken-hearted.

He died early in the next spring. He was buried by the side of the poor young lady for whom he had cherished those tender and unhappy regrets; and he left all he had to her sister. She lived to be a happy wife and mother; she married my sister's son, who succeeded poor Meltham; she is living now, and her children ride about the garden on my walking-stick when I go to see her.

Sir Arthur Conan Doyle
1859–1930

THE MAN WITH THE TWISTED LIP

Isa Whitney, brother of the late Elias Whitney, DD, Principal of the Theological College of St George's, was much addicted to opium. The habit grew upon him, as I understand, from some foolish freak when he was at college; for having read De Quincey's description of his dreams and sensations, he had drenched his tobacco with laudanum in an attempt to produce the same effects. He found, as so many more have done, that the practice is easier to attain than to get rid of, and for many years he continued to be a slave to the drug, an object of mingled horror and pity to his friends and relatives. I can see him now, with yellow, pasty face, drooping lids, and pin-point pupils, all huddled in a chair, the wreck and ruin of a noble man.

One night—it was in June, '89—there came a ring to my bell, about the hour when a man gives his first yawn and glances at the clock. I sat up in my chair, and my wife laid her needle-work down in her lap and made a little face of disappointment.

'A patient!' said she. 'You'll have to go out.'

I groaned, for I was newly come back from a weary day.

We heard the door open, a few hurried words, and then quick steps upon the linoleum. Our own door flew open, and a lady, clad in some dark-coloured stuff, with a black veil, entered the room.

'You will excuse my calling so late,' she began, and then, suddenly losing her self-control, she ran forward, threw her arms about my wife's neck, and sobbed upon her shoulder. 'Oh, I'm in such trouble!' she cried; 'I do so want a little help.'

'Why,' said my wife, pulling up her veil, 'it is Kate Whitney. How you startled me, Kate! I had not an idea who you were when you came in.'

'I didn't know what to do, so I came straight to you.' That was always the way. Folk who were in grief came to my wife like birds to a lighthouse.

'It was very sweet of you to come. Now, you must have some wine and water, and sit here comfortably and tell us all about it. Or should you rather that I sent James off to bed?'

'Oh, no, no! I want the doctor's advice and help, too. It's about Isa. He has not been home for two days. I am so frightened about him!'

It was not the first time that she had spoken to us of her husband's trouble, to me as a doctor, to my wife as an old friend and school companion. We soothed and comforted her by such words as we could find. Did she know where her husband was? Was it possible that we could bring him back to her?

It seems that it was. She had the surest information that of late he had, when the fit was on him, made use of an opium den in the farthest east of the City. Hitherto his orgies had always been confined to one day, and he had come back, twitching and shattered, in the evening. But now the spell had been upon him eight-and-forty hours, and he lay there, doubtless among the dregs of the docks, breathing in the poison or sleeping off the effects. There he was to be found, she was sure of it, at the Bar of Gold, in Upper Swandam Lane. But what was she to do? How could she, a young and timid woman, make her way into such a place and pluck her husband out from among the ruffians who surrounded him?

There was the case, and of course there was but one way out of it. Might I not escort her to this place? And then, as a second thought, why should she come at all? I was Isa Whitney's medical advisor, and as such I had influence over him. I could manage it better if I were alone. I promised her on my word that I would send him home in a cab within two hours if he were indeed at the address which she had given me. And so in ten minutes I had left my armchair and cheery sitting-room behind me, and was speeding eastward in a hansom on a strange errand, as it seemed to me at the time, though the future only could show how strange it was to be.

But there was no great difficulty in the first stage of my adventure. Upper Swandam Lane is a vile alley lurking behind the high wharves which line the north side of the river to the east of London Bridge. Between a slop-shop and a gin-shop, approached by a steep flight of steps leading down to a black gap like the mouth of a cave, I found the den of which I was in search. Ordering my cab to wait, I passed down the steps, worn hollow in the centre by the ceaseless tread of drunken feet; and by the light of a flickering oil-lamp above the door I found the latch and made my way into a long, low room, thick and heavy with the brown opium smoke, and terraced with wooden berths, like the forecastle of an emigrant ship.

Through the gloom one could dimly catch a glimpse of bodies lying in strange, fantastic poses, bowed shoulders, bent knees, heads thrown back, and chins pointing upward, with here and there a dark, lack-lustre eye turned upon the newcomer. Out of the black shadows there glimmered little red circles of light, now bright, now faint, as the burning poison waxed or waned in the bowls of the metal pipes. The most lay silent, but some muttered to themselves, and others talked together in a strange, low, monotonous voice, their conversation coming in gushes, and then suddenly tailing off into silence, each mumbling out his own thoughts and paying little heed to the words of his neighbour. At the farther end was a small brazier of burning charcoal, beside which on a three-legged wooden stool there sat a tall, thin old man, with his jaw resting upon his two fists, and his elbows upon his knees, staring into the fire.

As I entered, a sallow Malay attendant had hurried up with a pipe for me and a supply of the drug, beckoning me to an empty berth.

'Thank you. I have not come to stay,' said I. 'There is a friend of mine here, Mr Isa Whitney, and I wish to speak with him.'

There was a movement and an exclamation from my right, and peering through the gloom I saw Whitney, pale, haggard, and unkempt, staring out at me.

'My God! It's Watson,' said he. He was in a pitiable state of reaction, with every nerve in a twitter. 'I say, Watson, what o'clock is it?'

'Nearly eleven.'

'Of what day?'

'Of Friday, June 19th.'

'Good heavens! I thought it was Wednesday. It *is* Wednesday. What d'you want to frighten the chap for?' He sank his face onto his arms and began to sob in a high treble key.

'I tell you that it is Friday, man. Your wife has been waiting this two days for you. You should be ashamed of yourself!'

'So I am. But you've got mixed, Watson, for I have only been here a few hours, three pipes, four pipes—I forget how many. But I'll go home with you. I wouldn't frighten Kate—poor little Kate. Give me your hand! Have you a cab?'

'Yes, I have one waiting.'

'Then I shall go in it. But I must owe something. Find what I owe, Watson. I am all off colour. I can do nothing for myself.'

I walked down the narrow passage between the double row of sleepers, holding my breath to keep out the vile, stupefying fumes of the drug, and looking about for the manager. As I passed the tall man who sat by the brazier I felt a sudden pluck at my skirt, and a low voice whispered, 'Walk past me, and then look back at me.' The words fell quite distinctly upon my ear. I glanced down. They could only have come from the old man at my side, and yet he sat now as absorbed as ever, very thin, very wrinkled, bent with age, an opium pipe dangling down from between his knees, as though it had dropped in sheer lassitude from his fingers. I took two steps forward and looked back. It took all my self-control to prevent me from breaking out into a cry of astonishment. He had turned his back so that none could see him but I. His form had filled out, his wrinkles were gone, the dull eyes had regained their fire, and there, sitting by the fire and grinning at my surprise, was none other than Sherlock Holmes. He made a slight motion to me to approach him, and instantly, as he turned his face half round to the company once more, subsided into a doddering, loose-lipped senility.

'Holmes!' I whispered, 'what on earth are you doing in this den?'

'As low as you can,' he answered; 'I have excellent ears. If you would have the great kindness to get rid of that sottish friend of yours I should be exceedingly glad to have a little talk with you.'

'I have a cab outside.'

'Then pray send him home in it. You may safely trust him, for he appears to be too limp to get into any mischief. I should recommend you also to send a note by the cabman to your wife to say that you have thrown in your lot with me. If you will wait outside, I shall be with you in five minutes.'

It was difficult to refuse any of Sherlock Holmes's requests, for they were always so exceedingly definite, and put forward with such a quiet air of mastery. I felt, however, that when Whitney was once confined in the cab my mission was practically accomplished; and for the rest, I could not wish anything better than to be associated with my friend in one of those singular adventures which were the normal condition of his existence. In a few minutes I had written my note, paid Whitney's bill, led him out to the cab, and seen him driven through the darkness. In a very short time a decrepit figure had emerged from the opium den, and I was walking down the street with Sherlock Holmes. For two streets he shuffled along with a bent back and an uncertain foot. Then, glancing quickly round, he straightened himself out and burst into a hearty fit of laughter.

'I suppose, Watson,' said he, 'that you imagine that I have added opium smoking to cocaine injections, and all the other little weaknesses on which you have favoured me with your medical views.'

'I was certainly surprised to find you there.'

'But not more so than I to find you.'

'I came to find a friend.'

'And I to find an enemy.'

'An enemy?'

'Yes; one of my natural enemies, or, shall I say, my natural prey. Briefly, Watson, I am in the midst of a very remarkable inquiry, and I have hoped to find a clue in the incoherent ramblings of these sots, as I have done before now. Had I been recognised in that den my life would not have been worth an hour's purchase; for I have used it before now for my own purposes, and the rascally lascar who runs it has sworn to have vengeance upon me. There is a trap-door at the back of that building, near the corner of Paul's Wharf, which could tell some strange tales of what has passed through it upon the moonless nights.'

'What! You do not mean bodies?'

'Ay, bodies, Watson. We should be rich men if we had £1,000 for every poor devil who has been done to death in that den. It is the vilest murder-trap on the whole riverside, and I fear that Neville St Clair has entered it never to leave it more. But our trap should be here.' He put his two forefingers between his teeth and whistled shrilly—a signal which was answered by a similar whistle from the distance, followed shortly by the rattle of wheels and the clink of horses' hoofs.

'Now, Watson,' said Holmes, as a tall dog-cart dashed up through the gloom, throwing out two golden tunnels of yellow light from its side lanterns. 'You'll come with me, won't you?'

'If I can be of use.'

'Oh, a trusty comrade is always of use; and a chronicler still more so. My room at The Cedars is a double-bedded one.'

'The Cedars?'

'Yes; that is Mr St Clair's house. I am staying there while I conduct the inquiry.'

'Where is it, then?'

'Near Lee, in Kent. We have a seven-mile drive before us.'

'But I am all in the dark.'

'Of course you are. You'll know all about it presently. Jump up here. All right, John; we shall not need you. Here's half a crown. Look out for me to-morrow, about eleven. Give her her head. So long, then!'

He flicked the horse with his whip, and we dashed away through the endless succession of sombre and deserted streets, which widened gradually, until we were flying across a broad balustraded bridge, with the murky river flowing sluggishly beneath us. Beyond lay another dull wilderness of bricks and mortar, its silence broken only by the heavy, regular footfall of the policeman, or the songs and shouts of some belated party of revellers. A dull wrack was drifting slowly across the sky, and a star or two twinkled dimly here and there through the rifts of the clouds. Holmes drove in silence, with his head sunk upon his breast, and the air of a man who is lost in thought, while I sat beside him, curious to learn what this new quest might be which seemed to tax his powers so sorely, and yet afraid to break in upon the current of his thoughts. We had driven several miles, and were beginning to get to the fringe of the belt of suburban villas, when he shook himself, shrugged his shoulders, and lit up his pipe with the air of a man who has satisfied himself that he is acting for the best.

'You have a grand gift of silence, Watson,' said he. 'It makes you quite invaluable as a companion. 'Pon my word, it is a great thing for me to have someone to talk to, for my own thoughts are not over-pleasant. I was wondering what I should say to this dear little woman to-night when she meets me at the door.'

'You forget that I know nothing about it.'

'I shall just have time to tell you the facts of the case before we get to Lee. It seems absurdly simple, and yet, somehow, I can get nothing to go upon. There's plenty of thread, no doubt, but I can't get the end of it into my hand. Now, I'll state the case clearly and concisely to you, Watson, and maybe you can see a spark where all is dark to me.'

'Proceed, then.'

'Some years ago—to be definite, in May, 1884—there came to Lee a gentleman, Neville St Clair by name, who appeared to have plenty of money. He took a large villa, laid out the grounds very nicely, and lived generally in good style. By degrees he made friends in the neighbourhood, and in 1887 he married the daughter of a local brewer, by whom he now has two children. He had no occupation, but was interested in several companies and went into town as a rule in the morning, returning by the 5.14 from Cannon Street every night. Mr St Clair is now thirty-seven years of age, is a man of temperate habits, a good husband, a very affectionate father, and a man who is popular with all who know him. I may add that his whole debts at the present moment, as far as we have been able to ascertain, amount to £88 10s., while he has £220 standing to his credit in the Capital and Counties Bank. There is no reason, therefore, to think that money troubles have been weighing upon his mind.

'Last Monday Mr Neville St Clair went into town rather earlier than usual, remarking before he started that he had two important commissions to perform, and that he would bring his little boy home a box of bricks. Now, by the merest chance, his wife received a telegram upon this same Monday, very shortly after his departure, to the effect that a small parcel of considerable value which she had been expecting was waiting for her at the offices of the Aberdeen Shipping Company. Now, if you are well up in your London, you will know that the office of the company is in Fresno Street, which branches out of Upper Swandam Lane, where you found me to-night. Mrs St Clair had her lunch, started for the City, did some shopping, proceeded to the company's office, got her packet, and found herself at exactly 4.35 walking through Swandam Lane on her way back to the station. Have you followed me so far?'

'It is very clear.'

'If you remember, Monday was an exceedingly hot day, and Mrs St Clair walked slowly, glancing about in the hope of seeing a cab, as she did not like the neighbourhood in which she found herself. While she was walking in this way down Swandam Lane, she suddenly heard an ejaculation or cry, and was struck cold to see her husband looking down at her and, as it seemed to her, beckoning to her from a second-floor window. The window was open, and she distinctly saw his face, which she describes as being terribly agitated. He waved his hands frantically to her, and then vanished from the window so suddenly that it seemed to her that he had been plucked back by some irresistible force from behind. One singular point which struck her quick feminine eye was that although he wore some dark coat, such as he had started to town in, he had on neither collar nor necktie.

'Convinced that something was amiss with him, she rushed down the steps— for the house was none other than the opium den in which you found me to-night—and running through the front room she attempted to ascend the stairs which led to the first floor. At the foot of the stairs, however, she met this lascar scoundrel of whom I have spoken, who thrust her back and, aided by a Dane, who acts as assistant there, pushed her out into the street. Filled with the most maddening doubts and fears, she rushed down the lane and, by rare good-fortune, met in Fresno Street a number of constables with an inspector, all on their way to their beat. The inspector and two men accompanied her back, and in spite of the continued resistance of the proprietor, they made their way to the room in which Mr St Clair had last been seen. There was no sign of him there. In fact, in the whole of that floor there was no one to be found save a crippled wretch of hideous aspect, who, it seems, made his home there. Both he and the lascar stoutly swore that no one else had been in the front room during the afternoon. So determined was their denial that the inspector was staggered, and had almost come to believe that Mrs St Clair had been deluded when, with a cry, she sprang at a small deal box which lay upon the table and tore the lid from it. Out there fell a cascade of children's bricks. It was the toy which he had promised to bring home.

'This discovery, and the evident confusion which the cripple showed, made the inspector realise that the matter was serious. The rooms were carefully examined, and results all pointed to an abominable crime. The front room was plainly furnished as a sitting-room and led into a small bedroom, which looked out upon the back of one of the wharves. Between the wharf and the bedroom window is a narrow strip, which is dry at low tide but is covered at high tide with at least four and a half feet of water. The bedroom window was a broad one and opened from below. On examination traces of blood were to be seen upon the window-sill, and several scattered drops were visible upon the wooden floor of the bedroom. Thrust away behind a curtain in the front room were all the clothes of Mr Neville St Clair, with the exception of his coat. His boots, his socks, his hat, and his watch—all were there. There were no signs of violence upon any of these garments, and there were no other traces of Mr Neville St Clair. Out of the window he must apparently have gone, for no other exit could be discovered, and the ominous blood-stains upon the sill gave little promise that he could save himself by swimming, for the tide was at its very highest at the moment of the tragedy.

'And now as to the villains who seemed to be immediately implicated in the matter. The lascar was known to be a man of the vilest antecedents, but as, by Mrs St Clair's story, he was known to have been at the foot of the stair within a very few seconds of her husband's appearance at the window, he could hardly have been more than an accessory to the crime. His defence was one of absolute ignorance, and he protested that he had no knowledge as to the doings of Hugh Boone, his lodger, and that he could not account in any way for the presence of the missing gentleman's clothes.

'So much for the lascar manager. Now for the sinister cripple who lives upon the second floor of the opium den, and who was certainly the last human being whose eyes rested upon Neville St Clair. His name is Hugh Boone, and his hideous face is one which is familiar to every man who goes much to the City. He is a professional beggar, though in order to avoid the police regulations he pretends to a small trade in wax vestas. Some little distance down Threadneedle Street, upon the left-hand side, there is, as you may have remarked, a small angle in the wall. Here it is that this creature takes his daily seat, cross-legged, with his tiny stock of matches on his lap, and as he is a piteous spectacle a small rain of charity descends into the greasy leather cap which lies upon the pavement beside him. I have watched the fellow more than once before ever I thought of making his professional acquaintance, and I have been surprised at the harvest which he has reaped in a short time. His appearance, you see, is so remarkable that no one can pass him without observing him. A shock of orange hair, a pale face disfigured by a horrible scar, which, by its contraction, has turned up the outer edge of his upper lip, a bulldog chin, and a pair of very penetrating dark eyes, which present a singular contrast to the colour of his hair, all mark him out from amid the common crowd of mendicants, and so, too, does his wit, for he is ever ready with a reply to any piece of chaff which may be thrown at him by the passers-by. This is the man whom we now learn to have been the lodger at the opium den, and to have been the last man to see the gentleman of whom we are in quest.'

'But a cripple!' said I. 'What could he have done single-handed against a man in the prime of life?'

'He is a cripple in the sense that he walks with a limp; but in other respects he appears to be a powerful and well-nurtured man. Surely your medical experience would tell you, Watson, that weakness in one limb is often compensated for by exceptional strength in the others.'

'Pray continue your narrative.'

'Mrs St Clair had fainted at the sight of the blood upon the window, and she was escorted home in a cab by the police, as her presence could be of no help to them in their investigations. Inspector Barton, who had charge of the case, made a very careful examination of the premises, but without finding anything which threw any light upon the matter. One mistake had been made in not arresting Boone instantly, as he was allowed some few minutes during which he might have communicated with his friend the lascar, but this fault was soon remedied, and he was seized and searched, without anything being found which could incriminate him. There were, it is true, some blood-stains upon his right shirt-sleeve, but he pointed to his ring-finger, which had been cut near the nail, and explained that the bleeding came from there, adding that he had been to the window not long before, and that the stains which had been observed there came doubtless from the same source. He denied strenuously having ever seen Mr Neville St Clair and swore that the presence of the clothes in his room was as much a mystery to him as to the police. As to Mrs St Clair's assertion that she had actually seen her husband at the window, he declared that she must have been either mad or dreaming. He was removed, loudly protesting, to the police-station, while the inspector remained upon the premises in the hope that the ebbing tide might afford some fresh clue.

'And it did, though they hardly found upon the mud-bank what they had feared to find. It was Neville St Clair's coat, and not Neville St Clair, which lay uncovered as the tide receded. And what do you think they found in the pockets?'

'I cannot imagine.'

'No, I don't think you would guess. Every pocket stuffed with pennies and half-pennies—421 pennies and 270 half-pennies. It was no wonder that it had not been swept away by the tide. But a human body is a different matter. There is a fierce eddy between the wharf and the house. It seemed likely enough that the weighted coat had remained when the stripped body had been sucked away into the river.'

'But I understand that all the other clothes were found in the room. Would the body be dressed in a coat alone?'

'No, sir, but the facts might be met speciously enough. Suppose that this man Boone had thrust Neville St Clair through the window, there is no human eye which could have seen the deed. What would he do then? It would of course instantly strike him that he must get rid of the tell-tale garments. He would seize the coat, then, and be in the act of throwing it out, when it would occur to him that it would swim and not sink. He has little time, for he has heard the scuffle downstairs when the wife tried to force her way up, and perhaps he has already heard from his lascar confederate that the police are hurrying up the street. There is not an instant to be lost. He rushes to some secret hoard, where he has accumulated the fruits of his beggary, and he stuffs all the coins upon which he can lay his hands into the pockets to make sure of the coat's sinking. He throws it out, and would have done the same with the other garments had not he heard the rush of steps below, and only just had time to close the window when the police appeared.'

'It certainly sounds feasible.'

'Well, we will take it as a working hypothesis for want of a better. Boone, as I have told you, was arrested and taken to the station, but it could not be shown that there had ever before been anything against him. He had for years been known as a professional beggar, but his life appeared to have been a very quiet and innocent one. There the matter stands at present, and the questions which have to be solved—what Neville St Clair was doing in the opium den, what happened to him when there, where is he now, and what Hugh Boone had to do with his disappearance—are all as far from a solution as ever. I confess that I cannot recall any case within my experience which looked at the first glance so simple and yet which presented such difficulties.'

While Sherlock Holmes had been detailing this singular series of events, we had been whirling through the outskirts of the great town until the last straggling houses had been left behind, and we rattled along with a country hedge upon either side of us. Just as he finished, however, we drove through two scattered villages, where a few lights still glimmered in the windows.

'We are on the outskirts of Lee,' said my companion. 'We have touched on three English counties in our short drive, starting in Middlesex, passing over an angle of Surrey, and ending in Kent. See that light among the trees? That is The Cedars, and beside that lamp sits a woman whose anxious ears have already, I have little doubt, caught the clink of our horse's feet.'

'But why are you not conducting the case from Baker Street?' I asked.

'Because there are many inquiries which must be made out here. Mrs St Clair has most kindly put two rooms at my disposal, and you may rest assured that she will have nothing but a welcome for my friend and colleague. I hate to meet her, Watson, when I have no news of her husband. Here we are. Whoa, there, whoa!'

We had pulled up in front of a large villa which stood within its own grounds. A stable-boy had run out to the horse's head, and springing down I followed Holmes up the small, winding gravel-drive which led to the house. As we approached, the door flew open, and a little blonde woman stood in the opening, clad in some sort of light mousseline de soie, with a touch of fluffy pink chiffon at her neck and wrists. She stood with her figure outlined against the flood of light, one hand upon the door, one half-raised in her eagerness, her body slightly bent, her head and face protruded, with eager eyes and parted lips, a standing question.

'Well?' she cried, 'well?' And then, seeing that there were two of us, she gave a cry of hope which sank into a groan as she saw that my companion shook his head and shrugged his shoulders.

'No good news?'

'None.'

'No bad?'

'No.'

'Thank God for that. But come in. You must be weary, for you have had a long day.'

'This is my friend, Dr Watson. He has been of most vital use to me in several of my cases, and a lucky chance has made it possible for me to bring him out and associate him with this investigation.'

'I am delighted to see you,' said she, pressing my hand warmly. 'You will, I am sure, forgive anything that may be wanting in our arrangements, when you consider the blow which has come so suddenly upon us.'

'My dear madam,' said I, 'I am an old campaigner, and if I were not I can very well see that no apology is needed. If I can be of any assistance, either to you or to my friend here, I shall be indeed happy.'

'Now, Mr Sherlock Holmes,' said the lady as we entered a well-lit dining-room, upon the table of which a cold supper had been laid out, 'I should very much like to ask you one or two plain questions, to which I beg that you will give a plain answer.'

'Certainly, madam.'

'Do not trouble about my feelings. I am not hysterical, nor given to fainting. I simply wish to hear your real, real opinion.'

'Upon what point?'

'In your heart of hearts, do you think that Neville is alive?'

Sherlock Holmes seemed to be embarrassed by the question. 'Frankly, now!' she repeated, standing upon the rug and looking keenly down at him as he leaned back in a basket-chair.

'Frankly, then, madam, I do not.'

'You think that he is dead?'

'I do.'

'Murdered?'

'I don't say that. Perhaps.'

'And on what day did he meet his death?'

'On Monday.'

'Then perhaps, Mr Holmes, you will be good enough to explain how it is that I have received a letter from him to-day.'

Sherlock Holmes sprang out of his chair as if he had been galvanised. 'What!' he roared.

'Yes, to-day.' She stood smiling, holding up a little slip of paper in the air.

'May I see it?'

'Certainly.'

He snatched it from her in his eagerness, and smoothing it out upon the table he drew over the lamp and examined it intently. I had left my chair and was gazing at it over his shoulder. The envelope was a very coarse one and was stamped with the Gravesend postmark and with the date of that very day, or rather of the day before, for it was considerably after midnight.

'Coarse writing,' murmured Holmes. 'Surely this is not your husband's writing, madam.'

'No, but the enclosure is.'

'I perceive also that whoever addressed the envelope had to go and inquire as to the address.'

'How can you tell that?'

'The name, you see, is in perfectly black ink, which has dried itself. The rest is of the greyish colour, which shows that blotting-paper has been used. If it had been written straight off, and then blotted, none would be of a deep black shade. This man has written the name, and there has then been a pause before he wrote the address, which can only mean that he was not familiar with it. It is, of course, a trifle, but there is nothing so important as trifles. Let us now see the letter. Ha! there has been an enclosure here!'

'Yes, there was a ring. His signet-ring.'

'And you are sure that this is your husband's hand?'

'One of his hands.'

'One?'

'His hand when he wrote hurriedly. It is very unlike his usual writing, and yet, I know it well.'

'"Dearest do not be frightened. All will come well. There is a huge error which it may take some little time to rectify. Wait in patience.

'"NEVILLE".

'Written in pencil upon the fly-leaf of a book, octavo size, no water-mark. Hum! Posted to-day in Gravesend by a man with a dirty thumb. Ha! And the flap has been gummed, if I am not very much in error, by a person who had been chewing tobacco. And you have no doubt that it is your husband's hand, madam?'

'None. Neville wrote those words.'

'And they were posted to-day at Gravesend. Well, Mrs St Clair, the clouds lighten, though I should not venture to say that the danger is over.'

'But he must be alive, Mr Holmes.'

'Unless this is a clever forgery to put us on the wrong scent. The ring, after all, proves nothing. It may have been taken from him.'

'No, no; it is, it is his very own writing!'

'Very well. It may, however, have been written on Monday and only posted to-day.'

'That is possible.'

'If so, much may have happened between.'

'Oh, you must not discourage me, Mr Holmes. I know that all is well with him. There is so keen a sympathy between us that I should know if evil came upon him. On the very day that I saw him last he cut himself in the bedroom, and yet I in the dining-room rushed upstairs instantly with the utmost certainty that something had happened. Do you think that I would respond to such a trifle and yet be ignorant of his death?'

'I have seen too much not to know that the impression of a woman may be more valuable than the conclusion of an analytical reasoner. And in this letter you certainly have a very strong piece of evidence to corroborate your view. But if your husband is alive and able to write letters, why should he remain away from you?'

'I cannot imagine. It is unthinkable.'

'And on Monday he made no remarks before leaving you?'

'No.'

'And you were surprised to see him in Swandam Lane?'

'Very much so.'

'Was the window open?'

'Yes.'

'Then he might have called to you?'

'He might.'

'He only, as I understand, gave an inarticulate cry?'

'Yes.'

'A call for help, you thought?'

'Yes. He waved his hands.'

'But it might have been a cry of surprise. Astonishment at the unexpected sight of you might cause him to throw up his hands?'

'It is possible.'

'And you thought he was pulled back?'

'He disappeared so suddenly.'

'He might have leaped back. You did not see anyone else in the room?'

'No, but this horrible man confessed to having been there, and the lascar was at the foot of the stairs.'

'Quite so. Your husband, as far as you could see, had his ordinary clothes on?'

'But without his collar or tie. I distinctly saw his bare throat.'

'Had he ever spoken of Swandam Lane?'

'Never.'

'Had he ever showed any signs of having taken opium?'

'Never.'

'Thank you, Mrs St Clair. Those are the principal points about which I wished to be absolutely clear. We shall now have a little supper and then retire, for we may have a very busy day to-morrow.'

A large and comfortable double-bedded room had been placed at our disposal, and I was quickly between the sheets, for I was weary after my night of adventure. Sherlock Holmes was a man, however, who, when he had an unsolved problem upon his mind, would go for days, and even for a week, without rest, turning it over, rearranging his facts, looking at it from every point of view until he had either fathomed it or convinced himself that his data were insufficient. It was soon evident to me that he was now preparing for an all-night sitting. He took off his coat and waistcoat, put on a large blue dressing-gown, and then wandered about the room collecting pillows from his bed and cushions from the sofa and armchairs. With these he constructed a sort of Eastern divan, upon which he perched himself cross-legged, with an ounce of shag tobacco and a box of matches laid out in front of him. In the dim light of the lamp I saw him sitting there, an old briar pipe between his lips, his eyes fixed vacantly upon the corner of the ceiling, the blue smoke curling up from him, silent, motionless, with the light shining upon his strong-set aquiline features. So he sat as I dropped off to sleep, and so he sat when a sudden ejaculation caused me to wake up, and I found the summer sun shining into the apartment. The pipe was still between his lips, the smoke still curled upward, and the room was full of a dense tobacco haze, but nothing remained of the heap of shag which I had seen upon the previous night.

'Awake, Watson?' he asked.

'Yes.'

'Game for a morning drive?'

'Certainly.'

'Then dress. No one is stirring yet, but I know where the stable-boy sleeps, and we shall soon have the trap out.' He chuckled to himself as he spoke, his eyes twinkled, and he seemed a different man to the sombre thinker of the previous night.

As I dressed I glanced at my watch. It was no wonder that no one was stirring. It was twenty-five minutes past four. I had hardly finished when Holmes returned with the news that the boy was putting in the horse.

'I want to test a little theory of mine,' said he, pulling on his boots. 'I think, Watson, that you are now standing in the presence of one of the most absolute fools in Europe. I deserve to be kicked from here to Charing Cross. But I think I have the key of the affair now.'

'And where is it?' I asked, smiling.

'In the bathroom,' he answered. 'Oh, yes, I am not joking,' he continued, seeing my look of incredulity. 'I have just been there, and I have taken it out, and I have got it in this Gladstone bag. Come on, my boy, and we shall see whether it will not fit the lock.'

We made our way downstairs as quietly as possible, and out into the bright morning sunshine. In the road stood our horse and trap, with the half-clad stable-boy waiting at the head. We both sprang in, and away we dashed down the London Road. A few country carts were stirring, bearing in vegetables to the metropolis, but the lines of villas on either side were as silent and lifeless as some city in a dream.

'It has been in some points a singular case,' said Holmes, flicking the horse on into a gallop. 'I confess that I have been as blind as a mole, but it is better to learn wisdom late than never to learn it at all.'

In town the earliest risers were just beginning to look sleepily from their windows as we drove through the streets of the Surrey side. Passing down the Waterloo Bridge Road we crossed over the river, and dashing up Wellington Street wheeled sharply to the right and found ourselves in Bow Street. Sherlock Holmes was well known to the force, and the two constables at the door saluted him. One of them held the horse's head while the other led us in.

'Who is on duty?' asked Holmes.

'Inspector Bradstreet, sir.'

'Ah, Bradstreet, how are you?' A tall, stout official had come down the stone-flagged passage, in a peaked cap and frogged jacket. 'I wish to have a quiet word with you, Bradstreet.'

'Certainly, Mr Holmes. Step into my room here.'

It was a small, office-like room, with a huge ledger upon the table, and a telephone projecting from the wall. The inspector sat down at his desk.

'What can I do for you, Mr Holmes?'

'I called about that beggarman, Boone—the one who was charged with being concerned in the disappearance of Mr Neville St Clair, of Lee.'

'Yes. He was brought up and remanded for further inquiries.'

'So I heard. You have him here?'

'In the cells.'

'Is he quiet?'

'Oh, he gives no trouble. But he is a dirty scoundrel.'

'Dirty?'

'Yes, it is all we can do to make him wash his hands, and his face is as black as a tinker's. Well, when once his case has been settled, he will have a regular prison bath; and I think, if you saw him, you would agree with me that he needed it.'

'I should like to see him very much.'

'Would you? That is easily done. Come this way. You can leave your bag.'

'No, I think that I'll take it.'

'Very good. Come this way, if you please.' He led us down a passage, opened a barred door, passed down a winding stair, and brought us to a whitewashed corridor with a line of doors on each side.

'The third on the right is his,' said the inspector. 'Here it is!' He quietly shot back a panel in the upper part of the door and glanced through.

'He is asleep,' said he. 'You can see him very well.'

We both put our eyes to the grating. The prisoner lay with his face towards us, in a very deep sleep, breathing slowly and heavily. He was a middle-sized man, coarsely clad as became his calling, with a coloured shirt protruding through the rent in his tattered coat. He was, as the inspector had said, extremely dirty, but the grime which covered his face could not conceal its repulsive ugliness. A broad wheal from an old scar ran right across it from eye to chin, and by its contraction had turned up one side of the upper lip, so that three teeth were exposed in a perpetual snarl. A shock of very bright red hair grew low over his eyes and forehead.

'He's a beauty, isn't he?' said the inspector.

'He certainly needs a wash,' remarked Holmes. 'I had an idea that he might, and I took the liberty of bringing the tools with me.' He opened the Gladstone bag as he spoke, and took out, to my astonishment, a very large bath-sponge.

'He! he! You are a funny one,' chuckled the inspector.

'Now, if you will have the great goodness to open that door very quietly, we will soon make him cut a much more respectable figure.'

'Well, I don't know why not,' said the inspector. 'He doesn't look a credit to the Bow Street cells, does he?' He slipped his key into the lock, and we all very quietly entered the cell. The sleeper half turned, and then settled down once more into a deep slumber. Holmes stooped to the water-jug, moistened his sponge, and then rubbed it twice vigorously across and down the prisoner's face.

'Let me introduce you,' he shouted, 'to Mr Neville St Clair, of Lee, in the county of Kent.'

Never in my life have I seen such a sight. The man's face peeled off under the sponge like the bark from a tree. Gone was the coarse brown tint! Gone, too, was the horrid scar which had seamed it across, and the twisted lip which had given the repulsive sneer to the face! A twitch brought away the tangled red hair, and there, sitting up in his bed, was a pale, sad-faced, refined-looking man, black-haired and smooth-skinned, rubbing his eyes and staring about him with sleepy bewilderment. Then suddenly realising the exposure, he broke into a scream and threw himself down with his face to the pillow.

'Great heavens!' cried the inspector, 'it is, indeed, the missing man. I know him from the photograph.'

The prisoner turned with the reckless air of a man who abandons himself to his destiny. 'Be it so,' said he. 'And pray, what am I charged with?'

'With making away with Mr Neville St—Oh, come, you can't be charged with that unless they make a case of attempted suicide of it,' said the inspector with a grin. 'Well, I have been twenty-seven years in the force, but this really takes the cake.'

'If I am Mr Neville St Clair, then it is obvious that no crime has been committed, and that, therefore, I am illegally detained.'

'No crime, but a very great error has been committed,' said Holmes. 'You would have done better to have trusted your wife.'

'It was not the wife; it was the children,' groaned the prisoner. 'God help me, I would not have them ashamed of their father. My God! What an exposure! What can I do?'

Sherlock Holmes sat down beside him on the couch and patted him kindly on the shoulder.

'If you leave it to a court of law to clear the matter up,' said he, 'of course you can hardly avoid publicity. On the other hand, if you convince the police authorities that there is no possible case against you, I do not know that there is any reason that the details should find their way into the papers. Inspector Bradstreet would, I am sure, make notes upon anything which you might tell us and submit it to the proper authorities. The case would then never go into court at all.'

'God bless you!' cried the prisoner passionately. 'I would have endured imprisonment, ay, even execution, rather than have left my miserable secret as a family blot to my children.

'You are the first who have ever heard my story. My father was a school-master in Chesterfield, where I received an excellent education. I travelled in my youth, took to the stage, and finally became a reporter on an evening paper in London. One day my editor wished to have a series of articles upon begging in the metropolis, and I volunteered to supply them. There was the point from which all my adventures started. It was only by trying begging as an amateur that I could get the facts upon which to base my articles. When an actor I had, of course, learned all the secrets of making up, and had been famous in the green-room for my skill. I took advantage now of my attainments. I painted my face, and to make myself as pitiable as possible I made a good scar and fixed one side of my lip in a twist by the aid of a small slip of flesh-coloured plaster. Then with a red head of hair, and an appropriate dress, I took my station in the business part of the City, ostensibly as a match-seller but really as a beggar. For seven hours I plied my trade, and when I returned home in the evening I found to my surprise that I had received no less than 26s. 4d.

'I wrote my articles and thought little more of the matter until, some time later, I backed a bill for a friend and had a writ served upon me for £25. I was at my wits' end where to get the money, but a sudden idea came to me. I begged a fortnight's grace from the creditor, asked for a holiday from my employers, and spent the time in begging in the City under my disguise. In ten days I had the money and had paid the debt.

'Well, you can imagine how hard it was to settle down to arduous work at £2 a week when I knew that I could earn as much in a day by smearing my face with a little paint, laying my cap on the ground, and sitting still. It was a long fight between my pride and the money, but the dollars won at last, and I threw up reporting and sat day after day in the corner which I had first chosen, inspiring pity by my ghastly face and filling my pockets with coppers. Only one man knew my secret. He was the keeper of a low den in which I used to lodge in Swandam Lane, where I could every morning emerge as a squalid beggar and in the evenings transform myself into a well-dressed man about town. This fellow, a lascar, was well paid by me for his rooms, so that I knew that my secret was safe in his possession.

'Well, very soon I found that I was saving considerable sums of money. I do not mean that any beggar in the streets of London could earn £700 a year—which is less than my average takings—but I had exceptional advantages in my power of making up, and also in a facility of repartee, which improved by practice and made me quite a recognised character in the City. All day a stream of pennies, varied by silver, poured in upon me, and it was a very bad day in which I failed to take £2.

'As I grew richer I grew more ambitious, took a house in the country, and eventually married, without anyone having a suspicion as to my real occupation. My dear wife knew that I had business in the City. She little knew what.

'Last Monday I had finished for the day and was dressing in my room above the opium den when I looked out of my window and saw, to my horror and astonishment, that my wife was standing in the street, with her eyes fixed full upon me. I gave a cry of surprise, threw up my arms to cover my face, and, rushing to my confidant, the lascar, entreated him to prevent anyone from coming up to me. I heard her voice downstairs, but I knew that she could not ascend. Swiftly I threw off my clothes, pulled on those of a beggar, and put on my pigments and wig. Even a wife's eyes could not pierce so complete a disguise. But then it occurred to me that there might be a search in the room, and that the clothes might betray me. I threw open the window, reopening by my violence a small cut which I had inflicted upon myself in the bedroom that morning. Then I seized my coat, which was weighted by the coppers which I had just transferred to it from the leather bag in which I carried my takings. I hurled it out of the window, and it disappeared into the Thames. The other clothes would have followed, but at that moment there was a rush of constables up the stairs, and a few minutes after I found, rather, I confess, to my relief, that instead of being identified as Mr Neville St Clair, I was arrested as his murderer.

'I do not know that there is anything else for me to explain. I was determined to preserve my disguise as long as possible, and hence my preference for a dirty face. Knowing that my wife would be terribly anxious, I slipped off my ring and confided it to the lascar at a moment when no constable was watching me, together with a hurried scrawl, telling her that she had no cause to fear.'

'That note only reached her yesterday,' said Holmes.

'Good God! What a week she must have spent.'

'The police have watched this lascar,' said Inspector Bradstreet, 'and I can quite understand that he might find it difficult to post a letter unobserved. Probably he handed it to some sailor customer of his, who forgot all about it for some days.'

'That was it,' said Holmes, nodding approvingly; 'I have no doubt of it. But have you never been prosecuted for begging?'

'Many times; but what was a fine to me?'

'It must stop here, however,' said Bradstreet. 'If the police are to hush this thing up, there must be no more of Hugh Boone.'

'I have sworn it by the most solemn oaths which a man can take.'

'In that case I think that it is probable that no further steps may be taken. But if you are found again, then all must come out. I am sure, Mr Holmes, that we are very much indebted to you for having cleared the matter up. I wish I knew how you reach your results.'

'I reached this one,' said my friend, 'by sitting upon five pillows and consuming an ounce of shag. I think, Watson, that if we drive to Baker Street we shall just be in time for breakfast.'

Stanley Ellin
1916–1986

THE BETRAYERS

BETWEEN THEM was a wall. And since it was only a flimsy, jerry-built partition, a sounding board between apartments, Robert came to know the girl that way.

At first she was the sound of footsteps, the small firm rap of high heels moving in a pattern of activity around her room. She must be very young, he thought idly, because at the time he was deep in *Green Mansions*, pursuing the lustrous Rima through a labyrinth of Amazonian jungle. Later he came to know her voice, light and breathless when she spoke, warm and gay when she raised it in chorus to some popular song dinning from her radio. She must be very lovely, he thought then, and after that found himself listening deliberately, and falling more and more in love with her as he listened.

Her name was Amy, and there was a husband, too, a man called Vince who had a flat, unpleasant voice, and a sullen way about him. Occasionally there were quarrels which the man invariably ended by slamming the door of their room and thundering down the stairs as loud as he could. Then she would cry, a smothered whimpering, and Robert, standing close to the wall between them, would feel as if a hand had been thrust inside his chest and was twisting his heart. He would think wildly of the few steps that would take him to her door, the few words that would let her know he was her friend, was willing to do something—anything—to help her. Perhaps, meeting face to face, she would recognise his love. Perhaps—

So the thoughts whirled around and around, but Robert only stood there, taut with helplessness.

And there was no one to confide in, which made it that much harder. The only acquaintances he numbered in the world were the other men in his office, and they would never have understood.

He worked, prosaically enough, in the credit department of one of the city's largest department stores, and too many years there had ground the men around him to a fine edge of cynicism. The business of digging into people's records, of searching for the tax difficulties, the clandestine affairs with expensive women, the touch of larceny in every human being—all that was bound to have an effect, they told Robert, and if he stayed on the job much longer he'd find it out for himself.

What would they tell him now? *A pretty girl next door? Husband's away most of the time? Go on, make yourself at home!*

How could he make them understand that that wasn't what he was looking for? That what he wanted was someone to meet his love halfway, someone to put an end to the cold loneliness that settled in him like a stone during the dark hours each night.

So he said nothing about it to anyone, but stayed close to the wall, drawing from it what he could. And knowing the girl as he had come to, he was not surprised when he finally saw her. The mail for all the apartments was left on a table in the downstairs hallway, and as he walked down the stairs to go to work that morning, he saw her take a letter from the table and start up the stairway toward him.

There was never any question in his mind that this was the girl. She was small and fragile and dark-haired, and all the loveliness he had imagined in her from the other side of the wall was there in her face. She was wearing a loose robe, and as she passed him on the stairway she pulled the robe closer to her breast and slipped by almost as if she were afraid of him. He realised with a start that he had been staring unashamedly, and with his face red he turned down the stairs to the street. But he walked the rest of his way in a haze of wonderment.

He saw her a few times after that, always under the same conditions, but it took weeks before he mustered enough courage to stop at the foot of the stairs and turn to watch her retreating form above: the lovely fine line of ankle, the roundness of calf, the curve of body pressing against the robe. And then as she reached the head of the stairs, as if aware he was watching her, she looked down at him and their eyes met.

For a heart-stopping moment Robert tried to understand what he read in her face, and then her husband's voice came flat and belligerent from the room. 'Amy,' it said, 'what's holdin' you up!'—and she was gone, and the moment with her.

When he saw the husband he marveled that she had chosen someone like that. A small, dapper game-cock of a man, he was good-looking in a hard way, but with the skin drawn so tight over his face that the cheekbones jutted sharply and the lips were drawn into a thin menacing line. He glanced at Robert up and down out of the corners of blank eyes as they passed, and in that instant Robert understood part of what he had seen in the girl's face. This man was as danger-ous as some half-tamed animal that would snap at any hand laid on him, no matter what its intent. Just being near him you could smell danger, as surely the girl did her every waking hour.

The violence in the man exploded one night with force enough to waken Robert from a deep sleep. It was not the pitch of the voice, Robert realised, sitting up half-dazed in bed, because the words were almost inaudible through the wall; it was the vicious intensity that was so frightening.

He slipped out of bed and laid his ear against the wall. Standing like that, his eyes closed while he strained to follow the choppy phrases, he could picture the couple facing each other as vividly as if the wall had dissolved before him.

'*So you know,*' the man said. '*So what?*'

'*. . . getting out!*' the girl said.

'*And then tell everybody? Tell the whole world?*'

'*I won't!*' The girl was crying now. '*I swear I won't!*'

'*Think I'd take a chance?*' the man said, and then his voice turned soft and derisive. '*Ten thousand dollars,*' he said. '*Where else could I get it? Digging ditches?*'

'*Better that way! This way . . . I'm getting out!*'

His answer was not delivered in words. It came in the form of a blow so hard that when she reeled back and struck the wall, the impact stung Robert's face.

'*Vince!*' she screamed, the sound high and quavering with terror. '*Don't, Vince!*'

Every nerve in Robert was alive now with her pain as the next blow was struck. His fingernails dug into the wall at the hard-breathing noises of scuffling behind it as she was pulled away.

'*Ahh, no!*' she cried out, and then there was the sound of a breath being drawn hoarsely and agonisingly into lungs no longer responsive to it, the thud of a flaccid weight striking the floor, and suddenly silence. A terrible silence.

As if the wall itself were her cold, dead flesh Robert recoiled from it, then stood staring at it in horror. His thoughts twisted and turned on themselves insanely, but out of them loomed one larger and larger so that he had to face it and recognise it.

She had been murdered, and as surely as though he had been standing there beside her he was a witness to it! He had been so close that if the wall were not there he could have reached out his hand and touched her. Done something to help her. Instead, he had waited like a fool until it was too late.

But there was still something to be done, he told himself wildly. And long as this madman in the next room had no idea there was a witness he could still be taken red-handed. A call to the police, and in five minutes . . .

But before he could take the first nerveless step Robert heard the room next door stealthily come to life again. There was a sound of surreptitious motion, of things being shifted from their place, then, clearly defined, a lifeless weight being pulled along the floor, and the cautious creaking of a door opened wide. It was that last sound which struck Robert with a sick comprehension of what was happening.

The murderer was a monster, but he was no fool. If he could safely dispose of the body now during these silent hours of the night he was, to all intents and purposes, a man who had committed no crime at all!

At his door Robert stopped short. From the hallway came the deliberate thump of feet finding their way down the stairs with the weight dragging behind them. The man had killed once. He was reckless enough in this crisis to risk being seen with his victim. What would such a man do to anyone who confronted him at such a time?

Robert leaned back against his door, his eyes closed tight, a choking constriction in his throat as if the man's hands were already around it. He was a coward, there was no way around it. Faced with the need to show some courage he had discovered he was a rank coward, and he saw the girl's face before him now, not with fear in it, but contempt.

But—and the thought gave him a quick sense of triumph—he could still go to the police. He saw himself doing it, and the sense of triumph faded away. He had heard some noises, and from that he had constructed a murder. The body? There would be none. The murderer? None. Only a man whose wife had left him because he had quarreled with her. The accuser? A young man who had wild dreams. A perfect fool. In short, Robert himself.

It was only when he heard the click of the door downstairs that he stepped out into the hallway and started down, step by careful step. Halfway down he saw it, a handkerchief, small and crumpled and blotched with an ugly stain. He picked it up gingerly, and holding it up toward the dim light overhead let it fall open. The stain was bright sticky red almost obscuring in one corner the word *Amy* carefully embroidered there. Blood. *Her* blood. Wouldn't that be evidence enough for anyone?

Sure, he could hear the policeman answer him jeeringly, *evidence of a nose-bleed, all right*, and he could feel the despair churn in him.

It was the noise of the car that roused him, and then he flew down the rest of the stairs, but too late. As he pressed his face to the curtain of the front door the car roared away from the curb, its tail-lights gleaming like malevolent eyes, its license plate impossible to read in the dark. If he had only been an instant quicker, he raged at himself, only had sense enough to understand that the killer must use a car for his purpose, he could easily have identified it. Now, even that chance was gone. Every chance was gone.

He was in his room pacing the floor feverishly when within a half-hour he heard the furtive sounds of the murderer's return. *And why not*, Robert thought; *he's gotten rid of her, he's safe now, he can go on as if nothing at all had happened.*

If I were only someone who could go into the room and beat the truth out of him, the thought boiled on, *or someone with such wealth or position that I would be listened to . . .*

But all that was as unreal and vaporous as his passion for the girl had been. What weapon of vengeance could he possibly have at his command, a nobody working, in a . . .

Robert felt the sudden realisation wash over him in a cold wave. His eyes narrowed on the wall as if, word by word, the idea were being written on it in a minute hand.

Everyone has a touch of larceny in him—wasn't that what the old hands in his department were always saying? Everyone was suspect. Certainly the man next door, with his bent for violence, his talk of ten thousand dollars come by in some unlikely way, must have black marks on his record that the authorities, blind as they might be, could recognise and act on. If someone skilled in investigation were to strip the man's past down, layer by layer, justice would have to be done. That was the weapon: the dark past itself stored away in the man, waiting only to be ignited!

Slowly and thoughtfully Robert slipped the girl's crumpled handkerchief into an envelope and sealed it. Then, straining to remember the exact words, he wrote down on paper the last violent duologue between murderer and victim. Paper and envelope both went into a drawer of his dresser, and the first step had been taken.

But then, Robert asked himself, what did he know about the man? His name was Vince, and that was all. Hardly information which could serve as the starting point of a search through the dark corridors of someone's past. There must be something more than that, something to serve as a lead.

It took Robert the rest of a sleepless night to hit on the idea of the landlady. A stout and sleepy-eyed woman whose only interest in life seemed to lie in the prompt collection of her rent, she still must have some information about the man. She occupied the rear apartment on the ground floor, and as early in the morning as he dared Robert knocked on her door.

She looked more sleepy-eyed than ever as she pondered his question. 'Them?' she said at last. 'That's the Sniders. Nice people, all right.' She blinked at Robert. 'Not having any trouble with them, are you?'

'No. Not at all. But is that all you can tell me about them? I mean, don't you know where they're from, or anything like that?'

The landlady shrugged. 'I'm sure it's none of my business,' she said loftily. 'All I know is they pay on the first of the month right on the dot, and they're nice respectable people.'

He turned away from her heavily, and as he did so he saw the street door close behind the postman. It was as if a miracle had been passed for him. The landlady was gone, he was all alone with that little heap of mail on the table, and there staring up at him was an envelope neatly addressed to Mrs Vincent Snider.

All the way to his office he kept that envelope hidden away in an inside pocket, and it was only when he was locked in the seclusion of his cubicle that he carefully slit it open and studied its contents. A single page with only a few lines on it, a noncommittal message about the family's well-being, and the signature: *Your sister, Celia*. Not much to go on—but wait, there was a return address on the stationery, an address in a small upstate town.

Robert hesitated only a moment, then thrust letter and envelope into his pocket, straightened his jacket, and walked into the office of his superior. Mr Sprague, in charge of the department and consequently the most ulcerated and cynical member of it, regarded him dourly.

'Yes?' he said.

'I'm sorry, sir,' said Robert, 'but I'll need a few days off. You see, there's been a sudden death.'

Mr Sprague sighed at this pebble cast into the smooth pool of his department's routine, but his face fell into the proper sympathetic lines.

'Somebody close?'

'Very close,' said Robert.

THE WALK from the railroad station to the house was a short one. The house itself had a severe and forbidding air about it, as did the young woman who opened the door in answer to Robert's knock.

'Yes,' she said, 'my sister's name is Amy Snider. Her married name, that is. I'm Celia Thompson.'

'What I'm looking for,' Robert said, 'is some information about her. About your sister.'

The woman looked stricken. 'Something's happened to her?'

'In a way,' Robert said. He cleared his throat hard. 'You see, she's disappeared from her apartment, and I'm looking into it. Now, if you . . .'

'You're from the police?'

'I'm acting for them,' Robert said, and prayed that this ambiguity would serve in place of identification. The prayer was answered, the woman gestured him into the house, and sat down facing him in the bare and uninviting living room.

'I knew,' the woman said, 'I knew something would happen,' and she rocked piteously from side to side in her chair.

Robert reached forward and touched her hand gently. 'How did you know?'

'How? What else could you expect when you drive a child out of her home and slam the door in her face! When you throw her out into the world not even knowing how to take care of herself?'

Robert withdrew his hand abruptly. 'You did *that*?'

'My father did it. *Her* father.'

'But why?'

'If you knew him,' the woman said. 'A man who thinks anything pretty is sinful. A man who's so scared of hellfire and brimstone that he's kept us in it all our lives!

'When she started to get so pretty, and the boys pestering her all the time, he turned against her just like that. And when she had her trouble with that man he threw her out of the house, bag and baggage. And if he knew I was writing letters to her,' the woman said fearfully, 'he'd throw me out, too. I can't even say her name in front of him, the way he is.'

'Look,' Robert said eagerly, 'that man she had trouble with. Was that the one she married? That Vincent Snider?'

'I don't know,' the woman said vaguely. 'I just don't know. Nobody knows except Amy and my father, the way it was kept such a secret. I didn't even know she was married until all of a sudden she wrote me a letter about it from the city.'

'But if your father knows, I can talk to him about it.'

'No! You can't! If he even knew I told you as much as I did . . .'

'But I can't let it go at that,' he pleaded. 'I have to find out about this man, and then maybe we can straighten everything out.'

'All right,' the woman said wearily, 'there is somebody. But not my father, you've got to keep away from him for my sake. There's this teacher over at the high school, this Miss Benson. She's the one to see. And she liked Amy; she's the one Amy mails my letters to, so my father won't know. Maybe she'll tell you, even if she won't tell anybody else. I'll write you a note to her, and you go see her.'

At the door he thanked her, and she regarded him with a hard, straight look. 'You have to be pretty to get yourself in trouble,' she said, 'so its something that'll never bother me. But you find Amy, and you make sure she's all right.'

'Yes,' Robert said. 'I'll try.'

At the school he was told that Miss Benson was the typewriting teacher, that she had classes until three, and that if he wished to speak to her alone he would have to wait until then. So for hours he fretfully walked the few main streets of the town, oblivious of the curious glances of passers-by, and thinking of Amy. These were the streets she had known. These shop windows had mirrored her image. And, he thought with a sharp jealousy, not always alone. There had been boys. Attracted to her, as boys would be, but careless of her, never realising the prize they had. But if he had known her then, if he could have been one of them . . .

At three o'clock he waited outside the school building until it had emptied, and then went in eagerly. Miss Benson was a small woman, gray-haired and fluttering, almost lost among the grim ranks of hooded typewriters in the room. After Robert had explained himself and she had read Celia Thompson's note she seemed ready to burst into tears.

'It's wrong of her!' she said. 'It's dreadfully wrong of her to send you to me. She must have known that.'

'But why is it wrong?'

'Why? Because she knows I don't want to talk about it to anyone. She knows what it would cost me if I did, that's why!'

'Look,' Robert said patiently, 'I'm not trying to find out what happened. I'm only trying to find out about this man Amy had trouble with, what his name is, where he comes from, where I can get more information about him.'

'No,' Miss Benson quavered, 'I'm sorry.'

'Sorry,' Robert said angrily. 'A girl disappears, this man may be at the bottom of it, and, all you can do is say you're sorry!'

Miss Benson's jaw went slack. 'You mean that he—that he *did* something to her?'

'Yes,' Robert said, 'he did,' and had to quickly catch her arm as she swayed unsteadily, apparently on the verge of fainting.

'I should have known,' she said lifelessly. 'I should have known when it happened that it might come to this. But at the time . . .'

At the time the girl had been one of her students. A good student—not brilliant, mind you—but a nice girl always trying to do her best. And well brought-up, too, not like so many of the young snips you get nowadays.

That very afternoon when it all happened the girl herself had told Miss Benson she was going to the Principal's office after school hours to get her program straightened out. Certainly if she meant to do anything wicked she wouldn't have mentioned that, would she? Wasn't that all the evidence anyone needed?

'Evidence?' Robert said in bewilderment.

Yes, evidence. There had been that screaming in the Principal's office, and Miss Benson had been the only one left in the whole school. She had run to the office, flung open the door, and that was how she found them. The girl sobbing hysterically, her dress torn halfway down; Mr Price standing behind her, glaring at the open door, at the incredulous Miss Benson.

'Mr Price?' Robert said. He had the sense of swimming numbly through some gelatinous depths, unable to see anything clearly.

Mr Price, the Principal, of course. He stood glaring at her, his face ashen. Then the girl had fled through the door and Mr Price had taken one step after her, but had stopped short. He had pulled Miss Benson into the office, and closed the door, and then he had talked to her.

The long and the short of what he told her was that the girl was a wanton. She had waltzed into his office, threatened him with blackmail, and when he had put her into her place she had artfully acted out her little scene. But he would be merciful, very merciful. Rather than call in the authorities and blacken the name of the school and of her decent, respectable father he would simply expel her and advise her father to get her out of town promptly.

And, Mr Price had remarked meaningfully, it was a lucky thing indeed that Miss Benson had walked in just in time to be his witness. Although if Miss Benson failed him as a witness it could be highly unlucky for her.

'And he meant it,' Miss Benson said bitterly. 'It's his family runs the town and everything in it. If I said anything of what I really thought, if I dared open my mouth, I'd never get another job anywhere. But I should have talked up, I know I should have, especially after what happened next!'

She had managed to get back to her room at the far end of the corridor although she had no idea of where she got the strength. And as soon as she had entered the room she saw the girl there, lying on the floor beneath the bulletin board from which usually hung the sharp, cutting scissors. But the scissors were in the girl's clenched fist as she lay there, and blood over everything. All that blood over everything.

'She was like that,' Miss Benson said dully. 'If you reprimanded her for even the littlest thing she looked like she wanted to sink through the floor, to die on the spot. And after what she went through it must have been the first thing in her head; just to get rid of herself. It was a mercy of God that she didn't succeed then and there.'

It was Miss Benson who got the doctor, a discreet man, who asked no questions, and it was she who tended the girl after her father had barred his door to her.

'And when she could get around,' Miss Benson said, 'I placed her with this office over at the county seat. She wasn't graduated, of course, or really expert, but I gave her a letter explaining she had been in some trouble and needed a helping hand, and they gave her a job.'

Miss Benson dug her fingers into her forehead. 'If I had only talked up when I should have. I should have known he'd never feel safe, that he'd hound her and hound her until he . . .'

'But he isn't the one!' Robert said hoarsely. 'He isn't the right man at all!'

She looked at him wonderingly. 'But you said . . .'

'No,' Robert said helplessly. 'I'm looking for someone else. A different man altogether.'

She shrank back. 'You've been trying to fool me!'

'I swear I haven't.'

'But it doesn't matter,' she whispered. 'If you say a word about this nobody'll believe you. I'll tell them you were lying, you made the whole thing up!'

'You won't have to,' Robert said. 'All you have to do is tell me where you sent her for that job. If you do that you can forget everything else.'

She hesitated, studying his face with bright, frightened eyes. 'All right,' she said at last. 'All right.'

He was about to go when she placed her hand anxiously on his arm. 'Please,' she said. 'You don't think unkindly of me because of all this, do you?'

'No,' Robert said, 'I don't have the right to.'

The bus trip which filled the remainder of the day was a wearing one, the hotel bed that night was no great improvement over the bus seat, and Mr Pardee of *Grace, Grace, & Pardee* seemed to Robert the hardest of all to take. He was a cheery man, too loud and florid to be properly contained by his small office.

He studied Robert's business card with interest. 'Credit research, eh?' he said admiringly. 'Wonderful how you fellas track 'em down wherever they are. Sort of a Northwest Mounted Police just working to keep business healthy, that's what it comes to, doesn't it? And anything I can do to help . . .'

Yes, he remembered the girl very well.

'Just about the prettiest little thing we ever had around here,' he said pensively. 'Didn't know much about her job, of course, but you got your money's worth just watching her walk around the office.'

Robert managed to keep his teeth clenched. 'Was there any man she seemed interested in? Someone around the office, maybe, who wouldn't be working here any more? Or even someone outside you could tell me about?'

Mr Pardee studied the ceiling with narrowed eyes. 'No,' he said, 'nobody I can think of. Must have been plenty of men after her, but you'd never get anything out of her about it. Not with the way she was so secretive and all. Matter of fact, her being that way was one of the things that made all the trouble.'

'Trouble?'

'Oh, nothing serious. Somebody was picking the petty-cash box every so often, and what with all the rest of the office being so friendly except her it looked like she might be the one. And then that letter she brought saying she had already been in some trouble—well, we just had to let her go.'

'Later on,' continued Mr Pardee pleasantly, 'when we found out it wasn't her after all, it was too late. We didn't know where to get in touch with her.' He snapped his fingers loudly. 'Gone, just like that.'

Robert drew a deep breath to steady himself. 'But there must be somebody in the office who knew her,' he pleaded. 'Maybe some girl she talked to.'

'Oh, that,' said Mr Pardee. 'Well, as I said, she wasn't friendly, but now and then she did have her head together with Jenny Rizzo over at the switchboard. If you want to talk to Jenny go right ahead. Anything I can do to help . . .'

But it was Jenny Rizzo who helped him. A plain girl dressed in defiant bad taste, she studied him with impersonal interest and told him coolly that she had nothing to say about Amy. The kid had taken enough kicking around. It was about time they let her alone.

'I'm not interested in her,' Robert said. 'I'm trying to find out about the man she married. Someone named Vincent Snider. Did you know about him?'

From the stricken look on her face Robert realised exultantly that she did.

'Him!' she said. 'So she went and married him, anyhow!'

'What about it?'

'What about it? I told her a hundred times he was no good. I told her just stay away from him.'

'Why?'

'Because I know his kind. Sharp stuff hanging around with money in his pocket, you never knew where it came from. The kind of guy's always pulling fast deals, but he's too smart to get caught, that's why!'

'How well did you know him?'

'How well? I knew him from the time he was a kid around my neighborhood here. Look,' Jenny dug into a desk drawer deep laden with personal possessions. She came out with a handful of snapshots which she thrust at Robert, 'we even used to double-date together, Vince and Amy, and me and my boy friend. Plenty of times I told her right in front of Vince that he was no good, but he gave her such a line she wouldn't even listen. She was like a baby that way; anybody was nice to her she'd go overboard.'

They were not good photographs, but there were Vince and Amy clearly recognisable.

'Could I have one of these?' Robert asked, his voice elaborately casual.

Jenny shrugged. 'Just go ahead and help yourself,' she said, and Robert did.

'Then what happened?' he said. 'I mean, to Vince and Amy?'

'You got me there. After she got fired they both took off. She said something about Vince getting a job downstate a-ways, in Sutton, and that was the last I saw of them. I could just see him working at anything honest, but the way she said it she must have believed him. Anyhow, I never heard from her after that.'

'Could you remember exactly when you saw her last? That time she told you they were going to Sutton?'

Jenny could and did. She might have remembered more, but Robert was out of the door by then, leaving her gaping after him, her mouth wide open in surprise.

The trip to Sutton was barely an hour by bus, but it took another hour before Robert was seated at a large table with the Sutton newspaper files laid out before him. The town's newspaper was a large and respectable one, its files orderly and well kept. And two days after the date Jenny Rizzo had given him there was the news Robert had hoped to find. Headline news emblazoned all across the top of the first page.

Ten thousand dollars stolen, the news report said. A daring, lone bandit had walked into the Sutton Bank and Trust, had bearded the manager without a soul knowing it, and had calmly walked out with a small valise containing ten thousand dollars in currency. The police were on the trail. An arrest was expected momentarily . . .

Robert traced through later dates with his hands shaking. The police had given up in their efforts. No arrest was ever made . . .

ROBERT HAD CAREFULLY scissored the photograph so that Vince now stood alone in the picture. The bank manager irritably looked at the picture, and then swallowed hard.

'It's him!' he told Robert incredulously. 'That's the man! I'd know him anywhere. If I can get my hands on him . . .'

'There's something you'll have to do first,' said Robert.

'I'm not making any deals,' the manager protested. 'I want him, and I want every penny of the money he's got left.'

'I'm not talking about deals,' Robert said. 'All you have to do is put down on paper that you positively identify this man as the one who robbed the bank. If you do that the police'll have him for you tomorrow.'

'That's all?' the man said suspiciously.

'That's all,' Robert said.

HE SAT AGAIN in the familiar room, the papers, the evidence, arranged before him. His one remaining fear had been that in his absence the murderer had somehow taken alarm and fled. He had not breathed easy until the first small, surreptitious noises from next door made clear that things were as he had left them.

Now he carefully studied all the notes he had painstakingly prepared, all the reports of conversations held. It was all here, enough to see justice done, but it was more than that, he told himself bitterly. It was the portrait of a girl who, step by step, had been driven through a pattern of betrayal.

Every man she had dealt with had been an agent of betrayal. Father, school principal, employer, and finally her husband, each was guilty in his turn. Jenny Rizzo's words rang loud in Robert's ears.

Anybody was nice to her she'd go overboard. If he had spoken, if he had moved, he could have been the one. When she turned at the top of the stairs to look at him she might have been waiting for him to speak or move. Now it was too late, and there was no way of letting her know what these papers meant, what he had done for her . . .

The police were everything Robert had expected until they read the bank manager's statement. Then they read and re-read the statement, they looked at the photograph, and they courteously passed Robert from hand to hand until finally there was a door marked *Lieutenant Kyserling*, and behind it a slender, soft-spoken man.

It was a long story—Robert had not realised until then how long it was or how many details there were to explain—but it was told from start to finish without interruption. At its conclusion Kyserling took the papers, the handkerchief, and the photograph, and pored over them. Then he looked at Robert curiously.

'It's all here,' he said. 'The only thing you left out is why you did it, why you went to all this trouble. What's your stake in this?'

It was not easy to have your most private dream exposed to a complete stranger. Robert choked on the words. 'It's because of her. The way I felt about her.'

'Oh.' Kyserling nodded understandingly. 'Making time with her?'

'No,' Robert said angrily. 'We never even spoke to each other!'

Kyserling tapped his fingers gently on the papers before him.

'Well,' he said, 'it's none of my business anyhow. But you've done a pretty job for us. Very pretty. Matter of fact, yesterday we turned up the body in a car parked a few blocks away from your place. The car was stolen a month ago, there wasn't a stitch of identification on the clothing or anything; all we got is a body with a big wound in it. This business could have stayed up in the air for a hundred years if it wasn't for you walking in with a perfect case made out from A to Z.'

'I'm glad,' Robert said. 'That's the way I wanted it.'

'Yeah,' Kyserling said. 'Any time you want a job on the force you just come and see me.'

Then he was gone from the office for a long while, and when he returned it was in the company of a big, stolid plain-clothesman who smiled grimly.

'We're going to wrap it up now,' Kyserling told Robert, and gestured at the man.

They went softly up the stairs of the house and stood to the side of the door while Kyserling laid his ear against it for some assurance of sound. Then he briskly nodded to the plain-clothesman and rapped hard.

'Open up!' he called. 'It's the police.'

There was an ear-ringing silence, and Robert's mouth went dry as he saw Kyserling and the plain-clothesman slip the chill blue steel of revolvers from their shoulder holsters.

'I got no use for these cute little games,' growled Kyserling, and suddenly raised his foot and smashed the heel of his shoe hard against the lock of the door. The door burst open. Robert cowed back against the balustrade of the staircase—

And then he saw her.

She stood in the middle of the room facing him wildly, the same look on her face, he knew in that fantastic moment, that she must have worn each time she came face to face with a betrayer exposed. Then she took one backward step, and suddenly whirled toward the window.

'*Ahh*, no!' she cried, as Robert had heard her cry it out once before, and then she was gone through the window in a sheet of broken glass. Her voice rose in a single despairing shriek, and then was suddenly and mercifully silent.

Robert stood there, the salt of sweat suddenly in his eyes, the salt of blood on his lips. It was an infinity of distance to the window, but he finally got there, and had to thrust Kyserling aside to look down.

She lay crumpled on the sidewalk, and the thick black hair in loose disorder around her face shrouded her from the eyes of the curious.

The plain-clothesman was gone, but Kyserling was still there watching Robert with sympathetic eyes.

'I thought he had killed her,' Robert whispered. 'I could swear he had killed her!'

'It was his body we found,' said Kyserling. 'She was the one who did it.'

'But why didn't you tell me then!' Robert begged. 'Why didn't you let me know!'

Kyserling looked at him wisely. 'Yeah?' he said. 'And then what? You tip her off so that she gets away; then we really got troubles.'

There could be no answer to that. None at all.

'She just cracked up,' Kyserling said reasonably. 'Holed up here like she was, not knowing which way to turn, nobody she could trust . . . It was in the cards. You had nothing to do with it.'

He went downstairs then, and Robert was alone in her room. He looked around it slowly, at all the things that were left of her, and then very deliberately picked up a chair, held it high over his head, and with all his strength smashed it against the wall . . .

R. Austin Freeman

1862–1943

THE BLUE SEQUIN

THORNDYKE STOOD looking up and down the platform with anxiety that increased as the time drew near for the departure of the train.

'This is very unfortunate,' he said, reluctantly stepping into an empty smoking compartment as the guard executed a flourish with his green flag. 'I am afraid we have missed our friend.' He closed the door and, as the train began to move, thrust his head out of the window.

'Now I wonder if that will be he,' he continued. 'If so he has caught the train by the skin of his teeth, and is now in one of the rear compartments.'

The subject of Thorndyke's speculations was Mr Edward Stopford, of the firm of Stopford & Myers, of Portugal Street, solicitors, and his connection with us at present arose out of a telegram that had reached our chambers on the preceding evening. It was reply paid, and ran thus:

Can you come here tomorrow to direct defence? Important case. All costs undertaken by us.—STOPFORD & MYERS.

Thorndyke's reply had been in the affirmative, and early on this present morning a further telegram—evidently posted overnight—had been delivered:

Shall leave for Woldhurst by 8.25 from Charing Cross. Will call for you if possible.—EDWARD STOPFORD.

He had not called, however, and, since he was unknown personally to us both, we could not judge whether or not he had been among the passengers on the platform.

'It is most unfortunate,' Thorndyke repeated, 'for it deprives us of that preliminary consideration of the case which is so invaluable.' He filled his pipe thoughtfully and, having made a fruitless inspection of the platform at London Bridge, took up the paper that he had bought at the bookstall, and began to turn over the leaves, running his eye quickly down the columns, unmindful of the journalistic baits in paragraph or article.

'It is a great disadvantage,' he observed, while still glancing through the paper, 'to come plump into an inquiry without preparation—to be confronted with the details before one has a chance of considering the case in general terms. For instance . . .'

He paused, leaving the sentence unfinished, and as I looked up inquiringly I saw that he had turned over another page, and was now reading attentively.

'This looks like our case, Jervis,' he said presently, handing me the paper and indicating a paragraph at the top of the page. It was quite brief, and was headed 'Terrible Murder in Kent', the account being as follows:

A shocking crime was discovered yesterday morning at the little town of Woldhurst, which lies on the branch line from Halbury Junction. The discovery was made by a porter who was inspecting the carriages of the train which had just come in. On opening the door of a first-class compartment, he was horrified to find the body of a fashionably dressed woman stretched upon the floor. Medical aid was immediately summoned, and on the arrival of the divisional surgeon, Dr Morton, it was ascertained that the woman had not been dead more than a few minutes.

The state of the corpse leaves no doubt that a murder of a most brutal kind had been perpetrated, the cause of death being a penetrating wound of the head, inflicted with some pointed implement which must have been used with terrible violence since it had perforated the skull and entered the brain. That robbery was not the motive of the crime is made clear by the fact that an expensively fitted dressing-bag was found on the rack, and that the dead woman's jewellery, including several valuable diamond rings, was untouched. It is rumoured that an arrest has been made by the local police.

'A gruesome affair,' I remarked as I handed back the paper, 'but the report does not give us much information.'

'It does not,' Thorndyke agreed, 'and yet it gives us something to consider. Here is a perforating wound of the skull, inflicted with some pointed implement—that is, assuming that it is not a bullet wound. Now, what kind of implement would be capable of inflicting such an injury? How would such an implement be used in the confined space of a railway carriage, and what sort of person would be in possession of such an implement? These are preliminary questions that are worth considering, and I commend them to you, together with the further problems of the possible motive—excluding robbery—and any circumstances other than murder which might account for the injury.'

'The choice of suitable implements is not very great,' I observed.

'It is very limited, and most of them, such as a plasterer's pick or a geological hammer, are associated with certain definite occupations. You have a note-book?'

I had, and, accepting the hint, I produced it and pursued my further reflections in silence, while my companion, with his note-book also on his knee, gazed steadily out of the window. And thus he remained, wrapped in thought, jotting down an entry now and again in his book, until the train slowed down at Halbury Junction, where we had to change on to a branch line.

As we stepped out I noticed a well-dressed man hurrying up the platform from the rear and eagerly scanning the faces of the few passengers who had alighted. Soon he espied us and, approaching quickly, asked, as he looked from one of us to the other:

'Dr Thorndyke?'

'Yes,' replied my colleague, adding: 'And you, I presume, are Mr Edward Stopford?'

The solicitor bowed. 'This is a dreadful affair,' he said in an agitated manner. 'I see you have the paper. A most shocking affair. I am immensely relieved to find you here. Nearly missed the train, and feared I should miss you.'

'There appears to have been an arrest,' Thorndyke began.

'Yes—my brother. Terrible business. Let us walk up the platform; our train won't start for a quarter of an hour yet.'

We deposited our joint Gladstone and Thorndyke's travelling-case in an empty first-class compartment, and then, with the solicitor between us, strolled up to the unfrequented end of the platform.

'My brother's position', said Mr Stopford, 'fills me with dismay—but let me give you the facts in order, and you shall judge for yourself. This poor creature who has been murdered so brutally was a Miss Edith Grant. She was formerly an artist's model, and as such was a good deal employed by my brother, who is a painter—Harold Stopford, you know, A.R.A. now—'

'I know his work very well, and charming work it is.'

'I think so too. Well, in those days he was quite a youngster—about twenty— and he became very intimate with Miss Grant, in quite an innocent way, though not very discreet; but she was a nice, respectable girl, as most English models are, and no one thought any harm. However, a good many letters passed between them, and some little presents, amongst which was a beaded chain carrying a locket, and in this he was fool enough to put his portrait and the inscription, "Edith, from Harold".

'Later on Miss Grant, who had a rather good voice, went on the stage in the comic opera line, and in consequence her habits and associates changed somewhat; and, as Harold had meanwhile become engaged, he was naturally anxious to get his letters back, and especially to exchange the locket for some less compromising gift. The letters she eventually sent him, but refused absolutely to part with the locket.

'Now for the last month Harold has been staying at Halbury, making sketching excursions into the surrounding country, and yesterday morning he took the train to Shinglehurst, the third station from here, and the one before Woldhurst.

'On the platform here he met Miss Grant, who had come down from London and was going on to Worthing. They entered the branch train together, having a first-class compartment to themselves. It seems she was wearing his locket at the time, and he made another appeal to her to make an exchange, which she refused, as before. The discussion appears to have become rather heated and angry on both sides, for the guard and a porter at Munsden both noticed that they seemed to be quarrelling; but the upshot of the affair was that the lady snapped the chain and tossed it together with the locket to my brother, and they parted quite amiably at Shinglehurst, where Harold got out. He was then carrying his full sketching kit, including a large holland umbrella, the lower joint of which is an ash staff fitted with a powerful steel spike for driving into the ground.

'It was about half past ten when he got out at Shinglehurst; by eleven he had reached his pitch and got to work, and he painted steadily for three hours. Then he packed up his traps, and was just starting on his way back to the station when he was met by the police and arrested.

'And now, observe the accumulation of circumstantial evidence against him. He was the last person seen in company with the murdered woman—for no one seems to have seen her after they left Munsden; he appeared to be quarrelling with her when she was last seen alive, he had a reason for possibly wishing for her death, he was provided with an implement—a spiked staff—capable of inflicting the injury which caused her death, and, when he was searched, there was found in his possession the locket and the broken chain, apparently removed from her person with violence.

'Against all this is, of course, his known character—he is the gentlest and most amiable of men, and his subsequent conduct—imbecile to the last degree if he had been guilty; but, as a lawyer, I can't help seeing that appearances are almost hopelessly against him.'

'We won't say "hopelessly",' replied Thorndyke as we took our places in the carriage, 'though I expect the police are pretty cock-sure. When does the inquest open?'

'Today at four. I have obtained an order from the coroner for you to examine the body and be present at the post-mortem.'

'Do you happen to know the exact position of the wound?'

'Yes; it is a little above and behind the left ear—a horrible round hole, with a ragged cut or tear running from it to the side of the forehead.'

'And how was the body lying?'

'Right along the floor, with the feet close to the off-side door.'

'Was the wound on the head the only one?'

'No; there was a long cut or bruise on the right cheek—a contused wound the police surgeon called it, which he believes to have been inflicted with a heavy and rather blunt weapon. I have not heard of any other wounds or bruises.'

'Did anyone enter the train yesterday at Shinglehurst?' Thorndyke asked.

'No one entered the train after it left Halbury.'

Thorndyke considered these statements in silence, and presently fell into a brown study, from which he roused only as the train moved out of Shinglehurst station.

'It would be about here that the murder was committed,' said Mr Stopford; 'at least, between here and Woldhurst.'

Thorndyke nodded rather abstractedly, being engaged at the moment in observing with great attention the objects that were visible from the windows.

'I notice,' he remarked presently, 'a number of chips scattered about between the rails, and some of the chair-wedges look new. Have there been any plate-layers at work lately?'

'Yes,' answered Stopford, 'they are on the line now, I believe—at least, I saw a gang working near Woldhurst yesterday, and they are said to have set a rick on fire; I saw it smoking when I came down.'

'Indeed; and this middle line of rails is, I suppose, a sort of siding?'

'Yes, they shunt the goods trains and empty trucks on to it. There are the remains of the rick—still smouldering, you see.'

Thorndyke gazed absently at the blackened heap until an empty cattle-truck on the middle track hid it from view. This was succeeded by a line of goods-wagons, and these by a passenger coach, one compartment of which—a first-class—was closed up and sealed. The train now began to slow down rather suddenly, and a couple of minutes later we brought up in Woldhurst station.

It was evident that rumours of Thorndyke's advent had preceded us, for the entire staff—two porters, an inspector and the stationmaster—were waiting expectantly on the platform, and the latter came forward, regardless of his dignity, to help us with our luggage.

'Do you think I could see the carriage?' Thorndyke asked the solicitor.

'Not the inside, sir,' said the stationmaster, on being appealed to. 'The police have sealed it up. You would have to ask the inspector.'

'Well, I can have a look at the outside, I suppose?' said Thorndyke.

And to this the stationmaster readily agreed, and offered to accompany us.

'What other first-class passengers were there?' Thorndyke asked.

'None, sir. There was only one first-class coach, and the deceased was the only person in it. It has given us all a dreadful turn, this affair has,' he continued as we set off up the line. 'I was on the platform when the train came in. We were watching a rick that was burning up the line, and a rare blaze it made too; and I was just saying that we should have to move the cattle-truck that was on the mid track, because you see, sir, the smoke and sparks were blowing across, and I thought it would frighten the poor beasts. And Mr Felton, he don't like his beasts handled roughly. He says it spoils the meat.'

'No doubt he is right,' said Thorndyke. 'But now, tell me, do you think it is possible for any person to board or leave the train on the off-side unobserved? Could a man, for instance, enter a compartment on the off-side at one station and drop off as the train was slowing down at the next without being seen?'

'I doubt it,' replied the stationmaster. 'Still, I wouldn't say it is impossible.'

'Thank you. Oh, and there's another question. You have a gang of men at work on the line, I see. Now, do those men belong to the district?'

'No, sir; they are strangers, every one, and pretty rough diamonds some of 'em are. But I shouldn't say there was any real harm in 'em. If you was suspecting any of 'em of being mixed up in this—'

'I am not,' interrupted Thorndyke rather shortly. 'I suspect nobody; but I wish to get all the facts of the case at the outset.'

'Naturally, sir,' replied the abashed official; and we pursued our way in silence.

'Do you remember, by the way,' said Thorndyke as we approached the empty coach, 'whether the off-side door of the compartment was closed and locked when the body was discovered?'

'It was closed, sir, but not locked. Why, sir, did you think—'

'Nothing, nothing. The sealed compartment is the one of course?'

Without waiting for a reply he commenced his survey of the coach, while I gently restrained our two companions from shadowing him, as they were disposed to do.

The off-side footboard occupied his attention specially, and when he had scrutinised minutely the part opposite the fatal compartment he walked slowly from end to end with his eyes but a few inches from its surface, as though he was searching for something.

Near what had been the rear end he stopped and drew from his pocket a piece of paper; then with a moistened finger-tip he picked up from the footboard some evidently minute object, which he carefully transferred to the paper, folding the latter and placing it in his pocket-book.

He next mounted the footboard and, having peered in through the window of the sealed compartment, produced from his pocket a small insufflator or powder-blower, with which he blew a stream of impalpable smoke-like powder on to the edges of the middle window, bestowing the closest attention on the irregular dusty patches in which it settled, and even measuring one on the jamb of the window with a pocket rule.

At length he stepped down and, having carefully looked over the near-side footboard, announced that he had finished for the present.

As we were returning down the line we passed a working man who seemed to be viewing the chairs and sleepers with more than casual interest.

'That, I suppose, is one of the platelayers?' Thorndyke suggested to the stationmaster.

'Yes, the foreman of the gang,' was the reply.

'I'll just step back and have a word with him, if you will walk on slowly.' And my colleague turned back briskly and overtook the man, with whom he remained in conversation for some minutes.

'I think I see the police inspector on the platform,' remarked Thorndyke as we approached the station.

'Yes, there he is,' said our guide. 'Come down to see what you are after, sir, I expect.' Which was doubtless the case, although the officer professed to be there by the merest chance.

'You would like to see the weapon, sir, I suppose?' he remarked when he had introduced himself.

'The umbrella-spike,' Thorndyke corrected. 'Yes, if I may. We are going to the mortuary now.'

'Then you'll pass the station on the way; so, if you care to look in, I will walk up with you.'

This proposition being agreed to, we all proceeded to the police station, including the stationmaster, who was on the very tiptoe of curiosity.

'There you are, sir,' said the inspector, unlocking his office and ushering us in. 'Don't say we haven't given every facility to the defence. There are all the effects of the accused, including the very weapon the deed was done with.'

'Come, come,' protested Thorndyke; 'we mustn't be premature.'

He took the stout ash staff from the officer and, having examined the formidable spike through a lens, drew from his pocket a steel calliper-gauge, with which he carefully measured the diameter of the spike and the staff to which it was fixed.

'And now,' he said, when he had made a note of the measurements in his book, 'we will look at the colour-box and the sketch. Ha! A very orderly man, your brother, Mr Stopford. Tubes all in their places, palette-knives wiped clean, palette cleaned off and rubbed bright, brushes wiped—they ought to be washed before they stiffen—all this is very significant.'

He unstrapped the sketch from the blank canvas to which it was pinned, and, standing it on a chair in a good light, stepped back to look at it.

'And you tell me that that is only three hours' work!' he exclaimed, looking at the lawyer. 'It is a really marvellous achievement.'

'My brother is a very rapid worker,' replied Stopford dejectedly.

'Yes, but this is not only amazingly rapid; it is in his very happiest vein—full of spirit and feeling. But we mustn't stay to look at it longer.'

He replaced the canvas on its pins and, having glanced at the locket and some other articles that lay in a drawer, thanked the inspector for his courtesy and withdrew.

'That sketch and the colour-box appear very suggestive to me,' he remarked as we walked up the street.

'To me also,' said Stopford gloomily, 'for they are under lock and key, like their owner, poor old fellow.'

He sighed heavily, and we walked on in silence.

The mortuary-keeper had evidently heard of our arrival, for he was waiting at the door with the key in his hand and, on being shown the coroner's order, unlocked the door and we entered together.

But after a momentary glance at the ghostly, shrouded figure lying upon the slate table, Stopford turned pale and retreated, saying that he would wait for us outside with the mortuary-keeper.

As soon as the door was closed and locked on the inside Thorndyke glanced curiously round the bare whitewashed building.

A stream of sunlight poured in through the skylight and fell upon the silent form that lay so still under its covering sheet, and one stray beam glanced into a corner by the door where, on a row of pegs and a deal table, the dead woman's clothing was displayed.

'There is something unspeakably sad in these poor relics, Jervis,' said Thorndyke as we stood before them. 'To me they are more tragic, more full of pathetic suggestions, than the corpse itself. See the smart, jaunty hat and the costly skirts hanging there, so desolate and forlorn; the dainty lingerie on the table, neatly folded—by the mortuary-man's wife, I hope—the little French shoes and openwork silk stockings. How pathetically eloquent they are of harmless womanly vanity, and the gay, careless life snapped short in the twinkling of an eye. But we must not give way to sentiment. There is another life threatened, and it is in our keeping.'

He lifted the hat from its peg and turned it over in his hand. It was, I think, what is called a 'picture-hat'—a huge, flat, shapeless mass of gauze and ribbons and feathers, spangled over freely with dark blue sequins. In one part of the brim was a ragged hole, and from this the glittering sequins dropped off in little showers when the hat was moved.

'This will have been worn tilted over on the left side,' said Thorndyke, 'judging by the general shape and the position of the hole.'

'Yes,' I agreed. 'Like that of the Duchess of Devonshire in Gainsborough's portrait.'

'Exactly.'

He shook a few of the sequins into the palm of his hand and, replacing the hat on its peg, dropped the little disks into an envelope, on which he wrote, 'From the hat', and slipped it into his pocket. Then, stepping over to the table, he drew back the sheet reverently and even tenderly from the dead woman's face and looked down at it with grave pity.

It was a comely face, white as marble, serene and peaceful in expression, with half-closed eyes, and framed with a mass of brassy yellow hair; but its beauty was marred by a long linear wound, half-cut, half-bruise, running down the right cheek from the eye to the chin.

'A handsome girl,' Thorndyke commented; 'a dark-haired blonde. What a sin to have disfigured herself so with that horrible peroxide.'

He smoothed the hair back from her forehead and added: 'She seems to have applied the stuff last about ten days ago. There is about a quarter of an inch of dark hair at the roots. What do you make of that wound on the cheek?'

'It looks as if she had struck some sharp angle in falling, though, as the seats are padded in first-class carriages, I don't see what she could have struck.'

'No. And now let us look at the other wound. Will you note down the description?'

He handed me his note-book, and I wrote down as he dictated:

'A clean-punched circular hole in skull, an inch behind and above margin of left ear—diameter, an inch and seven-sixteenths; starred fracture of parietal bone; membranes perforated and brain entered deeply; ragged scalp-wound, extending forward to margin of left orbit; fragments of gauze and sequins in edges of wound. That will do for the present. Dr Morton will give us further details if we want them.'

He pocketed his callipers and rule, drew from the bruised scalp one or two loose hairs, which he placed in the envelope with the sequins, and, having looked over the body for other wounds or bruises (of which there were none), replaced the sheet and prepared to depart.

As we walked away from the mortuary Thorndyke was silent and deeply thoughtful, and I gathered that he was piecing together the facts that he had acquired.

At length Mr Stopford, who had several times looked at him curiously, said:

'The post-mortem will take place at three, and it is now only half past eleven. What would you like to do next?'

Thorndyke, who in spite of his mental preoccupation had been looking about him in his usual keen, attentive way, halted suddenly.

'Your reference to the post-mortem,' said he, 'reminds me that I forgot to put the ox-gall into my case.'

'Ox-gall!' I exclaimed, endeavouring vainly to connect this substance with the technique of the pathologist. 'What were you going to do with. . .'

But here I broke off, remembering my friend's dislike of any discussion of his methods before strangers.

'I suppose,' he continued, 'there would hardly be an artist's colourman in a place of this size?'

'I should think not,' said Stopford. 'But couldn't you get the stuff from a butcher? There's a shop just across the road.'

'So there is,' agreed Thorndyke, who had already observed the shop. 'The gall ought of course to be prepared, but we can filter it ourselves—that is, if the butcher has any. We will try him, at any rate.'

He crossed the road towards the shop, over which the name 'Felton' appeared in gilt lettering, and, addressing himself to the proprietor, who stood at the door, introduced himself and explained his wants.

'Ox-gall?' said the butcher. 'No, sir, I haven't any just now; but I am having a beast killed this afternoon, and I can let you have some then. In fact,' he added, after a pause, 'as the matter is of importance, I can have one killed at once if you wish it.'

'That is very kind of you,' said Thorndyke, 'and it would greatly oblige me. Is the beast perfectly healthy?'

'They're in splendid condition, sir. I picked them out of the herd myself. But you shall see them—ay, and choose the one that you'd like killed.'

'You are really very good,' said Thorndyke warmly. 'I will just run into the chemist's next door and get a suitable bottle, and then I will avail myself of your exceedingly kind offer.'

He hurried into the chemist's shop, from which he presently emerged carrying a white paper parcel; and we then followed the butcher down a narrow lane by the side of his shop.

It led to an enclosure containing a small pen, in which were confined three handsome steers, whose glossy black coats contrasted in a very striking manner with their long greyish-white, nearly straight horns.

'These are certainly very fine beasts, Mr Felton,' said Thorndyke as we drew up beside the pen, 'and in excellent condition too.'

He leaned over the pen and examined the beasts critically, especially as to their eyes and horns; then, approaching the nearest one, he raised his stick and bestowed a smart rap on the underside of the right horn, following it by a similar tap on the left one, a proceeding that the beast viewed with stolid surprise.

'The state of the horns,' explained Thorndyke as he moved on to the next steer, 'enables one to judge to some extent of the beast's health.'

'Lord bless you, sir,' laughed Mr Felton, 'they haven't got no feeling in their horns, else what good 'ud their horns be to 'em?'

Apparently he was right, for the second steer was as indifferent to a sounding rap on either horn as the first.

Nevertheless, when Thorndyke approached the third steer, I unconsciously drew near to watch; and I noticed that, as the stick struck the horn, the beast drew back in evident alarm, and that then the blow was repeated it became manifestly uneasy.

'He don't seem to like that,' said the butcher. 'Seems as if—hallo, that's queer!'

Thorndyke had just brought his stick up against the left horn, and immediately the beast had winced—and started back, shaking his head and moaning.

There was not, however, room for him to back out of reach, and Thorndyke, by leaning into the pen, was able to inspect the sensitive horn, which he did with the closest attention, while the butcher looked on with obvious perturbation.

'You don't think there's anything wrong with this beast, sir, I hope,' said he.

'I can't say without a further examination,' replied Thorndyke. 'It may be the horn only that is affected. If you will have it sawn off close to the head, and sent up to me at the hotel, I will look at it and tell you. And, by way of preventing any mistakes, I will mark it and cover it up to protect it from injury in the slaughterhouse.'

He opened his parcel and produced from it a wide-mouthed bottle labelled

'Ox-gall', a sheet of gutta-percha tissue, a roller bandage and a stick of sealing-wax.

Handing the bottle to Mr Felton, he encased the distal half of the horn in a covering by means of the tissue and the bandage, which he fixed securely with the sealing-wax.

'I'll saw the horn off and bring it up to the hotel myself, with the ox-gall,' said Mr Felton. 'You shall have them in half an hour.'

He was as good as his word, for in half an hour Thorndyke was seated at a small table by the window of our private sitting-room in the Black Bull Hotel.

The table was covered with newspaper, and on it lay the long grey horn and Thorndyke's travelling-case, now open and displaying a small microscope and its accessories.

The butcher was seated solidly in an armchair waiting, with a half-suspicious eye on Thorndyke, for the report; and I was endeavouring by cheerful talk to keep Mr Stopford from sinking into utter despondency, though I too kept a furtive watch on my colleague's rather mysterious proceedings.

I saw him unwind the bandage and apply the horn to his ear, bending it slightly to and fro.

I watched him as he scanned the surface closely through a lens and observed him as he scraped some substance from the pointed end on to a glass slide and, having applied a drop of some reagent, began to tease out the scraping with a pair of mounted needles.

Presently he placed the slide under the microscope and, having observed it attentively for a minute or two, turned round sharply.

'Come and look at this, Jervis,' said he.

I wanted no second bidding, being on tenterhooks of curiosity, but came over and applied my eye to the instrument.

'Well, what is it?' he asked.

'A multipolar nerve corpuscle—very shrivelled, but un-mistakable.'

'And this?'

He moved the slide to a fresh spot.

'Two pyramidal nerve corpuscles and some portions of fibres.'

'And what do you say the tissue is?'

'Cortical brain substance, I should say, without a doubt.'

'I entirely agree with you. And that being so,' he added, turning to Mr Stopford, 'we may say that the case for the defence is practically complete.'

'What in heaven's name do you mean?' exclaimed Stopford, starting up.

'I mean that we can now prove when and where and how Miss Grant met her death. Come and sit down here, and I will explain. No, you needn't go away, Mr Felton. We shall have to subpoena you. Perhaps,' he continued, 'we had better go over the facts and see what they suggest. And first we note the position of the body, lying with the feet close to the off-side door, showing that, when she fell, the deceased was sitting, or more probably standing, close to that door. Next there is this.'

He drew from his pocket a folded paper, which he opened, displaying a tiny blue disk.

'It is one of the sequins with which her hat was trimmed, and I have in this envelope several more which I took from the hat itself.

'This single sequin I picked up on the rear end of the off-side footboard, and its presence there makes it nearly certain that at some time Miss Grant had put her head out of the window on that side.

'The next item of evidence I obtained by dusting the margins of the off-side window with a light powder, which made visible a greasy impression three and a quarter inches long on the sharp corner of the right-hand jamb (right-hand from the inside, I mean).

'And now as to the evidence furnished by the body. The wound in the skull is behind and above the left ear, is roughly circular, and measures one inch and seven sixteenths at most, and a ragged scalp-wound runs from it towards the left eye. On the right cheek is a linear contused wound three and a quarter inches long. There are no other injuries.

'Our next facts are furnished by this.'

He took up the horn and tapped it with his fingers, while the solicitor and Mr Felton stared at him in speechless wonder.

'You notice it is a left horn, and you remember that it was highly sensitive. If you put your ear to it while I strain it, you will hear the grating of a fracture in the bony core.

'Now look at the pointed end, and you will see several deep scratches running lengthwise, and where those scratches end the diameter of the horn is, as you see by this calliper-gauge, one inch and seven-sixteenths. Covering the scratches is a dry bloodstain, and at the extreme tip is a small mass of a dried substance which Dr Jervis and I have examined with the microscope and are satisfied is brain tissue.'

'Good God!' exclaimed Stopford eagerly. 'Do you mean to say——'

'Let us finish with the facts, Mr Stopford,' Thorndyke interrupted. 'Now, if you look closely at that bloodstain, you will see a short piece of hair stuck to the horn, and through this lens you can make out the root-bulb. It is a golden hair, you notice, but near the root it is black, and our calliper-gauge shows us that the black portion is fourteen sixty-fourths of an inch long.

'Now in this envelope are some hairs that I removed from the dead woman's head. They also are golden hairs, black at the roots, and when I measure the black portion I find it to be fourteen sixty-fourths of an inch long. Then, finally, there is this.'

He turned the horn over and pointed to a small patch of dried blood. Embedded in it was a blue sequin.

Mr Stopford and the butcher gazed at the horn in silent amazement; then the former drew a deep breath and looked up at Thorndyke.

'No doubt,' said he, 'you can explain this mystery, but for my part I am utterly bewildered, though you are filling me with hope.'

'And yet the matter is quite simple,' returned Thorndyke, 'even with these few facts before us, which are only a selection from the body of evidence in our possession. But I will state my theory, and you shall judge.'

He rapidly sketched a rough plan on a sheet of paper and continued:

'These were the conditions when the train was approaching Woldhurst. Here was the passenger-coach, here was the burning rick, and here was a cattle-truck. This steer was in that truck. Now my hypothesis is that at that time Miss Grant was standing with her head out of the off-side window, watching the burning rick. Her wide hat, worn on the left side, hid from her view the cattle-truck which she was approaching, and then this is what happened.'

He sketched another plan to a larger scale.

'One of the steers—this one—had thrust its long horn out through the bars. The point of that horn struck the deceased's head, driving her face violently against the corner of the window, and then, in disengaging, ploughed its way through the scalp and suffered a fracture of its core from the violence of the wrench. This hypothesis is inherently probable, it fits all the facts, and those facts admit of no other explanation.'

The solicitor sat for a moment as though dazed; then he rose impulsively and seized Thorndyke's hands.

'I don't know what to say to you,' he exclaimed huskily, 'except that you have saved my brother's life, and for that may God reward you!'

The butcher rose from his chair with a slow grin.

'It seems to me,' said he, 'as if that ox-gall was what you might call a blind, eh, sir?'

And Thorndyke smiled an inscrutable smile.

WHEN WE RETURNED to town on the following day we were a party of four, which included Mr Harold Stopford.

The verdict of 'Death by misadventure', promptly returned by the coroner's jury, had been shortly followed by his release from custody, and he now sat with his brother and me, listening with rapt attention to Thorndyke's analysis of the case.

'So you see,' the latter concluded, 'I had six possible theories of the cause of death worked out before I reached Halbury, and it only remained to select the one that fitted the facts. And when I had seen the cattle-truck, had picked up that sequin, had heard the description of the steers, and had seen the hat and the wounds, there was nothing left to do but the filling in of details.'

'And you never doubted my innocence?' asked Harold Stopford.

Thorndyke smiled at his quondam client.

'Not after I had seen your colour-box and your sketch,' said he; 'to say nothing of the spike.'

Michael Gilbert

b. 1912

THE OYSTER CATCHER

THE TABLE WAS the first thing that caught your eye as you came into the room. Its legs were of green-painted angle-iron, bolted to the floor; its top, a block of polished teak. Overhead shone five white fluorescent lights.

On the wide, shadowless, aseptic surface the raincoat looked out of place, like some jolly, seedy old tramp who has strayed into an operating-theatre. A coat is such a personal thing, almost a second skin. As it loses its own shape and takes on the outlines of its wearer, as its pockets become a repository of tobacco flakes and sand and fragments of leaves, and its exterior spotted with more unexpected things than rain, so does it take on an intimate life all of its own.

There was an element of indecency, Petrella thought, in tearing this life from it. The earnest man in rimless glasses and a white laboratory overall had just finished going over the lining with a pocket-sized vacuum cleaner with a thimble-shaped container. Now he was at work on the exterior. He cut a broad strip of adhesive tape and laid it on the outside of the coat, pressing it firmly down. Then he marked the area with a special pencil, and pulled the tape off. There was nothing visible to the naked eye on the under-surface of the tape, but he seemed satisfied.

'We'll make a few micro-slides,' he said. 'They'll tell us anything we want to know. There's no need for you to hang about if you don't want to.'

Sergeant Petrella disliked being told, even indirectly, that he was wasting his time. Let the truth be told, he did not care for Scientific Assistant Worsley at all. Worsley had the very slightly patronising manner of one who has himself been admitted to the inner circles of knowledge and is speaking to unfortunates who are still outside the pale—a habit, Petrella had noticed, that was very marked at the outset of a scientific career, but diminished as a man gained more experience and realised how little certainty there was, even under the eye of the microscope.

'All right,' he said. 'I'll push off and come back in a couple of hours.'

'To do the job completely,' said Worsley, 'will take about six days.' He looked complacently at the neat range of Petri dishes round the table, and the samples he had so far extracted. 'Perhaps another three to tabulate the results.'

'All the same,' said Petrella, 'I'll look in this evening and see what you have got for me.'

'As long as you appreciate,' said Worsley, 'that the results I give you will be unchecked.'

'I'll take a chance on that.'

'That, of course, is for you to decide.' His voice contained a reproof. Impetuous people, police officers. Unschooled in the discipline of the laboratory. Jumpers to conclusions. People on whom careful, controlled research was usually wasted. Worsley sighed audibly.

Sergeant Petrella said nothing at all. He had long ago found out that it was a waste of time antagonising people who were in a position to help you.

He consulted his watch, his notebook, and his stomach. He had a call to make in Wandsworth, another in Acton, and a third in South Harrow. Then he would come back to the Forensic Science Laboratory to see what Worsley had got for them. Then he would go back to Highside and report to Superintendent Haxtell. He might have time for lunch between Acton and South Harrow. If not, the prospect of food was remote, for once he reached Highside, there was no saying that Haxtell would not have a lot more visits lined up for him.

All this activity—and, indirectly, the coat lying on Worsley's table—stemmed from a discovery made by a milkman at No. 39 Carhow Mansions. Carhow Mansions is a tall block of flats overlooking the southern edge of Helenwood Common.

Miss Martin, who lived alone at No. 39, was a woman of about thirty. Neither beautiful, nor clever; nor ugly, nor stupid. She was secretary to Dr Hunter, who had a house and consulting-room in Wimpole Street. She did her work well, and was well paid for it.

The flat, which was tucked away on the top storey and was smaller than the others in the block, was known as a 'single', which means that it had about as little accommodation as one person could actually exist in. A living-room that was also a dining-room; an annexe that served as a bedroom; one cupboard, called a kitchen, and another called a bathroom. Not that Miss Martin had ever been heard to complain. She had no time to waste on housework and ate most of her meals out. Her interests were Shakespeare and tennis.

Which brings us to the milkman, who, finding Friday's milk bottle still unused outside the door of Flat 39 on Saturday, mentioned the matter to the caretaker.

The caretaker was not immediately worried. Tenants often went away without telling him, although Miss Martin was usually punctilious about such matters. Later in the morning his rounds took him up to No. 39, and he looked at the two milk bottles and found the sight faintly disturbing. Fortunately, he had his passkey with him.

Which brought Superintendent Haxtell onto the scene in a fast car. And Chief Superintendent Barstow, from District Headquarters. And photographic and fingerprint detachments, and a well-known pathologist, and a crowd on the pavement, and a uniformed policeman to control them. And eventually, since Carhow Mansions was in his manor, Sergeant Petrella.

Junior detective sergeants do not conduct investigations into murders, but they are allowed to help, in much the same way as a junior officer helps to run a war. They are allowed to do the work, while their superiors do the thinking. In this case, there was a lot of work to do.

'I don't like it,' said Barstow, in the explosive rumble that was his normal conversational voice. 'Here's this girl, as ordinary as apples-and-custard. No one's got a word to say against her. Life's an open book. Then someone comes in and hits her on the head, not once, but five or six times.'

'Any one of the blows might have caused death,' agreed the pathologist. 'She's been dead more than twenty-four hours. Probably killed on Friday morning. And I think there's no doubt that that was the weapon.' He indicated a heavy long-handled screwdriver.

'It could have belonged to her,' said Haxtell. 'Funny thing to find in a flat, though. More like a piece of workshop equipment.'

'All right,' said Barstow. 'Suppose the murderer brought it with him. Ideal for the job. You could force a front door with a thing like that. Then, if the owner comes out, it's just as handy as a weapon. But it's still'—he boggled over the word and its implications—'it's still mad.'

And the further they looked, and the wider they spread their net, the madder it did seem.

Certain facts came to light at once. Haxtell was talking to Doctor Hunter, of Wimpole Street, within the hour. The doctor explained that Miss Martin had not come to work on Friday because he himself had ordered her to stay in bed.

'I think she'd been over-using her eyes,' said the doctor. 'That gave her a headache, and the headache in turn affected her stomach. It was a form of migraine. What she needed was forty-eight hours on her back, with the blinds down. I told her to take Friday off, and come back on Monday if she felt well enough. She's been with me for nearly ten years now. An excellent secretary, and such a nice girl.'

He spoke with so much warmth that Haxtell, who was a cynic, made a mental note of a possible line of inquiry. Nothing came of it. The doctor, it transpired, was very happily married.

'That part of it fits all right,' said Haxtell to Chief Superintendent Barstow. 'She was in bed when the intruder arrived. He hit her as she was coming out of her bedroom.'

'Then you think he was a housebreaker?'

'I'd imagined so, yes,' said Haxtell. 'The screwdriver looks like the sort of thing a housebreaker would carry. You could force an ordinary mortise lock right off with it. He didn't have to use it in this instance, because she'd got a simple catch-lock that a child of five could open. I don't doubt he slipped it with a piece of talc.'

'Why did he choose her flat?'

'Because it was an isolated one, on the top floor. Or because he knew her habits. Just bad luck that she should have been there at all.'

'Bad luck for her,' agreed Barstow sourly. 'Well, we've got the machine working. We may turn something up.'

Haxtell was an experienced police officer. He knew that investigating a murder was like dropping a stone into a pool of water. He started two inquiries at once. Everybody within a hundred yards of the flat was asked what they had been doing and whether they had noticed anything. And everyone remotely connected with Miss Martin, by ties of blood, friendship or business, was sought out and questioned.

It is a system that involves an enormous amount of work for a large number of people, and has got only one thing in its favour. It is nearly always successful in the end.

To Sergeant Petrella fell the task of questioning all the other tenants in the block. This involved seven visits. In each case at least one person, it appeared, had been at home all Friday morning. And no one had heard anything, which was disappointing. Had anything unusual happened on Friday morning? The first six people to whom this inquiry was addressed scratched their heads and said that they didn't think anything had. The seventh mentioned the gentleman who had left census papers.

Now Petrella was by then both hot and tired. He was, according to which way you looked at it, either very late for his lunch or rather early for his tea. He was on the point of dismissing the man with the census papers when the instinct that guides all good policemen drove him to persevere with one further inquiry. Had he not, the Martin case would probably have remained unsolved.

As he probed, a curious little story emerged. The man had not actually left any papers behind him. He had been making preliminary inquiries as to the number of people on the premises so that arrangements for the census could be put in hand. These papers would be issued later.

Petrella trudged down three flights of stairs—it is only in grave emergency that a policeman is allowed to use a private telephone—and rang up the Municipal Returning Officer from a call box.

After that he revisited the first six flats. The occupants unanimously agreed that a 'man from the Council' had called on them that Friday morning. They had not mentioned it because Petrella had asked if anything 'unusual' had happened. There was nothing in the least unusual in men from the Council snooping round.

Petrella asked for a description and collated, from his six informants, the following items. The man in question was young, youngish, sort of middle-aged—this was from the teen-aged daughter in No. 37. He was bareheaded and had tousled hair. He was wearing a hat. He had a shifty look No. 34; a nice smile—teen-aged daughter; couldn't say, didn't really look at him—the remainder. He was about six foot—five foot nine—five foot six—didn't notice. He had an ordinary sort of voice. He was wearing an Old Harrovian tie—gentleman in ground-floor flat No. 34. He seemed to walk with rather a stiff sort of leg, almost a limp—four out of six informants.

Petrella hurried back to Highside Police Station, where he found Haxtell and Barstow in conference.

'There doesn't seem to be much doubt,' he reported, 'that it was a sneak thief. Posing as a Council employee. I've checked with them and they are certain that he couldn't have been genuine. His plan would be to knock once or twice. If he got no answer he'd either slip the lock or force it. He drew a blank at the other seven. Someone answered the door in each of them. When he got to No. 39, I expect Miss Martin didn't hear him. The migraine must have made her pretty blind and deaf.'

'That's right,' said Barstow. 'And then she came out and caught him at it, and he hit her!'

'The descriptions aren't a lot of good,' said Haxtell, 'but we'll get all the pictures from the C.R.O. of people known to go in for this sort of lark. They may sort someone out for us.'

'Don't forget the most important item,' said Barstow. 'The limp.'

Petrella said, 'It did occur to me to wonder whether we ought to place much reliance on the limp, sir.'

He received a glare that would have daunted a less self-confident man.

'He would have to have somewhere to hide that big screwdriver. It was almost two foot long. The natural place would be a pocket inside his trouser leg. That might account for the appearance of a stiff leg.'

Haxtell avoided Barstow's eye. 'It's an idea,' he said. 'Now just get along and start checking on this list of Miss Martin's known relations.'

'There was one other thing—'

'Do you know,' observed Chief Superintendent Barstow unkindly, 'why God gave young policemen two feet but only one head?'

Petrella accepted the hint and departed.

NEVERTHELESS, the idea persisted; and later that day, when he was alone with Superintendent Haxtell, he voiced it to him.

'Do you remember,' he said, 'about six months ago, I think it was, we had an outbreak of this sort of thing in the Cholderton Road, Park Branch area? A man cleared out three or four blocks of flats, and we never caught him. He was posing as a pools salesman then.'

'The man who left his coat behind.'

'That's right,' said Petrella. 'With Colonel Wing.'

Colonel Wing was nearly ninety and rather deaf, but still spry. He had fought in the Afghan campaign, and one Zulu war, and the walls of his top-floor living-room in Cholderton Mansions were adorned with a fine selection of assegais, yataghans, and knopkieries. Six months before this story opens he had had an experience that might have unnerved a less seasoned warrior.

Pottering out of his bedroom one fine morning at about eleven o'clock—he was not an early riser—he had observed a man kneeling in front of his sideboard and quietly sorting out the silver. It was difficult to say who had been more taken aback. The man had jumped up, and run from the room. Colonel Wing had regretfully dismissed the idea of trying to spear him with an assegai from the balcony as he left the front door of the flats, and had rung up the police. They had made one curious discovery.

Hanging in the hall was a strange raincoat.

'Never seen it before in my life,' said Colonel Wing. 'D'you mean to say the damn feller had the cheek to hang his coat up before starting work? Wonder he didn't help himself to a whisky-and-soda while he was about it.'

Haxtell said that he had known housebreakers to do just that. He talked to the Colonel at length about the habits of criminals; and removed the coat for examination. Since the crime was only an attempted robbery, it was not thought worth while wasting too much time on it. A superficial examination produced no results in the way of name tabs or tailors' marks, the coat was carefully placed in a cellophane bag and stored.

'I'd better have a word with him,' said Petrella.

He found the Colonel engaged in writing a letter to the *United Services' Journal* on the comparative fighting qualities of Zulus and Russians. He listened to the descriptions of the intruder, and said that, as far as one could tell, they sounded like the same man. His intruder had been on the younger side of middle age, of medium height, and strongly built.

'There's one thing,' said the Colonel. 'I saw him in a good light, and I may be deaf but I've got excellent eyesight. There's a tiny spot on his left eye. A little red spot, like a fire opal. You couldn't mistake it. If you catch him, I'll identify him for you fast enough.'

'The trouble is,' said Petrella, 'that it looks as if he's never been through our hands. Almost the only real lead we've got is that coat he left behind him at your place. We're going over it again now, much more thoroughly.'

Thus had the coat grown in importance. It had improved its status. It had become a possible exhibit in a murder case.

'Give it everything,' said Haxtell to the scientists. And the scientists prepared to oblige.

THAT EVENING, after a weary afternoon spent interrogating Miss Martin's father's relatives in Acton and South Harrow, Petrella found himself back on the Embankment. The Forensic Science Laboratory observes civilised hours and Mr Worsley was on the point of removing his long white overall and replacing it with a rather deplorable green tweed coat with matching leather patches on the elbows.

'I've finished my preliminary work on the right-hand pocket,' he said. 'We have isolated arrowroot starch, pipe tobacco and a quantity of common silver sand.'

'Splendid,' said Petrella. 'Splendid. All I have got to do now is to find a house-wife who smokes a pipe and has recently been to the seaside and we shall be home and dry.'

'What use you make of the data we provide must be entirely a matter for you,' said Mr Worsley coldly. He was already late for a meeting of the South Wimbledon Medico-Legal Society, to whom he had promised a paper entitled, *The Part of the Laboratory in Modern Crime Detection*.

Petrella went back to Highside.

There he found a note from Superintendent Haxtell that ran: 'A friend of Miss Martin has suggested that some or other of these were, or might have been, boy-friends of the deceased. I am seeing ones marked with cross. Would you tackle the others?' There followed a list of names and addresses ranging from Welwyn Garden City to Morden.

He looked at his watch. It was half past seven. With any luck he could knock off a few of them before midnight.

In the ensuing days the ripples spread wider and wider, diminishing in size and importance as they became more distant from the centre of the disturbance.

Petrella worked his way from near relatives and close friends, who said, 'How terrible! Who ever would have thought of anything like that happening to Marjorie!' through more distant connections who said, 'Miss Martin? Yes, I know her. I haven't seen her for a long time,' right out to the circumference where there were people who simply looked bewildered and said, 'Miss Martin—I'm sorry, I don't think I remember anyone of that name,' and on being reminded that they had danced with her at a tennis club dance two years before said, 'If you say so, I expect it's right, but I'm dashed if I can remember what she looked like.'

It was in the course of the third day that Petrella called at a nice little house in Herne Hill. The name was Taylor. Mr Taylor was not at home, but the door was opened by his wife, a cheerful redhead, who banished her two children to the kitchen when she understood what Petrella was after.

Her reactions were the standard ones. Apprehension, followed, as soon as she understood that what Petrella wanted was nothing to do with her, by a cheerful communicativeness. Miss Martin was, she believed, her husband's cousin. That is to say not his cousin, but his second cousin, or something like that. Her husband's father's married sister's husband's niece. So far as she knew they had only met her once, and that was quite by chance, six months before, at the funeral of Miss Martin's mother who was, of course, sister to her husband's uncle by marriage.

Petrella disentangled this complicated relationship without difficulty. He was already a considerable expert on the Martin family tree. Unfortunately, Mrs

Taylor could tell him nothing. Her acquaintance with Miss Martin was confined to this single occasion and she had not set eyes on her since. Her husband, who was a commercial traveller for Joblox, the London paint firm, was unlikely to be back until very late. He was on a tour in the Midlands; and it depended on the traffic, when he got home. Petrella said he quite understood. The interview remained in his memory chiefly because it was on his way back from it that he picked up his copy of the laboratory report on the coat.

The scientists had done themselves proud. No inch of its surface, interior or exterior, had escaped their microscopic gaze. Petrella cast his eye desperately over the eight closely typed foolscap pages. Stains on the exterior had been isolated and chemically tested and proved beyond reasonable doubt to be in two cases ink, in one case rabbit blood and in one case varnish. A quantity of sisal-hemp fluff had been recovered from the seam of the left-hand cuff and some marmalade from the right-hand one.

A sliver of soft wood, originally identified on the Chaterton Key Card as ordinary *pinus sylvestris*, was now believed to be *chamaecyparis lawsoniana*. In the right-hand pocket had been discovered a number of fragments of oyster shell, and a stain of oil shown by quantitative analysis to be a thick oil of a sort much used in marine engineering.

Petrella read the report in the underground between Charing Cross and Highside. When he reached the Police Station he found Haxtell in the C.I.D. room. He had in front of him the reports of all visits so far made. There were two hundred and thirty of them. Petrella added the five he had completed that afternoon, and was about to retire when he remembered the laboratory report, and cautiously added that too to the pile. He was conscious of thunder in the air.

'Don't bother,' said Haxtell. 'I've had a copy.' His eyes were red-rimmed from lack of proper sleep. 'So has the Chief Superintendent. He's just been here. He wants us to take some action on it.'

'Action, sir?'

'He suggests,' said Haxtell, in ominously quiet tones, 'that we re-examine all persons interviewed so far'—his hand flickered for a moment over the pile of paper on the table—'to ascertain whether they have ever been interested in the oyster-fishing industry. He feels that the coincidence of oyster shell and marine oil must have some significance.'

'I see, sir,' said Petrella. 'When do we start?

Haxtell stopped himself within an ace of saying something that would have been both indiscreet and insubordinate. Then, to his eternal credit, he laughed instead. 'We are both,' he said, 'going to get one good night's rest first. We'll start tomorrow morning.'

'I wonder if I could borrow the reports until then,' said Petrella, wondering at himself as he did so.

'Do what you like with them,' said Haxtell, 'I've got three days' routine work to catch up with.'

Petrella took them back with him to Mrs Catt's, where that worthy widow had prepared a high tea for him, his first leisured meal for three days. Sustained by a mountainous dish of sausages and eggs and refreshed by his third cup of strong tea, he started on the task of proving to himself the theory that had come to him.

Each paper was skimmed, and put on one side. Every now and then he would stop, extract one, and add it to a much smaller pile beside his plate. At the end of an hour, Petrella looked at the results of his work with satisfaction. In the small pile were six papers, six summaries of interviews with friends or relations of the murdered girl. If his idea was right, he had thus, at a stroke, reduced the possibles from two hundred and thirty-five to six. And of those six possibles, only one, he knew in his heart of hearts, was a probable.

There came back into his mind the visit that he had made that afternoon. There it was, in that place and no other, that the answer lay. There he had glimpsed, without realising it, the end of the scarlet thread that led to the heart of this untidy, rambling labyrinth. He thought of a nice redheaded girl and two redheaded children, and unexpectedly he found himself shivering.

It was dusk before he got back to Herne Hill. The lights were on in the nice little house, upstairs and downstairs, and a muddy car stood in the gravel run-in in front of the garage. Sounds suggested that the redheaded children were being put to bed by both their parents and were enjoying it.

One hour went by, and then a second. Petrella had found an empty house opposite, and he was squatting in the garden, his back propped against a tree. The night was warm and he was quite comfortable, and his head was nodding on his chest when the front door of the house opposite opened, and Mr Taylor appeared.

He stood for a moment, outlined against the light from the hall, saying something to his wife. He was too far off for Petrella to make out the words. Then he came down the path. He ignored the car, and made for the front gate, for which Petrella was thankful. He had made certain arrangements to cope with the contingency that Mr Taylor might use his car, but it was much easier if he remained on foot.

A short walk took them both, pursuer and pursued, to the door of the King of France public house. Mr Taylor went into the saloon. Petrella himself chose the private bar. Like most private bars, it had nothing to recommend it save its privacy, being narrow, bare and quite empty. But it had the advantage of looking straight across the serving-counter into the saloon.

Petrella let his man order first. He was evidently a well-known character in the King of France. He called the landlord Sam, and the landlord called him Mr Taylor.

Petrella drank his own beer slowly. Ten minutes later the moment for which he had been waiting arrived. Mr Taylor picked up a couple of glasses and strolled across with them to the counter. Petrella also rose casually to his feet. For a moment they faced each other, a bare two paces apart, under the bright bar lights.

Petrella saw in front of him a man of early middle age, with a nondescript face and neutral-coloured tousled hair, perhaps five foot nine in height, and wearing some sort of old-school tie.

As if aware that he was being looked at, Mr Taylor raised his head; and Petrella observed, in the left eye, a tiny red spot. It was, as the Colonel had said, exactly the colour of a fire opal.

'WE SHOWED HIS photograph to everyone in the block,' said Haxtell with satisfaction, 'and they all of them picked it out straight away, out of a set of six. Also the Colonel.'

'Good enough,' said Chief Superintendent Barstow. 'Any background?'

'We made a very cautious inquiry at Joblox. Taylor certainly works for them. But he's what they call an outside commission man. He sells in his spare time, and gets a percentage on sales. Last year he made just under a hundred pounds.'

'Which wouldn't keep him in his present style.'

'Definitely not. And of course a job like that would be very useful cover for a criminal sideline. He would be out when and where he liked, and no questions asked by his family.'

Barstow considered the matter slowly. The decision was his.

'Pull him in,' he said. 'Charge him with the job at Colonel Wing's. The rest will sort itself out quick enough when we search his house. Take a search-warrant with you. By the way, I never asked how you got onto him. Has he some connection with the oyster trade?'

Petrella said, cautiously, 'Well . . . no, sir. As a matter of fact, he hadn't. But the report was very useful corroborative evidence.'

'Clever chaps, these scientists,' said Barstow.

'Come clean,' said Haxtell, when the Chief Superintendent had departed. 'It was nothing to do with that coat, was it?'

'Nothing at all,' said Petrella. 'What occurred to me was that it was a very curious murder. Presuming it was the same man both times. Take Colonel Wing—he's full of beans, but when all's said and done, he's a frail old man, over ninety. He saw the intruder in a clear light, and the man simply turned tail and bolted. Then he bumps into Miss Martin, who's a girl, but a muscular young tennis player, but he *kills* her, coldly and deliberately.'

'From which you deduced that Miss Martin knew him, and he was prepared to kill to preserve the secret of his identity. Particularly as he had never been in the hands of the police.'

'There was a bit more to it than that,' said Petrella. 'It had to be someone who knew Miss Martin, but so casually that he would have no idea where she lived. Mightn't even remember her name. If he'd had any idea that it was the flat of someone who knew him he wouldn't have touched it with a barge pole. What I was looking for was someone who was distantly connected with

Miss Martin, but happened to have renewed his acquaintance with her recently. He had to be a very distant connection, you see. But they had to know each other by sight. There were half a dozen who could have filled the bill. I had this one in my mind because I'd interviewed Mrs Taylor only that afternoon. Of course, I'd have tried all the others afterwards. Only it wasn't necessary.'

There was neither pleasure nor satisfaction in his voice. He was seeing nothing but a nice redheaded girl and two redheaded children.

IT WAS PERHAPS six months later that Petrella ran across Colonel Wing again. The Taylor case was now only an uncomfortable memory, for Mr Taylor had taken his own life in his cell, and the redheaded girl was now a widow. Petrella was on his way home, and he might not have noticed him, but the Colonel came right across the road to greet him, narrowly missing death at the hands of a motorcyclist of whose approach he had been blissfully unaware. 'Good evening, Sergeant,' the old man said. 'How are you keeping?'

'Very well, thank you, Colonel,' said Petrella. 'And how are you?'

'I'm not getting any younger,' said the Colonel. Petrella suddenly perceived to his surprise that the old man was covered with embarrassment. He waited patiently for him to speak.

'I wonder—' said the old man at last, 'it's an awkward thing to have to ask, but could you get that coat back—you remember?'

'Get it *back*?' said Petrella. 'I don't know. I suppose so.'

'If it was mine, I wouldn't bother. But it isn't. I find it's my cousin Tom's. I'd forgotten all about it, until he reminded me.'

Petrella stared at him.

'Do you mean to say—'

'Tom stayed the night with me—he does that sometimes, between trips. Just drops in. Of course, when he reminded me, I remembered—'

'Between trips . . .' said Petrella weakly. 'He isn't by any chance an oyster fisherman?'

It was the Colonel's turn to stare. 'Certainly not,' he said. 'He's one of the best-known breeders of budgerigars in the country.'

'Budgerigars?'

'Very well known for them. I believe I'm right in saying he introduced the foreign system of burnishing their feathers with oil. It's funny you should mention oysters, though. That's a thing he's very keen on. Powdered oyster shell in the feed. It improves their high notes.'

Petrella removed his hat in a figurative but belated salute to the Forensic Science Laboratory.

'Certainly you shall have your coat back,' he said. 'It'll need a thorough clean and a little stitching, but I am delighted to think that it is going to be of use to someone at last.'

Sue Grafton

b. 1940

LONG GONE

EPTEMBER IN SANTA TERESA. I've never known anyone yet who doesn't suffer a certain restlessness when autumn rolls around. It's the season of new school clothes, fresh notebooks, and finely sharpened pencils without any teeth marks in the wood. We're all eight years old again and anything is possible. The new year should never begin on 1 January. It begins in the fall and continues as long as our saddle oxfords remain unscuffed and our lunch boxes have no dents.

My name is Kinsey Millhone. I'm female, thirty-two, twice divorced, 'doing business' as Kinsey Millhone Investigations in a little town ninety-five miles north of Los Angeles. Mine isn't a walk-in trade like a beauty salon. Most of my clients find themselves in a bind and then seek my services, hoping I can offer a solution for a mere thirty bucks an hour, plus expenses. Robert Ackerman's message was waiting on my answering machine that Monday morning at nine when I got in.

'Hello. My name is Robert Ackerman and I wonder if you could give me a call. My wife is missing and I'm worried sick. I was hoping you could help me out.' In the background, I could hear whiny children, my favorite kind. He repeated his name and gave me a telephone number. I made a pot of coffee before I called him back.

A little person answered the phone. There was a murmured childsize hello and then I heard a lot of heavy breathing close to the mouthpiece.

'Hi,' I said, 'can I speak to your daddy?'

'Yes.' Long silence.

'Today?' I asked.

The receiver was clunked down on a tabletop and I could hear the clatter of footsteps in a room that sounded as if it didn't have any carpeting. In due course, Robert Ackerman picked up the phone.

'Lucy?'

'It's Kinsey Millhone, Mr Ackerman. I just got your message on my answering machine. Can you tell me what's going on?'

'Oh wow, yeah . . .'

He was interrupted by a piercing shriek that sounded like one of those policeman's whistles you use to discourage obscene phone callers. I didn't jerk back quite in time. 'Shit, that hurt.'

262

I listened patiently while he dealt with the errant child.

'Sorry,' he said when he came back on the line. 'Look, is there any way you could come out to the house? I've got my hands full and I just can't get away.'

I took his address and brief directions, then headed out to my car.

ROBERT AND THE MISSING Mrs Ackerman lived in a housing tract that looked like it was built in the 'forties before anyone ever dreamed up the notion of family rooms, country kitchens, and his 'n' hers solar spas. What we had here was a basic drywall box; cramped living-room with a dining L, a kitchen and one bathroom sandwiched between two nine-by-twelve-foot bedrooms. When Robert answered the door I could just about see the whole place at a glance. The only thing the builders had been lavish with was the hardwood floors, which, in this case, was unfortunate. Little children had banged and scraped these floors and had brought in some kind of foot grit that I sensed before I was even asked to step inside.

Robert, though harried, had a boyish appeal; a man in his early thirties per-haps, lean and handsome, with dark eyes and dark hair that came to a pixie point in the middle of his forehead. He was wearing chinos and a plain white T-shirt. He had a baby, maybe eight months old, propped on his hip like a gro-cery bag. Another child clung to his right leg, while a third rode his tricycle at various walls and doorways, making quite loud sounds with his mouth.

'Hi, come on in,' Robert said. 'We can talk out in the back yard while the kids play.' His smile was sweet.

I followed him through the tiny disorganised house and out to the back yard, where he set the baby down in a sandpile framed with two-by-fours. The second child held on to Robert's belt loops and stuck his thumb in its mouth, staring at me while the tricycle child tried to ride off the edge of the porch. I'm not fond of children. I'm really not. Especially the kind who wear hard brown shoes. Like dogs, these infants sensed my distaste and kept their distance, eyeing me with a mixture of rancor and disdain.

The back yard was scruffy, fenced in, and littered with the fifty-pound sacks the sand had come in. Robert gave the children homemade-style cookies out of a cardboard box and shooed them away. In fifteen minutes the sugar would prob-ably turn them into lunatics. I gave my watch a quick glance, hoping to be gone by then.

'You want a lawn chair?'

'No, this is fine,' I said and settled on the grass. There wasn't a lawn chair in sight, but the offer was nice anyway.

He perched on the edge of the sandbox and ran a distracted hand across his head. 'God, I'm sorry everything is such a mess, but Lucy hasn't been here for two days. She didn't come home from work on Friday and I've been a wreck ever since.'

'I take it you notified the police.'

'Sure. Friday night. She never showed up at the babysitter's house to pick the kids up. I finally got a call here at seven asking where she was. I figured she'd just stopped off at the grocery store or something, so I went ahead and picked 'em up and brought 'em home. By ten o'clock when I hadn't heard from her, I knew something was wrong. I called her boss at home and he said as far as he knew she'd left work at five as usual, so that's when I called the police.'

'You filed a missing persons report?'

'I can do that today. With an adult, you have to wait seventy-two hours, and even then, there's not much they can do.'

'What else did they suggest?'

'The usual stuff, I guess. I mean, I called everyone we know. I talked to her mom in Bakersfield and this friend of hers at work. Nobody has any idea where she is. I'm scared something's happened to her.'

'You've checked with hospitals in the area, I take it.'

'Sure. That's the first thing I did.'

'Did she give you any indication that anything was wrong?'

'Not a word.'

'Was she depressed or behaving oddly?'

'Well, she was kind of restless the past couple of months. She always seemed to get excited around this time of year. She said it reminded her of her old elementary school days.' He shrugged. 'I hated mine.'

'But she's never disappeared like this before.'

'Oh, heck no. I just mentioned her mood because you asked. I don't think it amounted to anything.'

'Does she have any problems with alcohol or drugs?'

'Lucy isn't really like that,' he said. 'She's petite and kind of quiet. A homebody, I guess you'd say.'

'What about your relationship? Do the two of you get along OK?'

'As far as I'm concerned, we do. I mean, once in a while we get into it but never anything serious.'

'What are your disagreements about?'

He smiled ruefully. 'Money, mostly. With three kids, we never seem to have enough. I mean, I'm crazy about big families, but it's tough financially. I always wanted four or five, but she says three is plenty, especially with the oldest not in school yet. We fight about that some . . . having more kids.'

'You both work?'

'We have to, just to make ends meet. She has a job in an escrow company downtown, and I work for the phone company.'

'Doing what?'

'Installer,' he said.

'Has there been any hint of someone else in her life?'

He sighed, plucking at the grass between his feet. 'In a way, I wish I could say yes. I'd like to think maybe she just got fed up or something and checked into a motel for the weekend. Something like that.'

'But you don't think she did.'

'Unh-uh and I'm going crazy with anxiety. Somebody's got to find out where she is.'

'Mr Ackerman . . .'

'You can call me Rob,' he said.

Clients always say that. I mean, unless their names are something else.

'Rob,' I said, 'the police are truly your best bet in a situation like this. I'm just one person. They've got a vast machinery they can put to work and it won't cost you a cent.'

'You charge a lot, huh?'

'Thirty bucks an hour plus expenses.'

He thought for a moment, then gave me a searching look. 'Could you maybe put in ten hours? I got three hundred bucks we were saving for a trip to the San Diego Zoo.'

I pretended to think about it, but the truth was, I knew I couldn't say no to that boyish face. Anyway, the kids were starting to whine and I wanted to get out of there. I waived the retainer and said I'd send him an itemised bill when the ten hours were up. I figured I could put a contract in the mail and reduce my contact with the short persons who were crowding around him now, begging for more sweets. I asked for a recent photograph of Lucy, but all he could come up with was a two-year-old snapshot of her with the two older kids. She looked beleaguered even then, and that was before the third baby came along. I thought about quiet little Lucy Ackerman whose three strapping sons had leg's the size of my arms. If I were she, I knew where I'd be. Long gone.

Lucy Ackerman was employed as an escrow officer for a small company on State Street not far from my office. It was a modest establishment of white walls, rust and brown plaid furniture with burnt orange carpeting. There were Gauguin reproductions all around and a live plant on every desk. I introduced myself first to the office manager, a Mrs Merriman, who was in her sixties, had tall hair, and wore lace-up boots with stiletto heels. She looked like a woman who'd trade all her pension monies for a head-to-toe body tuck.

I said, 'Robert Ackerman has asked me to see if I can locate his wife.'

'Well, the poor man. I heard about that,' she said with her mouth. Her eyes said, 'Fat chance!'

'Do you have any idea where she might be?'

'I think you'd better talk to Mr Sotherland.' She had turned all prim and officious, but my guess was she knew something and was dying to be asked. I intended to accommodate her as soon as I'd talked to him. The protocol in small offices, I've found, is ironclad.

Gavin Sotherland got up from his swivel chair and stretched a big hand across the desk to shake mine. The other member of the office force, Barbara Hemdahl, the book-keeper, got up from her chair simultaneously and excused herself. Mr Sotherland watched her depart and then motioned me into the same seat. I sank into leather still hot from Barbara Hemdahl's back-side, a curiously intimate effect. I made a mental note to find out what she knew, and then I looked, with interest, at the company vice president. I picked up all these names and job titles because his was cast in stand-up bronze letters on his desk, and the two women both had white plastic name tags affixed to their breasts, like nurses. As nearly as I could tell, there were only four of them in the office, including Lucy Ackerman, and I couldn't understand how they could fail to identify each other on sight. Maybe all the badges were for clients who couldn't be trusted to tell one from the other without the proper IDs.

Gavin Sotherland was large, an ex-jock to all appearances, maybe forty-five years old, with a heavy head of blond hair thinning slightly at the crown. He had a slight paunch, a slight stoop to his shoulders, and a grip that was damp with sweat. He had his coat off, and his once-starched white shirt was limp and wrin-kled, his beige gabardine pants heavily creased across the lap. Altogether, he looked like a man who'd crossed a continent by rail. Still, I was forced to credit him with good looks, even if he had let himself go to seed.

'Nice to meet you, Miss Millhone. I'm so glad you're here.' His voice was deep and rumbling, with confidence-inspiring undertones. On the other hand, I didn't like the look in his eyes. He could have been a conman, for all I knew. 'I understand Mrs Ackerman never got home Friday night,' he said.

'That's what I'm told,' I replied. 'Can you tell me anything about her day here?'

He studied me briefly. 'Well, now I'm going to have to be honest with you. Our book-keeper has come across some discrepancies in the accounts. It looks like Lucy Ackerman has just walked off with half a million dollars entrusted to us.'

'How'd she manage that?'

I was picturing Lucy Ackerman, free of those truck-busting kids, lying on a beach in Rio, slurping some kind of rum drink out of a coconut.

Mr Sotherland looked pained. 'In the most straightforward manner imagin-able,' he said. 'It looks like she opened a new bank account at a branch in Montebello and deposited ten checks that should have gone into other accounts. Last Friday, she withdrew over five hundred thousand dollars in cash, claiming we were closing out a big real estate deal. We found the passbook in her bottom drawer.' He tossed the booklet across the desk to me and I picked it up. The word "VOID" had been punched into the pages in a series of holes. A quick glance showed ten deposits at intervals dating back over the past three months and a zero balance as of last Friday's date.

'Didn't anybody else double-check this stuff?'

'We'd just undergone our annual audit in June. Everything was fine. We trusted this woman implicitly and had every reason to.'

'You discovered the loss this morning?'

'Yes, ma'am, but I'll admit I was suspicious Friday night when Robert Ackerman called me at home. It was completely unlike that woman to disappear without a word. She's worked here eight years, and she's been punctual and conscientious since the day she walked in.'

'Well, punctual at any rate,' I said. 'Have you notified the police?'

'I was just about to do that. I'll have to alert the Department of Corporations, too. God, I can't believe she did this to us. I'll be fired. They'll probably shut this entire office down.'

'Would you mind if I had a quick look around?'

'To what end?'

'There's always a chance we can figure out where she went. If we move fast enough, maybe we can catch her before she gets away with it.'

'Well, I doubt that,' he said. 'The last anybody saw her was Friday afternoon. That's two full days. She could be anywhere by now.'

'Mr Sotherland, her husband has already authorised three hundred dollars' worth of my time. Why not take advantage of it?'

He stared at me. 'Won't the police object?'

'Probably. But I don't intend to get in anybody's way, and whatever I find out, I'll turn over to them. They may not be able to get a fraud detective out here until late morning anyway. If I get a line on her, it'll make you look good to the company *and* to the cops.'

He gave a sigh of resignation and waved his hand. 'Hell, I don't care. Do what you want.'

When I left his office, he was putting the call through to the police department.

I SAT BRIEFLY at Lucy's desk, which was neat and well organised. Her drawers contained the usual office supplies; no personal items at all. There was a calendar on her desktop, one of those loose-leaf affairs with a page for each day. I checked back through the past couple of months. The only personal notation was for an appointment at the Women's Health Center, 2nd August, and a second visit last Friday afternoon. It must have been a busy day for Lucy, what with a doctor's appointment and ripping off her company for half a million bucks. I made a note of the address she'd pencilled in at the time of her first visit. The other two women in the office were keeping an eye on me, I noticed, though both pretended to be occupied with paperwork.

When I finished my search, I got up and crossed the room to Mrs Merriman's desk. 'Is there any way I can make a copy of the passbook for that account Mrs Ackerman opened?'

'Well, yes, if Mr Sotherland approves,' she said.

'I'm also wondering where she keeps her coat and purse during the day.'

'In the back. We each have a locker in the storage room.'

'I'd like to take a look at that, too.'

I waited patiently while she cleared both matters with her boss, and then I accompanied her to the rear. There was a door that opened on to the parking lot. To the left of it was a small rest room and, on the right, there was a storage room that housed four connecting upright metal lockers, the copy machine, and numerous shelves neatly stacked with office supplies. Each shoulder-high locker was marked with a name. Lucy Ackerman's was still securely padlocked. There was something about the blank look of that locker that seemed ominous some-how. I looked at the lock, fairly itching to have a crack at it with my little set of key picks, but I didn't want to push my luck with the cops on the way.

'I'd like for someone to let me know what's in that locker when it's finally opened,' I remarked while Mrs Merriman ran off the copy of the passbook pages for me.

'This, too,' I said, handing her a carbon of the withdrawal slip Lucy'd been required to sign in receipt of the cash. It had been folded and tucked into the back of the booklet. 'You have any theories about where she went?'

Mrs Merriman's mouth pursed piously, as though she were debating with herself about how much she might say.

'I wouldn't want to be accused of talking out of school,' she ventured.

'Mrs Merriman, it does look like a crime's been committed,' I suggested. 'The police are going to ask you the same thing when they get here.'

'Oh. Well, in that case, I suppose it's all right. I mean, I don't have the faintest idea where she is, but I do think she's been acting oddly the past few months.'

'Like what?'

'She seemed secretive. Smug. Like she knew something the rest of us didn't know about.'

'That certainly turned out to be the case,' I said.

'Oh, I didn't mean it was related to that,' she said hesitantly. 'I think she was having an affair.'

That got my attention. 'An affair? With whom?'

She paused for a moment, touching at one of the hairpins that supported her ornate hairdo. She allowed her gaze to stray back toward Mr Sotherland's office. I turned and looked in that direction, too.

'Really?' I said. 'No wonder he was in a sweat,' I thought.

'I couldn't swear to it,' she murmured, 'but his marriage has been rocky for years, and I gather she hasn't been that happy herself. She has those beastly little boys, you know, and a husband who seems determined to spawn more. She and Mr Sotherland . . . Gavie, she calls him . . . have . . . well, I'm sure they've been together. Whether it's connected to this matter of the missing money, I wouldn't presume to guess.' Having said as much, she was suddenly uneasy. 'You won't repeat what I've said to the police, I hope.'

'Absolutely not,' I said. 'Unless they ask, of course.'

'Oh. Of course.'

'By the way, is there a company travel agent?'

'Right next door,' she replied.

I HAD A BRIEF CHAT with the book-keeper, who added nothing to the general picture of Lucy Ackerman's last few days at work. I retrieved my VW from the parking lot and headed over to the health center eight blocks away, wondering what Lucy had been up to. I was guessing birth control and probably the permanent sort. If she were having an affair (and determined not to get pregnant again in any event), it would seem logical, but I hadn't any idea how to verify the fact. Medical personnel are notoriously stingy with information like that.

I parked in front of the clinic and grabbed my clipboard from the back seat. I have a supply of all-purpose forms for occasions like this. They look like a cross between a job application and an insurance claim. I filled one out now in Lucy's name and forged her signature at the bottom where it said "authorisation to release information". As a model, I used the Xerox copy of the withdrawal slip she'd tucked in her passbook. I'll admit my methods would be considered unorthodox, nay illegal, in the eyes of law-enforcement officers everywhere, but I reasoned that the information I was seeking would never actually be used in court, and therefore it couldn't matter *that* much how it was obtained.

I went into the clinic, noting gratefully the near-empty waiting room. I approached the counter and took out my wallet with my California Fidelity ID. I do occasional insurance investigations for CF in exchange for office space. They once made the mistake of issuing me a company identification card with my picture right on it that I've been flashing around quite shamelessly ever since.

I had a choice of three female clerks and, after a brief assessment, I made eye contact with the oldest of them. In places like this, the younger employees usually have no authority at all and are thus impossible to con. People without authority will often simply stand there, reciting the rules like mynah birds. Having no power, they also seem to take a vicious satisfaction in forcing others to comply.

The woman approached the counter on her side, looking at me expectantly. I showed her my CF ID and made the form on the clipboard conspicuous, as though I had nothing to hide.

'Hi. My name is Kinsey Millhone,' I said, 'I wonder if you can give me some help. Your name is what?'

She seemed wary of the request, as though her name had magical powers that might be taken from her by force. 'Lillian Vincent,' she said reluctantly. 'What sort of help did you need?'

'Lucy Ackerman has applied for some insurance benefits and we need verification of the claim. You'll want a copy of the release form for your files, of course.'

I passed the forged paper to her and then busied myself with my clipboard as though it was all perfectly matter-of-fact.

She was instantly alert. 'What is this?'

I gave her a look. 'Oh, sorry. She's applying for maternity leave and we need her due date.'

'Maternity leave?'

'Isn't she a patient here?'

Lillian Vincent looked at me. 'Just a moment,' she said, and moved away from the desk with the form in her hand. She went to a file cabinet and extracted a chart, returning to the counter. She pushed it over to me. 'The woman has had a tubal ligation,' she said, her manner crisp.

I blinked, smiling slightly as though she were making a joke. 'There must be some mistake.'

'Lucy Ackerman must have made it then if she thinks she can pull this off.' She opened the chart and tapped significantly at the 2 August date. 'She was just in here Friday for a final checkup and a medical release. She's sterile.'

I looked at the chart. Sure enough, that's what it said. I raised my eyebrows and then shook my head slightly. 'God. Well. I guess I better have a copy of that.'

'I should think so,' the woman said and ran one off for me on the desktop dry copier. She placed it on the counter and watched as I tucked it on to my clipboard.

She said, 'I don't know how they think they can get away with it.'

'People love to cheat,' I replied.

IT WAS NEARLY NOON by the time I got back to the travel agency next door to the place where Lucy Ackerman had worked. It didn't take any time at all to unearth the reservations she'd made two weeks before. Buenos Aires, first class on Pan Am. For one. She'd picked up the ticket Friday afternoon just before the agency closed for the weekend.

The travel agent rested his elbows on the counter and looked at me with interest, hoping to hear all the gory details, I'm sure. 'I heard about that business next door,' he said. He was young, maybe twenty-four, with a pug nose, auburn hair and a gap between his teeth. He'd make the perfect co-star on a wholesome family TV show.

'How'd she pay for the tickets?'

'Cash,' he said. 'I mean, who'd have thunk?'

'Did she say anything in particular at the time?'

'Not really. She seemed jazzed and we joked some about Montezuma's revenge and stuff like that. I knew she was married, and I was asking her all about who was keeping the kids and what her old man was going to do while she was gone. God, I never in a million *years* guessed she was pulling off a scam like that, you know?'

'Did you ask why she was going to Argentina by herself?'

'Well, yeah, and she said it was a surprise.' He shrugged. 'It didn't really make sense, but she was laughing like a kid, and I thought I just didn't get the joke.'

I asked for a copy of the itinerary, such as it was. She had paid for a round-trip ticket, but there were no reservations coming back. Maybe she intended to cash in the return ticket once she got down there. I tucked the travel docs on to my clipboard along with the copy of her medical forms. Something about this whole deal had begun to chafe, but I couldn't figure out quite why.

'Thanks for your help,' I said, heading towards the door.

'No problem. I guess the other guy didn't get it either,' he remarked.

I paused, midstride, turning back. 'Get what?'

'The joke. I heard 'em next door and they were fighting like cats and dogs. He was pissed.'

'Really?' I asked. I stared at him. 'What time was this?'

'Five-fifteen. Something like that. They were closed and so were we, but Dad wanted me to stick around for a while until the cleaning crew got here. He owns this place, which is how I got in the business myself. These new guys were starting and he wanted me to make sure they understood what to do.'

'Are you going to be here for a while?'

'Sure.'

'Good. The police may want to hear about this.'

I WENT BACK into the escrow office with mental alarm bells clanging away like crazy. Both Barbara Hemdahl and Mrs Merriman had opted to eat lunch in. Or maybe the cops had ordered them to stay where they were. The book-keeper sat at her desk with a sandwich, apple, and a carton of milk neatly arranged in front of her, while Mrs Merriman picked at something in a plastic container she must have brought in from a fast-food place.

'How's it going?' I asked.

Barbara Hemdahl spoke up from her side of the room. 'The detectives went off for a search warrant so they can get in all the lockers back there, collecting evidence.'

'Only one of 'em is locked,' I pointed out.

She shrugged. 'I guess they can't even peek without the paperwork.'

Mrs Merriman spoke up then, her expression tinged with guilt. 'Actually, they asked the rest of us if we'd open our lockers voluntarily, so of course we did.'

Mrs Merriman and Barbara Hemdahl exchanged a look.

'And?'

Mrs Merriman colored slightly. 'There was an overnight case in Mr Sotherland's locker, and I guess the things in it were hers.'

'Is it still back there?'

'Well, yes, but they left a uniformed officer on guard so nobody'd walk off with it. They've got everything spread out on the copy machine.'

I went through the rear of the office, peering into the storage room. I knew the guy on duty and he didn't object to my doing a visual survey of the items, as long as I didn't touch anything. The overnight case had been packed with all the personal belongings women like to keep on hand in case the rest of the luggage gets sent to Mexicali by mistake. I spotted a toothbrush and toothpaste, slippers, a filmy nightie, prescription drugs, hairbrush, extra eyeglasses in a case. Tucked under a change of underwear, I spotted a round plastic container, slightly convex, about the size of a compact.

Gavin Sotherland was still sitting at his desk when I stopped by his office. His skin tone was gray and his shirt was hanging out, big rings of sweat under each arm. He was smoking a cigarette with the air of a man who's quit the habit and has taken it up again under duress. A second uniformed officer was standing just inside the door to my right.

I leaned against the frame, but Gavin scarcely looked up.

I said, 'You knew what she was doing, but you thought she'd take you with her when she left.'

His smile was bitter. 'Life is full of surprises,' he said.

I was going to have to tell Robert Ackerman what I'd discovered, and I dreaded it. As a stalling maneuver, just to demonstrate what a good girl I was, I drove over to the police station first and dropped off the data I'd collected, filling them in on the theory I'd come up with. They didn't exactly pin a medal on me, but they weren't as pissed off as I thought they'd be, given the number of civil codes I'd violated in the process. They were even moderately courteous, which is unusual in their treatment of me. Unfortunately, none of it took that long and before I knew it, I was standing at the Ackermans' front door again.

I rang the bell and waited, bad jokes running through my head. Well, there's good news and bad news, Robert. The good news is we've wrapped it up with hours to spare so you won't have to pay me the full three hundred dollars we agreed to. The bad news is your wife's a thief, she's probably dead, and we're just getting out a warrant now, because we think we know where the body's stashed.

The door opened and Robert was standing there with a finger to his lips. 'The kids are down for their naps,' he whispered.

I nodded elaborately, pantomiming my understanding, as though the silence he'd imposed required this special behavior on my part.

He motioned me in and together we tiptoed through the house and out to the back yard, where we continued to talk in low tones. I wasn't sure which bedroom the little rugrats slept in, and didn't want to be responsible for waking them.

Half a day of playing papa to the boys had left Robert looking disheveled and sorely in need of relief.

'I didn't expect you back this soon,' he whispered.

I found myself whispering too, feeling anxious at the sense of secrecy. It reminded me of grade school somehow: the smell of autumn hanging in the air, the two of us perched on the edge of the sandbox like little kids, conspiring. I didn't want to break his heart, but what was I to do?

'I think we've got it wrapped up,' I said.

He looked at me for a moment, apparently guessing from my expression that the news wasn't good. 'Is she OK?'

'We don't think so,' I said. And then I told him what I'd learned, starting with the embezzlement and the relationship with Gavin, taking it right through to the quarrel the travel agent had heard. Robert was ahead of me.

'She's dead, isn't she?'

'We don't know it for a fact, but we suspect as much.'

He nodded, tears welling up. He wrapped his arms around his knees and propped his chin on his fists. He looked so young, I wanted to reach out and touch him. 'She was really having an affair?' he asked plaintively.

'You must have suspected as much,' I said. 'You said she was restless and excited for months. Didn't that give you a clue?'

He shrugged one shoulder, using the sleeve of his T-shirt to dash at the tears trickling down his cheeks. 'I don't know,' he said. 'I guess.'

'And then you stopped by the office Friday afternoon and found her getting ready to leave the country. That's when you killed her, isn't it?'

He froze, staring at me. At first, I thought he'd deny it, but maybe he realised there wasn't any point. He nodded mutely.

'And then you hired me to make it look good, right?'

He made a kind of squeaking sound in the back of his throat and sobbed once, his voice reduced to a whisper again. 'She shouldn't have done it . . . betrayed us like that. We loved her so much . . .'

'Have you got the money here?'

He nodded, looking miserable. 'I wasn't going to pay your fee out of that,' he said incongruously. 'We really did have a little fund so, we could go to San Diego one day.'

'I'm sorry things didn't work out,' I said.

'I didn't do so bad, though, did I? I mean, I could have gotten away with it, don't you think?'

I'd been talking about the trip to the zoo. He thought I was referring to his murdering his wife. Talk about poor communication. God.

'Well, you nearly pulled it off,' I said. Shit, I was sitting there trying to make the guy *feel* good.

He looked at me piteously, eyes red and flooded, his mouth trembling. 'But where did I slip up? What did I do wrong?'

'You put her diaphragm in the overnight case you packed. You thought you'd shift suspicion on to Gavin Sotherland, but you didn't realise she'd had her tubes tied.'

A momentary rage flashed through his eyes and then flickered out. I suspected that her voluntary sterilisation was more insulting to him than the affair with her boss.

'Jesus, I don't know what she saw in him,' he breathed. 'He was such a pig.'

'Well,' I said, 'If it's any comfort to you, she wasn't going to take *him* with her, either. She just wanted freedom, you know?'

He pulled out a handkerchief and blew his nose, trying to compose himself. He mopped his eyes, shivering with tension. 'How can you prove it, though, without a body? Do you know where she is?'

'I think we do,' I said softly. 'The sandbox, Robert. Right under us.'

He seemed to shrink. 'Oh, God,' he whispered, 'Oh, God, don't turn me in. I'll give you the money, I don't give a damn. Just let me stay here with my kids. The little guys need me. I did it for them. I swear I did. You don't have to tell the cops do you?'

I shook my head and opened my shirt collar, showing him the mike. 'I don't have to tell a soul. I'm wired for sound,' I said, and then I looked over toward the side yard.

For once, I was glad to see Lieutenant Dolan amble into view.

Dashiell Hammett
1894–1961

A MAN CALLED SPADE

Samuel Spade put his telephone aside and looked at his watch. It was not quite four o'clock. He called, 'Yoo-hoo!'

Effie Perine came in from the outer office. She was eating a piece of chocolate cake.

'Tell Sid Wise I won't be able to keep that date this afternoon,' he said.

She put the last of the cake into her mouth and licked the tips of forefinger and thumb.

'That's the third time this week.'

When he smiled, the v's of his chin, mouth and brows grew longer.

'I know, but I've got to go out and save a life.' He nodded at the telephone. 'Somebody's scaring Max Bliss.'

She laughed. 'Probably somebody named John D. Conscience.'

He looked up at her from the cigarette he had begun to make. 'Know anything I ought to know about him?'

'Nothing you don't know. I was just thinking about the time he let his brother go to San Quentin.'

Spade shrugged. 'That's not the worst thing he's done.' He lit his cigarette, stood up and reached for his hat. 'But he's all right now. All Samuel Spade clients are honest, God-fearing folk. If I'm not back at closing time just run along.'

He went to a tall apartment building on Nob Hill, pressed a button set in the frame of a door marked 10K. The door was opened immediately by a burly dark man in wrinkled dark clothes. He was nearly bald and carried a gray hat in one hand.

The burly man said, 'Hello, Sam.' He smiled, but his small eyes lost none of their shrewdness. 'What are you doing here?'

Spade said, 'Hello, Tom.' His face was wooden, his voice expressionless. 'Bliss in?'

'Is he!' Tom pulled down the corners of his thick-lipped mouth. 'You don't have to worry about that.'

Spade's brows came together. 'Well?'

A man appeared in the vestibule behind Tom. He was smaller than either Spade or Tom, but compactly built. He had a ruddy, square face and a close-trimmed, grizzled mustache. His clothes were neat. He wore a black bowler perched on the back of his head.

Spade addressed this man over Tom's shoulder:—

'Hello, Dundy.'

Dundy nodded briefly and came to the door. His blue eyes were hard and prying.

'What is it?' he asked Tom.

'B-l-i-s-s, M-a-x,' Spade spelled patiently. 'I want to see him. He wants to see me. Catch on?'

Tom laughed. Dundy did not.

Tom said, 'Only one of you gets your wish.' Then he glanced sidewise at Dundy and abruptly stopped laughing. He seemed uncomfortable.

Spade scowled. 'All right,' he demanded irritably; 'is he dead or has he killed somebody?'

Dundy thrust his square face up at Spade and seemed to push his words out with his lower lip:

'What makes you think either?'

Spade said, 'Oh, sure! I come calling on Mr Bliss and I'm stopped at the door by a couple of men from the police Homicide Detail, and I'm supposed to think I'm just interrupting a game of rummy.'

'Aw, stop it, Sam,' Tom grumbled, looking at neither Spade nor Dundy. 'He's dead.'

'Killed?'

Tom wagged his head slowly up and down. He looked at Spade now. 'What've you got on it?'

Spade replied in a deliberate monotone, 'He called me up this afternoon—say at five minutes to four—I looked at my watch after he hung up and there was still a minute or so to go—and said somebody was after his scalp. He wanted me to come over. It seemed real enough to him—it was up in his neck all right.' He made a small gesture with one hand. 'Well, here I am.'

'Didn't say who or how?' Dundy asked.

Spade shook his head. 'No. Just somebody had offered to kill him and he believed them, and would I come over right away.'

'Didn't he—?' Dundy began quickly.

'He didn't say anything else,' Spade said. 'Don't you people tell me anything?'

Dundy said curtly, 'Come in and take a look at him.'

Tom said, 'It's a sight.'

They went across the vestibule and through a door into a green and rose living-room.

A man near the door stopped sprinkling white powder on the end of a glass-covered small table to say, 'Hello, Sam.'

Spade nodded, said, 'How are you, Phels?' and then nodded at the two men who stood talking by a window.

The dead man lay with his mouth open. Some of his clothes had been taken off. His throat was puffy and dark. The end of his tongue showing in a corner of his mouth was bluish, swollen. On his bare chest, over the heart, a five-pointed star had been outlined in black ink and in the center of it a T.

Spade looked down at the dead man and stood for a moment silently studying him.

Then he asked, 'He was found like that?'

'About,' Tom said. 'We moved him around a little.' He jerked a thumb at the shirt, undershirt, vest and coat lying on a table. 'They were spread over the floor.'

Spade rubbed his chin. His yellow-gray eyes were dreamy.

'When?'

Tom said, 'We got it at four twenty. His daughter gave it to us.' He moved his head to indicate a closed door. 'You'll see her.'

'Know anything?'

'Heaven knows,' Tom said wearily. 'She's been kind of hard to get along with so far.' He turned to Dundy. 'Want to try her again now?'

Dundy nodded, then spoke to one of the men at the window. 'Start sifting his papers, Mack. He's supposed to've been threatened.'

Mack said, 'Right.' He pulled his hat down over his eyes and walked toward a green secrétaire in the far end of the room.

A man came in from the corridor, a heavy man of fifty with a deeply lined, grayish face under a broad-brimmed black hat.

He said, 'Hello, Sam,' and then told Dundy, 'He had company around half past two, stayed just about an hour. A big blond man in brown, maybe forty or forty-five. Didn't send his name up. I got it from the Filipino in the elevator that rode him both ways.'

'Sure it was only an hour?' Dundy asked.

The gray-faced man shook his head. 'But he's sure it wasn't more than half past three when he left. He says the afternoon papers came in then, and this man had ridden down with him before they came.'

He pushed his hat back to scratch his head, then pointed a thick finger at the design inked on the dead man's breast and asked somewhat plaintively, 'What the deuce do you suppose that thing is?'

Nobody replied.

Dundy asked, 'Can the elevator boy identify him?'

'He says he could, but that ain't always the same thing. Says he never saw him before.' He stopped looking at the dead man. 'The girl's getting me a list of his phone calls. How you been, Sam?'

Spade said he had been all right. Then he said slowly, 'His brother's big and blond and maybe forty or forty-five.'

Dundy's blue eyes were hard and bright.

'So what?' he asked.

'You remember the Graystone Loan swindle. They were both in it, but Max eased the load over on Theodore and it turned out to be one to fourteen years in San Quentin.'

Dundy was slowly wagging his head up and down. 'I remember now. Where is he?'

Spade shrugged and began to make a cigarette.

Dundy nudged Tom with an elbow. 'Find out.'

Tom said, 'Sure, but if he was out of here at half past three and this fellow was still alive at five to four—'

'And he broke his leg so he couldn't duck back in,' the gray-faced man said jovially.

'Find out,' Dundy repeated.

Tom said, 'Sure, sure,' and went to the telephone.

Dundy addressed the gray-faced man:

'Check up on the newspapers; see what time they were actually delivered this afternoon.'

The gray-faced man nodded and left the room.

The man who had been searching the secrétaire said, 'Uh-huh,' and turned around holding an envelope in one hand, a sheet of paper in the other.

Dundy held out his hand. 'Something?'

The man said, 'Uh-huh,' again and gave Dundy the sheet of paper.

Spade was looking over Dundy's shoulder.

It was a small sheet of common white paper bearing a penciled message in neat, undistinguished handwriting:

> *When this reaches you I will be too close for you to escape—this time. We will*
> *balance our accounts—for good.*

The signature was a five-pointed star enclosing a T, the design on the dead man's left breast.

Dundy held out his hand again and was given the envelope. Its stamp was French. The address was typewritten:

Max Bliss, Esq.
Amsterdam Apartments
San Francisco, Calif., USA

'Postmarked Paris,' he said, 'the second of the month.' He counted swiftly on his fingers. 'That would get it here today, all right.'

He folded the message slowly, put it in the envelope, put the envelope in his coat pocket:

'Keep digging,' he told the man who had found the message.

The man nodded and returned to the secrétaire.

Dundy looked at Spade. 'What do you think of it?'

Spade's brown cigarette wagged up and down with his words: 'I don't like it. I don't like any of it.'

Tom put down the telephone.

'He got out the fifteenth of last month,' he said. 'I got them trying to locate him.'

Spade went to the telephone, called a number, and asked for Mr Darrell. Then: 'Hello, Harry, this is Sam Spade . . . Fine. How's Lil? . . . Yes . . . Listen, Harry, what does a five-pointed star with a capital T in the middle mean? . . . What? How do you spell it? . . . Yes, I see . . . And if you found it on a body? . . . Neither do I . . . Yes, and thanks. I'll tell you about it—when I see you . . . Yes, give me a ring . . . Thanks . . . 'Bye.'

Dundy and Tom were watching him closely when he turned from the telephone.

He said, 'That's a fellow who knows things sometimes. He says it's a pentagram with a Greek tau—t-a-u—in the middle; a sign magicians used to use. Maybe Rosicrucians still do.'

'What's a Rosicrucian?' Tom asked.

'It could be Theodore's first initial, too,' Dundy said.

Spade moved his shoulders, said carelessly, 'Yes, but if he wanted to autograph the job it'd been just as easy for him to sign his name.'

He then went on more thoughtfully, 'There are Rosicrucians at both San José and Point Loma. I don't go much for this, but maybe we ought to look them up.'

Dundy nodded.

Spade looked at the dead man's clothes on the table. 'Anything in his pockets?'

'Only what you'd expect to find,' Dundy replied. 'It's on the table there.'

Spade went to the table and looked down at the little pile of watch and chain, keys, wallet, address book, money, gold pencil, handkerchief and spectacle case beside the clothing. He did not touch them, but slowly picked up, one at a time, the dead man's shirt, undershirt, vest and coat. A blue necktie lay on the table beneath them. He scowled irritably at it.

'It hasn't been worn,' he complained.

Dundy, Tom and the coroner's deputy, who had stood silent all this while by the window—he was a small man with a slim, dark, intelligent face—came together to stare down at the unwrinkled blue silk.

Tom groaned miserably.

Dundy cursed under his breath.

Spade lifted the necktie to look at its back. The label was a London haberdasher's. Spade said cheerfully, 'Swell. San Francisco, Point Loma, San José, Paris, London.'

Dundy glowered at him.

The gray-faced man came in.

'The papers got here at three-thirty, all right,' he said. His eyes widened a little. 'What's up?' As he crossed the room toward them he said, 'I can't find anybody that saw Blondy sneak back in here again.'

He looked uncomprehendingly at the necktie until Tom growled, 'It's brand-new'; then he whistled softly.

Dundy turned to Spade.

'The deuce with all this,' he said bitterly. 'He's got a brother with reasons for not liking him. The brother just got out of stir. Somebody who looks like his brother left here at half past three. Twenty-five minutes later he phoned you he'd been threatened. Less than half an hour after that his daughter came in and found him dead—strangled.' He poked a finger at the small, dark-faced man's chest. 'Right?'

'Strangled,' the dark-faced man said precisely, 'by a man. The hands were large.'

'OK.' Dundy turned to Spade again. 'We find a threatening letter. Maybe that's what he was telling you about, maybe it was something his brother said to him. Don't let's guess. Let's stick to what we know. We know he—'

The man at the secrétaire turned around and said, 'Got another one.' His mien was somewhat smug.

The eyes with which the five men at the table looked at him were identically cold, unsympathetic.

He, nowise disturbed by their hostility, read aloud:

'Dear Bliss: I am writing this to tell you for the last time that I want my money back, and I want it back by the first of the month, all of it. If I don't get it I am going to do something about it, and you ought to be able to guess what I mean. And don't think I am kidding. Yours truly, Daniel Talbot.'

He grinned. 'That's another T for you.' He picked up an envelope. 'Post-marked San Diego, the twenty-fifth of last month.' He grinned again. 'And that's another city for you.'

Spade shook his head. 'Point Loma's down that way,' he said.

He went over with Dundy to look at the letter. It was written in blue ink on white stationery of good quality, as was the address on the envelope, in a cramped, angular handwriting that seemed to have nothing in common with that of the penciled letter.

Spade said ironically, 'Now we're getting somewhere.'

Dundy made an impatient gesture. 'Let's stick to what we know,' he growled.

'Sure,' Spade agreed. 'What is it?'

There was no reply.

Spade took tobacco and cigarette papers from his pocket.

'Didn't somebody say something about talking to a daughter?' he asked.

'We'll talk to her.' Dundy turned on his heel, then suddenly frowned at the dead man on the floor. He jerked a thumb at the small, dark-faced man. 'Through with it?'

'I'm through.'

Dundy addressed Tom curtly: 'Get rid of it.'

He addressed the gray-faced man: 'I want to see both elevator boys when I'm finished with the girl.'

He went to the closed door Tom had pointed out to Spade and knocked on it.

A slightly harsh female voice within asked, 'What is it?'

'Lieutenant Dundy. I want to talk to Miss Bliss.'

There was a pause; then the voice said, 'Come in.'

Dundy opened the door and Spade followed him into a black, gray and silver room, where a big-boned and ugly middle-aged woman in black dress and white apron sat beside a bed on which a girl lay.

The girl lay, elbow on pillow, cheek on hand, facing the big-boned, ugly woman. She was apparently about eighteen years old. She wore a gray suit. Her hair was blond and short, her face firm-featured and remarkably symmetrical. She did not look at the two men coming into the room.

Dundy spoke to the big-boned woman, while Spade was lighting his cigarette: 'We want to ask you a couple of questions, too, Mrs Hooper. You're Bliss's housekeeper, aren't you?'

The woman said, 'I am.'

Her slightly harsh voice, the level gaze of her deep-set gray eyes, the stillness and size of her hands lying in her lap, all contributed to the impression she gave of resting strength.

'What do you know about this?'

'I don't know anything about it. I was let off this morning to go over to Oakland to my nephew's funeral, and when I got back you and the other gentlemen were here and—and this had happened.'

Dundy nodded, asked, 'What do you think about it?'

'I don't know what to think,' she replied simply.

'Didn't you know he expected it to happen?'

Now the girl suddenly stopped watching Mrs Hooper. She sat up in bed, turning wide, excited eyes on Dundy, and asked, 'What do you mean?'

'I mean what I said. He'd been threatened. He called up Mr Spade'—he indicated Spade with a nod—'and told him so just a few minutes before he was killed.'

'But who—?' she began.

'That's what we're asking you,' Dundy said. 'Who had that much against him?'

She stared at him in astonishment. 'Nobody would.'

This time Spade interrupted her, speaking with a softness that made his words seem less brutal than they were:

'Somebody did.' When she turned her stare on him he asked, 'You don't know of any threats?'

She shook her head from side to side with emphasis.

He looked at Mrs Hooper. 'You?'

'No, sir,' she said.

He returned his attention to the girl. 'Do you know Daniel Talbot?'

'Why, yes,' she said. 'He was here for dinner last night.'

'Who is he?'

'I don't know, except that he lives in San Diego, and he and father had some sort of business together. I'd never met him before.'

'What sort of terms were they on?'

She frowned a little, said slowly, 'Friendly.'

Dundy spoke: 'What business was your father in?'

'He was a financier.'

'You mean a promoter?'

'Yes, I suppose you could call it that.'

'Where is Talbot staying, or has he gone back to San Diego?'

'I don't know.'

'What does he look like?'

She frowned again, thoughtfully. 'He's kind of large, with a red face and white hair and a white mustache.'

'Old?'

'I guess he must be sixty; fifty-five at least.'

Dundy looked at Spade, who put the stub of his cigarette in a tray on the dressing table and took up the questioning:

'How long since you've seen your uncle?'

Her face flushed. 'You mean Uncle Ted?'

He nodded.

'Not since,' she began, and bit her lip. Then she said, 'Of course, you know. Not since he first got out of prison.'

'He came here?'

'Yes.'

'To see your father?'

'Of course.'

'What sort of terms were they on?'

She opened her eyes wide.

'Neither of them is very demonstrative,' she said, 'but they are brothers, and father was giving him money to set him up in business again.'

'Then they were on good terms?'

'Yes,' she replied in the tone of one answering an unnecessary question.

'Where does he live?'

'On Post Street,' she said, and gave a number.

'And you haven't seen him since?'

'No. He was shy, you know, about having been in prison—' She finished the sentence with a gesture of one hand.

Spade addressed Mrs Hooper: 'You've seen him since?'

'No, sir.'

He pursed his lips, asked slowly, 'Either of you know he was here this afternoon?'

They said, 'No,' together.

'Where did—?'

Someone knocked on the door.

Dundy said, 'Come in.'

Tom opened the door far enough to stick his head in.

'His brother's here,' he said.

The girl, leaning forward, called, 'Oh, Uncle Ted!'

A big blond man in brown appeared behind Tom. He was sunburned to an extent that made his teeth seem whiter, his clear eyes bluer, than they were.

He asked, 'What's the matter, Miriam?'

'Father's dead,' she said, and began to cry.

Dundy nodded at Tom, who stepped out of Theodore Bliss's way and let him come into the room.

A woman came in behind him, slowly, hesitantly. She was a tall woman in her late twenties, blond, not quite plump. Her features were generous, her face pleasant and intelligent. She wore a small brown hat and a mink coat.

Bliss put an arm around his niece, kissed her forehead, sat on the bed beside her. 'There, there,' he said awkwardly.

She saw the blond woman, stared through her tears at her for a moment, then said, 'Oh, how do you do, Miss Barrow.'

The blond woman said, 'I'm awfully sorry to—'

Bliss cleared his throat, and said, 'She's Mrs Bliss now. We were married this afternoon.'

Dundy looked angrily at Spade. Spade, making a cigarette, seemed about to laugh.

Miriam Bliss, after a moment's surprised silence, said, 'Oh, I do wish you all the happiness in the world.' She turned to her uncle while his wife was murmuring, 'Thank you,' and said, 'And you too, Uncle Ted.'

He patted her shoulder and squeezed her to him. He was looking questioningly at Spade and Dundy.

'Your brother died this afternoon,' Dundy said. 'He was murdered.'

Mrs Bliss caught her breath. Bliss's arm tightened around his niece with a little jerk, but there was not yet any change in his face.

'Murdered?' he repeated uncomprehendingly.

'Yes.' Dundy put his hands in his coat pockets. 'You were here this afternoon.'

Theodore Bliss paled a little under his sunburn, but said, 'I was,' steadily enough.

'How long?'

'About an hour. I got here about half past two and—' He turned to his wife. 'It was almost half past three when I phoned you, wasn't it?'

She said, 'Yes.'

'Well, I left right after that.'

'Did you have a date with him?' Dundy asked.

'No. I phoned his office'—he nodded at his wife—'and was told he'd left for home, so I came on up. I wanted to see him before Elise and I left, of course, and I wanted him to come to the wedding, but he couldn't. He said he was expecting somebody. We sat here and talked longer than I had intended, so I had to phone Elise to meet me at the Municipal Building.'

After a thoughtful pause, Dundy asked, 'What time?'

'That we met there?' Bliss looked inquiringly at his wife, who said:

'It was just quarter to four.' She laughed a little. 'I got there first and I kept looking at my watch.'

Bliss said very deliberately, 'It was a few minutes after four when we were married. We had to wait for Judge Whitefield—about ten minutes, and it was a few more before we got started—to get through with the case he was hearing. You can check it up—Superior Court, Part Two, I think.'

Spade whirled around and pointed at Tom. 'Maybe you'd better check it up.'

Tom said, 'Oke,' and went away from the door.

'If that's so, you're all right, Mr Bliss,' Dundy said, 'but I have to ask these things. Now, did your brother say who he was expecting?'

'No.'

'Did he say anything about having been threatened?'

'No. He never talked much about his affairs to anybody, not even to me. Had he been threatened?'

Dundy's lips tightened a little. 'Were you and he on intimate terms?'

'Friendly, if that's what you mean.'

'Are you sure?' Dundy asked. 'Are you sure neither of you held any grudge against the other?'

Theodore Bliss took his arm free from around his niece. Increasing pallor made his sunburned face yellowish.

He said, 'Everybody here knows about my having been in San Quentin.

You can speak out, if that's what you're getting at.'

'It is,' Dundy said, and then, after a pause, 'Well?'

Bliss stood up.

'Well, what?' he asked impatiently. 'Did I hold a grudge against him for that? No. Why should I? We were both in it. He could get out, I couldn't. I was sure of being convicted whether he was or not. Having him sent over with me wasn't going to make it any better for me. We talked it over and decided I'd go it alone, leaving him outside to pull things together. And he did. If you look up his bank account you'll see he gave me a check for twenty-five thousand dollars two days after I was discharged from San Quentin, and the registrar of the National Steel Corporation can tell you a thousand shares of stock have been transferred from his name to mine since then.'

He smiled apologetically and sat down on the bed again. 'I'm sorry. I know you have to ask things.'

Dundy ignored the apology.

'Do you know Daniel Talbot?' he asked.

Bliss said, 'No.'

His wife said, 'I do; that is, I've seen him. He was in the office yesterday.'

Dundy looked her up and down carefully before asking, 'What office?'

'I am—I was Mr Bliss's secretary, and—'

'Max Bliss's?'

'Yes, and a Daniel Talbot came in to see him yesterday afternoon, if it's the same one.'

'What happened?'

She looked at her husband, who said, 'If you know anything, for heaven's sake tell them.'

She said, 'But nothing really happened. I thought they were angry with each other at first, but when they left together they were laughing and talking, and before they went Mr Bliss rang for me and told me to have Trapper—he's the bookkeeper—make out a check to Mr Talbot's order.'

'Did he?'

'Oh, yes. I took it in to him. It was for seventy-five hundred and some dollars.'

'What was it for?'

She shook her head. 'I don't know.'

'If you were Bliss's secretary,' Dundy insisted, 'you must have some idea of what his business with Talbot was.'

'But I haven't,' she said. 'I'd never even heard of him before.'

Dundy looked at Spade. Spade's face was wooden. Dundy glowered at him, then put a question to the man on the bed:

'What kind of necktie was your brother wearing when you saw him last?'

Bliss blinked, then stared distantly past Dundy, and finally shut his eyes.

When he opened them he said, 'It was green with—I'd know it if I saw it. Why?'

Mrs Bliss said, 'Narrow diagonal stripes of different shades of green.

That's the one he had on at the office this morning.'

'Where does he keep his neckties?' Dundy asked the housekeeper.

She rose, saying, 'In a closet in his bedroom. I'll show you.'

Dundy and the newly married Blisses followed her out.

Spade put his hat on the dressing table and asked Miriam Bliss:

'What time did you go out?' He sat on the foot of her bed.

'Today? About one o'clock. I had a luncheon engagement for one and I was a little late, and then I went shopping, and then——' She broke off with a shudder.

'And then you came home at what time?' His voice was friendly, matter-of-fact.

'Some time after four, I guess.'

'And what happened?'

'I f-found father lying there and I phoned——I don't know whether I phoned downstairs or the police, and then I don't know what I did. I fainted or had hysterics or something, and the first thing I remember is coming to and finding those men here and Mrs Hooper.' She looked him full in the face now.

'You didn't phone a doctor?'

She lowered her eyes again. 'No, I don't think so.'

'Of course you wouldn't, if you knew he was dead,' he said casually.

She was silent.

'You knew he was dead?' he asked.

She raised her eyes and looked blankly at him.

'But he was dead,' she said.

He smiled. 'Of course; but what I'm getting at is, did you make sure before you phoned?'

She put a hand to her throat.

'I don't remember what I did,' she said earnestly. 'I think I just knew he was dead.'

He nodded understandingly. 'And if you phoned the police it was because you knew he had been murdered.'

She worked her hands together and looked at them and said, 'I suppose so. It was awful. I don't know what I thought or did.'

Spade leaned forward and made his voice low and persuasive. 'I'm not a police detective, Miss Bliss. I was engaged by your father—a few minutes too late to save him. I am, in a way, working for you now, so if there is anything I can do—maybe something the police wouldn't——' He broke off as Dundy, followed by the Blisses and the housekeeper, returned to the room. 'What luck?'

Dundy said, 'The green tie's not there.' His suspicious gaze darted from Spade to the girl. 'Mrs Hooper says the blue tie we found is one of half a dozen he just got from England.'

Bliss asked, 'What's the importance of the tie?'

Dundy scowled at him. 'He was partly undressed when we found him. The tie with his clothes had never been worn.'

'Couldn't he have been changing clothes when whoever killed him came,

285

and was killed before he had finished dressing?'

Dundy's scowl deepened. 'Yes, but what did he do with the green tie? Eat it?'

Spade said, 'He wasn't changing clothes. If you'll look at the shirt collar you'll see he must've had it on when he was choked.'

Tom came to the door.

'Checks all right,' he told Dundy. 'The judge and a bailiff named Kittredge say they were there from about a quarter to four till five or ten minutes after. I told Kittredge to come over and take a look at them to make sure they're the same ones.'

Dundy said, 'Right,' without turning his head and took the penciled threat signed with the T in a star from his pocket. He folded it so only the signature was visible.

Then he asked, 'Anybody know what this is?'

Miriam Bliss left the bed to join the others in looking at it. From it they looked at one another blankly.

'Anybody know anything about it?' Dundy asked.

Mrs Hooper said, 'It's like what was on poor Mr Bliss's chest, but—'

The others said, 'No.'

'Anybody ever seen anything like it before?'

They said they had not.

Dundy said, 'All right. Wait here. Maybe I'll have something else to ask you after a while.'

Spade said, 'Just a minute. Mr Bliss, how long have you known Mrs Bliss?'

Bliss looked curiously at Spade.

'Since I got out of prison,' he replied somewhat cautiously. 'Why?'

'Just since last month,' Spade said as if to himself. 'Meet her through your brother?'

'Of course—in his office. Why?'

'And at the Municipal Building this afternoon, were you together all the time?'

'Yes, certainly.' Bliss spoke sharply. 'What are you getting at?'

Spade smiled at him, a friendly smile.

'I have to ask things,' he said.

Bliss smiled too. 'It's all right.' His smile broadened. 'As a matter of fact, I'm a liar. We weren't actually together all the time. I went out into the corridor to smoke a cigarette, but I assure you every time I looked through the glass of the door I could see her still sitting in the courtroom where I had left her.'

Spade's smile was as light as Bliss's.

Nevertheless, he asked, 'And when you weren't looking through the glass you were in sight of the door? She couldn't've left the courtroom without your seeing her?'

Bliss's smile went away.

'Of course she couldn't,' he said, 'and I wasn't out there more than five minutes.'

Spade said, 'Thanks,' and followed Dundy into the living-room, shutting the door behind him.

Dundy looked sidewise at Spade. 'Anything to it?'

Spade shrugged.

MAX BLISS'S BODY had been removed. Besides the man at the secrétaire and the gray-faced man, two Filipino boys in plum-colored uniforms were in the room. They sat close together on the sofa.

Dundy said, 'Mack, I want to find a green necktie. I want this house taken apart, this block taken apart, and the whole neighborhood taken apart till you find it. Get what men you need.'

The man at the secrétaire rose, said, 'Right,' pulled his hat down over his eyes, and went out.

Dundy scowled at the Filipinos. 'Which of you saw the man in brown?'

The smaller stood up. 'Me, sir.'

Dundy opened the bedroom door and said, 'Bliss.'

Bliss came to the door.

The Filipino's face lighted up. 'Yes, sir, him.'

Dundy shut the door in Bliss's face. 'Sit down.'

The boy sat down hastily.

Dundy stared gloomily at the boys until they began to fidget. Then, 'Who else did you bring up to this apartment this afternoon?'

They shook their heads in unison from side to side.

'Nobody else, sir,' the smaller one said. A desperately ingratiating smile stretched his mouth wide across his face.

Dundy took a threatening step toward them.

'Nuts!' he snarled. 'You brought up Miss Bliss.'

The larger boy's head bobbed up and down. 'Yes, sir. Yes, sir. I bring them up. I think you mean other people.' He too tried a smile.

Dundy was glaring at him. 'Never mind what you think I mean. Tell me what I ask. Now, what do you mean by "them"?'

The boy's smile died under the glare. He looked at the floor between his feet and said, 'Miss Bliss and the gentleman.'

'What gentleman? The gentleman in there?' He jerked his head toward the door he had shut on Bliss.

'No, sir. Another gentleman, not an American gentleman.' He had raised his head again and now brightness came back into his face. 'I think he is Armenian.'

'Why?'

'Because he not like us Americans, not talk like us.'

Spade laughed, asked, 'Ever seen an Armenian?'

'No, sir. That is why I think he—' He shut his mouth with a click as Dundy made a growling noise in his throat.

'What'd he look like?' Dundy asked.

The boy lifted his shoulders, spread his hands. 'He tall, like this gentleman.' He indicated Spade. 'Got dark hair, dark mustache. Very'—he frowned earnestly—'very nice clothes. Very nice-looking man. Cane, gloves, spats, even, and—'

'Young?' Dundy asked.

The head went up and down again. 'Young. Yes, sir.'

'When did he leave?'

'Five minutes,' the boy replied.

Dundy made a chewing motion with his jaws, then asked, 'What time did they come in?'

The boy spread his hands, lifted his shoulders again. 'Four o'clock—maybe ten minutes after.'

'Did you bring anybody else up before we got here?'

The Filipinos shook their heads in unison once more.

Dundy spoke out the side of his mouth to Spade: 'Get her.'

Spade opened the bedroom door, bowed slightly, said, 'Will you come out a moment, Miss Bliss?'

'What is it?' she asked warily.

'Just for a moment,' he said, holding the door open. Then he suddenly added, 'And you'd better come along too, Mr Bliss.'

Miriam Bliss came slowly into the living-room followed by her uncle, and Spade shut the door behind them.

Miss Bliss's lower lip twitched a little when she saw the elevator boys. She looked apprehensively at Dundy.

He asked, 'What's this fiddlededee about the man that came in with you?'

Her lower lip twitched again. 'Wh-what?' She tried to put bewilderment on her face.

Theodore Bliss hastily crossed the room, stood for a moment before her as if he intended to say something, and then, apparently changing his mind, took up a position behind her, his arms crossed over the back of a chair.

'The man who came in with you,' Dundy said harshly, rapidly. 'Who is he? Where is he? Why'd he leave? Why didn't you say anything about him?'

The girl put her hands over her face and began to cry.

'He didn't have anything to do with it,' she blubbered through her hands. 'He didn't, and it would just make trouble for him.'

'Nice boy,' Dundy said. 'So, to keep his name out of the newspapers, he runs off and leaves you alone with your murdered father.'

She took her hands away from her face.

'Oh, but he had to,' she cried. 'His wife is so jealous, and if she knew he had been with me again she'd certainly divorce him, and he hasn't a cent in the world of his own.'

Dundy looked at Spade. Spade looked at the goggling Filipinos and jerked a thumb at the outer door.

'Scram,' he said.

They went out quickly.

'And who is this gem?' Dundy asked the girl.

'But he didn't have any—'

'Who is he?'

Her shoulders drooped a little and she lowered her eyes.

'His name is Boris Smekalov,' she said wearily.

'Spell it.'

She spelled it.

'Where does he live?'

'At the St Mark Hotel.'

'Does he do anything for a living except marry money?'

Anger came into her face as she raised it, but went away as quickly.

'He doesn't do anything,' she said.

Dundy wheeled to address the gray-faced man:

'Get him.'

The gray-faced man grunted and went out.

Dundy faced the girl again. 'You and this Smekalov in love with each other?'

Her face became scornful. She looked at him with scornful eyes and said nothing.

He said, 'Now your father's dead, will you have enough money for him to marry if his wife divorces him?'

She covered her face with her hands.

He said, 'Now your father's dead, will—?'

Spade, leaning far over, caught her as she fell. He lifted her easily and carried her into the bedroom. When he came back he shut the door behind him and leaned against it.

'Whatever the rest of it was,' he said, 'the faint's a phony.'

'Everything's a phony,' Dundy growled.

Spade grinned mockingly. 'There ought to be a law making criminals give themselves up.'

Mr Bliss smiled and sat down at his brother's desk by the window.

Dundy's voice was disagreeable.

'You got nothing to worry about,' he said to Spade. 'Even your client's dead and can't complain. But if I don't come across I've got to stand for riding from the captain, the chief, the newspapers, and heaven knows who all.'

'Stay with it,' Spade said soothingly; 'you'll catch a murderer sooner or later yet.' His face became serious except for the lights in his yellow-gray eyes. 'I don't want to run this job up any more alleys than we have to, but don't you think we ought to check up on the funeral the housekeeper said she went to? There's something funny about that woman.'

After looking suspiciously at Spade for a moment, Dundy nodded, and said, 'Tom'll do it.'

Spade turned about and, shaking his finger at Tom, said, 'It's a ten-to-one bet there wasn't any funeral. Check on it—don't miss a trick.'

Then he opened the bedroom door and called Mrs Hooper.

'Sergeant Polhaus wants some information from you,' he told her.

While Tom was writing down names and addresses that the woman gave him, Spade sat on the sofa and made and smoked a cigarette, and Dundy walked the floor slowly, scowling at the rug. With Spade's approval, Theodore Bliss rose and rejoined his wife in the bedroom.

Presently Tom put his notebook in his pocket, said, 'Thank you,' to the house-keeper, 'Be seeing you,' to Spade and Dundy, and left the apartment.

The housekeeper stood where he had left her, ugly, strong, serene, patient.

Spade twisted himself around on the sofa until he was looking into her deep-set, steady eyes.

'Don't worry about that,' he said, flirting a hand toward the door Tom had gone through. 'Just routine.' He pursed his lips, asked, 'What do you honestly think of this thing, Mrs Hooper?'

She replied calmly, in her strong, somewhat harsh voice, 'I think it's the judgment of God.'

Dundy stopped pacing the floor.

Spade said, 'What?'

There was certainty and no excitement in her voice: 'The wages of sin is death.'

Dundy began to advance toward Mrs Hooper in the manner of one stalking game.

Spade waved him back with a hand which the sofa hid from the woman. His face and voice showed interest, but were now as composed as the woman's.

'Sin?' he asked.

She said, '"Whosoever shall offend one of these little ones that believe in me, it were better for him that a millstone were hanged around his neck, and he were cast into the sea."' She spoke, not as if quoting, but as if saying something she believed.

Dundy barked a question at her: 'What little one?'

She turned her grave gray eyes on him, then looked past him at the bedroom door.

'Her,' she said; 'Miriam.'

Dundy frowned at her. 'His daughter?'

The woman said, 'Yes, his own adopted daughter.'

Angry blood mottled Dundy's square face.

'What the heck is this?' he demanded. He shook his head as if to free it from some clinging thing. 'She's not really his daughter?'

The woman's serenity was in no way disturbed by his anger. 'No. His wife was an invalid most of her life. They didn't have any children.'

Dundy moved his jaws as if chewing for a moment and when he spoke again his voice was cooler:

'What did he do to her?'

'I don't know,' she said, 'but I truly believe that when the truth's found out you'll see that the money her father—I mean her real father—left her has been—'

Spade interrupted her, taking pains to speak very clearly, moving one hand in small circles with his words:

'You mean you don't actually know he's been gypping her? You just suspect it?'

She put a hand over her heart.

'I know it here,' she replied calmly.

Dundy looked at Spade, Spade at Dundy, and Spade's eyes were shiny with not altogether pleasant merriment.

Dundy cleared his throat and addressed the woman again: 'And you think this'—he waved a hand at the floor where the dead man had lain—'was the judgment of God, huh?'

'I do.'

He kept all but the barest trace of craftiness out of his eyes. 'Then whoever did it was just acting as the hand of God?'

'It's not for me to say,' she replied.

Red began to mottle his face again.

'That'll be all right now,' he said in a choking voice, but by the time she had reached the bedroom door his eyes became alert again and he called, 'Wait a minute.' And when they were facing each other: 'Listen, do you happen to be a Rosicrucian?'

'I wish to be nothing but a Christian.'

He growled, 'All right, all right,' and turned his back on her. She went into the bedroom and shut the door. He wiped his forehead with the palm of his right hand and complained wearily, 'Great Scott, what a family!'

Spade shrugged. 'Try investigating your own some time.'

Dundy's face whitened. His lips, almost colorless, came back tight over his teeth. He balled his fists and lunged toward Spade.

'What do you—?'

The pleasantly surprised look on Spade's face stopped him. He averted his eyes, wet his lips with the tip of his tongue, looked at Spade again and away, essayed an embarrassed smile, and mumbled:

'You mean any family. Uh-huh, I guess so.' He turned hastily toward the corridor door as the doorbell rang.

The amusement twitching Spade's face accentuated his likeness to a blond Satan.

An amiable, drawling voice came in through the corridor door:

'I'm Jim Kittredge, Superior Court. I was told to come over here.'

Dundy's voice: 'Yes, come in.'

Kittredge was a roly-poly ruddy man in too-tight clothes with the shine of age on them. He nodded at Spade and said:

'I remember you, Mr Spade, from the Burke–Harris suit.'

Spade said, 'Sure,' and stood up to shake hands with him.

Dundy had gone to the bedroom door to call Theodore Bliss and his wife.

Kittredge looked at them, smiled at them amiably, said, 'How do you do?' and turned to Dundy. 'That's them, all right.' He looked around as if for a place to spit, found none, and said, 'It was just about ten minutes to four that the gentleman there came in the courtroom and asked me how long His Honor would be, and I told him about ten minutes, and they waited there; and right after court adjourned at four o'clock we married them.'

Dundy said, 'Thanks.' He sent Kittredge away, the Blisses back to the bedroom, scowled with dissatisfaction at Spade, and said:

'So what?'

Spade, sitting down again, replied, 'So you couldn't get from here to the Municipal Building in less than fifteen minutes on a bet, so he couldn't've ducked back here while he was waiting for the judge, and he couldn't have hustled over here to do it after the wedding and before Miriam arrived.'

The dissatisfaction in Dundy's face increased. He opened his mouth, but shut it in silence when the gray-faced man came in with a tall, slender, pale young man who fitted the description the Filipino had given of Miriam Bliss's companion.

The gray-faced man said, 'Lieutenant Dundy, Mr Spade, Mr Boris—uh—Smekalov.'

Dundy nodded curtly.

Smekalov began to speak immediately. His accent was not heavy enough to trouble his hearers much, though his r's sounded more like w's.

'Lieutenant, I must beg of you that you keep this confidential. If it should get out it will ruin me, Lieutenant, ruin me completely and most unjustly. I am most innocent, sir. I assure you, in heart, spirit, and deed, not only innocent, but in no way whatever connected with any part of the whole horrible matter. There is no—'

'Wait a minute.' Dundy prodded Smekalov's chest with a blunt finger. 'Nobody's said anything about you being mixed up in anything—but it'd looked better if you'd stuck around.'

The young man spread his arms, his palms forward, in an expansive gesture.

'But what can I do? I have a wife who—' He shook his head violently. 'It is impossible. I cannot do it.'

The gray-faced man said to Spade in an inadequately subdued voice, 'Goofy, these Russians.'

Dundy screwed up his eyes at Smekalov and made his voice judicial.

'You've probably,' he said, 'put yourself in a pretty tough spot.'

Smekalov seemed about to cry.

'But only put yourself in my place,' he begged. 'And you—'

'Wouldn't want to.' Dundy seemed, in his callous way, sorry for the young man. 'Murder's nothing to play with in this country.'

'Murder! But I tell you, Lieutenant, I happen to enter into this situation by the merest mischance only. I am not—'

'You mean you came in here with Miss Bliss by accident?'

The young man looked as if he would like to say, *Yes*. He said, 'No,' slowly, then went on with increasing rapidity: 'But that was nothing, sir, nothing at all. We had been to lunch. I escorted her home and she said, "Will you come in for a cocktail?" and I would. That is all, I give you my word.' He held out his hands, palms up. 'Could it not have happened so to you?' He moved his hands in Spade's direction. 'To you?'

Spade said, 'A lot of things happen to me. Did Bliss know you were running around with his daughter?'

'He knew we were friends, yes.'

'Did he know you had a wife?'

Smekalov said cautiously, 'I do not think so.'

Dundy said, 'You know he didn't.'

Smekalov moistened his lips and did not contradict the lieutenant.

Dundy asked, 'What do you think he'd've done if he found out?'

'I do not know, sir.'

Dundy stepped close to the young man and spoke through his teeth in a harsh, deliberate voice:

'What *did* he do when he found out?'

The young man retreated a step, his face white and frightened.

The bedroom door opened and Miriam Bliss came into the room.

'Why don't you leave him alone?' she asked indignantly. 'I told you he had nothing to do with it. I told you he didn't know anything about it.' She was beside Smekalov now and had one of his hands in hers. 'You're simply making trouble for him without doing a bit of good. I'm awfully sorry, Boris, I tried to keep them from bothering you.'

The young man mumbled unintelligibly.

'You tried, all right,' Dundy agreed. He addressed Spade: 'Could it've been like this, Sam? Bliss found out about the wife, knew they had the lunch date, came home early to meet them when they came in, threatened to tell the wife, and was choked to stop him.' He looked sidewise at the girl. 'Now, if you want to fake another faint, hop to it.'

The young man screamed and flung himself at Dundy, clawing with both hands.

Dundy grunted—'Uh!'—and struck him in the face with a heavy fist.

The young man went backward across the room until he collided with a chair. He and the chair went down on the floor together.

Dundy said to the gray-faced man, 'Take him down to the Hall— material witness.'

The gray-faced man said, 'Oke,' picked up Smekalov's hat, and went over to help pick him up.

Theodore Bliss, his wife, and the housekeeper had come to the door Miriam Bliss had left open.

Miriam Bliss was crying, stamping her foot, threatening Dundy:

'I'll report you, you coward. You had no right to—' and so on.

Nobody paid much attention to her; they watched the gray-faced man help Smekalov to his feet, take him away. Smekalov's nose and mouth were red smears.

Then Dundy said, 'Hush,' negligently to Miriam Bliss and took a slip of paper from his pocket. 'I got a list of the calls from here today. Sing out when you recognise them.'

He read a telephone number.

Mrs Hooper said, 'That is the butcher. I phoned him before I left this morning.' She said the next number Dundy read was the grocer's.

He read another.

'That's the St Mark,' Miriam Bliss said. 'I called up Boris.' She identified two more numbers as those of friends she had called.

The sixth number, Bliss said, was his brother's office. 'Probably my call to Elise to ask her to meet me.'

Spade said, 'Mine,' to the seventh number, and Dundy said:

'That last one's police emergency.' He put the slip back in his pocket.

Spade said cheerfully, 'And that gets us a lot of places.'

The doorbell rang.

Dundy went to the door. He and another man could be heard talking in voices too low for their words to be recognised in the living-room.

The telephone rang. Spade answered it:

'Hello . . . No, this is Spade. Wait a min—All right.' He listened. 'Right, I'll tell him . . . I don't know. I'll have him call you . . . Right.'

When he turned from the telephone Dundy was standing, hands behind him, in the vestibule doorway.

Spade said, 'O'Gar says your Russian went completely nuts on the way to the Hall. They had to shove him into a straight-jacket.'

'He ought to been there long ago,' Dundy growled. 'Come here.'

Spade followed Dundy into the vestibule. A uniformed policeman stood in the outer doorway.

Dundy brought his hands from behind him. In one was a necktie with narrow diagonal stripes in varying shades of green, in the other was a platinum scarfpin in the shape of a crescent set with small diamonds.

Spade bent over to look at three small, irregular spots on the tie.

'Blood?'

'Or dirt,' Dundy said. 'He found them crumpled up in a newspaper in the rubbish can on the corner.'

'Yes, sir,' the uniformed man said proudly; 'there I found them, all wadded up in—' He stopped because nobody was paying any attention to him.

'Blood's better,' Spade was saying. 'It gives a reason for taking the tie away. Let's go in and talk to people.'

Dundy stuffed the tie in one pocket, thrust his hand holding the pin into another. 'Right—and we'll call it blood.'

They went into the living-room.

Dundy looked from Bliss to Bliss's wife, to Bliss's niece, to the housekeeper, as if he did not like any of them. He took his fist from his pocket, thrust it straight out in front of him, and opened it to show the crescent pin lying in his hand.

'What's that?' he demanded.

Miriam Bliss was the first to speak.

'Why, it's father's pin,' she said.

'So it is?' he said disagreeably .'And did he have it on today?'

'He always wore it.' She turned to the others for confirmation.

Mrs Bliss said, 'Yes,' while the others nodded.

'Where did you find it?' the girl asked.

Dundy was surveying them one by one again, as if he liked them less than ever. His face was red.

'He always wore it,' he said angrily, 'but there wasn't one of you could say, "Father always wore a pin. Where is it?" No, we got to wait till it turns up before we can get a word out of you about it.'

Bliss said, 'Be fair. How were we to know—?'

'Never mind what you were to know,' Dundy said. 'It's coming around to the point where I'm going to do some talking about what I know.' He took the green necktie from his pocket. 'This is his tie?'

Mrs Hooper said, 'Yes, sir.'

Dundy said, 'Well, it's got blood on it, and it's not his blood, because he didn't have a scratch on him that we could see.' He looked narrow-eyed from one to another of them. 'Now, suppose you were trying to choke a man that wore a scarfpin and he was wrestling with you, and—'

He broke off to look at Spade.

Spade had crossed to where Mrs Hooper was standing. Her big hands were clasped in front of her. He took her right hand, turned it over, took the wadded handkerchief from her palm, and there was a two-inch-long fresh scratch in the flesh.

She had passively allowed him to examine her hand. Her mien lost none of its tranquillity now. She said nothing.

'Well?' he asked.

'I scratched it on Miss Miriam's pin fixing her on the bed when she fainted,' the housekeeper said calmly.

Dundy's laugh was brief, bitter.

'It'll hang you just the same,' he said.

There was no change in the woman's face.

'The Lord's will be done,' she replied.

Spade made a peculiar noise in his throat as he dropped her hand.

'Well, let's see how we stand.' He grinned at Dundy. 'You don't like that star-T, do you?'

Dundy said, 'Not by a long shot.'

'Neither do I,' Spade said. 'The Talbot threat was probably on the level, but that debt seems to have been squared. Now—Wait a minute.' He went to the telephone and called his office. 'The tie thing looked pretty funny, too, for a while,' he said while he waited, 'but I guess the blood takes care of that.'

He spoke into the telephone:

'Hello, Effie. Listen: Within half an hour or so of the time Bliss called me, did you get any call that maybe wasn't on the level? Anything that could have been a stall? ... Yes, before ... Think now.'

He put his hand over the mouthpiece and said to Dundy, 'There's a lot of deviltry going on in this world.'

He spoke into the telephone again:

'Yes? ... Yes ... Kruger? ... Yes. Man or woman? ... Thanks ... No, I'll be through in half an hour. Wait for me and I'll buy your dinner. 'Bye.'

He turned away from the telephone. 'About half an hour before Bliss phoned, a man called my office and asked for Mr Kruger.'

Dundy frowned. 'So what?'

'Kruger wasn't there.'

Dundy's frown deepened. 'Who's Kruger?'

'I don't know,' Spade said blandly. 'I never heard of him.' He took tobacco and cigarette papers from his pockets. 'All right, Bliss, where's your scratch?'

Theodore Bliss said, 'What?' while the others stared blankly at Spade.

'Your scratch,' Spade repeated in a consciously patient tone. His attention was on the cigarette he was making. 'The place where your brother's pin gouged you when you were choking him.'

'Are you crazy?' Bliss demanded. 'I was—'

'Uh-huh, you were being married when he was killed. You were not.'

Spade moistened the edge of his cigarette paper and smoothed it with his forefingers.

Mrs Bliss spoke now, stammering a little: 'But he—but Max Bliss called—'

'Who says Max Bliss called me?' Spade asked. 'I don't know that. I wouldn't know his voice. All I know is a man called me and said he was Max Bliss. Anybody could say that.'

'But the telephone records here show the call came from here,' she protested.

He shook his head and smiled. 'They show I had *a* call from here, and I did, but not that one. I told you somebody called up half an hour or so before the supposed Max Bliss call and asked for Mr Kruger.' He nodded at Theodore Bliss. 'He was smart enough to get a call from this apartment to my office on the record before he left to meet you.'

She stared from Spade to her husband with dumbfounded blue eyes.

Her husband said lightly, 'It's nonsense, my dear. You know—'

Spade did not let him finish that sentence. 'You know he went out to smoke a cigarette in the corridor while waiting for the judge, and he knew there were telephone booths in the corridor. A minute would be all he needed.' He lit his cigarette and returned his lighter to his pocket.

Bliss said, 'Nonsense!' more sharply. 'Why should I want to kill Max?' He smiled reassuringly to his wife's horrified eyes. 'Don't let this disturb you, dear. Police methods are sometimes—'

'All right,' Spade said, 'let's look you over for scratches.'

Bliss wheeled to face him more directly. 'Damned if you will!' He put a hand behind him.

Spade, wooden-faced and dreamy-eyed, came forward.

SPADE AND EFFIE PERINE sat at a small table in Julius's Castle on Telegraph Hill. Through the window beside them ferryboats could be seen carrying lights to and from the cities' lights on the other side of the bay.

'—hadn't gone there to kill him, chances are,' Spade was saying; 'just to shake him down for some more money; but when the fight started, once he got his hands on his throat, I guess, his grudge was too hot in him for him to let go till Max was dead. Understand, I'm just putting together what the evidence says, and what we got out of his wife, and the not much that we got out of him.'

Effie nodded. 'She's a nice, loyal wife.'

Spade drank coffee, shrugged. 'What for? She knows now that he made his play for her only because she was Max's secretary. She knows that when he took out the marriage license a couple of weeks ago it was only to string her along so she'd get him the photostatic copies of the records that tied Max up with the Graystone Loan swindle. She knows—Well, she knows she wasn't just helping an injured innocent to clear his good name.'

He took another sip of coffee. 'So he calls on his brother this afternoon to hold San Quentin over his head for a price again, and there's a fight, and he kills him, and gets his wrist scratched by the pin while he's choking him. Blood on the tie, a scratch on his wrist—that won't do. He takes the tie off the corpse and hunts up another, because the absence of a tie will set the police to thinking. He gets a bad break there. Max's new ties are on the front of the rack, and he grabs the first one he comes to. All right. Now he's got to put it around the dead man's neck—or wait—he gets a better idea. Pull off some more clothes and puzzle the police. The tie'll be just as inconspicuous off as on, if the shirt's off too. Undressing him, he gets another idea. He'll give the police something else to worry about, so he draws a mystic sign he has seen somewhere on the dead man's chest.'

Spade emptied his cup, set it down, and went on:

'By now he's getting to be a regular master-mind at bewildering the police. A threatening letter signed with the thing on Max's chest. The afternoon mail is on the desk. One envelope's as good as another so long as it's typewritten and has no return address, but the one from France adds a touch of the foreign, so out comes the original letter and in goes the threat. He's overdoing it now; see? He's giving us so much that's wrong that we can't help suspecting things that seem all right—the phone call, for instance.

'Well, he's ready for the phone calls now—his alibi. He picks my name out of the private detectives in the phone book and does the Mr Kruger trick; but that's after he calls the blond Elise and tells her that not only have the obstacles to their marriage been removed, but he's had an offer to go in business in New York and has to leave right away, and will she meet him in fifteen minutes and get married? There's more than just an alibi to that. He wants to make sure *she* is dead sure he didn't kill Max, because she knows he doesn't like Max, and he doesn't want her to think he was just stringing her along to get the dope on Max, because she might be able to put two and two together and get something like the right answer.

'With that taken care of, he's ready to leave. He goes out quite openly, with only one thing to worry about now—the tie and pin in his pocket. He takes the pin along because he's not sure the police mightn't find traces of blood around the setting of the stones, no matter how carefully he wipes it. On his way out he picks up a newspaper—buys one from the newsboy he meets at the street door—wads tie and pin up in a piece of it, and drops it in the rubbish can at the corner. That seems all right. No reason for the police to look for the tie. No reason for the street cleaner who empties the can to investigate a crumpled piece of newspaper, and if something does go wrong—what the deuce!—the murderer dropped it there, but he, Theodore, can't be the murderer, because he's going to have an alibi.

'Then he jumps in his car and drives to the Municipal Building. He knows there are plenty of phones there and he can always say he's got to wash his hands, but it turns out he doesn't have to. While they're waiting for the judge to get through with a case he goes out to smoke a cigarette, and there you are—"Mr Spade, this is Max Bliss and I've been threatened."'

Effie Perine nodded, then asked:

'Why do you suppose he picked on a private detective instead of the police?'

'Playing safe. If the body had been found, meanwhile, the police might've heard of it and traced the call. A private detective wouldn't be likely to hear about it till he read it in the papers.'

She laughed, then said, 'And that was your luck.'

'Luck? I don't know.' He looked gloomily at the back of his left hand. 'I hurt a knuckle stopping him and the job only lasted an afternoon. Chances are whoever's handling the estate'll raise hobs if I send them a bill for any decent amount of money.' He raised a hand to attract the waiter's attention. 'Oh, well, better luck next time. Want to catch a movie or have you got something else to do?'

Headon Hill

1857–1927

THE SAPIENT MONKEY

WOULD ADVISE every person whose duties take him into the field of 'private enquiry' to go steadily through the daily papers the first thing every morning. Personally I have found the practice most useful, for there are not many *causes célèbres* in which my services are not enlisted on one side or the other, and by this method I am always up in my main facts before I am summoned to assist. When I read the account of the proceedings at Bow Street against Franklin Gale in connection with the Tudways' bank robbery, I remember thinking that on the face of it there never was a clearer case against a misguided young man.

Condensed for the sake of brevity, the police-court report disclosed the following state of things:

Franklin Gale, clerk, aged twenty-three, in the employment of Messrs Tudways, the well-known private bankers of the Strand, was brought up on a warrant charged with stealing the sum of £500—being the moneys of his employers. Mr James Spruce, assistant cashier at the bank, gave evidence to the effect that he missed the money from his till on the afternoon of July 22. On making up his cash for the day he discovered that he was short of £300 worth of notes and £200 in gold. He had no idea how the amount had been abstracted. The prisoner was an assistant bookkeeper at the bank, and had access behind the counter. Detective sergeant Simmons said that the case had been placed in his hands for the purpose of tracing the stolen notes. He had ascertained that one of them—of the value of £5—had been paid to Messrs Crosthwaite & Co., tailors, of New Bond Street, on July 27th, by Franklin Gale. As a result, he had applied for a warrant, and had arrested the prisoner. The latter was remanded for a week, at the end of which period it was expected that further evidence would be forthcoming.

I had hardly finished reading the report when a telegram was put into my hands demanding my immediate presence at 'Rosemount', Twickenham. From the address given, and from the name of 'Gale' appended to the despatch, I concluded that the affair at Tudways' Bank was the cause of the summons. I had little doubt that I was to be retained in the interests of the prisoner, and my surmise proved correct.

'Rosemount' was by no means the usual kind of abode from which the ordinary run of bank clerks come gaily trooping into the great City in shoals by the early trains. There was nothing of cheap gentility about the 'pleasant suburban residence standing in its own-grounds of an acre', as the house-agent would say—with its lawns sloping down to the river, shaded by mulberry and chestnut trees, and plentifully garnished with the noble flower which gave it half its name. 'Rosemount' was assuredly the home either of some prosperous merchant or of a private gentleman, and when I crossed its threshold I did so quite prepared for the fuller enlightenment which was to follow. Mr Franklin Gale was evidently not one of the struggling genus bank clerk, but must be the son of well-to-do people, and not yet flown from the parent nest. When I left my office I had thought that I was bound on a forlorn hope, but at the sight of 'Rosemount'— my first real 'touch' of the case—my spirits revived. Why should a young man living amid such signs of wealth want to rob his employers? Of course I recognised that the youth of the prisoner precluded the probability of the place being his own. Had he been older, I should have reversed the argument. 'Rosemount' in the actual occupation of a middle-aged bank clerk would have been prima-facie evidence of a tendency to outrun the constable.

I was shown into a well-appointed library, where I was received by a tall, silver-haired old gentleman of ruddy complexion, who had apparently been pacing the floor in a state of agitation. His warm greeting towards me—a perfect stranger—had the air of one who clutches at a straw.

'I have sent for you to prove my son's innocence, Mr Zambra,' he said. 'Franklin no more stole that money than I did. In the first place, he didn't want it; and, secondly, if he had been ever so pushed for cash, he would rather have cut off his right hand than put it into his employer's till. Besides, if these thick-headed policemen were bound to lock one of us up, it ought to have been me. The five-pound note with which Franklin paid his tailor was one—so he assures me, and I believe him—which I gave him myself.'

'Perhaps you would give me the facts in detail?' I replied.

'As to the robbery, both my son and I are as much in the dark as old Tudway himself,' Mr Gale proceeded. 'Franklin tells me that Spruce, the cashier, is accredited to be a most careful man, and the very last to leave his till to take care of itself. The facts that came out in evidence are perfectly true. Franklin's desk is close to the counter, and the note identified as one of the missing ones was certainly paid by him to Crosthwaite & Co., of New Bond Street, a few days after the robbery. It bears his endorsement, so there can be no doubt about that.

'So much for their side of the case. Ours is, I must confess, from a legal point of view, much weaker, and lies in my son's assertion of innocence, coupled with the knowledge of myself and his mother and his sisters that he is incapable of such a crime. Franklin insists that the note he paid to Crosthwaite & Co., the tailors, was one that I gave him on the morning of the 22nd. I remember perfectly well giving him a five-pound note at breakfast on that day, just before he left for town, so that he must have had it several hours before the robbery was committed. Franklin says that he had no other bank-notes between the 22nd and 27th, and that he cannot, therefore, be mistaken. The note which I gave him I got fresh from my own bankers a day or two before, together with some others; and here is the most unfortunate point in the case. The solicitor whom I have engaged to defend Franklin has made the necessary enquiries at my bankers, and finds that the note paid to the tailors is *not* one of those which I drew from the bank.'

'Did not your son take notice of the number of the note you gave him?' I asked.

'Unfortunately, no. He is too much worried about the numbers of notes at his business, he says, to note those which are his own property. He simply sticks to it that he knows it must be the same note because he had no other.'

In the slang of the day, Mr Franklin Gale's story seemed a little too thin. There was the evidence of Tudways that the note paid to the tailor was one of those stolen from them, and there was the evidence of Mr Gale senior's bankers that it was not one of those handed to their client. What was the use of the prisoner protesting in the face of this that he had paid his tailor with his father's present? The notes stolen from Tudways were, I remembered reading, consecutive ones of a series, so that the possibility of young Gale having at the bank changed his father's gift for another note, which was subsequently stolen, was knocked on the head. Besides, he maintained that it was the *same* note.

'I should like to know something of your son's circumstances and position,' I said, trying to divest the question of any air of suspicion it might have implied.

'I am glad you asked me that,' returned Mr Gale, 'for it touches the very essence of the whole case. My son's circumstances and position are such that were he the most unprincipled scoundrel in creation he would have been nothing less than an idiot to have done this thing. Franklin is not on the footing of an ordinary bank clerk, Mr Zambra. I am a rich man, and can afford to give him anything in reason, though he is too good a lad ever to have taken advantage of me. Tudway is an old friend of mine, and I got him to take Franklin into the bank with a view to a partnership. Everything was going on swimmingly towards that end: the boy had perfected himself in his duties, and made himself valuable; I was prepared to invest a certain amount of capital on his behalf; and, lastly, Tudway, who lives next door to me here, got so fond of him that he allowed Franklin to become engaged to his daughter Maud. Would any young man in his senses go and steal a paltry £500 under such circumstances as that?'

I thought not, but I did not say so yet.

'What are Mr Tudway's views about the robbery?' I asked.

'Tudway is an old fool,' replied Mr Gale. 'He believes what the police tell him, and the police tell him that Franklin is guilty. I have no patience with him. I ordered him out of this house last night. He had the audacity to come and offer not to press the charge if the boy would confess.'

'And Miss Tudway?'

'Ah! she's a brick. Maud sticks to him like a true woman. But what is the use of our sticking to him against such evidence?' broke down poor Mr Gale, impotently. 'Can you, Mr Zambra, give us a crumb of hope?'

Before I could reply there was a knock at the library door, and a tall, graceful girl entered the room. Her face bore traces of weeping, and she looked anxious and dejected; but I could see that she was naturally quick and intelligent.

'I have just run over to see if there is any fresh news this morning,' she said, with an enquiring glance at me.

'This is Mr Zambra, my dear, come to help us,' said Mr Gale; 'and this,' he continued, turning to me, 'is Miss Maud Tudway. We are all enlisted in the same cause.'

'You will be able to prove Mr Franklin Gale's innocence, sir?' she exclaimed.

'I hope so,' I said; 'and the best way to do it will be to trace the robbery to its real author. Has Mr Franklin any suspicions on that head?'

'He is as much puzzled as we are,' said Miss Tudway. 'I went with Mr Gale here to see him in that horrible place yesterday, and he said there was absolutely no one in the bank he cared to suspect. But he *must* get off the next time he appears. My evidence ought to do that. I saw with my own eyes that he had only one £5 note in his purse on the 25th—that is two days before he paid the tailor, and three days after the robbery.'

'I am afraid that won't help us much,' I said. 'You see, he might easily have had the missing notes elsewhere. But tell me, under what circumstances did you see the £5 note?'

'There was a garden party at our house,' replied Miss Tudway, 'and Franklin was there. During the afternoon a man came to the gate with an accordion and a performing monkey, and asked permission to show the monkey's tricks. We had the man in, and after the monkey had done a lot of clever things the man said that the animal could tell a good banknote from a "flash" one. He was provided with spurious notes for the purpose; would any gentlemen lend him a good note for a minute, just to show the trick? The man was quite close to Franklin, who was sitting next to me. Franklin, seeing the man's hand held out towards him, took out his purse and handed him a note, at the same time calling my attention to the fact that it was his only one, and laughingly saying that he hoped the man was honest. The sham note and the good one were placed before the monkey, who at once tore up the bad note and handed the good one back to Franklin.'

'This is more important than it seems,' I said, after a moment's review of the whole case. 'I must find that man with the monkey, but it bids fair to be difficult. There are so many of them in that line of business.'

Miss Tudway smiled for the first time during the interview.

'It is possible that I may be of use to you there,' she said. 'I go in for amateur photography, and I thought that the man and his monkey made so good a "subject" that I insisted on taking him before he left. Shall I fetch the photograph?'

'By all means,' I said. 'Photography is of the greatest use to me in my work. I generally arrange it myself, but if you have chanced to take the right picture for me in this case so much the better.'

Miss Tudway hurried across to her father's house and quickly returned with the photograph. It was a fair effort for an amateur, and portrayed an individual of the usual seedy stamp, equipped with a huge accordion and a small monkey secured by a string. With this in my hand it would only be a matter of time before I found the itinerant juggler who had presented himself at the Tudways' garden party, and I took my leave of old Mr Gale and Miss Maud in a much more hopeful frame of mind. Every circumstance outside the terrible array of actual evidence pointed to my client's innocence, and if this evidence had been manufactured for the purpose, I felt certain that the 'monkey man' had had a hand in it.

On arriving at my office I summoned one of my assistants— a veteran of doubtful antecedents—who owns to no other name than 'Old Jemmy'. Old Jemmy's particular line of business is a thorough knowledge of the slums and the folk who dwell there; and I knew that after an hour or two on Saffron Hill my ferret, armed with the photograph, would bring me the information I wanted. Towards evening Old Jemmy came in with his report, to the effect that the party I was after was to be found in the top attic of 7 Little Didman's Fields, Hatton Garden, just recovering from the effects of a prolonged spree.

'He's been drunk for three or four days, the landlord told me,' Old Jemmy said. 'Had a stroke of luck, it seems, but he is expected to go on tramp tomorrow, now his coin has given out. His name is Pietro Schilizzi.'

I knew I was on the right scent now, and that the 'monkey man' had been made the instrument of *changing* the note which Franklin Gale had lent him for one of the stolen ones. A quick cab took me to Little Didman's Fields in a quarter of an hour, and I was soon standing inside the doorway of a pestilential apartment on the top floor of No. 7, which had been pointed out to me as the abode of Pietro Schilizzi. A succession of snores from a heap of rags in a corner told me the whereabouts of the occupier. I went over, and shaking him roughly by the shoulder, said in Italian:

'Pietro, I want you to tell me about that little juggle with a banknote at Twickenham the other day. You will be well rewarded.'

The fellow rubbed his eyes in half-drunken astonishment, but there certainly was no guilty fear about him as he replied:

'Certainly, signor; anything for money. There was nothing wrong about the note, was there? Anyhow, I acted innocently in the matter.'

'No one finds fault with you,' I said; 'but see, here is a five-pound note. It shall be yours if you will tell me exactly what happened.'

'I was with my monkey up at Highgate the other evening,' Mr Schilizzi began, 'and was showing Jacko's trick of telling a good note from a bad one. It was a small house in the Napier Road. After I had finished, the gentleman took me into a public house and stood me a drink. He wanted me to do something for him, he said. He had a young friend who was careless, and never took the number of notes, and he wanted to teach him a lesson. He had a bet about the number of a note, he said. Would I go down to Twickenham next day to a house he described, where there was to be a party, and do my trick with the monkey? I was to borrow a note from the young gentleman, and then, instead of giving him back his own note after the performance, I was to substitute one which the Highgate gentleman gave me for the purpose. He met me at Twickenham next day, and came behind the garden wall to point out the young gentleman to me. I managed it just as the Highgate gentleman wanted, and he gave me a couple of pounds for my pains. I have done no wrong; the note I gave back was a good one.'

'Yes,' I said, 'but it happens to have been stolen. Put on your hat and show me where this man lives in Highgate.'

The Napier Road was a shabby street of dingy houses, with a public house at the corner. Pietro stopped about half-way down the row and pointed out No. 21.

'That is where the gentleman lives,' he said.

We retraced our steps to the corner public house.

'Can you tell me who lives at No. 21?' I asked of the landlord, who happened to be in the bar.

'Certainly,' was the answer; 'it is Mr James Spruce—a good customer of mine, and the best billiard player hereabouts. He is a cashier at Messrs Tudways' bank, in the Strand, I believe.'

IT ALL CAME out at the trial—not of Franklin Gale, but of James Spruce, the fraudulent cashier. Spruce had himself abstracted the notes and gold entrusted to him, and his guilty conscience telling him that he might be suspected, he had cast about for a means of throwing suspicion on some other person. Chancing to witness the performance of Pietro's monkey, he had grasped the opportunity for foisting one of the stolen notes on Franklin Gale, knowing that sooner or later it would be traced to him. The other notes he had intended to hold over till it was safe to send them out of the country; but the gold was the principal object of his theft.

Mr Tudway, the banker, was, I hear, so cut up about the false accusation that he had made against his favourite that he insisted on Franklin joining him as a partner at once, and the marriage is to take place before very long. I am also told that the photograph of the 'monkey man', handsomely enlarged and mounted, will form one of the mural decorations of the young couple.

Michael Innes

1906–1994

A QUESTION OF CONFIDENCE

BOBBY APPLEBY (successful scrum-half retired, and author of that notable anti-novel *The Lumber Room*) had been down from Oxford for a couple of years. But he went back from time to time, sometimes for the day and sometimes on a week-end basis. He had a number of clever friends there who were now busily engaged in digging in for life. They had become, that is to say, junior dons of one or another more or less probationary sort, and had thereby risen from the austerities of undergraduate living to the fleshpots and the thrice-driven beds of down associated with Senior Common Rooms and High Tables. They liked entertaining Bobby, to whom *The Lumber Room* rather than his athletic prowess lent, in their circle, a certain prestige. One of these youths was a historian called Brian Button.

Button sometimes came home with Bobby to Long Dream. Sir John Appleby (policeman retired) rather liked this acquaintance of his son's, and was even accustomed to address him as B.B.—this seemingly with some elderly facetious reference to the deceased art historian Bernhard Berenson. Bobby's B.B. (unlike the real B.B.) came from Yorkshire, a region of which Bobby's father approved. So Appleby was quite pleased when, chancing to look up from his writing-table on a sunny Saturday morning, he saw Bobby's ancient Porsche stationary on the drive, with Bobby climbing out of the driver's seat and B.B. out of the other. But the young men were unprovided with suitcases, which was odd. The young men bolted for the front door as if through a thunder-storm, which was odder still. And seconds later—what was oddest of all—the young men burst without ceremony into the room.

'Daddy!' the distinguished novelist exclaimed—and he seemed positively out of breath—'here's an awful thing happened. Brian's got mixed up in a murder.'

'BOTH OF YOU sit down.' Appleby looked with considerably more interest at Mr Button than at his son. B.B. too was out of breath. But B.B. was also as pale as death. The lad—Appleby said to himself—is clean out of his comfortable academic depth. 'And might it be described'—Appleby asked aloud—'as a particularly gruesome murder?'

'Moderately,' Bobby replied judiciously. 'You see—'

'In Oxford?'

'Yes, of course. We've driven straight over. And you've damn well got to come and clear it up.'

'But, Bobby, it isn't my business to clear up homicides in Oxford: not even in the interest of B.B. Of course, I can be told about it.'

'Well, it seems to have been like this—'

'By B.B. himself, please. It will do him good. So do you go and fetch us drinks. And, Brian, go ahead.'

'Thank you, sir—thank you very much.' Mr Button clearly liked being called Brian for a change; it braced him. 'Perhaps you know the job I've been given. It's ordering and cataloguing the Cannongate Papers.'

'The Third Marquis's stuff?'

'Yes. I'm the Cannongate Lecturer.'

'You lecture on the Papers?'

'Of course not.' B.B. found this a foolish question. 'That's just what I'm called, since I've got to be called something. I get the whole bloody archive in order, and then it's to be edited and published in a grand way, and I shall be Number Two on the job. Quite a thing for me.'

'I'm delighted to hear it. Go on.'

'All Lord Cannongate's papers have been deposited with the college by the trustees. Masses and masses of them—and some of them as confidential as hell.'

'State papers, do you mean?'

'Well yes—but that's not exactly the rub. There's a certain amount of purely personal and family stuff. It hasn't been sieved out. I have to segregate it and lock it up. It has nothing to do with what can ever be published.'

'Then the trustees ought to have done that job themselves.'

'I couldn't agree more. But they're lazy bastards, and the responsibility has come on me. It's a question of confidence. If there's a leak, what follows is a complete shambles, so far as my career's concerned.'

'I see.' Appleby looked with decent sympathy at this agitated young man. 'But I think something has been said about murder? That sounds rather a different order of thing.'

'Yes, of course.' B.B. passed a hand across his brow. 'A sense of proportion, and all that. I must try to get it right.' B.B. took a big breath. 'So just listen.'

And B.B. began to tell his story.

He worked, it seemed, in a kind of commodious dungeon beneath the college library. The cavernous chamber was impregnable; so, within it, were the numerous steel filing cabinets in which the Cannongate Papers had arrived. B.B., coming and going, had only to deal faithfully with locks and keys, and nothing could go wrong. Unfortunately it is not easy, when living in a residential university, to bear at all constantly in mind that the world is inhabited by others as well as scholars and gentlemen, ancient faithful menservants of a quasi-hereditary sort, a few pretty secretaries and an excellent *chef*. One may differ sharply from one's colleagues over such issues as the problem of the historical Socrates; one may even be conscious that at times quite naked and shocking animosities can generate themselves out of less learned matters—as, for example, where to hang a picture or who shall look after the wine; but one doesn't—one simply doesn't—expect to have one's pocket picked or one's researches plagiarised. The concept of the felonious, in short, is one to which it is difficult to give serious thought.

These considerations—or something like them—B.B. did a little divagate to advance, as the early stages of his narrative now unfolded themselves. He had not always been too careful about those bloody keys, and he would look a pretty fool in a witness-box if this ghastly affair had the consequence of depositing him in one before a judge and jury.

Appleby's benevolent reception of the troubles of Bobby's friend didn't stand up to all this too well. He had a simple professional persuasion that keys exist to be turned in locks without fail at appropriate times, and that a young man who has gone vague on instructions he has received and accepted in such a matter ought not to be let off being told that he has been improperly negligent. On the other hand it was possible that B.B. was himself feeling very bad indeed. These were considerations that required balanced utterance.

'I hope,' Appleby said, 'that we needn't conclude your culpable carelessness over these things to have been the direct occasion of somebody's getting murdered. It sounds inherently improbable. But go on.'

'Well, sir, there's rather a difficult one there.' B.B. was recovering from the extreme disarray in which he had arrived at Dream. 'I suppose the original chunk of dirty work—a bit of thieving—couldn't have happened if I'd always been right on the ball over those rotten keys. But the murder's a different matter. That seems to have been the result of my having, as a matter of fact, a brighter moment.'

'Brian saw the significance of the electricity.' Bobby Appleby, who had returned to his father's study deftly carrying a decanter, three glasses and a plate of chocolate biscuits, offered this luminous remark. 'Absolutely top-detective stuff, if you ask me.'

'But I don't ask you. So just pour us that sherry and be quiet.' Appleby turned back to Mr Button. 'More about your brighter moment, please.'

'When I happen on any paper dealing with a certain delicate and purely family matter, I have instructions to photocopy it. There's some prospect of a law-suit, it seems, over whether a grandson of *my* Lord Cannongate was of legitimate birth or not; and a sort of dossier has to be got together for some solicitors.'

'You have to make only one copy?'

'Yes—and when I came on something relevant earlier this week I did just that. We have a machine on which we can do the job ourselves, you see, in one of the college offices. There were eight pages of the stuff, and when I'd made a copy I filed the eight sheets of it away in a special box with other photocopies of similar material. That was on Monday. Yesterday morning I had to go to that box again, and I happened to turn over those particular copies. Only, the sheets were pretty well stuck to each other still. So you see.'

'No, Brian, I *don't* see.' Appleby glanced from the Cannongate Lecturer to the creator of *The Lumber Room* (who was punishing the chocolate biscuits rather more heavily than the sherry). He might have been wondering whether England was exclusively populated by excessively clever young men. 'Why should they be stuck to each other?'

'Because of what Bobby says—the electricity.' B.B. seemed surprised that this had not been immediately apparent. 'Those photocopying machines are uncommonly lavish with it. Static electricity, I think it's called. If you stack your copies one on top of another as they come out of the contraption, they cling to one another like—'

'Like characters in a skin-flick.' Bobby had momentarily stopped munching to offer this helpful simile. 'And that's what Brian found.'

'I see.' Appleby was no longer mystified. 'The electrical phenomenon fades, and therefore the sheets manifesting it yesterday could not be those which you had filed away on Monday. Earlier yesterday, or just a little before that, somebody had extracted your copies from their box; photocopied them in turn; and then—inadvertently, perhaps—returned to the box not the older copies but the newer ones. And but for this curious electrical or magnetic effect on the paper, and but for your being alert enough to notice it and draw the necessary inference, nobody need ever have known that there had been any monkey-business at all.'

'That's it, sir. And, if I may say so, pretty hot of you to get there in one.'

'Thank you very much,' Appleby said a shade grimly. 'It doesn't exactly tax the intellect. And just what did you do, Brian, when you made this unfortunate discovery?'

'I went straight to our Master, Robert Durham, and told him the whole thing. There was nothing else for it but to confess to the head man.'

'That was thoroughly sensible of you.' Appleby spoke as a man mollified. 'And how has the Master taken it?'

'How *did* he take it,' Bobby corrected, and reached for another biscuit.

'*What?*' Appleby looked from one to the other young man aghast. 'Brian . . .?'

'Yes, sir. You see, the Master seemed to have ideas about what had happened, although he didn't tell me what they were. It appeared to ring a bell. And that must be why they've murdered him.'

'Good God!' Appleby had a passing acquaintance with the scholar thus summarily disposed of.

'We could have better spared a better man.' Bobby offered this improving quotation with some solemnity. 'Of course, the old boy had had his life. I did feel that. He must have been sixty, if he was a day. He'd toasted his bottom before the fire of life. It sank—'

'Possibly so.' Appleby made no attempt to find this out-of-turn mortuary humour diverting, but he did perhaps judge it, from Bobby, a shade mysterious.

'Still,' Bobby went on, 'even if the Master was a clear case for euthanasia, the thing must be cleared up. *You* must come and clear it up, as I've said. The fact is, they may be getting round to imagining things.'

'Who do you mean by "they"? B.B. seems to be applying the word to a gang of assassins.'

'What *I* mean is the police.' Bobby Appleby was suddenly speaking slowly and carefully. 'They may pitch on some quite unsuitable suspect. For instance, on B.B. himself. You see, there are one or two things you haven't yet heard.'

'To my confusion, Bobby means.' Mr Button, who had cheered up while retailing his acumen over the electrified photocopies, was again sunk in gloom, and he had blurted this out after a short expressive silence. 'I think the police believe I took the Master a cock-and-bull story, just as a cover-up for something else. I think they believe the Master spotted my deception, and that I killed him because otherwise I'd have been turfed out in disgrace and it would have been the end of me.'

'That's a succinct statement, at least.' Appleby was looking at his son's friend gravely. 'Does it mean that, in addition to being careless with those keys, you had been at fault in some other way as well?'

'I'm afraid it does. You see, I'd had the idea of writing a few popular articles on the side.'

'My dear young man! You were going to publicise this intimate Cannongate family scandal you've been talking about?'

'Of course not.' B.B. had flushed darkly. 'Just some purely political things. I'd have got permission, and all that, from the trustees. But I felt I wanted to have a definite proposition to put to them. So I had a newspaper chap up from London several times, and showed him this and that. It was a bit irregular, I suppose. It could have looked bad. As a matter of fact, our senior History Tutor came on us a couple of times, and didn't seem to like it. I expect he has told the pigs.'

'As it had undoubtedly now become his duty to do.' Appleby wasn't pleased by this manner of referring to the police. 'But this London contact of yours could at least substantiate your comparatively blameless intentions?'

'I suppose so.'

'On the other hand, if this journalist is an unscrupulous person, might he have come back into the college and done this thieving and copying himself? Had you told him about those more intimate papers? Even shown them to him?'

'Not shown them. And only mentioned them in a general way. A bit of talk over a pint. He may have gathered where they were kept.'

'Could he, as a stranger, have got swiftly at the photocopying machine?'

'Well, yes—in theory. I took him in there and copied something trivial for him—just to show him we're quite up to date. It's all a bit unfortunate.'

'I agree. And is there anything else that's unfortunate? For example, have you done any other indiscreet talking about this scandal-department in the Cannongate Papers?'

'No, of course not. Or only to Bruno.'

'Very well, B.B. Tell me about Bruno.'

'Bruno Bone is our English Tutor, although he's pretty well just a contemporary of Bobby and me. Teaches Wordsworth and Coleridge and all that sort of stuff. But, really, he wants to be a novelist. More junk yards, so to speak.' This impertinent glance at Bobby's masterpiece was accompanied by rather a joyless laugh on B.B.'s part. 'I told Bruno one evening that there was a whole novel in those damned private papers.'

'That was sheer nonsense, I suppose?'

'I'm afraid so. You know how it is, late at night and after some drinks. Talking for effect, and all that.'

'But at least your brilliant conversation apprised Mr Bone that these scandalous papers exist? Did he take any further interest in them?'

'Well, yes. Bruno came in one morning and asked to have a dekko. He was a bit huffed when I told him it couldn't be done.'

'Just how did you tell him?'

'Oh, I slapped the relevant box and said "Not for you, my boy".'

'I see.' Appleby gazed in some fascination at this unbelievably luckless youth. 'Tell me, B.B. Of course there isn't the material for a novel in your wretched dossier. But might there be material for blackmail?'

'Definitely, I'd say. It's not all exactly past history, you know. There are still people alive—'

'All right—we needn't go into details yet. But tell me this: might the Master have got to know about your chatter to Bruno Bone?'

'It's not unlikely. Bruno's an idiot. Talk about anything to anybody.'

'That's a habit I'm glad to feel you disapprove of. Do you think Bruno could have developed some morbid and irrational curiosity as a result of all this, and have actually abstracted that particular bunch of papers and made copies of them?'

'I suppose it's possible. Those literary characters are wildly neurotic.'

'And the Master might have found it—with the result that Bruno's own career would suddenly have been very much at risk?'

'Yes. The Master is—was—rather a dab at nosing things out.'

'And that brings us to the last relevant point at the moment. Just how did Dr Durham die?'

'Brains blown out.' Bobby Appleby (who had finished the last chocolate biscuit) produced this robustly. 'With some sort of revolver, it seems. Not something it's likely that Brian keeps handy, I'd have thought.'

'Nor Bruno,' B.B. said handsomely.

'Nor any stray blackmailer, either.' Appleby was frowning. 'You wouldn't know whether the police are claiming to have found the weapon?'

'Oh, yes.' Bobby nodded vigorously. 'It was just lying on the carpet in the Master's study.'

'That's where I'd expect it to be.' Appleby sounded faintly puzzled. 'You know, the great majority of men who are found with their brains blown out have effected the messy job themselves. And even in the moment of death some spasm or convulsion can result in the weapon's landing yards away. So, just for the moment, this story of yours sounds to me something of a mare's nest. Robert Durham is in some pathological state of depression and suddenly makes away with himself. And then in comes Brian's bad conscience about his handling of his archive. Bobby, wouldn't you agree? You've said something that makes me think you would agree.'

'Have I?' Bobby seemed not to make much of this. 'Durham wasn't *my* Master, you know. He got the job only when mine died a couple of years ago. But I've seen enough of him to know that he was a rum bird.'

'Secretive,' B.B. added. 'Nobody quite knew what he was up to. He was a bit remote. Brooding type. And a sick man, some said.'

'God bless my soul!' As he made use of this antique expression, Sir John Appleby got to his feet. 'Unless you're both having me up the garden path, you're describing a thoroughly persuasive candidate for suicide. Not that such don't get murdered from time to time. They may ingeniously elect liquidation in one way or another, without so much as being conscious of the fact. Which is psychologically interesting, no doubt, but murder it nevertheless remains.' Appleby paused, and looked searchingly from one young man to the other. 'Is there anything else I ought to know?'

'Not in the way of fact, I'd say.' For the moment, Bobby Appleby (so childishly addicted to chocolate biscuits) appeared to have taken charge of things. 'Of course, the people who may have extra facts are the police. And they *do* have something. I don't know what—but I know it's there. I was present when they talked to Brian early this morning. They kept mum, but I knew they had *something*.' Bobby grinned at his father. 'Family instinct, perhaps. It's why I brought Brian over to Dream. You *can* take a hand?'

'I can stroll around the college, and have a chat here and there. I'd tell the Chief Constable, and he wouldn't mind a bit—always provided I was tactful with his men on the spot. And being *that* is one of the things I keep a grip on even in senescence.' Appleby, as he momentarily adopted this humorous vein, let his glance stray out of the window. It fixed itself briefly, and then returned to the two young men. 'I'll make a call or two,' he said easily, and moved towards the door. 'Drink up the sherry meanwhile: there's about a thimbleful left for each of you.'

With this, Appleby left the room. But he was back before much in the way of telephone calls could have been achieved.

'We were talking about the police,' he said gently. 'As a matter of fact, they're here; and—Brian—they very probably have a warrant for your arrest.'

'THE PERSONALITIES of the people concerned?' The Vice-Master, who was called Fordyce, looked at Appleby doubtfully. 'That's not what the local police are asking. They want to know who had keys to what, and when who could have been where.'

'Quite right. Absolutely essential.' Appleby nodded approvingly. 'It's what gets the results—in nine cases out of ten. And, on this occasion, they appear to have got a result quite rapidly. Too rapidly, I think you'd say?'

'Of course I'd say. The notion of that young man Brian Button providing himself with a revolver and shooting the Master dead with it in his own study is simply too fantastic to stand up.'

'But just at the moment, Vice-Master, it seems to be standing up rather well. The police have no doubt about what Dr Durham was doing when he was shot down—and it's what they've discovered that has led them to question our young man. Durham was dictating a letter on his tape-recorder for his secretary to type out later. It was to the Cannongate trustees, and said flatly that Button had been guilty of professional misconduct of so scandalous a sort that he must be dismissed at once—even though it meant that all academic employment would henceforth be closed to him.'

'It was a very strange thing for the Master to propose to write, Sir John.'

'Well, there it is. The tape isn't to be denied. The Master appears to have flicked the switch that stops the machine simply because he was interrupted while on the job. So the record remained for the police to find.'

'I understand the police case. Button has admitted going to see the Master early yesterday morning and telling him a story about rifled papers. It is now supposed that he returned again in the late afternoon, armed and resolved. The Master told him of the step he proposed to take, but without saying that he had at that moment broken off from recording his letter. So Button killed him, hoping thus to smother up the whole thing. I repeat that it is utter nonsense, completely alien to Brian Button's character, such as it is. A somewhat irresponsible young man, perhaps. But not precisely bloody, bold and resolute.'

'It's Durham's character that interests me more. And aren't you saying that he too seems to have behaved out of character?'

'In a sense, that is so.' Fordyce had taken this point soberly. 'But perhaps I have to say that, although I knew Robert Durham long before he became Master, I never quite understood the man. I have sometimes thought of him as harbouring that degree of inner instability which is liable to produce what they call a personality-change. And yet that is a fantastic speculation.'

'At least a change of job, one supposes, may bring out something roughly of that sort. Was there any particular regard in which he appeared to you to be changing?'

'I can scarcely answer that without appearing very much at sea, Sir John. In one aspect Durham was a man growing detached, remote, fatigued. In another, he was becoming irascible, authoritarian and increasingly prone to flashes of odd behaviour. He could behave like an old-fashioned headmaster with a vindictive turn of mind.'

'Dear me! That sort of thing surely doesn't cut much ice with undergraduates today?'

'Decidedly not. They can be a very great nuisance, our young men. But it is reason alone that is of any avail with them. It's something they have a little begun to get the hang of. Talk sense patiently enough and without condescension—and round they always come.' Fordyce had delivered this high doctrine with an effect of sudden intellectual conviction. 'Durham had lost grip on that.'

'How did he get along with the younger dons?'

'Ah! Not too well.'

'To the extent of anything like feud? With Button himself, for instance?'

'With Button, I'd scarcely suppose so—although the lad may have annoyed him. Nor with any of them to what you might call a point of naked animosity. Bone might be an exception.'

'Bone? A young man called Bruno Bone?'

'Yes. I'm not sure that Bone, for whatever reason, hadn't got to the point of hating Durham in his guts.' It was rather unexpectedly that the Vice-Master had produced this strong expression.

'But Bone, too, would scarcely be bloody, bold and resolute?'

'Of course not. He—' The Vice-Master, who seemed to have produced this reply by rote, suddenly checked himself. 'Do you know,' he said, 'that I wouldn't be quite confident of that? But then I'm coming to wonder what I shall ever be robustly confident about again. This is an undermining affair, Sir John.'

BRUNO BONE, a lanky, prematurely bald young man, was spending his Saturday afternoon banging away on his typewriter. Perhaps he was writing a lecture, or perhaps he was writing a novel. Whichever it was, he didn't seem much to care for being interrupted by the mere father of the author of *The Lumber Room*.

'Yes, of course I know they've arrested Button,' Bone said. 'So what?'

'I'd rather suppose you might be distressed or concerned. Not that they have, perhaps, quite arrested him. He's helping them with their inquiries. They have to tread carefully, you know. But it's true they hold a document from a magistrate. It's in reserve. But I'd simply like to ask, Mr Bone, what you think of the affair.'

'Absolute poppycock. Brian Button's an irresponsible idiot, and I wouldn't trust him with looking after the beer in the buttery, let alone those Cannongate Papers. But he wouldn't shoot old bloody Durham. Wouldn't have the nerve.'

'Would you?'

'If you weren't old enough to be my father, I'd tell you that was a damned impertinent question.'

'Never mind the impertinence. Would you?'

'I don't know that I know.' Bruno Bone was of a sudden entirely amenable. 'It's an interesting speculation. On the whole—I'm ashamed to say—I guess not.'

'Or would anybody else in the college?'

'Can't think of anybody.'

'Then I'm left—so far as anybody who has been put a name to goes—with a London journalist whom Button sent for and talked to a shade rashly. There are journalists, I suppose, who are fit for anything.'

'This one may have scented a hopeful whiff of blackmail, or something of that kind? And the Master may have got on to what he was up to, and had his brains blown out for his pains? I wouldn't like to have to render such a course of events plausible in a novel.'

'If you ever try, I'll hope to read your attempt at it.' Appleby gave this quite a handsome sound. 'When did you last see Dr Durham?'

'When did I last see my father?' Bruno Bone was amused. 'Quite late in the day, really. I'm not a bad suspect, come to think of it. Smart of you to be chasing me up, Sir John. Quite Bobby's father, if I may say so. Bobby's bright.'

'I never judged him exactly dim—but the point's not of the first relevance. Be more precise, please.'

'Very well. I went to see the old brute about an hour before he was indubitably dead. Probably the last man in, so to speak. A breathless hush in the close, and all that. I wanted to sound him out about the prospects of my touching the college for a travel grant. California. Awful universities, but a marvellous climate. Durham treated me as if I was a ghost. Bizarre, wouldn't you say? Considering he was so well on the way to becoming one himself.'

'No doubt. What was the Master doing?'

'Concocting a letter.'

'On some sort of dictaphone?'

'Nothing of the sort. Laborious pen and ink. And putting a lot of concentration into it, I'd say. He made a civil pretence of listening to me for about thirty seconds, and then turfed me out. He was back on his job before I'd reached the door.'

'And that was the last you saw of him?'

'No, it wasn't.' Bruno Bone was sardonically triumphant. 'And here's where I get off the hook. I saw him ten minutes later—and so must plenty of other people—crossing the great quadrangle, with his letter in his hand. He went out through the main gate, crossed the road to the post office, shoved his letter into the box and came back.'

'There would be nothing particularly out of the way, would there, about all that?'

'Of course there would. He had only to leave the thing on a table in his hall, and it would have been collected and dealt with by a college messenger.'

'Thank you very much, Mr Bone. And I apologise for disturbing you.'

APPLEBY'S FINAL CALL was on the senior History Tutor, an elderly man called Farnaby. Farnaby, he supposed, was in some vague and informal fashion Brian Button's boss.

'One of Button's indiscretions,' Appleby said, 'appears to have been dreaming up some popular articles based on the documents in his charge, and calling in a man from some paper or other with whom to discuss the matter. Would you term his doing that a grave breach of confidence?'

'Certainly not. Button ought, no doubt, to have mentioned the proposal to the

Master or to myself in the first instance. It might even be said that there was a slight element of discourtesy in his conduct of the matter; and anything of the kind is, of course, greatly to be deprecated in a society like ours.'

'Of course.'

'But let us simply call it an error of judgement. Button has the makings of a complete scholar; but of what may be called *practical* judgement he has very little sense.'

'I see. Would you say, Mr Farnaby, that the young man's lack of practical judgement might extend to his supposing it judicious to murder Dr Durham?'

'Of course not. I am almost inclined, Sir John, to say that the question could be asked only in a frivolous spirit. It is utter nonsense.'

'So everybody except the police appears to feel. Might Button be described as a protégé of yours?'

'I don't think we go in for protégés.' Farnaby had frowned. 'But I certainly feel in some degree responsible for him. He was my pupil, and it was I who recommended him for his present employment.'

'Thank you. Now, it appears to me, Mr Farnaby, that we have at present just one hard fact in this affair. The day before yesterday, or thereabout, some person unknown abstracted eight sheets from a file of photocopies, photocopied those photocopies anew and then returned the newer and not the older photocopies to the file. The switch was almost certainly fortuitous rather than intentional. It could not have been designed to attract Button's attention, since there was no particular likelihood of his turning over those particular papers again before the static electricity had faded from them. At this specific point, then, we have no reason to suspect any sort of plot against the young man.'

'Clearly not.'

'Button went to the Master and told his story. The Master—if Button is to be believed, and if he didn't form a false impression—the Master responded to the story as if he had some inkling of what lay behind it. It rang a bell. That is Button's phrase for it. Does that suggest anything to you?'

'Nothing whatever, I fear.'

'I suppose everybody would have learnt almost at once about Button's cleverness in tumbling to the implications of that small electrical phenomenon?'

'Almost certainly. He's a young man who can't help chattering.'

'Do you think that his chatterbox quality, and perhaps other forms of tiresomeness, may have been irritating the Master in a manner, or to a degree, Button himself wasn't aware of?'

'I'm afraid it is only too probable. Poor Durham was becoming rather intolerant of folly.'

'That seems to be a view generally held—and it brings me to my last point. The Vice-Master has given me some impression of Durham as a man. And he judges it rather odd, for one thing, that Durham should have thought to dictate a letter to the Cannongate trustees that could only have resulted in Button's being sacked.

But again—and rather contradictorily—he represents Durham as increasingly irascible, indeed vindictive. How would you yourself describe the man?'

'He owned a certain complexity of character, I suppose. Sit beside him at dinner, and you might judge him rather a dull—even a morose man, particularly during his recent ill-health. But in solitude and at his desk he must have become something quite different, since his writing was often brilliantly witty. And maliciously witty, it may be added; whereas in all his college relations his sense of the academic proprieties extended almost to the rectitudinous.' Farnaby paused, and seemed to become aware of this speech as a shade on the heavy side. 'In fact,' he added, 'poor Robert Durham, barring occasional acts of almost alarming eccentricity, was a bit of a bore. But it would have been a safe bet that the memoirs he was working on would have been highly entertaining. You will recall that he was in political life as a younger man, and knew everybody there was to know. It was probably because he found Oxford a bit of a bore that *we* found *him* one. But I must not speak uncharitably. A horrifying mystery like this is a chastening thing.'

'It is, no doubt, horrifying.' Appleby stood up. 'Or, if not horrifying, at least distressing. Whether it is a mystery is another matter. We can only wait and see.'

'Wait and see, Sir John! I very much hope that the most active steps are being taken to clear the matter up.'

'In a sense, perhaps they are. A little patience is what is required, all the same.'

'And my unfortunate young colleague has to set us an example in the matter?' Farnaby spoke with asperity. 'Button has to rest content in his cell?'

'I think not. It is improbable that any very definitive step has been taken in regard to him. Perhaps I can make myself useful—in this way if in no other, my dear sir—by persuading my former colleagues to part with him. In fact, I'll take him back to Dream with me. He and Bobby can play tennis.'

'And for how long will they have to do *that*?' Although he uttered this question challengingly, Farnby was clearly much relieved.

'Oh, until Monday morning. It's my guess that between breakfast and lunch on that day Dr Durham's demise will effectively clear itself up.'

AND IT WAS at ten o'clock on Monday that Appleby strolled out to the tennis court. A police car had arrived at Dream and departed again, and Appleby now had some papers in his hand.

'Relax,' he said to the two young men. 'Your late Master wilfully sought his own salvation. Or that's how the First Grave Digger would put it. *Felo de se*. The letter has arrived, and all is clear.'

'The letter?' Brian Button repeated. 'The one he was dictating—'

'No, no, B.B. Have some sense, my dear boy. The one your friend Bruno came on him writing, and that he took over to the post office himself. Stamped, of course, as second-class mail.'

'I don't understand you, sir.' B.B. had sat down on a garden seat; he was almost as pale as when he had arrived at Dream in the first instance.

'And I'm blessed if I do either.' Bobby Appleby chucked his tennis racket on the grass at his feet. 'Explain—for goodness sake.'

'Come, come—where's all that absolutely top-detective stuff?' Appleby was in irritatingly good humour. 'And, Bobby, you had an instinct it was all a matter of Durham's calling it a day: don't you remember your prattle about the fire of life, and euthanasia, and whatever? As for the letter, it stared us in the face. The Master didn't want it to go out of his lodging through the college messenger service, so he took it to the post himself.'

'He was anxious,' B.B. demanded, 'to conceal whom he was writing to?'

'Not exactly that. *The letter was to somebody in college*. And he didn't want to risk its being delivered, after his death, more or less straightaway by hand. Despatched by second-class mail, it would be delivered this morning. And it was. To the Vice-Master.'

'And just what was this in aid of?' It was clear from his tone that Brian Button already dimly knew.

'It was in aid, my dear lad, of what his seemingly interrupted communication to the Cannongate trustees on that tape-recorder was also in aid of. Something quite extravagantly malevolent. For let's face it, B.B. You'd annoyed him. You'd annoyed him quite a lot. And he was maliciously resolved to make his departure from this life the occasion of your experiencing *un mauvais quart d'heure*. Or rather more.'

'He thought it was really me who had done that monkeying with the photocopies?'

'No, B.B. He couldn't have thought that. For the Master had done that copying turn himself. Incidentally, the photocopying machine has been in use this morning. By the police. And they've sent me out this.' Appleby handed a paper to B.B. 'From the Master to the Vice-Master. Robert Durham's testament, poor chap.'

> My dear Adrian,
>
> First, let me say how much I hope that the Fellows will elect you into the Mastership. If it should come about that I am permitted to look down upon the college from on high, or obliged to peer up at it from below, this will be the spectacle I shall most wish to view. Bless you, my dear man.
>
> Secondly, pray have the police release that wretched Button. (Is not this appropriately reminiscent of some of the last words of Shakespeare's Lear?) If he be not in custody as you read this, it is because they have been so stupid and negligent as to neglect the tape-recorder on my desk. But surely not even Dogberry and Verges could be so dull.
>
> Button needs a lesson in (as we used to say) pulling his socks up. He is also (what, most illogically, I cannot quite forgive him) the immediate occasion of the step I am about to take. The Cannongate Papers contain some fascinating things, and the censurable carelessness of this young man

prompted me to help myself in a clandestine fashion to certain material useful to—shall I say?—an historian of the intimate *mores* of the more elevated classes of society at least not so very long ago. Unfortunately the tiresome Button is very acute; he detected the theft, and came to tell me about it with a mingling of trepidation, uneasiness, complacency and self-congratulation which has extremely offended me.

I need not speak of my present state of health. What has told me that the time has come is really, and precisely, this Button business. He hasn't found me out but *I* have found *myself* out. And in an action of the weirdest eccentricity! As that equally tiresome Bruno Bone would tell you, the poet Pope speaks of Heads of Houses who beastly Skelton quote. But who ever heard of a Head of a House given to petty nocturnal pilferings?

Ave, Hadriane, moriturus te salutat.

ROBERT DURHAM, *Master*

H. R. F. Keating
b. 1926

CAUGHT AND BOWLED, MRS CRAGGS

MEMBERS OF THE Marylebone Cricket Club do not drop toffee papers on the floor of the Long Room at Lord's. Nevertheless during the course of a day's hard cricket-watching a certain amount of debris does appear on that wide expanse of marbled brown linoleum. So it has to be cleared up.

Which is how it comes about that that stretch of territory sacred by long tradition to the male of the species, sub-genus cricket-lover, is trodden daily by Mrs Craggs, cleaning lady, and her friend Mrs Milhorne, cleaning lady too if of a more refined sort.

But not only does Mrs Craggs vigorously sweep and yet more vigorously polish early in the mornings well before play begins (Mrs Milhorne does rather more artistic things with a feather duster), but later in the day in some cavern measureless to man within the Pavilion both these examples of womanhood are still actually to be found on the premises, chiefly cutting sandwiches.

And it was a good thing, on this particular day, that Mrs Craggs, female though she is, was there. Otherwise a murderer might have carried his bat all the way till the last great stumps are drawn.

It was the third day of the Test. England were batting with a small lead on the first innings and two wickets cheaply down. A good hour before the Indians were due to come out on to the field some of the older, more regular, more passionately devoted Members began to gather in the Long Room. In various ways, more or less sly, they set about bagging their favourites among those specially made, high-seated bentwood chairs that are ranged in front of the wide expanse of window looking out at the field of play.

To be in the sun on the terraced Pavilion steps was all right for youngsters who could still take the heat. But with advancing years the cool of the Long Room was the place for them, and the window chairs.

And for most of these early comers the years had advanced to an extraordinary extent, without, of course, in any way abating their fanatical interest in the game. There was the Member Who Saw Grace's Last Century, generally called Grace's Last for convenience. Even more ancient was a favourite of Mrs Craggs's, the Oldest Member But Three, a tortoise-like old boy never seen except in the season, never seen except in a frayed-sleeved blazer and time-creased M.C.C. tie. He was apt to be called But Three.

Indeed, proper names were seldom used in this circle. If it wasn't something connected with cricket, it was a nickname deriving from some disgraceful episode at a prep school in the early years of the century, like Boggers or Winkie. Or it was just 'That Feller in Wine'. Or 'The Yorkshire Chap', a Member who perversely delighted in extolling northern cricketers in this Middlesex stronghold.

And it was the Yorkshire Chap who began it all. He came striding up the Pavilion's wide stone stairs, wearing, of course, a Yorkshire blazer together with his M.C.C. tie (ties and jackets, thank heaven, are still mandatory in the Long Room), his ruddy bald head already glistening with sweat and his big belly protruding in front of him like a dangling sack of flour. And as soon as he saw the others he started holding forth.

'I bet you one thing,' he said, his voice reverberating from one end of the room by the painting of old Thomas Lord himself right down to the other where Don Bradman has been caught by the artist wearing a business suit and so looking, without white flannels and long-peaked green cap, like an utter fish out of water.

'I bet you one thing. I bet anybody here a hundred pound straight that there's a Yorkshireman's century before today's play's done.' There was a stir of interest among the little group he had addressed. Mrs Craggs, who at this very early hour was still within hearing of the Long Room, her polishing mop in hand, noticed it at once.

'But then,' she said later to Mrs Milhorne down among the sandwiches, 'money's money. It means something, money does. Not like all this scoring, an' centuries, an' leg before whatsit.'

'Oh, I like cricket,' Mrs Milhorne replied. 'I love it. Reely. All kind of restful. More like the bally, I always think. Like nice slow dancing. Romantic. I always was romantic, you know.'

Perhaps it was a good thing that the two of them were buried deep. If one of the Members had heard ... But Mrs Craggs paid it all no attention.

'Yerss,' she said, 'an' they took 'im up, they did. Every blessed one o' the old boys sitting together there. Seemed to think they was on to a good thing. "Why," said one of 'em, "the wicket's turning and your feller's still fiddling about in his twenties, he'll never do it." Don't know what he meant. That old wicket ain't turned to left nor right, far as I can see.'

'Oh, but he's right,' said Mrs Milhorne. 'I saw the headlines this morning. "England in Trouble", they said. I like that, I do. Old England's always at her best when there's trouble.'

Mrs Craggs thought of saying a word or two about Mrs Milhorne always being at her most depressed whenever a mite of trouble came her particular way. But she decided to be charitable. Besides, if she had spoken, Mrs Milhorne would have been at her pills in a moment, and then she'd be so dopey she'd never even get two sandwiches put together, never mind butter forty dozen.

So she pursued the theme of money rather than that of cricket. 'Mind you,' she said, 'there'll be trouble about those bets. I can smell it. A hundred pound either way. It don't match up to what it's all about. No wonder they call this the Nursery End, just a lot o' kids they are.'

'Oh, but gentlemen like them,' Mrs Milhorne protested. 'A hundred pounds don't mean nothing to them, not reely. It just shows they're interested, reely interested in the game.'

'Trouble,' Mrs Craggs replied tersely. 'Trouble. Mark my words.'

And indeed those bets were to be won and in an altogether extraordinary way lost too before play was over at Lord's that day. And murder was to be committed in the Long Room.

MEMBERS OF THE MARYLEBONE Cricket Club do not use the Long Room at Lord's as a common betting shop. Nevertheless when the great game of cricket rouses passions to a fever heat the verb 'I bet' can sometimes be heard. As it had been on the day murder was committed in the Long Room.

But that day seemed at its beginning tranquil enough. The headlines in the papers promising trouble for England did not prove exactly factual. The Indian bowlers were turning the ball a little and they toiled hard, but England steadily piled on the runs with the Yorkshireman distinctly aggressive.

So as it neared the lunch interval a Yorkshire century before the day was done began to look very likely. In the Long Room the Yorkshire Chap was openly jubilant, and his companions were finding it hard to keep looking sanguine.

Mrs Craggs, emerging for a breather from that deep cavern where sandwiches are cut (Mrs Milhorne had irritated her beyond endurance by refusing to work at the cheese variety on obscure medical grounds), spotted the Oldest Member But Three on his way to answer a call of nature looking really very glum indeed.

'Poor old duck,' she said to Mrs Milhorne, 'trotting off down there, trotting back again, not wanting to miss a single moment of it—an' nothing really happening as far as I can make out. Him an' his grimy old striped tie, been round his neck for fifty years by the look of it.'

'It's that Yorkshire one I can't stand,' Mrs Milhorne replied, without much logic. 'You can hear his voice right down here when he comes out. On about cheese sandwiches he was just now. Someone asked him if he wanted one for lunch. And you should have heard him saying no. Great healthy fellow like him. You'd of thought they was offering poison, you would.'

'I dare say there's some as'd like to do that,' Mrs Craggs said, with a chuckle. ''E's not exactly top o' the pops in there, the Yorkshire Chap.'

'No,' Mrs Milhorne agreed. 'Someone suggested a nice bit of Wensleydale just now. That's a Yorkshire cheese, and he ought to of liked it. But, do you know, I had to come right back down here to get away from his language. Right back down here.'

Mrs Craggs, who had suspected that her companion had not been hard at work during her absence, pursed her lips at this unwitting confirmation. But before she had a chance to comment something else distracted her attention.

She listened for a moment to sounds coming from the direction of the bar behind the Long Room. Then, instead of going back to the sandwiches, she moved a few paces nearer, regardless of the fact that in doing so she was intruding a female presence into at least semi-sacrosanct territory.

Then, as a waiter carried into the Long Room a tray on which there were half a dozen glasses and two bottles of wine, Italian wine in straw-covered plump bottles, she did something altogether unprecedented. She marched, feminine flowered apron flaunting, right into the Long Room itself.

The very moment she crossed the threshold, just under the disapproving look of old Thomas Lord himself, there was a stir of protest. She was quite well aware of it, but she tramped on. Straight up to the end of the long table where the Yorkshire Chap and his fellow cricket-lovers were gathered she went. And she looked the Yorkshire Chap full in the face.

'You're not to touch a drop o' that,' she said, pointing a lean brown finger at the two fat bottles of wine. 'Not a—'

She got no further. The Yorkshire Chap rose from his chair, big belly looming up like the first hint of an undersea atomic explosion, drew in a single deep breath and pronounced.

'A woman,' he said, voice bouncing off the glass cases of ancient bats and brownish shrivelled historical balls. 'You're a woman.'

'Course I'm a woman,' Mrs Craggs retorted. 'Do I look like I was anything else?'

And it was true that, if no longer the pretty girl who had forty and more years before captivated a certain Alf Craggs, she was still, crinkled and creased though her nut-brown face had been by the hard years, undoubtedly a woman. But women are not, are simply not, permitted in the Long Room, and in a minute a couple of post-war Members had politely swept her out.

She would not have let it happen, though. Only, as she went, she was able to hear the loud voice of the Yorkshire Chap demanding 'a bottle of decent burgundy, not this Italian pigswill'. And she even half-heard That Feller in Wine, who had been kind enough to stand his friends a rather good Chianti for lunch, murmur an unavailing protest.

And then, when the Yorkshire bat out in the sun-kissed field had got to within one run of his century and had stuck there, the umpires called for lunch. Still, it looked as if the big swaggering Yorkshire Chap's money was as safe as if it was already in the bank. Yet it was not.

Not that, with the second ball after lunch, the 99 on the scoreboard wasn't transformed with a sizzling four between the covers to 103. But by that time the Yorkshire Chap was dead, a dramatic seizure had laid him flat, his head just resting against one of the tall semi-circular wastepaper baskets on the back wall of the room, emptied that very morning by Mrs Craggs herself. So, of course, the bets were cancelled.

Down below, Mrs Craggs was taking a cuppa before pushing off home. When she heard the news she turned to Mrs Milhorne and said: 'Very convenient for some too, dear, 'im going like that. You know, I think I'll just stay on for a bit.'

MEMBERS OF THE MARYLEBONE Cricket Club do not expire on the floor of the Long Room at Lord's. Some things simply are not done. Except that occasionally they happen.

As death happened that third day of the Test to the man they called the Yorkshire Chap. So, quickly as they could, they scouted round for a doctor who was a Member. But no one was available, and at last after a loudspeaker appeal they had to make do with a young medico with no real right to enter the Long Room at all.

However, he seemed to know his business and before long he was saying that it appeared to be a case of simple heart failure. Though there would have to be an inquest and some undesirable publicity, there should be no need now for anything more than a discreet and rapid removal of 'the—er—body'.

But then Mrs Craggs, who despite her undoubted feminineness had been summoned, a little after the doctor, to deal with the mess of spilled wine and broken glasses on the long polished table in the centre of the room, spoke up. 'Only it's murder,' she said.

'Don't talk nonsense, woman.' 'Just get on with the clearing up, Mrs Harumph.' 'I don't think there's any need for that sort of talk.' Replies were quick to come. And every one of them pretty sharp.

Which perhaps made Mrs Craggs only the more determined to be heard. 'Murder, I said, and murder I meant. Tell you what the weapon was, too.'

'My good woman, there was no weapon and no murder. This is just a case of sudden heart failure.' The young doctor summoned from the proletarian huddle of the lunchtime Tavern did not appreciate having his expert opinion called in question,

Mrs Craggs put her hands on her hips and regarded him squarely. 'The weapon was some wine what they call Chianti,' she told him. 'An' that's a fact.'

But, quite unexpectedly, at the mention of the name of this common and excellent Italian table wine, the young doctor looked suddenly doubtful.

'Yes,' said Mrs Craggs. 'Chianti. Just look at them bottles with the straw stuff round 'em.'

'What the devil is the woman talking about?' said That Feller in Wine. 'Perfectly good Chianti that. Sell plenty of it myself.'

'Yes, of course, sir,' the young doctor replied. 'But I'm afraid it is true that in some circumstances Chianti can be a killer. If it's taken when you happen to be using what's called an MAOI anti-depressant. A few things react with those very strongly. Cheese, Chianti, Iranian or Russian caviar. Does anybody know if the gentleman was by any chance taking pills or tablets?'

No one replied. So Mrs Craggs spoke up again. 'He wouldn't touch cheese,' she said. 'My friend Mrs Milhorne heard him only today. Swore he wouldn't touch even a crumb o' Wensleydale, he did. That was when I tried to warn 'im about Chianti, an' got politely pushed out of here for me pains. 'Cept I did hear 'im order something else.'

'But how did *you* know Chianti can be dangerous?' the doctor demanded, a little nettled.

'My friend Mrs Milhorne,' said Mrs Craggs. 'Martyr to depression, she is. So she says. Wouldn't even touch the cheese for the sandwiches on account o' the pills she has. Told me about 'em many a time she has, all about 'em.'

But it was the M.C.C. Secretary himself, called to the scene before even the doctor, who put the really important question. 'Tell me, Mrs Craggs,' he said, 'is it because you heard him order some other wine that you think his death isn't as simple as it looked?'

'Got it in one, sir,' Mrs Craggs said to this mighty personage. 'Old Yorkshire knew for a cert he must never touch that stuff. An' there were people in this room just going to lose hundred pound bets. So ain't it likely that someone switched glasses on him? Ain't it, sir?'

And that was when the Secretary said that the very least they could do was to get in touch with Scotland Yard. And he added that perhaps it would be as well if nobody went home just yet.

But in any case, as the Oldest Member But Three pointed out, no one was going to go home at this juncture. England had really begun to knock up a commanding lead and the Yorkshireman's display was a joy to watch.

No one, however, was able to look on from those specially made high bentwood chairs in the Long Room. Now that such doubt had been cast on the manner of the Yorkshire Chap's death there could be no question of moving the body until the man from Scotland Yard had arrived.

So out into the heat on the steps in front of the Pavilion went all the little group who had been the Yorkshire Chap's companions during this momentous day, Boggers, Winkie, the Member Who Saw Grace's Last Century, the Oldest Member But Three and That Feller in Wine. Inside the Long Room only the Secretary and Mrs Craggs remained.

'Perhaps you could just clear up those glasses he knocked over, Mrs Craggs?' the Secretary suggested.

'I don't think as 'ow I'd better, sir,' said Mrs Craggs.

'Oh, come, I can't see any objection.' But Mrs Craggs shook her grey-curled head. 'Look at where he fell, sir. Right by that wastepaper basket there, yards away from the table. He never knocked no glasses over. Someone else did that.'

And, sure enough, when a certain Detective Superintendent Hutton arrived—he *would* share the name of that great cricketer on a case like this—he was quick to appreciate Mrs Craggs's point. He was more than ready, too, to take advantage of her sharp observations. ('It's on account of I keeps my eyes open fer dust, sir').

After quite a short conversation he was able to say, half to himself, half to this invaluable assistant he had acquired: 'So there were five of them with the deceased today, were there? Just five. Well, I think I'd better see each one of them before I do anything else.'

MEMBERS OF THE MARYLEBONE Cricket Club do not submit to police interrogation in the Long Room at Lord's. Unless there's been a murder in the Long Room.

But murder there had been—or at least a highly suspicious death—and Detective Superintendent Hutton was decidedly interested in the five Members who had spent most of the victim's last hours in his company. The two whom Mrs Craggs had identified by their prep school nicknames, Boggers and Winkie, the one she knew as That Feller in Wine, and the two extreme ancients, the Oldest Member But Three and the Member Who Saw Grace's Last Century.

The Superintendent was anxious to talk to them. But he did not share his unorthodox colleague's view on why any one of them might be a killer. 'Come now, Mrs Craggs,' he said. 'To take a life over a bet of a hundred pounds? I'm afraid it's just not on, you know.'

'If you say so, sir,' Mrs Craggs replied. 'But that Yorkshire Chap did die when those bets looked as if they was as good as money in his pocket. On 99 the feller out there was, one off that century. You can't get over that.'

Superintendent Hutton, who had clean bowled a fair number of murderers in his time, gave Mrs Craggs a smile which mingled a fair ration of sharp amusement with its outward kindliness. 'We'll see,' he said. 'But in the meantime there's nothing to stop you going off home now. Thanks very much.'

'As you say, sir,' said Mrs Craggs. But she did not go home. Instead she made her way to a quiet nook she knew of and there she sat and waited.

She had a long time to wait, too. Out on the green of the field England added run to run and the Indian bowlers slaved and sweated, neither side knowing that the death that had taken place in the Long Room at the lunch break had been anything other than an unfortunate incident. And in the cool of the Long Room Superintendent Hutton and his sergeant talked at length with each of five men.

Boggers—he turned out to be Major General E. H. Fitzharding—agreed that he had had this 'rather foolish' bet with the dead man. 'Jolly sorry he isn't here to collect actually.' But, no, beyond meeting him at Lord's from time to time he knew nothing about the chap.

Winkie—and he was Mr Arnold Boutley of the Foreign Office—said almost exactly the same. 'He was a good enough fellow in his way, you know. But naturally one didn't . . .'

The Oldest Member But Three, a Mr Charles Tilkinson, subjected to equally long, polite but persistent questioning, produced nothing more germane. 'I'm afraid I never actually knew his—er—name, you know. Funny thing, I suppose. But as one grows older . . .'

The Member Who Saw Grace's Last (Rear Admiral Sir Horace Virtonbright, K.C.V.O., C.M.G., D.S.O.) was more forthright but no more informative. 'Bit of a bounder really. Man was a Member and all that. But. Well, there it is.'

That Feller in Wine, or Mr Frederic Lowesmith, managing director of Lowesmith and Lowesmith, Duke Street, St James's, did have a little more to contribute. He had after all bought the circle the Chianti that looked as if it had been, as Mrs Craggs had called it, the murder weapon. 'Do you know, Superintendent, I've been in the wine trade all my life and my father before me, and I had no idea Chianti did that, not the least notion.'

But he was unable, like the others, to recall anything about what exactly had been happening at the table before suddenly the Yorkshire Chap had lunged forward, sent all the glasses crashing over and had died.

'He lunged forward, did he?' Superintendent Hutton asked quickly. 'Knocked over the glasses?'

Mr Lowesmith thought for a moment. 'Well, no, Superintendent, I'm not sure that he did. I seem to remember actually that he fell backwards. Yes, I'm sure he did. But then . . .?'

'You didn't see anyone knock over the glasses afterwards? Perhaps in the excitement of it all?'

'No. No, I'm afraid I didn't. You see, we were all looking at—at the poor chap.'

And though the questioning had gone on for some time after this, just as it had gone on with the others, apparently the Superintendent felt that he could get no further. A little later, tucked away in her nook, Mrs Craggs heard his sergeant telling everybody that they could now go.

Which was when she emerged, pushed past the sergeant without so much as a by-your-leave and went straight up to the Superintendent. 'Sir,' she said, 'there's something I got to put you right about.'

The Superintendent looked at her, plainly a good deal irked.

'It's Mrs Craggs, isn't it?' he said. 'I did tell you it was all right for you to be off, you know. Quite some time ago.'

'Yes,' said Mrs Craggs, 'you did. An' you told all the rest of 'em it's all right for them to go too. Well, it ain't, you know. It bloody ain't. You're letting go a murderer, an' I can tell you why.'

MEMBERS OF THE MARYLEBONE Cricket Club do not get arrested for murder in the Long Room at Lord's. Unless, of course, it becomes apparent to an investigating officer while the Member is answering a few extra questions in the Long Room that he has actually committed a murder.

And provided too, of course, that the investigating officer has been lucky enough to have been assisted by Mrs Craggs, cleaning lady. However unwillingly it had been at first.

'Mrs Craggs,' Superintendent Hutton had said when she had pushed her way in and told him it wasn't 'bloody right' for him to let go one of the five men who had made bets with the dead Yorkshire Chap in the Long Room that morning. 'Mrs Craggs, I dare say I owe something to your gift of observation, but I think you've long ago told me all you can.'

'Oh, no, I ain't. You didn't ask, so I didn't say. Thought you'd likely find out for yourself. That's what I thought then.'

'Find out what? Have you been withholding evidence? Because if so, let me warn you, you have been committing a very serious offence.'

'I wasn't withholding no evidence,' Mrs Craggs replied. 'I wasn't withholding one thing you couldn't of seen for yourself. If so as you'd opened your eyes and looked.'

The Superintendent's face froze then in an anger that had reduced many a junior in rank to abject silence, let alone many an outright villain. But it failed altogether to silence Mrs Craggs.

'Didn't you see?' she demanded. 'Didn't you see what was in front of your very eyes? 'Cos if you didn't you should be polishing this 'ere floor an' trying to get the dirt out of them little stud marks everywhere, an' I should be a-lording it down Scotland Yard.'

The insult ought to have had Mrs Craggs bundled out of the Long Room in less time than it takes to tell, and much less gently than she had been bundled out when she had tried to warn the Yorkshire Chap not to drink Chianti. But Superintendent Hutton had not notched up his half-century of caught murderers by being pig-headed.

'There was something to see, was there?' he asked with a sudden change-down in tone. 'Well, suppose you tell me just what that was, Mrs Craggs.'

There was more menace in his quietness than there had been in his anger, and for once Mrs Craggs sounded defensive when she answered.

'Well, I s'pose you never did see him stuff that old score-card into his shoe, same as I did once when he thought nobody wasn't looking,' she said.

'Stuff a score-card into his shoe? What on earth are you saying, woman?'

A glint of the sardonic came into Mrs Craggs's eyes in response. All right, if he couldn't see it when it was practically thrust under his nose . . .

'What you think a person would put a thick sheet o' paper into his shoe for?' she demanded. ''Cos he's got a hole in the sole, o' course. An' why would he have a hole in the sole of his shoe? 'Cos he couldn't afford to have 'em mended. An' if he couldn't afford that, he couldn't afford to fork up a hundred quid, could he? An' he'd gone an' made that bet, hadn't he? In the excitement o' the moment. Cricket mad as he is.'

But now Superintendent Hutton, who could after all very easily see a thing if it was thrust under his nose, was absolutely with her.

'Of course,' he said. 'That grimy old tie. And his blazer. The sleeves of his blazer were frayed. I saw them. Saw them, but I never thought that a Member of the M.C.C. didn't actually have to be well off. Of course, it's him.'

'Yes, dear,' said Mrs Craggs. 'You got it. Now. The Oldest Member But Three, poor old devil.'

Peter Lovesey
b. 1936

A CASE OF BUTTERFLIES

BEFORE CALLING THE POLICE, he had found a butterfly in the summerhouse. It had unsettled him. The wings had been purple, a rich, velvety purple. Soaring and swooping, it had intermittently come to rest on the wood floor. His assumption that it was trapped had proved to be false, because two of the windows had been wide open and it had made no move towards the open door. He knew what it was, a Purple Emperor, for there was one made of paper mounted in a perspex case in his wife Ann's study. As a staunch conservationist, Ann wouldn't have wanted to possess a real specimen. She had told him often enough that she preferred to see them flying free. She had always insisted that Purple Emperors were in the oak wood that surrounded the house. He had never spotted one until this morning, and it seemed like a sign from her.

'YOU DID THE RIGHT thing, sir.'

'The right thing?'

'Calling us in as soon as you knew about this. It takes courage.'

'I don't want your approval, Commander. I want my wife back.'

'We all want that, sir.'

Sir Milroy Shenton made it plain that he didn't care for the remark, mildly as it was put. He rotated his chair to turn his back on the two police officers and face the view along King's Reach where the City skyline rises above Waterloo Bridge. He stared at it superficially. The image of the butterfly refused to leave his mind, just as it had lingered in the summerhouse. Less than an hour ago he had called the emergency number from his house in Sussex. The police had suggested meeting in London in case the house was being observed, and he had nominated the Broad Wall Complex. He had the choice of dozens of company boardrooms across London and the Home Counties that belonged in his high-tech empire. The advantage of using Broad Wall was the proximity of the heliport.

He swung around again. 'You'll have to bear with me. I'm short of sleep. It was a night flight from New York.'

'Let's get down to basics, then. Did you bring the ransom note?'

Commander Jerry Glazier was primed for this. He headed the Special Branch team that was always on stand-by to deal with kidnapping incidents. International terrorism was so often involved in extortion that a decision had been taken to involve Special Branch from the beginning in major kidnap inquiries. Captains of industry like Shenton were obvious targets. They knew the dangers, and often employed private bodyguards. Not Shenton: such precautions would not square with his reputation in the city as a devil-may-care dealer in the stock market, known and feared for his dawn raids.

Glazier was assessing him with a professional eye, aware how vital in kidnap cases is the attitude and resolve of the 'mark'.

First impressions suggested that this was a man in his forties trying to pass for twenty-five, with a hairstyle that would once have been called short back and sides and was now trendy and expensive. A jacket of crumpled silk was hanging off his shoulders. The accent was Oxford turned cockney, a curious inversion Glazier had noted lately in the business world. Scarcely ten minutes ago he had read in *Who's Who* that Shenton's background was a rectory in Norfolk, followed by Winchester and Magdalen. He had married twice. The second wife, the lady now abducted, was Ann, the only daughter of Dr Hamilton Porter, deceased. Under *Recreations*, Shenton had entered *Exercising the wife*. It must have seemed witty when he thought of it.

Now he took a package from his pocket. 'Wrapped in a freezer bag, as your people suggested. My sweaty prints are all over it, of course. I didn't know it was going to be evidence until I'd read the bloody thing, did I?'

'It isn't just the prints.' Glazier glanced at the wording on the note. It read, IF YOU WANT HER BACK ALIVE GET ONE MILLION READY. INSTRUCTIONS FOLLOW.

'There's modern technology for you,' he commented. 'They do the old thing of cutting words from the papers, but now they dispense with paste. They use a photocopier.' He turned it over to look at the envelope. 'Indistinct postmark, wouldn't you know.'

'The bastards could have sent it any time in the last six days, couldn't they?' said Shenton. 'For all I know, they may have tried to phone me. She could be dead.'

Glazier wasn't there to speculate. 'So you flew in from New York this morning, returned to your house and found this on the mat?'

'And my wife missing.'

'You've been away from the house for how long, sir?'

'I told you—six days. Ann had been away as well, but she should have been back by now.'

'Then I dare say there was a stack of mail waiting.'

'Is that relevant?'

The pattern of the interview was taking shape. Shenton was using every opportunity to assert his status as top dog.

'It may be,' Glazier commented, 'if you can remember what was above or below it in the stack.' He wasn't to be intimidated.

'I just picked everything up, flipped through what was there and extracted the interesting mail from the junk.'

'*This* looked interesting?'

'It's got a stamp, hasn't it?'

'Fair enough. You opened it, read the note, and phoned us. Did you call anyone else?'

'Cressie.'

'Cressie?'

'Cressida Concannon, Ann's college friend. The two of them were touring.'

'Touring where, sir?'

'The Ring of Kerry.'

'*Ireland*?' Glazier glanced towards his assistant, then back at Shenton. 'That was taking a chance, wasn't it?'

'With hindsight, yes. I told Ann to use her maiden name over there.'

'Which is . . .?'

'Porter.'

'So what have you learned from her friend?'

'Cressie's still over there, visiting her sister. She last saw Ann on Wednesday at the end of their holiday, going in to Cork airport.'

'Have you called the airline to see if she was on the flight?'

Shenton shook his head. 'Tracing Cressie took the best part of half an hour. I flew straight up from Sussex after that.'

'Flew?'

'Chopper.'

'I see. Did your wife have a reservation?'

'Aer Lingus. The two-fifteen flight to Heathrow.'

Glazier nodded to his assistant, who left the room to check. 'This holiday in Ireland—when was it planned?'

'A month ago, when New York came up. She said she deserved a trip of her own.'

'So she got in touch with her friend. I shall need to know more about Miss Concannon, sir. She's an old and trusted friend, I take it?'

'Cressie? She's twenty-four carat. We've known her for twelve years, easily.'

'Well enough to know her political views?'

'Hold on.' Shenton folded his arms in a challenging way. 'Cressie isn't one of that lot.'

'But does she guard her tongue?'

'She's far too smart to mouth off to the micks.'

'They met at college, you say. What were they studying?'

'You think I'm going to say politics?' Shenton said as if he were scoring points at a board meeting. 'It was bugs. Ann and Cressie's idea of a holiday is kneeling in cowpats communing with dung-beetles.'

'Entomology,' said Glazier.

'Sorry, I was forgetting some of the fuzz can read without moving their lips.'

'Do you carry a picture of your wife, sir?'

'For the press, do you mean? She's been kidnapped. She isn't a missing person.'

'For our use, Sir Milroy.'

He felt for his wallet. 'I dare say there's one I can let you have.'

'If you're bothered about the media, sir, we intend to keep them off your back until this is resolved. The Press Office at the Yard will get their co-operation.'

'You mean an embargo?' He started to remove a photo from his wallet and then pushed it back into its slot. Second thoughts, apparently.

Glazier had glimpsed enough of the print to make out a woman in a see-through blouse. She seemed to be dancing. 'I mean a voluntary agreement to withhold the news until you've got your wife back. After that, of course . . .'

'If I get her back unharmed I'll speak to anyone.'

'Until that happens, you talk only to us, sir. These people, whoever they are, will contact you again. Do you have an answerphone at your house?'

'Of course.'

'Have you played it back?'

'Didn't have time.' Shenton folded the wallet and returned it to his pocket. 'I don't, after all, happen to have a suitable picture of Ann on me. I'll arrange to send you one.'

'Listen to your messages as soon as you get back, sir, and let me know if there's anything.'

'What do you do in these cases—tap my phone?'

'Is that what you'd recommend?'

'Commander Glazier, don't patronise me. I called you in. I have a right to know what to expect.'

'You can expect us to do everything within our powers to find your wife, sir.'

'You don't trust me, for God's sake?'

'I didn't say that. What matters is that you put your trust in us. Do you happen to have a card with your Sussex address?'

Shenton felt for the wallet again and opened it.

Glazier said at once, 'Isn't that a picture of your wife, sir, the one you put back just now?'

'That wasn't suitable. I told you.'

'If it's the way she's dressed that bothers you, that's no problem. I need the shot of her face, that's all. May I take it?'

Shenton shook his head.

'What's the problem?' asked Glazier.

'As it happens, that isn't Ann. It's her friend Cressida.'

BETWEEN TRAFFIC SIGNALS along the Embankment, Glazier told his assistant, Inspector Tom Salt, about the photograph.

'You think he's cheating with his wife's best friend?'

'It's a fair bet.'

'Does it have any bearing on the kidnap?'

'Too soon to tell. His reactions are strange. He seems more fussed about how we intend to conduct the case than what is happening to his wife.'

'High-flyers like him operate on a different level from you and me, sir. Life is all about flow-charts and decision-making.'

'They're not all like that. Did you get anything from the airline?'

'Everything he told us checks. There was a first class reservation in the name of Ann Porter. She wasn't aboard that Heathrow flight or any other.'

The next morning Glazier flew to Ireland for a meeting with senior officers in the *gardai*. Cork airport shimmered in the August heat. At headquarters they were served iced lemonade in preference to coffee. A full-scale inquiry was authorised.

He visited Cressida Concannon at her sister's, an estate house on the northern outskirts of Cork, and they talked outside, seated on patio chairs. She presented a picture distinctly different from the photo in Shenton's wallet; she was in a cream-coloured linen suit and brown shirt buttoned to the top. Her long brown hair was drawn back and secured with combs. Like Lady Ann, she was at least ten years younger than Shenton. She had made an itinerary of the tour around the Ring of Kerry. She handed Glazier a sheaf of hotel receipts.

He flicked through them. 'I notice you paid all of these yourself, Miss Concannon.'

'Yes. Ann said she would settle up with me later. She couldn't write cheques because she was using her maiden name.'

'Of course. Porter, isn't it? So the hotel staff addressed her as Mrs Porter?'

'Yes.'

'And was there any time in your trip when she was recognised as Lady Shenton?'

'Not to my knowledge.'

'You remember nothing suspicious, nothing that might help us to find her?'

'I've been over it many times in my mind, and I can't think of anything, I honestly can't.'

'What was her frame of mind? Did she seem concerned at any stage of the tour?'

'Not once that I recall. She seemed to relish every moment. You can ask at any of the hotels. She was full of high spirits right up to the minute we parted.'

'Which was . . .?'

'Wednesday, about twelve-thirty. I drove her to the airport and put her down where the cars pull in. She went through the doors and that was the last I saw of her. Surely they won't harm her, will they?'

Glazier said as if he hadn't listened to the question, 'Tell me about your relationship with Sir Milroy Shenton.'

She drew herself up. 'What do you mean?'

'You're a close friend, close enough to spend some time alone with him, I believe.'

'They are both my friends. I've known them for years.'

'But you do meet him, don't you?'

'I don't see what this has to do with it.'

'I'll tell you,' said Glazier. 'I'm just surprised that she went on holiday with you and relished every moment, as you expressed it. She's an intelligent woman. He carries your picture fairly openly in his wallet. He doesn't carry one of Lady Ann. Her behaviour strikes me as untypical, that's all.'

She said coolly, 'When you rescue her from the kidnappers, you'll be able to question her about it, won't you?'

Before leaving Ireland, Glazier had those hotels checked. Without exception the inquiries confirmed that the two women had stayed there on the dates in question. Moreover, they had given every appearance of getting on well together. One hotel waiter in Killarney recalled that they had laughed the evenings away together.

Within an hour of Glazier's return to London, there was a development. Sir Milroy Shenton called on the phone. His voice was strained. 'I've heard from them. She's dead. They've killed her, the bastards, and I hold you responsible.'

'Dead? You're sure?'

'*They're* sure.'

'Tell me precisely how you heard about this.'

'They just phoned me, didn't they? Irish accent.'

'A man?'

'Yes. Said they had to abort the operation because I got in touch with the filth. That's you. They said she's at the bottom of the Irish Sea. This is going to be on your conscience for the rest of your bloody life.'

'I need to see you,' said Glazier. 'Where are you now?'

'Manchester.'

'How do they know you're up there?'

'It was in the papers. One of my companies has a shareholders' meeting. Look, I can't tell you any more than I just did.'

'You want the killers to get away with it, sir?'

'What?'

'I'll be at Midhurst. Your house.'

'Why Midhurst?'

'Get there as soon as you can, Sir Milroy.' Glazier put an end to the call and stabbed out Tom Salt's number. 'Can you lay on a chopper, Tom?'

'What's this about?' Salt shouted over the engine noise after they were airborne.

'Shenton. His wife is dead.'

'Why would they kill her? While she was alive she was worth a million.'

'My thought exactly.'

Salt wrestled with that remark as they followed the ribbon of the Thames southwards, flying over Richmond and Kingston. 'Don't you believe what Shenton told you?'

'She's dead. I believe that much.'

'No kidnap?'

'No kidnap.'

'We're talking old-fashioned murder, then.'

'That's my reading of it.'

There was a break in the conversation that brought them across the rest of Surrey before Salt shouted, 'It's got to be Cressie Concannon, hasn't it?'

'Why?'

'She wasn't satisfied with her status as the mistress, so she snuffed her rival and sent the ransom note to cover up the crime.'

Glazier shook his head. 'Cressie is in Ireland.'

'What's wrong with that? Lady Shenton was last seen in Ireland. We know she didn't make the flight home.'

'Cressie didn't send the ransom note. The postage stamp was British.'

The pilot turned his head. 'The place should be coming up any minute, sir. Those are the South Downs ahead.'

Without much difficulty they located Shenton's house, a stone-built Victorian mansion in a clearing in an oak wood. The helicopter wheeled around it once before touching down on the forecourt, churning up dust and gravel.

'We've got at least an hour before he gets here,' Glazier said.

'Is there a pub?' asked Salt, and got a look from his superior that put him off drinking for a week.

Rather less than the estimated hour had passed when the clatter of a second helicopter disturbed the sylvan peace. Glazier crossed the drive to meet it.

'No more news, I suppose?' Sir Milroy Shenton asked as he climbed out. He spoke in a more reasonable tone than he'd used on the phone. He'd had time to compose himself.

'Not yet, sir.'

'Found your way in?'

'No, we've been out here in the garden.'

'Not much of a garden. Ann and I preferred to keep it uncultivated except for the lawns.'

'She must have wanted to study the insect life in its natural habitat.'

Shenton frowned slightly, as if he'd already forgotten about his wife's field of study. 'Shall we go indoors?'

A fine curved staircase faced them as they entered. The hall was open to three floors. 'Your wife had a study, I'm sure,' said Glazier. 'I'd like to see it, please.'

'To your left—but there's nothing in there to help you,' said Shenton.

'We'll see.' Glazier entered the room and moved around the desk to the book-shelves. 'Whilst we were waiting for you I saw a couple of butterflies I'd never spotted before. I used to collect them when I was a kid, little horror, before they were protected. Did you know you had Purple Emperors here?'

Shenton twitched and swayed slightly. Then he put his hand to his face and said distractedly, 'What?'

'Purple Emperors. There were two in the summerhouse just now. The windows were open, but they had no desire to leave. They settled on the floor in the joints between the boards.' Glazier picked a book off the shelf and thumbed through the pages, finally turning them open for Shenton's inspection. 'How about that? Isn't it superb? The colour on those wings! I'd have sold my electric train-set for one of these in my collection.' He continued to study the page.

'You must have lived in the wrong area,' said Shenton, with an effort to sound reasonable.

'I wouldn't say that,' said Glazier. 'There were oaks in the park where I played. They live high up in the canopy of the wood. You never see them normally, but they are probably more common than most of us realised then.'

'This isn't exactly helping to find my wife,' said Shenton.

'You couldn't be more wrong,' said Glazier. 'How long ago did you kill her, Sir Milroy?'

Shenton tensed. He didn't respond.

'She's been dead a few weeks, hasn't she, long before your trip to New York. She didn't visit Ireland at all. That was some friend of Cressida Concannon's, using the name of Ann Porter. A free trip around the Ring of Kerry. No wonder the woman was laughing. She must have thought the joke was on you, just as the expenses were. I don't suppose she knew that the real Lady Ann was dead.'

'I don't have to listen to this slanderous rubbish,' said Shenton. He'd recovered his voice, but he was ashen.

'You'd better. I'm going to charge you presently. Miss Concannon will also be charged as an accessory. The kidnapping was a fabrication. You wrote the ransom note yourself some time ago. You posted envelopes to this address until one arrived in the condition you required—with the indistinct date-stamp. Then all you had to do was slip the ransom note inside and hand it to me when you got back from New York and alerted us to your wife's so-called abduction. How long has she been dead—four or five weeks?'

Shenton said with contempt, 'What am I supposed to have done with her?'

'Buried her—or tried to. You weren't the first murderer to discover that digging a grave isn't so easy if the ground is unhelpful. It's always a shallow grave in the newspaper reports, isn't it? But you didn't let that defeat you. You jacked up the summerhouse and wedged her under the floorboards—which I suppose was easier than digging six feet down. The butterflies led me to her.'

Shenton latched on to this at once. Turning to Tom Salt he said, 'Is he all right in the head?'

Salt gave his boss a troubled glance.

Shenton flapped his hand in derision. 'Crazy.'

'You don't believe me?' said Glazier. 'Why else would a Purple Emperor come down from the trees? Listen to this.' He started reading from the book. '"They remain in the treetops feeding on sap and honeydew unless attracted to the ground by the juices of dung or decaying flesh. They seldom visit flowers:"' He looked up, straight into Shenton's stricken eyes. 'Not so crazy after all, is it?'

John D. MacDonald
1916–1986

THE HOMESICK BUICK

To get to Leeman, Texas, you go southwest from Beaumont on Route 90 for approximately thirty miles and then turn right on a two-lane concrete farm road. Five minutes from the time you turn, you will reach Leeman. The main part of town is six lanes wide and five blocks long. If the hand of a careless giant should remove the six gas stations, the two theaters, Willows' Hardware Store, the Leeman National Bank, the two big air-conditioned five-and-dimes, the Sears store, four cafés, Rightsinger's dress shop, and The Leeman House, a twenty-room hotel, there would be very little left except the supermarket and four assorted drugstores.

On October 3rd, 1949, a Mr Stanley Woods arrived by bus and carried his suitcase over to The Leeman House. In Leeman there is no social distinction of bus, train, or plane, since Leeman has neither airport facilities nor railroad station.

On all those who were questioned later, Mr Stanley Woods seemed to have made very little impression. They all spoke of kind of a medium-size fella in his thirties, or it might be his forties. No, he wasn't fat, but he wasn't thin either. Blue eyes? Could be brown. Wore a gray suit, I think. Can't remember whether his glasses had rims or not. If they did have rims, they were probably gold.

But all were agreed that Mr Stanley Woods radiated quiet confidence and the smell of money. According to the cards that were collected here and there, Mr Woods represented the Groston Precision Tool Company of Atlanta, Georgia. He had deposited in the Leeman National a certified check for twelve hundred dollars and the bank had made the routine check of looking up the credit standing of Groston. It was Dun & Bradstreet double-A, but, of course, the company explained later that they had never heard of Mr Stanley Woods. Nor could the fake calling cards be traced. They were of a type of paper and type face which could be duplicated sixty or a hundred times in every big city in the country.

Mr Woods' story, which all agreed on, was that he was '. . . nosing around to find a good location for a small plant. Decentralisation, you know. No, we don't want it right in town.'

He rented Tod Bishner's car during the day. Tod works at the Shell station on the corner of Beaumont and Lone Star Streets and doesn't have any use for his Plymouth sedan during the day. Mr Woods drove around all the roads leading out of town and, of course, real estate prices were jacked to a considerable degree during his stay.

Mr Stanley Woods left Leeman rather suddenly on the morning of October 17th under unusual circumstances.

The first person to note a certain oddness was Miss Trilla Price on the switchboard at the phone company. Her local calls were all right but she couldn't place Charley Anderson's call to Houston, nor, when she tried, could she raise Beaumont. Charley was upset because he wanted to wangle an invitation to go visit his sister over the coming weekend.

That was at five minutes of nine. It was probably at the same time that a car with two men in it parked on Beaumont Street, diagonally across from the bank, and one of the two men lifted the hood and began to fiddle with the electrical system.

Nobody agrees from what direction the Buick came into town. There was a man and a girl in it and they parked near the drugstore. No one seems to know where the third car parked, or even what kind of car it was.

The girl and the man got out of the Buick slowly, just as Stanley Woods came down the street from the hotel.

In Leeman the bank is open on weekdays from nine until two. And so, at nine o'clock, C. F. Hethridge, who is, or was, the chief teller, raised the green shades on the inside of the bank doors and unlocked the doors. He greeted Mr Woods, who went on over to the high counter at the east wall and began to ponder over his check book.

At this point, out on the street, a very peculiar thing happened. One of the two men in the first car strolled casually over and stood beside the Buick. The other man started the motor of the first car, drove down the street, and made a wide U-turn to swing in and park behind the Buick.

The girl and the man had gone over to Bob Kimball's window. Bob is second teller, and the only thing he can remember about the girl is that she was blonde and a little hard-looking around the mouth, and that she wore a great big alligator shoulder-bag. The man with her made no impression on Bob at all, except that Bob thinks the man was on the heavy side.

Old Rod Harrigan, the bank guard, was standing beside the front door, yawning, and picking his teeth with a broken match.

At this point C. F. Hethridge heard the buzzer on the big time-vault and went over and swung the door wide and went in to get the money for the cages. He was out almost immediately, carrying Bob's tray over to him. The girl was saying something about cashing a check and Bob had asked her for identification. She had opened the big shoulder-bag as her escort strolled over to the guard. At the same moment the girl pulled out a small vicious-looking revolver and aimed it between Bob's eyes, her escort sapped Old Rod Harrigan with such gusto that it was four that same afternoon before he came out of it enough to talk. And then, of course, he knew nothing.

C. F. Hethridge bolted for the vault and Bob, wondering whether he should step on the alarm, looked over the girl's shoulder just in time to see Stanley Woods aim carefully and bring Hethridge down with a slug through the head, catching him on the fly, so to speak.

Bob says that things were pretty confusing and that the sight of Hethridge dying so suddenly sort of took the heart out of him. Anyway, there was a third car and it contained three men, two of them equipped with empty black-leather suitcases. They went into the vault, acting as though they had been all through the bank fifty times. They stepped over Hethridge on the way in, and on the way out again.

About the only cash they overlooked was the cash right in front of Bob, in his teller's drawer.

As they all broke for the door, Bob dropped and pressed the alarm button. He said later that he held his hands over his eyes, though what good that would do him, he couldn't say.

Henry Willows is the real hero. He was fuddying around in his hardware store when he heard the alarm. With a reaction-time remarkable in a man close to seventy, he took a little twenty-two rifle, slapped a clip into it, trotted to his store door, and quickly analysed the situation. He saw Mr Woods, whom he recognised, plus three strangers and a blonde woman coming out of the bank pretty fast. Three cars were lined up, each one with a driver. Two of the men coming out of the bank carried heavy suitcases. Henry leveled on the driver of the lead car, the Buick, and shot him in the left temple, killing him outright. The man slumped over the wheel, his body resting against the horn ring, which, of course, added its blare to the clanging of the bank alarm.

At that point a slug, later identified as having come from a Smith & Wesson Police Positive, smashed a neat hole in Henry's plate-glass store window, radiating cracks in all directions. Henry ducked, and by the time he got ready to take a second shot, the two other cars were gone. The Buick was still there. He saw Bob run out of the bank, and later on he told his wife that he had his finger on the trigger and his sights lined up before it came to him that it was Bob Kimball.

It was agreed that the two cars headed out toward Route 90 and, within two minutes, Hod Abrams and Lefty Quinn had roared out of town in the same direction in the only police car. They were followed by belligerent amateurs to whom Henry Willows had doled out firearms. But on the edge of town all cars ran into an odd obstacle. The road was liberally sprinkled with metal objects shaped exactly like the jacks that little girls pick up when they bounce a ball, except they were four times normal size and all the points were sharpened. No matter how a tire hit one, it was certain to be punctured.

The police car swerved to a screaming stop, nearly tipping over. The Stein twins, boys of nineteen, managed to avoid the jacks in their souped-up heap until they were hitting eighty. When they finally hit one, the heap rolled over an estimated ten times, killing the twins outright.

So that made four dead. Hethridge, the Stein twins, and one unidentified bank robber.

Nobody wanted to touch the robber, and he stayed right where he was until the battery almost ran down and the horn squawked into silence. Hod Abrams commandeered a car, and he and Lefty rode back into town and took charge. They couldn't get word out by phone and within a very short time they found that some sharpshooter with a high-powered rifle had gone to work on the towers of local station WLEE and had put the station out of business.

Thus, by the time the Texas Rangers were alerted and ready to set up road blocks, indecision and confusion had permitted an entire hour to pass.

The Houston office of the FBI assigned a detail of men to the case and, from the Washington headquarters, two bank-robbery experts were dispatched by plane to Beaumont. Reporters came from Houston and Beaumont and the two national press services, and Leeman found itself on the front pages all over the country because the planning behind the job seemed to fascinate the average joe.

Mr Woods left town on that particular Thursday morning. The FBI from Houston was there by noon, and the Washington contingent arrived late Friday. Everyone was very confident. There was a corpse and a car to work on. These would certainly provide the necessary clues to indicate which outfit had pulled the job, even though the method of the robbery did not point to any particular group whose habits were known.

Investigation headquarters were set up in the local police station and Hod and Lefty, very important in the beginning, had to stand around outside trying to look as though they knew what was going on.

Hethridge, who had been a cold, reserved, unpopular man, had, within twenty-four hours, fifty stories invented about his human kindness and generosity. The Stein twins, heretofore considered to be trash who would be better off in prison, suddenly became proper sons of old Texas.

Special Agent Randolph A. Sternweister who, fifteen years before, had found a law office to be a dull place, was in charge of the case, being the senior of the two experts who had flown down from Washington. He was forty-one years old, a chain smoker, a chubby man with incongruous hollow cheeks and hair of a shade of gray which his wife, Claire, tells him is distinguished.

The corpse was the first clue. Age between thirty and thirty-two. Brown hair, thinning on top. Good teeth, with only four small cavities, two of them filled. Height, five foot eight and a quarter, weight a hundred and forty-eight. No distinguishing scars or tattoos. X-ray plates showed that the right arm had been fractured years before. His clothes were neither new nor old. The suit had been purchased in Chicago. The shirt, underwear, socks, and shoes were all national brands, in the medium-price range. In his pockets they found an almost full pack of cigarettes, a battered Zippo lighter, three fives and a one in a cheap, trick billclip, eighty-five cents in change, a book of matches advertising a nationally known laxative, a white bone button, two wooden kitchen matches with blue and white heads, and a penciled map, on cheap notebook paper, of the main drag of Leeman—with no indication as to escape route. His fingerprint classification was teletyped to the Central Bureau files and the answer came back that there was no record of him. It was at this point that fellow workers noted that Mr Sternweister became a shade irritable.

The next search of the corpse was more minute. No specific occupational calluses were found on his hands. The absence of laundry marks indicated that his linen, if it had been sent out, had been cleaned by a neighborhood laundress. Since Willows had used a .22 hollow-point, the hydraulic pressure on the brain fluids had caused the eyes of Mr X to bulge in a disconcerting fashion. A local undertaker, experienced in the damage caused by the average Texas automobile accident, replaced the bulging eyeballs and smoothed out the expression for a series of pictures which were sent to many points. The Chicago office reported that the clothing store which had sold the suit was large and that the daily traffic was such that no clerk could identify the customer from the picture; nor was the youngish man known to the Chicago police.

Fingernail scrapings were put in a labeled glassine envelope, as well as the dust vacuumed from pants cuffs and other portions of the clothing likely to collect dust. The excellent lab in Houston reported back that the dust and scrapings were negative to the extent that the man could not be tied down to any particular locality.

In the meantime the Buick had been the object of equal scrutiny. The outside was a mass of prints from the citizens of Leeman who had peered morbidly in at the man leaning against the horn ring. The plates were Mississippi license plates and, in checking with the Bureau of Motor Vehicle Registration, it was found that the plates had been issued for a 1949 Mercury convertible which had been almost totally destroyed in a head-on collision in June, 1949. The motor number and serial number of the Buick were checked against central records and it was discovered that the Buick was one which had disappeared from Chapel Hill, North Carolina, on the 5th of July, 1949. The insurance company, having already replaced the vehicle, was anxious to take possession of the stolen car.

Pictures of Mr X, relayed to Chapel Hill, North Carolina, and to myriad points in Mississippi, drew a large blank. In the meantime a careful dusting of the car had brought out six prints, all different. Two of them turned out to be on record. The first was on record through the cross-classification of Army prints. The man in question was found working in a gas station in Lake Charles, Louisiana. He had a very difficult two hours until a bright police officer had him demonstrate his procedure for brushing out the front of a car. Ex-Sergeant Golden braced his left hand against the dashboard in almost the precise place where the print had been found. He was given a picture of Mr X to study. By that time he was so thoroughly annoyed at the forces of law and order that it was impossible to ascertain whether or not he had ever seen the man in question. But due to the apparent freshness of the print it was established—a reasonable assumption—that the gangsters had driven into Texas from the East.

The second print on record was an old print, visible when dust was carefully blown off the braces under the dismantled front seat. It belonged to a garage mechanic in Chapel Hill who once had a small misunderstanding with the forces of law and order and who was able to prove, through the garage work orders, that he had repaired the front seat mechanism when it had jammed in April, 1949.

The samples of road dirt and dust taken from the fender wells and the frame members proved nothing. The dust was proved, spectroscopically, to be from deep in the heart of Texas, and the valid assumption, after checking old weather reports, was that the car had come through some brisk thunderstorms en route.

Butts in the ashtray of the car showed that either two women, or one woman with two brands of lipstick, had ridden recently as a passenger. Both brands of lipstick were of shades which would go with a fair-complexioned blonde, and both brands were available in Woolworth's, Kress, Kresge, Walgreens—in fact, in every chain outfit of any importance.

One large crumb of stale whole-wheat bread was found on the floor mat, and even Sternweister could make little of that, despite the fact that the lab was able to report that the bread had been eaten in conjunction with liverwurst.

Attention was given to the oversized jacks which had so neatly punctured the tires. An ex-OSS officer reported that similar items had been scattered on enemy roads in Burma during the late war and, after examining the samples, he stated confidently that the OSS merchandise had been better made. A competent machinist looked them over and stated with assurance that they had been made by cutting eighth-inch rod into short lengths, grinding them on a wheel, putting them in a jig, and spot-welding them. He said that the maker did not do much of a job on either the grinding or the welding, and that the jig itself was a little out of line. An analysis of the steel showed that it was a Jones & Laughlin product that could be bought in quantity at any wholesaler and in a great many hardware stores.

The auditors, after a careful examination of the situation at the bank, reported that the sum of exactly $94,725 had disappeared. They recommended that the balance remaining in Stanley Woods' account of $982.80 be considered as forfeited, thus reducing the loss to $93,742.20. The good citizens of Leeman preferred to think that Stanley had withdrawn his account.

Every person who had a glimpse of the gang was cross-examined. Sternweister was appalled at the difficulty involved in even establishing how many there had been. Woods, the blonde, and the stocky citizen were definite. And then there were two with suitcases—generally agreed upon. Total, so far— five. The big question was whether each car had a driver waiting. Some said no—that the last car in line had been empty. Willows insisted angrily that there had been a driver behind each wheel. Sternweister at last settled for a total of eight, seven of whom escaped.

No one had taken down a single license number. But it was positively established that the other two cars had been either two- or four-door sedans in dark blue, black, green, or maroon, and that they had been either Buicks, Nashes, Oldsmobiles, Chryslers, Pontiacs, or Packards—or maybe Hudsons. And one lone woman held out for convertible Cadillacs. For each person that insisted that they had Mississippi registration, there was one equally insistent on Louisiana, Texas, Alabama, New Mexico, and Oklahoma. And one old lady said that she guessed she knew a California plate when she saw one.

On Saturday morning, nine days after the sudden blow to the FDIC, Randolph Sternweister paced back and forth in his suite at the hotel, which he shared with the number two man from the Washington end, one Buckley Weed. Weed was reading through the transcripts of the testimony of the witnesses, in vain hope of finding something to which insufficient importance had been given, Weed, though lean, a bit stooped, and only thirty-one, had, through osmosis, acquired most of the personal mannerisms of his superior. Sternweister had noticed this and for the past year had been on the verge of mentioning it. As Weed had acquired Sternweister's habit of lighting one cigarette off the last half-inch of the preceding one, any room in which the two of them remained for more than an hour took on the look and smell of any hotel room after a Legion convention.

'Nothing,' Sternweister said. 'Not one censored, unmentionable, unprintable, unspeakable thing! My God, if I ever want to kill anybody, I'll do it in the Pennsy Station at five-fifteen.

'The Bureau has cracked cases when the only thing it had to go on was a human hair or a milligram of dust. My God, we've got a whole automobile that weighs nearly two tons, and a whole corpse! They'll think we're down here learning to rope calves. You know what?'

'What, Ran?'

'I think this was done by a bunch of amateurs. There ought to be a law restricting the practice of crime to professionals. A bunch of wise amateurs. And you can bet your loudest argyles, my boy, that they established identity, hideout, the works, before they knocked off that vault. Right now, blast their souls, they're being seven average citizens in some average community, making no splash with that ninety-four grand. People didn't used to move around so much. Since the war they've been migrating all over the place. Strangers don't stick out like sore thumbs any more. See anything in those transcripts?'

'Nothing.'

'Then stop rattling paper. I can't think. Since a week ago Thursday fifty-one stolen cars have been recovered in the South and Southwest. And we don't know which two, if any, belonged to this mob. We don't even know which route they took away from here. Believe it or not—nobody saw 'em!

As THE TWO SPECIALISTS stared bleakly at each other, a young man of fourteen named Pink Dee was sidling inconspicuously through the shadows in the rear of Louie's Garage. (Tow car service—open 24 hours.) Pink was considered to have been the least beautiful baby, the most unprepossessing child, in Leeman, and he gave frank promise of growing up to be a rather coarse joke on the entire human race. Born with a milk-blue skin, dead white hair, little reddish weak eyes, pipe-cleaner bones, narrow forehead, no chin, beaver teeth, a voice like an unoiled hinge, nature had made the usual compensation. His reaction-time was exceptional. Plenty of more rugged and more normal children had found out that Pink Dee could hit you by the time you had the word out of your mouth. The blow came from an outsize, knobbly fist at the end of a long thin arm, and he swung it with all the abandon of a bag of rocks on the end of a rope. The second important item about Pink Dee came to light when the Leeman School System started giving IQs. Pink's was higher than they were willing to admit the first time, as it did not seem proper that the only genius in Leeman should be old Homer Dee's only son. Pink caught on, and the second time he was rated he got it down into the cretin class. The third rating was ninety-nine and everybody seemed happy with that.

At fourteen Pink was six foot tall and weighed a hundred and twenty pounds. He peered at the world through heavy lenses and maintained, in the back room of his home on Fountain Street, myriad items of apparatus, some made, some purchased. There he investigated certain electrical and magnetic phenomena, having tired of building radios, and carried on a fairly virulent correspondence on the quantum theory with a Cal Tech professor who was under the impression that he was arguing with someone of more mature years.

Dressed in his khakis, the uniform of Texas, Pink moved through the shadows, inserted the key he had filched into the Buick door, and then into the ignition lock. He turned it on in order to activate the electrical gimmicks, and then turned on the car radio. As soon as it warmed up he pushed the selective buttons, carefully noting the dial. When he had the readings he tuned it to WLEE to check the accuracy of the dial. When WLEE roared into a farm report, Louis appeared and dragged Pink out by the thin scruff of his neck.

'What the hell?' Louie said.

Being unable to think of any adequate explanation, Pink wriggled away and loped out.

Pink's next stop was WLEE, where he was well known. He found the manual he wanted and spent the next twenty minutes with it.

Having been subjected to a certain amount of sarcasm from both Sternweister and Weed, Hod Abrams and Lefty Quinn were in no mood for the approach Pink Dee used.

'I demand to see the FBI,' Pink said firmly, the effect spoiled a bit by the fact that his voice change was so recent that the final syllable was a reversion to his childhood squeaky-hinge voice.

'He demands,' Hod said to Lefty.

'Go away, Pink,' Lefty growled, 'before I stomp on your glasses.'

'I am a citizen who wishes to speak to a member of a Federal agency,' Pink said with dignity.

'A citizen, maybe. A taxpayer, no. You give me trouble, kid, and I'm going to warm your pants right here in this lobby.'

Maybe the potential indignity did it. Pink darted for the stairs leading up from the lobby. Hod went roaring up the stairs after him and Lefty grabbed the elevator. They both snared him outside Sternweister's suite and found that they had a job on their hands. Pink bucked and contorted like a picnic on which a hornet's nest has just fallen.

The door to the suite opened and both Sternweister and Weed glared out, their mouths open.

'Just . . . just a fresh . . . kid,' Hod Adams panted.

'I know where the crooks are!' Pink screamed.

'He's nuts,' Lefty yelled.

'Wait a minute,' Randolph Sternweister ordered sharply. They stopped dragging Pink but still clung to him. 'I admit he doesn't look as though he knew his way home, but you can't tell. You two wait outside. Come in here, young man.'

343

Pink marched erectly into the suite, selected the most comfortable chair, and sank into it, looking smug.

'Where are they?'

'Well, I don't know exactly . . .'

'Outside!' Weed said with a thumb motion.

'. . . but I know how to find out.'

'Oh, you know how to find out, eh? Keep talking, I haven't laughed in nine days,' Sternweister said.

'Oh, I had to do a little checking first,' Pink said in a lofty manner. 'I stole the key to the Buick and got into it to test something.'

'Kid, experts have been over that car, half-inch by half-inch.'

'Please don't interrupt me, sir. And don't take that attitude. Because, if it turns out I have something, and I know I have, you're going to look as silly as anything.'

Sternweister flushed and then turned pale. He held hard to the edge of a table. 'Go ahead,' he said thickly.

'I am making an assumption that the people who robbed our bank started out from some hideout and then went back to the same one. I am further assuming that they were in their hideout some time, while they were planning the robbery.'

Weed and Sternweister exchanged glances. 'Go on.'

'So my plan has certain possible flaws based on these assumptions, but at least it uncovers one possible pattern of investigation. I know that the car was stolen from Chapel Hill. That was in the paper. And I know the dead man was in Chicago. So I checked Chicago and Chapel Hill a little while ago.'

'Checked them?'

'At the radio station, of course. Modern car radios are easy to set to new stations by altering the push buttons. The current settings of the push buttons do not conform either to the Chicago or the Chapel Hill areas. There are six stations that the radio in the Buick is set for and . . .'

Sternweister sat down on the couch as though somebody had clubbed him behind the knees. 'Agh!' he said.

'So all you have to do,' Pink said calmly, 'is to check areas against the push-button settings until you find an area *where all six frequencies are represented by radio stations in the immediate geographical vicinity*. It will take a bit of statistical work, of course, and a map of the country, and a supply of push pins should simplify things, I would imagine. Then, after the area is located, I would take the Buick there and, due to variations in individual sets and receiving conditions, you might be able to narrow it down to a mile or two. Then, by showing the photograph of the dead gangster around at bars and such places . . .'

AND THAT WAS WHY, on the following Wednesday, a repainted Buick with new plates and containing two agents of the Bureau roamed through the small towns near Tampa on the West Florida Coast, and how they found that the car radio in the repainted Buick brought in Tampa, Clearwater, St Pete, Orlando, Winter Haven, and Dunedin on the push buttons with remarkable clarity the closer they came to a little resort town called Tarpon Springs. On Thursday morning at four, the portable floodlights bathed three beach cottages in a white glare, and the metallic voice of the P.A. system said, 'You are surrounded. Come out with your hands high. You are surrounded.'

The shots, a few moments later, cracked with a thin bitterness against the heavier sighing of the Gulf of Mexico. Mr Stanley Woods, or, as the blonde later stated, Mr Grebbs Fainstock, was shot, with poetic justice, through the head, and that was the end of resistance.

On Pink Dee Day in Leeman, the president of the Leeman National Bank turned over the envelope containing the reward. It came to a bit less than six per cent of the recovered funds, and it is ample to guarantee, at some later date, a Cal Tech degree.

In December the Sternweisters bought a new car. When Claire demanded to know why Randolph insisted on delivery *sans* car radio, his only answer was a hollow laugh.

She feels that he has probably been working too hard.

Ngaio Marsh
1899–1982

CHAPTER AND VERSE: THE LITTLE COPPLESTONE MYSTERY

W HEN THE TELEPHONE RANG, Troy came in, sun-dazzled, from the cottage garden to answer it, hoping it would be a call from London.

'Oh,' said a strange voice uncertainly. 'May I speak to Superintendent Alleyn, if you please?'

'I'm sorry. He's away.'

'Oh, dear!' said the voice, crestfallen. 'Er—would that be—am I speaking to Mrs Alleyn?'

'Yes.'

'Oh. Yes. Well, it's Timothy Bates here, Mrs Alleyn. You don't know me,' the voice confessed wistfully, 'but I had the pleasure several years ago of meeting your husband. In New Zealand. And he did say that if I ever came home I was to get in touch, and when I heard quite by accident that you were here—well, I *was* excited. But, alas, no good after all.'

'I *am* sorry,' Troy said. 'He'll be back, I hope, on Sunday night. Perhaps—'

'Will he! Come, *that's* something! Because here I am at the Star and Garter, you see, and so—' The voice trailed away again.

'Yes, indeed. He'll be delighted,' Troy said, hoping that he would.

'I'm a bookman,' the voice confided. 'Old books, you know. He used to come into my shop. It was always such a pleasure.'

'But, of course!' Troy exclaimed. 'I remember perfectly now. He's often talked about it.'

'*Has* he? Has he, really! Well, you see, Mrs Alleyn, I'm here on business. Not to *sell* anything, please don't think that, but on a voyage of discovery; almost, one might say, of detection, and I think it might amuse him. He has such an eye for the curious. Not,' the voice hurriedly amended, 'in the trade sense. I mean curious in the sense of mysterious and unusual. But I mustn't bore you.'

Troy assured him that he was not boring her and indeed it was true. The voice was so much coloured by odd little overtones that she found herself quite drawn to its owner. 'I know where you are,' he was saying. 'Your house was pointed out to me.'

After that there was nothing to do but ask him to visit. He seemed to cheer up prodigiously. 'May I? May I, really? Now?'

'Why not?' Troy said. 'You'll be here in five minutes.'

She heard a little crow of delight before he hung up the receiver.

He turned out to he exactly like his voice—a short, middle-aged, bespectacled man, rather untidily dressed. As he came up the path she saw that with both arms he clutched to his stomach an enormous Bible. He was thrown into a fever over the difficulty of removing his cap.

'How ridiculous!' he exclaimed. 'Forgive me! One moment.'

He laid his burden tenderly on a garden seat. 'There!' he cried. 'Now! How do you do?'

Troy took him indoors and gave him a drink. He chose sherry and sat in the window seat with his Bible beside him. 'You'll wonder,' he said, 'why I've appeared with this unusual piece of baggage. I *do* trust it arouses your curiosity.'

He went into a long excitable explanation. It appeared that the Bible was an old and rare one that he had picked up in a job lot of books in New Zealand. All this time he kept it under his square little hands as if it might open of its own accord and spoil his story.

'Because,' he said, 'the *really* exciting thing to me is not its undoubted authenticity but—' He made a conspiratorial face at Troy and suddenly opened the Bible. 'Look!' he invited.

He displayed the flyleaf. Troy saw that it was almost filled with entries in a minute, faded copperplate handwriting.

'The top,' Mr Bates cried. 'Top left-hand. Look at *that*.'

Troy read: '*Crabtree Farm at Little Copplestone in the County of Kent*. Why, it comes from our village!'

'Ah, ha! So it does. Now, the entries, my dear Mrs Alleyn. The entries.'

They were the recorded births and deaths of a family named Wagstaff, beginning in 1705 and ending in 1870 with the birth of William James Wagstaff. Here they broke off but were followed by three further entries, close together.

Stewart Shakespeare Hadet. Died: Tuesday, 5th April, 1779. 2nd Samuel 1.10.

Naomi Balbus Hadet. Died: Saturday, 13th August, 1779. Jeremiah 50.24.

Peter Rook Hadet. Died: Monday, 12th September, 1779. Ezekiel 7.6.

Troy looked up to find Mr Bates's gaze fixed on her. 'And what,' Mr Bates asked, 'my dear Mrs Alleyn, do you make of *that*?'

'Well,' she said cautiously, 'I know about Crabtree Farm. There's the farm itself, owned by Mr De'ath, and there's Crabtree House, belonging to Miss Hart, and—yes, I fancy I've heard they both belonged originally to a family named Wagstaff.'

'You are perfectly right. Now! What about the Hadets? What about *them*?'

'I've never heard of a family named Hadet in Little Copplestone. But—'

'Of course you haven't. For the very good reason that there never have been any Hadets in Little Copplestone.'

'Perhaps in New Zealand, then?'

'The dates, my dear Mrs Alleyn, the dates! New Zealand was not colonised in 1779. Look closer. Do you see the sequence of double dots—ditto marks—under the address? Meaning, of course, "also of Crabtree Farm at Little Copplestone in the County of Kent".'

'I suppose so.'

'Of course you do. And how right you are. Now! You have noticed that throughout there are biblical references. For the Wagstaffs they are the usual pious offerings. You need not trouble yourself with them. But consult the text awarded to the three Hadets. Just you look *them* up! I've put markers.'

He threw himself back with an air of triumph and sipped his sherry. Troy turned over the heavy bulk of pages to the first marker. 'Second of Samuel, one, ten,' Mr Bates prompted, closing his eyes.

The verse had been faintly underlined.

'*So I stood upon him,*' Troy read, '*and slew him.*'

'That's Stewart Shakespeare Hadet's valedictory,' said Mr Bates. 'Next!'

The next was at the 50th chapter of Jeremiah, verse 24: '*I have laid a snare for thee and thou are taken.*'

Troy looked at Mr Bates. His eyes were still closed and he was smiling faintly.

'That was Naomi Balbus Hadet,' he said. 'Now for Peter Rook Hadet. Ezekiel, seven, six.'

The pages flopped back to the last marker.

'An end is come, the end is come: it watcheth for thee; behold it is come.'

Troy shut the Bible.

'How very unpleasant,' she said.

'And how very intriguing, don't you think?' And when she didn't answer, 'Quite up your husband's street, it seemed to me.'

'I'm afraid,' Troy said, 'that even Rory's investigations don't go back to 1779.'

'What a pity!' Mr Bates cried gaily.

'Do I gather that you conclude from all this that there was dirty work among the Hadets in 1779?'

'I don't know, but I'm dying to find out. *Dying* to. Thank you, I should enjoy another glass. Delicious!'

He had settled down so cosily and seemed to he enjoying himself so much that Troy was constrained to ask him to stay to lunch.

'Miss Hart's coming,' she said. 'She's the one who bought Crabtree House from the Wagstaffs. If there's any gossip to be picked up in Copplestone, Miss Hart's the one for it. She's coming about a painting she wants me to donate to the Harvest Festival raffle.'

Mr Bates was greatly excited. 'Who knows!' he cried. 'A Wagstaff in the hand may be worth two Hadets in the bush. I am your slave forever, my dear Mrs Alleyn!'

Miss Hart was a lady of perhaps sixty-seven years. On meeting Mr Bates she seemed to imply that some explanation should be advanced for Troy receiving a gentleman caller in her husband's absence. When the Bible was produced, she immediately accepted it in this light, glanced with professional expertise at the inscriptions and fastened on the Wagstaffs.

'No doubt,' said Miss Hart, 'it was their family Bible and much good it did them. A most eccentric lot they were. Very unsound. Very unsound, indeed. Especially Old Jimmy.'

'Who,' Mr Bates asked greedily, 'was Old Jimmy?'

Miss Hart jabbed her forefinger at the last of the Wagstaff entries. 'William James Wagstaff. Born 1870. And died, although it doesn't say so, in April, 1921. Nobody was left to complete the entry, of course. Unless you count the niece, which I don't. Baggage, if ever I saw one.'

'The niece?'

'Fanny Wagstaff. Orphan. Old Jimmy brought her up. Dragged would be the better word. Drunken old reprobate he was and he came to a drunkard's end. They said he beat her *and* I daresay she needed it.' Miss Hart lowered her voice to a whisper and confided in Troy. 'Not a *nice* girl. You know what I mean.'

Troy, feeling it was expected of her, nodded portentously.

'A drunken end, did you say?' prompted Mr Bates.

'Certainly. On a Saturday night after Market. Fell through the top landing stair rail in his nightshirt and split his skull on the flagstoned hall.'

348

'And your father bought it, then, after Old Jimmy died?' Troy ventured.

'Bought the house and garden. Richard De'ath took the farm. He'd been after it for years—wanted it to round off his own place. He and Old Jimmy were at daggers drawn over *that* business. And, of course, Richard being an atheist, over the Seven Seals.'

'I beg your pardon?' Mr Bates asked.

'Blasphemous!' Miss Hart shouted. 'That's what it was, rank blasphemy. It was a sect that Wagstaff founded. If the rector had known his business he'd have had him excommunicated for it.'

Miss Hart was prevented from elaborating this theory by the appearance at the window of an enormous woman, stuffily encased in black, with a face like a full moon.

'Anybody at home?' the newcomer playfully chanted. 'Telegram for a lucky girl! Come and get it!'

It was Mrs Simpson, the village postmistress. Miss Hart said, 'Well, *really*!' and gave an acid laugh.

'Sorry, I'm sure,' said Mrs Simpson, staring at the Bible which lay under her nose on the window seat. 'I didn't realise there was company. Thought I'd pop it in as I was passing.'

Troy read the telegram while Mrs Simpson, panting, sank heavily on the window ledge and eyed Mr Bates, who had drawn back in confusion. 'I'm no good in the heat,' she told him. 'Slays me.'

'Thank you so much, Mrs Simpson,' Troy said. 'No answer.'

'Righty-ho. Cheerie-bye,' said Mrs Simpson and with another stare at Mr Bates and the Bible, and a derisive grin at Miss Hart, she waddled away.

'It's from Rory,' Troy said. 'He'll he home on Sunday evening.'

'As that woman will no doubt inform the village,' Miss Hart pronounced. 'A busybody of the first water and ought to be taught her place. Did you ever!'

She fulminated throughout luncheon and it was with difficulty that Troy and Mr Bates persuaded her to finish her story of the last of the Wagstaffs. It appeared that Old Jimmy had died intestate, his niece succeeding. She had at once announced her intention of selling everything and had left the district to pursue, Miss Hart suggested, a life of freedom, no doubt in London or even in Paris. Miss Hart wouldn't, and didn't want to, know. On the subject of the Hadets, however, she was uninformed and showed no inclination to look up the marked Bible references attached to them.

After luncheon Troy showed Miss Hart three of her paintings, any one of which would have commanded a high price at an exhibition of contemporary art, and Miss Hart chose the one that, in her own phrase, really did look like something. She insisted that Troy and Mr Bates accompany her to the parish hall where Mr Bates would meet the rector, an authority on village folklore. Troy in person must hand over her painting to be raffled.

Troy would have declined this honour if Mr Bates had not retired behind

Miss Hart and made a series of beseeching gestures and grimaces. They set out therefore in Miss Hart's car which was crammed with vegetables for the Harvest Festival decorations.

'And if the woman Simpson thinks she's going to hog the lectern with *her* pumpkins,' said Miss Hart, 'she's in for a shock. Hah!'

St Cuthbert's was an ancient parish church round whose flanks the tiny village nestled. Its tower, an immensely high one, was said to be unique. Nearby was the parish hall where Miss Hart pulled up with a masterful jerk.

Troy and Mr Bates helped her unload some of her lesser marrows to be offered for sale within. They were observed by a truculent-looking man in tweeds who grinned at Miss Hart. 'Burnt offerings,' he jeered, 'for the tribal gods, I perceive.' It was Mr Richard De'ath, the atheist. Miss Hart cut him dead and led the way into the hall.

Here they found the rector, with a crimson-faced elderly man and a clutch of ladies engaged in preparing for the morrow's sale.

The rector was a thin gentle person, obviously frightened of Miss Hart and timidly delighted by Troy. On being shown the Bible he became excited and dived at once into the story of Old Jimmy Wagstaff.

'Intemperate, I'm afraid, in everything,' sighed the rector. 'Indeed, it would not be too much to say that he both preached and drank hellfire. He *did* preach, on Saturday nights at the crossroads outside the Star and Garter. Drunken, blasphemous nonsense it was and although he used to talk about his followers, the only one he could claim was his niece, Fanny, who was probably too much under his thumb to refuse him.'

'Edward Pilbrow,' Miss Hart announced, jerking her head at the elderly man who had come quite close to them. 'Drowned him with his bell. They had a fight over it. Deaf as a post,' she added, catching sight of Mr Bates's startled expression. 'He's the verger now. *And* the town crier.'

'What!' Mr Bates exclaimed.

'Oh, yes,' the rector explained. 'The village is endowed with a town crier.' He went over to Mr Pilbrow, who at once cupped his hand round his ear. The rector yelled into it.

'When did you start crying, Edward?'

'Twenty-ninth September, 'twenty-one,' Mr Pilbrow roared back.

'I thought so.'

There was something in their manner that made it difficult to remember, Troy thought, that they were talking about events that were almost fifty years back in the past. Even the year 1779 evidently seemed to them to be not so long ago, but, alas, none of them knew of any Hadets.

'By all means,' the rector invited Mr Bates, 'consult the church records, but I can assure you—no Hadets. Never any Hadets.'

Troy saw an expression of extreme obstinacy settle round Mr Bates's mouth.

The rector invited him to look at the church and as they both seemed to expect Troy to tag along, she did so. In the lane they once more encountered Mr Richard De'ath out of whose pocket protruded a paper-wrapped bottle. He touched his cap to Troy and glared at the rector, who turned pink and said, 'Afternoon, De'ath,' and hurried on.

Mr Bates whispered imploringly to Troy, '*Would* you mind? I *do* so want to have a word—' and she was obliged to introduce him. It was not a successful encounter. Mr Bates no sooner broached the topic of his Bible, which he still carried, than Mr De'ath burst into an alcoholic diatribe against superstition, and, on the mention of Old Jimmy Wagstaff, worked himself up into such a state of reminiscent fury that Mr Bates was glad to hurry away with Troy.

They overtook the rector in the churchyard, now bathed in the golden opulence of an already westering sun.

'There they all lie,' the rector said, waving a fatherly hand at the company of headstones. 'All your Wagstaffs, right back to the sixteenth century. But no Hadets, Mr Bates, I assure you.'

They stood looking up at the spire. Pigeons flew in and out of a balcony far above their heads. At their feet was a little flagged area edged by a low coping. Mr Bates stepped forward and the rector laid a hand on his arm.

'Not there,' he said. 'Do you mind?'

'Don't!' bellowed Mr Pilbrow from the rear. 'Don't you set foot on them bloody stones, Mister.'

Mr Bates backed away.

'Edward's not swearing,' the rector mildly explained. 'He is to be taken, alas, literally. A sad and dreadful story, Mr Bates.'

'Indeed?' Mr Bates asked eagerly.

'Indeed, yes. Some time ago, in the very year we have been discussing—1921, you know—one of our girls, a very beautiful girl she was, named Ruth Wall, fell from the balcony of the tower and was, of course, killed. She used to go up there to feed the pigeons and it was thought that in leaning over the low balustrade she overbalanced.'

'Ah!' Mr Pilbrow roared with considerable relish, evidently guessing the purport of the rector's speech. 'Terrible, terrible! And 'er sweetheart after 'er, too. Terrible!'

'Oh, no!' Troy protested.

The rector made a dabbing gesture to subdue Mr Pilbrow. 'I wish he wouldn't,' he said. 'Yes. It was a few days later. A lad called Simon Castle. They were to be married. People said it must be suicide but—it may have been wrong of me—I couldn't bring myself—in short, he lies beside her over there. If you would care to look.'

For a minute or two they stood before the headstones.

'Ruth Wall. Spinster of this Parish. 1903—1921. *I will extend peace to her like a river.*'

'Simon Castle. Bachelor of this Parish. 1900—1921. *And God shall wipe away all tears from their eyes*.'

The afternoon having by now worn on, and the others having excused themselves, Mr Bates remained alone in the churchyard, clutching his Bible and staring at the headstones. The light of the hunter's zeal still gleamed in his eyes.

TROY DIDN'T SEE Mr Bates again until Sunday night service when, on her way up the aisle, she passed him, sitting in the rearmost pew. She was amused to observe that his gigantic Bible was under the seat.

'*We plough the fields*,' sang the choir, '*and scatter*—' Mrs Simpson roared away on the organ, the smell of assorted greengrocery rising like some humble incense. Everybody in Little Copplestone except Mr Richard De'ath was there for the Harvest Festival. At last the rector stepped over Miss Hart's biggest pumpkin and ascended the pulpit, Edward Pilbrow switched off all the lights except one and they settled down for the sermon.

'A sower went forth to sow,' announced the rector. He spoke simply and well but somehow Troy's attention wandered. She found herself wondering where, through the centuries, the succeeding generations of Wagstaffs had sat until Old Jimmy took to his freakish practices; and whether Ruth Wall and Simon Castle, poor things, had shared the same hymn book and held hands during the sermon; and whether, after all, Stewart Shakespeare Hadet and Peter Rook Hadet had not, in 1779, occupied some dark corner of the church and been unaccountably forgotten.

Here we are, Troy thought drowsily, and there, outside in the churchyard, are all the others going back and back—

She saw a girl, bright in the evening sunlight, reach from a balcony towards a multitude of wings. She was falling—dreadfully—into nothingness. Troy woke with a sickening jerk.

'—on stony ground,' the rector was saying. Troy listened guiltily to the rest of the sermon.

MR BATES EMERGED on the balcony. He laid his Bible on the coping and looked at the moonlit tree tops and the churchyard so dreadfully far below. He heard someone coming up the stairway. Torchlight danced on the doorjamb.

'You were quick,' said the visitor.

'I am all eagerness and, I confess, puzzlement.'

'It had to be here, on the spot. If you *really* want to find out—'

'But I do, I do!'

'We haven't much time. You've brought the Bible?'

'You particularly asked—'

'If you open it at Ezekiel, chapter twelve. I'll shine my torch.'

Mr Bates opened the Bible.

'The thirteenth verse. There!'

Mr Bates leaned forward. The Bible tipped and moved.

'Look out!' the voice urged.

Mr Bates was scarcely aware of the thrust. He felt the page tear as the book sank under his hands. The last thing he heard was the beating of a multitude of wings.

'—AND FOREVERMORE,' said the rector in a changed voice, facing east. The congregation got to its feet. He announced the last hymn. Mrs Simpson made a preliminary rumble and Troy groped in her pocket for the collection plate. Presently they all filed out into the autumnal moonlight.

It was coldish in the churchyard. People stood about in groups. One or two had already moved through the lychgate. Troy heard a voice, which she recognised as that of Mr De'ath. 'I suppose,' it jeered, 'you all know you've been assisting at a fertility rite.'

'Drunk as usual, Dick De'ath,' somebody returned without rancour. There was a general laugh.

They had all begun to move away when, from the shadows at the base of the church tower, there arose a great cry. They stood, transfixed, turned towards the voice.

Out of the shadows came the rector in his cassock. When Troy saw his face she thought he must be ill and went to him.

'No, no!' he said. 'Not a woman! Edward! Where's Edward Pilbrow?'

Behind him, at the foot of the tower, was a pool of darkness; but Troy, having come closer, could see within it a figure, broken like a puppet on the flagstones. An eddy of night air stole round the church and fluttered a page of the giant Bible that lay pinned beneath the head.

It was nine o'clock when Troy heard the car pull up outside, the cottage. She saw her husband coming up the path and ran to meet him, as if they had been parted for months.

He said, 'This is mighty gratifying!' And then, 'Hullo, my love. What's the matter?'

As she tumbled out her story, filled with relief at telling him, a large man with uncommonly bright eyes came up behind them.

'Listen to this, Fox,' Roderick Alleyn said. 'We're in demand, it seems.' He put his arm through Troy's and closed his hand found hers. 'Let's go indoors, shall we? Here's Fox, darling, come for a nice bucolic rest. Can we give him a bed?'

Troy pulled herself together and greeted Inspector Fox. Presently she was able to give them a coherent account of the evening's tragedy. When she had finished, Alleyn said, 'Poor little Bates. He was a nice little bloke.' He put his hand on Troy's. 'You need a drink,' he said, 'and so, by the way, do we.'

While he was getting the drinks he asked quite casually, 'You've had a shock and a beastly one at that, but there's something else, isn't there?'

'Yes,' Troy swallowed hard, 'there is. They're all saying it's an accident.'

'Yes?'

'And, Rory, I don't think it is.'

Mr Fox cleared his throat. 'Fancy,' he said.

'Suicide?' Alleyn suggested, bringing her drink to her.

'No. Certainly not.'

'A bit of rough stuff, then?'

'You sound as if you're asking about the sort of weather we've been having.'

'Well, darling, you don't expect Fox and me to go into hysterics. Why not an accident?'

'He knew all about the other accidents, he *knew* it was dangerous. And then the oddness of it, Rory. To leave the Harvest Festival service and climb the tower in the dark, carrying that enormous Bible!'

'And he was hellbent on tracing these Hadets?'

'Yes. He kept saying you'd be interested. He actually brought a copy of the entries for you.'

'Have you got it?'

She found it for him. 'The selected texts,' he said, 'are pretty rum, aren't they, Br'er Fox?' and handed it over.

'Very vindictive,' said Mr Fox.

'Mr Bates thought it was in your line,' Troy said.

'The devil he did! What's been done about this?'

'The village policeman was in the church. They sent for the doctor. And— well, you see, Mr Bates had talked a lot about you and they hope you'll be able to tell them something about him—whom they should get in touch with and so on.'

'Have they moved him?'

'They weren't going to until the doctor had seen him.'

Alleyn pulled his wife's ear and looked at Fox. 'Do you fancy a stroll through the village, Foxkin?'

'There's a lovely moon,' Fox said bitterly and got to his feet.

THE MOON WAS HIGH in the heavens when they came to the base of the tower and it shone on a group of four men—the rector, Richard De'ath, Edward Pilbrow, and Sergeant Botting, the village constable. When they saw Alleyn and Fox, they separated and revealed a fifth, who was kneeling by the body of Timothy Bates.

'Kind of you to come,' the rector said, shaking hands with Alleyn. 'And a great relief to all of us.'

Their manner indicated that Alleyn's arrival would remove a sense of personal responsibility. 'If you'd like to have a look—?' the doctor said.

The broken body lay huddled on its side. The head rested on the open Bible. The right hand, rigid in cadaveric spasm, clutched a torn page. Alleyn knelt and

Fox came closer with the torch. At the top of the page Alleyn saw the word Ezekiel and a little farther down, Chapter 12.

Using the tip of his finger Alleyn straightened the page. 'Look,' he said, and pointed to the thirteenth verse. *'My net also will I spread upon him and he shall be taken in my snare.'*

The words had been faintly underlined in mauve.

Alleyn stood up and looked round the circle of faces.

'Well,' the doctor said, 'we'd better see about moving him.'

Alleyn said, 'I don't think he should be moved just yet.'

'Not!' the rector cried out. 'But surely—to leave him like this—I mean, after this terrible accident—'

'It has yet to be proved,' Alleyn said, 'that it was an accident.'

There was a sharp sound from Richard De'ath.

'—and I fancy,' Alleyn went on, glancing at De'ath, 'that it's going to take quite a lot of proving.'

AFTER THAT, EVENTS, as Fox observed with resignation, took the course that was to be expected. The local Superintendent said that under the circumstances it would be silly not to ask Alleyn to carry on, the Chief Constable agreed, and appropriate instructions came through from Scotland Yard. The rest of the night was spent in routine procedure. The body having been photographed and the Bible set aside for fingerprinting, both were removed and arrangements put in hand for the inquest.

At dawn Alleyn and Fox climbed the tower. The winding stair brought them to an extremely narrow doorway through which they saw the countryside lying vaporous in the faint light. Fox was about to go through to the balcony when Alleyn stopped him and pointed to the doorjambs. They were covered with a growth of stonecrop.

About three feet from the floor this had been brushed off over a space of perhaps four inches and fragments of the microscopic plant hung from the scars. From among these, on either side, Alleyn removed morsels of dark coloured thread. 'And here,' he sighed, 'as sure as fate, we go again. O Lord, O Lord!'

They stepped through to the balcony and there was a sudden whirr and beating of wings as a company of pigeons flew out of the tower. The balcony was narrow and the balustrade indeed very low. 'If there's any looking over,' Alleyn said, 'you, my dear Foxikin, may do it.'

Nevertheless he leaned over the balustrade and presently knelt beside it. 'Look at this. Bates rested the open Bible here—blow me down flat if he didn't! There's a powder of leather where it scraped on the stone and a fragment where it tore. It must have been moved—outward. Now, why, *why?*'

'Shoved it accidentally with his knees, then made a grab and overbalanced?'

'But why put the open Bible there? To read by moonlight? *My net also will I spread upon him and he shall be taken in my snare*. Are you going to tell me he underlined it and then dived overboard?'

'I'm not going to tell you anything,' Fox grunted and then: 'That old chap Edward Pilbrow's down below swabbing the stones. He looks like a beetle.'

'Let him look like a rhinoceros if he wants to, but for the love of Mike don't leer over the edge—you give me the willies. Here, let's pick this stuff up before it blows away.'

They salvaged the scraps of leather and put them in an envelope. Since there was nothing more to do, they went down and out through the vestry and so home to breakfast.

'Darling,' Alleyn told his wife, 'you've landed us with a snorter.'

'Then you *do* think—?'

'There's a certain degree of fishiness. Now, see here, wouldn't *somebody* have noticed little Bates get up and go out? I know he sat all alone on the back bench, but wasn't there *someone*?'

'The rector?'

'No. I asked him. Too intent on his sermon, it seems.'

'Mrs Simpson? If she looks through her little red curtain she faces the nave.'

'We'd better call on her, Fox. I'll take the opportunity to send a couple of cables to New Zealand. She's fat, jolly, keeps the shop-cum-post office, and is supposed to read all the postcards. Just your cup of tea. You're dynamite with post-mistresses. Away we go.'

MRS SIMPSON sat behind her counter doing a crossword puzzle and refreshing herself with liquorice. She welcomed Alleyn with enthusiasm. He introduced Fox and then he retired to a corner to write out his cables,

'What a catastrophe!' Mrs Simpson said, plunging straight into the tragedy. 'Shocking! As nice a little gentleman as you'd wish to meet, Mr Fox. Typical New Zealander. Pick him a mile away and a friend of Mr Alleyn's, I'm told, and if I've said it once I've said it a hundred times, Mr Fox, they ought to have put something up to prevent it. Wire netting or a bit of ironwork; but, no, they let it go on from year to year and now see what's happened—history repeating itself and giving the village a bad name. Terrible!'

Fox bought a packet of tobacco from Mrs Simpson and paid her a number of compliments on the layout of her shop, modulating from there into an appreciation of the village. He said that one always found such pleasant company in small communities. Mrs Simpson was impressed and offered him a piece of liquorice.

'As for pleasant company,' she chuckled, 'that's as may be, though by and large I suppose I mustn't grumble. I'm a cockney and a stranger here myself, Mr Fox. Only twenty-four years and that doesn't go for anything with this lot.'

'Ah,' Fox said, 'then you wouldn't recollect the former tragedies. Though to be sure,' he added, 'you wouldn't do that in any case, being much too young, if you'll excuse the liberty, Mrs Simpson.'

After this classic opening Alleyn was not surprised to hear Mrs Simpson embark on a retrospective survey of life in Little Copplestone. She was particularly lively on Miss Hart, who, she hinted, had had her eye on Mr Richard De'ath for many a long day.

'As far back as when Old Jimmy Wagstaff died, which was why she was so set on getting the next door house; but Mr De'ath never looked at anybody except Ruth Wall, and her head-over-heels in love with young Castle, which together with her falling to her destruction when feeding pigeons led Mr De'ath to forsake religion and take to drink, which he has done something cruel ever since.

'They do say he's got a terrible temper, Mr Fox, and it's well known he give Old Jimmy Wagstaff a thrashing on account of straying cattle and threatened young Castle, saying if he couldn't have Ruth, nobody else would, but fair's fair and personally I've never seen him anything but nice-mannered, drunk or sober. Speak as you find's my motto and always has been, but these old maids, when they take a fancy they get it pitiful hard. You wouldn't know a word of nine letters meaning "pale-faced lure like a sprat in a fishy story", would you?'

Fox was speechless, but Alleyn, emerging with his cables, suggested 'white bait'.

'Correct!' shouted Mrs Simpson. 'Fits like a glove. Although it's not a bit like a sprat and a quarter the size. Cheating, I call it. Still, it fits.' She licked her indelible pencil and triumphantly added it to her crossword.

They managed to lead her back to Timothy Bates. Fox, professing a passionate interest in organ music, was able to extract from her that when the rector began his sermon she had in fact dimly observed someone move out of the back bench and through the doors. 'He must have walked round the church and in through the vestry and little did I think he was going to his death,' Mrs Simpson said with considerable relish and a sigh like an earthquake.

'You didn't happen to hear him in the vestry?' Fox ventured, but it appeared that the door from the vestry into the organ loft was shut and Mrs Simpson, having settled herself to enjoy the sermon with, as she shamelessly admitted, a bag of chocolates, was not in a position to notice.

Alleyn gave her his two cables: the first to Timothy Bates's partner in New Zealand and the second to one of his own colleagues in that country asking for any available information about relatives of the late William James Wagstaff of Little Copplestone, Kent, possibly resident in New Zealand after 1921, and of any persons of the name of Peter Rook Hadet or Naomi Balbus Hadet.

Mrs Simpson agitatedly checked over the cables, professional etiquette and burning curiosity struggling together in her enormous bosom. She restrained herself, however, merely observing that an event of this sort set you thinking, didn't it?

'And no doubt,' Alleyn said as they walked up the lane, 'she'll be telling her customers that the next stop's bloodhounds and manacles.'

'Quite a tidy armful of lady, isn't she, Mr Alleyn?' Fox calmly rejoined.

THE INQUEST WAS at 10.20 in the smoking room of the Star and Garter. With half an hour in hand, Alleyn and Fox visited the churchyard. Alleyn gave particular attention to the headstones of Old Jimmy Wagstaff, Ruth Wall, and Simon Castle. 'No mention of the month or day,' he said. And after a moment: 'I wonder. We must ask the rector.'

'No need to ask the rector,' said a voice behind them. It was Miss Hart. She must have come soundlessly across the soft turf. Her air was truculent. 'Though why,' she said, 'it should be of interest, I'm sure I don't know. Ruth Wall died on August thirteenth, 1921. It was a Saturday.'

'You've a remarkable memory,' Alleyn observed.

'Not as good as it sounds. That Saturday afternoon I came to do the flowers in the church. I found her and I'm not likely ever to forget it. Young Castle went the same way almost a month later. September twelfth. In my opinion there was never a more glaring case of suicide. I believe,' Miss Hart said harshly, 'in facing facts.'

'She was a beautiful girl, wasn't she?'

'I'm no judge of beauty. She set the men by the ears. *He* was a fine-looking young fellow. Fanny Wagstaff did her best to get *him*.'

'Had Ruth Wall,' Alleyn asked, 'other admirers?'

Miss Hart didn't answer and he turned to her. Her face was blotted with an unlovely flush. 'She ruined two men's lives, if you want to know. Castle and Richard De'ath,' said Miss Hart. She turned on her heel and without another word marched away.

'September twelfth,' Alleyn murmured. 'That would be a Monday, Br'er Fox.'

'So it would,' Fox agreed, after short calculation, 'so it would. Quite a coincidence.'

'Or not, as the case may be. I'm going to take a gamble on this one. Come on.'

They left the churchyard and walked down the lane, overtaking Edward Pilbrow on the way. He was wearing his town crier's coat and hat and carrying his bell by the clapper. He manifested great excitement when he saw them.

'Hey!' he shouted, 'what's this I hear? Murder's the game, is it? What a go! Come on, gents, let's have it. Did 'e fall or was 'e pushed? Hor, hor, hor! Come on.'

'Not until after the inquest,' Alleyn shouted.

'Do we get a look at the body?'

'Shut up,' Mr Fox bellowed suddenly.

'I got to know, haven't I? It'll be the smartest bit of crying I ever done, this will! I reckon I might get on the telly with this. "Town crier tells old world village death stalks the churchyard." Hor, hor, hor!'

'Let us,' Alleyn whispered, 'leave this horrible old man.'

They quickened their stride and arrived at the pub, to be met with covert glances and dead silence.

THE SMOKING ROOM was crowded for the inquest. Everybody was there, including Mrs Simpson who sat in the back row with her candies and her crossword puzzle. It went through very quickly. The rector deposed to finding the body. Richard De'ath, sober and less truculent than usual, was questioned as to his sojourn outside the churchyard and said he'd noticed nothing unusual apart from hearing a disturbance among the pigeons roosting in the balcony. From where he stood, he said, he couldn't see the face of the tower.

An open verdict was recorded.

Alleyn had invited the rector, Miss Hart, Mrs Simpson, Richard De'ath, and, reluctantly, Edward Pilbrow, to join him in the Bar-Parlour and had arranged with the landlord that nobody else would be admitted. The Public Bar, as a result, drove a roaring trade.

When they had all been served and the hatch closed, Alleyn walked into the middle of the room and raised his hand. It was the slightest of gestures but it secured their attention.

He said, 'I think you must all realise that we are not satisfied this was an accident. The evidence against accident has been collected piecemeal from the persons in this room and I am going to put it before you. If I go wrong I want you to correct me. I ask you to do this with absolute frankness, even if you are obliged to implicate someone who you would say was the last person in the world to be capable of a crime of violence.'

He waited. Pilbrow, who had come very close, had his ear cupped in his hand. The rector looked vaguely horrified. Richard De'ath suddenly gulped down his double whisky. Miss Hart coughed over her lemonade and Mrs Simpson avidly popped a peppermint cream in her mouth and took a swig of her port and raspberry.

Alleyn nodded to Fox, who laid Mr Bates's Bible, open at the flyleaf, on the table before him.

'The case,' Alleyn said, 'hinges on this book. You have all seen the entries. I remind you of the recorded deaths in 1779 of the three Hadets—Stewart Shakespeare, Naomi Balbus, and Peter Rook. To each of these is attached a biblical text suggesting that they met their death by violence. There have never been any Hadets in this village and the days of the week are wrong for the given dates. They are right, however, for the year 1921 and *they fit the deaths*, all by falling from a height, of William Wagstaff, Ruth Wall, and Simon Castle.

'By analogy the Christian names agree. William suggests Shakespeare. Naomi—Ruth; Balbus—a wall. Simon—Peter; and a Rook is a Castle in chess. And Hadet,' Alleyn said without emphasis, 'is an anagram of Death.'

'Balderdash!' Miss Hart cried out in an unrecognisable voice.

'No, it's not,' said Mrs Simpson. 'It's jolly good crossword stuff.'

'Wicked balderdash. Richard!'

De'ath said, 'Be quiet. Let him go on.'

'We believe,' Alleyn said, 'that these three people met their deaths by one hand. Motive is a secondary consideration, but it is present in several instances, predominantly in one. Who had cause to wish the death of these three people? Someone whom old Wagstaff had bullied and to whom he had left his money and who killed him for it. Someone who was infatuated with Simon Castle and bitterly jealous of Ruth Wall. Someone who hoped, as an heiress, to win Castle for herself and who, failing, was determined nobody else should have him. Wagstaff's orphaned niece—Fanny Wagstaff.'

There were cries of relief from all but one of his hearers. He went on. 'Fanny Wagstaff sold everything, disappeared, and was never heard of again in the village. But twenty-four years later she returned, and has remained here ever since.'

A glass crashed to the floor and a chair overturned as the vast bulk of the post-mistress rose to confront him.

'Lies! *Lies!*' screamed Mrs Simpson.

'Did you sell everything again, before leaving New Zealand?' he asked as Fox moved forward. 'Including the Bible, Miss Wagstaff?'

'BUT,' TROY SAID, 'how could you be so sure?'

'She was the only one who could leave her place in the church unobserved. She was the only one fat enough to rub her hips against the narrow doorjambs. She uses an indelible pencil. We presume she arranged to meet Bates on the balcony, giving a cock-and-bull promise to tell him something nobody else knew about the Hadets. She indicated the text with her pencil, gave the Bible a shove, and, as he leaned out to grab it, tipped him over the edge.

'In talking about 1921 she forgot herself and described the events as if she had been there. She called Bates a typical New Zealander but gave herself out to be a Londoner. She said whitebait are only a quarter of the size of sprats. New Zealand whitebait are—English whitebait are about the same size.

'And as we've now discovered, she didn't send my cables. Of course she thought poor little Bates was hot on her tracks, especially when she learned that he'd come here to see me. She's got the kind of crossword-puzzle mind that would think up the biblical clues, and would get no end of a kick in writing them in. She's overwhelmingly conceited and vindictive.'

'Still—'

'I know. Not good enough if we'd played the waiting game. But good enough to try shock tactics. We caught her off her guard and she cracked up.'

'Not,' Mr Fox said, 'a nice type of woman.'

Alleyn strolled to the gate and looked up the lane to the church. The spire shone golden in the evening sun.

'The rector,' Alleyn said, 'tells me he's going to do something about the balcony.'

'Mrs Simpson, née Wagstaff,' Fox remarked, 'suggested wire netting.'

'And she ought to know,' Alleyn said and turned back to the cottage.

W. Somerset Maugham

1874–1965

FOOTPRINTS IN
THE JUNGLE

THERE IS NO PLACE in Malaya that has more charm than Tanah Merah. It lies on the sea, and the sandy shore is fringed with casuarinas. The government offices are still in the old Raad Huis that the Dutch built when they owned the land, and on the hill stand the grey ruins of the fort by aid of which the Portuguese maintained their hold over the unruly natives. Tanah Merah has a history and in the vast labyrinthine houses of the Chinese merchants, backing on the sea so that in the cool of the evening they may sit in their loggias and enjoy the salt breeze, families dwell that have been settled in the country for three centuries. Many have forgotten their native language and hold intercourse with one another in Malay and pidgin English. The imagination lingers here gratefully, for in the Federated Malay States the only past is within the memory for the most part of the fathers of living men.

Tanah Merah was for long the busiest mart of the Middle East and its harbour was crowded with shipping when the clipper and the junk still sailed the China seas. But now it is dead. It has the sad and romantic air of all places that have once been of importance and live now on the recollection of a vanished grandeur. It is a sleepy little town and strangers that come to it, losing their native energy, insensibly drop into its easy and lethargic ways. Successive rubber booms bring it no prosperity and the ensuing slumps hasten its decay.

The European quarter is very silent. It is trim and neat and clean. The houses of the white men—government servants and agents of companies— stand round an immense padang, agreeable and roomy bungalows shaded by great cassias, and the padang is vast and green and well cared for, like the lawn of a cathedral close, and indeed there is in the aspect of this corner of Tanah Merah something quiet and delicately secluded that reminds you of the precincts of Canterbury.

The club faces the sea; it is a spacious but shabby building; it has an air of neglect and when you enter you feel that you intrude. It gives you the impression that it is closed really, for alterations and repairs, and that you have taken indiscreet advantage of an open door to go where you are not wanted. In the morning you may find there a couple of planters who have come in from their estates on business and are drinking a gin-sling before starting back again; and latish in the

361

afternoon a lady or two may perhaps be seen looking with a furtive air through old numbers of the *Illustrated London News*. At nightfall a few men saunter in and sit about the billiard-room watching the play and drinking sukas. But on Wednesdays there is a little more animation. On that day the gramophone is set going in the large room upstairs and people come in from the surrounding country to dance. There are sometimes no less than a dozen couples and it is even possible to make up two tables of bridge.

It was on one of these occasions that I met the Cartwrights. I was staying with a man called Gaze who was head of the police and he came into the billiard-room, where I was sitting, and asked me if I would make up a four. The Cartwrights were planters and they came in to Tanah Merah on Wednesdays because it gave their girl a chance of a little fun. They were very nice people, said Gaze; quiet and unobtrusive, and played a very pleasant game of bridge. I followed Gaze into the card-room and was introduced to them. They were already seated at a table and Mrs Cartwright was shuffling the cards. It inspired me with confidence to see the competent way in which she did it. She took half the pack in each hand, and her hands were large and strong, deftly inserted the corners of one half under the corners of the other, and with a click and a neat bold gesture cascaded the cards together.

It had all the effect of a conjuring trick. The card-player knows that it can be done perfectly only after incessant practice. He can be fairly sure that anyone who can so shuffle a pack of cards loves cards for their own sake.

'Do you mind if my husband and I play together?' asked Mrs Cartwright. 'It's no fun for us to win one another's money.'

'Of course not.'

We cut for deal and Gaze and I sat down.

Mrs Cartwright drew an ace and while she dealt, quickly and neatly, chatted with Gaze of local affairs. But I was aware that she took stock of me. She looked shrewd, but good-natured.

She was a woman somewhere in the fifties (though in the East, where people age quickly, it is difficult to tell their ages), with white hair very untidily arranged, and a constant gesture with her was an impatient movement of the hand to push back a long wisp of hair that kept falling over her forehead. You wondered why she did not, by the use of a hairpin or two, save herself so much trouble. Her blue eyes were large, but pale and a little tired; her face was lined and sallow; I think it was her mouth that gave it the expression which I felt was characteristic of caustic but tolerant irony. You saw that here was a woman who knew her mind and was never afraid to speak it. She was a chatty player (which some people object to strongly, but which does not disconcert me, for I do not see why you should behave at the card-table as though you were at a memorial service) and it was soon apparent that she had an effective knack of badinage. It was pleasantly acid, but it was amusing enough to be offensive only to a fool. If now and then she uttered a remark so sarcastic that you wanted all your sense of humour to see the fun in it, you could not but quickly see that she was willing to take as much as she gave. Her large, thin mouth broke into a dry smile and her eyes shone brightly when by a lucky chance you brought off a repartee that turned the laugh against her.

I thought her a very agreeable person. I liked her frankness. I liked her quick wit. I liked her plain face. I never met a woman who obviously cared so little how she looked. It was not only her head that was untidy, everything about her was slovenly; she wore a high-necked silk blouse, but for coolness had unbuttoned the top buttons and showed a gaunt and withered neck; the blouse was crumpled and none too clean, for she smoked innumerable cigarettes and covered herself with ash. When she got up for a moment to speak to somebody I saw that her blue skirt was rather ragged at the hem and badly needed a brush, and she wore heavy, low-heeled boots. But none of this mattered. Everything she wore was perfectly in character.

And it was a pleasure to play bridge with her. She played very quickly, without hesitation, and she had not only knowledge but flair. Of course she knew Gaze's game, but I was a stranger and she soon took my measure. The team-work between her husband and herself was admirable; he was sound and cautious, but knowing him, she was able to be bold with assurance and brilliant with safety. Gaze was a player who founded a foolish optimism on the hope that his opponents would not have the sense to take advantage of his errors, and the pair of us were no match for the Cartwrights. We lost one rubber after another, and there was nothing to do but smile and look as if we liked it.

'I don't know what's the matter with the cards,' said Gaze at last, plaintively. 'Even when we have every card in the pack we go down.'

'It can't be anything to do with your play,' answered Mrs Cartwright, looking him full in the face with those pale blue eyes of hers, 'it must be bad luck pure and simple. Now if you hadn't had your hearts mixed up with your diamonds in that last hand you'd have saved the game.'

Gaze began to explain at length how the misfortune, which had cost us dear, occurred, but Mrs Cartwright, with a deft flick of the hand, spread out the cards in a great circle so that we should cut for deal. Cartwright looked at the time.

'This will have to be the last, my dear,' he said.

'Oh, will it?' She glanced at her watch and then called to a young man who was passing through the room. 'Oh, Mr Bullen, if you're going upstairs tell Olive that we shall be going in a few minutes.' She turned to me. 'It takes us the best part of an hour to get back to the estate and poor Theo has to be up at the crack of dawn.'

'Oh, well, we only come in once a week' said Cartwright, 'and it's the one chance Olive gets of being gay and abandoned.'

I thought Cartwright looked tired and old. He was a man of middle height, with a bald, shiny head, a stubbly grey moustache, and gold-rimmed spectacles. He wore white ducks and a black-and-white tie. He was rather neat and you could see he took much more pains with his clothes than his untidy wife. He talked little, but it was plain that he enjoyed his wife's caustic humour and some-times he made quite a neat retort. They were evidently very good friends. It was pleasing to see so solid and tolerant an affection between two people who were almost elderly and must have lived together for so many years.

It took but two hands to finish the rubber and we had just ordered a final gin and bitters when Olive came down.

'Do you really want to go already, Mumsey?' she asked.

Mrs Cartwright looked at her daughter with fond eyes.

'Yes, darling. Its nearly half past eight. It'll be ten before we get our dinner.'

'Damn our dinner,' said Olive gaily.

'Let her have one more dance before we go,' suggested Cartwright.

'Not one. You must have a good night's rest.'

Cartwright looked at Olive with a smile.

'If your mother has made up her mind, my dear, we may just as well give in without any fuss.'

'She's a determined woman,' said Olive, lovingly stroking her mother's wrinkled cheek.

Mrs Cartwright patted her daughter's hand, and kissed it.

Olive was not very pretty, but she looked extremely nice. She was nineteen or twenty, I suppose, and she had still the plumpness of her age; she would be more attractive when she had fined down a little. She had none of the determination that gave her mother's face so much character, but resembled her father; she had his dark eyes and slightly aquiline nose, and his look of rather weak good nature. It was plain that she was strong and healthy. Her cheeks were red and her eyes bright. She had a vitality that he had long since lost. She seemed to be the perfectly normal English girl, with high spirits, a great desire to enjoy her-self, and an excellent temper.

When we separated, Gaze and I set out to walk to his house.

'What did you think of the Cartwrights?' he asked me.

'I liked them. They must he a great asset in a place like this.'

'I wish they came oftener. They live a very quiet life.'

'It must be dull for the girl. The father and mother seem very well satisfied with one another's company.'

'Yes, it's been a great success.'

'Olive is the image of her father, isn't she?'

Gaze gave me a sidelong glance.

'Cartwright isn't her father. Mrs Cartwright was a widow when he married her. Olive was born four months after her father's death.'

'Oh!'

I drew out the sound in order to put in it all I could of surprise, interest, and curiosity. But Gaze said nothing and we walked the rest of the way in silence. The boy was waiting at the door as we entered the house and after a last gin pahit we sat down to dinner.

At first Gaze was inclined to be talkative. Owing to the restriction of the output of rubber there had sprung up a considerable activity among the smugglers and it was part of his duty to circumvent their knavishness. Two junks had been captured that day and he was rubbing his hands over his success. The go-downs were full of confiscated rubber and in a little while it was going to be solemnly burnt. But presently he fell into silence and we finished without a word. The boys brought in coffee and brandy and we lit our cheroots. Gaze leaned back in his chair. He looked at me reflectively and then looked at his brandy. The boys had left the room and we were alone.'

'I've known Mrs Cartwright for over twenty years,' he said slowly. 'She wasn't a bad-looking woman in those days. Always untidy, but when she was young it didn't seem to matter so much. It was rather attractive. She was married to a man called Bronson. Reggie Bronson. He was a planter. He was manager of an estate up in Selantan and I was stationed at Alor Lipis. It was a much smaller place than it is now; I don't suppose there were more than twenty people in the whole community, but they had a jolly little club, and we used to have a very good time. I remember the first time I met Mrs Bronson as though it was yesterday. There were no cars in those days and she and Bronson had ridden in on their bicycles. Of course then she didn't look so determined as she looks now. She was much thinner, she had a nice colour, and her eyes were very pretty—blue, you know—and she had a lot of dark hair. If she'd only taken more trouble with herself she'd have been rather stunning. As it was she was the best-looking woman there.'

I tried to construct in my mind a picture of what Mrs Cartwright—Mrs Bronson as she was then—looked like from what she was now and from Gaze's not very graphic description. In the solid woman, with her well-covered bones, who sat rather heavily at the bridge-table, I tried to see a slight young thing with buoyant movements and graceful, easy gestures. Her chin now was square and her nose decided, but the roundness of youth must have masked this: she must have been charming with a pink-and-white skin and her hair, carelessly dressed, brown and abundant. At that period she wore a long skirt, a tight waist, and a picture hat. Or did women in Malaya still wear the topees that you see in old numbers of the illustrated papers?

'I hadn't seen her for—oh, nearly twenty years,' Gaze went on. 'I knew she was living somewhere in the F.M.S., but it was a surprise when I took this job and came here to run across her in the club just as I had up in Selantan so many years before. Of course she's an elderly woman now and she's changed out of all recognition. It was rather a shock to see her with a grown-up daughter, it made me realise how the time had passed; I was a young fellow when I met her last and now, by Jingo, I'm due to retire on the age limit in two or three years. Bit thick, isn't it?'

Gaze, a rueful grin on his ugly face, looked at me with faint indignation, as though I could help the hurrying march of the years as they trod upon one another's heels.

'I'm no chicken myself,' I replied.

'You haven't lived out East all your life. It ages one before one's time. One's an elderly man at fifty and at fifty-five one's good for nothing but the scrap-heap.'

But I did not want Gaze to wander off into a disquisition on old age.

'Did you recognise Mrs Cartwright when you saw her again?' I asked.

'Well, I did and I didn't. At the first glance I thought I knew her, but couldn't quite place her. I thought perhaps she was someone I'd met on board ship when I was going on leave and had known only by sight. But the moment she spoke I remembered at once. I remembered the dry twinkle in her eyes and the crisp sound of her voice. There was something in her voice that seemed to mean: You're a bit of a damned fool, my lad, but you're not a bad sort and upon my soul I rather like you.'

'That's a good deal to read into the sound of a voice,' I smiled.

'She came up to me in the club and shook hands with me. "How do you do, Major Gaze? Do you remember me?" she said.

'"Of course I do."

'"A lot of water has passed under the bridge since we met last. We're none of us as young as we were. Have you seen Theo?"

'For a moment I couldn't think whom she meant. I suppose I looked rather stupid, because she gave a little smile, that chaffing smile that I knew so well, and explained.

'"I married Theo, you know. It seemed the best thing to do. I was lonely and he wanted it."

'"I heard you married him," I said. "I hope you've been very happy."

'"Oh, very. Theo's a perfect duck. He'll be here in a minute. He'll be so glad to see you."

'I wondered. I should have thought I was the last man Theo would wish to see. I shouldn't have thought she would wish it very much either. But women are funny.'

'Why shouldn't she wish him to see you?' I asked.

'I'm coming to that later,' said Gaze. 'Then Theo turned up. I don't know why I call him Theo; I never called him anything but Cartwright, I never thought of him as anything but Cartwright. Theo was a shock. You know what he looks like now; I remembered him as a curly-headed youngster, very fresh and clean-looking. He was always neat and dapper, he had a good figure, and he held himself well, like a man who's used to taking a lot of exercise. Now I come to think of it he wasn't bad-looking, not in a big, massive way, but graceful, you know, and lithe. When I saw this bowed, cadaverous, bald-headed old buffer with spectacles I could hardly believe my eyes. I shouldn't have known him from Adam. He seemed pleased to see me, at least, interested; he wasn't effusive, but he'd always been on the quiet side and I didn't expect him to be.

'"Are you surprised to find us here?" he asked me.

'"Well, I hadn't the faintest notion where you were."

'"We've kept track of your movements more or less. We've seen your name in the paper every now and then. You must come out one day and have a look at our place. We've been settled there a good many years, and I suppose we shall stay there till we go home for good. Have you ever been back to Alor Lipis?"

'"No, I haven't," I said.

'"It was a nice little place. I'm told it's grown. I've never been back."

'"It hasn't got the pleasantest recollections for us," said Mrs Cartwright.

'I asked them if they'd have a drink and we called the boy. I dare say you noticed that Mrs Cartwright likes her liquor; I don't mean that she gets tight or anything like that, but she drinks her stengah like a man. I couldn't help looking at them with a certain amount of curiosity. They seemed perfectly happy; I gathered that they hadn't done at all badly, and I found out later that they were quite well off. They had a very nice car, and when they went on leave they denied themselves nothing. They were on the best of terms with one another. You know how jolly it is to see two people who've been married a great many years obviously better pleased with their own company than anyone else's. Their marriage had evidently been a great success. And they were both of them devoted to Olive and very proud of her, Theo especially.'

'Although she was only his step-daughter?' I said.

'Although she was only his step-daughter,' answered Gaze. 'You'd think that she would have taken his name. But she hadn't. She called him Daddy, of course, he was the only father she'd ever known, but she signed her letters, Olive Bronson.'

'What was Bronson like, by the way?'

'Bronson? He was a great big fellow, very hearty, with a loud voice and a bellowing laugh, beefy, you know, and a fine athlete. There was not very much to him, but he was as straight as a die. He had a red face and red hair. Now I come to think of it I remember that I never saw a man sweat as much as he did. Water just poured off him, and when he played tennis he always used to bring a towel on the court with him.'

'It doesn't sound very attractive.'

'He was a handsome chap. He was always fit. He was keen on that. He hadn't much to talk about but rubber and games, tennis, you know, and golf and shooting; and I don't suppose he read a book from year's end to year's end. He was the typical public school boy. He was about thirty-five when I first knew him, but he had the mind of a boy of eighteen. You know how many fellows when they come out East seem to stop growing.'

I did indeed. One of the most disconcerting things to the traveller is to see stout, middle-aged gentlemen, with bald heads, speaking and acting like schoolboys. You might almost think that no idea has entered their heads since they first passed through the Suez Canal. Though married and the fathers of children, and perhaps in control of a large business, they continue to look upon life from the standpoint of the sixth form.

'But he was no fool,' Gaze went on. 'He knew his work from A to Z. His estate was one of the best managed in the country and he knew how to handle his labour. He was a damned good sort; and if he did get on your nerves a little you couldn't help liking him. He was generous with his money, and always ready to do anybody a good turn. That's how Cartwright happened to turn up in the first instance.'

'Did the Bronsons get on well together?'

'Oh, yes, I think so. I'm sure they did. He was good-natured and she was very jolly and gay. She was very outspoken, you know she can be damned amusing when she likes even now, but there's generally a sting lurking in the joke; when she was a young woman and married to Bronson it was just pure fun. She had high spirits and liked having a good time. She never cared a hang what she said, but it went with her type, if you understand what I mean; there was something so open and frank and careless about her that you didn't care what she said to you. They seemed very happy.

'Their estate was about five miles from Alor Lipis. They had a trap and they used to drive in most evenings about five. Of course it was a very small community and men were in the majority. There were only about six women. The Bronsons were a god-send. They bucked things up the moment they arrived. We used to have very jolly times in that little club. I've often thought of them since and I don't know that on the whole I've ever enjoyed myself more than I did when I was stationed there. Between six and eight-thirty the club at Alor Lipis twenty years ago was about as lively a place as you could find between Aden and Yokohama.

'One day Mrs Bronson told us that they were expecting a friend to stay with them and a few days later they brought Cartwright along. It appeared that he was an old friend of Bronson's, they'd been at school together, Marlborough, or some place like that, and they'd first come out East on the same ship. Rubber had taken a toss and a lot of fellows had lost their jobs. Cartwright was one of them. He'd been out of work for the greater part of a year and he hadn't anything to fall back on. In those days planters were even worse paid than they are now and a man had to be very lucky to put by something for a rainy day. Cartwright had gone to Singapore. They all go there when there's a slump, you know. It's awful then, I've seen it; I've known of planters sleeping in the street because they hadn't the price of a night's lodging. I've known them stop strangers outside the Europe and ask for a dollar to get a meal, and I think Cartwright had had a pretty rotten time.

'At last he wrote to Bronson and asked him if he couldn't do something for him. Bronson asked him to come and stay till things got better, at least it would be free board and lodging, and Cartwright jumped at the chance, but Bronson had to send him the money to pay his railway fare. When Cartwright arrived at Alor Lipis he hadn't ten cents in his pocket. Bronson had a little money of his own, two or three hundred a year, I think, and though his salary had been cut, he'd kept his job, so that he was better off than most planters. When Cartwright came Mrs Bronson told him that he was to look upon the place as his home and stay as long as he liked.'

'It was very nice of her, wasn't it?' I remarked.

'Very.'

Gaze lit himself another cheroot and filled his glass. It was very still and but for the occasional croak of the chik-chak the silence was intense. We seemed to be alone in the tropical night and heaven only knows how far from the habitations of men. Gaze did not speak for so long that at last I was forced to say something.

'What sort of a man was Cartwright at that time?' I asked. 'Younger, of course, and you told me rather nice-looking; but in himself?'

'Well, to tell you the truth, I never paid much attention to him. He was pleasant and unassuming. He's very quiet now, as I dare say you noticed; well, he wasn't exactly lively then. But he was perfectly inoffensive. He was fond of reading and he played the piano rather nicely. You never minded having him about, he was never in the way, but you never bothered very much about him. He danced well and the women rather liked that, but he also played billiards quite decently and be wasn't bad at tennis. He fell into our little groove very naturally. I wouldn't say that he ever became wildly popular, but everyone liked him. Of course we were sorry for him, as one is for a man who's down and out, but there was nothing we could do, and, well, we just accepted him and then forgot that he hadn't always been there. He used to come in with the Bronsons every evening and pay for his drinks like everyone else, I suppose Bronson had lent him a bit of money for current expenses, and he was always very civil. I'm rather vague about him, because really he didn't make any particular impression on me; in the East one meets such a lot of people, and he seemed very much like anybody else. He did everything he could to get something to do, but he had no luck; the fact is, there were no jobs going, and sometimes he seemed rather depressed about it. He was with the Bronsons for over a year. I remember his saying to me once:

'"After all I can't live with them for ever. They've been most awfully good to me, but there are limits."

'"I should think the Bronsons would be very glad to have you," I said. "It's not particularly gay on a rubber estate, and as far as your food and drink go, it must make precious little difference if you're there or not." '

Gaze stopped once more and looked at me with a sort of hesitation.

'What's the matter?' I asked.

'I'm afraid I'm telling you this story very badly,' he said. 'I seem to be just rambling on. I'm not a damned novelist, I'm a policeman, and I'm just telling you the facts as I saw them at the time; and from my point of view all the circumstances are important; it's important, I mean, to realise what sort of people they were.'

'Of course. Fire away.'

'I remember someone, a woman, I think it was, the doctor's wife, asking Mrs Bronson if she didn't get tired sometimes of having a stranger in the house. You know, in places like Alor Lipis there isn't very much to talk about, and if you didn't talk about your neighbours there'd be nothing to talk about at all.

'"Oh, no," she said, "Theo's no trouble." She turned to her husband, who was sitting there mopping his face. "We like having him, don't we?"

'"He's all right," said Bronson.

'"What does he do with himself all day long?"

'"Oh, I don't know," said Mrs Bronson. "He walks round the estate with Reggie sometimes, and he shoots a bit. He talks to me."

'"He's always glad to make himself useful," said Bronson. "The other day when I had a go of fever, he took over my work and I just lay in bed and had a good time." '

'Hadn't the Bronsons any children?' I asked.

'No,' Gaze answered. 'I don't know why, they could well have afforded it.'

Gaze leant back in his chair. He took off his glasses and wiped them. They were very strong and hideously distorted his eyes. Without them he wasn't so homely. The chik-chak on the ceiling gave its strangely human cry. It was like the cackle of an idiot child.

'Bronson was killed,' said Gaze suddenly.

'Killed?'

'Yes, murdered. I shall never forget that night. We'd been playing tennis, Mrs Bronson and the doctor's wife, Theo Cartwright and I; and then we played bridge. Cartwright had been off his game and when we sat down at the bridge-table Mrs Bronson said to him: "Well, Theo, if you play bridge as rottenly as you played tennis we shall lose our shirts."

'We'd just had a drink, but she called the boy and ordered another round.

'"Put that down your throat," she said to him, "and don't call without top honours and an outside trick."

'Bronson hadn't turned up, he'd cycled into Kabulong to get the money to pay his coolies their wages and was to come along to the club when he got back. The Bronsons' estate was nearer Alor Lipis than it was to Kabulong, but Kabulong was a more important place commercially, and Bronson banked there.

'"Reggie can cut in when he turns up," said Mrs Bronson.

'"He's late, isn't he?" said the doctor's wife.

'"Very. He said he wouldn't get back in time for tennis, but would be here for a rubber. I have a suspicion that he went to the club at Kabulong instead of coming straight home and is having drinks, the ruffian."

'"Oh, well, he can put away a good many without their having much effect on him," I laughed.

'"He's getting fat, you know. He'll have to be careful."

'We sat by ourselves in the card-room and we could hear the crowd in the billiard-room talking and laughing. They were all on the merry side. It was getting on to Christmas Day and we were all letting ourselves go a little. There was going to be a dance on Christmas Eve.

'I remembered afterwards that when we sat down the doctor's wife asked Mrs Bronson if she wasn't tired.

'"Not a bit," she said. "Why should I be?"

'I didn't know why she flushed.

'"I was afraid the tennis might have been too much for you," said the doctor's wife.

'"Oh, no," answered Mrs Bronson, a trifle abruptly, I thought, as though she didn't want to discuss the matter.

'I didn't know what they meant, and indeed it wasn't till later that I remembered the incident.

'We played three or four rubbers and still Bronson didn't turn up.

'"I wonder what's happened to him," said his wife. "I can't think why he should be so late."

'Cartwright was always silent, but this evening he had hardly opened his mouth. I thought he was tired and asked him what he'd been doing.

'"Nothing very much," he said. "I went out after tiffin to shoot pigeon."

'"Did you have any luck?" I asked.

'"Oh, I got half a dozen. They were very shy."

'But now he said: 'If Reggie got back late, I dare say he thought it wasn't worth while to come here. I expect he's had a bath and when we get in we shall find him asleep in his chair.'

'"It's a good long ride from Kabulong," said the doctor's wife. "He doesn't take the road, you know," Mrs Bronson explained. "He takes the short cut through the jungle."

'"Can he get along on his bicycle?" I asked.

'"Oh, yes, its a very good track. It saves about a couple of miles."

'We had just started another rubber when the bar-boy came in and said there was a police-sergeant outside who wanted to speak to me.

'"What does he want?" I asked.

'The boy said he didn't know, but he had two coolies with him.

'"Curse him," I said. "I'll give him hell if I find he's disturbed me for nothing."

'I told the boy I'd come and I finished playing the hand. Then I got up.

'"I won't be a minute," I said. "Deal for me, will you?" I added to Cartwright.

'I went out and found the sergeant with two Malays waiting for me on the steps. I asked him what the devil he wanted. You can imagine my consternation when he told me that the Malays had come to the police-station and said there was a white man lying dead on the path that led through the jungle to Kabulong. I immediately thought of Bronson.

'"Dead?" I cried.

'"Yes, shot. Shot through the head. A white man with red hair."

'Then I knew it was Reggie Bronson, and indeed, one of them naming his estate said he'd recognised him as the man. It was an awful shock. And there was Mrs Bronson in the card-room waiting impatiently for me to sort my cards and make a bid. For a moment I really didn't know what to do. I was frightfully upset. It was dreadful to give her such a terrible and unexpected blow without a word of preparation, but I found myself quite unable to think of any way to soften it. I told the sergeant and the coolies to wait and went back into the club. I tried to pull myself together. As I entered the card-room Mrs Bronson said: "You've been an awful long time." Then she caught sight of my face. "Is anything the matter?" I saw her clench her fists and go white. You'd have thought she had a presentiment of evil.

'"Something dreadful has happened," I said, and my throat was all closed up so that my voice sounded even to myself hoarse and uncanny. "There's been an accident. Your husband's been wounded."

'She gave a long gasp, it was not exactly a scream, it reminded me oddly of a piece of silk torn in two.

'"Wounded?"

'She leapt to her feet and with her eyes starting from her head stared at Cartwright. The effect on him was ghastly, he fell back in his chair and went as white as death.

'"Very, very badly, I'm afraid," I added.

'I knew that I must tell her the truth, and tell it then, but I couldn't bring myself to tell it all at once.

'"Is he," her lips trembled so that she could hardly form the words, "is he—conscious?"

'I looked at her for a moment without answering. I'd have given a thousand pounds not to have to.

'"No, I'm afraid he isn't."

'Mrs Bronson stared at me as though she were trying to see right into my brain.

'"Is he dead?"

'I thought the only thing was to get it out and have done with it.

'"Yes, he was dead when they found him."

'Mrs Bronson collapsed into her chair and burst into tears.

'"Oh, my God," she muttered. "Oh, my God."

'The doctor's wife went to her and put her arms round her. Mrs Bronson with her face in her hands swayed to and fro weeping hysterically. Cartwright, with that livid face, sat quite still, his mouth open, and stared at her. You might have thought he was turned to stone.

'"Oh, my dear, my dear," said the doctor's wife, "you must try and pull yourself together." Then, turning to me, "Get her a glass of water and fetch Harry."

'Harry was her husband and he was playing billiards. I went in and told him what had happened.

"'A glass of water be damned," he said. "What she wants is a good long peg of brandy."

'We took it in to her and forced her to drink it and gradually the violence of her emotion exhausted itself. In a few minutes the doctor's wife was able to take her into the ladies' lavatory to wash her face. I'd made up my mind now what had better be done. I could see that Cartwright wasn't good for much; he was all to pieces. I could understand that it was a fearful shock to him, for after all Bronson was his greatest friend and had done everything in the world for him.

"'You look as though you'd be all the better for a drop of brandy yourself, old man," I said to him.

'He made an effort.

"'It's shaken me, you know," he said. "I . . . I didn't . . ." He stopped as though his mind was wandering; he was still fearfully pale; he took out a packet of cigarettes and struck a match, but his hand was shaking so that he could hardly manage it.

"'Yes, I'll have a brandy."

"'Boy," I shouted, and then to Cartwright: "Now, are you fit to take Mrs Bronson home?"

"'Oh, yes," he answered.

"'That's good. The doctor and I will go along with the coolies and some police to where the body is."

"'Will you bring him back to the bungalow?" asked Cartwright.

"'I think he'd better be taken straight to the mortuary," said the doctor before I could answer. "I shall have to do a PM."

'When Mrs Bronson, now so much calmer that I was amazed, came back, I told her what I suggested. The doctor's wife, kind woman, offered to go with her and spend the night at the bungalow, but Mrs Bronson wouldn't hear of it. She said she would be perfectly all right, and when the doctor's wife insisted— you know how bent some people are on forcing their kindness on those in trouble—she turned on her almost fiercely.

"'No, no, I must be alone," she said. "I really must. And Theo will be there."

'They got into the trap. Theo took the reins and they drove off. We started after them, the doctor and I, while the sergeant and the coolies followed. I had sent my seis to the police-station with instructions to send two men to the place where the body was lying. We soon passed Mrs Bronson and Cartwright.

"'All right?" I called.

"'Yes," he answered.

'For some time the doctor and I drove without saying a word; we were both of us deeply shocked. I was worried as well. Somehow or other I'd got to find the murderers and I foresaw that it would be no easy matter.

"'Do you suppose it was gang robbery?" said the doctor at last.

'He might have been reading my thoughts.

"'I don't think there's a doubt of it," I answered. "They knew he'd gone into

Kabulong to get the wages and lay in wait for him on the way back. Of course he should never have come alone through the jungle when everyone knew he had a packet of money with him."

"'He'd done it for years,' said the doctor. "And he's not the only one."

"'I know. The question is, how we're going to get hold of the fellows that did it."

"'You don't think the two coolies who say they found him could have had anything to do with it?"

"'No. They wouldn't have the nerve. I think a pair of Chinks might think out a trick like that, but I don't believe Malays would. They'd be much too frightened. Of course we'll keep an eye on them. We shall soon see if they seem to have any money to fling about."

"'It's awful for Mrs Bronson,' said the doctor. "It would have been bad enough at any time, but now she's going to have a baby ...'

"'I didn't know that,' I said, interrupting him.

"'No, for some reason she wanted to keep it dark. She was rather funny about it, I thought."

'I recollected then that little passage between Mrs Bronson and the doctor's wife. I understood why that good woman had been so anxious that Mrs Bronson should not overtire herself.

"'It's strange her having a baby after being married so many years."

"'It happens, you know. But it was a surprise to her. When first she came to see me and I told her what was the matter she fainted, and then she began to cry. I should have thought she'd be as pleased as Punch. She told me that Bronson didn't like children and he'd be awfully bored at the idea, and she made me promise to say nothing about it till she had had a chance of breaking it to him gradually."

'I reflected for a moment.

"'He was the kind of breezy, hearty cove whom you'd expect to be as keen as mustard on having kids."

"'You never can tell. Some people are very selfish and just don't want the bother."

"'Well, how did he take it when she did tell him? Wasn't he rather bucked?"

"'I don't know that she ever told him. Though she couldn't have waited much longer; unless I'm very much mistaken she ought to be confined in about five months."

"'Poor devil,' I said. "You know, I've got a notion that he'd have been most awfully pleased to know."

'We drove in silence for the rest of the way and at last came to the point at which the short cut to Kabulong branched off from the road. Here we stopped and in a minute or two my trap, in which were the police-sergeant and the two Malays, came up. We took the head-lamps to light us on our way. I left the doctor's seis to look after the ponies and told him that when the policemen came they were to follow the path till they found us. The two coolies, carrying the lamps, walked ahead, and we followed them. It was a fairly broad track, wide enough for a small cart to pass, and before the road was built it had been the highway between Kabulong and Alor Lipis. It was firm to the foot and good walking. The surface here and there was sandy and in places you could see quite plainly the mark of a bicycle wheel. It was the track Bronson had left on his way to Kabulong.

'We walked twenty minutes, I should think, in single file, and on a sudden the coolies, with a cry, stopped sharply. The sight had come upon them so abruptly that notwithstanding they were expecting it they were startled. There, in the middle of the pathway lit dimly by the lamps the coolies carried, lay Bronson; he'd fallen over his bicycle and lay across it in an ungainly heap. I was too shocked to speak, and I think the doctor was, too. But in our silence the din of the jungle was deafening; those damned cicadas and the bull-frogs were making enough row to wake the dead. Even under ordinary circumstances the noise of the jungle at night is uncanny; because you feel that at that hour there should be utter silence it has an odd effect on you, that ceaseless and invisible uproar that beats upon your nerves. It surrounds you and hems you in. But just then, believe me, it was terrifying. That poor fellow lay dead and all round him the restless life of the jungle pursued its indifferent and ferocious course.

'He was lying face downwards. The sergeant and the coolies looked at me as though awaiting an order. I was a young fellow then and I'm afraid I felt a little frightened. Though I couldn't see the face I had no doubt that it was Bronson, but I felt that I ought to turn the body over to make sure. I suppose we all have our little squeamishnesses; you know, I've always had a horrible distaste for touching dead bodies. I've had to do it fairly often now, but it still makes me feel slightly sick.

'"It's Bronson, all right," I said.

'The doctor—by George, it was lucky for me he was there—the doctor bent down and turned the head. The sergeant directed the lamp on the dead face.

'"My God, half his head's been shot away," I cried.

'"Yes."

'The doctor stood up straight and wiped his hands on the leaves of a tree that grew beside the path.

'"Is he quite dead?" I asked.

'"Oh, yes. Death must have been instantaneous. Whoever shot him must have fired at pretty close range."

'"How long has he been dead, d'you think?"

'"Oh, I don't know, several hours."

'"He would have passed here about five o'clock, I suppose if he was expecting to get to the club for a rubber at six."

'"There's no sign of any struggle," said the doctor.

'"No, there wouldn't be. He was shot as he was riding along."

'I looked at the body for a little while. I couldn't help thinking how short a time ago it was since Bronson, noisy and loud-voiced. had been so full of hearty life.

'"You haven't forgotten that he had the coolies' wages on him," said the doctor.

'"No, we'd better search him."

'"Shall we turn him over?"

'"Wait a minute. Let us just have a look at the ground first."

'I took the lamp and as carefully as I could looked all about me. Just where he had fallen the sandy pathway was trodden and confused; there were our footprints and the footprints of the coolies who had found him. I walked two or three paces and then saw quite clearly the mark of his bicycle wheels; he had been riding straight and steadily. I followed it to the spot where he had fallen, to just before that, rather, and there saw very distinctly the prints on each side of the wheels of his heavy boots. He had evidently stopped there and put his feet to the ground, then he'd started off again, there was a great wobble of the wheel, and he'd crashed.

'"Now let's search him," I said.

'The doctor and the sergeant turned the body over and one of the coolies dragged the bicycle away. They laid Bronson on his back. I supposed he would have had the money partly in notes and partly in silver. The silver would have been in a bag attached to the bicycle and a glance told me that it was not there. The notes he would have put in a wallet. It would have been a good thick bundle. I felt him all over, but there was nothing; then I turned out the pockets, they were all empty except the right trouser pocket, in which there was a little small change.

'"Didn't he always wear a watch?" asked the doctor.

'"Yes, of course he did."

'I remembered that he wore the chain through the buttonhole in the lapel of his coat and the watch and some seals and things in his handkerchief pocket. But watch and chain were gone.

'"Well, there's not much doubt now, is there?" I said.

'It was clear that he had been attacked by gang robbers who knew he had money on him. After killing him they had stripped him of everything. I suddenly remembered the footprints that proved that for a moment he had stood still. I saw exactly how it had been done. One of them had stopped him on some pretext and then, just as he started off again, another, slipping out of the jungle behind him, had emptied the two barrels of a gun into his head.

'"Well," I said to the doctor, " it's up to me to catch them, and I'll tell you what, it'll be a real pleasure to me to see them hanged."

'Of course there was an inquest. Mrs Bronson gave evidence, but she had nothing to say that we didn't know already. Bronson had left the bungalow about eleven, he was to have tiffin at Kabulong and was to be back between five and six. He asked her not to wait for him, he said he would just put the money in the safe and come straight to the club. Cartwright confirmed this. He had lunched alone with Mrs Bronson and after a smoke had gone out with a gun to shoot pigeon. He had got in about five, a little before perhaps, had a bath and changed to play tennis. He was shooting not far from the place where Bronson was killed, but never heard a shot. That, of course, meant nothing; what with the cicadas and the frogs and the other sounds of the jungle, he would have had to be very near to hear anything; and besides, Cartwright was probably back in the bungalow before Bronson was killed. We traced Bronson's movements. He had lunched at the club, he had got money at the bank just before it closed, had gone to the club and had one more drink, and then started off on his bicycle. He had crossed the river by the ferry; the ferryman remembered distinctly seeing him, but was positive that no one else with a bicycle had crossed. That looked as though the murderers were not following, but lying in wait for him. He rode along the main road for a couple of miles and then took the path which was a short cut to his bungalow.

'It looked as though he had been killed by men who knew his habits, and suspicion, of course, fell immediately on the coolies of his estate. We examined them all—pretty carefully—but there was not a scrap of evidence to connect any of them with the crime. In fact, most of them were able satisfactorily to account for their actions and those who couldn't seemed to me for one reason and another out of the running. There were a few bad characters among the Chinese at Alor Lipis and I had them looked up. But somehow I didn't think it was the work of the Chinese; I had a feeling that Chinese would have used revolvers and not a shotgun. Anyhow, I could find out nothing there. So then we offered a reward of a thousand dollars to anyone who could put us in the way of discovering the murderers. I thought there were a good many people to whom it would appeal to do a public service and at the same time earn a tidy sum. But I knew that an informer would take no risks, he wouldn't want to tell what he knew till he knew he could tell it safely, and I armed myself with patience. The reward had brightened the interest of my police and I knew they would use every means they had to bring the criminals to trial. In a case like this they could do more than I.

'But it was strange, nothing happened; the reward seemed to tempt no one. I cast my net a little wider. There were two or three kampongs along the road and I wondered if the murderers were there; I saw the headmen, but got no help from them. It was not that they would tell me nothing, I was sure they had nothing to tell. I talked to the bad hats, but there was absolutely nothing to connect them with the murder. There was not the shadow of a clue.

'"Very well, my lads," I said to myself, as I drove back to Alor Lipis, "there's no hurry; the rope won't spoil by keeping."

'The scoundrels had got away with a considerable sum, but money is no good unless you spend it. I felt I knew the native temperament enough to be sure that the possession of it was a constant temptation. The Malays are an extravagant race, and a race of gamblers, and the Chinese are gamblers, too; sooner or later someone would start flinging his money about, and then I should want to know where it came from. With a few well directed questions I thought I could put the fear of God into the fellow and then, if I knew my business, it shouldn't be hard to get a full confession.

'The only thing now was to sit down and wait till the hue and cry had died down and the murderers thought the affair was forgotten. The itch to spend those ill-gotten dollars would grow more and more intolerable till at last it could be resisted no longer. I would go about my business, but I meant never to relax my watch, and one day, sooner or later, my time must come.

'Cartwright took Mrs Bronson down to Singapore. The company Bronson had worked for asked him if he would care to take Bronson's place, but he said, very naturally, that he didn't like the idea of it; so they put another man in and told Cartwright that he could have the job that Bronson's successor had vacated. It was the management of the estate that Cartwright lives on now. He moved in at once. Four months after this Olive was born at Singapore, and a few months later, when Bronson had been dead just over a year, Cartwright and Mrs Bronson were married. I was surprised; but on thinking it over I couldn't help confessing that it was very natural. After the trouble Mrs Bronson had leant much on Cartwright and he had arranged everything for her; she must have been lonely, and rather lost, and I dare say she was grateful for his kindness, he did behave like a brick; and so far as he was concerned I imagined he was sorry for her, it was a dreadful position for a woman, she had nowhere to go, and all they'd gone through must have been a tie between them. There was every reason for them to marry and it was probably the best thing for them both.

'It looked as though Bronson's murderers would never be caught, for that plan of mine didn't work; there was no one in the district who spent more money than he could account for, and if anyone had that hoard buried away under his floor he was showing a self-control that was superhuman. A year had passed and to all intents and purposes the thing was forgotten. Could anyone be so prudent as after so long not to let a little money dribble out? It was incredible. I began to think that Bronson had been killed by a couple of wandering Chinese who had got away, to Singapore perhaps, where there would be small chance of catching them. At last I gave it up. If you come to think of it, as a rule, it's just those crimes, crimes of robbery, in which there is least chance of getting the culprit; for there's nothing to attach suspicion to him, and if he's caught it can only be by his own carelessness. It's different with crimes of passion or vengeance, then you can find out who had a motive to put the victim out of the way.

'It's no use grizzling over one's failures, and bringing my common sense to bear I did my best to put the matter out of my mind. No one likes to be beaten, but beaten I was and I had to put as good a face on it as I could. And then a Chinaman was caught trying to pawn poor Bronson's watch.

'I told you that Bronson's watch and chain had been taken, and of course Mrs Bronson was able to give us a fairly accurate description of it. It was a half-hunter, by Benson, there was a gold chain, three or four seals, and a sovereign purse. The pawnbroker was a smart fellow and when the Chinaman brought the watch he recognised it at once. On some pretext he kept the man waiting and sent for a policeman. The man was arrested and immediately brought to me. I greeted him like a long-lost brother. I was never so pleased to see anyone in my life. I have no feeling about criminals, you know; I'm rather sorry for them, because they're playing a game in which their opponents hold all the aces and kings; but when I catch one it gives me a little thrill of satisfaction, like bringing off a neat finesse at bridge. At last the mystery was going to be cleared up, for if the Chinaman hadn't done the thing himself we were pretty sure through him to trace the murderers. I beamed on him.

'I asked him to account for his possession of the watch. He said he had bought it from a man he didn't know. That was very thin. I explained the circumstances briefly and told him he would be charged with murder. I meant to frighten him and I did. He said then that he'd found the watch.

'"Found it?" I said. "Fancy that. Where?"

'His answer staggered me; he said he'd found it in the jungle. I laughed at him; I asked him if he thought watches were likely to be left lying about in the jungle; then he said he'd been coming along the pathway that led from Kabulong to Alor Lipis, and had gone into the jungle and caught sight of something gleaming and there was the watch. That was odd. Why should he have said he found the watch just there? It was either true or excessively astute. I asked him where the chain and the seals were, and he produced them immediately. I'd got him scared, and he was pale and shaking; he was a knock-kneed little fellow and I should have been a fool not to see that I hadn't got hold of the murderer there. But his terror suggested that he knew something.

'I asked him when he'd found the watch.

'"Yesterday," he said.

'I asked him what he was doing on the short-cut from Kabulong to Alor Lipis. He said he'd been working in Singapore and had gone to Kabulong because his father was ill, and that he himself had come to Alor Lipis to work. A friend of his father, a carpenter by trade, had given him a job. He gave me the name of the man with whom he had worked in Singapore and the name of the man who had engaged him at Alor Lipis. All he said seemed plausible and could so easily be verified that it was hardly likely to be false. Of course it occurred to me that if he had found the watch as he said, it must have been lying in the jungle for more than a year. It could hardly be in very good condition; I tried to open it, but couldn't. The pawnbroker had come to the police station and was waiting in the next room. Luckily he was also something of a watch-maker. I sent for him and asked him to look at the watch; when he opened it he gave a little whistle, the works were thick with rust.

'"This watch no good," he said, shaking his head. "Him never go now."

'I asked him what had put it in such a state, and without a word from me he said that it had been long exposed to wet. For the moral effect I had the prisoner put in a cell and I sent for his employer. I sent a wire to Kabulong and another to Singapore. While I waited I did my best to put two and two together. I was inclined to believe the man's story true; his fear might be ascribed to no more guilt than consisted in his having found something and tried to sell it. Even quite innocent persons are apt to be nervous when they're in the hands of the police; I don't know what there is about a policeman, people are never very much at their ease in his company. But if he really had found the watch where he said, someone had thrown it there. Now that was funny. Even if the murderers had thought the watch a dangerous thing to possess, one would have expected them to melt down the gold case; that would be a very simple thing for any native to do; and the chain was of so ordinary a pattern they could hardly have thought it possible to trace that. There were chains like it in every jeweller's shop in the country. Of course there was the possibility that they had plunged into the jungle and having dropped the watch in their hurry had been afraid to go back and look for it. I didn't think that very likely: the Malays are used to keeping things tucked away in their sarongs, and the Chinese have pockets in their coats. Besides, the moment they got into the jungle they knew there was no hurry; they probably waited and divided the swag then and there.

'In a few minutes the man I had sent for came to the police station and confirmed what the prisoner had said, and in an hour I got an answer from Kabulong. The police had seen his father, who told them that the boy had gone to Alor Lipis to get a job with a carpenter. So far everything he had said seemed true. I had him brought in again, and told him I was going to take him to the place where he said he had found the watch and he must show me the exact spot. I handcuffed him to a policeman, though it was hardly necessary, for the poor devil was shaking with fright, and took a couple of men besides. We drove out to where the track joined the road and walked along it; within five yards of the place where Bronson was killed the Chinaman stopped.

'"Here," he said.

'He pointed to the jungle and we followed him in. We went in about ten yards and he pointed to a chink between two large boulders and said that he found the watch there. It could only have been by the merest chance that he noticed it, and if he really had found it there it looked very much as though someone had put it there to hide it.'

Gaze stopped and gave me a reflective look.

'What would you have thought then?' he asked.

'I don't know,' I answered.

'Well, I'll tell you what I thought. I thought that if the watch was there the money might be there, too. It seemed worth while having a look. Of course, to look for something in the jungle makes looking for a needle in a bundle of hay a drawing-room pastime. I couldn't help that. I released the Chinaman, I wanted all the help I could get, and set him to work. I set my three men to work, and I started in myself. We made a line—there were five of us—and we searched from the road; for fifty yards on each side of the place at which Bronson was murdered and for a hundred yards in we went over the ground foot by foot. We routed among dead leaves and peered in bushes, we looked under boulders and in the hollows of trees. I knew it was a foolish thing to do, for the chances against us were a thousand to one; my only hope was that anyone who had just committed a murder would be rattled and if he wanted to hide anything would hide it quickly; he would choose the first obvious hiding-place that offered itself. That is what he had done when he hid the watch. My only reason for looking in so circumscribed an area was that as the watch had been found so near the road, the person who wanted to get rid of the things must have wanted to get rid of them quickly.

'We worked on. I began to grow tired and cross. We were sweating like pigs. I had a maddening thirst and nothing in the world to drink. At last I came to the conclusion that we must give it up as a bad job, for that day at least, when suddenly the Chinaman—he must have had sharp eyes, that young man—uttered a guttural cry. He stooped down and from under the winding root of a tree drew out a messy, mouldering, stinking thing. It was a pocket-book that had been out in the rain for a year, that had been eaten by ants and beetles and God knows what, that was sodden and foul, but it was a pocket-book all right, Bronson's, and inside were the shapeless, mushed-up, fetid remains of the Singapore notes he had got from the bank at Kabulong. There was still the silver and I was convinced that it was hidden somewhere about, but I wasn't going to bother about that. I had found out something very important; whoever had murdered Bronson had made no money out of it.

'Do you remember my telling you that I'd noticed the print of Bronson's feet on each side of the broad line of the pneumatic tyre, where he had stopped, and presumably spoken to someone? He was a heavy man and the prints were well marked. He hadn't just put his feet on the soft sand and taken them off, but must have stopped at least for a minute or two. My explanation was that he had stopped to chat with a Malay or a Chinaman, but the more I thought of it the less I liked it. Why the devil should he? Bronson wanted to get home, and though a jovial chap, he certainly was not hail-fellow-well-met with the natives. His relations towards them were those of master and servants. Those footprints had always puzzled me. And now the truth flashed across me. Whoever had murdered Bronson hadn't murdered him to rob and if he'd stopped to talk with someone it could only be with a friend. I knew at last who the murderer was.'

I have always thought the detective story a most diverting and ingenious variety of fiction, and have regretted that I never had the skill to write one, but I have read a good many, and I flatter myself it is rarely that I have not solved the mystery before it was disclosed to me; and now for some time I had foreseen what Gaze was going to say, but when at last he said it I confess that it gave me, notwithstanding, somewhat of a shock.

'The man he met was Cartwright. Cartwright was pigeon shooting. He stopped and asked him what sport he had had, and as he rode on Cartwright raised his gun and discharged both barrels into his head. Cartwright took the money and the watch in order to make it look like the work of gang robbers and hurriedly hid them in the jungle, then made his way along the edge till he got to the road, went back to the bungalow, changed into his tennis things, and drove with Mrs Bronson to the club.

'I remembered how badly he'd played tennis, and how he'd collapsed when, in order to break the news more gently to Mrs Bronson, I said Bronson was wounded and not dead. If he was only wounded he might have been able to speak. By George, I bet that was a bad moment. The child was Cartwright's. Look at Olive: why, you saw the likeness yourself. The doctor had said that Mrs Bronson was upset when he told her she was going to have a baby and made him promise not to tell Bronson. Why? Because Bronson knew that he couldn't be the father of the child.'

'Do you think that Mrs Bronson knew what Cartwright had done?' I asked.

'I'm sure of it. When I look back on her behaviour that evening at the club I am convinced of it. She was upset, but not because Bronson was killed; she was upset because I said he was wounded; on my telling her that he was dead when they found him she burst out crying, but from relief. I know that woman. Look at that square chin of hers and tell me that she hasn't got the courage of the devil. She has a will of iron. She made Cartwright do it. She planned every detail and every move. He was completely under her influence; he is now.'

'But do you mean to tell me that neither you nor anyone else ever suspected that there was anything between them?'

'Never. Never.'

'If they were in love with one another and knew that she was going to have a baby, why didn't they just bolt?'

'How could they? It was Bronson who had the money; she hadn't a bean and neither had Cartwright. He was out of a job. Do you think he would have got another with that story round his neck? Bronson had taken him in when he was starving and he'd stolen his wife from him. They wouldn't have had a dog's chance. They couldn't afford to let the truth come out, their only chance was to get Bronson out of the way, and they got him out of the way.'

'They might have thrown themselves on his mercy.'

'Yes, but I think they were ashamed. He'd been so good to them, he was such a decent chap, I don't think they had the heart to tell him the truth. They preferred to kill him.'

There was a moment's silence while I reflected over what Gaze said.

'Well, what did you do about it?' I asked.

'Nothing. What was there to do? What was the evidence? That the watch and notes had been found? They might easily have been hidden by someone who was afterwards afraid to come and get them. The murderer might have been quite content to get away with the silver. The footprints? Bronson might have stopped to light a cigarette or there might have been a tree-trunk across the path and he waited while the coolies he met there by chance moved it away. Who could prove that the child that a perfectly decent, respectable woman had had four months after her husband's death was not his child? No jury would have convicted Cartwright. I held my tongue and the Bronson murder was forgotten.'

'I don't suppose the Cartwrights have forgotten,' I suggested.

'I shouldn't be surprised. Human memory is astonishingly short and if you want my professional opinion I don't mind telling you that I don't believe remorse for a crime ever sits very heavily on a man when he's absolutely sure he'll never be found out.'

I thought once more of the pair I had met that afternoon, the thin, elderly, bald man with gold-rimmed spectacles, and that white-haired untidy woman with her frank speech and kindly, caustic smile. It was almost impossible to imagine that in the distant past they had been swayed by so turbulent a passion, for that alone made their behaviour explicable, that it had brought them in the end to such a pass that they could see no other issue than a cruel and cold-blooded murder.

'Doesn't it make you feel a little uncomfortable to be with them?' I asked Gaze. 'For, without wishing to be censorious, I'm bound to say that I don't think they can be very nice people.'

'That's where you're wrong. They are very nice people; they're about the pleasantest people here. Mrs Cartwright is a thoroughly good sort and a very amusing woman. It's my business to prevent crime and to catch the culprit when crime is committed, but I've known far too many criminals to think that on the whole they're worse than anybody else. A perfectly decent fellow may be driven by circumstances to commit a crime and if he's found out he's punished; but he may very well remain a perfectly decent fellow. Of course society punishes him if he breaks its laws, and it's quite right, but it's not always his actions that indicate the essential man. If you'd been a policeman as long as I have, you'd know it's not what people do that really matters, it's what they are. Luckily a policeman has nothing to do with their thoughts, only with their deeds; if he had, it would be a very different, a much more difficult matter.'

Gaze flicked the ash from his cheroot and gave me his wry, sardonic, but agreeable smile.

'I'll tell you what, there's one job I *shouldn't* like,' he said.

'What is that?' I asked.

'God's, at the Judgement Day,' said Gaze. 'No, sir.'

Ed McBain

b. 1926

SADIE WHEN SHE DIED

'I'M VERY GLAD SHE'S DEAD,' the man said.

He wore a homburg, muffler, overcoat, and gloves. He stood near the night table, a tall man with a narrow face, and a well-groomed gray mustache that matched the graying hair at his temples. His eyes were clear and blue and distinctly free of pain or grief.

Detective Steve Carella wasn't sure he had heard the man correctly. 'Sir,' Carella said, 'I'm sure I don't have to tell you—'

'That's right,' the man said, 'you don't have to tell me. It happens I'm a criminal lawyer and am well aware of my rights. My wife was no good, and I'm delighted someone killed her.'

Carella opened his pad. This was not what a bereaved husband was supposed to say when his wife lay disemboweled on the bedroom floor in a pool of her own blood.

'Your name is Gerald Fletcher.'

'That's correct.'

'Your wife's name, Mr Fletcher?'

'Sarah. Sarah Fletcher.'

'Want to tell me what happened?'

'I got home about fifteen minutes ago. I called to my wife from the front door, and got no answer. I came into the bedroom and found her dead on the floor. I immediately called the police.'

'Was the room in this condition when you came in?'

'It was.'

'Touch anything?'

'Nothing. I haven't moved from this spot since I placed the call.'

'Anybody in here when you came in?'

'Not a soul. Except my wife, of course.'

'Is that your suitcase in the entrance hallway?'

'It is. I was on the coast for three days. An associate of mine needed advice on a brief he was preparing. What's your name?'

'Carella. Detective Steve Carella.'

'I'll remember that.'

While the police photographer was doing his macabre little jig around the body to make sure the lady looked good in the rushes, or as good as any lady *can* look in her condition, a laboratory assistant named Marshall Davies was in the kitchen of the apartment, waiting for the medical examiner to pronounce the lady dead, at which time Davies would go into the bedroom and with delicate care remove the knife protruding from the blood and slime of the lady, in an attempt to salvage some good latent prints from the handle of the murder weapon.

Davies was a new technician, but an observant one, and he noticed that the kitchen window was wide open, not exactly usual on a December night when the temperature outside hovered at twelve degrees. Leaning over the sink, he further noticed that the window opened on to a fire escape on the rear of the building. He could not resist speculating that perhaps someone had climbed up the fire escape and then into the kitchen.

Since there was a big muddy footprint in the kitchen sink, another one on the floor near the sink, and several others fading as they traveled across the waxed kitchen floor to the living room, Davies surmised that he was onto something hot. Wasn't it possible that an intruder *had* climbed over the windowsill, into the sink, and walked across the room, bearing the switchblade knife that had later been pulled viciously across the lady's abdomen from left to right? If the M.E. ever got through with the damn body, the boys of the 87th would be halfway home, thanks to Marshall Davies. He felt pretty good.

THE THREE POINTS of the triangle were Detective-Lieutenant Byrnes, and Detectives Meyer Meyer and Steve Carella. Fletcher sat in a chair, still wearing homburg, muffler, overcoat, and gloves as if he expected to be called outdoors at any moment. The interrogation was being conducted in a windowless cubicle labeled Interrogation Room.

The cops standing in their loose triangle around Gerald Fletcher were amazed but not too terribly amused by his brutal frankness.

'I hated her guts,' he said.

'Mr Fletcher,' Lieutenant Byrnes said, 'I *still* feel I must warn you that a woman has been murdered—'

'Yes. My dear, wonderful wife,' Fletcher said sarcastically.

'. . . which is a serious crime . . .' Byrnes felt tongue-tied in Fletcher's presence. Bullet-headed, hair turning from iron-gray to ice-white, blue-eyed, built like a compact linebacker, Byrnes looked to his colleagues for support. Both Meyer and Carella were watching their shoelaces.

'You have warned me repeatedly,' Fletcher said. 'I can't imagine why. My wife is dead—someone killed her—but it was not I.'

'Well, it's nice to have your assurance of that, Mr Fletcher, but this alone doesn't necessarily still our doubts,' Carella said, hearing the words and wondering where the hell they were coming from. He was, he realised, trying to impress Fletcher. He continued, 'How do we know it *wasn't* you who stabbed her?'

'To begin with,' Fletcher said, 'there were signs of forcible entry in the kitchen and hasty departure in the bedroom; witness the wide-open window in the aforementioned room and the shattered window in the latter. The drawers in the dining-room sideboard were open—'

'You're very observant,' Meyer said suddenly. 'Did you notice all this in the four minutes it took you to enter the apartment and call the police?'

'It's my *job* to be observant,' Fletcher said. 'But to answer your question, no. I noticed all this *after* I had spoken to Detective Carella here.'

Wearily, Byrnes dismissed Fletcher, who then left the room.

'What do you think?' Byrnes said.

'I think he did it,' Carella said.

'Even with all those signs of a burglary?'

'*Especially* with those signs. He could have come home, found his wife stabbed—but not fatally—and finished her off by yanking the knife across her belly. Fletcher had four minutes, when all he needed was maybe four seconds.'

'It's possible,' Meyer said.

'Or maybe I just don't like the guy,' Carella said.

'Let's see what the lab comes up with,' Byrnes said.

The laboratory came up with good fingerprints on the kitchen window sash and on the silver drawer of the dining-room sideboard. There were good prints on some of the pieces of silver scattered on the floor near the smashed bedroom window. Most important, there were good prints on the handle of the switchblade knife. The prints matched; they had all been left by the same person.

Gerald Fletcher graciously allowed the police to take *his* fingerprints, which were then compared with those Marshall Davies had sent over from the police laboratory. The fingerprints on the window sash, the drawer, the silverware, and the knife did not match Gerald Fletcher's.

Which didn't mean a damn thing if he had been wearing his gloves when he'd finished her off.

ON MONDAY MORNING, in the second-floor rear apartment of 721 Silvermine Oval, a chalked outline on the bedroom floor was the only evidence that a woman had lain there in death the night before. Carella sidestepped the outline and looked out the shattered window at the narrow alleyway below. There was a distance of perhaps twelve feet between this building and the one across from it.

Conceivably, the intruder could have leaped across the shaftway, but this would have required premeditation and calculation. The more probable likelihood was that the intruder had fallen to the pavement below.

'That's quite a long drop,' Detective Bert Kling said, peering over Carella's shoulder.

'How far do you figure?' Carella asked.

'Thirty feet. At least.'

'Got to break a leg taking a fall like that. You think he went through the window head first?'

'How else?'

'He might have broken the glass out first, then gone through,' Carella suggested.

'If he was about to go to all that trouble, why didn't he just open the damn thing?'

'Well, let's take a look,' Carella said.

They examined the latch and the sash. Kling grabbed both handles on the window frame and pulled up on them. 'Stuck.'

'Probably painted shut,' Carella said.

'Maybe he *did* try to open it. Maybe he smashed it only when be realised it was stuck.'

'Yeah,' Carella said. 'And in a big hurry, too. Fletcher was opening the front door, maybe already in the apartment by then.'

'The guy probably had a bag or something with him, to put the loot in. He must have taken a wild swing with the bag when he realised the window was stuck, and maybe some of the stuff fell out, which would explain the silverware on the floor. Then he probably climbed through the hole and dropped down feet first. In fact, what he could've done, Steve, was drop the bag down first, and *then* climbed out and hung from the sill before he jumped, to make it a shorter distance.'

'I don't know if he had all that much time, Bert. He must have heard that front door opening, and Fletcher coming in and calling to his wife. Otherwise, he'd have taken his good, sweet time and gone out the kitchen window and down the fire escape, the way he'd come in.'

Kling nodded reflectively.

'Let's take a look at that alley,' Carella said.

In the alleyway outside, Carella and Kling studied the concrete pavement, and then looked up at the shattered second-floor window of the Fletcher apartment.

'Where do you suppose he'd have landed?' Kling said.

'Right about where we're standing.' Carella looked at the ground. 'I don't know, Bert. A guy drops twenty feet to a concrete pavement, doesn't break anything, gets up, dusts himself off, and runs the fifty yard dash, right?' Carella shook his head. 'My guess is he stayed right where he was to catch his breath, giving Fletcher time to look out the window, which would be the natural thing to do, but which Fletcher didn't.'

'He was anxious to call the police.'

'I still think he did it.'

'Steve, be reasonable. If a guy's fingerprints are on the handle of a knife and the knife is still in the victim—'

'*And* if the victim's husband realises what a sweet set up he's stumbled into, wife lying on the floor with a knife in her, place broken into and burglarised, why *not* finish the job and hope the burglar will be blamed?'

'Sure,' Kling said. 'Prove it.'

'I can't,' Carella said. 'Not until we catch the burglar.'

WHILE CARELLA AND KLING went through the tedious routine of retracing the burglar's footsteps, Marshall Davies called the 87th Precinct and got Detective Meyer.

'I think I've got some fairly interesting information about the suspect,' Davies said. 'He left latent fingerprints all over the apartment and footprints in the kitchen. A very good one in the sink, when he climbed in through the window, and some middling-fair ones tracking across the kitchen floor to the dining room. I got some excellent pictures and some good blowups of the heel.'

'Good,' Meyer said.

'But more important,' Davies went on, 'I got a good walking picture from the footprints on the floor. If a man is walking slowly, the distance between his foot prints is usually about twenty-seven inches. Forty for running, thirty-five for fast walking. These were thirty-two inches. So we have a man's usual gait, moving quickly, but not in a desperate hurry, with the walking line normal and not broken.'

'What does that mean?'

'Well, a walking line should normally run along the inner edge of a man's heel prints. Incidentally, the size and type of shoe and angle of the foot clearly indicate that this *was* a man.'

'OK, fine,' Meyer said. He did not thus far consider Davies' information valuable nor even terribly important.

'Anyway, none of this is valuable nor even terribly important,' Davies said, 'until we consider the rest of the data. The bedroom window was smashed, and the Homicide men were speculating that the suspect had jumped through the window into the alley below. I went down to get some meaningful pictures, and got some pictures of where he must have landed—on both feet, incidentally—and I got another walking picture and direction line. He moved toward the basement door and into the basement. But the important thing is that our man is injured, and I think badly.'

'How do you know?' Meyer asked.

'The walking picture downstairs is entirely different from the one in the kitchen. When he got downstairs he was leaning heavily on the left leg and dragging the right leg. I would suggest that whoever's handling the case put out a physicians' bulletin. If this guy hasn't got a broken leg, I'll eat the pictures I took.'

A GIRL IN A GREEN coat was waiting in the apartment lobby when Carella and Kling came back in, still retracing footsteps, or trying to. The girl said, 'Excuse me, are you the detectives?'

'Yes,' Carella said.

'The super told me you were in the building,' the girl said. 'You're investigating the Fletcher murder, aren't you?' She was quite softspoken.

'How can we help you, miss?' Carella asked.

'I saw somebody in the basement last night, with blood on his clothes.'

Carella glanced at Kling and immediately said, 'What time was this?'

'About a quarter to eleven,' the girl said.

'What were you doing in the basement?'

The girl looked surprised. 'That's where the washing machines are. I'm sorry, my name is Selma Bernstein. I live here in the building.'

'Tell us what happened, will you?' Carella said.

'I was sitting by the machine, watching the clothes tumble, which is simply *fascinating*, you know, when the door leading to the back yard opened—the door to the alley. This man came down the stairs, and I don't even think he saw me. He went straight for the stairs at the other end, the ones that go up into the street. I never saw him before last night.'

'Can you describe him?' Carella asked.

'Sure. He was about twenty-one or twenty-two, your height and weight, well, maybe a little bit shorter, five ten or eleven, brown hair.'

Kling was already writing. The man was white, wore dark trousers, high-topped sneakers, and a poplin jacket with blood on the right sleeve and on the front. He carried a small red bag, 'like one of those bags the airlines give you'.

Selma didn't know if he had any scars. 'He went by in pretty much of a hurry, considering he was dragging his right leg. I think he was hurt pretty badly.'

WHAT THEY HAD in mind, of course, was identification from a mug shot, but the I.S. reported that none of the fingerprints in their file matched the ones found in the apartment. So the detectives figured it was going to be a tough one, and they sent out a bulletin to all of the city's doctors just to prove it.

Just to prove that cops can be as wrong as anyone else, it turned out to be a nice easy one after all.

The call came from a physician in Riverhead at 4.37 that afternoon, just as Carella was ready to go home.

'This is Dr Mendelsohn,' he said. 'I have your bulletin here, and I want to report treating a man early this morning who fits your description—a Ralph Corwin of 894 Woodside in Riverhead. He had a bad ankle sprain.'

'Thank you, Dr Mendelsohn,' Carella said.

Carella pulled the Riverhead directory from the top drawer of his desk and quickly flipped to the Cs. He did not expect to find a listing for Ralph Corwin. A man would have to be a rank amateur to burglarise an apartment without wearing gloves, then stab a woman to death, and then give his name when seeking treatment for an injury sustained in escaping from the murder apartment.

Ralph Corwin was apparently a rank amateur. His name was in the phone book, and he'd given the doctor his correct address.

CARELLA AND KLING kicked in the door without warning, fanning into the room, guns drawn. The man on the bed was wearing only undershorts. His right ankle was taped.

'Are you Ralph Corwin?' Carella asked.

'Yes,' the man said. His face was drawn, the eyes in pain.

'Get dressed, Corwin. We want to ask you some questions.'

'There's nothing to ask,' he said and turned his head into the pillow. 'I killed her.'

RALPH CORWIN made his confession in the presence of two detectives of the 87th, a police stenographer, an assistant district attorney, and a lawyer appointed by the Legal Aid Society.

Corwin was the burglar. He'd entered 721 Silvermine Oval on Sunday night, December 12, down the steps from the street where the garbage cans were. He went through the basement, up the steps at the other end, into the back yard, and climbed the fire escape, all at about ten o'clock in the evening. Corwin entered the Fletcher apartment because it was the first one he saw without lights. He figured there was nobody home. The kitchen window was open a tiny crack; Corwin squeezed his fingers under the bottom and opened it all the way. He was pretty desperate at the time because he was a junkie in need of cash. He swore that he'd never done anything like this before.

The man from the D.A.'s office was conducting the Q. and A. and asked Corwin if he hadn't been afraid of fingerprints, not wearing gloves. Corwin figured that was done only in the movies, and anyway, he said, he didn't own gloves.

Corwin used a tiny flashlight to guide him as he stepped into the sink and down to the floor. He made his way to the dining room, emptied the drawer of silverware into his airline bag. Then he looked for the bedroom, scouting for watches and rings, whatever he could take in the way of jewelry. 'I'm not a pro,' he said. 'I was just hung up real bad and needed some bread to tide me over.'

Now came the important part. The D.A.'s assistant asked Corwin what happened in the bedroom.

A. 'There was a lady in bed. This was only like close to ten-thirty, you don't expect nobody to be asleep so early.'

Q. 'But there was a woman in bed.'

A. 'Yeah. She turned on the light the minute I stepped in the room.'

Q. 'What did you do?'

A. 'I had a knife in my pocket. I pulled it out to scare her. It was almost comical. She looks at me and says, "What are you doing here?"'

Q. 'Did you say anything to her?'

A. 'I told her to keep quiet, that I wasn't going to hurt her. But she got out of bed and I saw she was reaching for the phone. That's got to be crazy, right?

A guy is standing there in your bedroom with a knife in his hand, so she reaches for the phone.'

Q. 'What did you do?'

A. 'I grabbed her hand before she could get it. I pulled her off the bed, away from the phone, you know? And I told her again that nobody was going to hurt her, that I was getting out of there right away, to just please calm down.'

Q. 'What happened next?'

A. 'She started to scream. I told her to stop. I was beginning to panic. I mean she was really yelling.'

Q. 'Did she stop?'

A. 'No.'

Q. 'What did you do?'

A. 'I stabbed her.'

Q. 'Where did you stab her?'

A. 'I don't know. It was a reflex. She was yelling. I was afraid the whole building would come down. I just . . . I just stuck the knife in her. I was very scared. I stabbed her in the belly. Someplace in the belly.'

Q. 'How many times did you stab her?'

A. 'Once. She . . . She backed away from me. I'll never forget the look on her face. And she . . . fell on the floor.'

Q. 'Would you look at this photograph please?'

A. 'Oh, no . . .'

Q. 'Is that the woman you stabbed?'

A. 'Oh, no . . . I didn't think . . . Oh, no!'

A moment after he stabbed Sarah Fletcher, Corwin heard the door opening and someone coming in. The man yelled, 'Sarah, it's me, I'm home.' Corwin ran past Sarah's body on the floor, and tried to open the window, but it was stuck. He smashed it with his airline bag, threw the bag out first to save the swag because, no matter what, he knew he'd need another fix, and he climbed through the broken window, cutting his hand on a piece of glass. He hung from the sill, and finally let go, dropping to the ground. He tried to get up, and fell down again. His ankle was killing him, his hand bleeding. He stayed in the alley nearly fifteen minutes, then finally escaped via the route Selma Bernstein had described to Carella and Kling. He took the train to Riverhead and got to Dr Mendelsohn at about nine in the morning. He read of Sarah Fletcher's murder in the newspaper on the way back from the doctor.

ON TUESDAY, DECEMBER 14, which was the first of Carella's two days off that week, he received a call at home from Gerald Fletcher. Fletcher told the puzzled Carella that he'd gotten his number from a friend in the D.A.'s office, complimented Carella and the boys of the 87th on their snappy detective work, and invited Carella to lunch at the Golden Lion at one o'clock. Carella wasn't happy about interrupting his Christmas shopping, but this was an unusual opportunity, and he accepted.

Most policemen in the city for which Carella worked did not eat very often in restaurants like the Golden Lion. Carella had never been inside. A look at the menu posted on the window outside would have frightened him out of six months' pay. The place was a faithful replica of the dining room of an English coach house, circa 1627: huge oaken beams, immaculate white cloths, heavy silver.

Gerald Fletcher's table was in a secluded corner of the restaurant. He rose as Carella approached, extended his hand, and said, 'Glad you could make it. Sit down, won't you?'

Carella shook Fletcher's hand, and then sat. He felt extremely uncomfortable, but he couldn't tell whether his discomfort was caused by the room or by the man with whom he was dining.

'Would you care for a drink?' Fletcher asked.

'Well, are you having one?' Carella asked.

'Yes, I am.'

'I'll have a Scotch and soda,' Carella said. He was not used to drinking at lunch.

Fletcher signaled the waiter and ordered the drinks, making his another whiskey sour. When the drinks came, Fletcher raised his glass. 'Here's to a conviction,' he said.

Carella lifted his own glass. 'I don't expect there'll be any trouble,' he said. 'It looks airtight to me.'

Both men drank. Fletcher dabbed his lips with a napkin and said, 'You never can tell these days. I hope you're right, though.' He sipped at the drink. 'I must admit I feel a certain amount of sympathy for him.'

'Do you?'

'Yes. If he's an addict, he's automatically entitled to pity. And when one considers that the woman he murdered was just nothing but a—'

'Mr Fletcher . . .'

'Gerry, please. And I know: it isn't very kind of me to malign the dead. I'm afraid you didn't know my wife, though, Mr Carella. May I call you Steve?'

'Sure.'

'My enmity might be a bit more understandable if you had. Still, I shall take your advice. She's dead, and no longer capable of hurting me, so why be bitter. Shall we order, Steve?'

Fletcher suggested that Carella try either the trout *au meunière* or the beef and kidney pie, both of which were excellent. Carella ordered prime ribs, medium rare, and a mug of beer.

As the men ate and talked, something began happening, or at least Carella *thought* something was happening; he might never be quite sure. The conversation with Fletcher seemed on the surface to be routine chatter, but rushing through this inane, polite discussion was an undercurrent that caused excitement, fear, and apprehension. As they spoke, Carella knew with renewed certainty that Gerald Fletcher had killed his wife. Without ever being told so, he knew it. *This* was why Fletcher had called this morning; *this* was why Fletcher had invited him to lunch; *this* was why he prattled on endlessly while every contradictory move of his body signaled on an almost extrasensory level that he *knew* Carella suspected him of murder, and was here to *tell* Carella (*without* telling him) that, 'Yes, you stupid cop, I killed my wife. However much the evidence may point to another man, however many confessions you get, I killed her and I'm glad I killed her. And there isn't a damn thing you can do about it.'

RALPH CORWIN was being held before trial in the city's oldest prison, known to law enforcers and lawbreakers alike as Calcutta. Neither Corwin's lawyer nor the district attorney's office felt that allowing Carella to talk to the prisoner would be harmful to the case.

Corwin was expecting him. 'What did you want to see me about?'

'I wanted to ask you some questions.'

'My lawyer says I'm not supposed to add anything to what I already said. I don't even *like* that guy.'

'Why don't you ask for another lawyer? Ask one of the officers here to call the Legal Aid Society. Or simply tell him. I'm sure he'd have no objection to dropping out.'

Corwin shrugged. 'I don't want to hurt his feelings. He's a little cockroach, but what the hell.'

'You've got a lot at stake here, Corwin.'

'But I killed her, so what does it matter *who* the lawyer is? You got it all in black and white.'

'You feel like answering some questions?' Carella said.

'I feel like dropping dead, is what I feel like. Cold turkey's never good, and it's worse when you can't yell.'

'If you'd rather I came back another time . . .'

'No, no, go ahead. What do you want to know?'

'I want to know exactly how you stabbed Sarah Fletcher.'

'How do you *think* you stab somebody? You stick a knife in her, that's how.'

'Where?'

'In the belly.'

'Left-hand side of the body?'

'Yeah. I guess so.'

'Where was the knife when she fell?'

'I don't know what you mean.'

'Was the knife on the *right*-hand side of her body or the *left*?'

393

'I don't know. That was when I heard the front door opening and all I could think of was getting out of there.'

'When you stabbed her, did she *twist* away from you?'

'No, she backed away, straight back, as if she couldn't believe what I done, and . . . and just wanted to get *away* from me.'

'And then she fell?'

'Yes. She . . . her knees sort of gave way and she grabbed for her belly, and her hands sort of—it was terrible—they just . . . they were grabbing *air*, you know? And she fell.'

'In what position?'

'On her side.'

'*Which* side?'

'I could still see the knife, so it must've been the opposite side. The side opposite from where I stabbed her.'

'One last question, Ralph. Was she dead when you went through that window?'

'I don't know. She was bleeding and . . . she was very quiet. I guess she was dead. I don't know. I guess so.'

AMONG SARAH FLETCHER's personal effects that were considered of interest to the police before they arrested Ralph Corwin was an address book found in the dead woman's handbag on the bedroom dresser. In the Thursday afternoon stillness of the squad room, Carella examined the book.

There was nothing terribly fascinating about the alphabetical listings. Sarah Fletcher had possessed a good handwriting, and most of the listings were obviously married couples (Chuck and Nancy Benton, Harold and Marie Spander, and so on), some were girlfriends, local merchants, hairdresser, dentist, doctors, restaurants in town or across the river. A thoroughly uninspiring address book—until Carella came to a page at the end of the book, with the printed word MEMORANDA at its top.

Under the word, there were five names, addresses, and telephone numbers written in Sarah's meticulous hand. They were all men's names, obviously entered at different times because some were in pencil and others in ink. The parenthetical initials following each entry were all noted in felt marking pens of various colors:

Andrew Hart, 1120 Hall Avenue, 622-8400 (PB&G) (TG)
Michael Thornton, 371 South Lindner, 881-9371 (TS)
Lou Kantor, 434 North 16 Street, FR 7-2346 (TPC) (TG)
Sal Decotto, 831 Grover Avenue, FR 5-3287 (F) (TG)
Richard Fenner, 110 Henderson, 593-6648 (QR) (TG)

If there was one thing Carella loved, it was a code. He loved a code almost as much as he loved German measles. He flipped through the phone book, and the address for Andrew Hart matched the one in Sarah's handwriting. He found an address for Michael Thornton. It, too, was identical to the one in her book. He kept turning pages in the directory, checking names and addresses. He verified all five.

At a little past eight the next morning, Carella got going on them. He called Andrew Hart at the number listed in Sarah's address book. Hart answered, and was not happy. 'I'm in the middle of shaving,' he said. 'I've got to leave for the office in a little while. What's this about?'

'We're investigating a homicide, Mr Hart.'

'A *what*? A homicide? Who's been killed?'

'A woman named Sarah Fletcher.'

'I don't know anyone named Sarah Fletcher,' he said.

'She seems to have known you, Mr Hart.'

'Sarah *who*? Fletcher, did you say?' Hart's annoyance increased.

'That's right.'

'I don't know anybody by that name. Who says she knew me? I never heard of her in my life.'

'Your name's in her address book.'

'*My* name? That's impossible.'

Nevertheless, Hart agreed to see Carella and Meyer at the office of Hart and Widderman, 480 Reed Street, sixth floor, at ten o'clock that morning.

At ten, Meyer and Carella parked the car and went into the building at 480 Reed, and up the elevator to the sixth floor. Hart and Widderman manufactured watchbands. A huge advertising display near the receptionist's desk in the lobby proudly proclaimed 'H&W Beats the Band!' and then backed the slogan with more discreet copy that explained how Hart and Widderman had solved the difficult engineering problems of the expansion watch bracelet.

'Mr Hart, please,' Carella said.

'Who's calling?' the receptionist asked. She sounded as if she were chewing gum, even though she was not.

'Detectives Carella and Meyer.'

'Just a minute, please,' she said, and lifted her phone, pushing a button in the base. 'Mr Hart,' she said, 'there are some cops here to see you.' She listened for a moment and then said, 'Yes, sir.' She replaced the receiver on its cradle, gestured toward the inside corridor with a nod of her golden tresses, said, 'Go right in, please. Door at the end of the hall,' and then went back to her magazine.

The gray skies had apparently infected Andrew Hart. 'You didn't have to broadcast to the world that the police department was here,' he said immediately.

'We merely announced ourselves,' Carella said.

'Well, OK, now you're here,' Hart said, 'let's get it over with.' He was a big man in his middle fifties, with iron-gray hair and black-rimmed eyeglasses. 'I told you I don't know Sarah Fletcher and I don't.'

'Here's her book, Mr Hart,' Carella said. 'That's your name, isn't it?'

'Yeah,' Hart said, and shook his head. 'But how it got there is beyond me.'

'Is it possible she's someone you met at a party, someone you exchanged numbers with?'

'No.'

'Are you married, Mr Hart?'

'No.'

'We've got a picture of Mrs Fletcher. I wonder——'

'Don't go showing me any pictures of a corpse,' Hart said.

'This was taken when she was still very much alive, Mr Hart.'

Meyer handed Carella a manila envelope. He opened the flap and removed from the envelope a framed picture of Sarah Fletcher, which he handed to Hart. Hart looked at the photograph, and then immediately looked up at Carella.

'What is this?' he said. He looked at the photograph again, shook his head, and said, 'Somebody killed her, huh?'

'Yes, somebody did,' Carella answered. 'Did you know her?'

'I knew her.'

'I thought you said you didn't.'

'I didn't know Sarah Fletcher, if that's who you think she was. But I knew *this* broad, all right.'

'Who'd *you* think she was?' Meyer asked.

'Just who she told me she was. Sadie Collins. She introduced herself as Sadie Collins, and that's who I knew her as, Sadie Collins.'

'Where was this, Mr Hart? Where'd you meet her?'

'A singles bar. The city's full of them.'

'Would you remember when?'

'At least a year ago.'

'Ever go out with her?'

'I used to see her once or twice a week.'

'When did you stop seeing her?'

'Last summer.'

'Did you know she was married?'

'Who, Sadie? You're kidding.'

'She never told you she was married?'

'Never.'

Meyer asked, 'When you were going out, where'd you pick her up? At her apartment?'

'No. She used to come to my place.'

'Where'd you call her when you wanted to reach her?'

'I didn't. She used to call me.'

'Where'd you go, Mr Hart? When you went out?'

'We didn't go out too much.'

'What *did* you do?'

'She used to come to my place. The truth is, we never went out. She didn't want to go out much.'

'Didn't you think that was strange?'

'No,' Hart shrugged. 'I figured she liked to stay home.'

'Why'd you stop seeing her, Mr Hart?'

'I met somebody else. A nice girl. I'm very serious about her.'

'Was there something wrong with Sadie?'

'No, no. She was a beautiful woman, beautiful.'

'Then why would you be ashamed—'

'Ashamed? Who said anything about being ashamed?'

'I gathered you wouldn't want your girlfriend—'

'Listen, what is this? I stopped seeing Sadie six months ago, wouldn't even talk to her on the phone after that. If the crazy babe got herself killed—'

'Crazy?'

Hart suddenly wiped his hand over his face, wet his lips and walked behind his desk. 'I don't think I have anything more to say to you gentlemen.'

'What did you mean by crazy?' Carella asked.

'Good day, gentlemen,' Hart said.

CARELLA WENT TO SEE Lieutenant Byrnes. In the lieutenant's corner office, Byrnes and Carella sat down over coffee. Byrnes frowned at Carella's request.

'Oh, come on, Pete!' Carella said. 'If Fletcher *did* it—'

'That's only *your* allegation. Suppose he *didn't* do it, and suppose *you* do something to screw up the D.A.'s case?'

'Like what?'

'I don't know like what. The way things are going these days, if you spit on the sidewalk, that's enough to get a case thrown out of court.'

'Fletcher hated his wife,' Carella said calmly.

'Lots of men hate their wives. Half the men in this city hate their wives.'

'But her little fling gives Fletcher a good reason for . . . Look, Pete, he had a motive; he had the opportunity, a golden one, in fact; and he had the means—another man's knife sticking in Sarah's belly. What more do you want?'

'Proof. There's a funny little system we've got here—it requires proof before we can arrest a man and charge him with murder.'

'Right. And all I'm asking is the opportunity to *try* for it.'

'Sure, by putting a tail on Fletcher. Suppose he sues the city?'

'Yes or no, Pete? I want permission to conduct a round-the-clock surveillance of Gerald Fletcher, starting Sunday morning. Yes or no?'

'I must be out of my mind,' Byrnes said, and sighed.

MICHAEL THORNTON LIVED in an apartment building several blocks from the Quarter, close enough to absorb some of its artistic flavor, distant enough to escape its high rents. A blond man in his apartment, Paul Wendling, told Kling and Meyer that Mike was in his jewelry shop.

In the shop, Thornton was wearing a blue work smock, but the contours of the garment did nothing to hide his powerful build. His eyes were blue, his hair black. A small scar showed white in the thick eyebrow over his left eye.

'We understand you're working,' Meyer said. 'Sorry to break in on you this way.'

'That's OK,' Thornton said. 'What's up?'

'You know a woman named Sarah Fletcher?'

'No,' Thornton said.

'You know a woman named Sadie Collins?'

Thornton hesitated. 'Yes,' he said.

'What was your relationship with her?' Kling asked.

Thornton shrugged. 'Why? Is she in trouble?'

'When's the last time you saw her?'

'You didn't answer my question,' Thornton said.

'Well, you didn't answer ours either,' Meyer said, and smiled. 'What was your relationship with her, and when did you see her last?'

'I met her in July, in a joint called The Saloon, right around the corner. It's a bar, but they also serve sandwiches and soup. It gets a big crowd on weekends, singles, a couple of odd ones for spice—but not a gay bar. I saw her last in August, a brief, hot thing, and then good-bye.'

'Did you realise she was married?' Kling said.

'No. Is she?'

'Yes,' Meyer said. Neither of the detectives had yet informed Thornton that the lady in question was now unfortunately deceased. They were saving that for last, like dessert.

'Gee, I didn't know she was married.' Thornton seemed truly surprised. 'Otherwise, nothing would've happened.'

'What *did* happen?'

'I bought her a few drinks and then I took her home with me. Later, I put her in a cab.'

'When did you see her next?'

'The following day. It was goofy. She called me in the morning, said she was on her way downtown. I was still in bed. I said, "So come on down, baby." And she did. *Believe* me, she did.'

'Did you see her again after that?' Kling asked.

'Two or three times a week.'

'Where'd you go?'

'To my pad on South Lindner.'

'Never went any place but there?'

'Never.'

'Why'd you quit seeing her?'

'I went out of town for a while. When I got back, I just didn't hear from her again. She never gave me her number, and she wasn't in the directory, so I couldn't reach her.'

'What do you make of this?' Kling asked, handing Thornton the address book.

Thornton studied it and said, 'Yes, what about it? She wrote this down the night we met—we were in bed, and she asked my address.'

'Did she write those initials at the same time, the ones in parentheses under your phone number?'

'I didn't actually see the page itself, I only saw her writing in the book.'

'Got any idea what the initials mean?'

'None at all.' Suddenly he looked thoughtful. 'She *was* kind of special, I have to admit it.' He grinned. 'She'll call again, I'm sure of it.'

'I wouldn't count on it,' Meyer said. 'She's dead.'

His face did not crumble or express grief or shock. The only thing it expressed was sudden anger. 'The stupid . . .' Thornton said. 'That's all she ever was, a stupid, crazy . . .'

ON SUNDAY MORNING, Carella was ready to become a surveillant, but Gerald Fletcher was nowhere in sight. A call to his apartment from a nearby phone booth revealed that he was not in his digs. He parked in front of Fletcher's apartment building until 5.00pm. when he was relieved by Detective Arthur Brown. Carella went home to read his son's latest note to Santa Claus, had dinner with his family, and was settling down in the living room with a novel he had bought a week ago and not yet cracked, when the telephone rang.

'Hello?' Carella said into the mouthpiece.

'Hello, Steve? This is Gerry. Gerry Fletcher.'

Carella almost dropped the receiver. 'How are you?'

'Fine, thanks. I was away for the weekend, just got back a little while ago, in fact. Frankly I find this apartment depressing as hell. I was wondering if you'd like to join me for a drink.'

'Well,' Carella said. 'It's Sunday night, and it's late—'

'Nonsense, it's only eight o'clock. We'll do a little old-fashioned pub crawling.'

It suddenly occurred to Carella that Gerald Fletcher had already had a few drinks before placing his call. It further occurred to him that if he played this *too* cozily, Fletcher might rescind his generous offer.

'Okay. I'll see you at eight-thirty, provided I can square it with my wife.'

'Good,' Fletcher said. 'See you.'

PADDY'S BAR AND GRILL was on the Stem, adjacent to the city's theater district. Carella and Fletcher got there at about nine o'clock while the place was still relatively quiet. The action began a little later, Fletcher explained.

Fletcher lifted his glass in a silent toast. 'What kind of person would you say comes to a place like this?'

'I would say we've got a nice lower-middle-class clientele bent on making contact with members of the opposite sex.'

'What would you say if I told you the blonde in the clinging jersey is a working prostitute?'

Carella looked at the woman. 'I don't think I'd believe you. She's a bit old for the young competition, and she's not *selling* anything. She's waiting for one of those two or three older guys to make their move. Hookers don't wait, Gerry. Is she a working prostitute?'

'I haven't the faintest idea,' Fletcher said. 'I was merely trying to indicate that appearances can sometimes be misleading. Drink up, there are a few more places I'd like to show you.'

He knew Fletcher well enough by now to realise that the man was trying to tell him something. At lunch last Tuesday, Fletcher had transmitted a message and a challenge: *I killed my wife, what can you do about it?* Tonight, in a similar manner, he was attempting to indicate something else, but Carella could not fathom exactly what.

Fanny's was only twenty blocks away from Paddy's Bar and Grill, but as far removed from it as the moon. Whereas the first bar seemed to cater to a quiet crowd peacefully pursuing its romantic inclinations, Fanny's was noisy and raucous, jammed to the rafters with men and women of all ages wearing plastic hippie gear purchased in head shops up and down Jackson Avenue.

Fletcher lifted his glass. 'I hope you don't mind if I drink myself into a stupor,' he said. 'Merely pour me into the car at the end of the night.' Fletcher drank. 'I don't usually consume this much alcohol, but I'm very troubled about that boy.'

'What boy?' Carella asked.

'Ralph Corwin,' Fletcher said. 'I understand he's having some difficulty with his lawyer and, well, I'd like to help him somehow.'

'*Help* him?'

'Yes. Do you think the D.A.'s office would consider it strange if I suggested a good defense lawyer for the boy?'

'I think they might consider it passing strange, yes.'

'Do I detect a note of sarcasm in your voice?'

'Not, at all.'

Fletcher squired Carella from Fanny's to, in geographical order, The Purple Chairs and Quigley's Rest. Each place was rougher, in its way, than the last. The Purple Chairs catered to a brazenly gay crowd, and Quigley's Rest was a dive, where Fletcher's liquor caught up with him, and the evening ended suddenly in a brawl. Carella was shaken by the experience, and still couldn't piece out Fletcher's reasons.

CARELLA RECEIVED a further shock when he continued to pursue Sarah Fletcher's address book. Lou Kantor was simply the third name in a now wearying list of Sarah's bedmates, until she turned out to be a tough and striking woman. She confirmed Carella's suspicions immediately.

'I only knew her a short while,' she said. 'I met her in September, I believe. Saw her three or four times after that.'

'Where'd you meet her?'

'In a bar called The Purple Chairs. That's right,' she added quickly. 'That's what I am.'

'Nobody asked,' Carella said. 'What about Sadie Collins?'

'Spell it out, Officer, I'm not going to help you. I don't like being hassled.'

'Nobody's hassling you, Miss Kantor. You practice your religion and I'll practice mine. We're here to talk about a dead woman.'

'Then talk about her, spit it out. What do you want to know? Was she straight? Everybody's straight until they're *not* straight any more, isn't that right? She was willing to learn. I taught her.'

'Did you know she was married?'

'She told me. So what? Broke down in tears one night, and spent the rest of the night crying. I knew she was married.'

'What'd she say about her husband?'

'Nothing that surprised me. She said he had another woman. Said he ran off to see her every weekend, told little Sadie he had out-of-town business. *Every* weekend, can you imagine that?'

'What do you make of this?' Carella said, and handed her Sarah's address book, opened to the MEMORANDA page.

'I don't know any of these people,' Lou said.

'The initials under your name.' Carella said. 'TPC and then TG. Got any ideas?'

'Well, the TPC is obvious, isn't it? I met her at The Purple Chairs. What else could it mean?'

Carella suddenly felt very stupid. 'Of course. What else could it mean?' He took back the book. 'I'm finished,' he said. 'Thank you very much.'

'I miss her,' Lou said suddenly. 'She was a wild one.'

CRACKING A CODE is like learning to roller-skate; once you know how to do it, it's easy. With a little help from Gerald Fletcher, who had provided a guided tour the night before, and a lot of help from Lou Kantor, who had generously provided the key, Carella was able to crack the code wide open—well, almost. Last night, he'd gone with Fletcher to Paddy's Bar and Grill, or PB&G under Andrew Hart's name; Fanny's, F under Sal Decotto; The Purple Chairs, Lou Kantor's TPC; and Quigley's Rest, QR for Richard Fenner on the list. Probably because of the fight, he hadn't taken Carella to The Saloon, TS under Michael Thornton's name—the place where Thornton had admitted first meeting Sarah.

Except, what the hell did TG mean, under all the names but Thornton's?'

By Carella's own modest estimate, he had been in more bars in the past twenty-four hours than he had in the past twenty-four years. He decided, nevertheless, to hit The Saloon that night.

The Saloon was just that. A cigarette-scarred bar behind which ran a mottled, flaking mirror; wooden booths with patched, fake leather seat cushions; bowls of pretzels and potato chips; jukebox gurgling; steamy bodies.

'They come in here,' the bartender said, 'at all hours of the night. Take yourself. You're here to meet a girl, am I right?'

'There *was* someone I was hoping to see. A girl named Sadie Collins. Do you know her?'

'Yeah. She used to come in a lot, but I ain't seen her in months. What do you want to fool around with her for?'

'Why? What's the matter with her?'

'You want to know something?' the bartender said. 'I thought she was a hooker at first. Aggressive. You know what that word means? Aggressive? She used to come dressed down to here and up to there, ready for action, selling everything she had, you understand? She'd come in here, pick out a guy she wanted, and go after him like the world was gonna end at midnight. And always the same type. Big guys. You wouldn't stand a chance with her, not that you ain't big, don't misunderstand me. But Sadie liked them gigantic, and mean. You know something?'

'What?'

'I'm glad she don't come in here any more. There was something about her— like she was compulsive. You know what that word means, compulsive?'

TUESDAY AFTERNOON, Arthur Brown handed in his surveillance report on Gerald Fletcher. Much of it was not at all illuminating. Prom 4.55pm to 8.45pm. Fletcher had driven home, and then to 812 North Crane and parked. The report *did* become somewhat illuminating when, at 8.46pm, Fletcher emerged from the building with a redheaded woman wearing a black fur coat over a green dress. They went to Rudolph's restaurant, ate, and drove back to 812 Crane, arrived at 10.35pm and went inside. Arthur Brown had checked the lobby mailboxes, which showed eight apartments on the eleventh floor, which was where the elevator indicator had stopped. Brown went outside to wait again, and Fletcher emerged alone at 11.40pm and drove home. Detective O'Brien relieved Detective Brown at 12.15am.

Byrnes said, 'This woman could be important.'

'That's just what I think,' Brown answered.

CARELLA HAD NOT yet spoken to either Sal Decotto or Richard Fenner, the two remaining people listed in Sarah's book, but saw no reason to pursue that trail any further. If the place listings in her book had been chronological, she'd gone from bad to worse in her search for partners.

Why? To give it back to her husband in spades? Carella tossed Sarah's little black book into the manila folder bearing the various reports on the case, and turned his attention to the information Artie Brown had brought in last night.

The redheaded woman's presence might be important, but Carella was still puzzling over Fletcher's behavior. Sarah's blatant infidelity provided Fletcher with a strong motive, so why take Carella to his wife's unhappy haunts, why *show* Carella that he had good and sufficient reason to kill her? Furthermore, why the offer to get a good defense attorney for the boy who had already been indicted for the slaying?

Sometimes Carella wondered who was doing what to whom.

At five o'clock that evening, Carella relieved Detective Hal Willis outside Fletcher's office building downtown, and then followed Fletcher to a department store in midtown Isola. Carella was wearing a false mustache stuck to his upper lip, a wig with hair longer than his own and of a different color, and a pair of sunglasses.

In the department store, he tracked Fletcher to the Intimate Apparel department. Carella walked into the next aisle, pausing to look at women's robes and kimonos, keeping one eye on Fletcher, who was in conversation with the lingerie salesgirl.

'May I help you, sir?' a voice said, and Carella turned to find a stocky woman at his elbow, with gray hair, black-rimmed spectacles, wearing army shoes and a black dress. Her suspicious smile accused him of being a junkie shoplifter or worse.

'Thank you, no,' Carella said. 'I'm just looking.'

Fletcher made his selections from the gossamer undergarments that the salesgirl had spread out on the counter, pointing first to one garment, then to another. The salesgirl wrote up the order and Fletcher reached into his wallet to give her either cash or a credit card; it was difficult to tell from an aisle away. He chatted with the girl a moment longer, and then walked off toward the elevator bank.

'Are you *sure* I can't assist you?' the woman in the army shoes said, and Carella answered, 'I'm positive,' and moved swiftly toward the lingerie counter. Fletcher had left the counter without a package in his arms, which meant he was *sending* his purchases. The salesgirl was gathering up Fletcher's selections and looked up when Carella reached the counter.

'Yes, sir,' she said. 'May I help you?'

Carella opened his wallet and produced his shield. 'Police officer,' he said. 'I'm interested in the order you just wrote up.'

The girl was perhaps nineteen years old, a college girl working in the store during the Christmas rush. Speechlessly, she studied the shield, eyes bugging.

'Are these items being sent?' Carella asked.

'Yes, *sir*,' the girl said. Her eyes were still wide. She wet her lips and stood up a little straighter, prepared to be a perfect witness.

'Can you tell me where?' Carella asked.

'Yes, *sir*,' she said, and turned the sales slip toward him. 'He wanted them wrapped separately, but they're all going to the same address. Miss Arlene Orton, 812 North Crane Street, right here in the city, and I'd guess it's a swell—'

'Thank you very much,' Carella said.

It felt like Christmas Day already.

THE MAN WHO PICKED the lock on Arlene Orton's front door ten minutes after she left her apartment on Wednesday morning, was better at it than any burglar in the city, and he happened to work for the Police Department. It took the technician longer to set up his equipment, but the telephone was the easiest of his jobs. The tap would become operative when the telephone company supplied the police with a list of so-called bridging points that located the pairs and cables for Arlene Orton's phone. The monitoring equipment would be hooked into these, and whenever a call went out of or came into the apartment, a recorder would automatically tape both ends of the conversation. In addition, whenever a call was made from the apartment, a dial indicator would ink out a series of dots that signified the number being called.

The technician placed his bug in the bookcase on the opposite side of the room. The bug was a small FM transmitter with a battery-powered mike that needed to be changed every twenty-four hours. The technician would have preferred running his own wires, but he dared not ask the building superintendent for an empty closet or workroom in which to hide his listener. A blabbermouth superintendent can kill an investigation more quickly than a squad of gangland goons.

In the rear of a panel truck parked at the curb some twelve feet south of the entrance to 812 North Crane, Steve Carella sat behind the recording equipment that was locked into the frequency of the bug. He sat hopefully, with a tuna sandwich and a bottle of beer, prepared to hear and record any sounds that emanated from Arlene's apartment.

At the bridging point seven blocks away and thirty minutes later, Arthur Brown sat behind equipment that was hooked into the telephone mike, and waited for Arlene Orton's phone to ring. He was in radio contact with Carella.

The first call came at 12.17pm. The equipment tripped in automatically and the spools of tape began recording the conversation, while Brown simultaneously monitored it through his headphone.

'Hello?'

'Hello, Arlene?'

'Yes, who's this?'

'Nan.'

'Nan? You sound so different. Do you have a cold or something?'

'Every year at this time. Just before the holidays. Arlene, I'm terribly rushed, I'll make this short. Do you know Beth's dress size?'

The conversation went on in that vein, and Arlene Orton spoke to three more girlfriends in succession. She then called the local supermarket to order the week's groceries. She had a fine voice, deep and forceful, punctuated every so often (when she was talking to her girlfriends) with a delightful giggle.

At 4.00pm, the telephone in Arlene's apartment rang again.

'Hello?'

'Arlene, this is Gerry.'

'Hello, darling.'

'I'm leaving here a little early. I thought I'd come right over.'

'Good.'

'I'll be there in, oh, half an hour, forty minutes.'

'Hurry.'

Brown radioed Carella at once. Carella thanked him, and sat back to wait.

ON THURSDAY MORNING, two days before Christmas, Carella sat at his desk in the squad room and looked over the transcripts of the five reels from the night before. The reel that interested him most was the second one. The conversation on that reel had at one point changed abruptly in tone and content. Carella thought he knew why, but he wanted to confirm his suspicion.

FLETCHER: 'I meant after the *holidays*, not the trial.'
MISS ORTON: 'I may be able to get away, I'm not sure. I'll have to check with my shrink.'
FLETCHER: 'What's he got to do with it?'
MISS ORTON: 'Well, I have to pay whether I'm there or not, you know.'
FLETCHER: 'Is he taking a vacation?'
MISS ORTON: 'I'll ask him.'
FLETCHER: 'Yes, ask him. Because I'd really like to get away.'
MISS ORTON: 'Ummm. When do you think the case (*inaudible*).'
FLETCHER: 'In March sometime. No sooner than that. He's got a new lawyer, you know.'
MISS ORTON: 'What does that mean, a new lawyer?'
FLETCHER: 'Nothing. He'll be convicted anyway.'
MISS ORTON: (*Inaudible*).
FLETCHER: 'Because the trial's going to take a lot out of me.'
MISS ORTON: 'How soon after the trial . . .?'
FLETCHER: 'I don't know.'
MISS ORTON: 'She's dead, Gerry, I don't see—'
FLETCHER: 'Yes, but—'
MISS ORTON: 'I don't see why we have to wait, do you?'
FLETCHER: 'Have you read this?'
MISS ORTON: 'No, not yet. Gerry. I think we ought to set a date now. A provisional date, depending on when the trial is. Gerry?'
FLETCHER: 'Mmmm?'

MISS ORTON: Do you think it'll be a terribly long, drawn-out trial?

FLETCHER: What?

MISS ORTON: Gerry?

FLETCHER: Yes?

MISS ORTON: Where are you?

FLETCHER: I was just looking over some of these books.

MISS ORTON: Do you think you can tear yourself away?

FLETCHER: Forgive me, darling.

MISS ORTON: If the trial starts in March, and we planned on April for it . . .

FLETCHER: Unless they come up with something unexpected, of course.

MISS ORTON: Like what?

FLETCHER: Oh, I don't know. They've got some pretty sharp people investigating this case.

MISS ORTON: What's there to investigate?

FLETCHER: There's always the possibility he didn't do it.

MISS ORTON: (*Inaudible*) A signed confession?

FLETCHER: One of the cops thinks I killed her.

MISS ORTON: You're not serious. Who?

FLETCHER: A detective named Carella. He probably knows about us by now. He's a very thorough cop. I have a great deal of admiration for him. I wonder if he realises that.

MISS ORTON: Where'd he even get such an idea?

FLETCHER: Well, I told him I hated her.

MISS ORTON: What? Gerry, why the hell did you do that?

FLETCHER: He'd have found out anyway. He probably knows by now that Sarah was sleeping around with half the men in this city. And he probably knows I knew it, too.

MISS ORTON: Who cares what he found out? Corwin's already confessed.

FLETCHER: I can understand his reasoning. I'm just not sure he can understand mine.

MISS ORTON: Some reasoning. If you were going to kill her, you'd have done it ages ago, when she refused to sign the separation papers. So let him investigate, who cares? Wishing your wife dead isn't the same thing as killing her. Tell that to Detective Copolla.

FLETCHER: Carella. (*Laughs*).

MISS ORTON: 'What's so funny?

FLETCHER: 'I'll tell him, darling.'

ACCORDING TO THE TECHNICIAN who had wired the Orton apartment, the living room bug was in the bookcase on the wall opposite the bar. Carella was interested in the tape from the time Fletcher had asked Arlene about a book—'Have you read this?'—and then seemed preoccupied. It was Carella's guess that Fletcher had discovered the bookcase bug. What interested Carella more, however, was what Fletcher had said *after* he knew the place was wired. Certain of an audience now, Fletcher had:

1. Suggested the possibility that Corwin was not guilty.
2. Flatly stated that a cop named Carella suspected him.
3. Expressed admiration for Carella, while wondering if Carella was aware of it.
4. Speculated that Carella had already doped out the purpose of the bar-crawling last Sunday night, was cognisant of Sarah's promiscuity, and knew Fletcher was aware of it.
5. Made a little joke about 'telling' Carella.

Carella felt as eerie as he had when lunching with Fletcher and later when drinking with him. Now he'd spoken, through the bug, directly to Carella. But what was he trying to say? And why?

Carella wanted very much to hear what Fletcher would say when he *didn't* know he was being overheard. He asked Lieutenant Byrnes for permission to request a court order to put a bug in Fletcher's automobile. Byrnes granted permission, and the court issued the order.

FLETCHER MADE A DATE with Arlene Orton to go to The Chandeliers across the river, and the bug was installed in Fletcher's 1972 car. If Fletcher left the city, the effective range of the transmitter on the open road would be about a quarter of a mile. The listener-pursuer had his work cut out for him.

By ten minutes to ten that night, Carella was drowsy and discouraged. On the way out to The Chandeliers, Fletcher and Arlene had not once mentioned Sarah nor the plans for their impending marriage. Carella was anxious to put them both to bed and get home to his family. When they finally came out of the restaurant and began walking toward Fletcher's automobile, Carella actually uttered an audible, 'At *last*,' and started his car.

They proceeded east on Route 701, heading for the bridge, and said nothing. Carella thought at first that something was wrong with the equipment, then finally Arlene spoke and Carella knew just what had happened. The pair had argued in the restaurant, and Arlene had been smoldering until this moment when she could no longer contain her anger.

'Maybe you don't want to marry me at all,' she shouted.

'That's ridiculous,' Fletcher said.

'Then why won't you set a date?'

'I have set a date.'

'You haven't set a date. All you've done is say after the trial. *When*, after the trial? Maybe this whole damn thing has been a stall. Maybe you *never* planned to marry me.'

'You know that isn't true, Arlene.'

'How do I know there really *were* separation papers?'

'There were. I told you there were.'

'Then why wouldn't she sign them?'

'Because she loved me.'

'If she loved you, then why did she do those horrible things?'

'To make me pay, I think.'

'Is that why she showed you her little black book?'

'Yes, to make me pay.'

'No. Because she was a slut.'

'I guess. I guess that's what she became.'

'Putting a little TG in her book every time she told you about a new one. *Told Gerry*, and marked a little TG in her book.'

'Yes, to make me pay.'

'A slut. You should have gone after her with detectives. Gotten pictures, threatened her, forced her to sign—'

'No, I couldn't have done that. It would have ruined me, Arl.'

'Your precious career.'

'Yes, my precious career.'

They both fell silent again. They were approaching the bridge now. Carella tried to stay close behind them, but on occasion the distance between the two cars lengthened and he lost some words in the conversation.

'She wouldn't sign the papers and I — adultery because — have come out.'

'And I thought—'

'I did everything I possibly could.'

'Yes, Gerry, but now she's dead. So what's your excuse now?'

'I'm suspected of having *killed* her, damn it!'

Fletcher was making a left turn, off the highway. Carella stepped on the accelerator, not wanting to lose voice contact now.

'What difference does that make?' Arlene asked.

'None at all, I'm sure,' Fletcher said. 'I'm sure you wouldn't mind at all being married to a convicted murderer.'

'What are you talking about?'

'I'm talking about the possibility . . . Never mind.'

'Let me hear it.'

'All right, Arlene. I'm talking about the possibility of someone accusing me of the murder. And of my having to stand trial for it.'

'That's the most paranoid—'

'It's not paranoid.'

'Then what is it? They've caught the murderer, they—'

'I'm only saying suppose. How could we get married if I killed her, if someone says I killed her?'

'No one has said that, Gerry.'

'Well, *if* someone should.'

Silence. Carella was dangerously close to Fletcher's car now, and risking discovery. Carella held his breath and stayed glued to the car ahead.

'Gerry, I don't understand this,' Arlene said, her voice low.

'Someone could make a good case for it.'

'Why would anyone do that? They know that Corwin—'

'They could say I came into the apartment and . . . They could say she was still alive when I came into the apartment. They could say the knife was still in her and I . . . I came in and found her that way and . . . finished her off.'

'Why would you do that?'

'To end it.'

'You wouldn't kill anyone, Gerry.'

'No.'

'Then why are you even suggesting such a terrible thing?'

'If she wanted it . . . If someone accused me . . . If someone said I'd done it . . . that I'd finished the job, pulled the knife across her belly, they could claim she *asked* me to do it.'

'What are you saying, Gerry?'

'I'm trying to explain that Sarah might have—'

'Gerry, I don't think I want to know.'

'I'm only trying to tell you—'

'No, I don't want to know. Please, Gerry, you're frightening me.'

'*Listen* to me, damn it! I'm trying to explain what *might* have happened. Is that so hard to accept? That she might have *asked* me to kill her?'

'Gerry, please, I—'

'I *wanted* to call the hospital, I was *ready* to call the hospital, don't you think I could *see* she wasn't fatally stabbed?'

'Gerry, please.'

'She begged me to kill her, Arlene, she begged me to end it for her, she . . . Damn it, can't *either* of you understand that? I tried to show him, I took him to all the places, I thought he was a man who'd understand. Is it that difficult?'

'Oh, my God, *did* you kill her? *Did* you kill Sarah?'

'No. Not Sarah. Only the woman she'd become, the slut I'd forced her to become. She was Sadie, you see, when I killed her—when she died.'

'Oh, my God,' Arlene said, and Carella nodded in weary acceptance.

Carella felt neither elated nor triumphant. As he followed Fletcher's car into the curb in front of Arlene's building, he experienced only a familiar nagging sense of repetition and despair. Fletcher was coming out of his car now, walking around to the curb side, opening the door for Arlene, who took his hand and stepped on to the sidewalk, weeping. Carella intercepted them before they reached the front door of the building. Quietly, he charged Fletcher with the murder of his wife, and made the arrest without resistance.

Fletcher did not seem at all surprised.

So IT WAS FINISHED, or at least Carella thought it was.

In the silence of his living room, the telephone rang at a quarter past one.

He caught the phone on the third ring.

'Hello?'

'Steve,' Lieutenant Byrnes said. 'I just got a call from Calcutta. Ralph Corwin hanged himself in his cell, just after midnight. Must have done it while we were still taking Fletcher's confession in the squad room.'

Carella was silent.

'Steve?' Byrnes said.

'Yeah, Pete.'

'Nothing,' Byrnes said, and hung up.

Carella stood with the dead phone in his hands for several seconds and then replaced it on the hook. He looked into the living room, where the lights of the tree glowed warmly, and thought of a despairing junkie in a prison cell, who had taken his own life without ever having known he had not taken the life of another.

It was Christmas day.

Sometimes none of it made any sense at all.

Marcia Muller
b. 1944

DEADLY FANTASIES

'**M**s McCone, I know what you're thinking. But I'm not paranoid. One of them—my brother or my sister—*is* trying to kill me!'

'Please, call me Sharon.' I said it to give myself time to think. The young woman seated across my desk at All Souls Legal Co-operative certainly sounded paranoid. My boss, Hank Zatin, had warned me about that when he'd referred her for private investigative services.

'Let me go over what you've told me, to make sure I've got it straight,' I said. 'Six months ago you were living here in the Mission district and working as a counselor for emotionally disturbed teenagers. Then your father died and left you his entire estate, something in the neighborhood of thirty million dollars.'

Laurie Newingham nodded and blew her nose. As soon as she'd come into my office she'd started sneezing. Allergies, she'd told me. To ease her watering eyes she'd popped out her contact lenses and stored them in their plastic case; in doing that she had spilled some of the liquid that the lenses soaked in over her fingers, then nonchalantly wiped them on her faded jeans. The gesture endeared her to me because I'm sloppy, too. Frankly, I couldn't imagine this freshly scrubbed young woman—she was about ten years younger than I, perhaps twenty-five—possessing a fortune. With her trim, athletic body, tanned, snub-nosed face, and carelessly styled blonde hair, she looked like a high school cheerleader. But Winfield Newingham had owned much of San Francisco's choice real estate, and Laurie had been the developer's youngest—and apparently favorite—child.

I went on, 'Under the terms of the will, you were required to move back into the family home in St Francis Wood. You've done so. The will also stipulated that your brother Dan and sister Janet can remain there as long as they wish. So you've been living with them, and they've both been acting hostile because you inherited everything.'

'Hostile? One of them wants to *kill* me! I keep having stomach cramps, throwing up—you know.'

'Have you seen a doctor?'

'I *hate* doctors! They're always telling me there's nothing wrong with me, when I know there is.'

'The police, then?'

'I like them a whole lot less than doctors. Besides, they wouldn't believe me.' Now she took out an inhaler and breathed deeply from it.

Asthma, as well as allergies, I thought. Wasn't asthma sometimes psychosomatic? Could the vomiting and other symptoms be similarly rooted?

'Either Dan or Janet is trying to poison me,' Laurie said, 'because if I die, the estate reverts to them.'

'Laurie,' I said, 'why did your father leave everything to you?'

'The will said it was because I'd gone out on my own and done something I believed in. Dan and Janet have always lived off him; the only jobs they've ever been able to hold down have been ones Dad gave them.'

'One more question: Why did you come to All Souls?' My employer is a legal services plan for people who can't afford the going rates.

Laurie looked surprised. 'I've *always* come here, since I moved to the Mission and started working as a counselor five years ago. I may be able to afford a downtown law firm, but I don't trust them anymore now than I did before I inherited the money. Besides, I talked it over with Dolph, and he said it would be better to stick with a known quantity.'

'Dolph?'

'Dolph Edwards. I'm going to marry him. He's director of the guidance center where I used to work—still work, as a volunteer.'

'That's the Inner Mission Self-Help Center?'

She nodded. 'Do you know them?'

'Yes.' The center offered a wide range of social services to a mainly Hispanic clientele—including job placement, psychological counseling, and short-term financial assistance. I'd heard that recently their programs had been drastically cut back due to lack of funding—as all too often happens in today's arid political climate.

'Then you know what my father meant about my having done something I believed in,' Laurie said. 'The center's a hopeless mess, of course; it's never been very well organised. But it's the kind of project I'd like to put my money to work for. After I marry Dolph I'll help him realise his dreams effectively—and in the right way.'

I nodded and studied her for a moment. She stared back anxiously. Laurie was emotionally ragged, I thought, and needed someone to look out for her. Besides, I identified with her in a way. At her age I'd also been the cheerleader type, and I'd gone out on my own and done something I believed in, too.

'Okay,' I said. 'What I'll do is talk with your brother and sister, feel the situation out. I'll say you've applied for a volunteer position here, counseling clients with emotional problems, and that you gave their names as character references.'

Her eyes brightened and some of the lines of strain smoothed. She gave me Dan's office phone number and Janet's private line at the St Francis Wood house. Preparing to leave, she clumsily dropped her purse on the floor. Then she located her contact case and popped a lens into her mouth to clean it; as she fitted it into her right eye, her foot nudged the bag, and the inhaler and a bottle of time-release vitamin capsules rolled across the floor. We went for them at the same time, and our heads grazed each other's.

She looked at me apologetically. One of her eyes was now gray, the other a brilliant blue from the tint of the contact. It was like a physical manifestation of her somewhat schizoid personality: down-to-earth wholesomeness warring with what I had begun to suspect was a dangerous paranoia.

DAN NEWINGHAM SAID, 'Why the hell does Laurie want to do that? She doesn't have to work anymore, even as a volunteer. She controls all the family's assets.'

We were seated in his office in the controller's department of Newingham Development, on the thirty-first floor of one of the company's financial district buildings. Dan was a big guy, with the same blond good looks as his sister, but they were spoiled by a petulant mouth and a body whose bloated appearance suggested an excess of good living.

'If she wants to work,' he added, 'there's plenty of positions she could fill right here. It's her company now, dammit, and she ought to take an interest in it.'

'I gather her interests run more to the social services.'

'More to the lowlife, you mean.'

'In what respect?'

Dan got up and went to look out the window behind the desk. The view of the bay was blocked by an upthrusting jumble of steel and plate glass—the legacy that firms such as Newingham Development had left a once old-fashioned and beautiful town.

After a moment Dan turned. 'I don't want to offend you, Ms . . . McCone, is it?' I nodded.

'I'm not putting down your law firm, or what you're trying to do,' he went on, 'but when you work on your end of the spectrum, you naturally have to associate with people who aren't quite . . . well, of our class. I wasn't aware of the kind of people Laurie was associating with during those years she didn't live at home, but now . . . her boyfriend, that Dolph, for instance. He's always around; I can't stand him. Anyway, my point is, Laurie should settle down now, come back to the real world, learn the business. Is that too much to ask in exchange for thirty million?'

'She doesn't seem to care about the money.'

Dan laughed harshly. 'Doesn't she? Then why did she move back into the house? She could have chucked the whole thing.'

'I think she feels she can use the money to benefit people who really need it.'

'Yes, and she'll blow it all. In a few years there won't be any Newingham Development. Oh, I know what was going through my father's mind when he made that will: Laurie's always been the strong one, the dedicated one. He thought that if he forced her to move back home, she'd eventually become involved in the business and there'd be real leadership here. Laurie can be very single-minded when she wants things to go a certain way, and that's what it takes to run a firm like this. But the sad thing is, Dad just didn't realise how far gone she is in her bleeding heart sympathies.'

'That aside, what do you think about her potential for counseling our disturbed clients?'

'If you really want to know, I think she'd be terrible. Laurie's a basket case. She has psychosomatic illnesses, paranoid fantasies. She needs counseling herself.'

'Can you describe these fantasies?'

He hesitated, tapping his fingers on the window frame. 'No, I don't think I care to. I shouldn't have brought them up.'

'Actually, Mr Newingham, I think I have an inkling of what they are. Laurie told her lawyer that someone's trying to poison her. She seemed obsessed with the idea, which is why we decided to check her references thoroughly.'

'I suppose she also told her lawyer who the alleged poisoner is?'

'In a way. She said it was either you or your sister Janet.'

'God, she's worse off than I realised. I suppose she claims one of us wants to kill her so he can inherit my father's estate. That's ridiculous—I don't need the damned money. I have a good job here, and I've invested profitably.' Dan paused, then added, 'I hope you can convince her to get into an intensive therapy program before she tries to counsel any of your clients. Her fantasies are starting to sound dangerous.'

JANET NEWINGHAM was the exact opposite of her sister: a tall brunette with a highly stylised way of moving and speaking. Her clothes were designer, her jewelry expensive, and her hair and nails told of frequent attention at the finest salons. We met at the St Francis Wood house—a great pile of stone reminiscent of an Italian villa that sat on a double lot near the fountain that crowned the area's main boulevard. I had informed Laurie that I would be interviewing her sister, and she had agreed to absent herself from the house; I didn't want my presence to trigger an unpleasant scene between the two of them.

I needn't have worried, however. Janet Newingham was one of those cool, reserved women who may smolder under the surface but seldom display anger. She seated me in a formal parlor overlooking the strip of park that runs down the center of St Francis Boulevard and served me coffee from a sterling silver pot. From all appearances, I might have been there to discuss the Junior League fashion show.

When I had gotten to the point of my visit, Janet leaned forward and extracted a cigarette from an ivory box on the coffee table. She took her time lighting it, then said, '*Another* volunteer position? It's bad enough she kept on working at that guidance center for nothing after they lost their federal funding last spring, but this . . . I'm surprised; I thought nothing would ever pry her away from her precious Dolph.'

'Perhaps she feels it's not a good idea to stay on there, since they plan to be married.'

'Did she tell you that? Laurie's always threatening to marry Dolph, but I doubt she ever will. She just keeps him around because he's her one claim to the exotic. He's one of these social reformers, you know. Totally devoted to his cause.'

'And what is that?'

'Helping people. Sounds very sixties, doesn't it? That center is his *raison d'être*. He founded it, and he's going to keep it limping along no matter what. He plays the crusader role to the hilt, Dolph does: dresses in Salvation Army cast-offs, drives a motorcycle. You know the type.'

'That's very interesting,' I said, 'but it doesn't have much bearing on Laurie's ability to fill our volunteer position. What do you think of her potential as a counselor?'

'Not a great deal. Oh, I know that's what she's been doing these past five years, but recently Laurie's been . . . a very disturbed young woman. But you know that. My brother told me of your visit to his office, and that you had already heard of her fantasy that one of us is trying to kill her.'

'Well, yes. It's odd—'

'It's not just odd, it's downright dangerous. Dangerous for her to walk around in such a paranoid state, and dangerous for Dan and me. It's our reputations she's smearing.'

'Because on the surface you both appear to have every reason to want her out of the way.'

Janet's lips compressed—a mild reaction, I thought, to what I'd implied. 'On the surface, I suppose that is how it looks,' she said. 'But as far as I'm concerned Laurie is welcome to our father's money. I had a good job in the public relations department in Newingham Development; I saved and invested my salary well.

After my father died, I quit working there, and I'm about to open my own public relations firm.'

'Did the timing of your quitting have anything to do with Laurie's inheriting the company?'

Janet picked up a porcelain ashtray and carefully stubbed her cigarette out. 'I'll be frank with you, Ms McCone: it did. Newingham Development had suddenly become not a very good place to work; people were running scared—they always do when there's no clear managerial policy. Besides . . .'

'Besides?'

'Since I'm being frank, I may as well say it. I did not want to work for my spoiled little bitch of a sister who's always had things her own way. And if that makes me a potential murderer—'

She broke off as the front door opened. We both looked that way. A man wearing a shabby tweed coat and a shocking purple scarf and aviator sunglasses entered. His longish black hair was windblown, and his sharp features were ruddy from the cold. He pocketed a key and started for the stairway.

'Laurie's not here, Dolph,' Janet said.

He turned. 'Where is she?'

'Gone shopping.'

'Laurie hates to shop.'

'Well, that's where she is. You'd better come back in a couple of hours.' Janet's tone did little to mask her dislike.

Nor did the twist of his mouth mask *his* dislike of his fiancée's sister. Without a word he turned and strode out the door.

I said, 'Dolph Edwards?'

'Yes. You can see what I mean.'

Actually, I hadn't seen enough of him, and I decided to take the opportunity to talk to him while it was presented. I thanked Janet Newingham for her time and hurried out.

DOLPH'S MOTORCYCLE was parked at the curb near the end of the front walk, and he was just revving it up when I reached him. At first his narrow lips pulled down in annoyance, but when I told him who I was, he smiled and shut the machine off. He remained astride it while we talked.

'Yes, I told Laurie it would be better to stick with All Souls,' he said when I mentioned the context in which I'd first heard of him. 'You've got good people there, and you're more likely to take Laurie's problem seriously than some downtown law firm.'

'You think someone *is* trying to kill her, then?'

'I know what I see. The woman's sick a lot lately, and those two'—he motioned at the house—'hate her guts.'

'You must see a great deal of what goes on here,' I said. 'I noticed you have a key.'

'Laurie's my fiancée,' he said with a puritanical stiffness that surprised me.

'So she said. When do you plan to be married?'

I couldn't make out his eyes behind the dark aviator glasses, but the lines around them deepened. Perhaps Dolph suspected what Janet claimed: that Laurie didn't really intend to marry him. 'Soon,' he said curtly.

We talked for a few minutes more, but Dolph could add little to what I'd already observed about the Newingham family. Before he started his bike he said apologetically, 'I wish I could help, but I'm not around them very much. Laurie and I prefer to spend our time at my apartment.'

I DIDN'T LIKE DAN or Janet Newingham, but I also didn't believe either was trying to poison Laurie. Still, I followed up by explaining the situation to my former lover and now good friend Greg Marcus, lieutenant with the SFPD homicide detail. Greg ran a background check on Dan for me, and came up with nothing more damning than a number of unpaid parking tickets. Janet didn't even have those to her discredit. Out of curiosity, I asked him to check on Dolph Edwards, too. Dolph had a record of two arrests involving political protests in the late seventies—just what I would have expected.

At that point I reported my findings to Laurie and advised her to ask her brother and sister to move out of the house. If they wouldn't, I said, she should talk to Hank about invalidating that clause of her father's will. And in any case she should also get herself some psychological counseling. Her response was to storm out of my office. And that, I assumed, ended my involvement with Laurie Newingham's problems.

But it didn't. Two weeks later Greg called to tell me that Laurie had been taken ill during a family cocktail party and had died at the St Francis Wood house, an apparent victim of poisoning.

I FELT TERRIBLE, thinking of how lightly I had taken her fears, how easily I'd accepted her brother's and sister's claims of innocence, how I'd let Laurie down when she'd needed and trusted me. So I waited until Greg had the autopsy results and then went to his office at the Hall of Justice.

'Arsenic,' Greg said when I'd seated myself on his visitor's chair. 'The murderer's perfect poison: widely available, no odor, little if any taste. It takes the body a long time to eliminate arsenic, and a person can be fed small amounts over a period of two or three weeks, even longer, before he or she succumbs. According to the medical examiner, that's what happened to Laurie.'

'But why small amounts? Why not just one massive dose? '

'The murderer was probably stupid enough that he figured if she'd been sick for weeks we wouldn't check for poisons. But why he went on with it after she started talking about someone trying to kill her . . .'

'He? Dan's your primary suspect, then?'

'I was using "he" generically. The sister looks good, too. They both had extremely strong motives, but we're not going to be able to charge either until we can find out how Laurie was getting the poison.'

'You say extremely strong motives. Is there something besides the money?'

'Something connected to the money; each of them seems to need it more badly than they're willing to admit. The interim management of Newingham Development has given Dan his notice; there'll be a hefty sever-ance payment, of course, but he's deeply in debt—gambling debts, to the kind of people who won't accept fifty-dollars-a-week installments. The sister had most of her savings tied up in one of those real estate investment partnerships; it went belly up, and Janet needs to raise additional cash to satisfy outstanding obligations to the other partners.'

'I wish I'd known about that when I talked with them. I might have pre-vented Laurie's death.'

Greg held up a cautioning hand. 'Don't blame yourself for something you could-n't know or foresee. That should be one of the cardinal rules of your profession.'

'It's one of the rules, all right, but I seem to keep breaking it. Greg, what about Dolph Edwards?'

'He didn't stand to benefit by her death. Laurie hadn't made her will, so everything reverts to the brother and sister.'

'No will? I'm surprised Hank didn't insist she make one.'

'According to your boss, she had an appointment with him for the day after she died. She mentioned something about a change in her circumstances, so I guess she was planning to make the will in favor of her future husband. Another reason we don't suspect Edwards.'

I sighed. 'So what you've got is a circumstantial case against one of two people.'

'Right. And without uncovering the means by which the poison got to her, we don't stand a chance of getting an indictment against either.'

'Well . . . the obvious means is in her food.'

'There's a cook who prepares all the meals. She, a live-in maid, and the family basically eat the same things. On the night she died, Laurie, her brother and sister, and Dolph Edwards all had the same hors d'oeuvres with cocktails. The leftovers tested negative.'

'And you checked what she drank, of course.'

'It also tested negative.'

'What about medications? Laurie probably took pills for her asthma. She had an inhaler—'

'We checked everything. Fortunately, I caught the call and remembered what you'd told me. I was more than thorough. Had the contents of the bedroom and bathroom inventoried, anything that could have contained poison was taken away for testing.'

'What about this cocktail party? I know for a fact that neither Dan nor Janet liked Dolph. And according to Dolph, they both hated Laurie. He wasn't fond of them, either. It seems like an unlikely group for a convivial gathering.'

'Apparently Laurie arranged the party. She said she had an announcement to make.'

'What was it?'

'No one knows. She died before she could tell them.'

THREE DAYS LATER Hank and I attended Laurie's funeral. It was in an old-fashioned churchyard in the little town of Tomales, near the bay of the same name northwest of San Francisco. The Newinghams had a summer home on the bay, and Laurie had wanted to be buried there.

It was one of those winter afternoons when the sky is clear and hard, and the sun is as pale as if it were filtered through water. Hank and I stood a little apart from the crowd of mourners on the knoll, near a windbreak of eucalyptus that bordered the cemetery. The people who had traveled from the city to lay Laurie to rest were an oddly assorted group: dark-suited men and women who repre-sented San Francisco's business community; others who bore the unmistakable stamp of high society; shabbily dressed Hispanics who must have been clients of the Inner Mission Self-Help Center. Dolph Edwards arrived on his motorcycle; his inappropriate attire—the shocking purple scarf seemed several shades too festive—annoyed me.

Dan and Janet Newingham arrived in the limousine that followed the hearse and walked behind the flower-covered casket to the graveside. Their pious pro-priety annoyed me, too. As the service went on, the wind rose. It rustled the leaves of the eucalyptus trees and brought with it dampness and the odor of the nearby sea. During the final prayer, a strand of my hair escaped the knot I'd fas-tened it in and blew across my face. It clung damply there, and when I licked my lips to push it away, I tasted salt—whether from the sea air or tears, I couldn't tell.

As soon as the service was concluded, Janet and Dan went back to the limou-sine and were driven away. One of the Chicana women stopped to speak to Hank; she was a client, and he introduced us. When I looked around for Dolph, I found he had disappeared. By the time Hank finished chatting with his client, the only other person left at the graveside besides us and the cemetery workers was an old Hispanic lady who was placing a single rose on the casket.

Hank said, 'I could use a drink.' We started down the uneven stone walk, but I glanced back at the old woman, who was following us unsteadily.

'Wait,' I said to Hank and went to take her arm as she stumbled.

The woman nodded her thanks and leaned on me, breathing heavily.

'Are you all right?' I asked. 'Can we give you a ride back to the city?' My old MG was the only car left beyond the iron fence.

'Thank you, but no,' she said. 'My son brought me. He's waiting down the street, there's a bar. You were a friend of Laurie?'

'Yes.' But not as good a friend as I might have been, I reminded myself. 'Did you know her through the center?'

'Yes. She talked with my grandson many times and made him stay in school when he wanted to quit. He loved her, we all did.'

'She was a good woman. Tell me, did you see her fiancé leave?' I had wanted to give Dolph my condolences.

The woman looked puzzled.

'The man she planned to marry—Dolph Edwards.'

'I thought he was her husband.'

'No, although they planned to marry soon.'

The old woman sighed. 'They were always together. I thought they were already married. But nowadays, who can tell? My son—Laurie helped his own son, but is he grateful? No. Instead of coming to her funeral, he sits in a bar. . . '

I WAS SILENT on the drive back to the city—so silent that Hank, who is usually oblivious to my moods, asked me twice what was wrong. I'm afraid I snapped at him, something to the effect of funerals not being my favorite form of entertainment, and when I dropped him at All Souls, I refused to have the drink he offered. Instead I went downtown to City Hall.

WHEN I ENTERED Greg Marcus's office at the Hall of Justice a couple of hours later, I said without preamble, 'The Newingham. case: you told me you inventoried the contents of Laurie's bedroom and bathroom and had anything that could have contained poison taken away for testing?'

'. . . Right.'

'Can I see the inventory sheet?'

He picked up his phone and asked for the file to be brought in. While he waited, he asked me about the funeral. Over the years, Greg had adopted a wait-and-see attitude toward my occasional interference in his cases. I've never been sure whether it's because he doesn't want to disturb what he considers to be my shaky thought processes, or that he simply prefers to leave the hard work to me.

When the file came, he passed it to me. I studied the inventory sheet, uncertain exactly what I was looking for. But something was missing there. What? I flipped the pages, then wished I hadn't. A photo of Laurie looked up at me, brilliant blue eyes blank and lifeless. No more cheerleader out to save the world—

Quickly I flipped back to the inventory sheet. The last item was "1 handbag, black leather, & contents." I looked over the list of things from the bathroom again and focused on the word *unopened*.

'Greg,' I said, 'what was in Laurie's purse?'

He took the file from me and studied the list. 'It should say here, but it doesn't. Sloppy work—new man on the squad.'

'Can you find out?'

Without a word he picked up the phone receiver, dialed, and made the inquiry. When he hung up he read off the notes he'd made. 'Wallet. Checkbook. Inhaler, sent to lab. Vitamin capsules, also sent to lab. Contact lens case. That's all.'

'That's enough. The contact lens case is a two-chambered plastic receptacle holding about half an ounce of fluid for the lenses to soak in. There was a brand-new, unopened bottle of the fluid on the inventory of Laurie's bathroom.'

'So?'

'I'm willing to bet the contents of that bottle will test negative for arsenic; the surface of it might or might not show someone's fingerprints, but not Laurie's. That's because the murderer put it there *after* she died, but *before* your people arrived on the scene.'

Greg merely waited.

'Have the lab test the liquid in that lens case for arsenic. I'm certain the results will be positive. The killer added arsenic to Laurie's soaking solution weeks ago, and then he removed that bottle and substituted the unopened one. We wondered why slow poisoning, rather than a massive dose; it was because the contact case holds so little fluid.'

'Sharon, arsenic can't be ingested through the eyes—'

'Of course it can't! But Laurie had the habit, as lots of contact wearers do—you're not supposed to, of course; it can cause eye infections—of taking her lenses out of the case and putting them into her mouth to clean before putting them on. She probably did it a lot because she had allergies and took the lenses off to rest her eyes. That's how he poisoned her, a little at a time over an extended period.'

'Dan Newingham?'

'No. Dolph Edwards.'

Greg waited, his expression neither doubting nor accepting.

'Dolph is a social reformer,' I said. 'He founded that Inner Mission Self-Help Center; it's his whole life. But its funding has been canceled and it can't go on much longer. In Janet Newingham's words, Dolph is intent on keeping it going "no matter what".'

'So? He was going to marry Laurie. She could have given him plenty of money—'

'Not for the center. She told me it was a "hopeless mess." When she married Dolph, she planned to help him, but in the "right way." Laurie has been described to me by both her brother and sister as quite single-minded and always getting what she wanted. Dolph must have realised that too, and knew her money would never go for his self-help center.'

'All right, I'll take your word for that. But Edwards still didn't stand to benefit.' They weren't married, she hadn't made a will—'

'They *were* married. I checked that out at City Hall a while ago. They were married last month, probably at Dolph's insistence when he realised the poisoning would soon have a fatal effect.'

Greg was silent for a moment. I could tell by the calculating look in his eyes that he was taking my analysis seriously. 'That's another thing we slipped up on—just like not listing the contents of her purse. What made you check?'

'I spoke with an old woman who was at the funeral. She thought they were married and made the comment that nowadays you can't tell. It got me thinking. . . Anyway, it doesn't matter about the will because under California's community property laws, Dolph inherits automatically in the absence of one.'

'It seems stupid of him to marry her so soon before she died. The husband automatically comes under suspicion—'

'But the poisoning started long *before* they were married. That automatically threw suspicion on the brother and sister.'

'And Dolph had the opportunity.'

'Plenty. He even tried to minimise it by lying to me: he said he and Laurie didn't spend much time at the St Francis Wood house, but Dan described Dolph as being around all the time. And even if he wasn't he could just as easily have poisoned her lens solution at his own apartment. He told another unnecessary lie to you when he said he didn't know what the announcement Laurie was going to make at the family gathering was. It could only have been the announcement of their secret marriage. He may even have increased the dosage of poison, in the hope she'd succumb before she could reveal it.'

'Why do you suppose they kept it secret?'

'I think Dolph wanted it that way. It would minimise the suspicion directed at him if he just let the fact of the marriage come out after either Dan or Janet had been charged with the murder. He probably intended to claim ignorance of the community property laws, say he'd assumed since there was no will he couldn't inherit. Why don't we ask him if I'm right?'

Greg's hand moved toward his phone. 'Yes—why don't we?'

WHEN DOLPH EDWARDS confessed to Laurie's murder, it turned out that I'd been absolutely right. He also added an item of further interest: he hadn't been in love with Laurie at all, had had a woman on the Peninsula whom he planned to marry as soon as he could without attracting suspicion.

It was too bad about Dolph; his kind of social crusader had so much ego tied up in their own individual projects that they lost sight of the larger objective. Had Laurie lived, she would have applied her money to any number of worthy causes, but now it would merely go to finance the lifestyles of her greedy brother and sister.

But it was Laurie I felt worst about. And it was a decidedly bittersweet satisfaction that I took in solving her murder, in fulfilling my final obligation to my client.

Baroness Orczy

1865–1947

THE MAN IN THE INVERNESS CAPE

1

I HAVE HEARD MANY people say—people, too, mind you, who read their daily paper regularly—that it is quite impossible for anyone to 'disappear' within the confines of the British Isles. At the same time these wise people invariably admit one great exception to their otherwise unimpeachable theory, and that is the case of Mr Leonard Marvell, who, as you know, walked out one afternoon from the Scotia Hotel in Cromwell Road and has never been seen or heard of since.

Information had originally been given to the police by Mr Marvell's sister Olive, a Scotchwoman of the usually accepted type: tall, bony, with sandy-coloured hair, and a somewhat melancholy expression in her blue-grey eyes.

Her brother, she said, had gone out on a rather foggy afternoon. I think it was the 3rd of February, just about a year ago. His intention had been to go and consult a solicitor in the City—whose address had been given him recently by a friend—about some private business of his own.

Mr Marvell had told his sister that he would get a train at South Kensington Station to Moorgate Street, and walk thence to Finsbury Square. She was to expect him home by dinner-time.

As he was, however, very irregular in his habits, being fond of spending his evenings at restaurants and music-halls, the sister did not feel the least anxious when he did not return home at the appointed time. She had her dinner in the *table d'hôte* room, and went to bed soon after ten.

She and her brother occupied two bedrooms and a sitting-room on the second floor of the little private hotel. Miss Marvell, moreover, had a maid always with her, as she was somewhat of an invalid. This girl, Rosie Campbell, a nice-looking Scotch lassie, slept on the top floor.

It was only on the following morning, when Mr Leonard did not put in an appearance at breakfast, that Miss Marvell began to feel anxious. According to her own account, she sent Rosie in to see if anything was the matter, and the girl, wide-eyed and not a little frightened, came back with the news that Mr Marvell was not in his room, and that his bed had not been slept in that night.

With characteristic Scottish reserve, Miss Olive said nothing about the matter at the time to anyone, nor did she give information to the police until two days later, when she herself had exhausted every means in her power to discover her brother's whereabouts.

She had seen the lawyer to whose office Leonard Marvell had intended going that afternoon, but Mr Statham, the solicitor in question, had seen nothing of the missing man.

With great adroitness Rosie, the maid, had made inquiries at South Kensington and Moorgate Street stations. At the former, the booking clerk, who knew Mr Marvell by sight, distinctly remembered selling him a first-class ticket to one of the City stations in the early part of the afternoon; but at Moorgate Street, which is a very busy station, no one recollected seeing a tall, red-haired Scotchman in an Inverness cape—such was the description given of the missing man. By that time the fog had become very thick in the City; traffic was disorganised, and everyone felt fussy, ill-tempered, and self-centred.

These, in substance, were the details which Miss Marvell gave to the police on the subject of her brother's strange disappearance.

At first she did not appear very anxious; she seemed to have great faith in Mr Marvell's power to look after himself; moreover, she declared positively that her brother had neither valuables nor money about his person when he went out that afternoon.

But as day succeeded day and no trace of the missing man had yet been found, matters became more serious, and the search instituted by our fellows at the Yard waxed more keen.

A description of Mr Leonard Marvell was published in the leading London and provincial dailies. Unfortunately, there was no good photograph of him extant, and descriptions are apt to prove vague.

Very little was known about the man beyond his disappearance, which had rendered him famous. He and his sister had arrived at the Scotia Hotel about a month previously, and subsequently they were joined by the maid Campbell.

Scotch people are far too reserved ever to speak of themselves or their affairs to strangers. Brother and sister spoke very little to anyone at the hotel. They had their meals in their sitting room, waited on by the maid, who messed with the staff. But, in face of the present terrible calamity, Miss Marvell's frigidity relaxed before the police inspector, to whom she gave what information she could about her brother.

'He was like a son to me,' she explained with scarcely restrained tears, 'for we lost our parents early in life, and as we were left very, very badly off, our relations took but little notice of us. My brother was years younger than I am—and though he was a little wild and fond of pleasure, he was as good as gold to me, and has supported us both for years by journalistic work. We came to London from Glasgow about a month ago, because Leonard got a very good appointment on the staff of the *Daily Post*.'

All this, of course, was soon proved to be true; and although, on minute inquiries being instituted in Glasgow, but little seemed to be known about Mr

Leonard Marvell in that city, there seemed no doubt that he had done some reporting for the *Courier*, and that latterly, in response to an advertisement, he had applied for and obtained regular employment on the *Daily Post*.

The latter enterprising halfpenny journal, with characteristic magnanimity, made an offer of £50 reward to any of its subscribers who gave information which would lead to the discovery of the whereabouts of Mr Leonard Marvell.

But time went by, and that £50 remained unclaimed.

2

LADY MOLLY had not seemed as interested as she usually was in cases of this sort. With strange flippancy—wholly unlike herself—she remarked that one Scotch journalist more or less in London did not vastly matter.

I was much amused, therefore, one morning about three weeks after the mysterious disappearance of Mr Leonard Marvell, when Jane, our little parlourmaid, brought in a card accompanied by a letter.

The card bore the name 'Miss Olive Marvell'. The letter was the usual formula from the chief, asking Lady Molly to have a talk with the lady in question, and to come and see him on the subject after the interview.

With a smothered yawn my dear lady told Jane to show in Miss Marvell.

'There are two of them, my lady,' said Jane, as she prepared to obey.

'Two what?' asked Lady Molly with a laugh.

'Two ladies, I mean,' explained Jane.

'Well! Show them both into the drawing room,' said Lady Molly, impatiently.

Then, as Jane went off on this errand, a very funny thing happened; funny, because during the entire course of my intimate association with my dear lady, I had never known her act with such marked indifference in the face of an obviously interesting case. She turned to me and said:

'Mary, you had better see these two women, whoever they may be; I feel that they would bore me to distraction. Take note of what they say, and let me know. Now, don't argue,' she added with a laugh, which peremptorily put a stop to my rising protest, 'but go and interview Miss Marvell and Co.'

Needless to say, I promptly did as I was told, and the next few seconds saw me installed in our little drawing room, saying polite preliminaries to the two ladies who sat opposite to me.

I had no need to ask which of them was Miss Marvell. Tall, ill-dressed in deep black, with a heavy crape veil over her face, and black cotton gloves, she looked the uncompromising Scotchwoman to the life. In strange contrast to her depressing appearance, there sat beside her an over-dressed, much behatted, peroxided young woman, who bore the stamp of *the* profession all over her pretty, painted face.

Miss Marvel, I was glad to note, was not long in plunging into the subject which had brought her here.

'I saw a gentleman at Scotland Yard,' she explained, after a short preamble, 'because Miss—er—Lulu Fay came to me at the hotel this very morning with a story which, in my opinion, should have been told to the police directly my brother's disappearance became known, and not three weeks later.'

The emphasis which she laid on the last few words, and the stern look with which she regarded the golden-haired young woman beside her, showed the disapproval with which the rigid Scotchwoman viewed any connection which her brother might have had with the lady, whose very name seemed unpleasant to her lips.

Miss—er—Lulu Fay blushed even through her rouge, and turned a pair of large, liquid eyes imploringly upon me.

'I—I didn't know. I was frightened,' she stammered.

'There's no occasion to be frightened now,' retorted Miss Marvell, 'and the sooner you try and be truthful about the whole matter, the better it will be for all of us.'

And the stern woman's lips closed with a snap, as she deliberately turned her back on Miss Fay and began turning over the leaves of a magazine which happened to be on a table close to her hand.

I muttered a few words of encouragement, for the little actress looked ready to cry. I spoke as kindly as I could, telling her that if indeed she could throw some light on Mr Marvell's present whereabouts it was her duty to be quite frank on the subject.

She 'hem'-ed and 'ha'-ed for a while, and her simpering ways were just beginning to tell on my nerves, when she suddenly started talking very fast.

'I am principal boy at the Grand,' she explained with great volubility; 'and I knew Mr Leonard Marvell well—in fact—er—he paid me a good deal of attention and—'

'Yes—and—?' I queried, for the girl was obviously nervous.

There was a pause. Miss Fay began to cry.

'And it seems that my brother took this young—er—lady to supper on the night of February 3rd, after which no one has ever seen or heard of him again,' here interposed Miss Marvell, quietly.

'Is that so?' I asked.

Lulu Fay nodded, whilst heavy tears fell upon her clasped hands.

'But why did you not tell this to the police three weeks ago?' I ejaculated, with all the sternness at my command.

'I—I was frightened,' she stammered.

'Frightened? Of what?'

'I am engaged to Lord Mountnewte and—'

'And you did not wish him to know that you were accepting the attentions of Mr Leonard Marvell—was that it? Well,' I added, with involuntary impatience, 'what happened after you had supper with Mr Marvell?'

'Oh! I hope—I hope that nothing happened,' she said through more tears; 'we had supper at the Trocadero, and he saw me into my brougham. Suddenly, just as I was driving away, I saw Lord Mountnewte standing quite close to us in the crowd.'

'Did the two men know one another?' I asked.

'No,' replied Miss Fay; 'at least, I didn't think so, but when I looked back through the window of my carriage I saw them standing on the kerb talking to each other for a moment, and then walk off together towards Piccadilly Circus. That is the last I have seen of either of them,' continued the little actress with a fresh flood of tears. 'Lord Mountnewte hasn't spoken to me since, and Mr Marvell has disappeared with my money and my diamonds.'

'Your money and your diamonds?' I gasped in amazement.

'Yes; he told me he was a jeweller, and that my diamonds wanted resetting. He took them with him that evening, for he said that London jewellers were clumsy thieves, and that he would love to do the work for me himself. I also gave him two hundred pounds, which he said he would want for buying the gold and platinum required for the settings. And now he has disappeared—and my diamonds—and my money! Oh! I have been very—very foolish—and—'

Her voice broke down completely. Of course, one often hears of the idiocy of girls giving money and jewels unquestioningly to clever adventurers who know how to trade upon their inordinate vanity. There was, therefore, nothing very out of the way in the story just told me by Miss—er—Lulu Fay, until the moment when Miss Marvell's quiet voice, with its marked Scotch burr, broke in upon the short silence which had followed the actress's narrative.

'As I explained to the chief detective inspector at Scotland Yard,' she said calmly, 'the story which this young—er—lady tells is only partly true. She may have had supper with Mr Leonard Marvell on the night of February 3rd, and he may have paid her certain attentions; but he never deceived her by telling her that he was a jeweller, nor did he obtain possession of her diamonds and her money through false statements. My brother was the soul of honour and loyalty. If, for some reason which Miss—er—Lulu Fay chooses to keep secret, he had her jewels and money in his possession on the fatal February 3rd, then I think his disappearance is accounted for. He has been robbed and perhaps murdered.'

Like a true Scotchwoman she did not give way to tears. but even her harsh voice trembled slightly when she thus bore witness to her brother's honesty, and expressed the fears which assailed her as to his fate.

Imagine my plight! I could ill forgive my dear lady for leaving me in this unpleasant position—a sort of peacemaker between two women who evidently hated one another, and each of whom was trying her best to give the other 'the lie direct'.

I ventured to ring for our faithful Jane and to send her with an imploring message to Lady Molly, begging her to come and disentangle the threads of this muddled skein with her clever fingers; but Jane returned with a curt note from my dear lady, telling me not to worry about such a silly case, and to bow the two women out of the flat as soon as possible and then come for a nice walk.

I wore my official manner as well as I could, trying not to betray the 'prentice hand. Of course, the interview lasted a great deal longer, and there was considerably more talk than I can tell you of in a brief narrative. But the gist of it all was just as I have said. Miss Lulu Fay stuck to every point of the story which she had originally told Miss Marvell. It was the latter uncompromising lady who had immediately marched the younger woman off to Scotland Yard in order that she might repeat her tale to the police. I did not wonder that the chief promptly referred them both to Lady Molly.

Anyway, I made excellent shorthand notes of the conflicting stories which I heard; and I finally saw, with real relief, the two women walk out of our little front door.

3

MISS—ER—LULU FAY, mind you, never contradicted in any one particular the original story which she had told me, about going out to supper with Leonard Marvell, entrusting him with £200 and the diamonds, which he said he would have reset for her, and seeing him finally in close conversation with her recognised *fiancé*, Lord Mountnewte. Miss Marvell, on the other hand, very commendably refused to admit that her brother acted dishonestly towards the girl. If he had her jewels and money in his possession at the time of his disappearance, then he had undoubtedly been robbed, or perhaps murdered, on his way back to the hotel, and if Lord Mountnewte had been the last to speak to him on that fatal night, then Lord Mountnewte must be able to throw some light on the mysterious occurrence.

Our fellows at the Yard were abnormally active. It seemed, on the face of it, impossible that a man, healthy, vigorous, and admittedly sober, should vanish in London between Piccadilly Circus and Cromwell Road without leaving the slightest trace of himself or of the valuables said to have been in his possession.

Of course, Lord Mountnewte was closely questioned. He was a young Guardsman of the usual pattern, and, after a great deal of vapid talk which irritated Detective Inspector Saunders not a little, he made the following statement:

'I certainly am acquainted with Miss Lulu Fay. On the night in question I was standing outside the Troc, when I saw this young lady at her own carriage window talking to a tall man in an Inverness cape. She had, earlier in the day, refused my invitation to supper, saying that she was not feeling very well, and would go home directly after the theatre; therefore I felt, naturally, a little vexed. I was just about to hail a taxi, meaning to go on to the club, when, to my intense astonishment, the man in the Inverness cape came up to me and asked me if I could tell him the best way to get back to Cromwell Road.'

'And what did you do?' asked Saunders.

'I walked a few steps with him and put him on his way,' replied Lord Mountnewte, blandly.

In Saunders' own expressive words, he thought that story 'fishy'. He could not imagine the arm of coincidence being quite so long as to cause these two men—who presumably were both in love with the same girl, and who had just met at a moment when one of them was obviously suffering pangs of jealousy—to hold merely a topographical conversation with one another. But it was equally difficult to suppose that the eldest son and heir of the Marquis of Loam should murder a successful rival and then rob him in the streets of London.

Moreover, here came the eternal and unanswerable questions: if Lord Mountnewte had murdered Leonard Marvell, where and how had he done it, and what had he done with the body?

I dare say you are wondering by this time why I have said nothing about the maid, Rosie Campbell.

Well, plenty of very clever people (I mean those who write letters to the papers and give suggestions to every official department in the kingdom) thought that the police ought to keep a very strict eye upon that pretty Scotch lassie. For she was very pretty, and had quaint, demure ways which rendered her singularly attractive, in spite of the fact that, for most masculine tastes, she would have been considered too tall. Of course, Saunders and Danvers kept an eye on her—you may be sure of that—and got a good deal of information about her from the people at the hotel. Most of it, unfortunately, was irrelevant to the case. She was maid-attendant to Miss Marvell, who was feeble in health, and who went out but little. Rosie waited on her master and mistress upstairs, carrying their meals to their private room, and doing their bedrooms. The rest of the day she was fairly free, and was quite sociable downstairs with the hotel staff.

With regard to her movements and actions on that memorable 3rd of February, Saunders—though he worked very hard—could glean but little useful information. You see, in an hotel of that kind, with an average of thirty to forty guests at one time, it is extremely difficult to state positively what any one person did or did not do on that particular day.

Most people at the Scotia remembered that Miss Marvell dined in the *table d'hôte* room on that 3rd of February; this she did about once a fortnight, when her maid had an evening 'out'.

The hotel staff also recollected fairly distinctly that Miss Rosie Campbell was not in the steward's room at supper-time that evening, but no one could remember definitely when she came in.

One of the chambermaids who occupied the bedroom adjoining hers, said that she heard her moving about soon after midnight; the hall porter declared that he saw her come in just before half-past twelve when he closed the doors for the night.

But one of the ground-floor valets said that, on the morning of the 4th, he saw Miss Marvell's maid, in hat and coat, slip into the house and upstairs, very quickly and quietly, soon after the front doors were opened, namely, about 7 a.m.

Here, of course, was a direct contradiction between the chambermaid and hall porter on the one side, and the valet on the other, whilst Miss Marvel said that Campbell came into her room and made her some tea long before seven o'clock every morning, including that of the 4th.

I assure you our fellows at the Yard were ready to tear their hair out by the roots, from sheer aggravation at this maze of contradictions which met them at every turn.

The whole thing seemed so simple. There was nothing 'to it' as it were, and but very little real suggestion of foul play, and yet Mr Leonard Marvel had disappeared, and no trace of him could be found.

Everyone now talked freely of murder. London is a big town, and this would not have been the first instance of a stranger—for Mr Leonard Marvell was practically a stranger in London—being enticed to a lonely part of the city on a foggy night, and there done away with and robbed, and the body hidden in an out-of-the-way cellar, where it might not be discovered for months to come.

But the newspaper reading public is notably fickle, and Mr Leonard Marvell was soon forgotten by everyone save the chief and the batch of our fellows who had charge of the case.

Thus I heard through Danvers one day that Rosie Campbell had left Miss Marvell's employ, and was living in rooms in Findlater Terrace, near Walham Green.

I was alone in our Maida Vale flat at the time, my dear lady having gone to spend the weekend with the Dowager Lady Loam, who was an old friend of hers; nor, when she returned, did she seem any more interested in Rosie Campbell's movements than she had been hitherto.

Yet another month went by, and I for one had absolutely ceased to think of the man in the Inverness cape, who had so mysteriously and so completely vanished in the very midst of busy London, when one morning early in January, Lady Molly made her appearance in my room, looking more like the landlady of a disreputable gambling-house than anything else I could imagine.

'What in the world—?' I began.

'Yes! I think I look the part,' she replied, surveying with obvious complacency the extraordinary figure which confronted her in the glass.

My dear lady had on a purple cloth coat and skirt of a peculiarly vivid hue, and of a singular cut, which made her matchless figure look like a sack of potatoes. Her soft brown hair was quite hidden beneath a 'transformation', of that yellow-reddish tint only to be met with in very cheap dyes.

As for her hat! I won't attempt to describe it. It towered above and around her face, which was plentifully covered with brick-red and with that kind of powder which causes the cheeks to look a deep mauve.

My dear lady looked, indeed, a perfect picture of appalling vulgarity.

'Where are you going in this elegant attire?' I asked in amazement.

'I have taken rooms in Findlater Terrace,' she replied lightly. 'I feel that the air of Walham Green will do us both good. Our amiable, if somewhat slatternly, landlady expects us in time for luncheon. You will have to keep rigidly in the background, Mary, all the while we are there. I said that I was bringing an invalid niece with me, and, as a preliminary, you may as well tie two or three thick veils over your face. I think I may safely promise that you won't be dull.'

And we certainly were not dull during our brief stay at 34, Findlater Terrace, Walham Green. Fully equipped, and arrayed in our extraordinary garments, we duly arrived there, in a rickety four-wheeler, on the top of which were perched two seedy-looking boxes.

The landlady was a toothless old creature, who apparently thought washing a quite unnecessary proceeding. In this she was evidently at one with every one of her neighbours. Findlater Terrace looked unspeakably squalid; groups of dirty children congregated in the gutters and gave forth discordant shrieks as our cab drove up.

Through my thick veils I thought that, some distance down the road, I spied a horsy-looking man in ill-fitting riding-breeches and gaiters, who vaguely reminded me of Danvers.

Within half an hour of our installation, and whilst we were eating a tough steak over a doubtful tablecloth, my dear lady told me that she had been waiting a full month, until rooms in this particular house happened to be vacant. Fortunately the population in Findlater Terrace is always a shifting one, and Lady Molly had kept a sharp eye on No. 34, where, on the floor above, lived Miss Rosie Campbell. Directly the last set of lodgers walked out of the ground-floor rooms, we were ready to walk in.

My dear lady's manners and customs, whilst living at the above aristocratic address, were fully in keeping with her appearance. The shrill, rasping voice which she assumed echoed from attic to cellar.

One day I heard her giving vague hints to the landlady that her husband, Mr Marcus Stein, had had a little trouble with the police about a small hotel which he had kept somewhere near Fitzroy Square, and where 'young gentlemen used to come and play cards of a night'. The landlady was also made to understand that the worthy Mr Stein was now living temporarily at His Majesty's expense, whilst Mrs Stein had to live a somewhat secluded life, away from her fashionable friends.

The misfortunes of the pseudo Mrs Stein in no way marred the amiability of Mrs Tredwen, our landlady. The inhabitants of Findlater Terrace care very little about the antecedents of their lodgers, so long as they pay their week's rent in advance, and settle their 'extras' without much murmur.

This Lady Molly did, with a generosity characteristic of an ex-lady of means. She never grumbled at the quantity of jam and marmalade which we were supposed to have consumed every week, and which anon reached titanic proportions. She tolerated Mrs Tredwen's cat, tipped Ermyntrude—the tousled lodging-house slavey—lavishly, and lent the upstairs lodger her spirit-lamp and curling-tongs when Miss Rosie Campbell's got out of order.

A certain degree of intimacy followed the loan of those curling-tongs. Miss Campbell, reserved and demure, greatly sympathised with the lady who was not on the best of terms with the police. I kept steadily in the background. The two ladies did not visit each other's rooms, but they held long and confidential conversations on the landings, and I gathered, presently, that the pseudo Mrs Stein had succeeded in persuading Rosie Campbell that, if the police were watching No. 34, Findlater Terrace, at all, it was undoubtedly on account of the unfortunate Mr Stein's faithful wife.

I found it a little difficult to fathom Lady Molly's intentions. We had been in the house over three weeks, and nothing whatever had happened. Once I ventured on a discreet query as to whether we were to expect the sudden reappearance of Mr Leonard Marvell.

'For if that's all about it,' I argued, 'then surely the men from the Yard could have kept the house in view, without all this inconvenience and masquerading on our part.'

But to this tirade my dear lady vouchsafed no reply.

She and her newly acquired friend were, about this time, deeply interested in the case known as the 'West End Shop Robberies', which no doubt you recollect, since they occurred such a very little while ago. Ladies who were shopping in the large drapers' emporiums during the crowded and busy sale time, lost reticules, purses, and valuable parcels, without any trace of the clever thief being found.

The drapers, during sale-time, invariably employ detectives in plain clothes to look after their goods, but in this case it was the customers who were robbed, and the detectives, attentive to every attempt at 'shop-lifting', had had no eyes for the more subtle thief.

I had already noticed Miss Rosie Campbell's keen look of excitement whenever the pseudo Mrs Stein discussed these cases with her. I was not a bit surprised, therefore, when, one afternoon at about tea time, my dear lady came home from her habitual walk, and, at the top of her shrill voice, called out to me from the hall:

'Mary! Mary! they've got the man of the shop robberies. He's given the silly police the slip this time, but they know who he is now, and I suppose they'll get him presently. Tisn't anybody I know,' she added, with that harsh, common laugh which she had adopted for her part.

I had come out of the room in response to her call, and was standing just outside our own sitting room door. Mrs Tredwen, too, bedraggled and unkempt, as usual, had sneaked up the area steps, closely followed by Ermyntrude.

But on the half-landing just above us the trembling figure of Rosie Campbell, with scared white face and dilated eyes, looked on the verge of a sudden fall.

Still talking shrilly and volubly, Lady Molly ran up to her, but Campbell met her halfway, and the pseudo Mrs Stein, taking vigorous hold of her wrist, dragged her into our own sitting room.

'Pull yourself together, now,' she said with rough kindness; 'that owl Tredwen is listening, and you needn't let her know too much. Shut the door, Mary. Lor'bless you, m'dear, I've gone through worse scares than these. There! you just lie down on this sofa a bit. My niece'll make you a cup o' tea; and I'll go and get an evening paper, and see what's going on. I suppose you are very interested in the shop robbery man, or you wouldn't have took on so.'

Without waiting for Campbell's contradiction to this statement, Lady Mary flounced out of the house.

Miss Campbell hardly spoke during the next ten minutes that she and I were left alone together. She lay on the sofa with eyes wide open, staring up at the ceiling, evidently still in a great state of fear.

I had just got tea ready when Lady Molly came back. She had an evening paper in her hand, but threw this down on the table directly she came in.

'I could only get an early edition,' she said breathlessly, 'and the silly thing hasn't got anything in it about the matter.'

She drew near to the sofa, and, subduing the shrillness of her voice, she whispered rapidly, bending down towards Campbell:

'There's a man hanging about at the corner down there. No, no; it's not the police,' she added quickly, in response to the girl's sudden start of alarm. 'Trust me, my dear, for knowing a 'tec when I see one! Why, I'd smell one half a mile off. No; my opinion is that it's your man, my dear, and that he's in a devil of a hole.'

'Oh! he oughtn't to come here,' ejaculated Campbell in great alarm. 'He'll get me into trouble and do himself no good. He's been a fool!' she added, with a fierceness wholly unlike her usual demure placidity, 'getting himself caught like that. Now I suppose we shall have to hook it—if there's time.'

'Can I do anything to help you?' asked the pseudo Mrs Stein. 'You know I've been through all this myself, when they was after Mr Stein. Or perhaps Mary could do something.'

'Well, yes,' said the girl, after a slight pause, during which she seemed to be gathering her wits together; 'I'll write a note, and you shall take it, if you will, to a friend of mine—a lady who lives in the Cromwell Road. But if you still see a man lurking about at the corner of the street, then, just as you pass him, say the word "Campbell", and if he replies "Rosie," then give *him* the note. Will you do that?'

'Of course I will, my dear. Just you leave it all to me.'

And the pseudo Mrs Stein brought ink and paper and placed them on the table. Rosie Campbell wrote a brief note, and then fastened it down with a bit of sealing-wax before she handed it over to Lady Molly. The note was addressed to Miss Marvell, Scotia Hotel, Cromwell Road.

'You understand?' she said eagerly. 'Don't give the note to the man unless he says "Rosie" in reply to the word "Campbell." '

'All right—all right!' said Lady Molly, slipping the note into her reticule. 'And you go up to your room, Miss Campbell; it's no good giving that old fool Tredwen too much to gossip about.'

Rosie Campbell went upstairs, and presently my dear lady and I were walking rapidly down the badly lighted street.

'Where is the man?' I whispered eagerly as soon as we were out of earshot of No. 34.

'There is no man,' replied Lady Molly, quickly.

'But the West End shop thief?' I asked.

'He hasn't been caught yet, and won't be either, for he is far too clever a scoundrel to fall into an ordinary trap.'

She did not give me time to ask further questions, for presently, when we had reached Reporton Square, my dear lady handed me the note written by Campbell, and said:

'Go straight on to the Scotia Hotel, and ask for Miss Marvell; send up the note to her, but don't let her see you, as she knows you by sight. I must see the chief first, and will be with you as soon as possible. Having delivered the note, you must hang about outside as long as you can. Use your wits; she must not leave the hotel before I see her.'

There was no hansom to be got in this elegant quarter of the town, so, having parted from my dear lady, I made for the nearest Underground station, and took a train for South Kensington.

Thus it was nearly seven o'clock before I reached the Scotia. In answer to my inquiries for Miss Marvell, I was told that she was ill in bed and could see no one. I replied that I had only brought a note for her, and would wait for a reply.

Acting on my dear lady's instructions, I was as slow in my movements as ever I could be, and was some time in finding the note and handing it to a waiter, who then took it upstairs.

Presently he returned with the message: 'Miss Marvell says there is no answer.'

Whereupon I asked for pen and paper at the office, and wrote the following brief note on my own responsibility, using my wits as my dear lady had bidden me to do.

'Please, madam,' I wrote, 'will you send just a line to Miss Rosie Campbell? She seems very upset and frightened at some news she has had.'

Once more the waiter ran upstairs, and returned with a sealed envelope, which I slipped into my reticule.

Time was slipping by very slowly. I did not know how long I have to wait about outside in the cold, when, to my horror, I heard a hard voice, with a marked Scotch accent, saying:

'I am going out, waiter, and shan't be back to dinner. Tell them to lay a little cold supper upstairs in my room.'

The next moment Miss Marvell, with coat, hat, and veil, was descending the stairs.

My plight was awkward. I certainly did not think it safe to present myself before the lady; she would undoubtedly recollect my face. Yet I had orders to detain her until the appearance of Lady Molly.

Miss Marvell seemed in no hurry. She was putting on her gloves as she came downstairs. In the hall she gave a few more instructions to the porter, whilst I, in a dark corner in the background, was vaguely planning an assault or an alarm of fire.

Suddenly, at the hotel entrance, where the porter was obsequiously holding open the door for Miss Marvell to pass through, I saw the latter's figure stiffen; she took one step back as if involuntarily, then, equally quickly, attempted to dart across the threshold, on which a group—composed of my dear lady, of Saunders, and of two or three people scarcely distinguishable in the gloom beyond—had suddenly made its appearance.

Miss Marvell was forced to retreat into the hall; already I had heard Saunders's hurriedly whispered words:

'Try and not make a fuss in this place, now. Everything can go off quietly, you know.'

Danvers and Cotton, whom I knew well, were already standing one each side of Miss Marvell, whilst suddenly amongst this group I recognised Fanny, the wife of Danvers, who is one of our female searchers at the Yard.

'Shall we go up to your own room?' suggested Saunders.

'I think that is quite unnecessary,' interposed Lady Molly. 'I feel convinced that Mr Leonard Marvell will yield to the inevitable quietly, and follow you without giving any trouble.'

Marvell, however, did make a bold dash for liberty. As Lady Molly had said previously, he was far too clever to allow himself to be captured easily. But my dear lady had been cleverer. As she told me subsequently, she had from the first suspected that the trio who lodged at the Scotia Hotel were really only a duo—namely, Leonard Marvell and his wife. The latter impersonated a maid most of the time; but among these two clever people the three characters were interchangeable. Of course, there was no Miss Marvell at all. Leonard was alternately dressed up as man or woman, according to the requirements of his villainies.

'As soon as I heard that Miss Marvell was very tall and bony,' said Lady Molly, 'I thought that there might be a possibility of her being merely a man in disguise. Then there was the fact—but little dwelt on by either the police or public—that no one seems ever to have seen brother and sister together, nor was the entire trio ever seen at one and the same time.

'On that 3rd of February Leonard Marvell went out. No doubt he changed his attire in a lady's waiting room at one of the railway stations; subsequently he came home, now dressed as Miss Marvell, and had dinner in the *table d'hôte* room so as to set up a fairly plausible alibi. But ultimately it was his wife, the pseudo Rosie Campbell, who stayed indoors that night, whilst he, Leonard Marvell, when going out after dinner, impersonated the maid until he was clear of the hotel; then he reassumed his male clothes once more, no doubt in the deserted waiting room of some railway station, and met Miss Lulu Fay at supper, subsequently returning to the hotel in the guise of the maid.

'You see the game of criss-cross, don't you? This interchanging of characters was bound to baffle everyone. Many clever scoundrels have assumed disguises, sometimes impersonating members of the opposite sex to their own, but never before have I known two people play the part of three. Thus, endless contradictions followed as to the hour when Campbell the maid went out and when she came in, for at one time it was she herself who was seen by the valet, and at another it was Leonard Marvel dressed in her clothes.'

He was also clever enough to accost Lord Mountnewte in the open street, thus bringing further complications into this strange case.

After the successful robbery of Miss Fay's diamonds, Leonard Marvell and his wife parted for a while. They were waiting for an opportunity to get across the Channel and there turn their booty into solid cash. Whilst Mrs Marvell, *alias* Rosie Campbell, led a retired life in Findlater Terrace, Leonard kept his hand in with West End shop robberies.

Then Lady Molly entered the lists. As usual, her scheme was bold and daring; she trusted her own intuition and acted accordingly.

When she brought home the false news that the author of the shop robberies had been spotted by the police, Rosie Campbell's obvious terror confirmed her suspicions. The note written by the latter to the so-called Miss Marvell, though it contained nothing in any way incriminating, was the crowning certitude that my dear lady was right, as usual, in all her surmises.

And now Mr Leonard Marvell will be living for a couple of years at the tax-payers' expense; he has 'disappeared' temporarily from the public eye.

Rosie Campbell—*i.e.* Mrs Marvell—has gone to Glasgow. I feel convinced that two years hence we shall hear of the worthy couple again.

Ellery Queen

MYSTERY AT THE LIBRARY OF CONGRESS

ELLERY RESPONDED to Inspector Terence Fineberg's invitation with pleasure. Fineberg, in charge of the Central Office, was one of Inspector Queen's ancient beat-buddies, and he used to slip Ellery candy bars. He detested amateur detectives, so the old mink must be desperate.

'Park it,' Inspector Fineberg said, blowing hot and cold. 'You know Inspector Pete Santoria of the Narcotics Squad?'

Ellery nodded to the stone-jawed Narcotics man.

'Well skip the protocol, Ellery,' Fineberg went on, gnashing his dentures. 'Calling you in wasn't our idea. The big brass thought this case could use your screwb—your God-given talents.'

'I'm ever at the beck of the law enforcement arm,' Ellery said kindly, 'especially when it's grasping at straws. You may fire when ready, Finey.'

'The buck,' Fineberg shouted to Inspector Santoria, 'is yours.'

Santoria said in tooth-sucking tones, 'We got a line on a new dope ring, Queen. The junk is coming in, we think, from France, and in kilo lots. New York is the distribution depot. None of the lower echelons knows any of the others except the few in immediate contact. We want the big boy on the New York end. That this gang aren't regulars is about all we know for sure!'

'Of course they're no regulars,' the Central Office head grumbled. 'Who ever heard of a regular dope-running crumbum who could read?'

'Read?' Ellery came to a point like a bird-dog. 'Read what, Finey?'

'Books, for gossakes!'

'Don't tell me we authors are now being blamed for the narcotics traffic, too,' Ellery said coldly. 'How do books come into this?'

'Using 'em as a code!' Terence Fineberg implored the ceiling to witness. 'An information-passing operation is going on down in Washington that's an intermediate step between shipment and delivery. The Federal Bureau of Narcotics got on the trail of the D.C. members of the ring—two of 'em, anyway—and they're both being watched.'

'One of the two,' Inspector Santoria took it up, 'is a colorless little shnook named Balcom who works for a Washington travel agency. He used to be a high school English teacher. The other—a girl named Norma Shuffing—is employed at the Library of Congress.'

'The Library's being used as the contact rendezvous?'

'Yes. Balcom's job is to pass along the information as to when, where, and how a new shipment is coming into New York. The contact to whom he has to pass the information is identified for Balcom by the Shuffing girl. They play it cool—a different contact is used every time.'

Ellery shrugged. 'All you have to do is spot one as the Shuffing girl points him out to Balcom—'

'Yes, sir, Mr Queen,' the Narcotics chief said, sounding like the Witch in *Hansel and Gretel*. 'Want a go at it?'

'Just what takes place?' Ellery asked intently.

Inspector Fineberg's glance quelled Santoria. 'Balcom visits the Library only when the girl is on duty—she works out of the main desk filling call slips and bringing the books onto the floor. Balcom takes either Desk One Forty-seven or, if that's occupied, the nearest one that's vacant. When Shuffing spies him she brings him some books conforming to slips filled out by her in advance. It's the titles of the books that tip him off—she never communicates with him in any other way.'

'Titles,' Ellery said, nuzzling the word. 'What does Balcom do?'

'He looks the books over, then takes an easy gander around his immediate neighborhood. And that's all. After that he just sits there reading, doesn't take his eyes off his books, till closing time, when he gets up and goes home.'

'The Library bit is just so Balcom can identify the messenger,' Inspector Santoria said. 'The actual passage of the information is made at a different meet.'

'But if Balcom's being watched—'

'He works for a travel agency, I told you! Any idea how many people he comes in contact with daily?'

'We figure it works like this, Ellery,' the Central Office head explained. 'After a session at the Library—the next morning, say—the messenger that this Norma Shuffing identified for Balcom through the book titles shows up at the travel agency as a customer. Balcom recognises him and passes him a legitimate ticket envelope, only it contains not just plane or railroad tickets, but the dope shipment info, too.'

'And if you could spot one of these contacts—'

'We could track Balcom's message to its destination. That would be Big Stuff himself, who's sure as hell covered behind a smart front here in New York.'

A contact and shipment, Ellery learned, occurred about once every ten days. The Federals had set up their first stakeout a month before, and at that time Miss Shuffing had brought three books to Balcom's desk.

'What were they?'

Inspector Santoria fished a report from a folder. 'Steve Allen's *The Funny Men*, Count Leo Tolstoy's *War and Peace*, and Sigmund Freud's *Interpretation of Dreams*.'

'Lovely!' Ellery murmured. 'Allen, Tolstoy, Freud. Well.' He seemed disappointed. 'It's simple enough. A kindergarten acrostic—'

'Sure,' Terence Fineberg retorted. 'F for Freud, A for Allen, T for Tolstoy. F-A-T. There was a three-hundred-pound character sitting near Balcom.'

'The trouble was,' Santoria said, 'the Feds and we weren't on to the system that first time, and by the time we'd figured it out the fat guy had already got his info from Balcom and taken off.'

'What about the second contact?'

'Three books again. Chekhov's *The Cherry Orchard*, George R. Stewart's *Fire*, and Ben Hecht's *Actor's Blood*.'

'C-S-H. No acrostic there. Changed the system . . .' Ellery frowned. 'Must be in the titles—something in common . . . Was there an American Indian sitting near Balcom on that visit? Or someone with red hair?'

'Quick, isn't he, Pete?' Inspector Fineberg asked sourly. 'Yeah, we saw that— cherries, fire, blood are all red. It was an old dame with dyed red hair sitting a couple seats from Balcom. Only again we doped it out too late to cover the actual contact. The third time we missed clean.'

'Ah, couldn't find the common denominator.'

'What common denominator?' Santoria asked angrily. 'You got to have at least two items for that!'

'There was only one book the third time?'

'Right! I still say the doll got suspicious and never brought the other books. But do you think the brass would listen to me? No, they got to call in a screwb— an expert!'

'The thing is, Ellery,' Inspector Fineberg said, 'we do have evidence that a third shipment was picked up, which means a contact *was* made after that one-book deal.'

'They did it some other way, Terence!' Santoria snapped.

'Sure, Pete, sure,' Fineberg said soothingly. 'I go along with you. Only the brass don't. They want Brains working on this. Who are we to reason why?'

'What was the book?' Ellery asked.

'Rudyard Kipling's *The Light That Failed*.'

Santoria growled. 'We waited around the whole damn afternoon while people came and went—what a turnover they get down there—and our boy Balcom sits there at Desk One Forty-seven reading the Kipling book from cover to cover like he was enjoying it!'

'*The Light That Failed* was about a man who went blind. Was there someone in the vicinity wearing dark glasses, or immersed in a volume of Braille?'

'No blind people, no cheaters, no Braille, no nothing.'

Ellery mused. 'Do you have a written report of that visit?'

Santoria dug out another folder. Ellery glanced through it. It was a detailed account of the third Balcom-Shuffing contact, complete with descriptions of suspects, unclassified incidents, and so on. Ellery emerged from this rubble bearing a nugget.

'Of course,' he said gently. 'The one book by Kipling was all Balcom needed that day. A saintly-looking old gent wearing a clerical collar was consulting a card catalogue within view of Balcom and absently filled his pipe. He was flipping the wheel of his pocket lighter—flipped it unsuccessfully several times, it says here, boys—when a guard walked over and stopped him. The old fellow apologised for his absent-mindedness, put the lighter and pipe away, and went on consulting the index cards. *The Light That Failed*.'

'Lemme see that!' Fineberg snatched the folder, red in the face. 'Pete,' he howled, 'how the devil did we miss that?'

'We thought sure there'd be more books, Terence,' Inspector Santoria stammered. 'And the old guy was a preacher—'

'The old guy was a phony! Look, Ellery, maybe you can help us at that. We've been slow on the uptake—books yet! If on the next meet you could be sitting near Balcom and spot the contact man right away—how about it?'

'You couldn't keep me out of this with a court order, Finey,' Ellery assured him. 'What's more, it won't cost the City of New York a plugged subway token—I'll pay my own expenses to Washington. Can you arrange it with the Feds?'

INSPECTOR FINEBERG arranged it with the Feds, and on Monday of the following week Ellery was snugged down one desk behind and to the right of Desk 147 in the main reading room of the venerable gray Renaissance building east of the Capitol in downtown Washington. One of his fellow stakeout men, a balding Federal Narcotics agent named Hauck, who looked like a senior accountant in a wholesale drygoods firm, was parked in the outermost concentric circle of desks, near the entrance; they could signal each other by a half turn of the head. Another Federal agent and Inspector Santoria lounged around outside making like camera bugs.

Ellery's desk was loaded with reference books, for he was being an Author in Search of Material, a role he had often played at the Library of Congress in earnest.

He had filed his slips at the main desk with Norma Shuffing, whose photo— along with Balcom's—he had studied at the Federal Bureau.

When she brought the books to his desk he was able to get a close look. Tense and sad-looking, she was a pretty, dark-eyed girl who had been at some pains to camouflage her prettiness. Ellery wondered how she had come to be mixed up in an international dope operation; she could not have been more than twenty years old.

The little travel agent, Balcom, did not appear that day. Ellery had not expected him to, for the Federal men had said that Balcom visited the Library only on his days off, which were unpredictable. Today he was reported swamped at the office by a tidal wave of travel orders.

'But it's got to be soon, Queen,' Inspector Santoria said Monday night in Ellery's room at the Hotel Mayflower. 'Tomorrow's the eleventh day since the last meet, and they've never gone this long before.'

'Balcom may not be able to get away from his office.'

'He'll manage it,' Agent Hauck said grimly.

Early the next morning Ellery's phone rang. It was Santoria. 'I just got the word from Hauck. It's today.'

'How's Balcom managing it?'

'He's reported out sick. Better get on over to the Library.'

NORMA SHUFFING was bringing Ellery an armful of books when a little man with mousy eyes and mousy hair, dressed in a mousy business suit, pat-patted past Ellery's desk and slipped into the seat of Desk 147.

Ellery did not need Hauck's pencil-to-nose signal to identify the newcomer. It was Balcom.

The Shuffing girl passed Desk 147 without a glance. She placed Ellery's books softly before him and returned to her station. Ellery began to turn pages.

It was fascinating to watch them. Balcom and the girl might have inhabited different planets. Balcom stared at the encircling walls, the very picture of a man waiting. Not once did he look toward the main desk. There, her back to him, the pretty girl was quietly busy.

The reading room began to fill.

Ellery continued to study the two of them from above his book. Balcom had his dainty hands clasped on his desk now; he seemed to be dozing. Norma Shuffing was fetching books, working on the floor dozens of feet away.

A quarter of an hour passed.

Ellery sneaked an inventory of the readers in the vicinity. To Balcom's left sat a buxom woman in a smart strawberry silk suit; she wore bifocals and was raptly reading a volume of industrial reports.

To Balcom's right a very large man with wrestler's shoulders and no hair was absorbed in a three-volume set on African lovebirds.

Beyond the bird-lover a sloppily dressed Latin who looked like Fidel Castro's double was making secretive notes from some ancient *National Geographic*s.

Near the Cuban-looking man sat a thin elongated lady with a lavender-rinse hairdo who reminded Ellery of Miss Hildegarde Withers; she was intent on the *Congressional Record*.

Also in the neighborhood were a scowling young priest who was leafing through a book on demonology; a Man of Distinction with a gray crew-cut and an egg-spattered necktie who was frankly dozing, and a young lady with hearing-aid eyeglasses and some blue ink on one nostril who was coping something from a book on naval ordnance as if her life depended on it.

Suddenly the Shuffing girl started up the aisle. She was carrying a thick, oversized book.

Ellery turned a page. Was this it?

It was!

Miss Shuffing paused at Desk 147, placed the book deftly before Balcom, and walked away.

Balcom unclasped his little hands and opened the book to the title page.

The Complete Shakespeare.

The Complete Shakespeare?

Balcom began to idle through the volume. He made no attempt to survey his fellow readers.

Shakespeare . . . Some relevant quotation? Not likely, with thousands to cull.

Ellery concentrated.

Plays? A playwright? An actor? Nothing about anyone in the vicinity suggested the theater. Moreover, Balcom seemed obviously to be waiting.

Ten minutes later Miss Shuffing silently laid another book on Desk 147 and as silently took herself off. This time Balcom reached for the book with something like eagerness. Ellery craned.

Shaw . . . Shaw's *Man and Superman*.

A playwright again! But how could you make an instant identification of a playwright—or an actor, for that matter? Ellery glanced about under the pretext of stretching. No one within eyeshot was even reading a play.

Shakespeare—Shaw. Initials? S, S. SS! An ex-Nazi Storm Trooper? The big bald wrestlerish character who was interested in African lovebirds? Possibly, but how could anyone be sure? It had to be something Balcom could interpret with certainty at a glance. Besides, the fellow didn't look Teutonic, but Slavic.

Shakespeare, Shaw . . . English literature. An Englishman? No one Ellery could see looked English, although any of them might be. Besides, Shaw was really Irish.

Man and Superman? Somehow that didn't fit in with Shakespeare.

Ellery shook his head. What the deuce was the girl trying to convey to Balcom?

Balcom was now reading Shaw with concentration. But then he had to keep doing something. Was he waiting for another volume? Or would he soon look around and spot the contact?

If he does, Ellery thought with exasperation, he's a better man than I am!

But Balcom did not look up from the Shaw book. He was showing no curiosity about his neighbors, so Ellery decided that he was expecting another book . . .

Yes, a third book was coming!

The Shuffing girl placed it on Desk 147. Ellery could barely contain himself.

He read the title almost simultaneously with Balcom, blessing his sharp eyesight.

Personal Memoirs of U.S. Grant.

Blam went his theories! Shakespeare and Shaw, playwrights; Grant, a military man. S, S, now G. One Englishman, one Irishman, one American.

What did it all add up to?

Ellery couldn't think of a thing. He could feel Agent Hauck's eyes boring critical holes in his back.

And the minutes went bucketing by.

He now studied Balcom with ferocity. Did the three books mean anything to *him*? Not yet. Balcom was in trouble, too, as he pretended to glance through the Grant autobiography. Puzzlement showed in every slightest movement.

Shakespeare . . . Shaw . . . General Grant . . .

Balcom had it!

He was now looking around casually, his gaze never lingering, as if one glimpse was all he needed.

Ellery struggled with panic. Any moment Balcom's contact might get up and leave, knowing Balcom had spotted him. People were constantly coming and going; it would be impossible to identify the right one without the clue conveyed by the books. Ellery could already hear Inspector Santoria's horse laugh . . .

And then—O blessed!—he had it, too!

Ellery rose. He plucked his hat from the desk, strolled up the aisle past Agent Hauck, who had chewed his pencil eraser to crumbs, and went out into the Washington sunshine.

Inspector Santoria and the other Federal man were seated in an unmarked car now, and Ellery slipped into the rear seat.

'Well?' the Federal man demanded. The Feds had been polite, but skeptical, over the New York brass's inspiration.

'Wait for Hauck!'

Agent Hauck came out two minutes later. He paused near the car to light a cigarette, and Ellery said, 'Get set for the tail. The contact is sitting two seats over to Balcom's right in the same row. He's the sloppy little Cuban type.'

'AFTERNOON, FINEY,' Ellery said on Friday of that week. Don't tell me. You're stumped again.'

'No, no, haha, sit down, my boy,' Inspector Terence Fineberg said cordially. 'You're ace-high around here! Thought you'd like to know Pete Santoria collared Big Stuff two hours ago in the act of taking possession of a shipment of H. The Feds are out right now picking up Balcom and the girl. By the way, that little Havana number who led us to him was never closer to Cuba than an El Stinko cigar. He's a poolroom punk name of Harry Hummelmayer from the Red Hook section of Brooklyn.'

Ellery nodded unenthusiastically. The spirit of the chase had long since left him. 'Well, Finey, congratulations and all that. Was there something else? I have a date with four walls and an empty typewriter!'

'Wait, Ellery, for gossakes! I've been going Nutsville trying to figure out a connection between Shakespeare, Shaw, and old man Grant. Even knowing the contact was Hummelmayer, I can't see what the three have in common.'

'With Hummelmayer looking like Fidel Castro?' Ellery reached over the desk and, gripping Inspector Fineberg's knotty chin firmly, waggled it. 'Beards, Finey, beards.'

Ian Rankin
b. 1960

CONCRETE EVIDENCE

'IT'S AMAZING what you find in these old buildings,' said the contractor, a middle-aged man in safety helmet and overalls. Beneath the overalls lurked a shirt and tie, the marks of his station. He was the chief, the gaffer. Nothing surprised him any more, not even unearthing a skeleton.

'Do you know,' he went on, 'in my time, I've found everything from ancient coins to a pocket watch. How old do you reckon he is then?'

'We're not even sure it is a he, not yet. Give us a chance, Mr Beesford.'

'Well, when can we start work again?'

'Later on today.'

'Must be gey old though, eh?'

'How do you make that out?'

'Well, it's got no clothes on, has it? They've perished. Takes time for that to happen, plenty of time . . .'

Rebus had to concede, the man had a point. Yet the concrete floor beneath which the bones had been found . . . *it* didn't look so old, did it? Rebus cast an eye over the cellar again. It was situated a storey or so beneath road-level, in the basement of an old building off the Cowgate. Rebus was often in the Cowgate; the mortuary was just up the road. He knew that the older buildings here were a veritable warren; long narrow tunnels ran here, there, and, it seemed, every-where, semicylindrical in shape and just about high enough to stand up in. This present building was being given the full works—gutted, new drainage system, rewiring. They were taking out the floor in the cellar to lay new drains and also because there seemed to be damp—certainly there was a fusty smell to the place and its cause needed to be found.

They were expecting to find old drains, open drains perhaps. Maybe even a trickle of a stream, something which would lead to damp. Instead, their pneumatic drills found what remained of a corpse, perhaps hundreds of years old. Except, of course, for that concrete floor. It couldn't be more than fifty or sixty years old, could it? Would clothing deteriorate to a visible noth-ing in so short a time? Perhaps the damp could do that. Rebus found the cellar oppressive. The smell, the shadowy lighting provided by portable lamps, the dust.

But the photographers were finished, and so was the pathologist, Dr Curt. He didn't have too much to report at this stage, except to comment that he preferred it when skeletons were kept in cupboards, not confined to the cellar. They'd take the bones away, along with samples of the earth and rubble around the find, and they'd see what they would see.

'Archaeology's not really my line,' the doctor added. 'It may take me some time to bone up on it.' And he smiled his usual smile.

IT TOOK SEVERAL DAYS for the telephone call to come. Rebus picked up the receiver.

'Hello?'

'Inspector Rebus? Dr Curt here. About our emaciated friend.'

'Yes?'

'Male, five feet ten inches tall, probably been down there between thirty and thirty-five years. His left leg was broken at some time, long before he died. It healed nicely. But the little finger on his left hand had been dislocated and it did *not* heal so well. I'd say it was crooked all his adult life. Perfect for afternoon tea in Morningside.'

'Yes?' Rebus knew damned well Curt was leading up to something. He knew, too, that Curt was not a man to be hurried.

'Tests on the soil and gravel around the skeleton show traces of human tissue, but no fibres or anything that might have been clothing. No shoes, socks, underpants, nothing. Altogether, I'd say he was buried there in the altogether.'

'But did he die there?'

'Can't say.'

'All right, what did he die *of*?'

There was an almost palpable smile in Curt's voice. 'Inspector, I thought you'd never ask. Blow to the skull, a blow of considerable force to the back of the head. Murder I'd say. Yes, definitely murder.'

THERE WERE, OF COURSE, ways of tracing the dead, of coming to a near infallible identification. But the older the crime, the less likely this outcome became. Dental records, for example. They just weren't *kept* in the fifties and sixties the way they are today. A dentist practising then would most probably be playing near-full-time golf by now. And the record of a patient who hadn't been in for his check-up since 1960? Discarded, most probably. Besides, as Dr Curt pointed out, the man's teeth had seen little serious work, a few fillings, a single extraction.

The same went for medical records, which didn't stop Rebus from checking. A broken left leg, a dislocated left pinkie. Maybe some aged doctor would recall? But then again, maybe not. Almost certainly not. The local papers and radio were interested, which was a bonus. They were given what information the police had, but no memories seemed to be jogged as a result.

Curt had said he was no archaeologist; well, Rebus was no historian either. He knew other cases—contemporary cases—were yammering for his attention. The files stacked up on his desk were evidence enough of that. He'd give this one a few days, a few hours of his time. When the dead ends started to cluster around him, he'd drop it and head back for the here and now.

Who owned the building back in the 1950s? That was easy enough to discover: a wine importer and merchant. Pretty much a one-man operation, Hillbeith Vintners had held the premises from 1948 until 1967. And yes, there was a Mr Hillbeith, retired from the trade and living over in Burntisland, with a house gazing out across silver sands to the grey North Sea.

He still had a cellar, and insisted that Rebus have a 'wee taste' from it. Rebus got the idea that Mr Hillbeith liked visitors—a socially acceptable excuse for a drink. He took his time in the cellar (there must have been over 500 bottles in there) and emerged with cobwebs hanging from his cardigan, holding a dusty bottle of something nice. This he opened and set on the mantelpiece. It would be half an hour or so yet at the very least before they could usefully have a glass.

Mr Hillbeith was, he told Rebus, seventy-four. He'd been in the wine trade for nearly half a century and had 'never regretted a day, not a day, nor even an hour'. Lucky you, Rebus thought to himself.

'Do you remember having that new floor laid in the cellar, Mr Hillbeith?'

'Oh yes. That particular cellar was going to be for best claret. It was just the right temperature, you see, and there was no vibration from passing buses and the like. But it was damp, had been ever since I'd moved in. So I got a building firm to take a look. They suggested a new floor and some other alterations. It all seemed fairly straightforward and their charges seemed reasonable, so I told them to go ahead.'

'And when was this, sir?'

'Nineteen sixty. The spring of that year. There you are, I've got a great memory where business matters are concerned.' His small eyes beamed at Rebus through the thick lenses of their glasses. 'I can even tell you how much the work cost me . . . and it was a pretty penny at the time. All for nothing, as it turned out. The cellar was still damp, and there was always that *smell* in it, a very unwholesome smell. I couldn't take a chance with the claret, so it became the general stockroom, empty bottles and glasses, packing cases, that sort of thing.'

'Do you happen to recall, Mr Hillbeith, was the smell there *before* the new floor was put in?'

'Well, certainly there was *a* smell there before the floor was laid, but the smell afterwards was different somehow.' He rose and fetched two crystal glasses from the china cabinet, inspecting them for dust. 'There's a lot of nonsense talked about wine, Inspector. About decanting, the type of glasses you must use, and so on. Decanting can help, of course, but I prefer the feel of the bottle. The bottle, after all, is part of the wine, isn't it?' He handed an empty glass to Rebus. 'We'll wait a few minutes yet.'

Rebus swallowed drily. It had been a long drive. 'Do you recall the name of the firm, sir, the one that did the work?'

Hillbeith laughed. 'How could I forget? Abbot & Ford, they were called. I mean, you just don't forget a name like that, do you? Abbot & Ford. You see, it sounds like Abbotsford, doesn't it? A small firm they were, mind. But you may know one of them, Alexander Abbot.'

'Of Abbot Building?'

'The same. He went on to make quite a name for himself, didn't he? Quite a fortune. Built up quite a company, too, but he started out small like most of us do.'

'How small, would you say?'

'Oh, small, small. Just a few men.' He rose and stretched an arm towards the mantelpiece. I think this should be ready to taste, Inspector. If you'll hold out your glass—'

Hillbeith poured slowly, deliberately, checking that no lees escaped into the glass. He poured another slow, generous measure for himself. The wine was reddish-brown. 'Robe and disc not too promising,' he muttered to himself. He gave his glass a shake and studied it. 'Legs not promising either.' He sighed. 'Oh dear.' Finally, Hillbeith sniffed the glass anxiously, then took a swig.

'Cheers,' said Rebus, indulging in a mouthful. A mouthful of vinegar. He managed to swallow, then saw Hillbeith spit back into the glass.

'Oxidisation,' the old man said, sounding cruelly tricked. 'It happens. I'd best check a few more bottles to assess the damage. Will you stay, Inspector?' Hillbeith sounded keen.

'Sorry, sir,' said Rebus, ready with his get-out clause. 'I'm still on duty.'

ALEXANDER ABBOT, aged fifty-five, still saw himself as the force behind the Abbot Building Company. There might be a dozen executives working furiously beneath him, but the company had grown from *his* energy and from *his* fury. He was chairman, and a busy man, too. He made this plain to Rebus at their meeting in the executive offices of ABC. The office spoke of business confidence, but then in Rebus's experience this meant little in itself. Often, the more dire straits a company was in, the healthier it tried to look. Still, Alexander Abbot seemed happy enough with life.

'In a recession,' he explained, lighting an overlong cigar, 'you trim your work force pronto. You stick with regular clients, good payers, and don't take on too much work from clients you don't know. They're the ones who're likely to welch on you or go bust, leaving nothing but bills. Young businesses . . . they're always hit hardest in a recession, no backup, you see. Then, when the recession's over for another few years, you dust yourself off and go touting for business again, rehiring the men you laid off. That's where we've always had the edge over Jack Kirkwall.'

Kirkwall Construction was ABC's main competitor in the Lowlands; when it came to medium-sized contracts. Doubtless Kirkwall was the larger company. It too was run by a 'self-made' man, Jack Kirkwall. A larger-than-life figure. There was, Rebus quickly realised, little love lost between the two rivals.

The very mention of Kirkwall's name seemed to have dampened Alexander Abbot's spirits. He chewed on his cigar like it was a debtor's finger.

'You started small though, didn't you, sir?'

'Oh aye, they don't come much smaller. We were a pimple on the bum of the construction industry at one time.' He gestured to the walls of his office. 'Not that you'd guess it, eh?'

Rebus nodded. 'You were still a small firm back in nineteen sixty, weren't you?'

'Nineteen sixty. Let's think. We were just starting out. It wasn't ABC then, of course. Let's see. I think I got a loan from my dad in nineteen fifty-seven, went into partnership with a chap called Hugh Ford, another self-employed builder. Yes, that's right. Nineteen sixty, it was Abbot & Ford. Of course it was.'

'Do you happen to remember working at a wine merchant's in the Cowgate?'

'When?'

'The spring of nineteen sixty.'

'A wine merchant's?' Abbot furrowed his brow. 'Should be able to remember that. Long time ago, mind. A wine merchant's.'

'You were laying a new floor in one of the cellars, amongst other work. Hillbeith Vintners.'

'Oh aye, Hillbeith, it's coming back now. I remember him. Little funny chap with glasses. Gave us a case of wine when the job was finished. Nice of him, but the wine was a bit off as I remember.'

'How many men were working on the job?'

Abbot exhaled noisily. 'Now you're asking. It was over thirty years ago, Inspector.'

'I appreciate that, sir. Would there be any records?'

Abbot shook his head. 'There might have been up to about ten years ago, but when we moved into this place a lot of the older stuff got chucked out. I regret it now. It'd be nice to have a display of stuff from the old days, something we could set up in the reception. But no, all the Abbot & Ford stuff got dumped.'

'So you don't remember how many men were on that particular job? Is there anyone else I could talk to, someone who might—'

'We were small back then, I can tell you that. Mostly using casual labour and part-timers. A job that size, I wouldn't think we'd be using more than three or four men, if that.'

'You don't recall anyone going missing? Not turning up for work, that sort of thing?'

Abbot bristled. 'I'm a stickler for time-keeping, Inspector. If anyone had done a bunk, I'd remember, I'm pretty sure of that. Besides, we were careful about who we took on. No lazy buggers, nobody who'd do a runner halfway through a job.'

Rebus sighed. Here was one of the dead ends. He rose to his feet. 'Well, thanks anyway, Mr Abbot. It was good of you to find time to see me.' The two men shook hands, Abbot rising to his feet.

'Not at all, Inspector. Wish I could help you with your little mystery. I like a good detective story myself.' They were almost at the door now.

'Oh,' said Rebus, 'just one last thing. Where could I find your old partner, Mr Ford?'

Abbot's face lost its animation. His voice was suddenly that of an old man. 'Hugh died, Inspector. A boating accident. He was drowned. Hell of a thing to happen. Hell of a thing.'

Two dead ends.

MR HILLBEITH'S TELEPHONE call came later that day, while Rebus was ploughing through the transcript of an interview with a rapist. His head felt full of foul-smelling glue, his stomach acid with caffeine.

'Is that Inspector Rebus?'

'Yes, hello, Mr Hillbeith. What can I do for you?' Rebus pinched the bridge of his nose and screwed shut his eyes.

'I was thinking all last night about that skeleton.'

'Yes?' In between bottles of wine, Rebus didn't doubt.

'Well, I was trying to think back to when the work was being done. It might not be much, but I definitely recall that there were four people involved. Mr Abbot and Mr Ford worked on it pretty much full time, and there were two other men, one of them a teenager, the other in his forties. They worked on a more casual basis.'

'You don't recall their names?'

'No, only that the teenager had a nickname. Everyone called him by that. I don't think I ever knew his real name.'

'Well, thanks anyway, Mr Hillbeith. I'll get back to Mr Abbot and see if what you've told me jogs his memory.'

'Oh, you've spoken to him then?'

'This morning. No progress to report. I didn't realise Mr Ford had died.'

'Ah, well, that's the other thing.'

'What is?'

'Poor Mr Ford. Sailing accident, wasn't it?'

'That's right.'

'Only I remember that too. You see, that accident happened just after they'd finished the job. They kept talking about how they were going to take a few days off and go fishing. Mr Abbot said it would be their first holiday in years.'

Rebus's eyes were open now. 'How soon was this after they'd finished your floor?'

'Well, directly after, I suppose.'

'Do you remember Mr Ford?'

'Well, he was very quiet. Mr Abbot did all the talking, really. A very quiet man. A hard worker though, I got that impression.'

'Did you notice anything about his hands? A misshapen pinkie?'

'Sorry, Inspector, it *was* a long time ago.'

Rebus appreciated that. 'Of course it was, Mr Hillbeith. You've been a great help. Thank you.'

He put down the receiver. A long time ago, yes, but still murder, still calculated and cold-blooded murder. Well, a path had opened in front of him. Not much of a path perhaps, a bit overgrown and treacherous. Nevertheless . . . Best foot forward, John. Best foot forward.

OF COURSE, he kept telling himself, he was still ruling possibilities out rather than ruling them in, which was why he wanted to know a little more about the boating accident. He didn't want to get the information from Alexander Abbot.

Instead, the morning after Hillbeith's phone call, Rebus went to the National Library of Scotland on George IV Bridge. The doorman let him through the turnstile and he climbed an imposing staircase to the reading room. The woman on the desk filled in a one-day reader's card for him and showed him how to use the computer. There were two banks of computers being used by people to find the books they needed. Rebus had to go into the reading room and find an empty chair, note its number, and put this on his slip when he'd decided which volume he required. Then he went to his chair and sat, waiting.

There were two floors to the reading room, both enveloped by shelves of reference books. The people working at the long desks downstair's seemed bleary. Just another morning's graft for them; but Rebus found it all fascinating. One person worked with a card index in front of him, to which he referred frequently. Another seemed asleep, head resting on arms. Pens scratched across countless sheets of paper. A few souls, lost for inspiration, merely chewed on their pens and stared at the others around them, as Rebus was doing.

Eventually, his volume was brought to him. It was a bound edition of the *Scotsman*, containing every issue for the months from January to June, 1960. Two thick leather buckles kept the volume closed. Rebus untied these and began to turn the pages.

He knew what he was looking for, and pretty well where to find it, but that didn't stop him browsing through football reports and front-page headlines. 1960. He'd been fifteen, preparing to leave school and go into the army. He'd been busy trying to lose his virginity and supporting Hearts. Yes, a long time ago.

The story hadn't quite made the front page. Instead, there were two paragraphs on page three.

'Drowning Off Lower Largo.' The victim, Mr Hugh Ford, was described as being twenty-six years of age (a year older than the survivor, Mr Alex Abbot) and a resident of Duddingston, Edinburgh. The men, on a short fishing holiday, had taken a boat out early in the morning, a boat hired from a local man, Mr John Thomson. There was a squall, and the boat capsized. Mr Abbot, a fair swimmer, had made it back to the shore. Mr Ford, a poor swimmer, had not. Mr Ford was further described as a 'bachelor, a quiet man, shy according to Mr Abbot, who was still under observation at the Victoria Hospital, Kirkcaldy.' There was a little more, but not much. Apparently, Ford's parents were dead, but he had a sister, Mrs Isabel Hammond, somewhere out in Australia.

Why hadn't Abbot mentioned any of this? Maybe he wanted to forget. Maybe it still gave him the occasional bad dream. And of course he would have forgotten all about the Hillbeith contract precisely because this tragedy happened so soon afterwards. So soon. Just the one line of print really bothered Rebus; just that one sentence niggled.

'Mr Ford's body has still not been recovered.'

RECORDS MIGHT GET lost in time, but not by Fife Police. They sent on what they had, much of it written in fading ink on fragile paper, some of it typed—badly. The two friends and colleagues, Abbot and Ford, had set out on Friday evening to the Fishing-Net Hotel in Largo, arriving late. As arranged, they'd set out early next morning on a boat they'd hired from a local man, John Thomson. The accident had taken place only an hour or so after setting out. The boat was recovered. It had been overturned, but of Ford there was no sign. Inquiries were made. Mr Ford's belongings were taken back to Edinburgh by Mr Abbot, after the latter was released from hospital, having sustained a bump to the head when the boat turned over. He was also suffering from shock and exhaustion. Mr Ford's sister, Mrs Isabel Hammond, was never traced.

They had investigated a little further. The business run jointly by Messrs Abbot and Ford now became Mr Abbot's. The case notes contained a good amount of information and suspicion—between the lines, as it were. Oh yes, they'd investigated Alexander Abbot, but there had been no evidence. They'd searched for the body, had found none. Without a body, they were left with only their suspicions and their nagging doubts.

'Yes,' Rebus said quietly to himself, 'but what if you were looking for the body in the wrong place?' The wrong place at the wrong time. The work on the cellar had ended on Friday afternoon, and by Saturday morning Hugh Ford had ceased to exist.

The path Rebus was on had become less overgrown, but it was still rock-strewn and dangerous, still a potential dead end.

THE FISHING-NET HOTEL was still in existence, though apparently much changed from its 1960 incarnation. The present owners told Rebus to arrive in time for lunch if he could and it would be on the house. Largo was north of Burntisland but on the same coastline. Alexander Selkirk, the original of Defoe's Robinson Crusoe, had a connection with the fishing village. There was a small statue of him somewhere which Rebus had been shown as a boy (but only after much hunting, he recalled). Largo was picturesque, but then so were most, if not all, of the coastal villages in Fife's 'East Neuk'. But it was not yet quite the height of the tourist season and the customers taking lunch at the Fishing-Net Hotel were businessmen and locals.

It was a good lunch, as picturesque as its surroundings but with a bit more flavour. And afterwards, the owner, an Englishman for whom life in Largo was a long-held dream come true, offered to show Rebus round, including 'the very room your Mr Ford stayed in the night before he died'.

'How can you be sure?'

'I looked in the register.'

Rebus managed not to look too surprised. The hotel had changed hands so often since 1960, he despaired of finding anyone who would remember the events of that weekend.

'The register?'

'Yes, we were left a lot of old stuff when we bought this place. The storerooms were chock-a-block. Old ledgers and what have you going back to the nineteen twenties and thirties. It was easy enough to find nineteen sixty.'

Rebus stopped in his tracks. 'Never mind showing me Mr Ford's room, would you mind letting me see that register?'

He sat at a desk in the manager's office with the register open in front of him, while Mr Summerson's finger stabbed the line. 'There you are, Inspector, H.

Ford. Signed in at eleven-fifty p.m., address given as Duddingston. Room number seven.'

It wasn't so much a signature as a blurred scrawl and above it, on a separate line, was Alexander Abbot's own more flowing signature.

'Bit late to arrive, wasn't it?' commented Rebus.

'Agreed.'

'I don't suppose there's anyone working here nowadays who worked in the hotel back then?'

Summerson laughed quietly. 'People do retire in this country, Inspector.'

'Of course, I just wondered.' He remembered the newspaper story. 'What about John Thomson? Does the name mean anything to you?'

'Old Jock? Jock Thomson? The fisherman?'

'Probably.'

'Oh yes, he's still about. You'll almost certainly find him down by the dock-side, or else in the Harbour Tavern.'

'Thanks. I'd like to take this register with me if I may?'

Jock Thomson sucked on his pipe and nodded. He looked the archetype of the 'old salt', from his baggy cord trousers to his chiselled face and silvery beard. The only departure from the norm was, perhaps, the Perrier water in front of him on a table in the Harbour Tavern.

'I like the fizz,' he explained after ordering it, 'and besides, my doctor's told me to keep off the alcohol. Total abstinence, he said, total abstinence. Either the booze goes, Jock, or the pipe does. No contest.'

And he sucked greedily on the pipe. Then complained when his drink arrived without 'the wee slice of lemon.' Rebus returned to the bar to fulfil his mission.

'Oh aye,' said Thomson, 'remember it like it was yesterday. Only there's not much to remember, is there?'

'Why do you say that?'

'Two inexperienced laddies go out in a boat. Boat tips. End of story.'

'Was the weather going to be bad that morning?'

'Not particularly. But there *was* a squall blew up. Blew up and blew out in a matter of minutes. Long enough though.'

'How did the two men seem?'

'How do you mean?'

'Well, were they looking forward to the trip?'

'Don't know, I never saw them. The younger one, Abbot was it? He phoned to book a boat from me, said they'd be going out early, six or thereabouts. I told him he was daft, but he said there was no need for me to be on the dockside, if I'd just have the boat ready and tell him which one it was. And that's what I did. By the time I woke up that morning, he was swimming for the shore and his pal was food for the fish.'

'So you never actually saw Mr Ford?'

'No, and I only saw the lad Abbot afterwards, when the ambulance was taking him away.'

It was fitting into place almost too easily now. And Rebus thought, sometimes these things are only visible with hindsight, from a space of years. I don't suppose,' he ventured, 'you know anyone who worked at the hotel back then?'

'Owner's moved on,' said Thomson, 'who knows where to. It might be that Janice Dryman worked there then. Can't recall if she did.'

'Where could I find her?'

Thomson peered at the clock behind the bar. 'Hang around here ten minutes or so, you'll bump into her. She usually comes in of an afternoon. Meantime, I'll have another of these if you're buying.'

Thomson pushed his empty glass over to Rebus. Rebus, most definitely, was buying.

MISS DRYMAN—'never married, never really saw the point'—was in her early fifties. She worked in a gift shop in town and after her stint finished usually nipped into the Tavern for a soft drink and 'a bit of gossip'. Rebus asked what she would like to drink.

'Lemonade, please,' she said, 'with a drop of whisky in it.' And she laughed with Jock Thomson, as though this were an old and cherished joke between them. Rebus, not used to playing the part of straight man, headed yet again for the bar.

'Oh yes,' she said, her lips poised above the glass. 'I was working there at the time all right. Chambermaid and general dogsbody, that was me.'

'You wouldn't see them arrive though?'

Miss Dryman looked as though she had some secret to impart. '*Nobody* saw them arrive, I know that for a fact. Mrs Dennis who ran the place back then, she said she'd be buggered if she'd wait up half the night for a couple of fishermen. They knew what rooms they were in and their keys were left at reception.'

'What about the front door?'

'Left unlocked, I suppose. The world was a safer place back then.'

'Aye, you're right there,' added Jock Thomson, sucking on his sliver of lemon.

'And Mr Abbot and Mr Ford knew this was the arrangement?'

'I suppose so. Otherwise it wouldn't have worked, would it?'

So Abbot knew there'd be nobody around at the hotel, not if he left it late enough before arriving.

'And what about in the morning?'

'Mrs Dennis said they were up and out before she knew anything about it. She was annoyed because she'd already cooked the kippers for their breakfast before she realised.'

So nobody saw them in the morning either. In fact . . .

'In fact,' said Rebus, 'nobody saw Mr Ford at all. Nobody at the hotel, not you, Mr Thomson, nobody.' Both drinkers conceded this.

'I saw his stuff though,' said Miss Dryman.

'What stuff?'

'In his room, his clothes and stuff. That morning. I didn't know anything about the accident and I went in to clean.'

'The bed had been slept in?'

'Looked like it. Sheets all rumpled. And his suitcase was on the floor, only half unpacked. Not that there was much *to* unpack.'

'Oh?'

'A single change of clothes, I'd say. I remember them because they seemed mucky, you know, not fresh. Not the sort of stuff *I'd* take on holiday with me.'

'What? Like he'd been working in them?'

She considered this. 'Maybe.'

'No point wearing clean clothes for fishing,' Thomson added. But Rebus wasn't listening.

Ford's clothes, the clothes he had been working in while laying the floor. It made sense. Abbot bludgeoned him, stripped him, and covered his body in fresh cement. He'd taken the clothes away with him and put them in a case, opening it in the hotel room, ruffling the sheets. Simple, but effective. Effective these past thirty years.

The motive? A falling-out perhaps, or simple greed. It was a small company, but growing, and perhaps Abbot hadn't wanted to share.

Rebus placed a five-pound note on the table.

'To cover the next couple of rounds,' he said, getting to his feet. 'I'd better be off. Some of us are still on duty.'

THERE WERE THINGS to be done. He had to speak to his superior, Chief Inspector Lauderdale. And that was for starters. Maybe Ford's Australian sister could be traced this time round. There had to be someone out there who could acknowledge that Ford had suffered from a broken leg in youth, and that he had a crooked finger. So far, Rebus could think of only one person—Alexander Abbot. Somehow, he didn't think Abbot could be relied on to tell the truth, the whole truth.

Then there was the hotel register. The forensics lab could ply their cunning trade on it. Perhaps they'd be able to say for certain that Ford's signature was merely a bad rendition of Abbot's. But again, he needed a sample of Ford's handwriting in order to substantiate that the signature was not genuine. Who did he know who might possess such a document? Only Alexander Abbot. Or Mr Hillbeith, but Mr Hillbeith had not been able to help.

'No, Inspector, as I told you, it was Mr Abbot who handled all the paperwork, all that side of things. If there is an invoice or a receipt, it will be in his hand, not Mr Ford's. I don't recall ever seeing Mr Ford writing anything.'

No through road.

Chief Inspector Lauderdale was not wholly sympathetic. So far all Rebus had to offer were more suppositions to add to those of the Fife Police at the time.

There was no proof that Alexander Abbot had killed his partner. No proof that the skeleton was Hugh Ford. Moreover, there wasn't even much in the way of circumstantial evidence. They could bring in Abbot for questioning, but all he had to do was plead innocence. He could afford a good lawyer; and even bad lawyers weren't stupid enough to let the police probe too deeply.

'We need proof, John,' said Lauderdale, 'concrete evidence. The simplest proof would be that hotel signature. If we prove it's not Ford's, then we have Abbot at that hotel, Abbot in the boat, and Abbot shouting that his friend has drowned, *all* without Ford having been there. That's what we need. The rest of it, as it stands, is rubbish. You know that.'

Yes, Rebus knew. He didn't doubt that, given an hour alone with Abbot in a darkened alley, he'd have his confession. But it didn't work like that. It worked through the law. Besides, Abbot's heart might not be too healthy. BUSINESSMAN, 55, DIES UNDER QUESTIONING. No, it had to be done some other way.

The problem was, there *was* no other way. Alexander Abbot was getting away with murder. Or was he? Why did his story have to be false? Why did the body have to be Hugh Ford's? The answer was: because the whole thing seemed to fit. Only, the last piece of the jigsaw had been lost under some sofa or chair a long time ago, so long ago now that it might remain missing for ever.

HE DIDN'T KNOW why he did it. If in doubt, retrace your steps . . . something like that. Maybe he just liked the atmosphere. Whatever, Rebus found himself back in the National Library, waiting at his desk for the servitor to bring him his bound volume of old news. He mouthed the words of 'Yesterday's Papers' to himself as he waited. Then, when the volume appeared, he unbuckled it with ease and pulled open the pages. He read past the April editions, read through into May and June. Football results, headlines—and what was this? A snippet of business news, barely a filler at the bottom right-hand corner of a page. About how the Kirkwall Construction Company was swallowing up a couple of smaller competitors in Fife and Midlothian.

'"The nineteen sixties will be a decade of revolution in the building industry," said Managing Director Mr Jack Kirkwall, "and Kirkwall Construction aims to meet that challenge through growth and quality. The bigger we are, the better we are. These acquisitions strengthen the company, and they're good news for the work force, too."'

It was the kind of sentiment which had lasted into the 1980s. Jack Kirkwall, Alexander Abbot's bitter rival. Now there was a man Rebus ought to meet . . .

THE MEETING, HOWEVER, had to be postponed until the following week. Kirkwall was in hospital for a minor operation.

'I'm at that age, Inspector,' he told Rebus when they finally met, 'when things go wrong and need treatment or replacing. Just like any bit of well-used machinery.'

And he laughed, though the laughter, to Rebus's ears, had a hollow centre.

Kirkwall looked older than his sixty-two years, his skin saggy, complexion wan. They were in his living room, from where, these days, he did most of his work.

'Since I turned sixty, I've only really wandered into the company headquarters for the occasional meeting. I leave the daily chores to my son, Peter. He seems to be managing.' The laughter this time was self-mocking.

Rebus had suggested a further postponement of the meeting, but when Jack Kirkwall knew that the subject was to be Alexander Abbot, he was adamant that they should go ahead.

'Is he in trouble then?'

'He might be,' Rebus admitted.

Some of the colour seemed to reappear in Kirkwall's cheeks and he relaxed a little further into his reclining leather chair. Rebus didn't want to give Kirkwall the story. Kirkwall and Abbot were still business rivals, after all. Still, it seemed, enemies. Given the story, Kirkwall might try some underhand tactic, some rumour in the media, and if it got out that the story originally came from a police inspector, well. Hello, being sued and goodbye, pension.

No, Rebus didn't want that. Yet he did want to know whether Kirkwall knew anything, knew of any reason why Abbot might wish, might *need* to kill Ford.

'Go on, Inspector.'

'It goes back quite a way, sir. Nineteen sixty, to be precise. Your firm was at that time in the process of expansion.'

'Correct.'

'What did you know about Abbot & Ford?'

Kirkwall brushed the palm of one hand over the knuckles of the other. 'Just that they were growing, too. Of course, they were younger than us, much smaller than us. ABC still is much smaller than us. But they were cocky, they were winning some contracts ahead of us. I had my eye on them.'

'Did you know Mr Ford at all?'

'Oh yes. Really, he was the cleverer of the two men. I've never had much respect for Abbot. But Hugh Ford was quiet, hardworking. Abbot was the one who did the shouting and got the firm noticed.'

'Did Mr Ford have a crooked finger?'

Kirkwall seemed bemused by the question. 'I've no idea,' he said at last. 'I never actually met the man, I merely knew *about* him. Why? Is it important?'

Rebus felt at last his meandering, narrowing path had come to the lip of the chasm. Nothing for it but to turn back.

'Well,' he said, 'it would have clarified something.'

'You know, Inspector, my company *was* interested in taking Abbot & Ford under our wing.'

'Oh?'

'But then with the accident, that tragic accident. Well, Abbot took control and he wasn't at all interested in any offer we had to make. Downright rude, in fact. Yes,

I've always thought that it was such a *lucky* accident so far as Abbot was concerned.'

'How do you mean, sir?'

'I mean, Inspector, that Hugh Ford was on our side. He wanted to sell up. But Abbot was against it.'

So Rebus had his motive. Well, what did it matter? He was still lacking that concrete evidence Lauderdale demanded.

'. . . Would it show up from his handwriting?'

Rebus had missed what Kirkwall had been saying. 'I'm sorry, sir, I didn't catch that.'

'I said, Inspector, if Hugh Ford had a crooked finger, would it show from his handwriting?'

'Handwriting?'

'Because I had his agreement to the takeover. He'd written to me personally to tell me. Had gone behind Abbot's back, I suppose. I bet Alex Abbot was mad as hell when he found out about that.' Kirkwall's smile was vibrant now. 'I always thought that accident was a bit too lucky where Abbot was concerned. A bit too neat. No proof though. There was never any proof.'

'Do you still have the letter?'

'What?'

'The letter from Mr Ford, do you still have it?'

Rebus was tingling now, and Kirkwall caught his excitement. 'I never throw anything away, Inspector. Oh yes, I've got it. It'll be upstairs.'

'Can I see it? I mean, can I see it now?'

'If you like,' Kirkwall made to stand up, but paused. '*Is* Alex Abbot in trouble, Inspector?'

'If you've still got that letter from Hugh Ford, then yes, sir, I'd say Mr Abbot could be in very grave trouble indeed.'

'Inspector, you've made an old man very happy.'

IT WAS THE LETTER against Alex Abbot's word, of course, and he denied everything. But there was enough now for a trial. The entry in the hotel's ledger, while it was *possibly* the work of Alexander Abbot, was *certainly* not the work of the man who had written the letter to Jack Kirkwall. A search warrant gave the police the powers to look through Abbot's home and the ABC headquarters. A contract, drawn up between Abbot and Ford when the two men had gone into partnership, was discovered to be held in a solicitor's safe. The signature matched that on the letter to Jack Kirkwall. Kirkwall himself appeared in court to give evidence. He seemed to Rebus a different man altogether from the person he'd met previously: sprightly, keening, enjoying life to the full.

From the dock, Alexander Abbot looked on almost reproachfully, as if this were just one more business trick in a life full of them. Life, too, was the sentence of the judge.

Ruth Rendell

b. 1930

WHEN THE WEDDING WAS OVER

'**M**ATRIMONY,' said Chief Inspector Wexford, 'begins with dearly beloved and ends with amazement.'

His wife, sitting beside him on the bridegroom's side of the church, whispered, 'What did you say?'

He repeated it. She steadied the large floral hat which her husband had called becoming but not exactly conducive to sotto voce intimacies. 'What on earth makes you say that?'

'Thomas Hardy. He said it first. But look in your Prayer Book.'

The bridegroom waited, hangdog, with his best man. Michael Burden was very much in love, was entering this second marriage with someone admirably suited to him, had agreed with his fiancée that nothing but a religious ceremony would do for them, yet at forty-four was a little superannuated for what Wexford called 'all this white wedding gubbins'. There were two hundred people in the church. Burden, his best man and his ushers were in morning dress. Madonna lilies and stephanotis and syringa decorated the pews, the pulpit and the chancel steps. It was the kind of thing that is properly designed for someone twenty years younger. Burden had been through it before when he was twenty years younger. Wexford chuckled silently, looking at the anxious face above the high white collar. And then as Dora, leafing through the marriage service, said, 'Oh, I *see*,' the organist went from voluntaries into the opening bars of the Lohengrin march and Jenny Ireland appeared at the church door on her father's arm.

A beautiful bride, of course. Seven years younger than Burden, blonde, gentle, low-voiced, and given to radiant smiles. Jenny's father gave her hand into Burden's and the Rector of St Peter's began:

'Dearly beloved, we are gathered together . . .'

While bride and groom were being informed that marriage was not for the satisfaction of their carnal lusts, and that they must bring up their children in a Christian manner, Wexford studied the congregation. In front of himself and Dora sat Burden's sister-in-law, Grace, whom everyone had thought he would marry after the death of his first wife. But Burden had found consolation with a red-headed woman, wild and sweet and strange, gone now God knew where,

457

and Grace had married someone else. Two little boys now sat between Grace and that someone else, giving their parents a full-time job keeping them quiet.

Burden's mother and father were both dead. Wexford thought he recognised, from one meeting a dozen years before, an aged aunt. Beside her sat Dr Crocker and his wife, beyond them and behind were a crowd whose individual members he knew either only by sight or not at all. Sylvia, his elder daughter, was sitting on his other side, his grandsons between her and their father, and at the central aisle end of the pew, Sheila Wexford of the Royal Shakespeare Company. Wexford's actress daughter, who on her entry had commanded nudges, whispers, every gaze, sat looking with unaccustomed wistfulness at Jenny Ireland in her clouds of white and wreath of pearls.

'I, Michael George, take thee, Janina, to my wedded wife, to have and to hold from this day forward . . .'

Janina. *Janina?* Wexford had supposed her name was Jennifer. What sort of parents called a daughter Janina? Turks? Fans of Dumas? He leaned forward to get a good look at these philonomatous progenitors. They looked ordinary enough, Mr Ireland apparently exhausted by the effort of giving the bride away, Jenny's mother making use of the lace handkerchief provided for the specific purpose of crying into it those tears of joy and loss. What romantic streak had led them to dismiss Elizabeth and Susan and Anne in favour of—Janina?

'Those whom God hath joined together, let no man put asunder. Forasmuch as Michael George and Janina have consented together in holy wedlock . . .'

Had they been as adventurous in the naming of their son? All Wexford could see of him was a broad back, a bit of profile, and now a hand. The hand was passing a large white handkerchief to his mother. Wexford found himself being suddenly yanked to his feet to sing a hymn.

'O, Perfect Love, all human thought transcending,
Lowly we kneel in prayer before Thy throne . . .'

These words had the effect of evoking from Mrs Ireland audible sobs. Her son—hadn't Burden said he was in publishing?—looked embarrassed, turning his head. A young woman, strangely dressed in black with an orange hat, edged past the publisher to put a consoling arm round his mother.

'O Lord, save Thy servant and Thy handmaid.'

Who put their trust in Thee,' said Dora and most of the rest of the congregation.

'O Lord, send them help from Thy holy place.'

Wexford, to show team spirit, said, 'Amen,' and when everyone else said, 'And evermore defend them,' decided to keep quiet in future.

Mrs Ireland had stopped crying. Wexford's gaze drifted to his own daughters, Sheila singing lustily, Sylvia, the Women's Liberationist, with less assurance as if she doubted the ethics of lending her support to so archaic and sexist a ceremony. His grandsons were beginning to fidget.

'Almighty God, who at the beginning did create our first parents, Adam and Eve . . .'

Dear Mike, thought Wexford with a flash of sentimentality that came to him perhaps once every ten years, you'll be OK now. No more carnal lusts conflicting with a puritan conscience, no more loneliness, no more worrying about those selfish kids of yours, no more temptation-of-St-Anthony stuff. For is it not ordained as a remedy against sin, and to avoid fornication, that such persons as have not the gift of continency may marry and keep themselves undefiled?

'For after this manner in the old time the holy women who trusted in God . . .'

He was quite surprised that they were using the ancient form. Still, the bride had promised to obey. He couldn't resist glancing at Sylvia.

'. . . being in subjection to their own husbands . . .'

Her face was a study in incredulous dismay as she mouthed at her sister 'unbelievable' and 'antique'.

'. . . Even as Sarah obeyed Abraham, calling him Lord, whose daughters ye are as long as ye do well, and are not afraid with any amazement.'

AT THE OLIVE AND DOVE hotel there was a reception line to greet guests, Mrs Ireland smiling, rerouged and restored, Burden looking like someone who has had an operation and been told the prognosis is excellent, Jenny serene as a bride should be.

Dry sherry and white wine on trays. No champagne. Wexford remembered that there was a younger Ireland daughter, absent with her husband in some dreadful place—Botswana? Lesotho? No doubt all the champagne funds had been expended on her. It was a buffet lunch, but a good one. Smoked salmon and duck and strawberries. Nobody, he said to himself, has ever really thought of anything better to eat than smoked salmon and duck and strawberries unless it might be caviar and grouse and syllabub. He was weighing the two menus against one another, must without knowing it have been thinking aloud, for a voice said:

'Asparagus, trout, apple pie.'

'Well, maybe,' said Wexford, 'but I do like meat. Trout's a bit insipid. You're Jenny's brother, I'm sorry I don't remember your name. How d'you do?'

'How d'you do? I know who you are. Mike told me. I'm Amyas Ireland.'

So that funny old pair hadn't had a one-off indulgence when they had named Janina. Again Wexford's thoughts seemed revealed to this intuitive person.

'Oh, I know,' said Ireland, 'but how about my other sister? She's called Cunegonde. Her husband calls her Queenie. Look, I'd like to talk to you. Could we get together a minute away from all this crush? Mike was going to help me out, but I can't ask him now, not when he's off on his honeymoon. It's about a book we're publishing.'

The girl in black and orange, Burden's nephews, Sheila Wexford, Burden's best man and a gaggle of children, all carrying plates, passed between them at this point. It was at least a minute before Wexford could ask, 'Who's we?' and another half-minute before Amyas Ireland understood what he meant.

459

'Carlyon Brent,' he said, his mouth full of duck. 'I'm with Carlyon Brent.'

One of the largest and most distinguished of publishing houses. Wexford was impressed. 'You published the Vandrian, didn't you, and the de Coverley books?'

Ireland nodded. 'Mike said you were a great reader. That's good. Can I get you some more duck? No? I'm going to. I won't be a minute.' Enviously Wexford watched him shovel fat-rimmed slices of duck breast onto his plate, take a brioche, have second thoughts and take another. The man was as thin as a rail too, positively emaciated.

'I look after the crime list,' he said as he sat down again. 'As I said, Mike half promised . . . This isn't fiction, it's fact. The Winchurch case?'

'Ah.'

'I know it's a bit of a nerve asking, but would you read a manuscript for me?'

Wexford took a cup of coffee from a passing tray. 'What for?'

'Well, in the interests of truth. Mike was going to tell me what he thought.' Wexford looked at him dubiously. He had the highest respect and the deepest affection for Inspector Burden but he was one of the last people he would have considered as a literary critic. 'To tell me what he thought,' the publisher said once again. 'You see, it's worrying me. The author has discovered some new facts and they more or less prove Mrs Winchurch's innocence.' He hesitated. 'Have you ever heard of a writer called Kenneth Gandolph?'

Wexford was saved from answering by the pounding of a gavel on the top table and the beginning of the speeches. A great many toasts had been drunk, several dozen telegrams read out, and the bride and groom departed to change their clothes before he had an opportunity to reply to Ireland's question. And he was glad of the respite, for what he knew of Gandolph, though based on hearsay, was not prepossessing.

'Doesn't he write crime novels?' he said when the enquiry was repeated. 'And the occasional examination of a real-life crime?'

Nodding, Ireland said, 'It's good, this script of his. We want to do it for next spring's list. It's an eighty-year-old murder, sure, but people are still fascinated by it. I think this new version could cause quite a sensation.'

'Florence Winchurch was hanged,' said Wexford, 'yet there was always some margin of doubt about her guilt. Where does Gandolph get his fresh facts from?'

'May I send you a copy of the script? You'll find all that in the introduction.'

Wexford shrugged, then smiled. 'I suppose so. You do realise I can't do more than maybe spot mistakes in forensics? I did say maybe, mind.' But his interest had already been caught. It made him say, 'Florence was married at St Peter's, you know, and she also had her wedding reception here.'

'And spent part of her honeymoon in Greece.'

'No doubt the parallels end there,' said Wexford as Burden and Jenny came back into the room.

Burden was in a grey lounge suit, she in pale-blue sprigged muslin. Wexford felt an absurd impulse of tenderness towards him. It was partly caused by

Jenny's hat which she would never wear again, would never have occasion to wear, would remove the minute they got into the car. But Burden was the sort of man who could never be happy with a woman who didn't have a hat as part of her 'going-away' costume. His own clothes were eminently unsuitable for flying to Crete in June. They both looked very happy and embarrassed.

Mrs Ireland seized her daughter in a crushing embrace.

'It's not for ever, Mother,' said Jenny. 'It's only for two weeks.'

'Well, in a way,' said Burden. He shook hands gravely with his own son, down from university for the weekend, and planted a kiss on his daughter's forehead. Must have been reading novels, Wexford thought, grinning to himself.

'Good luck, Mike,' he said.

The bride took his hand, put a soft cool kiss onto the corner of his mouth. Say I'm growing old but add, Jenny kissed me. He didn't say that aloud. He nodded and smiled and took his wife's arm and frowned at Sylvia's naughty boys like the patriarch he was. Burden and Jenny went out to the car which had Just Married written in lipstick on the rear window and a shoe tied on the back bumper.

There was a clicking of handbag clasps, a flurry of hands, and then a tempest of confetti broke over them.

IT WAS AN ISOLATED HOUSE, standing some twenty yards back from the Myringham road. Plumb in the centre of the façade was a plaque bearing the date 1896. Wexford had often thought that there seemed to have been positive intent on the part of late-Victorian builders to design and erect houses that were not only ugly, complex and inconvenient, but also distinctly sinister in appearance. The Limes, though well maintained and set in a garden as multicoloured, cushiony and floral as a quilt, nevertheless kept this sinister quality. Khaki-coloured brick and grey slate had been the principal materials used in its construction. Without being able to define exactly how, Wexford could see that, in relation to the walls, the proportions of the sash windows were wrong. A turret grew out of each of the front corners and each of these turrets was topped by a conical roof, giving the place the look of a cross between Balmoral Castle and a hotel in Kitzbühel. The lime trees which gave it its name had been lopped so many times since their planting at the turn of the century that now they were squat and misshapen.

In the days of the Winchurches it had been called Paraleash House. But this name, of historical significance on account of its connection with the ancient manor of Paraleash, had been changed specifically as a result of the murder of Edward Winchurch. Even so, it had stood empty for ten years. Then it had found a buyer a year or so before the First World War, a man who was killed in that war. Its present owner had occupied it for half a dozen years, and in the time intervening between his purchase of it and 1918 it had been variously a nursing home, the annexe of an agricultural college and a private school. The owner was a retired brigadier. As he emerged from the front door with two

Sealyhams on a lead, Wexford retreated to his car and drove home.

It was Monday evening and Burden's marriage was two days old. Monday was the evening of Dora's pottery class, the fruits of which, bruised-looking and not invariably symmetrical, were scattered haphazardly about the room like windfalls. Hunting along the shelves for G. Hallam Saul's *When the Summer is Shed* and *The Trial of Florence Winchurch* from the Notable British Trials series, he nearly knocked over one of those rotund yet lopsided objects. With a sigh of relief that it was unharmed, he set about refreshing his memory of the Winchurch case with the help of Miss Saul's classic.

FLORENCE MAY ANSTRUTHER had been nineteen at the time of her marriage to Edward Winchurch and he forty-seven. She was a good-looking fair-haired girl, rather tall and Junoesque, the daughter of a Kingsmarkham chemist—that is, a pharmacist, for her father had kept a shop in the High Street. In 1895 this damned her as of no account in the social hierarchy, and few people would have bet much on her chances of marrying well. But she did. Winchurch was a barrister who, at this stage of his life, practised law from inclination rather than from need. His father, a Sussex landowner, had died some three years before and had left him what for the last decade of the nineteenth century was an enormous fortune, £200,000. Presumably, he had been attracted to Florence by her youth, her looks and her ladylike ways. She had been given the best education, including six months at a finishing school, that the chemist could afford. Winchurch's attraction for Florence was generally supposed to have been solely his money.

They were married in June 1895 at the parish church of St Peter's, Kingsmarkham, and went on a six-month honeymoon, touring Italy, Greece and the Swiss Alps. When they returned home Winchurch took a lease of Sewingbury Priory while building began on Paraleash House, and it may have been that the conical roofs on those turrets were inspired directly by what Florence had seen on her alpine travels. They moved into the lavishly furnished new house in May 1896, and Florence settled down to the life of a Victorian lady with a wealthy husband and a staff of indoor and outdoor servants. A vapid life at best, even if alleviated by a brood of children. But Florence had no children and was to have none.

Once or twice a week Edward Winchurch went up to London by the train from Kingsmarkham, as commuters had done before and have been doing ever since. Florence gave orders to her cook, arranged the flowers, paid and received calls, read novels and devoted a good many hours a day to her face, her hair and her dress. Local opinion of the couple at that time seemed to have been that they were as happy as most people, that Florence had done very well for herself and knew it, and Edward not so badly as had been predicted.

In the autumn of 1896 a young doctor of medicine bought a practice in Kingsmarkham and came to live there with his unmarried sister. Their name was Fenton. Frank Fenton was an extremely handsome man, twenty-six years old, six feet tall, with jet-black hair, a Byronic eye and an arrogant lift to his chin. The sister was called Ada, and she was neither good-looking nor arrogant, being partly crippled by poliomyelitis which had left her with one leg badly twisted and paralysed.

It was ostensibly to befriend Ada Fenton that Florence first began calling at the Fentons' house in Queen Street. Florence professed great affection for Ada, took her about in her carriage and offered her the use of it whenever she had to go any distance. From this it was an obvious step to persuade Edward that Frank Fenton should become the Winchurches' doctor. Within another few months young Mrs Winchurch had become the doctor's mistress.

It was probable that Ada knew nothing, or next to nothing, about it. In the 1890s a young girl could be, and usually was, very innocent. At the trial it was stated by Florence's coachman that he would be sent to the Fentons' house several times a week to take Miss Fenton driving, while Ada's housemaid said that Mrs Winchurch would arrive on foot soon after Miss Fenton had gone out and be admitted rapidly through a french window by the doctor himself. During the winter of 1898 it seemed likely that Frank Fenton had performed an abortion on Mrs Winchurch, and for some months afterwards they met only at social gatherings and occasionally when Florence was visiting Ada. But their feelings for each other were too strong for them to bear separation and by the following summer they were again meeting at Fenton's house while Ada was out, and now also at Paraleash House on the days when Edward had departed for the law courts.

Divorce was difficult but by no means impossible or unheard-of in 1899. At the trial Frank Fenton said he had wanted Mrs Winchurch to ask her husband for a divorce. He would have married her in spite of the disastrous effect on his career. It was she, he said, who refused to consider it on the grounds that she did not think she could bear the disgrace.

In January 1900 Florence went to London for the day and, among other purchases, bought at a grocer's two cans of herring fillets marinaded in a white wine sauce. It was rare for canned food to appear in the Winchurch household, and when Florence suggested that these herring fillets should be used in the preparation of a dish called *Filets de hareng marinés à la Rosette*, the recipe for which she had been given by Ada Fenton, the cook, Mrs Eliza Holmes, protested that she could prepare it from fresh fish. Florence, however, insisted, one of the cans was used, and the dish was made and served to Florence and Edward at dinner. It was brought in by the parlourmaid, Alice Evans, as a savoury or final course to a four-course meal. Although Florence had shown so much enthusiasm about the dish, she took none of it. Edward ate a moderate amount and the rest was removed to the kitchen where it was shared between Mrs Holmes, Alice Evans and the housemaid, Violet Stedman. No one suffered any ill effects. The date was 30 January 1900.

Five weeks later on 5 March Florence asked Mrs Holmes to make the dish again, using the remaining can, as her husband had liked it so much. This time Florence too partook of the marinaded herrings, but when the remains of it were about to be removed by Alice to the kitchen, she advised her to tell the others not to eat it as she 'thought it had a strange taste and was perhaps not quite fresh'. However, although Mrs Holmes and Alice abstained, Violet Stedman ate a larger quantity of the dish than had either Florence or Edward.

Florence, as was her habit, left Edward to drink his port alone. Within a few minutes a strangled shout was heard from the dining room and a sound as of furniture breaking. Florence and Alice Evans and Mrs Holmes went into the room and found Edward Winchurch lying on the floor, a chair with one leg wrenched from its socket tipped over beside him and an overturned glass of port on the table. Florence approached him and he went into a violent convulsion, arching his back and baring his teeth, his hands grasping the chair in apparent agony.

John Barstow, the coachman, was sent to fetch Dr Fenton. By this time Florence was complaining of stomach pains and seemed unable to stand. Fenton arrived, had Edward and Florence removed upstairs and asked Mrs Holmes what they had eaten. She showed him the empty herring fillets can, and he recognised the brand as that by which a patient of a colleague of his had recently been infected with botulism, a virulent and usually fatal form of food poisoning. Fenton immediately assumed that it was *bacillus botulinus* which had attacked the Winchurches, and such is the power of suggestion that Violet Stedman now said she felt sick and faint.

Botulism causes paralysis, difficulty in breathing and a disturbance of the vision. Florence appeared to be partly paralysed and said she had double vision. Edward's symptoms were different. He continued to have spasms, was totally relaxed between spasms, and although he had difficulty in breathing and other symptoms of botulism, the onset had been exceptionally rapid for any form of food poisoning. Fenton, however, had never seen a case of botulism, which is extremely rare, and he supposed that the symptoms would vary greatly from person to person. He gave jalap and cream of tartar as a purgative and, in the absence of any known relatives of Edward Winchurch, he sent for Florence's father, Thomas Anstruther.

If Fenton was less innocent than was supposed, he had made a mistake in sending for Anstruther, for Florence's father insisted on a second opinion, and at ten o'clock went himself to the home of that very colleague of Fenton's who had recently witnessed a known case of botulism. This was Dr Maurice Waterfield, twice Fenton's age, a popular man with a large practice in Stowerton. He looked at Edward Winchurch, at the agonised grin which overspread his features, and as Edward went into his last convulsive seizure, pronounced that he had been poisoned not by *bacillus botulinus* but by strychnine.

Edward died a few minutes afterwards. Dr Waterfield told Fenton that there was nothing physically wrong with either Florence or Violet Stedman. The former was suffering from shock or 'neurasthenia', the latter from indigestion brought on by overeating. The police were informed, an inquest took place, and after it Florence was immediately arrested and charged with murdering her husband by administering to him a noxious substance, to wit *strychnos nux vomica*, in a decanter of port wine.

Her trial took place in London at the Central Criminal Court. She was twenty-four years old, a beautiful woman, and was by then known to have been having a love affair with the young and handsome Dr Fenton. As such, she and her case attracted national attention. Fenton had by then lost his practice, lost all hope of succeeding with another in the British Isles, and even before the trial his name had become a byword, scurrilous doggerel being sung about him and Florence in the music halls. But far from increasing his loyalty to Florence, this seemed to make him the more determined to dissociate himself from her. He appeared as the prosecution's principal witness, and it was his evidence which sent Florence to the gallows.

Fenton admitted his relationship with Florence but said that he had told her it must end. The only possible alternative was divorce and ultimately marriage to himself. In early January 1900 Florence had been calling on his sister Ada, and he had come in to find them looking through a book of recipes. One of the recipes called for the use of herring fillets marinaded in white wine sauce, the mention of which had caused him to tell them about a case of botulism which a patient of Dr Waterfield was believed to have contracted from eating the contents of a can of just such fillets. He had named the brand and advised his sister not to buy any of that kind. When, some seven weeks later, he was called to the dying Edward Winchurch, the cook had shown him an empty can of that very brand. In his opinion, Mrs Winchurch herself was not ill at all, was not even ill from 'nerves' but was shamming. The judge said that he was not there to give his opinion, but the warning came too late. To the jury the point had already been made.

Asked if he was aware that strychnine had therapeutic uses in small quantities, Fenton said he was but that he kept none in his dispensary. In any case, his dispensary was kept locked and the cupboards inside it locked, so it would have been impossible for Florence to have entered it or to have appropriated anything while on a visit to Ada. Ada Fenton was not called as a witness. She was ill, suffering from what her doctor, Dr Waterfield, called 'brain fever'.

The prosecution's case was that, in order to inherit his fortune and marry Dr Fenton, Florence Winchurch had attempted to poison her husband with infected fish, or fish she had good reason to suppose might be infected. When this failed she saw to it that the dish was provided again, and herself added strychnine to the port decanter. It was postulated that she obtained the strychnine from her father's shop, without his knowledge, where it was kept in stock for the destruction of rats and moles. After her husband was taken ill, she herself simulated symptoms of botulism in the hope that the convulsions of strychnine poisoning would be confused with the paralysis and impeded breathing caused by the bacillus.

The defence tried to shift the blame to Frank Fenton, at least to suggest a conspiracy with Florence, but it was no use. The jury were out for only forty minutes. They pronounced her guilty, the judge sentenced her to death, and she was hanged just twenty-three days later, this being some twenty years before the institution of a Court of Appeal.

After the execution Frank and Ada Fenton emigrated to the United States and settled in New England. Fenton's reputation had gone before him. He was never again able to practise as a doctor but worked as the travelling representative of a firm of pharmaceutical manufacturers until his death in 1932. He never married. Ada, on the other hand, surprisingly enough, did. Ephraim Hurst fell in love with her in spite of her sickly constitution and withered leg. They were married in the summer of 1902 and by the spring of 1903 Ada Hurst was dead in childbirth.

By then Paraleash House had been renamed The Limes and lime trees planted to conceal its forbidding yet fascinating façade from the curious passer-by.

THE PARCEL from Carlyon Brent arrived in the morning with a very polite covering letter from Amyas Ireland, grateful in anticipation. Wexford had never before seen a book in this embryo stage. The script, 100,000 words long, was bound in red, and through a window in its cover appeared the provisional title and the author's name: *Poison at Paraleash, A Reappraisal of the Winchurch Case* by Kenneth Gandolph.

'Remember all that fuss about Gandolph?' Wexford said to Dora across the coffeepot. 'About four years ago?'

'Somebody confessed a murder to him, didn't they?'

'Well, maybe. While a prison visitor, he spent some time talking to Paxton, the bank robber, in Wormwood Scrubs. Paxton died of cancer a few months later, and Gandolph then published an article in a newspaper in which he said that during the course of their conversations, Paxton had confessed to him that he was the perpetrator of the Conyngford murder in 1962. Paxton's widow protested, there was a heated correspondence, MPs wanting the libel laws extended to libelling the dead, Gandolph shouting about the power of truth. Finally, the by then retired Detective Superintendent Warren of Scotland Yard put an end to all further controversy by issuing a statement to the press. He said Paxton couldn't have killed James Conyngford because on the day of Conyngford's death in Brighton Warren's sergeant and a constable had had Paxton under constant surveillance in London. In other words, he was never out of their sight.'

'Why would Gandolph invent such a thing, Reg?' said Dora.

'Perhaps he didn't. Paxton may have spun him all sorts of tales as a way of passing a boring afternoon. Who knows? On the other hand, Gandolph does rather set himself up as the elucidator of unsolved crimes. Years ago, I believe, he did find a satisfactory and quite reasonable solution to some murder in Scotland, and maybe it went to his head. Marshall, Groves, Folliott used to be his publishers. I wonder if they've refused this one because of the Paxton business, if it was offered to them and they turned it down?'

'But Mr Ireland's people have taken it,' Dora pointed out.

'Mm-hm. But they're not falling over themselves with enthusiasm, are they? They're scared. Ireland hasn't sent me this so that I can check up on the police procedural part. What do I know about police procedure in 1900? He's sent it to me in the hope that if Gandolph's been up to his old tricks I'll spot what they are.'

The working day presented no opportunity for a look at *Poison at Paraleash*, but at eight o'clock that night Wexford opened it and read Gandolph's long introduction.

Gandolph began by saying that as a criminologist he had always been aware of the Winchurch case and of the doubt which many felt about Florence Winchurch's guilt. Therefore, when he was staying with friends in Boston, Massachusetts, some two years before and they spoke to him of an acquaintance of theirs who was the niece of one of the principals in the case, he had asked to be introduced to her. The niece was Ada Hurst's daughter, Lina, still Miss Hurst, seventy-four years old and suffering from a terminal illness.

Miss Hurst showed no particular interest in the events of March 1900. She had been brought up by her father and his second wife and had hardly known her uncle. All her mother's property had come into her possession, including the diary which Ada Fenton Hurst had kept for three years prior to Edward Winchurch's death. Lina Hurst told Gandolph she had kept the diary for sentimental reasons but that he might borrow it and after her death she would see that it passed to him.

Within weeks Lina Hurst did die and her stepbrother, who was her executor, had the diary sent to Gandolph. Gandolph had read it and had been enormously excited by certain entries because in his view they incriminated Frank Fenton and exonerated Florence Winchurch. Here Wexford turned back a few pages and noted the author's dedication: *In memory of Miss Lina Hurst, of Cambridge, Massachusetts, without whose help this reappraisal would have been impossible.*

More than this Wexford had no time to read that evening, but he returned to it on the following day. The diary, it appeared, was a five-year one. At the top of each page was the date, as it might be 1 April, and beneath that five spaces each headed 18 . . . There was room for the diarist to write perhaps forty or fifty words in each space, no more. On the 1 January page in the third heading down, the number of the year, the eight had been crossed out and a nine substituted, and so it went on for every subsequent entry until March 6, after which no more entries were made until the diarist resumed in December 1900, by which time she and her brother were in Boston.

Wexford proceeded to Gandolph's first chapters. The story he had to tell was substantially the same as Hallam Saul's, and it was not until he came to chapter five and the weeks preceding the crime that he began to concentrate on the character of Frank Fenton. Fenton, he suggested, wanted Mrs Winchurch for the money and property she would inherit on her husband's death. Far from encouraging Florence to seek a divorce, he urged her never to let her husband suspect her preference for another man. Divorce would have left Florence penniless and homeless and have ruined his career. Fenton had known that it was only by making away with Winchurch and so arranging things that the death appeared natural, that he could have money, his profession and Florence.

There was only his word for it, said Gandolph, that he had spoken to Florence of botulism and had warned her against these particular canned herrings. Of course he had never seriously expected those cans to infect Winchurch, but that the fish should be eaten by him was necessary for his strategy. On the night before Winchurch's death, after dining with his sister at Paraleash House, he had introduced strychnine into the port decanter. He had also, Gandolph suggested, contrived to bring the conversation round to a discussion of food and to fish dishes. From that it would have been a short step to get Winchurch to admit how much he had enjoyed *Filets de hareng marinés à la Rosette* and to ask Florence to have them served again on the following day. Edward, apparently, would have been highly likely to take his doctor's advice, even when in health, even on such a matter as what he should eat for the fourth course of his dinner, while Edward's wife did everything her lover, if not her husband, told her to do.

It was no surprise to Frank Fenton to be called out on the following evening to a man whose spasms only he would recognise as symptomatic of having swallowed strychnine. The arrival of Dr Waterfield was an unlooked-for circumstance. Once Winchurch's symptoms had been defined as arising from strychnine poisoning there was nothing left for Fenton to do but shift the blame onto his mistress. Gandolph suggested that Fenton attributed the source of the strychnine to Anstruther's chemist's shop out of revenge on Anstruther for calling in Waterfield and thus frustrating his hopes.

And what grounds had Gandolph for believing all this? Certain entries in Ada Hurst's diary. Wexford read them slowly and carefully.

For 27 February 1900, she had written, filling the entire small space: *Very cold. Leg painful again today. FW sent round the carriage and had John drive me to Pomfret. Compton says rats in the cellars and the old stables. Dined at home with F who says rats carry leptospiral jaundice, must be got rid of.*

28 February: *Drove in FW's carriage to call on old Mrs Paget. FW still here, having tea with F when I returned. I hope there is no harm in it. Dare I warn F?*

29 February: *F destroyed twenty rats with strychnine from his dispensary. What a relief!*

1 March: *Poor old Mrs Paget passed away in the night. A merciful release. Compton complained about the rats again. Warmer this evening and raining.*

There was no entry for 2 March.

3 March: *Annie gave notice, she is getting married. Shall be sorry to lose her. Would not go out in carriage for fear of leaving FW too much alone with F. To bed early as leg most painful.*

4 March: *My birthday. 26 today and an old maid now, I think. FW drove over, brought me beautiful Indian shawl. She is always kind. Invited F and me to dinner tomorrow.*

There was no entry for 5 March, and the last entry for nine months was the one for 6 March: *Dined last night at Paraleash House, six guests besides ourselves and the Ws. F left cigar case in the dining room, went back after seeing me home. I hope and pray there is no harm.*

GANDOLPH WAS evidently basing his case on the entries for 29 February and 6 March. In telling the court he had no strychnine in his dispensary, Fenton had lied. He had had an obvious opportunity for the introduction of strychnine into the decanter when he returned to Paraleash House in pursuit of his mislaid cigar case, and when he no doubt took care that he entered the dining room alone.

The next day Wexford reread the chapters in which the new information was contained and he studied with concentration the section concerning the diary. But unless Gandolph were simply lying about the existence of the diary or of those two entries—things which he would hardly dare to do—there seemed no reason to differ from his inference. Florence was innocent, Frank Fenton the murderer of Edward Winchurch. But still Wexford wished Burden were there so that they might have one of their often acrimonious but always fruitful discussions. Somehow, with old Mike to argue against him and put up opposition, he felt things might have been better clarified.

And the morning brought news of Burden, if not the inspector himself, in the form of a postcard from Agios Nikolaios. The blue Aegean, a rocky escarpment, green pines. Who but Burden, as Wexford remarked to Dora, would send postcards while on his honeymoon? The post also brought a parcel from Carlyon Brent. It contained books, a selection from the publishing house's current list as a present for Wexford, and on the compliments slip accompanying them, a note from Amyas Ireland. *I shall be in Kingsmarkham with my people at the weekend. Can we meet? AI.* The books were the latest novel about Regency London by Camilla Barnet; *Put Money in Thy Purse*, the biography of Vassili Vandrian, the financier; the memoirs of Sofya Bolkinska, Bolshoi ballerina; an omnibus version of three novels of farming life by Giles de Coverley; the *Cosmos Book of Stars and Calendars*, and Vernon Trevor's short stories, *Raise me up Samuel*. Wexford wondered if he would ever have time to read them, but he enjoyed looking at them, their handsome glossy jackets, and smelling the civilised, aromatic, slightly acrid print smell of them. At ten he phoned Amyas Ireland, thanked him for the present and said he had read *Poison at Paraleash*.

'We can talk about it?'

'Sure. I'll be at home all Saturday and Sunday.'

'Let me take you and Mrs Wexford out to dinner on Saturday night,' said Ireland.

But Dora refused. She would be an embarrassment to both of them, she said, they would have their talk much better without her, and she would spend the evening at home having a shot at making a coil pot on her own. So Wexford went alone to meet Ireland in the bar of the Olive and Dove.

'I suppose,' he said, accepting a glass of Moselle, 'that we can dispense with the fiction that you wanted me to read this book to check on police methods and court procedure? Not to put too fine a point on it, you were apprehensive Gandolph might have been up to his old tricks again?'

'Oh, well now, come,' said Ireland. He seemed thinner than ever. He looked about him, he looked at Wexford, made a face, wrinkling up nose and mouth. 'Well, if you must put it like that—yes.'

'There may not have been any tricks, though, may there? Paxton couldn't have murdered James Conyngford, but that doesn't mean he didn't tell Gandolph he did murder him. Certainly the people who give Gandolph information seem to die very conveniently soon afterwards. He picks on the dying, first Paxton, then Lina Hurst. I suppose you've seen this diary?'

'Oh, yes. We shall be using prints of the two relevant pages among the illustrations.'

'No possibility of forgery?'

Ireland looked unhappy. 'Ada Hurst wrote a very stylised hand, what's called a *ronde* hand, which she had obviously taught herself. It would be easy to forge. I can't submit it to handwriting experts, can I? I'm not a policeman. I'm just a poor publisher who very much wants to publish this reappraisal of the Winchurch case if it's genuine—and shun it like the plague if it's not.'

'I think it's genuine.' Wexford smiled at the slight lightening in Ireland's face. 'I take it that it was usual for Ada Hurst to leave blanks as she did for March 2nd and March 5th?'

Ireland nodded. 'Quite usual. Every month there'd have been half a dozen days on which she made no entries.' A waiter came up to them with two large menus. 'I'll have the *bouillabaisse* and the lamb *en croûte* and the *médaillon* potatoes and french beans.'

'Consommé and then the Parma ham,' said Wexford austerely. When the waiter had gone he grinned at Ireland. 'Pity they don't do *Filets de hareng marinés à la Rosette*. It might have provided us with the authentic atmosphere.' He was silent for a moment, savouring the delicate tangy wine. 'I'm assuming you've checked that 1900 genuinely was a Leap Year?'

'All first years of a century are.'

Wexford thought about it. 'Yes, of course, all years divisible by four are Leap Years.'

'I must say it's a great relief to me you're so happy about it.'

'I wouldn't quite say that,' said Wexford.

They went into the dining room and were shown, at Ireland's request, to a sheltered corner table. A waiter brought a bottle of Château de Portets 1973. Wexford looked at the basket of rolls, croissants, little plump brioches, miniature wholemeal loaves, Italian sticks, swallowed his desire and refused with an abrupt shake of the head. Ireland took two croissants.

'What exactly do you mean?' he said.

'It strikes me as being odd,' said the chief inspector, 'that in the entry for February 29th Ada Hurst says that her brother destroyed twenty rats with strychnine, yet in the entry for March 1st that Compton, whom I take to be the gardener, is still complaining about the rats. Why wasn't he told how effective the strychnine had been? Hadn't he been taken into Fenton's confidence about the poisoning? Or was twenty only a very small percentage of the hordes of rats which infested the place?'

'Right. It is odd. What else?'

'I don't know why, on March 6th, she mentions Fenton's returning for the cigar case. It wasn't interesting and she was limited for space. She doesn't record the name of a single guest at the dinner party, doesn't say what any of the women wore, but she carefully notes that her brother had left his cigar case in the Paraleash House dining room and had to go back for it. Why does she?'

'Oh, surely because by now she's nervous whenever Frank is alone with Florence.'

'But he wouldn't have been alone with Florence, Winchurch would have been there.'

They discussed the script throughout the meal, and later pored over it, Ireland with his brandy, Wexford with coffee. Dora had been wise not to come. But the outcome was that the new facts were really new and sound and that Carlyon Brent could safely publish the book in the spring. Wexford got home to find Dora sitting with a wobbly-looking half-finished coil pot beside her and deep in the *Cosmos Book of Stars and Calendars*.

'Reg, did you know that for the Greeks the year began on Midsummer Day? And that the Chinese and Jewish calendars have twelve months in some years and thirteen in others?'

'I can't say I did.'

'We avoid that, you see, by using the Gregorian Calendar and correct the error by making every fourth year a Leap Year. You really must read this book, it's fascinating.'

But Wexford's preference was for the Vassili Vandrian and the farming trilogy, though with little time to read he hadn't completed a single one of these works by the time Burden returned on the following Monday week. Burden had a fine even tan but for his nose which had peeled.

'Have a good time?' asked Wexford with automatic politeness.

'What a question,' said the inspector, 'to ask a man who has just come back from his honeymoon. Of course I had a good time.' He cautiously scratched his nose. 'What have you been up to?'

'Seeing something of your brother-in-law. He got me to read a manuscript.'

'Ha!' said Burden. 'I know what that was. He said something about it but he knew Gandolph'd get short shrift from me. A devious liar if ever there was one. It beats me what sort of satisfaction a man can get out of the kind of fame that comes from foisting on the public stories he *knows* aren't true. All that about Paxton was a pack of lies, and I've no doubt he bases this new version of the Winchurch case on another pack of lies. He's not interested in the truth. He's only interested in being known as the great criminologist and the man who shows the police up for fools.'

'Come on, Mike, that's a bit sweeping. I told Ireland I thought it would be OK to go ahead and publish.'

Burden's face wore an expression that was almost a caricature of sophisticated scathing knowingness. 'Well, of course, I haven't seen it, I can't say. I'm basing my objection to Gandolph on the Paxton affair. Paxton never confessed to any murder and Gandolph knows it.'

'You can't say that for sure.'

Burden sat down. He tapped his fist lightly on the corner of the desk. 'I *can* say. I knew Paxton, I knew him well.'

'I didn't know that.'

'No, it was years back, before I came here. In Eastbourne, it was, when Paxton was with the Garfield gang. In the force down there we knew it was useless ever trying to get Paxton to talk. He *never* talked. I don't mean he just didn't give away any info, I mean he didn't answer when you spoke to him. Various times we tried to interrogate him he just maintained this total silence. A mate of his told me he'd made it a rule not to talk to policemen or social workers or lawyers or any what you might call Establishment people, and he never had. He talked to his wife and his kids and his mates all right. But I remember once he was in the dock at Lewes Assizes and the judge addressed him. He just didn't answer—he wouldn't—and the judge, it was old Clydesdale, sent him down for contempt. So don't tell me Paxton made any sort of confession to Kenneth Gandolph, not *Paxton*.'

The effect of this was to reawaken all Wexford's former doubts. He trusted Burden, he had a high opinion of his opinion. He began to wish he had advised Ireland to have tests made to determine the age of the ink used in the 29 February and 6 March entries, or to have the writing examined by a handwriting expert. Yet if Ada Hurst had had a stylised hand self-taught in adulthood . . . What good were handwriting experts anyway? Not much, in his experience. And of course Ireland couldn't suggest to Gandolph that the ink should be tested without offending the man to such an extent that he would refuse publication of *Poison at Paraleash* to Carlyon Brent. But Wexford was suddenly certain that those entries were false and that Gandolph had forged them. Very subtly and cunningly he had forged them, having judged that the addition to the diary of just thirty-four words would alter the whole balance of the Winchurch case and shift the culpability from Florence to her lover.

Thirty-four words. Wexford had made a copy of the diary entries and now he looked at them again. 29 February: *F destroyed twenty rats with strychnine from his dispensary. What a relief!* 6 March: *F left cigar case in the dining room, went back after seeing me home. I hope and pray there is no harm.* There were no anachronisms—men certainly used cigar cases in 1900—no divergence from Ada's usual style. The word 'twenty' was written in letters instead of two figures. The writer, on 6 March, had written not about that day but about the day before. Did that amount to anything? Wexford thought not, though he pondered on it for most of the day.

That evening he was well into the last chapter of *Put Money in Thy Purse* when the phone rang. It was Jenny Burden. Would he and Dora come to dinner on Saturday? Her parents would be there and her brother.

Wexford said Dora was out at her pottery class, but yes, they would love to, and had she had a nice time in Crete?

'How sweet of you to ask,' said the bride. 'No one else has. Thank you, we had a lovely time.'

He had meant it when he said they would love to, but still he didn't feel very happy about meeting Amyas Ireland again. He had a notion that once the book was published some as yet unimagined Warren or Burden would turn up and denounce it, deride it, laugh at the glaring giveaway he and Ireland couldn't see. When he saw Ireland again he ought to say, don't do it, don't take the risk, publish and be damned can have another meaning than the popular one. But how to give such a warning with no sound reason for giving it, with nothing but one of those vague feelings, this time of foreboding, which had so assisted him yet run him into so much trouble in the past? No, there was nothing he could do. He sighed, finished his chapter and moved on to the farmer's fictionalised memoirs.

Afterwards Wexford was in the habit of saying that he got more reading done during that week than he had in years. Perhaps it had been a way of escape from fretful thought. But certainly he had passed a freakishly slack week, getting home most nights by six. He even read Miss Camilla Barnet's *The Golden Reticule*, and by Friday night there was nothing left but the *Cosmos Book of Stars and Calendars*.

IT WAS A LARGE PARTY, Mr and Mrs Ireland and their son, Burden's daughter Pat, Grace and her husband and, of course, the Burdens themselves. Jenny's face glowed with happiness and Aegean sunshine. She welcomed the Wexfords with kisses and brought them drinks served in their own wedding present to her.

The meeting with Amyas Ireland wasn't the embarrassment Wexford had feared it would be—had feared, that is, up till a few minutes before he and Dora had left home. And now he knew that he couldn't contain himself till after dinner, till the morning, or perhaps worse than that—a phone call on Monday morning. He asked his hostess if she would think him very rude if he spoke to her brother alone for five minutes.

She laughed. 'Not rude at all. I think you must have got the world's most wonderful idea for a crime novel and Ammy's going to publish it. But I don't know where to put you unless it's the kitchen. And you,' she said to her brother, 'are not to eat anything, mind.'

'I couldn't wait,' Wexford said as they found themselves stowed away into the kitchen where every surface was necessarily loaded with the constituents of dinner for ten people. 'I only found out this evening at the last minute before we were due to come out.'

'It's something about the Winchurch book?'

Wexford said eagerly, 'It's not too late, is it? I was worried I might be too late.'

'Good God, no. We hadn't planned to start printing before the autumn.' Ireland, who had seemed about to disobey his sister and help himself to a maca-roon from a silver dish, suddenly lost his appetite. 'This is serious?'

'Wait till you hear. I was waiting for my wife to finish dressing.' He grinned. 'You should make it a rule to read your own books, you know. That's what I was doing, reading one of those books you sent me and that's where I found it. You won't be able to publish *Poison at Paraleash.*' The smile went and he looked almost fierce. 'I've no hesitation in saying Kenneth Gandolph is a forger and a cheat and you'd be advised to have nothing to do with him in future.'

Ireland's eyes narrowed. 'Better know it now than later. What did he do and how do you know?'

From his jacket pocket Wexford took the copy he had made of the diary entries. 'I can't prove that the last entry, the one for March 6th that says, *F left cigar case in the dining room, went back after seeing me home*, I can't prove that's forged, I only think it is. What I know for certain is a forgery is the entry for February 29th.'

'Isn't that the one about strychnine?'

'F destroyed twenty rats with strychnine from his dispensary. What a relief!'

'How do you know it's forged?'

'Because the day itself didn't occur,' said Wexford. 'In 1900 there was no February 29th, it wasn't a Leap Year.'

'Oh, yes, it was. We've been through all that before.' Ireland sounded both relieved and impatient. 'All years divisible by four are Leap Years. All century years are divisible by four and 1900 was a century year. 1897 was the year she began the diary, following 1896 which was a Leap Year. Needless to say, there was no February 29th in 1897, 1898 or 1899 so there must have been one in 1900.'

'It wasn't a Leap Year,' said Wexford. 'Didn't I tell you I found this out through that book of yours, the *Cosmos Book of Stars and Calendars*? There's a lot of useful information in there, and one of the bits of information is about how Pope Gregory composed a new civil calendar to correct the errors of the Julian Calendar. One of his rulings was that every fourth year should be a Leap Year except in certain cases—'

Ireland interrupted him. 'I don't believe it!' he said in the voice of someone who knows he believes every word.

Wexford shrugged. He went on, 'Century years were not to be Leap Years unless they were divisible not by four but by four hundred. Therefore, 1600 would have been a Leap Year if the Gregorian Calendar had by then been adopted, and 2000 will be a Leap Year, but 1800 was not and 1900 was not. So in 1900 there was no February 29th and Ada Hurst left the space on that page blank for the very good reason that the day following February 28th was March 1st. Unluckily for him, Gandolph, like you and me and most people, knew nothing of this as otherwise he would surely have inserted his strychnine entry into the blank space of March 2nd and his forgery might never have been discovered.'

Ireland slowly shook his head at man's ingenuity and perhaps his chicanery. 'I'm very grateful to you. We should have looked fools, shouldn't we?'

'I'm glad Florence wasn't hanged in error,' Wexford said as they went back to join the others. 'Her marriage didn't begin with dearly beloved, but if she was afraid at the end it can't have been with any amazement.'

Dorothy L. Sayers
1893–1957

THE ADVENTUROUS EXPLOIT OF THE CAVE OF ALI BABA

IN THE FRONT ROOM of a grim and narrow house in Lambeth a man sat eating kippers and glancing through the *Morning Post*. He was smallish and spare, with brown hair rather too regularly waved and a strong, brown beard, cut to a point. His double-breasted suit of navy blue and his socks, tie and handkerchief, all scrupulously matched, were a trifle more point-device than the best taste approves, and his boots were slightly too bright a brown. He did not look a gentleman, not even a gentleman's gentleman, yet there was something about his appearance which suggested that he was accustomed to the manner of life in good families. The breakfast table, which he had set with his own hands, was arrayed with the attention to detail which is exacted of good-class servants. His action, as he walked over to a little side table and carved himself a plate of ham, was the action of a superior butler; yet he was not old enough to be a retired butler; a footman, perhaps, who had come into a legacy.

He finished the ham with good appetite, and, as he sipped his coffee, read through attentively a paragraph which he had already noticed and put aside for consideration.

LORD PETER WIMSEY'S WILL

BEQUEST TO VALET

£10,000 TO CHARITIES

The will of Lord Peter Wimsey, who was killed last December while shooting big game in Tanganyika, was proved yesterday at £500,000. A sum of £10,000 was left to various charities, including [here followed a list of bequests]. To his valet, Mervyn Bunter, was left an annuity of £500 and the lease of the testator's flat in Piccadilly. [Then followed a number of personal bequests.] The remainder of the estate, including the valuable collection of books and pictures at 110a Piccadilly, was left to the testator's mother, the Dowager Duchess of Denver.

Lord Peter Wimsey was thirty-seven at the time of his death. He was the younger brother of the present Duke of Denver, who is the wealthiest peer in the United Kingdom. Lord Peter was distinguished as a criminologist and took an active part in the solution of several famous mysteries. He was a well-known book collector and man-about-town.

The man gave a sigh of relief.

'No doubt about that,' he said aloud. 'People don't give their money away if they're going to come back again. The blighter's dead and buried right enough. I'm free.'

He finished his coffee, cleared the table, and washed up the crockery, took his bowler hat from the hall stand, and went out.

A bus took him to Bermondsey. He alighted, and plunged into a network of gloomy streets, arriving after a quarter of an hour's walk at a seedy looking public house in a low quarter. He entered and called for a double whisky.

The house had only just opened, but a number of customers, who had apparently been waiting on the doorstep for this desirable event, were already clustered about the bar. The man who might have been a footman reached for his glass, and in doing so jostled the elbow of a flash person in a check suit and regrettable tie.

'Here!' expostulated the flash person, 'what d'yer mean by it? We don't want your sort here. Get out!'

He emphasised his remarks with a few highly coloured words, and a violent push in the chest.

'Bar's free to everybody, isn't it?' said the other, returning the shove with interest.

'Now then!' said the barmaid, 'none o' that. The gentleman didn't do it intentional, Mr Jukes.'

'Didn't he?' said Mr Jukes. 'Well I *did*.'

'And you ought to be ashamed of yourself,' retorted the young lady, with a toss of the head. 'I'll have no quarrelling in my bar—not this time in the morning.'

'It was quite an accident,' said the man from Lambeth. 'I'm not one to make a disturbance, having always been used to the best houses. But if any gentleman wants to make trouble—'

'All right, all right,' said Mr Jukes, more pacifically. 'I'm not keen to give you a new face. Not but what any alteration wouldn't be for the better. Mind your manners another time, that's all. What'll you have?'

'No, no,' protested the other, 'this one must be on me. Sorry I pushed you. I didn't mean it. But I didn't like to be taken up so short.'

'Say no more about it,' said Mr Jukes generously. 'I'm standing this. Another double whisky, miss, and one of the usual. Come over here where there isn't so much of a crowd, or you'll be getting yourself into trouble again.'

He led the way to a small table in the corner of the room.

'That's all right,' said Mr Jukes. 'Very nicely done. I don't think there's any danger here, but you can't be too careful. Now, what about it, Rogers? Have you made up your mind to come in with us?'

'Yes,' said Rogers, with a glance over his shoulder, 'yes, I have. That is, mind you, if everything seems all right. I'm not looking for trouble, and I don't want to get let in for any dangerous games. I don't mind giving you information, but it's understood as I take no active part in whatever goes on. Is that straight?'

'You wouldn't be allowed to take an active part if you wanted to,' said Mr Jukes. 'Why, you poor fish, Number One wouldn't have anybody but experts on his jobs. All you have to do is to let us know where the stuff is and how to get it. The Society does the rest. It's some organisation, I can tell you. You won't even know who's doing it, or how it's done. You won't know anybody, and nobody will know you—except Number One, of course. He knows everybody.'

'And you,' said Rogers.

'And me, of course. But I shall be transferred to another district. We shan't meet again after today, except at the general meetings, and then we shall all be masked.'

'Go on!' said Rogers incredulously.

'Fact. You'll be taken to Number One—he'll see you, but you won't see him. Then, if he thinks you're any good, you'll be put on the roll, and after that you'll be told where to make your reports to. There is a divisional meeting called once a fortnight, and every three months there's a general meeting and share out. Each member is called up by number and has his whack handed over to him. That's all.'

'Well, but suppose two members are put on the same job together?'

'If it's a daylight job, they'll be so disguised their mothers wouldn't know 'em. But it's mostly night work.'

'I see. But, look here—what's to prevent somebody following me home and giving me away to the police?'

'Nothing, of course. Only I wouldn't advise him to try it, that's all. The last man who had that bright idea was fished out of the river down Rotherhithe way,

477

before he had time to get his precious report in. Number One knows everybody, you see.'

'Oh!—and who is this Number One?'

'There's lots of people would give a good bit to know that.'

'Does nobody know?'

'Nobody. He's a fair marvel, is Number One. He's a gentleman, I can tell you that, and a pretty high-up one, from his ways. *And* he's got eyes all round his head. *And* he's got an arm as long as from here to Australia. *But* nobody knows anything about him, unless it's Number Two, and I'm not even sure about her.'

'There are women in it, then?'

'You can bet your boots there are. You can't do a job without 'em nowadays. But that needn't worry you. The women are safe enough. They don't want to come to a sticky end, no more than you and me.'

'But look here, Jukes—how about the money? It's a big risk to take. Is it worth it?'

'Worth it?' Jukes leaned across the little marble-topped table and whispered.

'Coo!' gasped Rogers. 'And how much of that would I get, now?'

'You'd share and share alike with the rest, whether you'd been in that particular job or not. There's fifty members, and you'd get one-fiftieth, same as Number One and same as me.'

'Really? No kidding?'

'See that wet, see that dry!' Jukes laughed. 'Say, can you beat it? There's never been anything like it. It's the biggest thing ever been known. He's a great man, is Number One.'

'And do you pull off many jobs?'

'Many? Listen. You remember the Carruthers necklace, and the Gorleston Bank robbery? And the Faversham burglary? And the big Rubens that disappeared from the National Gallery? And the Frensham pearls? All done by the Society. And never one of them cleared up.'

Rogers licked his lips.

'But now, look here,' he said cautiously. 'Supposing I was a spy, as you might say, and supposing I was to go straight off and tell the police about what you've been saying?'

'Ah!' said Jukes, 'suppose you did, eh? Well, supposing something nasty didn't happen to you on the way there—which I wouldn't answer for, mind—'

'Do you mean to say you've got me watched?'

'You can bet your sweet life we have. Yes. Well, *supposing* nothing happened on the way there, and you was to bring the slops to this pub, looking for yours truly—'

'Yes?'

'You wouldn't find me, that's all. I should have gone to Number Five.'

'Who's Number Five?'

'Ah! I don't know. But he's the man that makes you a new face while you wait. Plastic surgery, they call it. And new fingerprints. New everything. We go in for up-to-date methods in our show.'

Rogers whistled.

'Well, how about it?' asked Jukes, eyeing his acquaintance over the rim of his tumbler.

'Look here—you've told me a lot of things. Shall I be safe if I say "no"?'

'Oh, yes—if you behave yourself and don't make trouble for us.'

'H'm, I see. And if I say "yes"?'

'Then you'll be a rich man in less than no time, with money in your pocket to live like a gentleman. And nothing to do for it, except to tell us what you know about the houses you've been to when you were in service. It's money for jam if you act straight by the Society.'

Rogers was silent, thinking it over.

'I'll do it!' he said at last.

'Good for you. Miss! The same again, please. Here's to it, Rogers! I knew you were one of the right sort the minute I set eyes on you. Here's to money for jam, and take care of Number One! Talking of Number One, you'd better come round and see him tonight. No time like the present.'

'Right you are. Where'll I come to? Here?'

'Nix. No more of this little pub for us. It's a pity, because it's nice and comfortable, but it can't be helped. Now, what you've got to do is this. At ten o'clock tonight exactly, you walk across Lambeth Bridge.' (Rogers winced at this intimation that his abode was known), 'and you'll see a yellow taxi standing there, with the driver doing something to his engine. You'll say to him, "Is your bus fit to go?" and he'll say, "Depends where you want to go to." And you'll say, "Take me to Number One, London." There's a shop called that, by the way, but he won't take you there. You won't know where he is taking you, because the taxi windows will be covered up, but you mustn't mind that. It's the rule for the first visit. Afterwards, when you're regularly one of us, you'll be told the name of the place. And when you get there, do as you're told and speak the truth, because, if you don't, Number One will deal with you. See?'

'I see.'

'Are you game? You're not afraid?'

'Of course I'm not afraid.'

'Good man! Well, we'd better be moving now. And I'll say goodbye, because we shan't see each other again. Goodbye—and good luck!'

'Goodbye.'

They passed through the swing doors, and out into the mean and dirty street.

THE TWO YEARS subsequent to the enrolment of the ex-footman Rogers in a crook society were marked by a number of startling and successful raids on the houses of distinguished people. There was the theft of the great diamond tiara from the Dowager Duchess of Denver; the burglary at the flat formerly occupied by the late Lord Peter Wimsey, resulting in the disappearance of £7,000 worth of silver and gold plate; the burglary at the country mansion of Theodore Winthrop, the millionaire—which, incidentally, exposed that thriving gentleman as a confirmed society blackmailer and caused a reverberating scandal in Mayfair; and the snatching of the famous eight-string necklace of pearls from the neck of the Marchioness of Dinglewood during the singing of the "Jewel Song" in *Faust* at Covent Garden. It is true that the pearls turned out to be imitation, the original string having been pawned by the noble lady under circumstances highly painful to the Marquis, but the coup was nevertheless a sensational one.

On a Saturday afternoon in January, Rogers was sitting in his room in Lambeth, when a slight noise at the front door caught his ear. He sprang up almost before it had ceased, dashed through the small hallway, and flung the door open. The street was deserted. Nevertheless, as he turned back to the sitting room, he saw an envelope lying on the hat stand. It was addressed briefly to 'Number Twenty-one'. Accustomed by this time to the somewhat dramatic methods used by the Society to deliver its correspondence, he merely shrugged his shoulders, and opened the note.

It was written in cipher, and, when transcribed, ran thus:

> *Number Twenty-one,—An Extraordinary General Meeting will be held tonight at the house of Number One at 11.30. You will be absent at your peril. The word is FINALITY.*

Rogers stood for a little time considering this. Then he made his way to a room at the back of the house, in which there was a tall safe, built into the wall. He manipulated the combination and walked into the safe, which ran back for some distance, forming, indeed, a small strong room. He pulled out a drawer marked 'Correspondence', and added the paper he had just received to the contents.

After a few moments he emerged, reset the lock to a new combination, and returned to the sitting room.

'Finality,' he said. 'Yes—I think so.' He stretched out his hand to the telephone—then appeared to alter his mind.

He went upstairs to an attic, and thence climbed into a loft close under the roof. Crawling among the rafters, he made his way into the farthest corner; then carefully pressed a knot on the timberwork. A concealed trap door swung open. He crept through it, and found himself in the corresponding loft of the next house. A soft cooing noise greeted him as he entered. Under the skylight stood three cages, each containing a carrier pigeon.

He glanced cautiously out of the skylight, which looked out upon a high blank wall at the back of some factory or other. There was nobody in the dim little courtyard, and no window within sight. He drew his head in again, and, taking a small fragment of thin paper from his pocketbook, wrote a few letters and numbers upon it. Going to the nearest cage, he took out the pigeon and attached the message to its wing. Then he carefully set the bird on the window ledge. It hesitated a moment, shifted its pink feet a few times, lifted its wings, and was gone. He saw it tower up into the already darkening sky over the factory roof and vanish into the distance.

He glanced at his watch and returned downstairs. An hour later he released the second pigeon, and in another hour the third. Then he sat down to wait.

At half past nine he went up to the attic again. It was dark, but a few frosty stars were shining, and a cold air blew through the open window. Something pale gleamed faintly on the floor. He picked it up—it was warm and feathery. The answer had come.

He ruffled the soft plumes and found the paper. Before reading it, he fed the pigeon and put it into one of the cages. As he was about to fasten the door, he checked himself.

'If anything happens to me,' he said, 'there's no need for you to starve to death, my child.'

He pushed the window a little wider open and went downstairs again. The paper in his hand bore only the two letters, 'OK'. It seemed to have been written hurriedly, for there was a long smear of ink in the upper left-hand corner. He noted this with a smile, put the paper in the fire, and, going out into the kitchen, prepared and ate a hearty meal of eggs and corned beef from a new tin. He ate it without bread, though there was a loaf on the shelf near at hand, and washed it down with water from the tap, which he let run for some time before venturing to drink it. Even then he carefully wiped the tap, both inside and outside, before drinking.

When he had finished, he took a revolver from a locked drawer, inspecting the mechanism with attention to see that it was in working order, and loaded it with new cartridges from an unbroken packet. Then he sat down to wait again.

At a quarter before eleven, he rose and went out into the street. He walked briskly, keeping well away from the wall, till he came out into a well-lighted thoroughfare. Here he took a bus, securing the corner seat next to the conductor, from which he could see everybody who got on and off. A succession of buses eventually brought him to a respectable residential quarter of Hampstead. Here he alighted and, still keeping well away from the walls, made his way up to the Heath.

The night was moonless, but not altogether black, and, as he crossed a deserted part of the Heath, he observed one or two other dark forms closing in upon him from various directions. He paused in the shelter of a large tree, and adjusted to his face a black velvet mask, which covered him from brow to chin. At its base the number 21 was clearly embroidered in white thread.

At length a slight dip in the ground disclosed one of those agreeable villas which stand, somewhat isolated, among the rural surroundings of the Heath. One of the windows was lighted. As he made his way to the door, other dark figures, masked like himself, pressed forward and surrounded him. He counted six of them.

The foremost man knocked on the door of the solitary house. After a moment, it was opened slightly. The man advanced his head to the opening; there was a murmur, and the door opened wide. The man stepped in, and the door was shut.

When three of the men had entered, Rogers found himself to be the next in turn. He knocked, three times loudly, then twice faintly. The door opened to the extent of two or three inches, and an ear was presented to the chink. Rogers whispered 'Finality'. The ear was withdrawn, the door opened, and he passed in.

Without any further word of greeting, Number Twenty-one passed into a small room on the left, which was furnished like an office, with a desk, a safe, and a couple of chairs. At the desk sat a massive man in evening dress, with a ledger before him. The new arrival shut the door carefully after him; it clicked to, on a spring lock. Advancing to the desk, he announced, 'Number Twenty-one, sir,' and stood respectfully waiting. The big man looked up, showing the number 1 startlingly white on his mask. His eyes, of a curious hard blue, scanned Rogers attentively. At a sign from him, Rogers removed his mask. Having verified his identity with care, the President said, 'Very well, Number Twenty-one,' and made an entry in the ledger. The voice was hard and metallic, like his eyes. The close scrutiny from behind the immovable black mask seemed to make Rogers uneasy; he shifted his feet, and his eyes fell. Number One made a sign of dismissal, and Rogers, with a faint sigh as though of relief, replaced his mask and left the room. As he came out, the next comer passed in in his place.

The room in which the Society met was a large one, made by knocking the two largest of the first-floor rooms into one. It was furnished in the standardised taste of twentieth-century suburbia and brilliantly lighted. A gramophone in one corner blared out a jazz tune, to which about ten couples of masked men and women were dancing, some in evening dress and others in tweeds and jumpers.

In one corner of the room was an American bar. Rogers went up and asked the masked man in charge for a double whisky. He consumed it slowly, leaning on the bar. The room filled. Presently somebody moved across to the gramophone and stopped it. He looked round. Number One had appeared on the threshold. A tall woman in black stood beside him. The mask, embroidered with a white 2, covered hair and face completely; only her fine bearing and her white arms and bosom and the dark eyes shining through the eye-slits proclaimed her a woman of power and physical attraction.

'Ladies and gentlemen.' Number One was standing at the upper end of the room. The woman sat beside him; her eyes were cast down and betrayed nothing, but her hands were clenched on the arms of the chair and her whole figure seemed tensely aware.

'Ladies and gentlemen. Our numbers are two short tonight.' The masks moved; eyes were turned, seeking and counting. 'I need not inform you of the disastrous failure of our plan for securing the plans of the Court-Windlesham helicopter. Our courageous and devoted comrades, Number Fifteen and Number Forty-eight, were betrayed and taken by the police.'

An uneasy murmur arose among the company.

'It may have occurred to some of you that even the well-known steadfastness of these comrades might give way under examination. There is no cause for alarm. The usual orders have been issued, and I have this evening received the report that their tongues have been effectually silenced. You will, I am sure, be glad to know that these two brave men have been spared the ordeal of so great a temptation to dishonour, and that they will not be called upon to face a public trial and the rigours of a long imprisonment.'

A hiss of intaken breath moved across the assembled members like the wind over a barley field.

'Their dependants will be discreetly compensated in the usual manner. I call upon Numbers Twelve and Thirty-four to undertake this agreeable task. They will attend me in my office for their instructions after the meeting. Will the Numbers I have named kindly signify that they are able and willing to perform this duty?'

Two hands were raised in salute. The President continued, looking at his watch:

'Ladies and gentlemen, please take your partners for the next dance.'

The gramophone struck up again. Rogers turned to a girl near him in a red dress. She nodded, and they slipped into the movement of a foxtrot. The couples gyrated solemnly and in silence. Their shadows were flung against the blinds as they turned and stepped to and fro.

'What has happened?' breathed the girl in a whisper, scarcely moving her lips. 'I'm frightened, aren't you? I feel as if something awful was going to happen.'

'It does take one a bit short, the President's way of doing things,' agreed Rogers, 'but it's safer like that.'

'Those poor men—'

A dancer, turning and following on their heels, touched Rogers on the shoulder.

'No talking, please,' he said. His eyes gleamed sternly; he twirled his partner into the middle of the crowd and was gone. The girl shuddered.

The gramophone stopped. There was a burst of clapping. The dancers again clustered before the President's seat.

'Ladies and gentlemen. You may wonder why this extraordinary meeting has been called. The reason is a serious one. The failure of our recent attempt was no accident. The police were not on the premises that night by chance. We have a traitor among us.'

Partners who had been standing close together fell distrustfully apart. Each member seemed to shrink, as a snail shrinks from the touch of a finger.

'You will remember the disappointing outcome of the Dinglewood affair,' went on the President, in his harsh voice. 'You may recall other smaller matters which have not turned out satisfactorily. All these troubles have been traced to their origin. I am happy to say that our minds can now be easy. The offender has been discovered and will be removed. There will be no more mistakes. The misguided member who introduced the traitor to our Society will be placed in a position where his lack of caution will have no further ill effects. There is no cause for alarm.'

Every eye roved about the company, searching for the traitor and his unfortunate sponsor. Somewhere beneath the black masks a face must have turned white; somewhere under the stifling velvet there must have been a brow sweating, not with the heat of the dance. But the masks hid everything.

'Ladies and gentlemen, please take your partners for the next dance.'

The gramophone struck into an old and half-forgotten tune: 'There ain't nobody loves me.' The girl in red was claimed by a tall mask in evening dress. A hand laid on Rogers's arm made him start. A small, plump woman in a green jumper slipped a cold hand into his. The dance went on.

When it stopped, amid the usual applause, everyone stood, detached, stiffened in expectation. The President's voice was raised again.

'Ladies and gentlemen, please behave naturally. This is a dance, not a public meeting.'

Rogers led his partner to a chair and fetched her an ice. As he stooped over her, he noticed the hurried rise and fall of her bosom.

'Ladies and gentlemen.' The endless interval was over. 'You will no doubt wish to be immediately relieved from suspense. I will name the persons involved. Number Thirty-seven!'

A man sprang up with a fearful, strangled cry.

'Silence!'

The wretch choked and gasped.

'I never—I swear—I never—I'm innocent.'

'Silence. You have failed in discretion. You will be dealt with. If you have anything to say in defence of your folly, I will hear it later. Sit down.'

Number Thirty-seven sank down upon a chair. He pushed his handkerchief under the mask to wipe his face. Two tall men closed in upon him. The rest fell back, feeling the recoil of humanity from one stricken by mortal disease.

The gramophone struck up.

'Ladies and gentlemen, I will now name the traitor. Number Twenty-one, stand forward.'

Rogers stepped forward. The concentrated fear and loathing of forty-eight pairs of eyes burned upon him. The miserable Jukes set up a fresh wail.

'Oh, my God! Oh, my God!'

'Silence! Number Twenty-one, take off your mask.'

The traitor pulled the thick covering from his face. The intense hatred of the eyes devoured him.

'Number Thirty-seven, this man was introduced here by you, under the name of Joseph Rogers, formerly second footman in the service of the Duke of Denver, dismissed for pilfering. Did you take steps to verify that statement?'

'I did—I did! As God's my witness, it was all straight. I had him identified by two of the servants. I made enquiries. The tale was straight—I'll swear it was.'

The President consulted a paper before him, then he looked at his watch again.

'Ladies and gentlemen, please take your partners . . .'

Number Twenty-one, his arms twisted behind him and bound, and his wrists handcuffed, stood motionless, while the dance of doom circled about him. The clapping, as it ended, sounded like the clapping of the men and women who sat, thirsty-lipped beneath the guillotine.

'Number Twenty-one, your name has been given as Joseph Rogers, footman, dismissed for theft. Is that your real name?'

'No.'

'What is your name?'

'Peter Death Bredon Wimsey.'

'We thought you were dead.'

'Naturally. You were intended to think so.'

'What has become of the genuine Joseph Rogers?'

'He died abroad. I took his place. I may say that no real blame attaches to your people for not having realised who I was. I not only took Rogers's place; I *was* Rogers. Even when I was alone, I walked like Rogers, I sat like Rogers, I read Rogers's books, and wore Rogers's clothes. In the end, I almost thought Rogers's thoughts. The only way to keep up a successful impersonation is never to relax.'

'I see. The robbery of your own flat was arranged?'

'Obviously.'

'The robbery of the Dowager Duchess, your mother, was connived at by you?'

'It was. It was a very ugly tiara—no real loss to anybody with decent taste. May I smoke, by the way?'

'You may not. Ladies and gentlemen . . .'

The dance was like the mechanical jigging of puppets. Limbs jerked, feet faltered. The prisoner watched with an air of critical detachment.

'Numbers Fifteen, Twenty-two, and Forty-nine. You have watched the prisoner. Has he made any attempts to communicate with anybody?'

'None.' Number Twenty-two was the spokesman. 'His letters and parcels have been opened, his telephone tapped, and his movements followed. His water pipes have been under observation for Morse signals.'

'You are sure of what you say?'

'Absolutely.'

'Prisoner, have you been alone in this adventure? Speak the truth, or things will be made somewhat more unpleasant for you than they might otherwise be.'

'I have been alone. I have taken no unnecessary risks.'

'It may be so. It will, however, be as well that steps should be taken to silence the man at Scotland Yard—what is his name?—Parker. Also the prisoner's manservant, Mervyn Bunter, and possibly also his mother and sister. The brother is a stupid oaf, and not, I think, likely to have been taken into the prisoner's confidence. A precautionary watch will, I think, meet the necessities of his case.'

The prisoner appeared, for the first time, to be moved.

'Sir, I assure you that my mother and sister know nothing which could possibly bring danger on the Society.'

'You should have thought of their situation earlier. Ladies and gentlemen, please take—'

'No—no!' Flesh and blood could endure the mockery no longer. 'No! Finish with him. Get it over. Break up the meeting. It's dangerous. The police—'

'Silence!'

The President glanced round at the crowd. It had a dangerous look about it. He gave way.

'Very well. Take the prisoner away and silence him. He will receive Number 4 treatment. And be sure you explain it to him carefully first.'

'Ah!'

The eyes expressed a wolfish satisfaction. Strong hands gripped Wimsey's arms.

'One moment—for God's sake let me die decently.'

'You should have thought this over earlier. Take him away. Ladies and gentlemen, be satisfied—he will not die quickly.'

'Stop! Wait!' cried Wimsey desperately. 'I have something to say. I don't ask for life—only for a quick death. I—I have something to sell.'

'To sell?'

'Yes.'

'We make no bargains with traitors.'

'No—but listen! Do you think I have not thought of this? I am not so mad. I have left a letter.'

'Ah! now it is coming. A letter. To whom?'

'To the police. If I do not return tomorrow—'

'Well?'

'The letter will be opened.'

'Sir,' broke in Number Fifteen. 'This is bluff. The prisoner has not sent any letter. He has been strictly watched for many months.'

'Ah! but listen. I left the letter before I came to Lambeth.'

'Then it can contain no information of value.'

'Oh, but it does.'

'What?'

'The combination of my safe.'

'Indeed? Has this man's safe been searched?'

'Yes, sir.'

'What did it contain?'

'No information of importance, sir. An outline of our organisation—the name of this house—nothing that cannot be altered and covered before morning.'

Wimsey smiled.

'Did you investigate the inner compartment of the safe?'

There was a pause.

'You hear what he says,' snapped the President sharply. 'Did you find this inner compartment?'

'There was no inner compartment, sir. He is trying to bluff.'

'I hate to contradict you,' said Wimsey, with an effort at his ordinary pleasant tone, 'but I really think you must have overlooked the inner compartment.'

'Well,' said the President, 'and what do you say is in this inner compartment, if it does exist?'

'The names of every member of this Society, with their addresses, photographs, and fingerprints.'

'What?'

The eyes round him now were ugly with fear. Wimsey kept his face steadily turned towards the President.

'How do you say you have contrived to get this information?'

'Well, I have been doing a little detective work on my own, you know.'

'But you have been watched.'

'True. The fingerprints of my watchers adorn the first page of the collection.'

'This statement can be proved?'

'Certainly. I will prove it. The name of Number Fifty, for example—'

'Stop!'

A fierce muttering arose. The President silenced it with a gesture.

'If you mention names here, you will certainly have no hope of mercy. There is a fifth treatment—kept specially for people who mention names. Bring the prisoner to my office. Keep the dance going.'

The President took an automatic from his hip pocket and faced the tightly fettered prisoner across the desk.

'Now speak!' he said.

'I should put that thing away, if I were you,' said Wimsey contemptuously. 'It would be a much pleasanter form of death than treatment Number 5, and I might be tempted to ask for it.'

'Ingenious,' said the President, 'but a little too ingenious. Now, be quick; tell me what you know.'

'Will you spare me if I tell you?'

'I make no promises. Be quick.'

Wimsey shrugged his bound and aching shoulders.

'Certainly. I will tell you what I know. Stop me when you have heard enough.'

He leaned forward and spoke low. Overhead the noise of the gramophone and the shuffling of feet bore witness that the dance was going on. Stray passers by crossing the Heath noted that the people in the lonely house were making a night of it again.

'WELL,' SAID WIMSEY, 'am I to go on?'

From beneath the mask the President's voice sounded as though he were grimly smiling.

'My lord,' he said, 'your story fills me with regret that you are not, in fact, a member of our Society. Wit, courage, and industry are valuable to an association like ours. I fear I cannot persuade you? No—I supposed not.'

He touched a bell on his desk.

'Ask the members kindly to proceed to the supper room,' he said to the mask who entered.

The 'supper room' was on the ground floor, shuttered and curtained. Down its centre ran a long, bare table, with chairs set about it.

'A Barmecide feast, I see,' said Wimsey pleasantly. It was the first time he had seen this room. At the far end, a trap door in the floor gaped ominously.

The President took the head of the table.

'Ladies and gentlemen,' he began, as usual—and the foolish courtesy had never sounded so sinister—'I will not conceal from you the seriousness of the situation. The prisoner has recited to me more than twenty names and addresses which were thought to be unknown, except to their owners and to me. There has been great carelessness'—his voice rang harshly—'which will have to be looked into. Fingerprints have been obtained—he has shown me the photographs of some of them. How our investigators came to overlook the inner door of this safe is a matter which calls for enquiry.'

'Don't blame them,' put in Wimsey. 'It was meant to be overlooked, you know. I made it like that on purpose.'

The President went on, without seeming to notice the interruption.

'The prisoner informs me that the book with the names and addresses is to be found in this inner compartment, together with certain letters and papers stolen from the houses of members, and numerous objects bearing authentic fingerprints. I believe him to be telling the truth. He offers the combination of the safe in exchange for a quick death. I think the offer should be accepted. What is your opinion, ladies and gentlemen?'

'The combination is known already,' said Number Twenty-two.

'Imbecile! This man has told us, and has proved to me, that he is Lord Peter Wimsey. Do you think he will have forgotten to alter the combination? And then there is the secret of the inner door. If he disappears tonight and the police enter his house—'

'I say,' said a woman's rich voice, 'that the promise should be given and the information used—and quickly. Time is getting short.'

A murmur of agreement went round the table.

'You hear,' said the President, addressing Wimsey. 'The Society offers you the privilege of a quick death in return for the combination of the safe and the secret of the inner door.'

'I have your word for it?'

'You have.'

'Thank you. And my mother and sister?'

'If you in your turn will give us your word—you are a man of honour—that these women know nothing that could harm us, they shall be spared.'

'Thank you, sir. You may rest assured, upon my honour, that they know nothing. I should not think of burdening any woman with such dangerous secrets—particularly those who are dear to me.'

'Very well. It is agreed—yes?'

The murmur of assent was given, though with less readiness than before.

'Then I am willing to give you the information you want. The word of the combination is UNRELIABILITY.'

'And the inner door?'

'In anticipation of the visit of the police, the inner door—which might have presented difficulties—is open.'

'Good! You understand that if the police interfere with our messenger—'

'That would not help me, would it?'

'It is a risk,' said the President thoughtfully, 'but a risk which I think we must take. Carry the prisoner down to the cellar. He can amuse himself by contemplating apparatus Number 5. In the meantime, Numbers Twelve and Forty-six—'

'No, no!'

A sullen mutter of dissent arose and swelled threateningly.

'No,' said a tall man with a voice like treacle. 'No—why should any members be put in possession of this evidence? We have found one traitor among us tonight and more than one fool. How are we to know that Numbers Twelve and Forty-six are not fools and traitors also?'

The two men turned savagely upon the speaker, but a girl's voice struck into the discussion, high and agitated.

'Hear, hear! That's right, I say. How about us? We ain't going to have our names read by somebody we don't know nothing about. I've had enough of this. They might sell the 'ole lot of us to the narks.'

'I agree,' said another member. 'Nobody ought to be trusted, nobody at all.'

The President shrugged his shoulders.

'Then what, ladies and gentlemen, do you suggest?'

There was a pause. Then the same girl shrilled out again:

'I say Mr President oughter go himself. He's the only one as knows all the names. It won't be no cop to him. Why should we take all the risk and trouble and him sit at home and collar the money? Let him go himself, that's what I say.'

A long rustle of approbation went round the table.

'I second that motion,' said a stout man who wore a bunch of gold seals at his fob. Wimsey smiled as he looked at the seals; it was that trifling vanity which had led him directly to the name and address of the stout man, and he felt a certain affection for the trinkets on that account.

The President looked round.

'It is the wish of the meeting, then, that I should go?' he said, in an ominous voice.

Forty-five hands were raised in approbation. Only the woman known as

Number Two remained motionless and silent, her strong white hands clenched on the arm of the chair.

The President rolled his eyes slowly round the threatening ring till they rested upon her.

'Am I to take it that this vote is unanimous?' he enquired.

The woman raised her head.

'Don't go,' she gasped faintly.

'You hear,' said the President, in a faintly derisive tone. 'This lady says, don't go.'

'I submit that what Number Two says is neither here nor there,' said the man with the treacly voice. 'Our own ladies might not like us to be going, if they were in madam's privileged position.' His voice was an insult.

'Hear, hear!' cried another man. 'This is a democratic society, this is. We don't want no privileged classes.'

'Very well,' said the President. 'You hear, Number Two. The feeling of the meeting is against you. Have you any reasons to put forward in favour of your opinion?'

'A hundred. The President is the head and soul of our Society. If anything should happen to him—where should we be? You'—she swept the company magnificently with her eyes—'you have all blundered. We have your carelessness to thank for all this. Do you think we should be safe for five minutes if the President were not here to repair your follies?'

'Something in that,' said a man who had not hitherto spoken.

'Pardon my suggesting,' said Wimsey maliciously, 'that, as the lady appears to be in a position peculiarly favourable for the reception of the President's confidences, the contents of my modest volume will probably be no news to her. Why should not Number Two go herself?'

'Because I say she must not,' said the President sternly, checking the quick reply that rose to his companion's lips. 'If it is the will of the meeting, I will go. Give me the key of the house.'

One of the men extracted it from Wimsey's jacket pocket and handed it over.

'Is the house watched?' he demanded of Wimsey.

'No.'

'That is the truth?'

'It is the truth.'

The President turned at the door.

'If I have not returned in two hours' time,' he said, 'act for the best to save yourselves, and do what you like with the prisoner. Number Two will give orders in my absence.'

He left the room. Number Two rose from her seat with a gesture of command.

'Ladies and gentlemen. Supper is now considered over. Start the dancing again.'

Down in the cellar the time passed slowly, in the contemplation of apparatus Number 5. The miserable Jukes, alternately wailing and raving, at length shrieked himself into exhaustion. The four members guarding the prisoners whispered together from time to time.

'An hour and a half since the President left,' said one.

Wimsey glanced up. Then he returned to his examination of the room. There were many curious things in it, which he wanted to memorise.

Presently the trap door was flung open. 'Bring him up!' cried a voice. Wimsey rose immediately, and his face was rather pale.

The members of the gang were again seated round the table. Number Two occupied the President's chair, and her eyes fastened on Wimsey's face with a tigerish fury, but when she spoke it was with a self-control which roused his admiration.

'The President has been two hours gone,' she said. 'What has happened to him? Traitor twice over—what has happened to him?'

'How should I know?' said Wimsey. 'Perhaps he has looked after Number One and gone while the going was good!'

She sprang up with a little cry of rage, and came close to him.

'Beast! Liar!' she said, and struck him on the mouth. 'You know he would never do that. He is faithful to his friends. What have you done with him? Speak—or I will make you speak. You two, there—bring the irons. He *shall* speak!'

'I can only form a guess, madame,' replied Wimsey, 'and I shall not guess any the better for being stimulated with hot irons, like Pantaloon at the circus. Calm yourself, and I will tell you what I think. I think—indeed, I greatly fear—that Monsieur le Président in his hurry to examine the interesting exhibits in my safe may, quite inadvertently, no doubt, have let the door of the inner compartment close behind him. In which case—'

He raised his eyebrows, his shoulders being too sore for shrugging, and gazed at her with a limpid and innocent regret.

'What do you mean?'

Wimsey glanced round the circle.

'I think,' he said, 'I had better begin from the beginning by explaining to you the mechanism of my safe. It is rather a nice safe,' he added plaintively. 'I invented the idea myself—not the principle of its working, of course; that is a matter for scientists—but just the idea of the thing.

'The combination I gave you is perfectly correct as far as it goes. It is a three-alphabet thirteen-letter lock by Bunn & Fishett—a very good one of its kind. It opens the outer door, leading into the ordinary strong room, where I keep my cash and my Froth Blower's cuff links and all that. But there is an inner compartment with two doors, which open in a quite different manner. The outermost of these two inner doors is merely a thin steel skin, painted to look like the back of the safe and fitting closely, so as not to betray any join. It lies in the same plane as the wall of the room, you understand, so that if you were to measure the outside and the inside of the safe you would discover no discrepancy. It opens outwards with an ordinary key, and, as I truly assured the President, it was left open when I quitted my flat.'

'Do you think,' said the woman sneeringly, 'that the President is so simple as to be caught in a so obvious trap? He will have wedged open that inner door undoubtedly.'

'Undoubtedly, madame. But the sole purpose of that outer inner door, if I may so express myself, is to appear to be the only inner door. But hidden behind the hinge of that door is another door, a sliding panel, set so closely in the thickness of the wall that you would hardly see it unless you knew it was there. This door was also left open. Our revered Number One had nothing to do but to walk straight through into the inner compartment of the safe, which, by the way, is built into the chimney of the old basement kitchen, which runs up the house at that point. I hope I make myself clear?'

'Yes, yes—get on. Make your story short.'

Wimsey bowed, and, speaking with even greater deliberation than ever, resumed:

'Now, this interesting list of the Society's activities, which I have had the honour of compiling, is written in a very large book—bigger, even, than Monsieur le Président's ledger which he uses downstairs. (I trust, by the way, madame, that you have borne in mind the necessity of putting that ledger in a safe place. Apart from the risk of investigation by some officious policeman, it would be inadvisable that any junior member of the Society should get hold of it. The feeling of the meeting would, I fancy, be opposed to such an occurrence.)'

'It is secure,' she answered hastily. '*Mon Dieu!* Get on with your story.'

'Thank you—you have relieved my mind. Very good. This big book lies on a steel shelf at the back of the inner compartment. Just a moment. I have not described this inner compartment to you. It is six feet high, three feet wide, and three feet deep. One can stand up in it quite comfortably, unless one is very tall. It suits me nicely—as you may see, I am not more than five feet eight and a half. The President has the advantage of me in height; he might be a little cramped, but there would be room for him to squat if he grew tired of standing. By the way, I don't know if you know it, but you have tied me up rather tightly.'

'I would have you tied till your bones were locked together. Beat him, you! He is trying to gain time.'

'If you beat me,' said Wimsey, 'I'm damned if I'll speak at all. Control yourself, madame; it does not do to move hastily when your king is in check.'

'Get on!' she cried again, stamping with rage.

'Where was I? Ah, the inner compartment. As I say, it is a little snug—the more so that it is not ventilated in any way. Did I mention that the book lay on a steel shelf?'

'You did.'

'Yes. The steel shelf is balanced on a very delicate concealed spring. When the weight of the book—a heavy one, as I said—is lifted, the shelf rises almost imperceptibly. In rising it makes an electrical contact. Imagine to yourself, madame; our revered President steps in—propping the false door open behind him—he sees the book—quickly he snatches it up. To make sure that it is the right one, he opens it—he studies the pages. He looks about for the other objects I have mentioned, which bear the marks of fingerprints. And silently, but very, very quickly—you can imagine it, can you not—the secret panel, released by the rising of the shelf, leaps across like a panther behind him. Rather a trite simile, but apt, don't you think?'

'My God! Oh, my God!' Her hand went up as though to tear the choking mask from her face. 'You—you devil—devil! What is the word that opens the inner door? Quick! I will have it torn out of you—the word!'

'It is not a hard word to remember, madame—though it has been forgotten before now. Do you recollect, when you were a child, being told the tale of "Ali Baba and the Forty Thieves"? When I had that door made, my mind reverted, with rather a pretty touch of sentimentality, in my opinion, to the happy hours of my childhood. The words that open the door are—"Open Sesame".'

'Ah! How long can a man live in this devil's trap of yours?'

'Oh,' said Wimsey cheerfully, 'I should think he might hold out a few hours if he kept cool and didn't use up the available oxygen by shouting and hammering. If we went there at once, I dare say we should find him fairly all right.'

'I shall go myself. Take this man and—do your worst with him. Don't finish him till I come back. I want to see him die!'

'One moment,' said Wimsey, unmoved by this amiable wish. 'I think you had better take me with you.'

'Why—why?'

'Because, you see, I'm the only person who can open the door.'

'But you have given me the word. Was that a lie?'

'No—the word's all right. But, you see, it's one of these new-style electric doors. In fact, it's really the very latest thing in doors. I'm rather proud of it. It opens to the words "Open Sesame" all right—*but to my voice only.*'

'Your voice? I will choke your voice with my own hands. What do you mean—your voice only?'

'Just what I say. Don't clutch my throat like that, or you may alter my voice so that the door won't recognise it. That's better. It's apt to be rather pernickety about voices. It got stuck up for a week once, when I had a cold and could only implore it in a hoarse whisper. Even in the ordinary way, I sometimes have to try several times before I hit on the exact right intonation.'

She turned and appealed to a short, thickset man standing beside her.

'Is this true? Is it possible?'

'Perfectly, ma'am, I'm afraid,' said the man civilly. From his voice Wimsey took him to be a superior workman of some kind—probably an engineer.

'Is it an electrical device? Do you understand it?'

'Yes, ma'am. It will have a microphone arrangement somewhere, which converts the sound into a series of vibrations controlling an electric needle. When the needle has traced the correct pattern, the circuit is completed and the door opens. The same thing can be done by light vibrations equally easily.'

'Couldn't you open it with tools?'

'In time, yes, ma'am. But only by smashing the mechanism, which is probably well protected.'

'You may take that for granted,' interjected Wimsey reassuringly.

She put her hands to her head.

'I'm afraid we're done in,' said the engineer, with a kind of respect in his tone for a good job of work.

'No—wait! Somebody must know—the workmen who made this thing?'

'In Germany,' said Wimsey briefly.

'Or—yes, yes, I have it—a gramophone. This—this—*he*—shall be made to say the word for us. Quick—how can it be done?'

'Not possible, ma'am. Where should we get the apparatus at half past three on a Sunday morning? The poor gentleman would be dead long before—'

There was a silence, during which the sounds of the awakening day came through the shuttered windows. A motor horn sounded distantly.

'I give in,' she said. 'We must let him go. Take the ropes off him. You will free him, won't you?' she went on, turning piteously to Wimsey. 'Devil as you are, you are not such a devil as that! You will go straight back and save him!'

'Let him go, nothing!' broke in one of the men. 'He doesn't go to peach to the police, my lady, don't you think it. The President's done in, that's all, and we'd all better make tracks while we can. It's all up, boys. Chuck this fellow down the cellar and fasten him in, so he can't make a row and wake the place up. I'm going to destroy the ledgers. You can see it done if you don't trust me. And you, Thirty, you know where the switch is. Give us a quarter of an hour to clear, and then you can blow the place to glory.'

'No! You can't go—you can't leave him to die—your President—your leader—my—I won't let it happen. Set this devil free. Help me, one of you, with the ropes—'

'None of that, now,' said the man who had spoken before. He caught her by the wrists, and she twisted, shrieking, in his arms, biting and struggling to get free.

'Think, think,' said the man with the treacly voice. 'It's getting on to morning. It'll be light in an hour or two. The police may be here any minute.'

'The police!' She seemed to control herself by a violent effort. 'Yes, yes, you are right. We must not imperil the safety of all for the sake of one man. *He* himself would not wish it. That is so. We will put this carrion in the cellar where it cannot harm us, and depart, every one to his own place, while there is time.'

'And the other prisoner?'

'He? Poor fool—he can do no harm. He knows nothing. Let him go,' she answered contemptuously.

In a few minutes' time Wimsey found himself bundled unceremoniously into the depths of the cellar. He was a little puzzled. That they should refuse to let him go, even at the price of Number One's life, he could understand. He had taken the risk with his eyes open. But that they should leave him as a witness against them seemed incredible.

The men who had taken him down strapped his ankles together and departed, switching the lights out as they went.

'Hi! Kamerad!' said Wimsey. 'It's a bit lonely sitting here. You might leave the light on.'

'It's all right, my friend,' was the reply. 'You will not be in the dark long. They have set the time fuse.'

The other man laughed with rich enjoyment, and they went out together. So that was it. He was to be blown up with the house. In that case the President would certainly be dead before he was extricated. This worried Wimsey; he would rather have been able to bring the big crook to justice. After all, Scotland Yard had been waiting six years to break up this gang.

He waited, straining his ears. It seemed to him that he heard footsteps over his head. The gang had all crept out by this time . . .

There was certainly a creak. The trap door had opened; he felt, rather than heard, somebody creeping into the cellar.

'Hush!' said a voice in his ear. Soft hands passed over his face, and went fumbling about his body. There came the cold touch of steel on his wrists. The ropes slackened and dropped off. A key clicked in the handcuffs. The strap about his ankles was unbuckled.

'Quick! quick! they have set the timeswitch. The house is mined. Follow me as fast as you can. I stole back—I said I had left my jewellery. It was true. I left it on purpose. *He* must be saved—only you can do it. Make haste!'

Wimsey, staggering with pain, as the blood rushed back into his bound and numbed arms, crawled after her into the room above. A moment, and she had flung back the shutters and thrown the window open.

'Now go! Release him! You promise?'

'I promise. And I warn you, madame, that this house is surrounded. When my safe door closed it gave a signal which sent my servant to Scotland Yard. Your friends are all taken—'

'Ah! But you go—never mind me—quick! The time is almost up.'

'Come away from this!'

He caught her by the arm, and they went running and stumbling across the little garden. An electric torch shone suddenly in the bushes.

'That you, Parker?' cried Wimsey. 'Get your fellows away. Quick! the house is going up in a minute.'

The garden seemed suddenly full of shouting, hurrying men. Wimsey, floundering in the darkness, was brought up violently against the wall. He made a leap at the coping, caught it, and hoisted himself up. His hands groped for the woman; he swung her up beside him. They jumped; everyone was jumping; the woman caught her foot and fell with a gasping cry. Wimsey tried to stop himself, tripped over a stone, and came down headlong. Then, with a flash and a roar, the night went up in fire.

WIMSEY PICKED HIMSELF painfully out from among the debris of the garden wall. A faint moaning near him proclaimed that his companion was still alive. A lantern was turned suddenly upon them.

'Here you are!' said a cheerful voice. 'Are you all right, old thing? Good Lord! what a hairy monster!'

'All right,' said Wimsey. 'Only a bit winded. Is the lady safe? H'm—arm broken, apparently—otherwise sound. What's happened?'

'About half a dozen of 'em got blown up; the rest we've bagged.' Wimsey became aware of a circle of dark forms in the wintry dawn. 'Good lord, what a day! What a comeback for a public character! You old stinker—to let us go on for two years thinking you were dead! I bought a bit of black for an armband. I did, really. Did anybody know, besides Bunter?'

'Only my mother and sister. I put it in a secret trust—you know, the thing you send to executors and people. We shall have an awful time with the lawyers, I'm afraid, proving I'm me. Hello! Is that friend Sugg?'

'Yes, my lord,' said Inspector Sugg, grinning and nearly weeping with excitement. 'Damned glad to see your lordship again. Fine piece of work, your lordship. They're all wanting to shake hands with you, sir.'

'Oh, Lord! I wish I could get washed and shaved first. Awfully glad to see you all again, after two years' exile in Lambeth. Been a good little show, hasn't it?'

'Is he safe?'

Wimsey started at the agonised cry.

'Good Lord!' he cried. 'I forgot the gentleman in the safe. Here, fetch a car, quickly. I've got the great big top Moriarty of the whole bunch quietly asphyxiating at home. Here—hop in, and put the lady in too. I promised we'd get back and save him—though' (he finished the sentence in Parker's ear) 'there may be murder charges too, and I wouldn't give much for his chance at the Old Bailey. Whack her up. He can't last much longer shut up there. He's the bloke you've been wanting, the man at the back of the Morrison case and the Hope-Wilmington case, and hundreds of others.'

THE COLD MORNING had turned the streets grey when they drew up before the door of the house in Lambeth. Wimsey took the woman by the arm and helped her out. The mask was off now, and showed her face, haggard and desperate, and white with fear and pain.

'Russian, eh?' whispered Parker in Wimsey's ear.

'Something of the sort. Damn! the front door's blown shut, and the blighter's got the key with him in the safe. Hop through the window, will you?'

Parker bundled obligingly in, and in a few seconds threw open the door to them. The house seemed very still. Wimsey led the way to the back room, where the strong room stood. The outer door and the second door stood propped open with chairs. The inner door faced them like a blank green wall.

'Only hope he hasn't upset the adjustment with thumping at it,' muttered Wimsey. The anxious hand on his arm clutched feverishly. He pulled himself together, forcing his tone to one of cheerful commonplace.

'Come on, old thing,' he said, addressing himself conversationally to the door. 'Show us your paces. Open Sesame, confound you. Open Sesame!'

The green door slid suddenly away into the wall. The woman sprang forward and caught in her arms the humped and senseless thing that rolled out from the safe. Its clothes were torn to ribbons, and its battered hands dripped blood.

'It's all right,' said Wimsey, 'it's all right! He'll live—to stand his trial.'

Georges Simenon
1903–1989

THE MAN IN
THE STREET

THE FOUR MEN were packed close together in the taxi. Paris was in the grip of frost. At half-past seven in the morning, the city looked leaden, and the wind drove powdery rime across the ground.

The thinnest of the four men, on a folding seat, had a cigarette stuck to his lower lip and handcuffs on his wrists. The biggest of them, a heavy-jawed man in a thick overcoat and a bowler hat, was smoking a pipe and watching the railings of the Bois de Boulogne race past.

'Would you like me to put up a lovely fight?' the handcuffed man proposed amiably. 'With writhing, cursing, foaming at the mouth, the lot?'

And Maigret growled, as he took the cigarette from the man's lips and opened the car door, since they had now reached the Porte de Bagatelle:

'Don't you try and be too clever!'

The avenues in the Bois were deserted, as white as limestone and as hard. A dozen people were kicking their heels at the corner of a woodland ride, and a photographer attempted to take a picture of the group as they approached. But Louis the Kid, as he had been instructed, held his arms in front of his face.

Maigret looked slowly round like a sulky bear, noticing everything, the new blocks of flats in the Boulevard Richard-Wallace, with their shuttered windows, a few workmen on bicycles coming in from Puteaux, a tram with its lights on, a couple of concierges approaching, their hands purple with cold.

'All set?' he asked.

The day before, he had had the following paragraph inserted in the newspapers:

THE CRIME AT BAGATELLE

This time the police have not been slow in clearing up a case that appeared to present insuperable difficulties. As has already been stated, on Monday morning a park-keeper in the Bois de Boulogne discovered on one of the walks, some hundred metres from the Torte de Bagatelle, a body which was identified on the spot as that of Ernest Borms, a well-known Viennese doctor, who had been living in Neuilly for some years.

Borms was in evening dress. He must have been attacked during the Sunday night as he was returning to his flat in the Boulevard Richard-Wallace.

He was shot point-blank through the heart with a small-calibre revolver.

Borms was a youngish man, handsome and very well dressed, who moved in fashionable society.

Scarcely forty-eight hours after this murder, the Criminal investigation Department have made an arrest. Tomorrow morning, between seven and eight, a reconstitution of the crime will take place on the spot.

LATER ON, at Police Headquarters, this case was to be cited as particularly characteristic of Maigret's method; but when it was spoken of in his presence, he had a peculiar habit of averting his head with a growl.

Well! Everything was ready. Almost no loiterers, as he had foreseen. It was not without good reason that he had chosen such an early hour. In fact, among the ten or fifteen people who were kicking their heels were a number of detectives wearing their most innocent air; one of them, Torrence, who adored dressing up, had disguised himself as a milkman, which caused Maigret to shrug his shoulders.

Provided Louis the Kid didn't overdo things! . . . He was an old acquaintance of the police and had been arrested the day before for picking pockets in the métro . . .

'You can lend us a hand tomorrow morning and we'll see to it that you get off lightly this time . . .'

He had been taken out of the cells.

'Let's go! growled Maigret. 'When you heard footsteps you were hiding in this corner, weren't you?'

'Just as you say, Superintendent . . . I was starving, you see . . . Absolutely broke! . . . So I said to myself that a big shot in a dinner jacket on his way home must have plenty of dough on him . . . "Your money or your life," I breathe in his ear . . . And I give you my word it wasn't my fault if the gun went off. I think it was the cold that made my finger press the trigger . . .'

11.00AM. MAIGRET was prowling about his room in the Quai des Orfèvres, smoking his pipe and fiddling endlessly with the telephone.

'Hello! is that you, Chief? it's Lucas . . . I followed the old boy who seemed to be interested in the reconstruction . . . Nothing doing there . . . He's a crank who goes for a walk in the Bois every morning . . .'

'All right! You can come back.'

11.15am. 'Hello, Chief? This is Torrence. I shadowed the young man you tipped me the wink about . . . He's a salesman in a Champs-Elysées shop, who's hoping to become a private inquiry agent . . . Shall I come back?'

Not until 11.55 was there a call from Janvier.

'I'm working fast, Chief . . . I'm afraid the bird may get away. . . I'm watching him in the little mirror set in the door of the phone box. I'm at the *Nain Jaune* bar in the Boulevard Rochechouart . . . Yes . . . He spotted me . . . He's not got a clear conscience . . . As we crossed the Seine he threw something into the river. He's tried to lose me about ten times . . . Shall I wait for you here?'

And thus began a chase which was to go on for five days and five nights, through a city that was unaware of it, among hurrying pedestrians, from bar to bar, from bistro to bistro, Maigret and his detectives taking it in turns to pursue a solitary man and becoming, in the end, as exhausted as their quarry.

Maigret alighted from his taxi in front of the *Nain Jaune*, at apéritif time, and found Janvier leaning against the counter. He made no effort to assume an innocent air; quite the reverse!

'Which is he?'

With a jerk of his chin the detective indicated a man sitting at a small table in a corner. The man was watching them with pale blue-grey eyes that gave his face a foreign look. A Scandinavian or a Slav? Probably the latter. He wore a grey overcoat, a well-cut suit, a soft felt hat.

'What'll you drink, Chief? A hot *picon*?'

'Hot *picon* be it . . . What's he drinking?'

'A brandy . . . the fifth since this morning . . . You mustn't mind if my speech is a bit slurred, but I've had to follow him into every bistro . . . He's tough, you know. Look at him . . . he's been like that all morning. He wouldn't drop his eyes for the world.'

It was quite true. And it was odd. One could not call it arrogance or defiance. The man was simply looking at them. If he was feeling anxious, he did not show it. His face expressed sadness, rather; but a calm, thoughtful sadness.

'At Bagatelle, when he noticed that you were watching him, he immediately moved away and I followed suit. He turned round before he'd gone a hundred metres. Then instead of leaving the Bois as he had apparently meant to, he strode off down the first walk he came to. He turned round again. He recognised me. He sat down on a bench, in spite of the cold, and I stopped . . . On several occasions I had the feeling that he wanted to speak to me, but he always ended by shrugging his shoulders and moving off again . . .

'At the Porte Dauphine I nearly lost him, for he jumped into a taxi, and it was only by sheer luck that I found another almost immediately. He got out in the Place de Opéra and rushed into the metro. One behind the other, we changed lines five-times, and he began to understand that he wouldn't get rid of me that way.

'We came up above ground again. We were in the Place Clichy. Since then we've been going from bar to bar . . . I was waiting for a convenient place with a telephone booth from which I could keep an eye on him. When he saw me telephoning he gave a sort of bitter little laugh . . . And afterwards one would have sworn he was expecting you . . .'

'Ring them up at the "office" . . . Tell Lucas and Torrence to be ready to join me at short notice . . . And a photographer from the Records Department with a very small camera . . .'

'Waiter!' the stranger called out. 'How much?'

'Three francs fifty.'

'I'm willing to bet he's a Pole,' Maigret whispered to Janvier. 'Let's go . . .'

They did not get far. In the Place Blanche they followed the man into a small restaurant and sat down at the table next to his. It was an Italian restaurant, and they ate pasta.

At three o'clock Lucas came to take over from Janvier, who was sitting with Maigret in a brasserie opposite the Gare du Nord.

'The photographer?' Maigret inquired.

'He's waiting to catch the man when he comes out.'

And when the Pole left the place, after reading the newspapers, a detective stepped up briskly towards him. When he was less than a yard away the click of a camera was heard. The man swiftly covered his face with his hand, but it was too late, and then, showing that he had understood, he cast a reproachful glance at the Superintendent.

'It's clear, my friend,' Maigret soliloquised, 'that you've some good reasons for not taking us to your home. But however much patience you have, mine's at least equal to yours . . .'

By evening a few snowflakes were drifting in the streets, while the stranger walked about, his hands in his pockets, waiting for bed-time.

'Shall I relieve you for the night, Chief?' Lucas proposed.

'No! I'd rather you saw to the photograph. Consult the files first of all. Then ask around in foreigners' circles. He's no recent arrival; somebody must know him.'

'Suppose we published his picture in the papers?'

Maigret gave his subordinate a contemptuous glance. So Lucas, who had worked with him for so many years, didn't understand? Had the police got a single piece of evidence? Not one! A man had been killed at night in the Bois de Boulogne; no weapon had been found, no fingerprints; Dr Borms lived alone and his one servant did not know where he had been the night before.

'Do as I tell you. Off with you . . .'

Finally, at midnight, the man brought himself to enter a hotel. Maigret followed. It was a second-rate, indeed a third-rate hotel.

'I want a room . . .'

'Will you fill in the form?'

He did so, hesitantly, his fingers numb with cold. He looked Maigret up and down, as if to say:

'If you think this worries me! . . . I can write whatever I fancy.'

And he put down a name at random: Nicolas Slaatkovitch, arrived in Paris the previous day.

It was obviously false. Maigret rang the Police Judiciaire. The records, of lodging, houses and registers of foreigners were searched; inquiries were made to frontier police. There was no sign of any Nicolas Slaatkovitch.

'A room for you too?' asked the proprietor somewhat resentfully, for he had recognised a policeman.

'No, thanks. I shall spend the night on the stairs.'

It seemed safer. He sat down on a step in front of the door of room number seven. Twice the door opened. The man peered into the darkness, caught sight of Maigret's figure and eventually went back to bed. In the morning his beard had grown and his cheeks were rough. He had not been able to change his shirt. He had not even a comb with him, and his hair was dishevelled.

Lucas appeared.

'Shall I take over, Chief?'

But Maigret could not bring himself to leave the stranger. He watched him pay for his room. He saw him turn pale, and he guessed.

A little later, in fact, in a bar where, practically side by side, they drank *café crème* and ate croissants, the man openly counted his store of wealth. One hundred-franc note, two twenty-franc pieces and one piece of ten, plus some small change. His lips twisted in a bitter grin.

Well, he wouldn't get far with that. When he came to the Bois de Boulogne he must just have left home, for he had freshly shaven cheeks and clothes without a speck of dust or a crease. He had probably expected to be back shortly afterwards; he hadn't even looked to see what money he had in his pockets.

What he had thrown into the Seine, Maigret guessed, must have been identity papers and possibly visiting cards.

At all costs, he wanted to prevent anyone finding out where he lived.

And he set off again on the long, weary ramble of the homeless, lingering in front of shops and stalls, entering bars from time to time for somewhere to sit and take refuge from the cold, reading newspapers in brasseries.

A hundred and fifty francs! No restaurant for him at midday; he had to content himself with hard-boiled eggs, which he ate standing up at a bar counter, washed down with a glass of beer, while Maigret devoured sandwiches.

The man hesitated for a long time in front of a cinema, wondering whether to go in. He fingered the coins in his pocket. Better try and last out . . . He went on walking, walking. . .

In fact, one detail struck Maigret: this exhausting ramble always followed the same course, through the same districts: between the Trinité and Place Clichy, between Place Clichy and Barbès by way of the Rue Caulaincourt, then from Barbès to the Gare du Nord and the Rue La Fayette . . .

Was the man afraid of being recognised elsewhere? Surely, he had chosen the districts farthest from his home or his hotel, those which he did not habitually visit . . .

Did he, like so many foreigners, frequent the Montparnasse district? The neighbourhood of the Panthéon?

To judge by his clothes, he was moderately well off; they were comfortable, quiet and well cut. A professional man, no doubt. Maigret noticed that he wore a wedding ring.

Maigret had had to resign himself to handing over his place to Torrence. He had hurried home. Madame Maigret was disappointed, because her sister had come on a visit from Orléans and she had prepared a special dinner, and now her husband, after shaving and changing, was off again, announcing that he didn't know when he would he back.

He made straight for the Quai des Orfèvres.

'Anything for me from Lucas?'

Yes. There was a message from the inspector. He had passed round the photograph in a number of Polish and Russian circles. Nobody knew the man. Nor was there anything to be learnt from the various political groups. As a last resort he had had a great many copies of the photograph printed; in every part of Paris, policemen went from door to door, inquiring from concierges, and showing the document to the landlords of bars and the waiters in cafés.

'Hello! Superintendent Maigret? I'm an usherette at the news-cinema in the Boulevard de Strasbourg . . . There's a gentleman here, Monsieur Torrence . . . He told me to call you to say that he's here, but daren't leave the hall . . .'

It was cunning of the man; he had reckoned that this was the warmest place to spend a number of hours at little expense . . . Two francs entry . . . and you could stay on for several performances!

A CURIOUS INTIMACY had sprung up between the hunter and the hunted, between the man with the unshaven chin and rumpled clothes and Maigret, who kept stubbornly on his trail. There was even one comical detail; they had both caught colds. Their noses were red. Almost rhythmically they pulled out their handkerchiefs, and once the man gave an involuntary smile on seeing Maigret give a whole series of sneezes.

After sitting through five consecutive programmes at the news-cinema, they moved on to a squalid hotel in the Boulevard de la Chapelle. The man signed the same name on the register. And Maigret, once again, settled down on the staircase. But since this was a hotel frequented by prostitutes, he was disturbed every ten minutes by couples who stared at him with curiosity, and the women felt uneasy.

Would the man make up his mind to go home once his money was spent or when he was at the end of his tether? In a brasserie where he stayed for some length of time and took off his grey overcoat, Maigret seized hold of this without hesitation and examined the inside of the collar. It bore the label of the 'Old England' shop in the Boulevard des Italiens. It was a ready-made garment, and the shop must have sold dozens like it. Maigret noticed one significant piece of evidence: it was a year old. So the stranger must have been in Paris for a year at least. And during that year he must have stayed somewhere . . .

Maigret had begun drinking toddies to get rid of his cold. The stranger was becoming close-fisted; he drank only coffee, not even laced with spirits, and ate hard-boiled eggs and croissants.

The news from the 'office' was still the same: nothing to report! Nobody had recognised the photograph of the Pole, and no missing person had been reported.

Nor was there any further information about the dead man. He had earned a good income, took no interest in politics, led a busy social life, and since he specialised in nervous diseases his patients were chiefly women.

MAIGRET HAD NEVER yet had occasion to study the question of how long it takes for a well-bred, well-dressed, well-groomed man to lose his gloss once he is turned out into the streets.

He knew, now, that it took four days. The beard, for one thing. The first morning the man looked like a lawyer, a doctor, an architect or an industrialist, and one could imagine him living in a comfortable flat. A four-day beard had transformed him so much that if his picture had been published in connection with the Bois de Boulogne affair people would have declared: 'He's obviously a murderer!'

The cold air and the lack of sleep had reddened his eyelids, and there was a hectic flush on his cheekbones. His shoes were unpolished and shapeless, his overcoat looked shabby and his trousers bagged at the knees.

Even his gait . . . He no longer walked in the same way . . . He slunk along by the wall . . . He lowered his eyes when people looked at him as they passed . . . One further point: he averted his head when he went past a restaurant where customers were sitting in front of well-filled plates . . .

'Your last twenty francs, poor fellow!' Maigret reckoned. 'And what next?'

Lucas, Torrence and Janvier relieved him from time to time, but he gave up his post to them as seldom as possible. He would burst into his chief's office at Police Headquarters. 'You ought to take a rest, Maigret . . .'

Peevish and prickly, Maigret seemed torn by conflicting feelings. 'Is it or isn't it my job to catch the murderer?'

'Obviously . . .'

'Then I'm off!' he sighed with a touch of resentment in his voice. 'I wonder where we shall go to bed tonight?'

Only twenty francs left, not even that! When he rejoined Torrence, the latter informed him that the man had eaten three hard-boiled eggs and drunk two coffees, laced with brandy, in a bar at the corner of the Rue Montmartre.

'Eight francs fifty . . . He's got eleven fifty left . . .'

He admired the man. Far from trying to conceal himself he walked level with him, sometimes right beside him, and had to control an impulse to speak to him.

'Come on, old chap! Don't you think it's time for a meal? . . . Somewhere or other there's a warm home waiting for you, a bed, slippers, a razor . . . eh? And a good dinner . . .'

The man, however, went on prowling aimlessly under the arc lamps of the Halles, among the heaps of cabbages and carrots, stepping aside when he heard the whistle of a train, avoiding market gardeners' trucks.

'You won't be able to afford a room!'

The Meteorological Office that evening registered eight degrees below zero. The man treated himself to hot sausages from an open-air stall. He would reek of garlic and burnt fat all night!

At one point he tried to slip into a shed and lie down in one corner. A policeman, to whom Maigret had not had time to give instructions, sent him packing. Now he was limping. The Quais. The Pont des Arts—provided he didn't take it into his head to throw himself into the Seine! Maigret felt he would not have the courage to jump in after him into the black water, where ice was beginning to drift.

He walked along the tow-path. Some tramps were grumbling; under the bridges, the best places were already taken.

In a little street near the Place Maubert, through the windows of a strange tavern, old men could be seen asleep, their heads on the table. For twenty sous, a glass of red wine included! The man looked at Maigret through the darkness. Then, with a fatalistic shrug, he pushed open the door. Before it had closed, Maigret caught a nauseating whiff; he decided to remain outside. Summoning a constable on the beat, he posted him as sentry on the pavement while he went off to ring Lucas, who was on duty that night.

'We've been hunting for you for the past hour, Chief! We've found out who the man is, thanks to a concierge . . . His name's Stephan Strevzki, thirty-four years old, born in Warsaw; he's been living in France for the past three years . . .'

He's married to a fine-looking Hungarian girl called Dora . . . They rent a twelve thousand franc flat in Passy, in the Rue de la Pompe . . . Nothing to do with politics . . . The concierge has never seen the murdered man . . . Stephan went out on Monday morning earlier than usual . . . She was surprised not to see him come back, but she didn't worry because . . .'

'What's the time now?'

'Half-past three . . . I'm alone at Headquarters . . . I've had some beer brought up, but it's very cold!'

'Listen, Lucas . . . You're to . . . Yes, I know! Too late for the morning ones, but in the evening ones . . . Understood?'

THAT MORNING an indefinable odour of poverty seemed to cling to the man's very clothes. His eyes were more sunken. The glance he threw at Maigret, in the pale dawn, was one of pathetic reproachfulness.

Had he not been brought, gradually but yet at a dizzying speed, to the lowest rung of the ladder? He pulled up the collar of his overcoat. He did not leave the district. He dived into a bistro which had just opened, and there drank four brandies in quick succession, as though to drive away the appalling aftertaste that the night had left in his throat and his breast.

Now there was nothing left for him but to keep on walking along streets slippery with frost. He must be aching in every limb; he was limping with the left leg. From time to time he halted and looked around despairingly.

Since he no longer went into cafés where there was a telephone, Maigret could not be relieved. Back to the Quais! And there the man almost automatically fingered the secondhand books, turning their pages, occasionally checking the authenticity of a print or an engraving. An icy wind swept the Seine. As the barges moved forward, the water made a clinking sound due to the clashing of tiny fragments of ice.

From afar, Maigret could see the Police Judiciaire building and the window of his office. His sister-in-law must have gone back to Orléans. If only Lucas . . .

He did not know, as yet, that this appalling case was going to become a classic, and that generations of detectives would relate it in every detail to their juniors. Absurdly, what disturbed him most was a trivial detail; the man had a spot on his forehead, which, looked at closely, would probably prove to be a boil, and which was turning from red to purple.

If only Lucas . . .

At midday, the man, who unquestionably knew his Paris well, made his way towards the paupers' soup kitchen at the far end of the Boulevard Saint-Germain. He joined the queue of down-and-outs. An old man spoke to him, but he pretended not to understand. Then another, whose face was pitted with smallpox, addressed him in Russian.

Maigret crossed over to the pavement on the other side of the street, and after a moment's hesitation yielded to the irresistible urge to enter a bistro and eat sandwiches; he turned away so that the man, if he looked through the window, should not see him eating.

The poor fellows moved on slowly, and were let in four or five at a time to the hall where they were given bowls of hot soup. The queue grew longer. From time to time someone would push at the back, and the others protested.

1.00pm. The newsboy came running from the far end of the street, leaning forward eagerly.

'Paper! Paper! *L'intransigeant* . . . *L'intran*. . .'

He too was trying to forestall his rivals. He could spot likely purchasers from afar. He paid no attention to the line of paupers.

'Paper . . .'

Humbly the man raised his hand, saying 'Pssstt!'

People in the queue looked at him. So he still had a few sous for a paper?

Maigret, too, hailed the newsboy, unfolded the paper, and found to his relief, on the front page, what he was looking for: the photograph of a young woman, smiling and beautiful.

MISSING WOMAN

A young Polish woman, Mme Dora Strevzki, is said to have disappeared four days ago from her home in Passy, 17 Rue de la Pompe. A disturbing factor in the case is that the husband of the missing woman, M. Stephan Strevzki, also disappeared from his home the day before, Monday, and the concierge, who informed the police, stated . . .

THE MAN, borne forward by the moving queue, had only five or six paces more to go to get his bowl of steaming soup. At that very moment he stepped out of line, crossed the street, nearly got knocked over by a bus, but reached the pavement just as Maigret stood in front of him.

'I'm all yours,' he declared quite simply. 'Take me off . . . I'll answer all your questions.'

Everyone was waiting in the passage at Police Headquarters, Lucas, Janvier, Torrence, and others who had not been working on the case but knew about it. As they passed, Lucas gave Maigret a sign that meant: 'It's all right!'

A door opened and then shut. Beer and sandwiches were on the table.

'Have something to eat first . . .'

Embarrassed, the man could scarcely swallow. Then at last he said,

'Since she's gone away and is safe somewhere . . .'

Maigret felt impelled to turn and poke the stove.

'When I read about the murder in the paper . . . I'd suspected for quite some time that Dora was having an affair with that man . . . I knew she was not his only mistress. . . I knew Dora with her impulsive character. . . D'you under-stand? If he had tried to get rid of her, I knew she was capable of . . . And she had a pearl-handled revolver, she always carried it in her bag . . . When the papers announced the capture of the murderer and the reconstruction of the crime, I wanted to watch . . .'

Maigret would have liked to say, like an English policeman: 'I warn you that anything you say may be taken down and used in evidence . . .'

The man had kept on his hat and overcoat.

'Now that she's safe . . . For I suppose . . .' He cast an anxious look around, as a sudden suspicion crossed his mind. 'She must have understood, when she saw that I'd not come back . . . I knew it would end like that, I knew Borms was not the man for her and that she'd come back to me . . . She went out alone on Sunday evening, as she had taken to doing recently . . . She must have killed him when. . .'

Maigret blew his nose; he took a long time blowing it. A ray of sunlight, that bleak winter sunlight that goes with icy weather, came in through the window. The boil was gleaming on the man's forehead; Maigret could only think of him as 'the man'.

'Yes, your wife killed him . . . When she realised that he was not serious about her . . . And *you* realised that she had killed him . . . And you didn't want . . .'

He suddenly went up close to the Pole.

'I'm sorry, old fellow,' he muttered as though he was speaking to an old friend, 'I had to get at the truth, hadn't I? It was my duty to . . .'

He opened the door.

'Bring in Madame Dora Strevzki . . . Lucas, you carry on, I'm going to . . .'

And nobody saw him again at Headquarters for two days. The director rang him up at home.

'Look here, Maigret . . . You know that she's confessed everything and that . . . By the way, how's your cold? I gather . . .'

'It's nothing at all. It's all right . . . In twenty-four hours . . . And how is he?'

'What? . . . Who? . . .'

'The man!'

'Ah, I follow . . . He's engaged the best lawyer in Paris . . . He hopes . . . You know, crimes of passion . . .'

Maigret went back to bed and doped himself with aspirin and hot toddies. Later on, when anyone asked him about the investigation, he would growl dis-couragingly:

'What investigation?'

And the man came to see him once or twice a week to keep him informed about the lawyer's hopes.

The result was not outright acquittal: a year with remission of sentence.

And it was from this man that Maigret learnt to play chess.

Julian Symons

1912–1994

PICKUP ON
THE DOVER ROAD

THE MILESTONE, just visible in the rain, said Dover 41. Donald's mouth pursed and he began to whistle *The Song of the Skye Boatmen*:

> 'Speed, bonny boat, like a bird on the wing,
> "Onward" the sailors cry.
> Carry the man who was born to be King
> Over the sea to Skye.'

Not to Skye, but to Calais. In a light pleasant voice he fitted words to the tune:

> 'Carry the man who was born to be young
> Over the sea to France.'

To be young, he thought, to be young and happy. He remembered for a moment the row with Charles, but nothing could keep down for long the bubble of his high spirits. Rain splashed on the car's windshield, the tyres made sucking noises on the wet road, the wipers echoed his thoughts by saying *a new life, a new life*.

Quite wrong, of course; he would return to England—this was nothing but a short holiday. He said aloud, 'One of the *things* about you, Donald, is that every time you do something fresh you think it's the beginning of a new life.'

Perfectly true, but a little silent reproach was in order. He knew that talking to himself was a bad habit, so he turned on the radio and found the plum-voiced announcer halfway through the news:

'. . . *yet another government scandal. Mr Michael Foot called on the government to resign.*' Pause, slight change of tone. '*A murder in Kent. An elderly woman, Mrs Mary Ford, was found murdered this evening in her house on the outskirts of the village of Oastley in Kent. She had been brutally attacked and beaten, and the house had been ransacked. Mrs Ford was something of a recluse, and it is believed that she kept a considerable sum of money in the house. Police investigations are continuing.*'

Oastley, he thought, can't be more than five miles from there now. He was listening abstractedly to an interview with a beauty queen when he became aware

508

of something in the road and in the next moment he realised that the something was human. He began to go into a skid, corrected it, stopped, opened his window, and shouted, 'What the hell do you think you're doing?'

A grinning face appeared, wet, snub-nosed, cheerful. 'Flashing a torch.'

'I didn't see it. I might have—'

'Can you help me? I've had a breakdown.' There was no car visible in the headlights. As though answering an unspoken question the man said, 'Down that side road you've just passed. I think the rear axle's gone,' he said and laughed again, the sound loud and meaningless. His voice was deep, coarse. 'Look, can you give me a lift? There's a café a few miles down the road. If you drop me off there I can make a phone call.'

Donald felt a momentary reluctance to let the man into the car, overcame it, leaned over, and opened the passenger door. The man took off a wet raincoat, threw it on the back seat, and got in. The interior light showed him as a rather squat figure, perhaps in his late twenties, a little younger than Donald, with thick brows and the corner of a thick mouth turned up in what seemed a perpetual smile. Then the door closed, the light went out, and he became just a darkly anonymous figure in the next seat.

'Dripping all over your car,' he said. 'Sorry.'

Donald did not reply. The incident had somehow disturbed his serenity. He drove off and found himself whistling the song again. Then the voice beside him revived the euphoria he had felt a few minutes ago by saying, 'Going far?'

'Into the sunset and beyond,' Donald said gaily. 'That's if it weren't night and raining. Dover, then across to France. Driving off the quay in another country, that's a wonderful feeling.'

'Must be. Never done it myself. You can do with a bit of change in this weather.'

Sheer pleasure in what lay ahead made Donald talk. 'You know, in England we always talk about the weather, I do it myself, it shows what a boring nation we are. In France that sort of thing simply couldn't happen— there are a thousand better things to talk about. God, I shall be pleased to get out of this smug country.'

As soon as the words had been spoken he regretted them. 'Not that I'm unpatriotic, mind you. This is just a holiday. Still, I shan't be sorry to get out of England in March. It's just that I know everything will be different in France—hotels, food, even the weather.'

'I know what you mean. Wish I was coming with you. Haven't been abroad for five years, and then it was just for the firm to a sales conference in Frankfurt. Trouble is, when you've got a wife and two kids it comes expensive, going abroad. So it's Littlehampton instead. Every year. Relatives there. You married?'

'No,' Donald said, a trifle sharply.

'Lucky man.' Again that laugh, loud and meaningless and somehow unlikable. 'Why lucky?'

'Don't know, really. It's just when I think of you single chaps, with a flat in London, time your own, do what you like, go where you like, I feel envious sometimes.'

'I didn't say I had a flat in London.' Again Donald spoke more sharply than he had intended. 'And I work too. I'm a writer. A free-lance journalist.'

'Freelance, there you are. Freelance, freedom.' A smell of drying clothes pervaded the air. Donald could almost feel them steaming. 'This breakdown's serious for me, I can tell you. I'm a knight of the road.'

'What's that? I didn't quite—'

'Commercial traveller, old man, and the bus is my steed, as you might say. Without it I'm sunk. Point is, I've got to get to Folkestone tonight—got an appointment there in the morning. If they can get my car going, well and good, but I doubt it and if not I'm in trouble. I was wondering.' Donald sensed what was coming. 'I was wondering if you could drop me off at Folkestone. Not out of your way, and it would be the most tremendous help to me.'

There was something about the man that did not seem genuine, and instinct told Donald to refuse; but that seemed churlish. 'I suppose if your car's still out of action—well, all right.'

'Very very decent of you, old man. We'll just look in at the café for five minutes so I can phone a garage. Must go through the motions.'

Something was troubling Donald and suddenly he realised what it was. 'What do you travel in?'

'Woollens, all sorts of woollens.'

A flurry of rain blurred his vision. Headlights loomed up dazzlingly and were gone. 'Samples?' Donald asked.

'How d'you mean?'

'You've got no samples.'

The pause was fractional. 'Left my case in the car. Overnight bag too. Didn't want to drag 'em up the lane. You get used to travelling light, you know, in my game.' Another pause, a longer one this time. Then, as though to divert Donald's attention from the missing sample case, the stranger said, 'Shocking business, that murder.'

For a moment Donald could not believe his ears. 'What murder?'

'Just a few miles away, place called Oastley. Old woman had her head bashed in, nasty business from the sound of it. They'll get the chap though. I wouldn't mind betting somebody saw him leaving the house, and then we shall get "Police are anxious to interview Joe Doakes," and we all know what that means.'

Donald said absently, 'You seem to know a lot about it.'

'Only what I've heard. But I'm interested. I'll tell you why. Murder is easy.' He gave that mechanical laugh, then said in a different tone, almost of alarm, 'What are you stopping for?'

'You should keep your eyes open.' Donald could not keep a tinge of malice out of his tone. 'There was a sign that said single lane traffic. Part of the road's under construction.'

'Oh, is that all. Well, as I say, murder's easy. I mean, look at the two of us. You give me a lift, you don't know me from Adam. Nobody sees me get in. I put a gun in your ribs, tell you to pull over and stop. I shoot you, toss you out of the car, drive off, leave the car somewhere, take two or three train and bus rides to get rid of the fuss, and I'm away. With whatever's in your wallet, of course. Don't worry, old man.' His loud bark sounded like the rattling of keys. 'But it's been done, you know. Think of that A6 job.'

'Hanratty, you mean? They caught him.'

'If he was the one who did it.' The laugh again, but this time it was only a chuckle. Then Donald felt a pressure on his arm from which he jerked away. 'Sorry. Am I putting you off your stroke?'

'Every murderer makes a mistake. Fingerprints, footprints.'

'I ought to have put my gloves on.' The laugh now was like a donkey's bray. 'You've got to forgive me, it's just my sense of humour. That café's round the next bend if I remember right, on the left, stands back a bit. But murder is fascinating, don't you agree?'

Donald did not reply. I want to get the night ferry, he told himself; whatever he says I must avoid becoming involved. He found himself whistling the song in an attempt to drown the other man's words.

'I mean, the psychology of it,' his passenger said. 'A chap goes in a house, bashes up an old woman in the hall, gets her money, fifty or a hundred quid. Do you reckon it's going to worry him, what he did? I don't.'

Along the road to the left, lights shone. It had stopped raining. There was no sound when he switched off the wipers, except the engine's throb and the suck of the tyres. Donald cut off the tune in mid-whistle.

'A case like that,' the other man went on, 'it could be the good old tramp at the door who leaves his dirty paw marks or footprints over everything. Or it could be the real artist, the kind of thing that interests me. But as I say, this one doesn't impress me that way. I reckon it was just run-of-the-mill and we'll be reading that the police want to talk to a one-eyed farm labourer from Rutland.' He broke off and said in a tone of some anxiety, 'Hey, here it is, here's Joe's.'

Donald took the car into the open space in front of the café. He sat with his hands on the wheel, uncertain what to do.

'Thought you'd missed it.' His companion stepped out. 'Coming?'

Donald decided there were things wrong with the man's story. He would have to do something about it. Reluctantly, he got out. The night air was fresh, cool. As he followed the other man into Joe's he could not help noticing his shoes. They were thickly caked with mud. Had that come just from walking up a lane?

PLASTIC-TOPPED tables with sauce bottles on them, a few truck drivers sitting on tubular chairs, a smell of frying food—Joe's was not the sort of place to which Donald was accustomed. His companion, however, seemed quite at home.

'Two cups of tea, nice and strong. And can you do us sausages and chips?'

The man behind the counter had a squashed nose and a cauliflower ear. 'Right away.'

As his passenger turned, red-faced and smiling, Donald felt angry. 'Nothing to eat, thank you.'

'We'll both feel better with something hot inside us.' Sitting down at a corner table, smiling across it, his face was revealed as round and ingenuous. It was given a slightly sinister look by a cast in the left eye.

'I told you,' Donald said, ' I don't want anything to eat. And anyway, I never eat sausages.' He was dismayed to hear his own voice come out as shrill, pettish.

'Right, old man, don't fret. Just one order of bangers and chips, not two,' he shouted across the room. The ex-boxer raised a hand like a veined slab of beef in acknowledgement. 'The name's Golightly, by the way. Bill before it, but friends call me Golly.'

That is a familiarity to which I should never aspire, Donald thought. The phrase pleased him. He said rather less acidulously, 'I thought you came in here to telephone.'

'That's right.' Golightly got up, but seemed reluctant to leave the table. 'I'll just make that call, ask Joe there if he knows a garage.' He went over and spoke to Joe, nodded, and crossed to a telephone in a corner. Was he really intending to make a call? Would it be a good thing just to walk out and leave him, or would that be too barbarously uncivilised? Donald liked to think of himself as above all a civilised man, and as Joe brought over the sausages and chips, with two cups of tea in thick mugs, he remembered something Golightly had said that jarred on him.

'Do you have an evening paper, by any chance?' Donald asked the café owner.

'Yeah, a driver brought one in. Late edition you want, is it, got the racing results?' Donald said that was what he wanted. Joe waddled across the room, came back with the paper, leaned over the table, and said confidentially, 'Had Rolling Home for the second leg of a double. Third at a hundred to eight. Still, you can't beat the bookies all the time, can you? Know what I took off 'em last-week? Forty nicker.'

'Oh. Congratulations. You said this is the last edition?'

'That's what I said, mate.'

He really did not know how to talk to people like Joe. He looked through the paper carefully, then folded it, still not knowing quite what to do. Was Golightly—if that was his ridiculous name—telephoning or just standing there pretending to do so? Donald pursed his mouth in thought, stopped himself from whistling, sipped his strong tea. Golightly came over, rubbing his hands and smiling.

'Bangers and chips, I love you.' He poured purplish sauce around and over them, began to ply knife and fork, spoke between mouthfuls. 'Tried a couple of garages—the second one's going to tow my old bus away and look after it for the night. I'll go on to Folkestone with you, since you were kind enough to offer. I mean, it's going on for eleven now, and I don't want to get stranded.'

'What are you going to do, stay at a hotel?'

'Not exactly. I've got a friend there.'

'Like your relatives in Littlehampton?'

'No, no.' Golightly did not seem to appreciate that this was sarcasm. He closed the eye with the cast in it. 'This is a lady friend. A commercial traveller's a bit like a sailor, you know, a girl in every port. As a matter of fact, that's the real reason I want to get to Folkestone tonight, and can you blame me? Why should you single men have all the fun? I suppose you've got a little bit o' fluff waiting for you across the Channel? Or perhaps you're not that way inclined.'

'What do you mean?'

'Nothing. No offence meant and none taken, I hope. Talking too much. I always do. Shan't be a couple of minutes now.'

There was sweat on Golightly's forehead.

'I'm not taking you,' Donald said flatly.

'Not taking me!' The knife and fork clattered on the table. The hand that held the cup shook slightly. Donald felt calm, in complete control of the situation.

'Don't worry,' he said. 'I'm not going to do anything about it. I've thought it out and I don't want to get involved.'

There was a blast of cold air as the door opened to let in two truck drivers in overalls. Golightly looked down at the table and spoke in a low voice. 'What d'you mean, involved?'

'I mean you've been telling me a pack of lies. Come along now, admit it.' Donald cocked one leg over the other, admired the sheen on his shoes.

'How d'you make that out, old man?'

'I'll tell you, *old man*. You say you're a commercial traveller and you've got an important appointment tomorrow morning. Now, I've met one or two commercial travellers, and I've never known one who let himself be parted from his sample case. Natural enough, because without it they've got nothing to show. But you not only leave it in your car—so you say—but you don't even bother to have the garage that's collecting the car drop the bag in here.'

'I shan't need the samples tomorrow.' Golightly spoke without conviction.

'And then you don't really *sound* like a traveller. All that knight-of-the-road and girl-in-every-port stuff, it's out of date. You sound like an actor, not a very good one, *pretending* to be a commercial traveller. I don't believe you've got a car, let alone a sample case. What's your car number?'

'AKT 113 H.'

'Make?'

'Triumph Herald.'

'Firm?'

'Universal Woollens.'

'Prove it.' Donald uncrossed his legs. 'Show me your business card.'

Slowly Golightly's hand went into his jacket. He kept his eyes on Donald, those slightly crossed eyes, until he had drawn out a wallet. He looked through the contents, wiped his brow with his sleeve, then said, 'No business card.'

'No card! Why, without a card a commercial traveller doesn't exist.'

'All right, I haven't told the exact truth, but I still want to get to Folkestone. I still need a lift.'

It was the moment at which Donald had planned to walk out, but something about Golightly's manner made him abruptly change his mind. 'Come on then.'

His reward was the other man's startled look. 'You're taking me?'

'That's what it looks like, doesn't it.'

Golightly said nothing more. He paid the bill and they walked to the car in silence, with Donald a couple of steps behind. The ruddiness had drained from Golightly's face, leaving it pale. Donald, as he drove away, said, 'There's more to come.'

'How do you mean?'

'About you. Who you are, what you've been doing. I want an explanation.'

'I don't know what you're talking about.'

'Your shoes. The mud on them. That hasn't come from walking up a lane. More like walking, or maybe running, across fields.'

'It was a muddy lane.'

Donald took his right hand from the wheel, felt in his jacket pocket, then took it out again. 'I pick you up near Oastley where that old Mrs Ford was murdered. You tell me this cock-and-bull story about being a commercial traveller and you talk about murder in a very queer way. How did you know about the murder?'

'Read it in the paper.'

'No. I borrowed the last edition in the café and there was nothing in it. How could there be, when it didn't happen till seven o'clock. I heard it on the ten o'clock news, on my car radio. But how about you?'

'Must have heard it the same way. On my car radio.'

'That won't wash. I picked you up a couple of minutes after I heard it. And I'll tell you something else. On the radio they didn't say anything about her being killed in the hall.'

Silence. The lights showed Ashford ahead, the Folkestone bypass to the left. They took the left turn to the dual carriageway. Donald thought triumphantly: that's shown him, that's shaken him up, now perhaps I'll get the truth. And sure enough, it was in a tone much less boisterous than usual, in a tone almost meek, that Golightly said, 'I made a mistake there, didn't I?'

'You certainly did.' Donald began to whistle sweetly, melodiously. And then—he could hardly believe it—Golightly's voice took on a jeering tone.

'You think I was the one who did for her, so why not tell the police then?'

Donald was so shaken that he could not reply.

'All right, I did it. I killed the old girl,' Golightly said.

'You—'

'Let's say I did. So why not ring the police from Joe's, when you've got it worked out so nice and logical?'

'I'll tell you why,' Donald said. His voice shook with the emotion he had been suppressing. 'I hate England—everything about this smug country, the filthy weather, places like that disgusting café, people like you. If I call the police it means I'll have to make a statement, give evidence. I shan't be able to leave for—oh, perhaps not for days, weeks. So I don't care, I just don't care what you've done.'

'Very decent of you, old man.' Still that jeering tone. 'We haven't been introduced, have we? I mean, you know my name, you haven't told me yours. But I think I know it.'

'What is it?'

'Donald Grant, right?'

With anger that was half assumed and half real Donald said, 'You've been looking at my logbook.'

'I haven't, you know.' Somewhere in the far distance there was furious hooting, then it stopped. 'I'll tell you a bit of a story, shall I? About an old lady named Mrs Ford. Quite a nice old lady, but a bit close with her money. No sons, no daughters, so what did it matter, who cared? Nobody, you might think.'

Donald pressed his foot on the accelerator. He did not usually drive fast, but it was as if pushing up the needle from 70 to 80 and nearly to 90 helped him to get away from the voice, although of course in fact it didn't; the voice was like a needle digging into his skin.

'One person did care, though. That was her nephew. I expect the sort of thing she said was, "You'll get everything when I'm gone, dear, now here's a five-pound note to be going on with." Very annoying to a young man, especially one without much money. He was a sort of freelance writer, though people don't seem to think he made much of a living at it. Not enough to keep up the nice little pad he shared with his boy friend.

'So one fine evening—a wet evening, as a matter of fact—Mrs Ford is murdered. Quite a nasty murder—everything turned upside down to try and make it look like a hurried job. Wasn't, though.' With a sound like a sigh he added, 'I don't have to tell you the name of the nephew.'

Donald's mind was empty of thought, except that of the need for action. Golightly went on talking.

'We found out quite a bit about you when we rang your flat, and the young man you share it with—Charles is his name? He said you'd decided to take off quite suddenly on a holiday abroad. Seemed peeved you didn't take him along too—quite a row you had, according to him. So we've been looking for you. You'd have done better to stay put. Didn't know which road you'd take, so there was poor Golly, Detective Sergeant Golightly as you'll have guessed by this time, getting wet. Could have taken you in for questioning, but I thought you might have a gun. Have you, by the way?'

Behind were the lights of a car, flashing on, off, on again. Donald's fingers moved over the hard curves of the metal in his pocket, and he kept one

515

comforting hand there while he said in a distressed falsetto: 'Why shouldn't I go abroad? It's not a crime.'

'No, but you made one or two mistakes. Not deliberate ones like mine. You said Mrs Ford was killed around seven o'clock. So she was, but it didn't say so on the radio.'

'Your word against mine. I should deny saying it.'

'Something else. A witness saw you leave the cottage. Didn't know you, but gave us a description, said he'd know you again.'

'One witness. A good counsel would—'

'You were whistling that catchy little tune. Favourite of yours, isn't it? The witness got it loud and clear.' Golightly began to sing, loudly, but in tune:

> 'Carry the man who was born to be King
> Over the sea to Skye.'

Two things happened together. The car that had been flashing drew level, switched on a spotlight, began blaring away with a hooter. And Golightly, in a quite different voice, loud and angry, cried, 'Give me that gun,' and threw himself across the steering wheel, pinioning Donald's right arm to his pocket.

Donald just had time to realise that he was not able to control the car with his left hand, and to think about the bad luck that seemed to have dogged his whole life, and then there was nothing . . .

GOLIGHTLY WOKE up in a hospital bed. The Superintendent was glaring down at him. 'You're a fool, Golly. Only cuts and bruises, but you're lucky to be alive. Grant isn't.'

'He bought it?'

'A sliver of glass through the neck when you crashed. You had no need to get into his car, no need at all. Just let us know what road he was on, that's all you had to do.'

'Yes, sir. It seemed a good idea at the time.'

'And why the hell did you have to leave that café with him?'

'He'd have taken me along anyway, sir. I'd been needling him and I made a slip. He was on to me.'

'Don't expect any medals. What was the slip?'

Golightly told him. 'He made one too—mentioned the time she was killed; but of course he'd have denied it. He broke when I told him we had a witness who'd seen him leave the house and heard him whistling that song—you know, song of the Skye boatmen. One of the villagers said he was fond of it.'

'We had no witness.'

'No, sir. But he didn't know that. And he *was* fond of that song, kept whistling it in the car.' Virtuously Golightly said, 'I don't like whistling. Bad manners, bad habit. Can get you into trouble.'

THE AUTHORS

Margery Allingham
Born in London, Margery Allingham (1904–1966) was brought up in Essex and later settled at Tolleshunt d'Arcy on the coast. Her first novel was written while she was still in her teens and she went on to produce twenty-four novels and over sixty short stories. Her most famous creation is Albert Campion, her brilliant but seemingly frivolous amateur sleuth, who made his first appearance in a novel called *The Crime at Black Dudley*.

Page 13

H. C. Bailey
Henry Christopher Bailey (1878–1961) enjoyed a successful career as a journalist, working as a drama critic and later as a war correspondent and leader writer for the *Daily Telegraph*. He was also the author of many novels and short stories, including the mind-teasing puzzles featuring police surgeon Reggie Fortune, which made him one of Britain's most popular mystery writers during the thirties and early forties.

Page 27

Linda Barnes
Linda Barnes (*b*. 1949) used her background in the theatre to good effect when creating her first fictional detective, actor Michael Spraggue. She is best known however for her novels featuring Carlotta Carlyle, a tough and independent private investigator who, between cases, works as a part-time cab-driver on the streets of Boston. Carlyle made her first appearance in 'Lucky Penny', the story included in this collection.

Page 44

Arnold Bennett
Arnold Bennett (1867–1931) made his reputation with novels about life in his native Potteries, which he called the Five Towns. During a prodigiously busy career Bennett also found time for successful plays, influential newspaper columns and voluminous private journals, as well as short stories such as the one included in this collection, 'Murder', a timely burlesque of the great detective.

Page 58

E. C. Bentley
Journalist Edmund Clerihew Bentley (1875–1956) has two claims to be remembered today. The first is for inventing the form of humorous verse known as the 'clerihew'. The second is for creating the amateur detective and painter Philip Trent, introduced in the ironically titled *Trent's Last Case* (1905) and the hero of the story in this collection, 'The Clever Cockatoo'.

Page 71

Ernest Bramah
Ernest Bramah Smith (1868–1942), a reclusive man of whom few personal details are known, dropped his surname when publishing two series of short stories in the decades following Sir Arthur Conan Doyle's success with Sherlock Holmes. His mock-Chinese tales about Kai Lung have lasted less well than those featuring Max Carrados, a blind amateur sleuth, and his Watson-like friend, Louis Carlyle.

Page 84

John Dickson Carr
An American who spent much of his writing life in Britain, John Dickson Carr (1906–1977) mixed a sense of the macabre with a love of farce. The detective in 'The Silver Curtain', selected for this volume, is the amiable Colonel March, head of Scotland Yard's Department of Queer Complaints. Carr's most famous creation was Dr Gideon Fell, modelled on G. K. Chesterton. This prolific author also published under the pseudonym Carter Dickson.

Page 100

Raymond Chandler
Boyhood in England and a career in the oil business made an unlikely background for Raymond Chandler (1888–1959), a writer who, in middle age, followed Dashiell Hammett in establishing a tough, authentically American detective fiction. Chandler's stories for the 'pulp' magazines, such as *Goldfish*, included in this collection and featuring the private eye Carmady, rehearse the plots and characters he polished to perfection in novels featuring Philip Marlowe.

Page 111

G. K. Chesterton
His poetry and essays are almost forgotten and his fantasies, *The Man Who Was Thursday* and *The Napoleon of Notting Hill*, are unfairly overlooked. The world has chosen instead to remember Gilbert Keith Chesterton (1874–1936) for creating Father Brown, a Catholic priest whose innocent manner belies his acquaintance with evil, and who is the hero of stories that are as much moral parables as detective puzzles.

Page 142

Agatha Christie

Agatha Christie (1890–1976) made her reputation in the 1920s, when *The Murder of Roger Ackroyd* not only served notice of her skill in devising plots to outwit the most experienced reader of detective fiction but also introduced her comically vain Belgian detective Hercule Poirot, who features in the story in this collection. She was later to create the equally enduring Miss Marple.

Page 157

Wilkie Collins

His novel *The Moonstone*, published in 1868, was hailed by T. S. Eliot as 'the first, the longest and the best of modern English detective novels'. Wilkie Collins (1824–1889) never repeated its success, but 'Who Killed Zebedee?'—reprinted here from his collection *Little Novels* (1887)—is just one reminder that he never completely lost his touch in presenting a mystery.

Page 168

Edmund Crispin

Edmund Crispin was the pen-name adopted by Robert Bruce Montgomery (1921–1978), otherwise known as a composer of music for, among other films, the *Carry On* series. Although he worked in the post-war years, his stories about Gervase Fen, Professor of English at Oxford and amateur sleuth, look back to an earlier period in their high spirits and playful erudition.

Page 184

Charles Dickens

Popular Victorian novelist Charles Dickens (1812–1870) was also the author of many short stories, notable for the intensity with which they isolate the different effects woven together in the tapestry of his novels. He is represented here by 'Hunted Down', which pursues his interest in murder, mystery and suspense— striking elements of *Oliver Twist*, *Bleak House* and the tantalisingly unfinished *Mystery of Edwin Drood*.

Page 191

Sir Arthur Conan Doyle

A writer of science fiction, historical novels and adventure stories, as well as military history and, in later life, works on spiritualism, Arthur Conan Doyle (1859–1930) grew to resent the success of his Sherlock Holmes stories in eclipsing his other achievements. But he could not prevent it and to many readers detection is still a meerschaum pipe, a deerstalker hat and an 'Elementary, my dear Watson'.

Page 207

Stanley Ellin

Although he published many novels, including a highly original contribution to private-eye fiction in *The Eighth Circle* (1958), Stanley Ellin (1916–1986) was unusual among recent crime and mystery writers in concentrating on the short story. In this field he earned himself a major reputation right from the start, with his collection *The Specialty of the House* from which the title story has been taken for this collection.

Page 225

R. Austin Freeman

Richard Austin Freeman (1862–1943) trained as a doctor, qualifying in 1887 and spent some time in the army before becoming a general practitioner. Of all the detective writers who flourished in the wake of Conan Doyle's success with the Sherlock Holmes stories, Freeman was one of the most accomplished at working within the exacting confines of the short story and his tales of Dr Thorndyke are admirably tight exercises in scientific method.

Page 238

Michael Gilbert

Though he began his writing career after the second world war, with *Close Quarters* published in 1947, Michael Gilbert (*b*. 1912) has always cultivated the virtues of an earlier generation of detective novelists: meticulous plotting, varied and imaginatively chosen settings, and a pervasive dry wit. His cheerfully amoral acceptance of human frailty and wrongdoing strikes a distinctively personal note.

Page 251

Sue Grafton

Like Marcia Muller and Linda Barnes, Sue Grafton (*b*. 1940) has challenged the male tradition of the American private-eye novel as pioneered by Hammett and Chandler. Her series about California investigator Kinsey Millhone began with *'A' is for Alibi* (1982); subsequent titles are systematically working their way through the alphabet.

Page 262

Dashiell Hammett

The tales that Dashiell Hammett (1894–1961) began to publish in the 1920s are tough, violent and told in the street slang of the characters they describe. A former private investigator himself, Hammett brought a new mood and a new hero to a form that had previously been genteel and cerebral, and his work signalled the emergence of a distinctively American, 'hard-boiled' school of fiction that still flourishes today.

Page 274

Headon Hill

Francis Edward Grainger (1857–1927) used the pseudonym of Headon Hill for more than fifty popular novels, now largely forgotten. They include *The Spies of the Wight* (1899), a tale of German espionage that is a forerunner of the tradition that produced Erskine Childers's *The Riddle of the Sands* (1903) and John Buchan's *The Thirty-Nine Steps* (1915).

Page 299

Michael Innes

Under his own name the Oxford don J. I. M. Stewart (1906–1994) wrote literary criticism and, in later years, novels of university life. By then he was already better known for the detective fiction he had been publishing since the 1930s as Michael Innes, usually featuring the deceptively modest policeman John Appleby, and always distinguished by its elegance and witty erudition.

Page 305

H. R. F. Keating

A journalist who worked for fifteen years as the crime books reviewer for *The Times*, Henry Reymond Fitzwalter Keating (*b*. 1926) is best known for his novels about Inspector Ghote of the Bombay Police, who was introduced in *The Perfect Murder* (1960). 'Caught and Bowled Mrs Craggs', chosen for this collection, is set against that most venerable of British institutions, Lord's cricket ground.

Page 318

Peter Lovesey

Peter Lovesey (*b*. 1936) served as an Education Officer in the RAF before becoming a full-time writer. His prize-winning first novel, *Wobble to Death*, published in 1970, began a series of Victorian mysteries involving Sergeant Cribb and Constable Thackeray, while with *Bertie and the Tinman* he started a series with the future Edward VII as detective. His recent novels feature a contemporary detective called Peter Diamond.

Page 327

John D. MacDonald

John Dann MacDonald (1916–1986) earned his reputation with a long-running series that began with *The Deep Blue Good-By* (1964). The novels featured detective Travies McGee, an amiable ex-footballer, and always included a colour in the title. A prolific writer of pulp fiction he is best known today for his novel *The Executioners*, which has been filmed twice, most recently by director Martin Scorsese as *Cape Fear*.

Page 335

Ngaio Marsh

Dame Ngaio Marsh (1899–1982) combined two long and distinguished careers, as a theatre producer in her native New Zealand and as a detective novelist. Virtually all her work features the suave policeman Roderick Alleyn, usually accompanied by his assistant Inspector 'Br'er' Fox and often by his painter wife Troy. She was made a Dame Commander of the British Empire in 1966 for her services to theatre.

Page 345

W. Somerset Maugham

Born at the British Embassy in Paris, William Somerset Maugham (1874–1965) eventually settled on the Riviera after a lifetime of travelling that gave a cosmopolitan flavour to his writing. Like many of his other short stories, 'Footsteps In the Jungle', selected for this collection, shows his familiarity with Southeast Asia; its apparently casual approach conceals a tight command of narrative structure.

Page 361

Ed McBain

The American writer who started life as Salvatore Lombino (b. 1926) is known to readers under several pen names. As Evan Hunter he has produced serious fiction that includes *The Blackboard Jungle* (1954). As Ed McBain he has created Steve Carella and his team of cops from the 87th Precinct, who feature in a memorable series of 'police procedurals', starting with the novel *Cop Hater* (1965).

Page 384

Marcia Muller

In her novel *Edwin of the Iron Shoes* (1977), Marcia Muller (*b*. 1944) introduced Sharon McCone, who appears in this collection in 'Deadly Fantasies'. McCone is a San Francisco private investigator and the first of the independent-minded women detectives who play so large a role in current writing. Muller has also created two other detectives: Elena Oliverez, introduced in *Tree of Death* (1983) and Joanna Stark, in *The Cavalier in White* (1986).

Page 410

Baroness Orczy

Everyone remembers Baroness Orczy (1865–1947) for creating Sir Percy Blakeney, the Scarlet Pimpernel whose gallant adventures extended from novels to stage and film. Crime and mystery readers also know her for her stories about the enigmatic and sometimes sinister 'Old Man in the Corner' and about one of the first women detectives, Lady Molly of Scotland Yard, who appears in this collection.

Page 422

Ellery Queen

Ellery Queen was the pseudonym adopted by the American writers Frederick Dannay (1905–1982) and Manfred B. Lee (1905–1971) for their work featuring a well-connected amateur detective who is also called Ellery Queen. Beginning in the late 1920s, Queen's fictional career lasted until 1971. *Ellery Queen's Mystery Magazine*, founded by the two men, has flourished for over forty years as a distinguished outlet for crime short stories.

Page 435

Ian Rankin

Although he has also written spy thrillers, Ian Rankin (*b*. 1960) has largely built his reputation with a tough, realistic series of novels and short stories about an all-too-human Edinburgh detective, Inspector Rebus, who was introduced in *Knots and Crosses* (1987) and features here in 'Concrete Evidence'. His eighth Rebus novel, *Black and Blue*, was awarded a Golden Dagger by the Crime Writers' Association.

Page 442

Ruth Rendell

Her position as one of Britain's leading crime writers has won Ruth Rendell (*b*. 1930) many honours, including a Diamond Dagger for lifetime achievement from the Crime Writers' Association and a life peerage. Sharp social observation and tight plotting distinguish her series about Chief Inspector Wexford, who appears in this collection. The work she publishes as 'Barbara Vine' explores the psychology of the criminal mind.

Page 457

Dorothy L. Sayers

The creator of amateur detective Lord Peter Wimsey, Dorothy Leigh Sayers (1893–1957) also had a strong reputation as the author of a number of works on religion and as a translator of Dante. Wimsey, introduced as a facetious young clubman in *Whose Body?* (1923) was transformed into a more complex figure by his final appearance in *Busman's Honeymoon* (1937), and has proved one of the most enduringly popular creations of detective fiction's Golden Age.

Page 475

Georges Simenon

Belgian author Georges Simenon (1903–1989) was astonishingly prolific, publishing nearly four hundred titles under at least a dozen different pseudonyms. He remains popular today for the stories he wrote about Inspector Jules Maigret of the Paris Police, whose humanity and conscience make him a universal hero. Maigret, who features in this collection in 'The Man in the Street', appeared in more than eighty titles published between 1931 and 1972.

Page 497

Julian Symons

Poet, biographer and popular historian as well as novelist, Julian Symons (1912–1994) took an idiosyncratic approach to detective fiction that avoided the familiar formulas and cultivated a bleak irony. *Bloody Murder*, the lively and opinionated history of the genre which he first issued in 1972 and several times updated, advocates social and psychological realism rather than mere technical ingenuity.

Page 508

Acknowledgments

The Publishers would like to thank the following for kind permission to reprint copyright material:

Curtis Brown London, for THE LONGER VIEW by Marjorie Allingham, © P and M. Youngman Carter Ltd 1939, from *Mr Campion and Others* by Marjorie Allingham, first published by William Heinemann Ltd, 1939.

Tessa Sayle Agency for THE LITTLE HOUSE by H. C. Bailey © H. C. Bailey 1927 from *Mr Fortune, Please*, Methuen, 1927.

Gina Maccoby Literary Agency for LUCKY PENNY by Linda Barnes, © Linda Barnes 1985, first published in *The New Black Mask, no. 3*, 1985.

A. P. Watt Ltd on behalf of Mme V. M. Eldin for MURDER by Arnold Bennett.

Nicholas Bentley and Alfred A. Knopf Inc., for THE CLEVER COCKATOO by E. C. Bentley, © E. C. Bentley 1938, from *Trent Intervenes* by E. C. Bentley.

A. P. Watt Ltd on behalf of the Estate of the late Mr W. P. Watt for THE TRAGEDY AT BROOKBEND COTTAGE by Edward Bramah, from *Max Carrados*, 1914.

David Higham Associates for THE SILVER CURTAIN by John Dickson Carr, collected in *Merrivale, March and Murder*, International Polygonics Ltd, 1991.

Ed Victor Ltd and Alfred A. Knopf on behalf of College Trustees Ltd for GOLDFISH by Raymond Chandler, first published in book form in the USA in 1946, first published in Great Britain in *Trouble is my Business and Other Stories*, Penguin Books, 1950.

A. P. Watt Ltd on behalf of The Royal Literary Fund for THE CHIEF MOURNER OF MARNE by G. K. Chesterton, © G. K. Chesterton 1927, renewed by Oliver Chesterton 1954, from *The Secret of Father Brown*, first published in Great Britain as *The Father Brown Stories*, Cassell, 1929.

Aitken & Stone Ltd for THE MYSTERY OF THE BAGHDAD CHEST by Agatha Christie, © Agatha Christie Limited 1997, from *While the Light Lasts and Other Stories*, HarperCollins, 1997.

A. P. Watt Ltd on behalf of Jean Bell for WITHIN THE GATES by Edmund Crispin, © Bruce Montgomery 1953. First published by Victor Gollancz Ltd, 1953.

Jonathan Clowes Ltd on behalf of Andrea Plunket, Administrator of The Sir Arthur Conan Doyle Copyrights, for THE MAN WITH THE TWISTED LIP, by Sir Arthur Conan Doyle from *The Adventures of Sherlock Holmes*, first published in 1892. © The Sir Arthur Conan Doyle Copyright Holders 1996.

Curtis Brown New York for THE BETRAYERS by Stanley Ellin, © Stanley Ellin 1956, from *The Specialty of the House and Other Stories* by Stanley Ellin, first published in the US as *Mystery Stories*, 1956.

A. P. Watt Ltd on behalf of Winifred Lydia Briant for THE BLUE SEQUIN by R. Austin Freeman, from *Dr Thorndyke's Cases* by R. Austin Freeman, Chatto & Windus 1909.

Curtis Brown London for THE OYSTER CATCHER by Michael Gilbert, first published in *Ellery Queen's Mystery Magazine*.

Aaron Priest Literary Agency for LONG GONE by Sue Grafton, © Sue Grafton 1986, first published in *Redbook* as "She Didn't Come Home".

Random House Inc. for A MAN CALLED SPADE by Dashiell Hammett, © American Mercury, Inc. 1932, renewed by Dashiell Hammett 1960.

Macmillan Publishers Ltd for A QUESTION OF CONFIDENCE by Michael Innes, © Michael Innes 1972, from *Winter's Crimes 4*, Macmillan London Ltd, 1972.

Peters Fraser & Dunlop Ltd for CAUGHT AND BOWLED MRS CRAGGS by H. R. F. Keating, © H. R. F. Keating 1981. First published in *John Creasey's Crime Collection*, Victor Gollancz Ltd, 1981.

Vanessa Holt Ltd for A CASE OF BUTTERFLIES by Peter Lovesey, © Peter Lovesey 1989. First published in *Winter's Crimes 21*, Macmillan, 1989.

John D. MacDonald for THE HOMESICK BUICK by John D. MacDonald, first published in *Ellery Queen's Mystery Magazine*.

10-088-040

HarperCollins Publishers Ltd for CHAPTER AND VERSE: THE LITTLE COPPLESTONE MYSTERY by Ngaio Marsh © Ngaio Marsh (Jersey) Ltd 1989, from *Death on the Air and Other Stories* by Ngaio Marsh, first published in Great Britain by HarperCollins Publishers, 1995.

A. P. Watt Ltd on behalf of The Royal Literary Fund for FOOTPRINTS IN THE JUNGLE by W. Somerset Maugham, © W. Somerset Maugham, first published in *The Complete Short Stories*, Heinemann, 1951.

Curtis Brown London for SADIE WHEN SHE DIED by Ed McBain © Evan Hunter 1972.

Berkley Publishing Group, a member of Penguin Putnam Inc. for DEADLY FANTASIES by Marcia Muller, © Marcia Muller 1989. First published in *Alfred Hitchcock's Mystery Magazine*, reprinted from *Sisters in Crime 4*, edited by Marilyn Wallace, © Marilyn Wallace 1991. All rights reserved.

A. P. Watt Ltd on behalf of Sara Orczy-Barstow Brown for THE MAN IN THE INVERNESS CAPE by Baroness Orczy.

A. M. Heath & Co Ltd for MYSTERY AT THE LIBRARY OF CONGRESS by Ellery Queen, originally published as ENTER, ELLERY QUEEN, © Popular Publications Inc. 1960, © renewed by Ellery Queen.

Ian Rankin for CONCRETE EVIDENCE by Ian Rankin, © Ian Rankin 1993. First published in *Ellery Queen's Mystery Magazine*.

Peters Fraser & Dunlop Ltd for WHEN THE

WEDDING WAS OVER by Ruth Rendell, © Kingsmarkham Enterprises Ltd 1979, from *Collected Short Stories* by Ruth Rendell, Hutchinson, 1987.

David Higham Associates for THE CAVE OF ALI BABA by Dorothy L. Sayers, from *Lord Peter Views the Body*, by Dorothy L. Sayers, first published in Great Britain by Victor Gollancz, 1928.

Penguin Books Ltd and Administration de L'Oeuvre de Georges Simenon for THE MAN IN THE STREET by Georges Simenon, © Georges Simenon, 1947, 1950. Translation by Jean Stewart © Georges Simenon 1976. From *Maigret's Christmas* by Georges Simenon, Hamish Hamilton, 1976.

Curtis Brown London for PICK UP ON THE DOVER ROAD by Julian Symons, collected in *John Creasey's Crime Collection*, Victor Gollancz, 1981.

Publishing details for the remaining stories are as follows:

WHO KILLED ZEBEDEE? by Wilkie Collins, first published in *Seaside Library*, 26 January 1881.

HUNTER DOWN by Charles Dickens, first published in *New York Ledger*, 20/27 August, 3 September 1859.

THE SAPIENT MONKEY by Headon Hill, first published in *The Million*, 22 October 1892.